Praise for the Safehold series

"A nice blend of historical combat and survival fiction . . . Very satisfying . . . Safehold is in store for some interesting times in the coming years."
—*SFRevu* on *At the Sign of Triumph*

"Marvelously entertaining!" —Vernor Vinge
on *Off Armageddon Reef*

"Vast, complex, intricate, subtle, and unlaydownable. This looks like the start of the biggest thing in science fiction since Isaac Asimov's Foundation series."
—Dave Duncan on the Safehold series

"A complex and fascinating epic about change, identity, and the nature of faith." —*Publishers Weekly*
on *Like a Mighty Army*

"A superb cast of characters and plenty of action . . . This fine book gives new luster to Weber's reputation and new pleasure to his fans." —*Booklist* (starred review)
on *By Schism Rent Asunder*

"Weber brings the political maneuvering, past and future technologies, and vigorous protagonists together for a cohesive, engrossing whole."
—*Publishers Weekly* (starred review)
on *Off Armageddon Reef*

"Effortlessly exceeds the magnificence of its predecessor . . . I cannot emphasize how much I want to read the next chapter in the Safehold saga."
—*Fantasy Book Critic*
on *By Schism Rent Asunder*

TOR BOOKS BY DAVID WEBER

THROUGH FIERY TRIALS

✦

DAVID WEBER

A TOM DOHERTY ASSOCIATES BOOK
NEW YORK

This is a work of fiction. All of the characters, organizations, and events portrayed in this novel are either products of the author's imagination or are used fictitiously.

THROUGH FIERY TRIALS

Copyright © 2018 by David Weber

A Tor Book
Published by Tom Doherty Associates
120 Broadway
New York, NY 10271

www.tor-forge.com

Tor® is a registered trademark of Macmillan Publishing Group, LLC.

ISBN 978-0-7653-6464-7

Our books may be purchased in bulk for promotional, educational, or business use. Please contact your local bookseller or the Macmillan Corporate and Premium Sales Department at 1-800-221-7945, extension 5442, or by email at MacmillanSpecialMarkets@macmillan.com.

First Edition: January 2019
First Mass Market Edition: January 2020

Printed in the United States of America

0 9 8 7 6 5 4 3 2 1

For everyone who takes Maikel Staynair's advice and makes the courageous decision to decide *for yourself* what you believe. Whatever you finally decide, you are precious beyond belief.

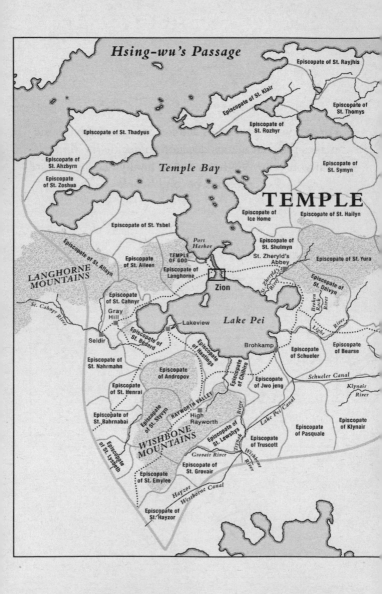

Hsing-wu's Passage

Episcopate of St. Rayjhis

Episcopate of St. Klair

Episcopate of St. Thomys

Episcopate of St. Thadyus

Episcopate of St. Rozhyr

Episcopate of St. Symyn

Episcopate of St. Ahzbyrn

Temple Bay

TEMPLE

Episcopate of St. Zoshua

Episcopate of St. Hailyn

Episcopate of Ice Home

Episcopate of St. Ysbel

Episcopate of St. Allayn

Port Harbor

Episcopate of St. Shulmyn

Episcopate of St. Aileen

TEMPLE OF GOD

St. Zheryld's Abbey

Episcopate of St. Yura

LANGHORNE MOUNTAINS

Episcopate of Langhorne

Zion

Episcopate of St. Dalvyn

St. Cahnyr River

Episcopate of St. Cahnyr

Gray Hill

Lake Pei

Broken Rock River

Light River

Seldir

Lakeview

Episcopate of St. Bedard

Brohkamp

Episcopate of Bearse

Episcopate of St. Nahrmahn

Episcopate of Hastings

Episcopate of Chihiro

Episcopate of Schueler

Episcopate of Andropov

Schueler Canal

Episcopate of St. Henrai

Episcopate of Jwo jeng

Klynair River

Episcopate of St. Styvyn

RAYWORTH VALLEY

High Rayworth

Tyryn River

Lake Pei Canal

Episcopate of St. Bahrnabai

WISHBONE MOUNTAINS

Episcopate of St. Lewhys

Episcopate of Pasquale

Episcopate of Klynair

Episcopate of St. Lysbeth

Episcopate of Truscott

Wishbone River

Grovair River

Episcopate of St. Grovair

Episcopate of St. Emylee

Hayzor

Westborne Canal

Episcopate of St. Hayzor

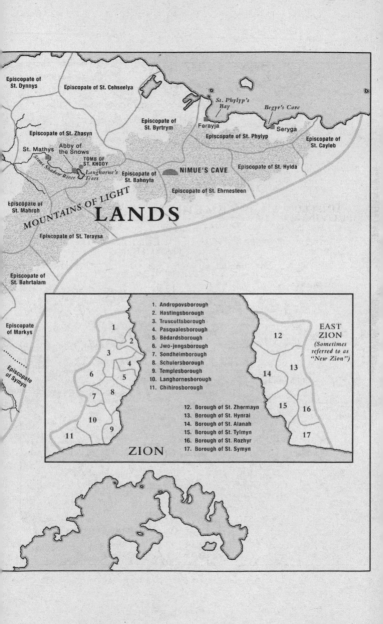

Episcopate of St. Dynnys

Episcopate of St. Cehseelya

St. Phylyp's Bay

Begyr's Cove

Episcopate of St. Zhasyn

Episcopate of St. Byrtrym

Ferayja

Seryga

Episcopate of St. Phylyp

Episcopate of St. Cayleb

St. Mathys

Abby of the Snows

TOMB OF ST. KHODY

Stone Shadow River

Langhorne's Tears

Episcopate of St. Bahnyta

NIMUE'S CAVE

Episcopate of St. Hylda

Episcopate of St. Mahroh

Episcopate of St. Ehrnesteen

MOUNTAINS OF LIGHT LANDS

Episcopate of St. Teraysa

Episcopate of St. Bahrtalam

Episcopate of Markys

Episcopate of Symyn

EAST ZION
(Sometimes referred to as "New Zion")

1. Andropovsborough
2. Hastingsborough
3. Truscottsborough
4. Pasqualesborough
5. Bédardsborough
6. Jwo-jengsborough
7. Sondheimborough
8. Schulersborough
9. Templesborough
10. Langhornesborough
11. Chihirosborough

12. Borough of St. Zhermayn
13. Borough of St. Hynrai
14. Borough of St. Alanah
15. Borough of St. Tylmyn
16. Borough of St. Rozhyr
17. Borough of St. Symyn

ZION

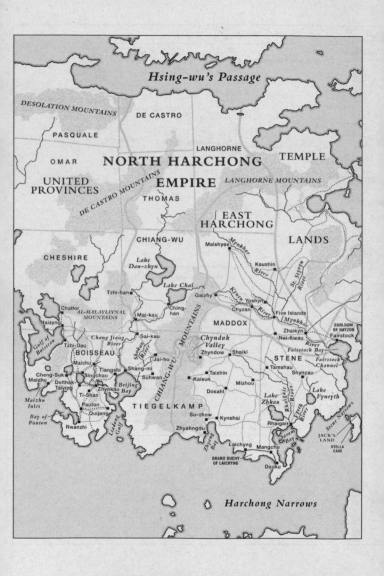

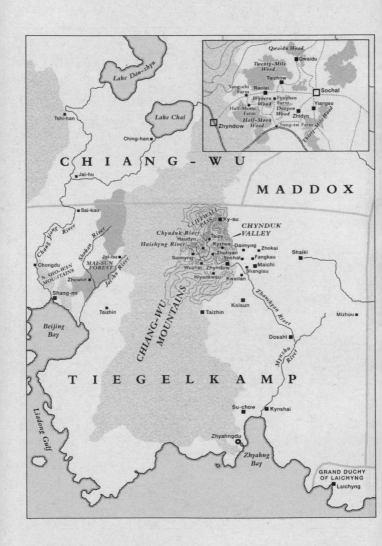

THROUGH FIERY TRIALS

An Introduction to the History of Safehold

In 2091, the sublight colony ship *Galileo* established the first extra-solar colony in the Alpha Centauri System.

In 2123, Doctor Samantha Adenauer and her team developed the first practical hyperdrive.

In 2350, the Malachai System, with a population of 436,000, became the fifteenth voting member system of the Terran Federation.

In 2367, the survey ship *Adenauer* discovered the first evidence of an advanced nonhuman species. Christened the Alphanes, they had achieved a three-star civilization, their technology had been substantially inferior to humanity's current level . . . and they had been exterminated in a massive interstellar war. The scientific community's majority view was that the Alphanes, who'd clearly been a militant species, had destroyed themselves. A minority, however, led by anthropologist Anton Sugawara, argued that the evidence suggested the Alphane civilization had been destroyed by an external force.

Sugawara was pilloried by the press—which christened his putative interstellar predators the Gbaba—for his paranoia. No one in government took the ridiculous notion seriously . . . but the Federation began expanding its navy—which had been little more than a police and rescue force—and building genuine warships. Not that anyone really *believed* in genocidal alien menaces, of course. Everyone in government was very clear about that! Still, one had to take some precautions, even if it *was* solely to assuage the dread of those who might have been frightened by Sugawara's absurd theories.

Everyone in government was very clear about that, too.

In 2370 Anton Sugawara was very quietly named the first cabinet-level Navy Minister and naval expansion was even more quietly—but enormously—accelerated.

In 2378, in the Crestwell System, the heavy cruiser TFNS *Swiftsure* discovered Sugawara had been right.

▼ ▼ ▼

Swiftsure was destroyed with all hands. The outpost in Crestwell was destroyed. Within seven months, every single human in three of the Federation's fourteen major extra-solar star systems was dead.

Sugawara's navy fought back hard, stopped the incursion, and—over the next couple of years—retook the lost star systems and drove the Gbaba back into their own space. Until, in 2381, in what came to be known as the Starfall System, Admiral Ellen Thomas' First Fleet, the TFN's major combat force, discovered that all humanity had seen so far were the Gbaba's light frontier forces. Now the *real* Gbaba navy had mobilized, and the result was massacre.

First Fleet's tattered survivors carried the warning home . . . and arrived upon the wings of Apocalypse.

The Federation had begun quietly fortifying its star systems at the same time it created its new navy. That process had been driven with frantic speed from the moment of *Swiftsure*'s destruction, and any star system made an awesome fortress. But *no* fortification could stand against the forces the Gbaba were willing to commit, the losses they were prepared to accept.

In 2406, the Federation's last major extra-solar star system was overwhelmed.

In 2411, all human population enclaves outside the Sol System's asteroid belt were withdrawn to the "Final Redoubt" inside the orbit of Mars.

In 2421, the last surviving Federation fleet launched a desperate effort to break through the Gbaba blockade.

It was hunted down. Its units were destroyed to the last ship.

In 2430, the Gbaba cracked the Final Redoubt and all human life in the Sol System ceased to exist.

In 3249, a young woman named Nimue Alban awakened in a cavern on a planet named Safehold . . . and discovered that she'd been dead for 828 years.

▼ ▼ ▼

Lieutenant Commander Alban had no memory of how she'd come to that cavern, but Commodore Pei Kau-yung, her mentor and commanding officer, had left a recording to explain. The fleet which had died in 2421 had actually succeeded in its true mission, which had been to cover Operation Ark, the Federation's last-ditch effort to establish a hidden colony among the distant stars where humanity might survive. Commodore Pei had commanded the colony ships' close escort when the rest of the Navy deliberately drew the Gbaba pursuit in upon itself and fought to the last man and woman to conceal the colony fleet's existence.

Nimue Alban had volunteered to serve on that sacrificial fleet's flagship, giving up her opportunity to accompany her commodore and his beloved wife, Pei Shan-wei, the scientist assigned to lead Operation Ark's terraforming fleet, to the colony which had become Safehold. And she'd done so because they and a core of their colleagues in Operation Ark's command crew had come to believe that Eric Langhorne, Operation Ark's senior administrator, intended to violate Operation Ark's mission plan.

That mission plan had called for the colony to abandon advanced technology for three hundred years, long enough—according to all of the Federation's projections, based on forty years of combat and analysis of Gbaba operational patterns—for the Gbaba to complete any scouting sweeps of the region in which the colony might lie. The command crew was to preserve humanity's knowledge and technology in small, carefully concealed enclaves. They and their immediate children were to be the custodians of that knowledge until the threat of discovery had passed, and then they were to restore that technology—and, *above all,* the warning of the Gbaba's existence—to the colonists' descendants.

But, as Kau-yung and Shan-wei had feared, Langhorne—traumatized by the brutal destruction of his entire species, obsessed by the knowledge that the eight million colonists in cryo-suspension aboard his forty mammoth transports represented every surviving human being—rejected that plan. He concluded that only the *permanent* renunciation of advanced technology could prevent humankind from someday venturing once again into space and, inevitably, encountering the Gbaba once more. And so, while Pei Shan-wei terraformed Safehold into humanity's new home, and while Pei Kau-yung and his handful of warships guarded the terraforming fleet, Eric Langhorne and Adorée Bédard, his chief psychologist—in hiding with the main fleet, ten light-years from Safehold—reprogrammed those colonists' memories. They erased all knowledge of any previous life. They programmed the colonists to believe that the moment in which they first opened their eyes on Safehold was the very first day of creation . . . and that the command crew were archangels, sent by God to educate them into the lives He had designed them to live.

The Peis were horrified but not taken unaware. Shan-wei and her fellows in the Alexandria Enclave, on Safehold's southernmost continent, fought Langhorne openly, arguing against his policy, vowing to follow the original mission plan. Aware that the Alexandrians were heavily outnumbered in the command crew staff Langhorne had stacked with people as traumatized—and determined to kill technology—as himself, she and her husband separated after a violent public disagreement in which he ostensibly accepted Langhorne's new plan. They became estranged, embittered opponents for the next fifty-seven years, with Shan-wei retreating to Alexandria and Kau-yung remaining Langhorne's chief military advisor.

In order to kill technology once and for all, Langhorne, Bédard, and Maruyama Chihiro, Langhorne's Assistant Administrator, created the *Holy Writ,* the seminal scripture of the Church of God Awaiting. The *Writ* consisted of books by the various "Archangels" which provided religious explanations specifically designed to prevent the reemergence of the scientific method. In addition, it contained the Proscriptions—the list of specifically proscribed knowledge and a religious limitation only to technologies powered by wind, water, or muscle.

Shan-wei and her supporters believed it would be impossible to prevent technology from someday reemerging, whatever constraints Langhorne and Bédard might have created. Although they'd retreated to Alexandria and outwardly accepted Langhorne's *legal* authority, they continued to work quietly towards the original mission plan and its goals. However, they also feared they would ultimately be forcibly constrained to accept Langhorne's anti-technology policies. What they did *not* expect was for them and everyone in the Alexandria Enclave to be murdered in a kinetic strike which obliterated the enclave and transformed the small continent on which it had been located into Armageddon Reef, the most desolate and accursed location on all of Safehold. Heartbroken and furious—and determined, above all, that Langhorne *must not succeed* in erasing all memory of the Gbaba—Pei Kau-yung carried a miniaturized nuclear device to his next meeting with Langhorne and his council . . . and detonated it.

▼ ▼ ▼

Alexandria's destruction had occurred 750 standard years (824 Safeholdian years) before Nimue awoke in that cavern and discovered the reason she had volunteered to die. Lieutenant Commander Alban had been the only member of Commodore Pei's staff who possessed a PICA: a Personality Integrated Cybernetic Avatar. In essence, a PICA was a robotic/android body, many times as strong as any human, virtually indestructible without the use of heavy crew-served weapons, and effectively immortal. A PICA's user could upload his or her personality into it for dangerous extreme sports, for example, then download the PICA's experiences into his or her own memory afterward.

Full-capability PICAs such as Nimue's were rare and extremely expensive; hers had been a gift from her billionaire father, bestowed upon a daughter he'd known would die before she was forty. By leaving her PICA aboard Commodore Pei's flagship while she transferred to the sacrificial covering force she had removed it from any equipment inventory Langhorne might have accessed, and Shan-wei's terraforming crew had excavated the cavern complex in which that PICA had been hidden beneath the roots of Mount Olympus, Safehold's tallest mountain. From the beginning, that PICA had been intended as the Peis' hidden weapon. Nimue's mission was to ensure that the Gbaba were not, in fact, forgotten, despite anything Langhorne's anti-technology plan might accomplish.

Nimue herself had no memory of having volunteered. There'd been no time to record an updated personality which would have remembered, and so in a very real sense, the Nimue Alban who awakened had *not* volunteered. It never occurred to her to reject her mission, however . . . even though the challenges she faced were more daunting than anything the original Nimue could possibly have imagined.

The Church of God Awaiting had survived. Pei Kau-yung's final attack had, indeed, killed Langhorne and the majority of his administrative council's "Archangels." Unfortunately, it had not killed them all. Maruyama Chihiro and Androcles Schueler had survived, and the bitter fighting against the "lesser angels" who had supported Shan-wei, even after her death, had produced a *Holy Writ* even more repressive than Langhorne's original. Safehold's population had increased enormously, to well over a billion, but Mother Church controlled all those millions upon millions, and her authority was unquestioned.

Unlike murdered Terra, Safehold had no atheists, not even agnostics, in large part because the eight million

"Adams" and "Eves" who had awakened on the Day of Creation were all literate. Hundreds of thousands of them left personal accounts, journals, diaries, and every single word of *The Testimonies* supported the *Holy Writ* in its totality. There were no disputed texts, no breaks in a written historical record which covered *everything* since—literally—the beginning of time. And every word of *The Testimonies* was a completely honest—and accurate—account of what had happened, left by eyewitnesses to the events they described.

Not only did the secular historical record support the *Writ*, but Mother Church controlled all education on the planet, and the Inquisition decided what was taught. And if education proved insufficient, there was always coercion. The *Book of Schueler* specifically required the Inquisition to mercilessly hunt down and punish heresy or apostasy in any form. The gruesome tortures it prescribed as a portion of that Punishment were hideous beyond belief.

And, to make Nimue's challenge complete, the kinetic bombardment system which had turned the Alexandria Enclave into Armageddon Reef remained active in orbit and apparently—or at least possibly—in communication with a high-tech presence buried under the Temple, the Church of God Awaiting's equivalent of the Vatican or Mecca, located in the heart of Safehold's largest city.

Nimue possessed some advantages, in addition to the capabilities of her PICA. Shan-wei had administratively "lost" or "expended" enough hardware to provide a limited manufacturing base, a supply of advanced weapons and other tools, the memory core of a major Federation library, and the services of a tactical (if none too bright) AI named Owl, in the caverns she christened "Nimue's Cave."

It wasn't much, set against the scope of her mission.

After evaluating her resources and familiarizing herself with Safehold, she concluded that she must somehow attack and destroy Safehold's faith in the Archangels and the *Holy Writ*. She had no way of knowing what was buried beneath the Temple, but if it was any sort of monitoring system, it could easily use the kinetic bombardment platforms to destroy any threat to the *Writ*'s anti-technology prohibitions, which meant she could not openly use advanced technology.

Safehold's technological capabilities were a strange mix of the 15th century and techniques from much later periods of history, courtesy of instructions the "Archangels" had recorded in the *Holy Writ*. Those techniques were applied by guilds of skilled artisans in small shops, not in vast factories, and they had been shorn of all scientific explanation when they were recorded. Like the surprisingly capable Safeholdian practice of medicine, they had become religious instructions delivered directly from God through the Archangels, and eight centuries of experience had validated them because they *always* worked exactly as the *Writ* said they would. That meant they provided building blocks, starting points, from which she might begin. But it also meant she must operate only within those allowable parameters and slowly, gradually push their boundaries until their expansion eroded the *Holy Writ*'s foundations to the point of collapse.

And that must, inevitably, provoke a religious war against the Church's authority. As a historian, she knew what that might entail, and her heart quailed at the thought. As the only individual who remembered the Gbaba, she knew she had no choice.

Her study of Safehold had focused in on the island kingdom of Charis. Charis was the smallest of Safehold's major kingdoms, but it was extremely wealthy, a nation of mariners and merchants, of entrepreneurs and skilled artisans. Despite the Proscriptions' limitations, Charis stood on the very brink of an industrial revolution—powered, like Terra's own, by waterwheels—albeit without the critical ability to question received authority or look for scientific explanations for processes. In addition, Charis, ruled by the Ahrmahk Dynasty, supported a tradition in which individual rights and freedoms—within the limitations of the *Writ,* of course—were strongly protected.

And it was a kingdom in which, if Nimue was not mistaken, some of those forbidden questions were on the brink of being asked.

▼ ▼ ▼

After identifying Charis, Nimue reconfigured her PICA to become *Seijin* Merlin Athrawes. The *seijins* were legendary figures, the "warrior saints" of the War Against the Fallen. They were warriors, teachers, mentors, and tradition—and *The Testimonies*—ascribed superhuman abilities to them, which would provide cover for "Merlin's" use of his PICA's capabilities.

Merlin introduced himself to the Ahrmahks by saving nineteen-year-old Crown Prince Cayleb from assassination and then offering his services to Cayleb's father, King Haarahld.

The king was a man beset. Charis' wealth and enormous merchant fleet had evoked growing resentment and envy among many of the other realms of Safehold for years. Now it seemed clear those other realms were marching towards open war against Charis . . . with the support of Mother Church, and—especially—of Grand Inquisitor Zhaspahr Clyntahn, who clearly distrusted Charisian orthodoxy. King Haarahld saw Merlin's arrival as a heaven-sent advantage in that looming conflict. Among other things, *Seijin* Merlin "saw visions," courtesy of the highly stealthy reconnaissance remotes he could deploy from orbit. And he had a vast store of knowledge he could impart—none of which *quite* violated the Proscriptions—from the reintroduction of arabic numerals and algebra to the invention of the cotton gin, spinning jenny, and a new design for cannon-armed sailing warships to replace the oared galleys of Safehold. Before Merlin's arrival, Haarahld had seen only death, ruin, and the brutal subjugation of his people. Now he saw at least a chance of survival, despite the enormous odds against Charis.

Merlin warned Haarahld that he had his own mission. "I respect you, and in many ways, I admire you," he told the king. "But my true loyalty? That belongs not to you, or to Cayleb, but to the future. I *will* use you, if I can, Your Majesty. Use you to create the day in which no man owns another, no man thinks men born less nobly than he are cattle or sheep."

Haarahld Ahrmahk accepted that warning . . . and Merlin Athrawes' service.

▼ ▼ ▼

Over the next nine Safeholdian years, Merlin and King Haarahld—and after Haarahld's death in battle, King Cayleb—fought shoulder to shoulder. Haarahld died protecting his people before Merlin ever discovered that he and the Bishop of Tellesberg, Maikel Staynair, had known the truth about the "Archangels" from the very beginning, thanks to the Monastery of Saint Zherneau, where a man named Jeremiah Knowles, one of the original "Adams" whose loyalty had been to Pei Shanwei, had left a journal . . . and copies of books which predated the Creation. Merlin learned that only after Haarahld's death, only after Cayleb had assumed the crown. And only after Maikel Staynair—with Cayleb's unwavering support—had proclaimed the Church of Charis, based upon the defiant proposition that every human being had the right—indeed, the *responsibility*—to decide for himself or herself what he or she believed.

Even then, Staynair dared not share the truth of the monumental lie behind the *Holy Writ*. Safehold might be prepared to entertain a schism within the Church, so long as that schism was aimed at *reforming* the obvious corruption of the Temple and, especially, the Group of Four, the quartet of Vicars who controlled it. The planet wasn't prepared—couldn't *be* prepared—to accept open, incontrovertible heresy against the ironclad authority of the *Writ* and *The Testimonies*. Charis must fight an incremental campaign to reach that point . . . and first and foremost, it must survive.

It did. Over the course of nine brutal, savage years of war—a war which saw armies millions of men strong, fleets counting hundreds of artillery-armed galleons, and unspeakable atrocities and extermination camps in the name of Zhaspahr Clyntahn's twisted vision of God—it did. It grew from a single small island nation to the most powerful single realm in Safeholdian history. It grew from a kingdom ruled by a young, untested king to a vast empire, governed jointly by Emperor Cayleb Ahrmahk and his beloved wife, Empress Sharleyan, the Queen of Chisholm, who voluntarily embraced Cayleb's cause and made it her own before they had even met. It grew through sacrifice, grew because it was protected by men and women willing to die where they stood in its defense. And it grew because the *Church* of Charis offered the freedom of conscience that demanded human beings decide what they truly believed, what they were prepared to die to defend.

But it did not destroy the Church of God Awaiting or discredit the *Holy Writ*.

Perhaps it might have done those things if not for Rhobair Duchairn, one of the Group of Four. For all its lies, all the brutality of the *Book of Schueler*, there was an enormous amount of good in the *Writ*, and it taught that the Church was the servant of God, the *shepherd* and protector of godly men and women, charged to love and nourish them, not abuse them in the name of personal power. And brought face-to-face with the carnage, the devastation, the proof of Zhaspahr Clyntahn's cruelty and quest for absolute power, Rhobair Duchairn *remembered* that. He remembered he was a priest and a servant of God, and in the end—in the full knowledge of the hideous way he would die if Clyntahn decided to remove him—Duchairn and a few allies organized and then led an uprising which overthrew Clyntahn and drove the Grand Inquisitor from Zion . . . and directly into the hands of Merlin Athrawes.

Clyntahn was tried and executed for the millions of murders he had ordered, but Rhobair Duchairn—destined to be known to Safeholdian history as "Saint Rhobair" and "the Good Shepherd"—accepted the Church of Charis' demands. He promised to truly reform the Church of God Awaiting, and in the face of that promise, Charis and its allies could not justify continuing the war. The inner circle of Cayleb and Sharleyan's allies might know the truth about Langhorne and the "Archangels," but they still dared not proclaim it, and Duchairn had promised all of the reforms they'd sought.

And so the war ended with just a few . . . unresolved issues. Like what to do about the bombardment platform still in orbit. What to do about whatever the high-tech presence under the Temple might be. How to reconstitute peaceful international relations on a planet which had torn itself apart in bitter religious strife. How to continue the industrialization process which had given Charis the war-fighting advantage it had needed to prevail without violating the Proscriptions' limitations.

And, of course, what to do about the Archangels' promise to "return in glory" a thousand years after the Day of Creation.

▼ ▼ ▼

Merlin Athrawes and his allies and friends had won their war against the Group of Four, but not their struggle against the Church of God Awaiting's fundamental doctrine.

That promised to be just a bit more difficult. . . .

—from *The Life of Merlin Athrawes*,
Zhakleen Wylsynn, Tellesberg,
Royal University Press, 4217.

NOVEMBER YEAR OF GOD 900

✦

. I .
Nimue's Cave,
The Mountains of Light,
Episcopate of St. Ehrnesteen,
The Temple Lands.

"No matter how many times Owl and I look at it, it keeps coming up the same," Nahrmahn Baytz said. "*Something*'s obviously gone wrong with Langhorne and Chihiro's master plan. We just don't know what, and that's what may kill us all in the end. Well, kill everyone *else,* I suppose, given your and my . . . ambiguous status."

The hologram of the rotund little Emeraldian prince who'd been dead for almost five years sat on the other side of the enormous, round table. Nimue Alban (who'd been dead *far* longer than he had) had instructed Owl to manufacture that table—and make it round—even before she'd reconfigured her PICA into Merlin Athrawes for the very first time. Now Merlin sat tipped back in one of the reclining chairs with his boot heels parked inelegantly on the polished surface and waved a beer stein at the hologram.

"If it was easy, anyone could play and we wouldn't need *you*," he observed, and Nahrmahn chuckled a bit sourly.

"I don't think most people would object if it wasn't *easy* as long as they knew what the rules were!" he said.

"Nahrmahn, you spent your entire adult life playing the 'Great Game.' *Now* you're going to complain about not having rules?"

"There's a difference between creatively breaking the rules and not knowing what the damned things are in the first place!" Nahrmahn shot back. "The former is a case of polished and elegant strategies. The latter is a case of floundering around in the dark."

"Point," Merlin conceded.

He sipped from the stein in his right hand (a PICA had no need for alcohol, but he liked the flavor) and checked his internal chronometer. Fourteen minutes yet until the "inner circle" convened by com to discuss his and Nahrmahn's recommendations. Finding a time when people in every time zone of the planet could coordinate com conversations without anyone noticing they were sitting in a corner talking to themselves was a nontrivial challenge, and usually only a relatively small percentage of the entire—and growing—inner circle could be "present." More of them than usual would be making it tonight, however, and he wished the two of them had been able to come up with something more . . . proactive to share with them.

"I'm going to call it the 'Nahrmahn Plan,' you know," he said now, smiling crookedly at the electronic ghost of his friend.

"Hey! Why do *I* get the blame?"

"Because you're our designated Schemer-in-Chief. If there's skulduggery afoot, *your* foot's usually in it up to the knee, or at least the ankle. And because I believe in giving credit where it's due."

"And because you think the uncertainties built into its foundation comport poorly with your status as the all-knowing, ever-prepared *Seijin* Merlin?"

"Well, of course, if you're going to be tacky about it."

Nahrmahn chuckled again, but he also shook his head.

"I just wish there weren't so many complete unknowns. Especially given what we *do* know. For example, we know the bombardment system's still up there, we know its maintenance systems are still operable, we've proved there's a two-way com link between it and *something* under the Temple, and we know its automated defenses took out the probes Owl sent towards it right after you woke up and started flailing around in your ignorance."

"Hey!" Merlin protested with a pained expression.

"Well, you did!" Nahrmahn shook his head again. "If whatever's missing in the command loop hadn't been missing, how do you think it would've responded to the evidence of a competing source of high-tech goodies? You're just damned lucky the system never even noticed, beyond swatting the pesky flies buzzing around its platforms!"

"All right," Merlin conceded. "That's fair."

"Thank you." Nahrmahn sniffed. "Now, as I was saying, we know all of that, but why in God's name did Chihiro leave it set up that way? Operating so . . . half-arsed? Why isn't it doing anything about all the steam engines and blast furnaces we've strewn across the planet? That's got to be a flare-lit tip-off that technology is reemerging, so why no kinetic bombardments? Why don't Charis and Emerald look like Armageddon Reef?"

"Because it's looking for electricity?" Merlin suggested. "I've always thought it's significant that the *Book of Jwo-jeng* specifically anathematizes electricity whereas the Proscriptions are defined in terms of what's *allowable*. They don't say 'You can't do A, B, or C'; they say 'You can't do anything *besides* A or B.' But not about electricity. And in addition to what she had to say about it, Chihiro says 'You shall not profane nor lay impious hands upon the power the Lord your God bestowed upon his servant Langhorne.'" His lips curled in distaste as he quoted from the *Book of Chihiro*. "That's why I've always assumed electricity would almost have to be a red line as far as any automated system under the Temple was concerned."

"And I tend to agree with you. But don't forget your own point—Chihiro anathematized it in terms of the 'Rakurai' Langhorne used to punish Shan-wei for her defiance of God's law. Lightning's sacred, unlike wind, water, or muscle power, so its use in any way is expressly forbidden."

"But Chihiro goes on to specifically describe *electricity,* not just lightning," Merlin pointed out. "People may call the damned things rakurai fish, but they don't flash like rakurai bugs. They just shock the hell out of anything that threatens them! But Chihiro uses them as a 'mortal avatar' of Langhorne's 'Holy Rakurai' placed on earth to remind humans of the awesome power entrusted to him by God. That's why the *Writ* says rakurai fish are sacred in the eyes of God, but where's the 'lightning bolt' in their case? He flat out tells people they have the same power as the Rakurai, and he didn't have to. For that matter, the *Writ* even talks about static electricity and links that to Langhorne's Rakurai, too." It was his turn to shake his head. "There's got to be a reason that Chihiro gassed on about it that long and that thoroughly, and the most likely one was to make *damned* sure no one even *thought* about fooling around with it."

"I said I agree with you, and there's no way in hell *I* want us playing around with electricity, because you may well be right. That could be the one-step-too-far that triggers some sort of auto response. I'm just saying any sort of threat analysis looking for the emergence of 'dangerous' technology should already have been triggered even *without* electricity. And that I don't understand why someone as paranoid as Langhorne—or, especially, Chihiro—didn't set up that threat analysis."

"Unless he did and the system's just broken," Merlin suggested.

"Which certainly seems to be what's happening, yes." Nahrmahn's avatar stood and began pacing around the conference room, apparently oblivious to the fact that its feet were at least an inch above the floor. "The problem is that it seems to be the *only* part of the system that's broken. I *wish* we could get a sensor array inside the Temple, but everything we can see from the outside—and all of the stories about the routine 'miracles' that go on inside it—seem to confirm that everything else is working just fine, even if no one has a clue how. So is the system really broken? And if it is, is there something we might do that could reset it? The last thing we want to do is turn it back on if it's gotten itself switched off somehow!"

"Nahrmahn, we've been over this—what, a dozen times? Two dozen?" Merlin said patiently. "Of course there may be an 'on button' we don't know a thing about. But whatever it might be, we obviously haven't hit it yet. And you're right, we've been scattering stuff all over Safehold for nine or ten years now. So it doesn't look like sheer scale's the critical factor. The threshold has to be something qualitative, not quantitative. Assuming there *is* a threshold, of course."

"Oh?" Nahrmahn paused in his pacing, hands folded behind him, and raised an eyebrow at the far taller *seijin*. "Are you suggesting we might assume there isn't one?"

"Of course not!" Merlin rolled his eyes. "I'm just saying it would appear we can go on doing what we're currently doing without getting blown up for our pains. And there are a lot more innovations we can introduce without going beyond water, steam, hydraulics, and pneumatics."

"I'll agree that that's most probably true," Nahrmahn said after a moment. "Whether it is or not, we have to assume it is or sit around with our thumbs up our arses without getting a damned thing done, anyway, and the clock's ticking."

"Damn, I *wish* we could get into the Key," Merlin sighed, and Nahrmahn snorted harshly in agreement.

The Key of Schueler was the most maddening clue they had—or *didn't* have, actually—about Safehold's future. According to the Wylsynn family tradition, the Key had been left by the Archangel Schueler as both the repository of his inspirational message to the family he'd established as the special guardians of Mother Church and as a weapon to be used by the Church in its time of greatest need. What it actually was was a memory module: a two-inch-diameter sphere of solid molecular circuitry which could have contained the contents of every book ever written on Safehold. What it actually did contain, aside from the recorded hologram of Androcles Schueler delivering his exhortation to the Church's guardians, remained a mystery. Owl, the artificial intelligence who resided in the computers in Nimue's Cave along with Nahrmahn's electronic personality, had determined that at least one of the files tucked away inside it contained over twelve petabytes of data, but no one had a clue what was in it and the Key's security protocols precluded accessing it without the password no one possessed.

It was entirely possible that the answer to every question facing them was contained inside the Key.

And they couldn't get at it.

"That *would* be nice, for a lot of reasons," Nahrmahn agreed. "Especially if the damned thing would tell us exactly what the *hell* Schueler meant by 'a thousand years'!"

Merlin grunted, because Androcles Schueler's promise to the Wylsynns that the "Archangels" would return "in a thousand years" was the true crux of their problem. If they *weren't* coming back, the time pressure came off and the inner circle could take however long it needed to find the right solution. But if someone—or some*thing*—actually was coming back to check on the progress of Eric Langhorne's grand scheme, whatever they or it might be would undoubtedly command the kinetic bombardment system, at a minimum.

That could be . . . bad.

Of course, there was no way of knowing if the Wylsynn family tradition that he'd promised anything of the sort was accurate. No one had been going to write something like that down, so it had been passed purely orally for almost nine centuries, and a few little details—like the password for the Key, for example, assuming the Wylsynns had ever known it—had gotten lost along the way. No one was certain if Schueler had meant that he and the other "Archangels" themselves would return—although that seemed unlikely, since most of them had been dead even before he recorded his message—or if something else would return. Or where whatever it was would return *from,* for that matter, although given all of those active power sources in the Temple, Merlin knew where *he* expected it to come from.

And had he meant the return of whoever or whatever was coming back would occur a thousand years after the Day of Creation when the first Adams and Eves had awakened here on Safehold? Or had he meant from the time he left the Key, at the end of the War Against the Fallen? Mother Church had begun counting years from her victory against the Fallen, but the war hadn't ended until seventy-plus Safeholdian years after the Day of Creation. So, if Schueler had meant a thousand years after Creation, he'd been talking about sometime around the middle of July of 915. If he'd meant a thousand years from the time he left the Key with the Wylsynns' distant ancestor, he'd been talking about the year 996 or so. Or he could simply have been talking about the year 1000, a thousand years after the start of the Church's post-Jihad calendar.

So we have fifteen years . . . or ninety-six . . . or a hundred and ten, Merlin thought now. *Nothing like a little ambiguity to liven up the day.*

"You know Domynyk's going to argue in favor of a fullbore onslaught on Church doctrine because we only have fifteen years," he said out loud.

"And I imagine Ahlfryd will support him," Nahrmahn agreed.

"And not just because he wants the Church kicked out on its ass." Merlin chuckled. It was not a sound of unalloyed mirth. "Braiahn was right about Ahlfryd's . . . impatience. Mind you, I still think Sharley was right and we needed to tell him, but he wants to tear down the Temple yesterday, if only so he can start playing openly with Federation tech!"

"I'm sure, but Maikel and Nynian—and, to be fair, you—are right. We can't go straight for an attack on the Church this soon after the Jihad." Nahrmahn's expression darkened. "Too many millions are dead already, and what looks like starting up in North Harchong's likely to be bad enough without cranking an overt religious war back into it. God knows, nobody in the North's going to be a candidate for industrialization, so it's not going to affect that side of things much, but the violence is going to be ugly as hell, and I'm pretty sure the divide between Zion and Shang-mi will already put religion front and center in it for a lot of those people. The Spears may be keeping the lid more or less screwed down so far, but when Waisu—or his ministers, anyway—decided the Mighty Host could never come home, they lit a fuse nobody's going to be able to put out. Sooner or later, the spark's reaching the Lywysite, and an awful lot of people will get killed when it does, if Owl and Nynian and Kynt and I are reading the tea leaves accurately."

The hologram gazed broodingly at something only Nahrmahn could see. Then he shook himself.

"It's going to be bad enough without *our* injecting religion back into the mess by attacking Church doctrine in the middle of it," he repeated, and chuckled mirthlessly. "Besides, the one thing we absolutely can't afford is to reopen that whole can of worms about demonic influence on Charisian innovation."

"Which only leaves the nefarious, unscrupulous, underhanded 'Nahrmahn Plan.'"

Merlin smiled as Nahrmahn perked back up visibly at his choice of adjectives, but then the little Emeraldian shook his head with a chiding expression.

"That's *really* not fair," he replied. "Especially since the original idea came from *you*."

"I think it occurred pretty much simultaneously to several of us," Merlin countered, "but I do like some of the . . . refinements you've incorporated. It's nice to see a little thing like dying hasn't diminished your devious quotient."

"To quote *Seijin* Merlin, 'One tries,'" Nahrmahn said, and bowed in gracious acknowledgment of the compliment.

Merlin chuckled again. Not that there was anything all that humorous about their options. Given ten years or so to openly deploy the capabilities of Owl's manufacturing capacity here in Nimue's Cave—and for it to clone itself and begin producing Federation-level technology *outside* the Cave—any belligerent "Archangels" who returned would find themselves promptly transformed into glowing clouds of gas, and their most pessimistic estimate gave them at least *fifteen* years before the return. The existence of the bombardment system, however, meant they couldn't deploy their own industry without almost certainly triggering that "reset" Nahrmahn feared. So, since they couldn't defeat any return by the Archangels, the best they could hope for was to create a situation in which those Archangels recognized the technology genie was irretrievably out of the bottle. If a native Safeholdian tech base could be spread broadly enough across the planet to make its eradication by bombardment impossible without killing enormous numbers of Safeholdians, any semi-sane "Archangel" would settle for a soft landing that accepted the inevitable. If the returnees *weren't* at least semi-sane, they might well opt to repeat the Armageddon Reef bombardment on a planetwide basis and damn the casualties, of course, but as Cayleb had put it with typical pithiness, "If they're that far gone, we're screwed whatever we do. All we can do is hope they aren't and plan accordingly."

So, assuming the earlier return date, the inner circle had fifteen years to spread Charis-style industrialization as broadly as possible around the planet. From the purely selfish viewpoint of the Charisian Empire's economic power, "giving away" its technological innovations would be a very poor business model. From the viewpoint of trying to keep everyone on the planet *alive*, however, it would make perfect sense, although that wasn't something they'd be explaining to anyone.

Nothing could be allowed to interfere with that process, and that was the reason, more even than the staggering potential casualties of a renewed Jihad, why any headlong assault on the Church of God Awaiting's fundamental doctrine had to be avoided . . . or at least postponed. Nahrmahn was right about what looked like firing up in Harchong, no matter what else happened, but he was also right about the need to keep any doctrinal conflict out of the equation. They *couldn't* afford to reawaken the charge that all of these innovations were the handiwork of Shan-wei, spreading her evil among humankind. If 915 came and went without any angelic reappearance, they'd have another eighty-five years to work on doctrinal revolutions.

And in the long run, that's as important as any piece of hardware, Merlin reflected. *"Archangels" who turn up and discover that everyone's laughing at them or giving them the finger instead of bowing down to worship them are a lot less likely to think they can cram the genie back into the bottle, and that has to be a good thing from our perspective. And I* do *like Nahrmahn's notion about the opening round if we decide a time's come when we* can *go after the inerrancy of the* Writ.

"It's going to dump a lot of responsibility on Ehdwyrd's shoulders," he said out loud, "and he's going to have to come up with some fancy footwork to convince his board and his fellow investors to let him more or less give away their technology."

"I'm sure he'll be up to the task," Nahrmahn said dryly. "And if he isn't, there's always Cayleb and Sharleyan. Or you could go stand behind him at the next board meeting and loom menacingly."

"I *do* do a nice 'ominous,' if I say so myself," Merlin conceded. "And Nynian's been helping me work on a proper curled lip."

"Has she really?" Nahrmahn looked the far taller *seijin* up and down. "I admire her willingness to tackle challenges. Especially when she's working with such . . . unprepossessing material."

MARCH YEAR OF GOD 901

✦

.I.
Tellesberg Palace,
City of Tellesberg,
Kingdom of Old Charis,
Empire of Charis.

"God, I hope this works out," Sharleyan Ahrmahk murmured fervently, standing beside her husband and gazing out a palace window into the steady, warm rain of Tellesberg.

"Sweetheart, we can still change our minds," Cayleb Ahrmahk replied. He wrapped one arm around her, hugging her tightly, and she leaned her head against his shoulder. "If you aren't on board with this, just say so."

"I can't. I can't!" Uncharacteristic uncertainty hazed Sharleyan's tone, but she shook her head firmly. "You're right about how much more effective he could be knowing the truth. I mean, Lord knows he's been pretty damned 'effective' already, but if he could access the SNARCs directly, tie his com into the net so we could discuss things in real time . . ." She shook her head again. "It's just that I've already lost Uncle Byrtrym, and he and Ruhsyl were always so close."

"I know, but Ruhsyl's also a lot more flexible than he was," Cayleb pointed out. "And there was never any doubt about his commitment during the Jihad."

"As far as reforming the Church, yes. And he's been wholehearted in supporting the Church of Charis, too. But this is going an awfully long step beyond that!"

"Sharley, stop." Cayleb kissed her forehead. "We can

always do this another time. Or not do it at all. We can just go ahead and have the family dinner we asked him to stop over for, then put him back aboard ship and send him on home to Cherayth. Or Maikelberg, anyway. And then we can think about it some more and brief him when we transfer the court back to Chisholm in June, if we decide we need to go ahead after all."

She looked up at him for a moment, but then she drew a deep breath and shook her head one more time.

"No. I've dithered about this for over two years already. If we don't bite the bullet and go ahead and do it, I'll go on dithering for the next twenty!"

"Only if you're sure," he said. "I've been pushing for this, and I know I have. But I want you to be sure you're on board with it because it's the right thing to do, not just because you know how in favor of it *I* am."

"Have I ever hesitated to disagree with you when I thought something was a bad idea?" she challenged with a familiar glint. He chuckled at the very thought and shook his head. "Well, I'm not hesitating because I think this is a bad idea. I'm hesitating because even *good* ideas can go wrong and because I love him so much. That's the real reason."

He put his other arm around her, capturing her in the circle of his embrace, and they leaned their foreheads together while the rain pattered steadily outside the window.

▼ ▼ ▼

"That was delicious," Ruhsyl Thairis, Duke Eastshare, said.

He sat back from the table with his snifter of after-dinner brandy and smiled at his hosts. Darkness had fallen, and the rain fell even harder than before. Outside the window overlooking the palace gardens the gas jet lamps burned like wet diamonds in the rain and a pleasant breeze—damp but gentle—fluttered the edges of the tablecloth.

"It certainly should've been," Cayleb replied with

a grin. "I made it clear enough heads would roll if it wasn't, anyway!"

"Oh, a paragon of ruthlessness if ever I met one!" Eastshare chuckled. "No wonder everyone's so terrified of you here in Tellesberg."

"Actually, I really can be ruthless, when I have to," Cayleb said, and Eastshare's eyebrows rose, because the emperor's tonc had turned unwontedly serious.

"I know you can," the duke said after a moment. "But I've never known you to be trivial about it. Admittedly, dinner isn't a trivial affair, but still—"

He shrugged, and Cayleb flickered a smile. But he also shook his head.

"I'm serious, Ruhsyl. And the truth is that Sharley and I didn't ask you to stop off in Tellesberg on your way home just because we wanted to have dinner with you. Oh, that would've been reason enough! And you saw how happy Alahnah was to see you. But the truth is, there's something we need to discuss."

"Of course." Eastshare set his brandy glass on the table and looked back and forth between his emperor and empress. "What is it?"

"This is going to be difficult, Ruhsyl," Sharleyan said. She reached out and took his hand in hers. "I'm afraid it's going to be painful, too. Not because of anything *you've* done," she added quickly as his eyes narrowed. "Cayleb and I couldn't possibly have a finer general or a better friend. But there's something we have to share with you, and I'm afraid it may be hard for you."

"Sharley," Eastshare said, covering their clasped hands with his free hand, "I can't imagine anything you could tell me or ask of me that I couldn't give you."

"I hope you still feel that way in about an hour, Your Grace," another voice said, and Eastshare looked over his shoulder to see that Merlin Athrawes had just entered the room. The tall *seijin* looked unusually sober this evening, and the duke cocked his head.

"Should I assume, then, that this is more *seijin* business, Merlin?"

"In a lot of ways, yes," Merlin replied. "But, actually, it starts well before the first *seijin* ever set foot on Safehold. In fact, it begins before the Day of Creation itself."

Eastshare's nostrils flared and he looked quickly back at Sharleyan. She only nodded, and he returned his gaze to Merlin. His brown eyes held Merlin's eyes of *seijin* blue for a long, steady second.

"That . . . sounds ominous," he said then. "On the other hand, I've never known you to lie to me. So why don't you get started?"

"Of course." Merlin dipped his head in a curiously formal little bow. Then he straightened and squared his broad shoulders.

"First," he began, "you have to know *why* there was a 'Day of Creation' here on Safehold at all. You see—"

▼ ▼ ▼

"You really mean it," an ashen-faced Ruhsyl Thairis said the better part of ninety minutes later. "You *really* mean it."

"Yes, we do, Ruhsyl," Sharleyan said softly. "And it's not just Merlin's word for it, either. Not just the 'coms' or the 'holograms.' Not even that." She waved at the fireplace poker Merlin had twisted into a pretzel in a casual demonstration of his "PICA's" superhuman strength. "We've been to 'Nimue's Cave.' We've seen it. And Merlin's used his 'technology' to save both our lives more than once. The proof is there, Ruhsyl. It truly is."

"No, Sharley." He shook his head, his voice sad, but there was no hesitation in his tone. "The *evidence* may be there, but not the proof."

"Ruhsyl—" Cayleb began, but Eastshare raised his hand, far more demandingly than he ever had to Cayleb Ahrmahk before, and shook his head again, harder.

"*Don't,* Cayleb." His tone was harder, flatter, than it had been. "I believe you're a good man. I believe— I've *always* believed—you love Sharleyan dearly, and that you're a man of honor, doing what you believe you must. But not this. *Never* this!"

"Ruhsyl, it's not—"

"Not one more word, Merlin! Or . . . Nimue. Or whoever—or *whatever*—the hell else you may be!" Eastshare snapped, glaring at the man who'd been his friend for years. "I *trusted* you. More than that, the people I *love* trusted you! Spare me any more lies, any more perversions!"

"Ruhsyl," tears gleamed in Sharleyan's eyes, "*no one's* lied to you, I swear it!"

"You haven't, and Cayleb hasn't," Eastshare grated, "but this demon sure as *Shan-wei* has!" He emphasized Shan-wei's name heavily and deliberately. "And he's lied to you, and he's lied to Maikel Staynair, and he's lied to the entire *world*! Can't you *see* that?"

"No, I can't," she told him. "Because he hasn't. I told you this would be hard, but it's the *truth*, Ruhsyl. It's nothing but the truth, and we've told you because we're so tired of *not* telling you. Because we owe you the truth."

"I believe that's exactly what you've done, but the fact that this . . . this *thing* has convinced you to believe its lies doesn't make a lie the truth and doesn't change blasphemy into something else."

"But the evidence is right here in front of your eyes," Sharleyan said pleadingly. She touched the twisted poker and stared into his eyes. "The proof is right here!"

"I don't see anything that one of Shan-wei's demons couldn't have produced!" Eastshare retorted. "And the *Writ* didn't call her 'Mother of Lies' for nothing! Am I supposed to believe that what he has to say and to show me here turns *nine centuries* of the truth into a lie? Oh, it's a *clever* lie, I'll give 'Nimue' that! But compared to the *Writ, The Testimonies,* every written word of history for nine hundred years, to the miracles that happen *every single day* in the Temple? Sharley, how could you and Cayleb fall for this? Have you forgotten what Chihiro said about Shan-wei? Forgotten how she deceived and seduced our entire world into evil?"

"But—"

"No." Eastshare's nostrils flared and he rose from his chair, facing Merlin with fiery eyes. "If *this* is what

Byrtrym had come to suspect, no wonder he joined forces with the Temple Loyalists." Tears glistened on his own cheeks. "And, God help me, if this is what he was trying to stop, Sharley, I wish to *God* he'd succeeded. I love you, but if this is what he was trying to stop, then at least you'd have died as one of God's own."

"I'm still one of God's own." Sharleyan's mouth quivered and her face was wet, but she raised her head and met his eyes without flinching when he darted another look at her. "I will *always* be God's own, Ruhsyl. And that's why I have *no choice* but to bring this world back to Him and away from the filthy lie Eric Langhorne and Adorée Bédard and Maruyama Chihiro told a thousand years ago!"

"*Listen* to yourself, Sharley!" Eastshare pled.

"I have listened, Ruhsyl," she said softly. "I've listened not just to Merlin, not just to Maikel, not just to Jeremiah Knowles and thousands upon *thousands* of years of recorded history from long before 'Creation' here. Not even just to Cayleb. I've listened to my own *heart,* my own soul. And you're right, if I'm wrong I've given myself to damnation and I'm leading this entire world into it right along with me. But I'm not wrong. And Merlin's no liar, no demon. And Pei Shan-wei was a good woman—not an archangel; a *woman*—who was murdered as the very first victim of the lie which has kept this entire world in chains for a thousand years."

"And you're not going to retreat one step from that, are you?" Eastshare's voice was quiet, and she shook her head. "No, of course you aren't," he said. "Because you're a brave woman, and—like Cayleb—a woman of *honor*. And of faith. And this is what you truly believe, but, oh, Sharley, you're so *wrong*. And I can only pray that in the end you fail. Because the thought of what this world will become if you succeed is more than I can stand."

Silence hovered against the backdrop of the pounding rain, and then Ruhsyl Thairis, Duke of Eastshare, looked back at Merlin Athrawes.

"I won't damn you to hell, because that's where you

came from in the first place," he said. "But I will tell you this. I will *never* bow my head or bend my knee to your foul mistress, and I curse the day I helped you defeat Zhaspahr Clyntahn. I know I'll face the price for that someday—someday very soon—but I know the truth now. So you go ahead and do what you have to do, because if you let me walk out that door alive, I will denounce you from the steps of Tellesberg Cathedral!"

"Of course you will," Merlin said sadly. "It takes a man of honor to know a man of honor, and I can't tell you how deeply I regret what I see in your eyes when you look at me now. I know you don't want to hear this, but I have always been—and I remain now, despite what you believe, what you think—honored by your friendship."

Eastshare's lips twisted, but he said nothing, only glared.

"Ruhsyl, we wouldn't have risked telling you this if our only option had been to kill you if you couldn't accept it," Merlin told him. "Sharleyan and Cayleb love you too much for that. *I* love you too much for that."

"It *is* the only option you have," Eastshare said flatly.

"No, it isn't." Merlin reached into his belt pouch and extracted a small, cylindrical rod of glittering crystal. "And someday, when the time comes, we'll have another conversation, you and I. Until that day, I can only say I respect and admire you as much as I've ever respected or admired another human being and I would give anything in the universe to not have to do this."

. II .
Tellesberg Cathedral,
City of Tellesberg,
Kingdom of Old Charis,
Empire of Charis,
and
Nimue's Cave,
The Mountains of Light,
Episcopate of St. Ehrnesteen,
The Temple Lands.

I am the resurrection and the life, says the Archangel Langhorne: he that believes in me, though he were dead, yet shall he live: and whosoever lives and believes in me and keeps the Law I have given, shall never die.

"'I know that the Archangels live, and that they shall stand at the latter day upon the world, and though this body be destroyed, yet shall I see God: whom I shall see for myself, and my eyes shall behold Him, and not as a stranger.

"'We brought nothing into this world, and it is certain we can carry nothing out. The Lord gave and the Lord has taken away: blessed be the name of the Lord and his servants, the Archangels.'"

Maikel Staynair's deep voice rolled out across the hushed pews of Tellesberg Cathedral in the ancient Office of the Dead. There was not another sound as the people of Tellesberg gathered to support their empress in the moment of her grief. Every man and woman in that cathedral knew how deeply Sharleyan Ahrmahk had loved her aunt's brother. And now, here in Charis, she'd lost both her uncle Byrtrym and his brother-in-law. And to lose him so suddenly, with so little warning, to a heart attack when he'd always been so healthy, so fit!

Small wonder she sat silent and white-faced in the imperial box, clinging to her husband's hand with one hand and crushing a tear-soaked handkerchief in the other.

"Hear now the words of Chihiro, from the second *Book of Chihiro,* in the third chapter," Staynair continued.

"'Out of the deep have I called unto you, O Lord; hear my voice. O let your ears consider well the voice of my complaint. If you, Lord, will be extreme to mark what is done amiss, O Lord, who may abide it? For there is mercy with you; therefore will you be feared. I look for the Lord; my soul waits for him; in his word is my trust. My soul flees on to the Lord before the morning watch; I say, before the morning watch. O Safehold, trust in the Lord, for with the Lord there is mercy, and with him is plenteous redemption. And he shall redeem Safehold from all the sins of the Fallen.'"

The archbishop looked up from the gem-encrusted volume before him and closed it gently. He gazed out across the cathedral, and his expression was sad despite the serenity of his own faith.

"My children," he said, "our brother Ruhsyl lived his life in fearless faith and worshipful obedience to the Law we have all been taught. He was, as I can tell you of my own sure and certain knowledge, a faithful servant of Langhorne and of God. I have never known a man of whose integrity, whose honesty and strength of spirit, I was more positive, and it has been one of the deep and abiding honors of my life to have known him and to have called him friend, as well as brother in God. We are gathered today not to mourn his death, but to celebrate his life, and so I ask you now to join with me, and with our beloved Empress, as we say farewell to the mortal shell of one who was, and is, and always will be alive in our hearts and a faithful servant unto God.

"Let us pray."

▼ ▼ ▼

Ruhsyl Thairis opened his eyes.

For a moment, he simply lay there on a padded surface that was almost unbelievably comfortable, staring up at a smooth, polished stone ceiling he'd never seen before. Then his nostrils flared, he inhaled deeply and explosively, and jerked into a sitting position on the bed.

"Hello, Ruhsyl," a voice he'd never heard before said, and his head whipped around and his eyes went wide as he saw a very tall woman—at least six inches taller than he was—in a black-and-gold uniform unlike any he'd ever seen before. He stared at her, and then his jaw clenched as he recognized those sapphire eyes.

"I know you believe 'Merlin' is a demon," the woman said in that same contralto, and as he listened to it he heard an eerie echo of Merlin's deep voice. "He's not. Neither am I. But this is who I was born to be, so if I'm going to tell you the truth and you'll ever believe me, I thought I should introduce you to Nimue."

"It doesn't change anything," he said harshly.

"Probably not." The woman smiled sadly. "But I have to try, Ruhsyl. I have to try because of how much Sharley and Cayleb love you and because of how much you mean to me. And because whether you believe me or not, everything I've told you is true and I know that you're a man who believes in the difference between truth and lies."

"You're right, I do. And that's why nothing you can say to me will change the truth I already know. I don't know why I'm still alive or why you've brought me to this place." He waved one hand in a choppy gesture. "I suppose this is the 'Nimue's Cave' the three of you were talking about."

"Yes, it is."

"Then I don't know why you've brought me here, because it won't make any difference in the end."

"Maybe not, but I've got to try."

The woman—Nimue Alban—stepped closer to him, and he made himself stand motionless, not shrinking away from her, as she pressed a button set into the wall. The entire end of the chamber disappeared and he found himself looking out over a vast cavern crowded with shapes and . . . *things* the likes of which he'd never seen before.

"These are the tools Shan-wei left me," she said steadily. "And if you genuinely think I'm a demon and if I can't convince you otherwise, then I'm sure you'll simply write them off as more of her 'demonic' inventions. But I'd like to show them to you, like to give you a chance to see what they truly are. And I'd like to open the archives to you, let you compare the written record of Safehold's history to the other records here in the Cave. You aren't the only person we've told about this who's had trouble accepting it, but most of them eventually recognized we'd told them only the truth and learned to handle it. I truly hope—wish—you can do the same."

"No," he said flatly.

"Ruhsyl, *please*." There were tears in her eyes, he realized, and despite himself he wavered before the pleading in her voice. "We love you. We *need* you. Just . . . just open your mind a tiny crack, to the *possibility* that we're telling you the truth."

"And the crack will become a leak, and the leak will become a torrent, and before I know it, my soul will've drowned in the tide of your lies, just like Sharleyan's and Cayleb's." He shook his head firmly, fiercely. "No. I'll *die* before I do that, Nimue or Merlin or whatever you are. Do your worst."

"That's what the lie you cling to does, Ruhsyl, not us!" For the first time those sapphire eyes flashed angrily. "We've *never* tortured, or maimed, or killed in God's name! Not like the lie you believe in!"

For an instant, he wavered, but then he stiffened his knees.

"No, you haven't. But then again, every single person who died in the Jihad died because of the war you started."

"*Bullshit!*" Nimue Alban snapped, her eyes glittering. "Whatever else you may believe, Ruhsyl, you *damned* well know better than that! Zhaspahr Clyntahn started that killing, those murders, long before anyone in Zion could possibly know a thing about me. All I did was prevent him from slaughtering his way clear across Charis and then, eventually, starting in on Chisholm because you didn't share his perverted view of what God wanted, either!"

"And how do I know how long you and Shan-wei have been working on this? Whether or not you're the ones who turned Clyntahn that direction in the first place?!" Eastshare demanded. There was a defensive edge in his voice—he heard it himself—but he shook his head angrily. "You say Clyntahn was already launched against Charis. Maybe that was because God had told him something the rest of us didn't know. I'm not defending Zhaspahr Clyntahn! The man was a monster. But even monsters can be used to do God's will."

"And God chose someone like Zhaspahr Clyntahn instead of someone like Merlin Athrawes . . . or Sharleyan Tayt Ahrmahk?" Nimue asked in a soft, deadly tone.

"It's not my job to tell God who to choose. It's my job to believe what He and His Archangels taught me as His Law! The fact that Zhaspahr Clyntahn and the Group of Four twisted Mother Church into something she wasn't supposed to be doesn't mean God gave you free rein to simply destroy Her forever! Cayleb and Sharleyan only wanted to repair what was wrong, the evil men had allowed to creep in. But *you!* You came along and twisted their devotion, their dedication to purging Mother Church, into something totally different."

"I'm sorry you feel that way," she said quietly. "I'm sorrier than I can ever say. But whatever you may think of me, whatever you may think of the truth I'm trying to tell you, I can't and I won't harm you, Ruhsyl. I'm sorry if you want to die a martyr, but I'm not much into making martyrs and, to be honest, I don't think God really wants any more of them. Even Zhaspahr Clyntahn's God has to've had a bellyful of that here on Safehold. So I will be *damned* if I give Him one more death than I absolutely have to, and I'll never give Him *yours.*"

"You don't have a choice." His voice was ribbed in iron. "I'll never change my mind, never renounce God and the Archangels. And I won't pretend otherwise. I *will* fight you, Merlin. Nimue. I'll fight you with every breath of my life. So sooner or later, you *will* have to kill me."

"No," she said. "I won't. I can't ever let you go home again—or not until we've settled accounts, one way or the other, with Langhorne and Bédard and their lies. I hate that, because I know how much Zhilyahn and Zohzet and Zohzef and Alahnah are all going to miss you. But I can't. That doesn't mean I have to kill you, though, and I won't. Even if Cayleb and Sharleyan would—and you know, deep inside, that they wouldn't agree to that in a million years if there was a single viable option—*I* won't. Me, the one you think is Shan-wei's own demon. I can't." She shook her head. "I've killed so many people, Ruhsyl. And a lot of them were *good* people, people who believed exactly what *you* believe, but if I hadn't killed them, other good people would have died . . . and the truth would have died with them. Nimue Alban died a thousand years ago to see that that never happened, and I won't let it. But I weep inside for every one of those people, and I won't—I will *not*—weep for you, Ruhsyl Thairis. Not that way."

He looked at her, and despite himself, despite his steel-spined faith, he sensed the sincerity in her voice. Yet—

"Maybe you really feel that way. And maybe I should encourage you to. But if you do, it will be the worst mistake you've ever made."

"We'll see." She smiled sadly. "Ultimately, the decision's up to you, but what I would prefer to do is to make you a . . . prisoner of state. We can keep you confined here in the Cave indefinitely, Thairis, and not in some filthy cell in a cellar somewhere. You'll be able to communicate freely with Cayleb and Sharleyan—any member of the inner circle, really—and you'll have complete freedom of Owl's library files. The one thing you won't be able to do is go home again, and unless we tell Zhilyahn the truth, you won't be able to speak to her or your children. And to be honest, we don't tell anyone unless we think we have to because every time we do, we put that person in the same position we've just put you in. So we think about it—*hard*—every time."

"No." He shook his head. "I believe that's what you want to do, and I'm not going to accept your offer. All I

have to do is look around me to see how hellishly convincing you and all of this 'Cave' of yours can be. Hell,
for all I know you *are* completely sincere! Maybe you're
not Shan-wei's knowing servant but her dupe. I don't
know about that. Listening to you, hearing you, you're
either the greatest actor ever born or telling the truth as
you know it. But it *isn't* the truth, Merlin, and I'm not
giving you the chance to dupe me, as well. No prisoners
of state, no libraries, no more 'convincing.' So you're going to have to do something else with me, and at least I
know that whatever else you are, you aren't Zhaspahr
Clyntahn. So I'm pretty sure it'll at least be quick."

He met her eyes fearlessly, and her nostrils flared.

"And that's your last word, isn't it?" she said sadly.
"*Damn* you, Ruhsyl! Why couldn't you have at least an
ounce of give in your integrity? Do you have any idea
how much *I'm* going to miss you?"

"I am who I am, and in the end, I am a son of Mother
Church," he said. "I can't—I won't—be anyone or anything else. Not for you. Not even for Sharley . . . or Zhilyahn and the kids. So get it over with."

"If you insist. But I'm still not going to kill you. I'm
not sure that wouldn't be kinder in the long run, but I
can't do that."

"Then do whatever it is you *are* going to do," he said
harshly. But then his voice gentled. "And tell Sharley she
has my love."

▼ ▼ ▼

"He wouldn't even listen?"

"No, Sharleyan," Merlin Athrawes replied over the
com. He could hear the tears in her voice, but there
wasn't any surprise. Not really. "You know Ruhsyl.
He'd made his decision."

"Oh, I *wish* he hadn't," she half whispered. "But then
he wouldn't have been the man he is, would he?"

"No."

Merlin stood with one hand on the bronze-sheened,
coffin-shaped cryo unit. It was featureless, aside from a
small panel of brightly lit LEDs.

"The procedure went smoothly?" Cayleb asked.

"Yes." Merlin patted the cryo unit. "And he never hesitated. I don't know if he really believed I wasn't going to kill him, but he looked me straight in the eye and said goodbye before the first injection. And he told me to tell you both that he loved you."

"Oh, Ruhsyl." This time the tears had escaped her voice, running down her cheeks while Cayleb's arms enfolded her. "Oh, Ruhsyl, I'm *so* sorry."

There was silence for a very long time, and then Cayleb cleared his throat.

"Will you be home in time for that council meeting tomorrow, Merlin?"

"No," Merlin said, and knew they could hear the unshed tears in his voice. "No. I'll be staying here to say goodbye to my friend for a little longer, Cayleb."

AUGUST YEAR OF GOD 903

·✦·

. I .
Show-wan Hills,
Tiegelkamp Province,
North Harchong.

The gunshot came with no warning.

It also didn't hit anything.

Captain of Swords Dauzhi Pauzho jerked fully erect in the saddle, his head snapping towards the sudden, explosive crack of sound. It took him a second to realize what it had been, but then he relaxed. Only slightly, of course. Since it had been a shot, it had to have come from someone in the column, and he damned well meant to find out how one of his troopers could have been careless—or stupid—enough to accidentally discharge his carbine. For that matter, why had the idiot even been playing around with it? Captain of Horse Nyangzhi was going to have someone's arse for it, and Pauzho fully intended for it to be someone else's!

But then his eyes narrowed. Gunpowder made Shanwei's own smoke—enough to guarantee it would be easy to identify the culprit. But where was it? Pauzho was near the head of the column. From his position, he could see almost half its length, despite the high road's twisty path through the Show-wan Hills. And in all that field of view, there wasn't a single puffball of smoke.

Maybe it hadn't been a shot after all?

His brow furrowed. That was certainly what it had *sounded* like. But—

His eyes rose from the roadway, sweeping the scrub wood of the steep slopes above the roadbed, and he stiffened. There *was* a smoke cloud, after all, but it was far up the hillside, at least eighty yards beyond the chest-high stone walls built to retain the loose scree that often slithered down those slopes during the spring thaws. What in Chihiro's name was one of their men doing scrambling around up there and accidentally discharging his weapon? There'd be hell to pay when Nyangzhi found out about that! And when he did, Pauzho hoped to Shan-wei he'd—

Dauzhi Pauzho never finished that thought. A flash of movement at the corner of his eye brought his gaze back down from the hillside just in time to see the first serf rise out of concealment less than sixty yards from him. The staff sling snapped around once, then released, and the sharp point of the three-ounce, ovoid sling bullet struck him just above the left eye with forty-five percent more velocity than a crossbow bolt.

His head snapped back in a grisly spray of red and gray and his horse reared as its rider was hurled abruptly from the saddle.

He was dead by the time he hit the ground, so he never saw the rest of the slingers—over a hundred of them—who'd come to their feet in response to the signal of that single shot. He never heard the screams as the lethal, whizzing bullets peasants and serfs weren't supposed to have smashed into the men of Captain of Horse Ruwahn Nyangzhi's column. He never saw the wave of other crudely armed serfs and peasants explode out of the retaining walls' concealment, vault across them, and sweep down across the column. Most of them had nothing better than converted agricultural implements, but however clumsy it might be, a straightened scythe blade at the end of an eight-foot shaft was as lethal as any sword ever forged.

The slingers had concentrated on the column's officers, not that it really mattered in the end. Surprise was total. The first warning the men on the flanks had was the sudden eruption of roughly dressed madmen screaming at the tops of their lungs, swinging clubs and threshing flails, stabbing with those horrible straightened scythes, thrusting with manure-encrusted pitch-forks. The serfs swarmed over them, bellowing their hate, dragging them from the saddle, beating them to death, cutting their throats.

The mounted men were professional soldiers, members of the Emperor's Spears, the elite branch of the Imperial Harchongese Army specifically dedicated to keeping the peace internally. That meant suppressing any serfs' pretension to be more than two-legged animals producing for their betters, and they'd done that job for years with brutal efficiency. In fact, they'd been kept home from the Mighty Host of God and the Archangels during the Jihad precisely because the Emperor—or, rather, his ministers—had realized how badly they'd need the Spears' bedrock reliability.

But they were accustomed to sporadic, spontaneous explosions, the desperate spasms of violence of men and women who'd been driven beyond the limit of what they could endure. Men and women who knew their resistance would be futile, that they and their families would be savagely punished for it, but who simply didn't *care* anymore. The Spears knew how to deal ruthlessly with uncoordinated, isolated outbreaks like that.

They had no clue how to deal with *this* one . . . and none of Captain of Horse Nyangzhi's men lived long enough to learn.

▼ ▼ ▼

"Didn't any of these stupid bastards ever even *hear* about watching your flanks?" Zhouhan Husan growled.

"Not so's anyone'd notice," Tangwyn Syngpu replied, slinging the Saint Kylmahn rifle which had fired the shot to signal the start of the attack as the two of them scrambled down from their perch above the roadway where nine hundred and two of the Emperor's Spears had just been slaughtered. From the sound of the screams, the remaining forty-three troopers would be a long, agonizing time joining their comrades, and Syngpu grimaced as he listened to the shrieks.

"Wouldn't've lasted five minutes on the Tarikah Line,"

Husan continued. The ex-corporal couldn't seem to decide whether he was more satisfied, contemptuous, or simply disgusted.

"Didn't seem to me they lasted a lot longer *here*," ex-Sergeant Syngpu observed. "Still, I'll give you that they didn't know their arse from their elbow. Just like the Captain of Foot said they wouldn't."

Husan grunted in acknowledgment as the two noncoms climbed over the retaining wall. Neither of them had been actual serfs—they'd been technically free peasants, not that there was much difference between the two, here in Harchong—and they were more focused on their command responsibilities than most of their followers. On the other hand, those followers were far more disciplined and well-trained than anything the Spears had ever before encountered, thanks in no small part to Husan and Syngpu's experience in the Mighty Host of God and the Archangels.

Some of that discipline showed as the six-limbed draft dragons harnessed to the four massive freight wagons stamped and tossed their heads. They were obviously anxious at the smell of blood and the screams of dying men, but the experienced drovers Syngpu had assigned to the wagons had already jogged over to them, begun murmuring to them in calming tones. They quieted quickly, although their eyes continued to roll, and Syngpu nodded in approval and relief. They needed those wagons, and that meant they needed the dragons, at least long enough to reach the crossroads five miles closer to Shang-mi, where the rest of the agricultural wagons and pack-dragons waited.

"Think we should stop them?" Husan asked as two officers who'd survived the initial massacre were dragged, twisting and fighting desperately, towards a knot of serfs gathered around eight nervous horses.

One of those officers wore a captain of horse's insignia, and Syngpu wondered if the column's commander had been stupid enough to let himself be taken alive.

"I remember something Allayn—Allayn Tahlbaht—said to me back when the Temple assigned its noncoms to the Host," Syngpu replied, never taking his pitiless eyes from the frantically struggling officers as they were hurled to the ground and ropes were tied to their wrists and ankles. "He said a really smart officer did two things. He always listened to his sergeants . . . and he never gave an order he knew wouldn't be obeyed." He hawked up a glob of phlegm and spat into the roadside drainage ditch. "'Pears to me this'd be a good time for you and me to pretend we're officers."

"I can live with that," Husan said grimly. Then he rested one hand on Syngpu's shoulder and squeezed briefly.

Husan's wife and two children had survived after he'd been conscripted for the Mighty Host. Syngpu's family had been less fortunate. His wife, their son, and his younger daughter had starved to death two winters ago, in the most recent famine to sweep Thomas Province. There was no way to prove they'd have survived the winter which had virtually wiped out their entire village if Syngpu had been there, but the sergeant would never know that. And he *did* know his seventeen-year-old daughter had lived only because she'd no *longer* been there. And that was because Earl Crimson Sky's eye had fallen upon her just after her fifteenth birthday. After he'd finished raping her for a month or two, he'd handed her over to one of his trusted barons, who'd been raping her ever since.

Syngpu hadn't learned about that—or about the rest of his family—for over five months after his wife's death. After all, who cared about letters to a peasant shepherd who'd been forbidden ever to return home, anyway? When he did learn, it had taken him another three and a half months to travel the fifteen hundred miles home on foot, evading the patrolling Spears charged with keeping desperate men like him from doing exactly that.

By the time he got there, his daughter had endured her second forced abortion. After all, what Harchongese noble needed a bastard half-peasant child to complicate the succession? Or a pregnancy to get in the way of his pleasure?

She was determined to keep her *third* child, though, whoever its father was, and neither Baron White Tree nor the Pasqualate monk who'd aborted Pauyin Syngpu's first two children would be around to prevent it.

Her father had seen to that.

Zhouhan Husan had known Syngpu for almost eight years now. The big sergeant was as tough as they came and only a fool tried to settle things with him physically, yet if there was a vicious bone in his body, Husan had never seen it. But he understood exactly why Tangwyn Syngpu felt no desire to intervene as the other ends of those ropes were tied to the saddle horns of the captured horses. For that matter, neither did Husan. It was one of the Spears' favorite "lessons" for serfs who got out of line, after all. If ripping parents' bodies apart in front of their children to encourage those children's better behavior was good enough for them, then he could indeed live with it when their turn came around.

Whips cracked, horses snorted, reared, and lunged forward, and the spread-eagled men shrieked as they were literally pulled—slowly and terribly—limb-from-limb while their cheering executioners jeered at their agony.

"Going to be ugly," he said quietly to Syngpu as the two of them climbed up into one of the freight wagons, and both men knew he was talking about far more than just this bloody day.

"Lot of that going around," Syngpu replied as he used a bayonet to pry the top off of one of the hundreds of long, heavy crates stacked in the thirty-ton wagon. The smell of lubricating grease rose to meet him and he smiled grimly.

"A lot of that going around," he repeated, gazing down into the crate, "and these beauties are about to make sure there's a lot *more* of it."

"It's all that bastard Rainbow Waters' fault!"

Lord of Foot Runzheng Zhou, Baron of Star Rising, suppressed a stillborn sigh before it ever touched his expression. He paused long enough to be sure it was staying suppressed, then glanced up from his conversation with Baron Blue River. Controlling reactions like that was second nature to anyone who wanted to survive long at the imperial court. It was a bit harder than usual this time, though.

"We should have called the fucking traitor home and made an example out of him and his entire family!" Earl White Fountain continued with a snarl. "And *he* should've told Maigwair to take a flying fuck!"

White Fountain's earldom lay in southeastern Tiegelkamp, and he'd been raging against Rainbow Waters for almost three years now, ever since three of his manors had been gutted by a serf insurrection. That particular outburst had been purely local and the Spears had suppressed it quickly, with all their customary, brutal finesse, but one of White Fountain's cousins and his wife had been caught by the serfs before the Spears could intervene. The cousin had at least died relatively quickly; his wife had been less fortunate as the serfs vented their hatred for all the generations of *their* wives and daughters who'd been casually raped by their betters.

Star Rising understood White Fountain's rage. He simply had zero sympathy for the man. He did feel a certain degree of compassion for White Fountain's cousin-in-law, but it was precisely White Fountain's sort of idiocy that had guaranteed the sporadic outbursts which had speckled the map of North Harchong ever since. There were times—a lot of them, and they'd been growing steadily more frequent since well before the Jihad—when Star Rising felt nothing but despair as he contemplated his fellow aristocrats' attitudes.

"He wouldn't have come," someone else pointed out to White Fountain. "Whatever else he may be, he wasn't *that* stupid! He knew damned well what would've happened to him."

"Then it should damned well happen to him where he is!" White Fountain snapped. "Are you telling me we don't have any assassins who could get to him even in Saint Cahnyr?"

I'm pretty sure that's been tried, Star Rising thought caustically. *Bit hard to get an assassin through to a man who's got several hundred fanatically devoted veterans watching his back, though. And more power to him!*

"I understand why you're upset, My Lord," a third courtier said. Star Rising couldn't remember his name, but the fellow was attached to Grand Duke North Wind Blowing's staff somehow. "And I deeply sympathize with your losses. But the Empire is huge, and there have always been some . . . unfortunate incidences of insurrection, even without any outside incendiaries. That's simply a fact of life, and it's one we've all learned to deal with. I agree it's past time something was done about Rainbow Waters, but it's not as if these scattered incidents pose any *significant* threat."

Several other voices muttered in agreement. There was, Star Rising noted, a certain lack of confidence in them.

"Well, I don't like what just happened to Captain of Horse Nyangzhi," someone else muttered. "That was less than fifty miles from the capital, for Chihiro's sake!"

"I know it was," North Wind Blowing's man said, and Star Rising frowned as he tried again to remember the idiot's name. "But the city guard has the situation well in hand here in Shang-mi; there haven't been any additional incidents in over a five-day; and if the rabble haven't taken to their heels and found deep, dark holes to hide in by the time Earl Winter Glory's column gets here *next* five-day, they'll learn a lesson they won't have *time* to forget!"

The mutter of agreement was louder and more fervent than before, and Star Rising shook his head ever so slightly.

"Do you think White Fountain has a point?" Blue River asked him very, very quietly, and Star Rising arched a thoughtful eyebrow.

His family had known the other man's for a long time and the two of them had always maintained a reasonably friendly relationship. That didn't mean as much as it might once have, though, and he rather regretted the headshake which had probably prompted Blue River's question.

"About Rainbow Waters?" he asked after a moment.

"White Fountain's had a bug up his arse about Rainbow Waters for *years* now," Blue River snorted. "I'm pretty sure he thinks Rainbow Waters is the reason Hsing-wu's Passage freezes every winter!" Star Rising's eyes widened ever so slightly at the searing contempt in the other baron's quiet voice. "No, what I'm worried about is whether or not he's right to be as scared shitless as he is about the other shoe."

Now that's an interesting insight, Star Rising thought. *And here I thought I was the only fellow at court smart enough to figure out just how scared White Fountain really is.*

"I don't know," he said out loud, equally quietly but rather more frankly than he'd intended. "I'm pretty sure Rainbow Waters isn't directly involved in any of this, though."

Blue River cocked his head with an air of polite skepticism, and Star Rising shrugged.

"Oh, he's got plenty of reason to be pissed off with North Wind Blowing and the rest of His Majesty's ministers. That's certainly true! But I've met the man. I think he's probably more sympathetic to the serfs than anybody here in Shang-mi. For that matter, after his time commanding the Mighty Host, I'm pretty sure he's a lot more sympathetic to them than he ever was before he left the Empire himself. But however true that might be, he knows as well as anyone—probably better, considering what he saw in the Temple Lands after the Sword of Schueler—just how ugly any general insurrection could get." Star Rising shook his head. "There's no way he'd knowingly contribute to something like that."

"All right," Blue River said after a moment. "I see your point. But the fact that White Fountain couldn't find his arse with both hands when it comes to figuring out who's behind it doesn't really address my original question. Do you think we *all* ought to be scared shitless?"

Star Rising looked at him levelly, considering very carefully. Then he shrugged mentally. He and Blue River *had* known one another a long time, so he nodded towards one of the many discreet alcoves which were always in quiet demand at any gathering at court.

The two of them stepped into it and Star Rising stood where he could keep an eye out for any curious ears that might wander into proximity.

"I don't know how scared we ought to be," he said then, softly, behind the cover of his fluted wineglass, "but we damned well ought to be *more* scared than North Wind Blowing or any of His Majesty's councilors are willing to admit."

"That's what I was afraid of," Blue River said equally quietly, "but I don't have any military background. How bad *is* it?"

"It's not like I've got decades of 'military experience' of my own," Star Rising snorted, lifting his left arm slightly. It ended just above the elbow. "I lost this and got invalided home less than six months after Rainbow Waters took over the Mighty Host." His lips twitched in a humorless smile. "Probably the best thing that ever happened to me, even if I didn't think so at the time! But I'll tell you this, the Spears don't have a clue how war's changed. And they aren't remotely as well equipped as they ought to be."

Blue River was an experienced courtier. His expression never changed, but his eyes were dark and worried, and Star Rising shrugged.

"Every rifle we managed to build during the Jihad—muzzleloaders and Saint Kylmahns alike—went to the Mighty Host. I think His Majesty's councilors managed to overlook that minor point when they convinced him to issue the decree against the Mighty Host's return."

Blue River nodded. Both of them knew precisely why North Wind Blowing, Waisu VI's first councilor, had issued that decree over the Emperor's signature, but Star Rising wondered if Blue River fully appreciated just how stupidly shortsighted it had been. From the look in his eyes, he probably did.

"Practically none of them, especially the Saint Kylmahns, were issued to the Spears or the other Army units retained at home," Star Rising continued. "And, to be honest, Duke Silver Meadow's acquisition programs since the Jihad have met with only . . . limited success."

This time Blue River's mouth twisted in bitter understanding, and Star Rising nodded ever so slightly. Mangchywan Zhyung, Duke Silver Meadow, Waisu VI's Minister of the Exchequer, was ostensibly in charge of the Empire's spending. In fact, Zyingfu Ywahn, who could claim only the modest title of First Permanent Underclerk, not only supervised the Empire's spending but formulated the policy for it. He was new in his job—he'd replaced Yang Zhyanchi in late 899 when Zhyanchi was fired as his nominal superiors' scapegoat for the ruinous state of the imperial treasury—but he'd been making up for lost time. His rapaciousness was almost as great as that of the aristocracy to which he would never be admitted, and vast sums which should have gone to reequipping the Harchongese Army had gone into his own pockets—and those of his aristocratic patrons—over the last four years.

"I have to say, that's what worries me the most," Star Rising said, although that wasn't strictly speaking true. What worried him the *most* was the reason the Army was likely to need all those weapons it didn't have. "And it's what makes these latest rumors especially . . . bothersome."

"What?" Blue River's eyes narrowed. "Why?"

Star Rising's eyebrows rose, then he took another precautionary glance out of the alcove. From his fellow baron's expression, he truly hadn't heard.

"I don't know if this is accurate," he said softly, "but if it is, I'm pretty damn sure that 'spontaneous attack' on Captain of Horse Nyangzhi's column was anything *but* spontaneous."

Blue River swallowed visibly. The capital had buzzed with rumors about the extermination of Nyangzhi's entire force—almost a thousand of the Emperor's Spears slaughtered to the man—for the last seven days, and the whispers about what had happened to Nyangzhi and his senior officers had been especially disquieting. But that obviously wasn't what Star Rising was talking about.

"From everything I've been able to turn up, the serfs had plenty of reason to want Nyangzhi dead," Star Rising continued, "but what he was doing when they caught up with him—according to my sources—was escorting a convoy to the capital from the Jai-hu manufactory. A convoy of *rifles*."

Blue River's jaw tightened. The city of Jai-hu, on the western flank of the Chiang-wu Mountains, was home to one of the relative handful of foundries which had been established in North Harchong during the Jihad. North Harchong's rivers and rugged terrain had never lent themselves to the sorts of canals which served most of Howard and both Havens. That was why the vast bulk of the Jihad's foundries and manufactories had been built in *South* Harchong, where the huge amounts of coke and iron ore they required could be freighted in by water and the weapons they produced could be freighted back out again. The transportation argument had been irrefutable, at least until the Imperial Charisian Navy cut all shipping routes across the Gulf of Dohlar, and even the imperial bureaucracy had had no choice but to bend to then-Treasurer Rhobair Duchairn and Captain General Maigwair's insistence that the foundries be built where they would be most efficient.

It was unfortunate that His Majesty's bureaucrats could collect such a smaller slice of graft off of contracts placed in South Harchong, but as the Grand Inquisitor had pointed out at the time, sometimes God's service required sacrifice. In the case of the imperial bureaucracy's pockets, that sacrifice had probably amounted to several million marks. Which had nothing at all to do with why all of the Army's current orders were being placed with the far smaller, far less efficient, far more *corrupt* manufactories in *North* Harchong, of course.

"How many rifles?" Blue River's voice was barely above a whisper, and Star Rising shrugged.

"That I don't know," he acknowledged. "But in fairness to North Wind Blowing and Ywahn, they have managed to substantially increase Jai-hu's capacity. I'd be surprised if it was less than several thousand."

Blue River paled, and Star Rising didn't blame him one bit if this was all coming at him cold. The thought of "several thousand" modern rifles in the hands of serfs ought to scare *any* aristocrat "shitless," he reflected.

"Langhorne," the other baron muttered, then moved so that he, too, could look out over the crowded chamber from Star Rising's side.

"I hadn't heard *that*," he murmured, "but it makes sense out of something I did overhear yesterday."

"What?" Star Rising asked, equally quietly.

"One of His Majesty's gentlemen-in-waiting was having a very quiet but . . . heated discussion with one of North Wind Blowing's people. I couldn't linger to hear all of it, of course. But apparently, His Majesty thinks this would be a good time for him and the entire imperial family to pay a long overdue state visit to Yu-kwau."

Their eyes met, and Star Rising grimaced. Yu-kwau was almost three thousand miles from Shang-mi as a wyvern might fly. It was also in South Harchong, where there'd been none of the unrest which had begun to flicker across North Harchong.

"North Wind Blowing's man assured him there was

no cause for alarm with Winter Glory on his way. From what you're saying, though. . . ."

"For all I know, he was absolutely right about that," Star Rising said. "On the other hand, he might be wrong, too."

"My family is visiting my wife's parents," Blue River said. "At Zhowlin."

Their eyes met. Zhowlin was one of Shang-mi's satellite summer vacation cities, thirty miles southeast of the capital on the Shang-mi–Suwhan High Road. Its city wall was rudimentary, little more than decorative, and it was surrounded by the estates of both the wealthy and the modestly well-to-do . . . which had no walls at all.

"If you have relatives in Boisseau, you might want to send them on a visit there," Star Rising said softly. "Unless you have relatives in the South, of course."

. III .
Shang-mi–Jai-hu High Road,
Mai-sun Forest,
Tiegelkamp Province,
North Harchong.

"Can you believe this *crap*," Lyangbau Saiyang snarled. The Earl of Winter Glory was not noted for his equable temper at the best of times, but his expression was savage as he thrust the message at Lord of Foot Chyang, his second in command.

Chyang took it a bit gingerly. Unlike Winter Glory's, Chyang's birth barely qualified him for inclusion in the Harchongese squirearchy. His family were small landholders in Stene Province, and there were times when he was acutely aware of his humble origins. Like the times when the Earl launched one of his tirades against their superiors. Not agreeing with Winter Glory was always a bad idea, but depending on who was listening, *agreeing* with one of his diatribes might be an even worse one.

The Lord of Foot unfolded the crumpled message and scanned it quickly, ignoring the totally blank expression of the mounted courier who'd delivered it. Then his nostrils flared, and he shook his head.

This time the Earl had a point.

"They're only getting around to telling us this *now*, My Lord?" he asked, looking up with an incredulous expression.

"You saw me open the dispatch!" Winter Glory half snapped, and Chyang nodded quickly. When the Earl was in one of his moods, rhetorical questions could go right past him.

"I'm sorry, My Lord. I meant to say they damned well should have told us sooner."

"Umph." Winter Glory scowled, but at least some of the irritation leached out of his expression. He snatched the message back and read it again, as if he hoped its contents could somehow become more palatable the second time around.

They didn't.

"It's probably the damned insurrectionists," he growled. "Bastards've been burning semaphore towers, I expect. For that matter, we've been out of contact with the chain for the last couple of days, anyway. Can't see crap with all these trees."

He waved irritably at the dense, unconsecrated forest stretching away on either hand. Aside from the high road's relatively narrow right-of-way, they were surrounded by a dense-growing, all but impenetrable sea of cone wood and northern oil tree. In fact, the right-of-way itself was much narrower and far more badly overgrown—not just with saplings, in all too many cases—than it ought to have been. Keeping the roadbed clear, especially of the fast-growing evergreen cone wood, was a nontrivial task, and in Chyang's opinion, this entire stretch was long overdue for another periodic logging back. For that matter, it was even farther overdue for consecration. Unfortunately, the terrain hereabout offered very little to incentivize the effort. Aside from the occasional hostel serving travelers to and from the capital, there weren't even any villages, since there was no agricultural land to support them. For that matter, there was already more farmland than anyone had serfs to work—especially after the Jihad's drafts had swept so many of those serfs off, never to return—and no one had the available labor to start logging off the unconsecrated trees. The local nobles were none too plump in the pocket, so they restricted themselves to the bare minimum of maintenance the *Holy Writ* required—and skimped even on *that,* if their local clergy let them get away with it—while they pinched their marks towards other ends.

"I don't suppose the delay's going to matter much, anyway," Winter Glory continued. "Not in the short term. We're only three days from the capital now, and it doesn't change anything about *our* situation. But not having Nyangzhi waiting for us when we get there. . . . *That's* going to be a royal pain in the arse."

"If you'll forgive me, My Lord, I'd call that a bit of an understatement," Chyang said, still grappling with the news himself. "But it happened a full *five-day* ago. That's what I can't get over. They could've gotten a post rider to us three days ago even if every tower in the semaphore chain is down!"

"The only thing that would surprise *me* would be to discover there really is someone in the capital who doesn't have his head squarely up his arse." Winter Glory handed the message to one of his aides. "File this piece of shit somewhere."

"Yes, My Lord! At once!"

Chyang watched with a certain amusement as the aide took advantage of the opportunity to remove himself from the Earl's presence.

"It's all part of the same kind of thinking that's fucked up everything else for the last six or seven years," Winter Glory went on, glowering at the deeply shaded high road as they rode along. "First sending every frigging rifle, artillery piece, and bayonet to that idiot Rainbow Waters just so he could *lose* them to the Shan-wei damned heretics. Then not dragging him home to Answer for the way he bungled the Jihad. So now everybody's playing catch-up, trying to make up for all the time we've lost. And what are *we* armed with? Arbalests and matchlocks, *that's* what we're armed with. Except, of course, for the fifteen *thousand* rifles that were supposed to be waiting for us at Shang-mi. Langhorne only knows how long it's going to take to put together another shipment that size!"

"Agreed, My Lord," Chyang said. He hesitated a moment, then cleared his throat. "I can't say I'm very happy about the possibility of serfs getting their hands on that many Saint Kylmahns, either," he said in a carefully neutral tone.

"I'm not doing any handsprings of joy over it, myself," Winter Glory growled. "On the other hand, they're *serfs*, Dzhungnan. Stupid bastards probably haven't even figured out which end the bullet comes out of yet! Even if they have, it'll take them a while to figure out anything *else* about how to use them." He shook his head. "Like I said, we're only three days from the capital now and at least the idiots-that-be haven't managed to lose any *artillery* to them yet! We've got plenty of time to get there, and rifles or no rifles, our men will do just fine from behind the walls with arbalests."

Chyang nodded, keeping his expression merely thoughtful, and hoped to hell the Earl was right about that.

▼ ▼ ▼

"Smell that, Sir?" Sergeant Mangzhin Pau said suddenly.

"Smell what?" Captain of Spears Sywangwan Zhu-chi asked, lowering the sausage he'd been gnawing on as they rode along in the cool shadows of the forest on either side of the high road.

"Dunno, Sir," Sergeant Pau frowned. "Smells almost like . . . smoke?"

Zhu-chi sat suddenly straighter in his saddle. His platoon was point for the entire column, and if the sergeant *was* smelling smoke, then it was coming to them on the wind out of the west . . . directly into their faces.

He looked around, and the cool shade was suddenly far less welcome than it had been.

"Send a scout ahead," he said.

▼ ▼ ▼

Corporal Hangdau Yungdan cantered briskly along the high road. At twenty-eight, he considered himself fortunate to have avoided assignment to the Mighty Host. He'd been only twenty when the first wave of the Mighty Host was hastily conscripted, and the Emperor's Spears had been forced to give up almost a third of their total manpower. The Spears hadn't liked that, and they'd opted to keep their more senior and experienced personnel close to home. That meant most of the troopers Yungdan's age had wound up in the Republic of Siddarmark, and precious few of them had come home again.

At the moment, his good fortune in that respect was rather secondary to his thinking, because he'd come to the conclusion Sergeant Pau had been right. At first, he'd been able to tell himself the sergeant was imagining things, although he couldn't remember the last time Sergeant Pau had allowed his imagination to run away with him. Still, *he* hadn't smelled any smoke. Not at first.

But as he'd moved ahead of the column, he'd begun to catch whiffs of something that certainly *could* be smoke, and now there was a fine haze of it drifting eastward, right into his face on a slowly but steadily strengthening wind. His horse knew it, too. It was snorting and tossing its head, obviously uneasy, and Yungdan reached down to pat it reassuringly on the shoulder.

He'd have felt better if someone had been reassuring *him*.

And then he rounded the bend and drew his mount to an abrupt halt.

He sat for a moment, staring into the abruptly denser, thicker wall of smoke, and fear was a sudden, icy boulder in his belly. He looked at that arc of flame, still distant enough that he saw it like the bowels of hell through the pickets of green treetops and branches, and swallowed hard. It stretched as far as he could see on either side of the high road . . . and it was coming for him.

▼ ▼ ▼

"Sweet Langhorne."

Earl Winter Glory stared at the hastily scrawled note the rider on the sweat-lathered horse had just handed him. Then he lowered it, passed it across to Lord of Foot Chyang, and turned in his saddle, staring up and down as much of the column as he could see. There were fifteen thousand troopers in that column. Along with its transport elements, it was over six miles long.

Chyang finished reading the dispatch and looked up, his face ashen.

"Get a courier off to Captain of Horse Tugpang!" Winter Glory snapped. "He's to stop, turn around, and immediately begin moving east at his best possible speed. He's authorized to abandon any of his baggage train if it slows him down, as long as he keeps the roadbed clear when he does. Then I want additional couriers to every regimental commander in the column. They're to halt in place immediately and turn back east as soon as the formation to *their* east stops and begins moving that direction!"

"Yes, My Lord! Immediately!" Chyang replied and began snapping orders of his own.

Winter Glory left him to it. He nodded to his immediate bodyguard and started cantering east himself. He needed to get closer to what was about to become the head of his column if he was going to control it.

At least a little of his initial panic—and that was what it had been, he acknowledged—began to ease as he considered his situation. There was no time to waste, that was certain, and the flames might very well overtake what had been his vanguard. That would be ugly. Winter Glory himself had grown up on the high northern plains of Maddox. He'd never actually seen a forest fire, but he'd seen plenty of bonfires. He knew how quickly seasoned cone wood and oil tree took fire, and he strongly doubted that *green* cone wood, with all of its waxy, resinous needles still attached, caught fire any more slowly . . . or burned with any less ferocity. For that matter, the oil trees' pods were ripe and swollen with their fiercely combustible oil.

There's time, he told himself firmly. *There has to be time. Maybe you're going to lose some of the men, and a lot's going to depend on how well the horses hold up to this when we really start to run for it. Probably have to abandon the draft dragons, for that matter. But if you can get them moving, surely you can save* most *of them!*

The courier to Tugpang went past him at a dead gallop, thundering along the verge of the high road, and the earl sprigged his own mount to a brisker pace.

▼ ▼ ▼

"'Bout time, I guess," Tangwyn Syngpu said, snapping shut the pocket watch Captain of Foot Giaupan had given him when he'd realized he couldn't keep his regiment's sergeant major from going home despite the emperor's ban. Syngpu knew Giaupan had been torn, that a part of him had wanted to go with the sergeant with whom he'd shared so much. But the captain of foot had sworn to abide by the ban . . . which hadn't kept him from giving Syngpu a lot of very sound advice. Including the need to coordinate things carefully . . . and keep even complicated operations as brutally simple as possible.

Now the ex-sergeant stood in the welcome cool of the forest's dense shade. The sky immediately above the high road was a brilliant blue canopy, dusted with distant white clouds, and there'd been no rain in five-days. The trees were dry as tinder, he thought, and shivered somewhere deep inside at his own choice of simile.

He couldn't smell any smoke yet, but he knew what had happened twelve miles to the west, where the only other watch they had showed the same time his did. And now it was his turn.

"Light 'em up," he said harshly, and Zhouhan Husan

struck one of the Shan-wei's candles on his belt buckle and lit the torch. Twenty yards away, another serf did the same thing. And twenty yards beyond him, another—and another. The chain of blazing torches spread out, racing away from the high road in either direction, and then Husan thrust his into the cone wood to the north of the high road while Syngpu did the same to the south.

Within less than ten minutes, a wall of fire four miles long blazed directly across the high road. The wind pushed it to the east, but not strongly enough to prevent it from creeping *west*, as well, and the vengeful serfs who'd ignited that holocaust took to their heels, racing to the horses they'd captured from Captain of Horse Nyangzhi.

The Shokan River was too shallow over most of its length to be navigable for anything much larger than canoes or rowboats, but it was broad, especially where it cut across the high road in the middle of the Mai-sun. It should provide an ample firebreak, once they got across it, Syngpu thought.

And unlike Earl Winter Glory's column, there would be no fire blazing across their path when they tried to.

. IV .
Zhynkau-Ti-Shan High Road,
Boisseau Province,
North Harchong.

Kanzheng Gwanzhi's right hand flew up in a sudden, imperative gesture.

Baron Star Rising had been riding lost in his thoughts, but the movement of his senior armsman's hand snatched him out of his reverie. He stiffened in the saddle, more aware than usual of his missing left hand as he drew rein. Fortunately, his mount was well trained. When he released the reins and let them fall on the horse's neck, it stopped instantly and its ears pricked as it waited for him to guide it by the pressure of knees and heels alone.

Most Harchongese warhorses had received similar training, but there was a reason South Wind had been particularly well schooled. It left the baron's remaining hand free for the double-barreled pistols in his saddle holsters.

Gwanzhi glanced at the much younger man riding to Star Rising's right, who looked a great deal like the armsman. Now Gwanzhi flicked a gesture that sent his son, Kanzheng, still farther to the right and twenty yards behind Star Rising. The third member of the baron's personal guard dropped back and to the left, and Gwanzhi touched a heel to his own horse and moved to Star Rising's side.

"What?" the baron asked quietly.

"Not sure, My Lord," Gwanzhi replied without a flicker of expression. The armsman took particular pride in his unflappable demeanor. That didn't mean there was anything slow about his mental processes, as Star Rising knew better than most. "But I heard something from behind," he added.

Star Rising's eyebrows began to rise, but then they lowered as he, too, heard the beat of galloping hooves. A moment later, a single rider thundered around the bend behind them, head down and riding hard.

The baron and his retainers were well to one side of the broad roadway, and the rider was on the broad swath of turf that paralleled the high road, reserved for imperial post-riders. Star Rising felt himself relax—a little—as he recognized the horseman's distinctive uniform, but then the rider looked up, saw him, and brought his mount to a slithering, sweating stop.

"My Lord Star Rising!" he gasped. "Thank Langhorne I've found you!"

Star Rising stiffened and glanced quickly at Gwanzhi. The armsman looked back with his usual lack of expression, but the sudden darkness in his eyes belied his calm. He shrugged his chain mail-armored shoulders ever so slightly, and the baron turned back to the post-rider.

"Why?" he asked.

"I have dispatches for you," the man said, and for the first time Star Rising truly realized how exhausted he was. He couldn't have been much older than Star Rising's own older son, Laiouzhyn, but the strain and fatigue in his face made him look far closer to Gwanzhi's forty-plus years as he unbuckled his dispatch case.

He extracted three envelopes and handed them across, and Star Rising glanced at them. The biggest—and least smudged—was addressed to him from Captain of Horse Hauzhwo Zhanma, the commander of the Zhynkau city guard. A second was simply addressed to him, with no sender noted, but bore the wax seal of an imperial dispatch. The third bore only his hastily scrawled name above an all but illegible signature that looked elusively familiar. It took him several seconds to realize it was Baron Blue River's.

He looked down at all three of them for a long moment, and then—moved by an impulse he couldn't have explained even to himself—handed the other two to Gwanzhi while he opened the one from Blue River with his remaining hand.

It was a very short note.

"I owe you my family's lives."

That was all it said, but an icy chill went through Star Rising as those words sank home. Then he looked up at the exhausted post-rider.

"I'm sure there's a lot of information in your dispatches, Captain of Bows, and I'll read them all," he said. "But I'm also sure Captain of Horse Zhanma told you why he wanted you to ride your horse half to death catching up with me. So now tell *me* why he did."

"My Lord, the dispatches—"

"I said tell me," Star Rising said flatly, and the younger man swallowed hard.

"My Lord, I'm not sure about the imperial dispatch. From what Captain of Horse Zhanma said, though, I expect it's an order to proceed home and begin arming and organizing Ti-Shan's garrison."

Something in his tone tightened Star Rising's stomach.

"Why?" he asked, and the young officer swallowed again.

"My Lord," he said, like a man who'd just heard his arm had to be amputated, "the serfs . . . the serfs have stormed Shang-mi. Most of the city was in flames when the galley that carried word to Zhynkau left."

The baron heard the unflappable Gwanzhi inhale suddenly, almost explosively. He was surprised that he himself felt so *little* surprise. Perhaps it was simply the anesthesia of shock.

"How?" he asked.

"I'm not sure, My Lord. The dispatch may tell you more. All the crew of the galley could tell us was that somehow a group of rifle-armed serfs stormed West Gate. They got inside—no one knows exactly how—and the street fighting began. The galley captain says he thinks the guard might have contained the attack if the dockside labor gangs hadn't rioted. From there, it spread. It sounds like . . . it sounds like a lot of the other labor gangs joined in, and then the street rabble started burning and looting."

Star Rising's expression tightened. The labor gangs were serfs—in some cases, outright slaves—whose owners rented them to businesses and individuals in Shang-mi who needed cheap labor. In most cases, they were "troublemakers" whose owners were relieved to pack them off, get them away from the estates where they might contribute to unrest. That meant they didn't really want them back, so they weren't going to complain very loudly about anything their renters might do with them.

And it also means far too many of the most bitter, hopeless "troublemakers" in the entire Empire are concentrated in one place, he thought grimly. *No wonder they rioted as soon as they had the chance!*

As for the captain of bows' "street rabble," that probably described better than half of Shang-mi's total population. The wretched, poverty-stricken inhabitants of the capital's tenement stews, hidden away in all their squalor behind the magnificent façades of aristocratic palaces and mansions that fronted the city's broad avenues. The people who never knew if they'd survive the next winter, how they'd clothe their children. Who worked their fingers to the bone for whatever wretched pittance they could earn because it was that or starve.

And who all too often starved, anyway.

"The captain couldn't tell us who actually started the fires, My Lord," the post-rider continued. "He *thinks* they started in the warehouses around the southern docks, but he's not sure. What he *is* sure of—" he braced himself visibly "—is that they spread rapidly. And that the Palace was heavily afire before his galley left the harbor."

"*Shan-wei,*" Gwanzhi muttered at Star Rising's elbow. The baron doubted he even realized he'd spoken.

"And His Majesty?" he heard someone else ask with his own voice.

"We . . . don't know," the captain of bows admitted wretchedly, but something in his tone made Star Rising look at him very sharply. The younger man looked away.

"Tell me," the baron commanded.

"My Lord," the captain of bows looked back at him, and his eyes glistened with what might have been unshed tears, "we *don't* know. But . . . but the galley captain says he heard that . . . that His Majesty's carriage and its escort never reached the galleon waiting for him."

Star Rising felt as if someone had just punched him in the belly.

"What about Earl Winter Glory? Where was *he* while all this was happening?!"

"My Lord, we don't know. He never reached Shang-mi."

"*What?!*" Star Rising stared at him. "He had *fifteen thousand* men! What do you mean 'he never reached Shang-mi'?!"

"*None* of his men reached the city, My Lord. We . . . don't know why."

It was Star Rising's turn to suck in a shocked, disbelieving draft of air. He sat staring at the white-faced young rider for several seconds, then shook himself.

"I see why Captain of Horse Zhanma sent you after me," he said. "What are your instructions now that you've found me?"

"My Lord, I'm at your service for the immediate future. I'm to accompany you the rest of the way to Ti-Shan, wait until you've read all of your dispatches and consulted with the mayor and the garrison commander, and then take your written response back to Zhynkau. If . . . if there's still no word of His Majesty, Captain of Horse Zhanma and Mayor Zhengtu will send their own reports to . . . to Yu-kwau."

Star Rising nodded in acknowledgment of what the captain of bows hadn't said. Emperor Waisu might still have been in the capital, but Crown Prince Zhyou-Zhwo and the rest of the imperial family had taken that "vacation trip" south after all. And if the worst had happened, he was no longer *Crown Prince* Zhyou-Zhwo.

"I understand, Captain of Bows," he said. "In that case, I think you'd better join us. We'll get you a fresh mount at the next posting station. For that matter," he looked at Gwanzhi, "we may requisition fresh mounts for *all* of us."

. V .
The Temple,
City of Zion,
The Temple Lands.

"How much of this is confirmed?" Grand Vicar Rhobair II asked, looking around the table in the quiet comfort of a council chamber that was rather less luxurious than it once had been.

"Almost all of it, I'm afraid," Vicar Allayn Maigwair replied heavily. The Captain General of Mother Church was six years younger than the Grand Vicar. He looked older, however. The last thirteen years had been less than kind to him.

"We know what happened to Winter Glory, at any rate," Maigwair continued with the grim expression of a man who'd seen—and been responsible for—far more carnage than he'd ever wanted to. "It was . . . ugly, Holiness."

In private, it remained "Rhobair" and "Allayn." In official settings or in front of others, Maigwair was always careful to observe every point of formal etiquette. As he'd said to the man who'd been Rhobair Duchairn on the day of his formal elevation to Grand Vicar, "The last thing we need is anyone wondering whether or not you're the one in charge, and you damned well *are* . . . praise God and all the Archangels!"

There were times—many of them—when Rhobair II wished with all his heart that he wasn't. It looked like this was going to be another of them.

"Tell me," he said, and Maigwair's nostrils flared.

"They caught his entire column in the middle of the Mai-sun Forest, Holiness. If I had to guess, he didn't have scouts out on his flanks. The terrain's incredibly constricted, and it would have slowed him down when he was under orders to reach Shang-mi as quickly as possible. Besides, he was a Spear, not a regular. I doubt it would even have occurred to him to worry about a bunch of 'rabble' attacking *him,* no matter what the terrain was like.

"Anyway, they must have surprised him completely. They set the woods on fire in front of him and the wind was in his face. Then they set the woods on fire *behind* him, as well." Rhobair's face tightened, and Maigwair continued in the same flat tone. "There was nowhere they could go. Fifteen thousand men, not counting their supply echelon, caught strung out on the high road in the middle of a roaring forest fire. None of them got out."

"None, Allayn?" Vicar Zherohmy Awstyn asked. Awstyn was young—ten years younger than Maigwair. Then again, a lot of Rhobair's vicars were young.

"If they did, the rebels finished them off," Maigwair said grimly. "To be honest, though, I doubt any of them did." He shook his head. "No, they were all burned to death, Zherohmy. Unless they were fortunate enough to die of smoke inhalation first. Or shot themselves or cut their own throats."

His voice was harsh, his eyes haunted. Every man sitting around that table had seen far too many people burned to death by Zhaspahr Clyntahn and his inquisitors. When Rhobair looked around their faces, his own guilt for letting that go on so long looked back at him from behind their eyes, as well.

"Do we know how they managed that?" Vicar Tymythy Symkyn, the man who'd become Rhobair's Chancellor, asked. Maigwair looked at him, and the Chancellor shrugged. "The timing, I mean. How did serfs separated by so much distance—what? Five miles? Ten miles? How did they . . . coordinate, I guess, so well." He shook his head. "That sounds a lot more *sophisticated,* for want of a better word, than anything we've seen out of Harchong since the Jihad."

He spoke from a certain personal experience, and in more ways than one, Maigwair thought. He'd served as Rhobair's representative to Shang-mi for two years before being recalled to assume the chancellorship after old Vicar Raiyn's death. And like the Grand Vicar himself, Tymythy Symkyn was a Chihirite. But whereas Rhobair Duchairn was a Brother of the Quill, Symkyn was a Brother of the Sword. Like Maigwair, he'd been a soldier, not a clerk. In fact, he'd served under Archbishop Militant Gustyv Walkyr during some of the most desperate fighting of the Jihad's final campaign. That meant he'd had the chance not simply to see the corruption and arrogance of the present court, but also the results of Earl Rainbow Waters' decision to turn the serfs under his command into effective soldiers. And *that* meant—

"I see where you're going, Tymythy," the Captain General said. "And you're right, 'sophisticated' is exactly the right word, at least where the timing's concerned. I think burning fifteen thousand men to death is about as *un*sophisticated as a tactic comes, but getting both sets of fires lit in the right window of time took some forethought. They certainly weren't in direct communication with one another across that many miles of woods. I've never been there myself, but some of the officers I've talked to tell me the Mai-sun is even worse than the Kyplyngyr or the Tarikah, and with a lot more oil trees. That's what made the damned fire so effective—and so *hot*. It was like soaking the entire forest in lamp oil and then dropping one of the Charisians' candles into it. But if you're suggesting Rainbow Waters was involved in this, I'm positive he wasn't. This is the *last* thing he'd be trying to do."

"Which doesn't mean some of his ex-officers and men weren't involved," Awstyn pointed out. Maigwair looked at him, and he shrugged. "I've been in close contact with the Earl, Allayn, and I'm sure you're right about *him*. But as much as all of his veterans respect him, no one could possibly expect them not to be looking for ways to go home. Or at least to rescue their families, for Langhorne's sake!"

Rhobair nodded. Awstyn was one of Symkyn's senior deputies, included in this conference because he was the vicar responsible for Mother Church's contacts with the two million—*two million*—Harchongians who'd been summarily denied the right to return to their own homes, their own families. Men who'd fought their hearts out for Mother Church and then been told they could never come home again lest they *contaminate* their fellow peasants and serfs with all those dangerous, radical notions they'd absorbed when they were treated as human beings in a foreign land.

Of all the many atrocities which had resulted from the Jihad, all the crimes he had yet to expiate, that one weighed upon him even more heavily than most, because he and Allayn Maigwair were directly responsible for the training which had turned the Mighty Host of God and the Archangels into the most effective military force Mother Church had. *They* were the ones who'd convinced Zhaspahr Clyntahn to support the very measures which had made the Mighty Host too dangerous for Waisu VI's ministers to ever let it come home. And, despite all his own power as the Grand Vicar of Mother

Church, God and Langhorne's deputy on Safehold, he'd been unable to shift that bedrock intransigence a single inch.

It's not like you didn't see this coming, Rhobair, he told himself drearily. *The idiots—the* idiots!*—can't even* consider *any response but to double down. To actually ramp up their brutality any time the serfs even* look *like they're getting "uppity," and the* Church *is supporting them! My God, those poor people think* I *support what's happening to them!*

His eyes burned, and he thought again about the decision he'd made when Waisu issued his decree. Maigwair had argued against it, and maybe he should have listened. If Mother Church had supported Rainbow Waters, launched him and that superbly trained Mighty Host into Harchong as an avenging, liberating army, nothing in the Empire could have stood up to him. It was simply impossible to conceive of the Emperor's Spears lasting a single summer against Rainbow Waters' veterans, especially with the downsized but still potent Army of God in support.

But if he'd done that it would have tainted his efforts to bind up all of the Jihad's other wounds. He would have ended the Jihad against the Church of Charis and Mother Church's own Reformists only to inaugurate a fresh *civil* war against the recalcitrant Harchongese church. He'd told himself he couldn't do that, not when so many millions had already died. And, he knew, he'd told himself that because he'd realized exactly how a war like that, even under a commander like Rainbow Waters, must engender a million fresh atrocities as the serfs who'd been abused, tormented, and brutally oppressed for so many generations took vengeance upon the ones who'd done that to them. There was no point pretending human nature could have allowed any other outcome.

And is it going to be any better this *way, Rhobair?* he asked himself bitterly. *Fifteen* thousand *human beings burned to death in a single afternoon. And if the reports coming out of Shang-mi are anything like accurate, two-*

thirds of the capital's gone up in flames all its own! And in the middle of all that, do you really think the rioters and the serf "army" that took the city didn't slake its appetite for blood and rape just as horribly as anything you could possibly imagine?

"You were right, Allayn," he said. "Four years ago, you were right."

"Maybe I was," Maigwair said, but he also shook his head. "On the other hand, so were you, Holiness. I wouldn't want to say anything about the Grand Vicar's infallibility when he speaks from Langhorne's Throne," the Captain General actually managed a smile, "but if we'd armed and supported Rainbow Waters and sent him home—and that's assuming he'd have been *willing* to invade his own homeland, which he probably wouldn't have been—this is exactly what would've happened anyway. Oh, not where his own troops or ours were concerned," he said quickly, waving one hand as Rhobair opened his mouth. "He'd never have allowed it, and neither would our men! But out in front of him, as he advanced, do you really think the serfs who heard he was coming wouldn't have done exactly what these people are doing? Langhorne, Holiness! Who *wouldn't* do what they're doing after the way they've been treated?"

"Vicar Allayn has a point, Holiness," Symkyn said, and there was a note of personal experience in his voice. The experience of Bishop Militant Tymythy, not Vicar Tymythy.

"And I'm pretty sure Zherohmy's right about where these people's 'sophistication' comes from," he continued. "There were over two million men in the Mighty Host. There's no way under God's sun Rainbow Waters could keep tabs on all of them, even if he'd tried. And if only a couple of thousand—even only a couple of *hundred*—of them got past the Spears, found men and women desperate enough to listen to them, that could explain everything we've heard so far."

"Exactly, Holiness," Awstyn said. His voice was firm, but his expression was oddly gentle. "I know you still blame yourself for it," he continued, "but you didn't have any good options. All you had were bad and worse."

"I know," Rhobair sighed. "I know."

And he did know. That was why, despite Mother Church's ravaged exchequer, he'd insisted she had a moral and religious responsibility to see to it that her two million marooned defenders were cared for. He'd paid their salaries, somehow, for over half a year, and then he'd settled them on largely empty land in the western episcopates. They'd had to clear and consecrate much of that land, but the vast majority of Rainbow Waters' veterans had been born serfs. They'd never owned *anything*, not even themselves, and the ferocity with which they'd attacked the task that would let them become *landowners*, on however small a scale, had been staggering to behold.

One thing he had held out for, though. If Waisu and his ministers—and his archbishops—refused to allow the Mighty Host's return, then any of the Host's officers' families who wanted to join them in the Temple Lands must be allowed to do so. He'd sent Maigwair to make that point clear in person, and the Captain General had summoned Waisu's ambassador to his office and flatly informed him that if those officers' families were *not* allowed to join them, Mother Church would arm, supply, and support the Mighty Host when it came to get them.

Rhobair had meant it. In fact, he'd longed to make that an across-the-board demand, for the noncommissioned officers and the men in the ranks, but he'd known he couldn't push that far. Not unless he really did want to invade. Waisu would let the officers' families go, if that was what they wanted. After all, then he could expropriate their lands for the Crown or distribute them to new, more reliable favorites. But that was as far as he would go. Letting millions upon millions of serfs flee the land to join their husbands and brothers and fathers and sons in the Temple Lands' freedom would have decimated his labor force . . . and left the still greater number of serfs who *couldn't* flee even more embittered and restive. Waisu would let him have the officers' families; if he'd wanted more, he'd have had no choice but to unleash the Mighty Host, and he'd settled for the best he could get.

"All right," he said finally. "I think it's obvious our worst fears are about to be realized. So, what can we do about it?"

"I don't think there's a lot we *can* do, unfortunately, Holiness," Symkyn said. "We could always send money and supplies to the archbishops, but you and I both know where that money and those supplies would end up."

Rhobair grimaced unhappily. The Harchongese clergy had officially accepted him as Grand Vicar Erek's legitimate successor after Erek's "spontaneous" abdication, but they'd stubbornly resisted all of his efforts to reform Mother Church's abuses. They'd been careful to avoid statements of outright defiance, but Harchongese bureaucrats—and, it seemed, prelates—had no peers when it came to obstructionism. Every one of his reform initiatives had been stymied, stalled and ignored amid a gathering tension between the Temple and the Church in Harchong. Instead, the senior Harchongese clergy, almost without exception, had thrown its support behind the oppressive policies of Waisu's ministers. After all, that was what Mother Church had done in Harchong since time out of mind! Any "humanitarian relief" Mother Church might send to Harchong would be diverted to the support of those same policies . . . or into the pockets of corrupt clerical and secular bureaucrats.

"What about Charis?" he asked and saw both Symkyn and Awstyn stiffen, although for rather different reasons, he suspected.

"I assume you mean what about the *Church* of Charis, Holiness?" the Chancellor said after a moment. Rhobair nodded, and Symkyn raised both hands in front of himself. "How would you approach them, Holiness?"

"I don't know," Rhobair said frankly. "I do know we can't trust our own archbishops and bishops—even our parish priests—to do what we know needs to be done in Harchong." His voice was as bitter as his eyes. "I've come to the conclusion that I should have been more . . . proactive about dismissing some of those archbishops and bishops from their sees. I know all the arguments about provoking another schism, and you were probably right, Tymythy. It *would* have created an official 'Church of Harchong' right alongside the Church of Charis. But that's what we got anyway, no matter what they call it!"

Symkyn nodded unhappily, and Rhobair shrugged angrily. Not at Symkyn, but at the problem—the *fresh* problem—he faced.

"The fact that we can't use our own clergy doesn't absolve us of our responsibility to care for God's children wherever they are," he continued, "but I don't see very many avenues open to us. To be brutally honest, I think that even if we tried to go around 'our' clergy and make direct contact with the rebels—assuming we could figure out a way to do that—they wouldn't trust us. Why should they? The only Church they've ever known supports the very people they're rebelling against! They'd probably murder anyone we sent to contact them!"

"You're thinking about using Staynair and his people?" Maigwair said.

"Well, given that the rebels have every reason—from their perspective—to hate and distrust Mother Church, I think it's only reasonable to assume they'd be more likely to at least give the Charisians a chance. After all, who did we just spend seven or eight years trying to massacre?" He shook his head. "As they say, my enemy's enemy is my friend."

"Holiness, with the deepest respect, I think that would be a mistake," Awstyn said after a long, still moment. Rhobair raised an eyebrow, inviting the younger vicar to continue.

"Holiness, I can't refute your logic but there are other implications. Please don't think I'm offering a *better* solution, because I'm not. I don't think there *is* one. But if we . . . I don't know, *delegate* our responsibility as Harchong's shepherds to Charis, then we *give* Harchong to the Church of Charis. I don't see how it could work any other way. I know how the argument that souls matter more than bodies enabled Clyntahn's madness, but that was because however he twisted it, it's ultimately true. It can't be an excuse for murdering and torturing, but it can't be simply *ignored*, either. Would the amount of good the Church of Charis could accomplish against such enormous need justify consigning so many of God's children to the other side of the schism?"

Awstyn's brown eyes were deeply and sincerely troubled, and Rhobair sympathized. Vicar Zherohmy was a man of warmth and deep compassion, yet he was also one of the new vicarate's conservative voices. Rhobair had made a point of incorporating both Conservative and Reformist viewpoints in the Church's bureaucratic hierarchy, and Awstyn was one of those Conservatives. He accepted Rhobair's decision that the Church of Charis must be allowed to go in peace, but he found it more difficult to accept the Grand Vicar's view that any church which accepted the *fundamentals* of the *Holy Writ* couldn't truly be heretical. His reason for that was simple—and inarguable: "fundamentals" was an inherently and dangerously elastic term. He supported the vast majority of Rhobair's internal reforms, yet the Charisians' refusal to acknowledge the paramount authority of the Grand Vicar, as Langhorne's direct—and *only*—successor upon Safehold, to define right doctrine was farther than he could go. He could respect their sincerity, their piety, the strength of their faith; he could *not* accept that they might be right.

"Zherohmy, I understand what you're saying," the Grand Vicar said now. "You may even be right. But I can't help the people, the children of God, I'm supposed to help as God's steward and shepherd in this mortal world. The *Holy Writ* underscores that responsibility in every chapter of the *Book of Bédard* and the *Book of Langhorne*. We have no choice—we're not given the *option* to do nothing for our brothers and sisters in God while they and their children *starve*." His eyes burned as he remembered how many millions of other parents and children had already starved while Mother Church stood by. "If the only way we can do that is to . . . coordinate with the Church of Charis, then I think that's what God and Langhorne are telling us to do."

Awstyn's internal struggle showed in his eyes, and Symkyn reached out and laid a hand on his forearm.

"I share many of your concerns, Zherohmy," he said quietly. "To be honest, if I'd truly understood what sorts of decisions we'd face when we were called to the orange, I'd have stayed a simple soldier and run the other way! But we're here, and His Holiness is right. We don't have any option but to do whatever we *can*."

Awstyn looked at the Chancellor. Then, slowly, he nodded. Not in agreement, but in acceptance.

"At the same time," Symkyn continued, turning back to Rhobair, "I have to say that I think Archbishop Maikel will also understand our concerns, Holiness. I may not see eye-to-eye with him on every issue, but you can't read the man's sermons or correspond with him as often as I have and not sense the depth and sincerity of his personal faith. He'd be more than human if he didn't see the opportunity to make inroads for the Church of Charis, but I believe he'd be more than willing to publicly, firmly, and *sincerely* acknowledge that this is a joint, ecumenical initiative of Mother Church and the Church of Charis. That we're both responding to a humanitarian crisis, not seeking converts . . . or to prevent anyone *from* converting."

"I'm sure he will," Rhobair said, and smiled sadly at Awstyn. "And I'm equally sure that whatever we proclaim we're doing, the Church of Charis *will* make ground in Harchong, Zherohmy. We'll just have to do our best to win some of those souls back in the fullness of time."

"Of course, Holiness," Awstyn said.

"In the meantime, though, Holiness," Maigwair said, "I think we need to consider a more secular string to our bow, as well."

"Somehow, I'm not surprised," Rhobair said, smiling

a bit crookedly at his old ally. "Should I assume this has something to do with Earl Rainbow Waters?"

"Of course you should." Maigwair smiled back, then his expression sobered. "I think Gustyv and I need to have a talk with him. With your permission, I propose to tell him Mother Church is ready to provide funds and arms for him to organize a body of troops from the Mighty Host's veterans. If what's happening in Harchong continues to spread, it's only a matter of time until it hits their eastern provinces, and that's right on the other side of our border. God only knows how that might spill over into the western episcopates, especially with so many of the Mighty Host's veterans settled there. At the very least, we need to organize a sufficiently powerful 'local militia' to deal with anything that does cross the border. And, if the situation continues to worsen, I think we have to very carefully consider the possibility of actually using him and those veterans of his to establish as much security as we can in Langhorne and Maddox and Stene, as well. There's no way he could come up with the manpower to 'pacify' the rest of North Harchong, but maybe—*maybe*—we can at least minimize the carnage in those provinces. And I think we'd be far wiser to use Rainbow Waters' Harchongians instead of inserting the Army of God into the mix. Shan-wei only knows where sending Mother Church's army into armed conflict with Mother Church's own, "true" bishops—which is *exactly* how the bastards will portray themselves if we do send in our own troops—would end."

Rhobair looked at him, thinking about it. Then, finally, he nodded.

"You're right," he said. "I wish you weren't, but you are. And you and Gustyv are definitely the best people to discuss that with him."

"I really should have come to Manchyr," a profoundly pregnant Sharleyan Ahrmahk said as Sergeant Edwyrd Seahamper opened the private Audience Chamber's door and bowed the wiry young man through it. A young woman, taller than he and with hazel eyes but the same determined chin, if in a somewhat more delicate version, followed him.

"Oh no, you shouldn't have, Empress Sharley," the young man said with a huge smile, waving her back as she started to lever herself upright. "Not this close!"

He crossed the chamber with quick, springy strides, bent over her comfortably padded chair, put his arms around her, and kissed her cheek. She reached up and patted his cheek in reply, then sighed as she settled back into the cushions.

"I won't pretend it wasn't a relief when you insisted I stay here," she admitted. "And at least Cayleb came personally to get you in the *Ahlfryd*. Maybe your subjects will forgive us for taking your formal investiture out of Manchyr Cathedral. I really *meant* for us to come to Manchyr for it. Truly I did, Daivyn, but this time. . . ."

She shook her head,

"Everyone back home understands," Prince Daivyn Daikyn told her, settling to perch on the ottoman beside her chair. "I think they're just fine about it."

"I'm *sure* they are," his sister, Princess Irys Aplyn-Ahrmahk, Duchess Darcos, said. "There's not a soul in Corisande who wants you taking any chances with your health, Sharley. On the other hand, there's no point pretending he wouldn't have insisted even if they hadn't felt that way," she added, as she reached Sharleyan's chair.

She moved rather more sedately than her brother's habitual headlong rush, and Sharleyan shook her head.

"He *is* aware that I'm not the only one who's pregnant, isn't he?" she asked, glancing rather pointedly at Irys' remarkably flat midsection before she opened her arms to her daughter-in-law.

"True, but *I'm* only two months along, Mother," Irys said demurely. "Unlike some people, who look ready to pop any minute."

"I'm not as big as I was with the boys!" Sharleyan protested. "And that was *your* fault, young lady!"

"*My* fault?" Irys hugged her briefly, then straightened. "Unless I'm mistaken, I don't believe *I* was involved in that bit of procreation at all."

"No, but it was *your* twins that inspired Cayleb to emulate you and Hektor," the Empress said severely. "There are no twins in my family, and precious few in his. But after you and Hektor got so carried away with the first pair and jumped ahead of Alahnah, he was determined to take the lead back."

"And you didn't have anything to do with the whole process? Do I have that right?" Irys inquired with a quizzical expression.

"*He* does the preliminary work, *I* do the heavy lifting. If anybody's going to get blamed for it, it's going to be him. Besides, I'm pregnant. I don't have to be logical."

"Wonderful, isn't it?" Irys grinned. "Mind you, the rest of it's a nuisance. Oh, the 'preliminary work' is a lot of fun—and the final product is wonderful!—but I *could* do without the 'heavy lifting' bit."

"Which is why we get to be irrational, emotional, weepy, snappish, and temperamental. Oh, and start craving all sorts of insane foods at ridiculous hours of the night and day until we drive our beloved spouses to frothing madness. It's simply a just dispensation of nature, righting the scales after the cads do this to us."

"You two do realize you're giving away all your secrets, don't you?" Daivyn looked back and forth between them. "I mean, Phylyp and Uncle Rysel keep telling me 'forewarned is forearmed.' If *my* wife—assuming we can ever find one who could put up with me—finds out the two of you 'forewarned' me about what to expect when she's pregnant, I don't think she'll be very happy with you."

"It would only matter if knowing would do you one bit of good, Daivy." Irys ran a hand affectionately over his hair, the way she had when he was much younger. "It won't. She's going to make you *just* as miserable as I've ever made Hektor or Empress Sharley's ever made Cayleb."

"Actually," the Duke of Darcos said as he and a fair-haired, immaculately dressed older man came into the room on Irys' heels, "I don't recall your ever actually making me *miserable,* love. A tad . . . impatient, once or twice, maybe. But if you'd really made me miserable, I'm sure I could've gotten Domynyk or Dunkyn to send me back to sea while you got on with all that 'heavy lifting.'"

"And would've done it, too," Irys shook her head darkly. "But Daivy won't have that unfair defensive weapon. He's a prince. He *has* to stay home."

"She's got you there, Hektor," Phylyp Ahzgood, the Earl of Coris and Prince Daivyn's first councilor, observed. He smiled approvingly at his prince's older sister. "She always knew how to go for the jugular!"

"Well, if I didn't climb out of this chair for a reigning prince, I'm not climbing out of it for a mere earl or a duke," Sharleyan declared, opening her arms to Hektor. Her adopted son leaned over her, embracing her with his functional arm. Then it was Coris' turn, and she shook her head as he straightened.

"What?" the earl asked.

"Just thinking about how impossible to imagine this entire scene once would've been," she replied. "It still sneaks up on me sometimes."

"I don't think any of us will ever be happy about the price we paid to get here, Sharley," Irys said. "But I don't think any of us would want to be anywhere else, either."

"I know *I* wouldn't." Daivyn's expression had gone unwontedly serious. "I miss Father, and Hektor. In fact,

I miss them a *lot* sometimes, and it worries me when I feel their memories starting to . . . fade, I guess." He shook his head, his brown eyes dark, then drew a deep breath. "I miss them, but I've still got you—and Hektor and Empress Sharley and Cayleb, Merlin and Nimue. Who else has a family like *that*? And my political tutors haven't been all *that* bad, either. Even counting Phylyp."

He smiled suddenly, and Coris chuckled, looking at the young man who would turn eighteen in eleven days. And on his birthday, Prince Daivyn of Corisande would reaffirm his oath of fealty to Cayleb and Sharleyan Ahrmahk and take up the crown of Corisande in his own right. There were times Coris could scarcely believe they'd made it to this point, but young Daivyn was right about his tutors. Coris himself was no slouch, but he knew even he had learned a lot watching Cayleb and Sharleyan in action. He couldn't think of two finer examples for any young ruler who took his responsibilities seriously, and Daivyn did.

He's going to be one of the good ones, the earl thought, smiling at the boy—no, the young man, now—who was the closest thing he'd ever had to a son. *He's got his father's political instincts, his sister's compassion, his brother-in-law's sense of duty and integrity, and Cayleb and Sharleyan's example. God, I wish his father could see him! He's what Hektor could have been—should have been, if he hadn't lost Raichynda so early—and I think he'd recognize that. I'm sure he'd still be pissed off over losing to them*—the earl's lips quirked ever so briefly—*but he loved his kids to pieces. He'd have to approve of how well Cayleb and Sharleyan have done by Daivyn and Irys. And by Corisande as a whole, for that matter.*

"It's good of you to be so gentle about my shortcomings, Your Highness," he said out loud, and Daivyn chuckled.

"It is turning into rather a *large* family, though, isn't it?" Hektor Aplyn-Ahrmahk buffed the fingernails of his right hand—the only one that functioned properly—on his doublet, then blew on them complacently. "I wouldn't want to say anything about Old Charisian virility, but still—!"

He shrugged modestly, then "oofed" as Irys smacked him in the stomach.

Sharleyan chuckled, but she had to admit he had a point. One thing Crown Princess Alahnah *definitely* wasn't going to lack were siblings and cousins to support her future reign. Her twin brothers, Gwylym and Bryahn, had turned three in April, about the same time she'd turned nine. Her half-Corisandian cousins, Princess Raichynda and Prince Hektor (universally known as Hektor Merlin, to avoid confusion with his father, his deceased uncle, and his deceased maternal grandfather) would be six in another four months. And her Uncle Zhan and Aunt Mahrya had provided two more cousins—Prince Haarahld Cayleb, a sturdy two-and-a-half-year-old, and Prince Nahrmahn Merlin, who was barely two months old—while Owl had already confirmed that Irys was expecting twins yet again, even if the Pasqualate obstetricians hadn't heard the heartbeats yet.

And that doesn't even count all of the Breygarts, especially now that Mairah's started popping out babies of her own! she thought.

Hauwerd Breygart, the Earl of Hanth and now Duke of Thesmar, and his first wife had produced five children. His second wife, Mairah, was seven years older than Sharleyan. She'd started late and been delayed by the minor fact that he'd been off fighting a war for the first three years of their marriage, but she'd been making up for it since. She'd already produced a son and daughter of her own, and she was due to deliver her third child in October.

All in all, Alahnah could count on a veritable phalanx of support when the time came, including her new baby sister. Princess Nynian Zhorzhet was due any day now, which explained why Father Ohmahr Arthmyn had made the trip to Chisholm with them this year. Arthmyn trusted Sister Fahnycis Sawyairm, who'd midwifed all of Sharleyan's children, implicitly and it might be only eleven days from Tellesberg to Port Royal aboard HMS *Ahlfryd Hyndryk,* the Imperial family's twenty-three-knot yacht, but this pregnancy truly had been harder than the others. That was the reason Arthmyn hadn't been going to let her out of his sight that far from any properly equipped hospital for two full five-days. It was also the reason Sharleyan was secretly so grateful for Daivyn's insistence she stay seated and for his insistence on coming to Cherayth rather than subjecting her to the trip to Manchyr, even aboard *Ahlfryd Hyhndryk.*

"Yes, it is turning into a large family," she said now, with the soft smile of an only-child princess who'd lost her own father when she was barely twelve. "And I'm glad. But speaking of large families, Hektor, what did you do with the patriarch?"

"*Patriarch!*" Hektor hooted. "Oh, wait till I tell your ancient and decrepit husband you dropped *that* one on him! Especially when you're two years more ancient—or would that be ancienter?—than *he* is!"

Sharleyan's lips twitched. It was true that at thirty-three (only thirty in the years of long-dead Terra) Cayleb was scarcely an antique. On the other hand, he *was* approaching patriarch status, given the enthusiastic manner in which his family and its allies had embraced the admonition to be fruitful and multiply.

"Don't try to change the subject!" She shook a severe finger at him. "Just be a dutiful son and tell me what you did with your father!"

"He'll be along shortly," Hektor said without pointing out that everyone in the room—except Daivyn—already knew precisely where Cayleb was, thanks to the Self-Navigating Autonomous Reconnaissance and Communications platforms of an artificial intelligence named Owl. "He and Dunkyn and Admiral Tartarian had a matter they urgently needed to discuss. I believe it had something to do with Glynfych or Seijin Kohdy's Blend."

"Well," Sharleyan said philosophically, "at least he's considerate enough not to drink the good stuff in front of me now that I'm pregnant again."

"I think the word you want is 'prudent,' not 'considerate,'" Irys said thoughtfully. "It took Hektor a while to acquire the same degree of prudence."

"I'm not surprised." Sharleyan shook her head. Then she squared her shoulders, gripped the arms of her chair and pushed herself steadily—if a bit ponderously—to her feet.

Daivyn popped to his own feet, offering her his arm, and she took it gratefully. This pregnancy really was taking more out of her than the earlier ones had, and she was grateful they'd been in Chisholm, with its cooler climate, for the last three months. Her Chisholmians were, too. In their opinion, it was past time for one of their Empress' children to be born on *their* soil for a change.

She smiled at the thought, but then the smile faded as she reflected on all the other reasons it was fortunate she and Cayleb had moved back to the kingdom of her own birth for the half-year mandated by the imperial constitution.

"I think it's time we went and disturbed those reprobates who are currently enjoying some of the finer things in life denied to the pregnant mothers of their children. Well, not Dunkyn's children, perhaps, but still. And then the cooks can go ahead and serve, now that the lot of you have finally arrived from Manchyr." She smiled warmly at all of them. "It's *good* to see you," she said with simple sincerity, "and we have a lot of catching up to do."

▼ ▼ ▼

Much later that evening, Sharleyan leaned back in the huge armchair beside her bed with her bare feet in her husband's lap and stretched like a pregnant cat-lizard as his strong fingers worked on her aching ankles and weary calves.

"You really do that very well," she sighed. "I think I'll keep you."

"I'm flattered," he replied, "but I think you're drifting a little from the point of this gathering, dear."

"And if you think any of us are going to argue with

her, you have another think coming," a deep voice said over the invisible plug in his ear. "Some things are more important than others."

"Or more likely to get us thumped if we say they aren't, at least," a voice which sounded suspiciously like Hektor Aplyn-Ahrmahk's added.

"I don't understand why everyone is so concerned about my temper," Sharleyan said a bit plaintively.

"'Everyone' *isn't* worried about your temper." Cayleb Ahrmahk leaned forward to kiss her forehead. "Just those of us in range of it."

"Which I'm not," Trahvys Ohlsyn put in from far distant Tellesberg. The Earl of Pine Hollow sat gazing out his Tellesberg Palace office window across the sunlit roofs of the Old Charisian capital. "And I'm afraid Cayleb's right about staying focused in my case, Sharleyan. I'm truly sorry to say that, but I have a Council meeting in about two hours."

"I know," Sharleyan admitted. "I think I'm trying to waste time because of how much I really don't want to think about any of this right now." She inhaled deeply and looked at Cayleb almost apologetically. "You know I get disgustingly weepy in the last month or so."

"Love, this is enough to make *anybody* cry," Cayleb replied. "Not that Trahvys doesn't have a point about time marching on. So, does anyone have anything to add to Nahrmahn's observations?"

There was silence over the heavily stealthed com network connecting the members of the inner circle. It lingered for several moments, and then the deep voice spoke again.

"I don't think I have anything to add to Nahrmahn's *observations,*" Merlin Athrawes said. "He and Owl called this from the beginning, and thanks to the remotes, we even know who the main players are . . . at least for now. But I have to say I don't like the consequences I see coming one bit." Cayleb's and Sharleyan's contacts showed his image as he shook his head, his expression grim. "I was afraid all along that the Jihad would make something like this inevitable, but then those idiots in Shang-mi did every damned thing they could to make sure it did! And now that it's finally happened, it's going to be even worse than it might have because they managed to keep the lid on it, more or less, for so long." He shook his head again. "If everyone involved was as organized as Syngpu amd Husan I might be less concerned, but they've lit a fire that's going to be a hell of a lot worse than the one that killed Winter Glory and all his men. I'll be surprised if Nahrmahn's not right about this killing *at least* as many people as the Sword of Schueler did, once the real 'grassroots' rebellion starts."

The slender woman sitting comfortably beside him on the couch in their quarters with her feet tucked up under her lifted her head from his shoulder to look at him.

"You are *not* going to add this to your 'Things I Am Responsible For' list," she told him severely. "Harchong—especially *North* Harchong—was a catastrophe waiting to happen before anyone on this planet, aside from you and Nimue, was ever born! Yes, the Jihad finally pushed it over the edge, but this was bound to happen anyway—later, if not sooner—and you know it."

"You're right, love." He smiled crookedly. "And I promise not to beat myself up over it. Not much, anyway. Doesn't change how bad it's going to be, though."

"No, it doesn't," Nynian Athrawes acknowledged, and her magnificent eyes darkened. Very few humans in history had ever been tougher minded than Nynian Rychtair Athrawes, but she hadn't been able to bring herself to watch the unspeakable atrocities being inflicted in Harchong.

"I can't disagree, either," Maikel Staynair said from Tellesberg. The Archbishop of Charis' voice was as powerful as ever, his eye as clear, but the grief in his expression was profound. "I know it's foolish of me, but I can't help wishing that anyone who's suffered as much as Harchongese serfs have would show at least a little compassion!"

"Some of them—a handful of them—*have* shown

compassion, Your Eminence," Sir Koryn Gahrvai said heavily. "Expecting more than that—?"

His image shrugged on the others' contact lenses, and the slender, red-haired woman sitting on the other side of his desk nodded somberly.

"I wish we had a magic wand that could make it all stop, but we don't." Her eyes—the same deep sapphire as Merlin's—were dark. "And I know a lot of the people this is happening to, especially the children, don't deserve it. But some of them *do*, Maikel." Her face tightened. "Some of them deserve every damned *second* of it."

"Of course they do, but it's not about 'just deserts,' Nimue." Staynair shook his head sadly. "The fact that some of them *don't* deserve it is terrible, but I pray as much for the people torturing and murdering them as I do for the innocent victims. Nothing else in this world can damn and destroy souls as effectively as our need to inflict vengeance and call it justice."

"You're probably right," the Earl of Coris acknowledged, "but I don't see any way to change human nature, Maikel. So I suppose the question is whether or not there's anything we can do to minimize its consequences. If we can't stop it, is there some way we can at least limit the carnage?"

"Not one *I* can see yet." Cayleb cocked an eyebrow at Sharleyan, but his wife only shook her head in sorrowful agreement.

"Officially, we still only have rumors of what's going on," the Emperor continued, refocusing his attention on the rest of the group. "I know confirmation's on the way, and we're going to have to formulate an official policy of some sort when it gets here, but until it does, there's nothing we could do even if we could think of something *to* do."

"Actually, I think I may have some hope for Baron Star Rising's initiative," Prince Nahrmahn said from the computer in which he and his virtual reality resided.

"You really think he'll be able to pull that off?" Pine Hollow sounded skeptical, and Nahrmahn's computer-generated image shrugged.

"I truly think he *may* . . . if he's luckier than hell, pardon the language, Maikel." Staynair's lips twitched, and Nahrmahn grinned. Then his own expression sobered. "Owl and I couldn't predict something like him coming along, Trahvys—or, rather, we deliberately refused to engage in wishful thinking and *hope* someone like him turned up. But I think he's really going to try rather than cutting and running for it with his family, and Doctor Johnson had a point. God knows Star Rising's got enough horrible examples next door in Tiegelkamp to concentrate *anyone's* thinking! Not only that, serfdom in western Harchong's never been quite as brutal as in the rest of North Harchong."

"Mostly because that's where so many of North Harchong's craftsmen and artisans are concentrated," Nynian pointed out. "Especially in Boisseau and southern Cheshire. Not so much in Omar and Pasquale, of course. And there's not much of *anything* in Bedard Province, aside from a few fishermen along the coast."

"But the guilds have been just as much in bed with the aristocracy in western Harchong as anywhere else," Ehdwyrd Howsmyn, the Duke of Delthak, countered. "They're just as invested in the old system as anyone else."

"Not really," Nahrmahn disagreed. "Oh, they *are* invested in it, I don't think anyone could argue about that, Ehdwyrd. For that matter, I know they don't want to see your style of manufactories move in on their turf. But I doubt they want to see their families massacred, either. And not even the aristocracy's interests are as tied to the land as they are for the major power holders in, say, Tiegelkamp or Chiang-wu, given how many more smaller landholders there are in Boisseau and Cheshire."

Delthak nodded, albeit with a doubtful expression. Some of those "smaller landholders"—like Baron Star Rising himself—were among the most ancient of Harchong's aristocratic families, given the initial pattern of human colonization, moving into those provinces from the original enclaves around Beijing Bay and the Yalu Inlet. However, they'd also moved into them before the great nobles managed to monopolize power. In fact, those ancient families had been largely squeezed out of the Harchongese power structure's top slots by the more recently ennobled families spreading out eastward from their new capital in Shang-mi into Tiegelkamp and Chiang-wu.

That probably helped explain why serfdom was less oppressive in Boisseau and Cheshire. Some of the peasant freeholds in those two provinces were almost as ancient as Star Rising's title, and the huge estates with hundreds, even thousands, of serfs bound to the soil were rare.

That was also the reason wealthy families there were more invested in trade than elsewhere in North Harchong. *South* Harchong was another matter entirely, of course, with fewer great nobles of any sort and a much more open mind where commerce was concerned. But not only were Star Rising and his fellows excluded from the lucrative perquisites of office by the more powerful aristocrats who monopolized the imperial government and bureaucracy, they couldn't generate sufficient income from farming their smaller estates, especially given the inefficiency of Harchongese agriculture. So they'd had no option but to seek other avenues . . . which, of course, allowed the great, land-rich members of the aristocracy to despise them as mere tradesmen.

"I'm not saying the odds are in Star Rising's favor," Nahrmahn continued. "I'm only saying he *might* pull it off. And if he does, I'm sure he will follow up on the suggestion that he seek Charisian aid."

"How much 'aid' could we actually give them?" Delthak asked skeptically.

"A valid question," Cayleb said. "Care to take a swing at it, Kynt?"

"If we're talking about military aid," Kynt Clareyk, Baron Green Valley and Duke Serabor, replied, "I'll have to give it some serious thought before I could give you any sort of definitive answer. But I can already tell you there's no way we have sufficient military capability to intervene on any broad scale in Harchong. That kind of rolling disaster sucks up manpower like a sponge, and we're still building down from Jihad levels."

"None of us think we can do that," Merlin said. "But what about in just the western provinces? Assuming Star Rising and his friends can keep a lid on things?"

"Unless the 'lid' includes something besides suppression, I think the technical phrase is 'not a chance in hell,'" Serabor said bluntly. "If he's able to bring the free peasants and what little middle class he has into some kind of genuine power-sharing relationship with the aristocracy, and if the lot of them manage to convince the majority of serfs they're truly willing to implement real reforms, we could *probably* find the strength to provide at least some islands of stability. But that's a lot of ifs, Merlin!"

"That's true," Staynair said. "But they may have a better chance of managing all that than you think, Kynt, given how much less hardline the local Church has been about resisting Duchairn's reforms. In fact, there's a strong Reformist element in both Boisseau and Cheshire—especially Boisseau. You know how severely Bishop Yaupang's been hammered by both Shang-mi and Shynkau because of his support for it."

"And that's exactly why I think they might be able to pull it off," Nahrmahn agreed. "Star Rising's being careful to get the bishop on board, and now that Zhynchi's run for it, I think Lyauyan has the inside track in the Church, at least in Boisseau."

Serabor considered that for several seconds, then nodded.

Archbishop Baudang Zhynchi, the Archbishop of Boisseau, was a Church apparatchik of the old school, bitterly opposed to Rhobair II's reforms. But he was also over eighty years old and increasingly frail. In fact, he would have retired at least two or three years ago if the Harchongese Church hierarchy had been one iota less determined to prevent Rhobair from replacing any more of its members. As it was, Zhynchi hadn't been about to request replacement, and none of his fellow archbishops would have been at all happy if he had. At the same time, age, ill health, and a gathering loss of mental focus had precluded him from keeping a firm grip on the Reformists in his own archbishopric.

And Zhynchi had panicked when the first reports of the sack of Shang-mi reached his cathedral in Zhynkau. It was probably unfair to blame a man his age and whose mind was increasingly fuddled even when it came to dealing with routine matters, but he'd been on the first galley south, and his unceremonious departure had created an abrupt vacuum at the very apex of the province's religious hierarchy. More than that, his cowardice—which was the only word for it, whatever excuses one might make for him—had further undermined the Church's hardliners.

Yaupang Lyauyan, the Bishop of Pauton, was quite a different sort of prelate. He was only forty-seven, thirty-plus years younger than Zhynchi, and one of those Reformists Zhynchi had been unable to repress properly. His see wasn't wealthy, but Pauton was the province's third-oldest diocese, after those of Zhynkau and Quijang. That gave him more seniority than his youth might otherwise have suggested, and he was not only younger than either of those other two bishops, he was far more charismatic, as well. In fact, unlike them, he was actually trusted by the peasants and serfs of his diocese. If Star Rising could enlist him in the nascent provisional government he was trying to create. . . .

"I still think it would be iffy," the duke said, "but you and Maikel have a point about Lyauyan."

"And bayonets aren't the only way to keep the peace," a soprano voice pointed out.

Lady Elayn Clareyk, Duchess Serabor, was ten years younger than her husband, with exotic—by Old Charisian standards—golden hair, green eyes, and a pronounced Siddarmarkian accent. They'd met following the Tarikah Campaign which had ended the Jihad, and there were dark places behind those green eyes, left by the things she'd had to do to keep herself and her younger sister Lyzbyt alive after the Sword of Schueler massacred every other member of their family.

Lyzbyt had taken vows with the Bédardists of the Church of Charis as Sister Lyzbyt, and she was emerging as a brilliant young psychologist. There was still too much anger inside Elayn for that sort of rapprochement with the Church, even in Charis, but she'd been a member of the inner circle almost from the day of her marriage and she'd grasped both the challenge that circle faced—and its capabilities—with almost frightening clarity.

"What do you mean, Elayn?" Sharleyan asked.

"I think I'm the only member of the conversation who's seen this kind of madness from the inside." Lady Elayn's voice was as dark as her eyes. "When it started in Harchong, I prayed to God that it wouldn't be as bad as it was in Siddarmark. Now it looks like it's actually going to be worse. And that means we have to do anything we can—*anything,* Your Majesty—to . . . to mitigate it. I know exactly why you don't want to send troops into the middle of this, Kynt. For that matter, I don't think any purely military solution would work. I think you're right that they could help provide at least your 'islands of stability,' but we need more than islands. We need to give Star Rising and the others *hope,* not just soldiers. We need to give them the kind of hope they can extend to other people—to those artisans and guild masters, to the peasants. Even to the serfs."

"I think all of us agree with that," Cayleb said soberly, and the others nodded. Young Elayn might be, by other people's standards, but she was only a year younger than Cayleb himself, with a hard-won wisdom far beyond her years. "The problem is how we do that."

"We do what Charisians do best, Your Majesty." She gave him a quirky smile. "We invest. We take those islands of stability and expand them into islands of *prosperity.*"

"Who do we invest *with*?" Delthak asked. "You're right, Elayn. If we could do that—if we could find someone to partner with and Kynt could buy us a big enough window of stability—it would help enormously! Some of the families involved in trade, especially in Boisseau, would see the opportunity in a heartbeat, but I don't think they have enough capital or enough time to take advantage of it."

Several heads nodded in agreement with that. The "Nahrmahn Plan"—Merlin's teasing name for it had actually stuck—seemed to be succeeding, but it was working far better in some places than in others. Charis' own rate of industrial expansion continued to accelerate, driven by an exuberant tide of innovations utterly foreign to Safehold's traditional mind-set, and Charisian investors had found scores of partners in the Kingdom of Dohlar, under the auspices of First Councilor Thirsk. The Grand Duchy of Silkiah was another success story, with Silkiahan investors almost trampling one another to buy shares in the new Silkiah Canal Company and import Charisian manufactory techniques. South Harchong, unlike the northern half of the empire, had also embraced the new opportunities, although the Harchongians had so far chosen to go largely their own way, with minimal Charisian involvement. After all, everyone knew how the Emperor and his heir felt about Charis, and no one wanted to be pasting any targets to their own backs. There were a handful of quiet partnerships underway in the south, but nothing like the scale in Dohlar and Silkiah.

Yet if the effort was succeeding in those places, it was going less well in the rest of Safehold, including North Harchong and, unfortunately, the Republic of Siddarmark.

"I don't pretend to understand economics as well as you and Baron Ironhill do, Your Grace," Elayn said, looking at Duke Delthak's image. "I do understand that promoting stable economic and industrial growth requires local investors and the local rule of law, though, especially if we want that growth to be sustainable. And I realize Delthak Enterprises is only one investor. Admittedly, you're the biggest in the entire world, but only one, and not all Charisian investors are as . . . altruistic as Delthak. I know that, too. But surely there has to be *some* way!"

"Altruism's not the best word to describe even my investment strategies, Elayn," Delthak said. "I do have partners and investors, and I do need to earn them a healthy return if I expect to hang onto them. And especially if I want to attract *more* of them!"

"You actually said that with a straight face, Ehdwyrd," Cayleb said in an admiring tone, and Sharleyan stifled a giggle, then poked him with an admonishing toe.

"All right, that's fair," the duke acknowledged. "But I haven't told my shareholders about our real objective. I can't, now can I? And none of the others—the ones Elayn is pointing out aren't as noble and altruistic as your humble servant—care a damned thing about spreading our technical infrastructure. Most of them would be just *delighted* to maintain a total monopoly on it as long as they frigging well can, actually! They're looking purely at the profit factor when they consider any overseas investment, and if they can't find local partners or some other damned convincing incentive, they won't be able—or willing—to free up enough risk capital to do any good. Especially not somewhere where they don't know if the local authorities are going to be able to *stay* the local authorities. Elayn's absolutely right about how important stable, law-abiding local governance is if we expect anyone else to come along for the ride. Hell, that's a big part of the problem—in a different way, of course—in *Siddarmark*!"

"Fair enough," Cayleb said in return.

They'd counted heavily on Siddarmarkian participation in their expansion effort. The fact that it didn't seem likely to be forthcoming, and that the chaos and catastrophe in North Harchong was likely to impact *South* Harchong, made all of them unpleasantly aware of the cold, fetid breath of apocalypse on the backs of their necks, and—

"Wait a minute," Merlin said suddenly. "Wait just one minute."

His wife looked at him, her eyes intent. He didn't seem to notice. He simply sat there, obviously thinking hard, and then as his expression began to change, she smiled.

"I know that look," she said. He blinked, then shook himself and gave her a crooked smile of his own. "Out with it!" she commanded.

"Well," he said, "it's just occurred to me that all we're seeing right now in Harchong is the devastation and massacres. At least, that's all we're *looking* at, because it's so horrible and there doesn't seem to be anything we can do to stop it. Which, unfortunately, is probably true for most of North Harchong. But you and Nahrmahn are right about Boisseau and Cheshire's social matrix. And that means that what we have in *those* provinces is actually an opportunity."

"An *opportunity*?" Cayleb's expression made it clear that only his respect for Merlin's past accomplishments had kept the incredulity out of his tone, and Merlin smiled again.

"We're all in agreement that we need to actively involve everyone we can in this industrialization effort, which is why we're letting the 'private sector' carry the primary burden. None of us like how some of our more unscrupulous Charisians are doing that, but Ehdwyrd's right that relying on the profit motive—and basic greed—means *somebody* will exploit every opportunity out there. He's also right about the situation in Harchong. The way it's headed, no private investor's going to risk the capital to accomplish anything in time to keep Star Rising and his effort from sinking. But we've got the Mohryah Lode."

Cayleb frowned, then his eyebrows arched, and Merlin nodded.

The enormous wealth under Silverlode Island's Mohryah Mountains had come as quite a shock when Nahrmahn found a description of it in the notes Pei Shan-wei's survey crews had left in Owl's memory. It dwarfed Old Earth's Comstock Lode. So far, the prospecting crews, working without benefit of Shan-wei's notes for obvious reasons, had found considerably less than a third of the major ore bodies under the mountains, yet those same notes indicated that what they *had* found would ultimately produce in excess of ten million tons of silver and six and a half million tons of gold.

And that was barely the tip of an iceberg that belonged—in toto—not to the Charisian Empire, but specifically to the House of Ahrmahk. In terms of real buying power, Cayleb and Sharleyan Ahrmahk were undoubtedly the wealthiest individuals in the history of the human race.

Period.

Obviously, they couldn't simply dump that kind of gold and silver into their own economy without fatally overheating it. But. . . .

"Are you suggesting what I *think* you're suggesting?" Cayleb asked after a moment.

"I'm suggesting a variant on what was once called the 'Marshall Plan' back on Old Earth. If we don't have Harchongese investors, we *create* them. We make Crown-guaranteed loans to qualified Harchongians—and we define 'qualified' as loosely as we can get away with—at a zero interest rate, or damned close to it. Face it, we've got money to burn in the Mohryah Lode. Even if half of them default, we can write it off the books and keep right on going. But by making the loans available in the first place, we provide a route to that prosperity Elayn was just talking about. Plus, we get all the good-will for having ridden to the rescue, and having been mighty generous when we did. And it gives us the opportunity to create a huge opening for industrial expansion in *North Harchong*, of all places!"

"I like it," Delthak said after a moment, then grinned suddenly. "We can call it the Ahrmahk Plan!"

"I like it, too," Archbishop Maikel said. "But if we're going to do that, we need to set up the mechanism very carefully to make sure it doesn't turn into something totally dominated by the local nobles. Ehdwyrd and Elayn's point about the need for stability and the assurance of the rule of law will be essential for outside investors. And if we want to convince peasants and serfs that this offers prosperity for *them*, as well, we can't create a situation that simply reinforces the existing elites' control!"

"Agreed." Merlin nodded firmly. "I'm sure we can draft terms to mandate the conditions—both of governance and of broad-based participation—under which we make them available, though. And since we're guaranteeing the loans, I think it'd be reasonable to assign Charisian administrators to them to make sure that Harchongese propensity for graft doesn't get a toehold. Offering to provide Charisian industrial advisors—like Brahd Stylmyn, if you can spare him, Ehdwyrd—for any project we underwrite would probably be a good idea, too. As long as we make it clear those advisors are being paid by the Crown, not by the people they're advising, at least."

"Excellent idea," Nahrmahn approved. "If we're paying them, the Harchongians will know their 'advisors' aren't skimming anything from their cash flow." The dead little Emeraldian chuckled suddenly. "Graft-free administration! I wonder how many Harchongians will drop dead from sheer shock when they hear about that!"

. UII .
Manchyr Palace,
City of Manchyr,
Princedom of Corisande,
Empire of Charis.

"Do you need anything else, My Lord?"

"No, Sailys. Thank you, I think we have everything we need . . . as always," Koryn Gahrvai said with a smile.

"Well, it's good of you to say so, anyway, Sir," Sailys Kylmohr said. He looked around the sun-filled dining room again, checking the arrangements, giving the table one last examination, then bowed. "If you discover that you do need anything else, just ring," he said.

"We will, I promise," Gahrvai told him.

Kylmohr nodded and withdrew, and Gahrvai looked across the table.

"Maybe we should find something to complain about—or demand, anyway," he said. "I think he feels . . . underutilized with Daivyn and Irys and the kids gone."

Nimue Chwaeriau chuckled. Over the last two or three years, she'd discovered she really liked Koryn Gahrvai, and part of it was their shared sense of humor. And of the absurd, she acknowledged, thinking about how . . . unlikely it was that the two of them should be sitting here in this sunny room over nine hundred years after her own death.

"I don't know if *he* feels 'underutilized,'" she said out loud. "But judging from this spread, the cooks certainly do. Look at all this food! What? They don't know how to cook for less than *twenty*?"

Gahrvai laughed, but she did have a point. The breakfast table was spread with melon balls, cut fruit, toast *and* biscuits, a side platter of sliced cheeses and smoked fish, half a dozen different sauces and dressings, an enormous warming pan heaped with scrambled eggs, another containing enough bacon for at least six people, and two steaming pots—one of chocolate for him and one of cherrybean for Nimue.

"If you don't want to break their hearts, you're going to have to help me eat at least some of this," he pointed out.

"I know. And it's not as if I can't enjoy the taste," she said, pouring herself a cup of cherrybean and adding a miserly dollop of cream. "There are times I wish I could actually feel hungry, though," she went on a bit wistfully, looking down into the cup as she stirred it. "It's really true that hunger is the best spice."

"You can't program yourself to feel that?" he asked curiously, and she shrugged.

"I can, but it's not the same, somehow. It's like I'm fooling myself and my brain knows it." She frowned, still stirring but more for something to do than because the cherrybean needed it. "It's not an *actual* sensation, I suppose. Not like my sense of touch or smell, when I'm absorbing real stimuli." She finished stirring and laid the spoon aside. "It's just *different* at the end of the day. I never played with my PICA as much as a lot of people who owned them did, so I never really realized that particular difference existed . . . before."

"I imagine there are a lot of differences," he observed, and she looked up quickly, arching an eyebrow. "It's just that you don't talk very much about what I guess you might call 'before and after,'" he said with a small shrug.

"Aren't very many people I *could* talk about it with."

"Not outside the circle, anyway," he replied, but it was an acknowledgment of what she'd said, she realized. Not agreement with it.

Irys and Hektor, with Nimue's strong backing, had nominated him for the inner circle shortly after Zhaspahr Clyntahn's execution, and he'd taken the truth in stride better than many other nominees. And he'd also cast the deciding vote against recruiting his father. Much as he loved Sir Rysel, he feared the true nature of the inner circle's war against the Church of God Awaiting would have pushed Earl Anvil Rock's flexibility one push too far, the same way it had Ruhsyl Thairis. He'd also proven even more perceptive than Nimue had thought he was.

"I suppose you're right," she said after a moment. "I *can't* talk about it with anyone outside the circle. I just . . . *don't* talk about it with the rest of you. Not even Merlin, really."

"Why not?" he asked, sitting back in his chair, and her eyes widened at the . . . gentleness of that simple, two-word question.

Gahrvai breakfasted with Daivyn, Irys and Hektor, and the royal children two or three times each five-day, and Major Chwaeriau had become a part of the royal family of Corisande, not simply its most deadly bodyguard. As such, she normally joined them at the table, for breakfast, at least, and the adults had gotten into the habit of turning those occasions into working sessions as well as meals, although the twins were getting old enough to pick up on conversations around them, which meant they'd have to change that soon. But she'd been a little surprised when she'd realized that Gahrvai had become a close friend, not just a colleague. Indeed, she hadn't realized until recently how much she looked forward to the days when he joined them, as well.

Normally, she would have traveled with Daivyn and Irys, although she had complete faith in Tobys Raimair and Hairahm Bahnystyr, who officially headed their security details. This time, however, she'd stayed home, ostensibly to assist Gahrvai in the expansion of the Royal Guard in the face of the growing royal family, so it made sense for the two of them to continue to share breakfasts. Technically, she was an officer of the *Imperial* Guard, not the Corisandian Royal Guard, but she'd been detailed to Manchyr for over six years now. In that time, she'd become one of the Royal Guard's own by adoption, and as a *seijin,* it was reasonable for her to remain in Manchyr, available to Gahrvai if he needed her, especially when all her royal charges would be safely in Merlin's hands from the moment they stepped off the ship in Cherayth. Of course, the real reason she'd been left home was that with Irys, Hektor, and Phylyp Ahzgood all off to Chisholm, the inner circle had wanted at least two of its members in Corisande in case something came up.

Something like the carnage in Harchong, for example, she thought darkly. But for all its grimness, the thought was fleeting, banished by something else as she heard the gentleness in that question.

"Mostly, I guess, because there's not much point," she said finally. "The only person who'd really understand is Merlin, and I don't have to discuss it with him." She quirked a bittersweet smile. "After all, I *am* him."

"No, you aren't," Gahrvai disagreed, spooning a portion of the scrambled eggs onto her plate before he served himself. "You started as the same person. I understand that—intellectually, at least; my brain still has a little trouble processing it. But you're very different people now, Nimue." The badly scarred cheek he'd acquired the day of Hektor and Irys' marriage pulled his quick grin off center. "For example, I can't really imagine Merlin as a woman."

"He's not." Nimue shrugged. "Now at least. Not even in his own mind, I'm pretty sure. I mean, I can't be positive about that, and in the Federation, it wasn't unusual for people who had last-generation PICAs to experiment with shifted genders. I was never tempted, though. I guess I'm pretty firmly heterosexual. And because we used to be the same person, I know Merlin had never been inclined to experiment that way before it was his turn to wake up in Nimue's Cave, either. But his PICA's chassis's height meant he didn't have any choice but to reconfigure himself as a man . . . and it looks like he's *still* just as heterosexual as I am, if in a somewhat different way." She shook her head with a smile. "I'm happy for him—happy he's adjusted so well, I mean. He's way too tall to ever pass as a woman on Safehold, even if he wanted to. Which, now that he's found Nynian, I can't imagine him wanting!"

She took a slice of toast and passed the bread basket across to him.

"It must be odd to realize there's someone else—a man, in this case—who has all of your memories and life experience right up to the moment you opened your eyes here on Safehold," Gahrvai said, spooning marmalade onto his own toast.

"I'll admit, it's not something I ever expected," she conceded. "It's . . . comforting though, in a lot of ways. The Federation—everyone and everything Nimue Alban ever knew—is dead." Her eyes turned shadowed. "It's good to know there's someone else who remembers them the way I do. It's sort of like they're not really all gone as long as someone remembers them."

"I can see how that could work," he said thoughtfully. "I haven't been through anything remotely like that—not on that scale. But we've all lost a lot of people right here on Safehold since the start of the Jihad. And you're right. As long as we remember them, they're not completely gone, are they?"

"And then there's Nahrmahn," Nimue said dryly, deliberately injecting humor into the conversation, and smiled as she watched him laugh.

"Nahrmahn is . . . unique, in *so* many ways!" he agreed. "I imagine there were quite a few people—electronic personalities, I mean—back in the Federation, but somehow I doubt any of them were quite like him."

"I think that's a fairly safe assumption."

"But, then again, I don't think there was ever anyone quite like you, either," he said. "Back in the Federation *or* here on Safehold."

She stiffened because that gentleness was back in his tone.

"What makes you say that?" she asked slowly.

"I've been thinking it for quite some time," he replied a bit obliquely. "Actually, I've been thinking about it since the first day I met you standing outside Irys and Hektor's door!" He snorted. "I couldn't decide whether I was more pissed off because no one had told me you were coming or because you'd managed to waltz right through all of my security arrangements without a single soul even spotting you." He shook his head. "Little did I realize that you were even more of a *seijin* than the *seijins*!"

"Well, I told you Merlin and I had certain unfair advantages. But what's brought this up this morning, Koryn?"

His smile faded, as if he'd realized she wasn't going to let him evade her question. Or, perhaps, as if he didn't *want* to evade it.

"Because it's taken me until this morning to get up the courage to bring it up," he said, looking across the table into her eyes.

"Am I that fearsome?" She tried to make it a joke, but she didn't fully succeed, because the look in his eyes . . . frightened her.

"One of the most fearsome people I know," he told her. "And not just because I know you could slice and dice your way through the entire Royal Guard any time you chose. I mean, I suppose that *is* a bit . . . sobering. But it's not really part of how I think of you. Not anymore."

"How do you think of me, then?"

"As the most beautiful woman I've ever met," he said, and there was no banter at all in his tone.

She stared at him across the table, and the heart she no longer had raced as she felt herself falling into that dark, steady brown gaze. Then she shook her head.

"I'm not," she said. "I can think of a dozen women right here in Manchyr who are a lot more beautiful than I am, Koryn."

"Far be it for me to tell a *seijin* she's wrong, but you are. Wrong, I mean, as *well* as the most beautiful woman I've ever met."

"Koryn, I'm not even really a woman," she said, and wondered why she'd put it that way even as she said it.

"In the words of Lieutenant Raimair, that's dragon shit, Nimue." His voice was firm. "You just said Merlin is a man, and he is. One of the most masculine men I've ever met, actually. I sometimes think that's because he was once a woman and it gives him a perspective most mere men can never have. But you, my dear, most assuredly *are* a woman."

That long vanished heart seemed to leap in her synthetic chest at the words "my dear," but there was enormous pain behind that leap, as well, and she shook her head again, harder than before.

"Don't go there, Koryn," she said quietly.

"Why not?" His voice was equally soft, but his eyes held her.

"Because you're talking to a machine with a ghost living inside it," she told him sharply. The bitterness in her own tone shocked her, but she continued unflinchingly. "It's not a woman, it's a *machine*. One I can configure to *pretend* to be anything I want it to. I've been a man, just as much as Merlin, when I needed to. I can't make myself taller or shorter, but what else would you like to see, Koryn? A brunette? A blonde? An old woman?" She cracked a laugh. "Oh, I can pretend on a lot of levels, Koryn. A last-generation PICA is *fully* functional, after all. But whatever it might look like at any given moment, it's only a machine pretending it's a woman!"

"I wasn't talking about the purely physical," he said calmly, "but I'm well aware of your . . . chameleon abilities. I've *seen* you being those other people, remember? And I'll admit that, in some ways, that makes you even more fascinating to a simple Safeholdian boy. But I've seen the file imagery of Nimue Alban, too. Aside from the hair color—and the height—you're identical to her, and I don't want anything else. Mind you, I'd feel the same way about you however you happened to look at the moment—well, except for the man part, maybe. And the reason I would is that I'm *not* talking to a machine with a ghost living inside it, however . . . configurable you may be. I'm talking to an artificial body with a *person* inside it. A *soul* inside it, just as much as there's a person or a soul inside *me*."

"Really?" She looked down at the piece of toast in her hand, then waved it almost angrily as she looked back up at him. "This isn't even *fuel* for me, Koryn. I've got a *fusion reactor* inside me with years' worth of reactor mass. I could walk across the bottom of the damned ocean without *breathing* for months, much less eating! This is just raw material to be available the *next* time I change into someone else entirely."

"And you eat it because you enjoy the flavor," he countered. "That's a very human motivation, and maybe that means you do need it for more than just raw material. But it's also completely beside the point. And the point is that I've always admired and respected you, even when you were 'just' *Seijin* Nimue. When I found out who you really are, what Nimue Alban sacrificed for you to be here at this moment, doing what you're doing, what I felt was a lot more like awe. Over the last several months, though, I've discovered I feel something else, as well."

She looked at him, refusing to speak, not certain herself why she felt so frightened, and he let the silence linger for two or three seconds before he reached across the table and touched her wrist gently.

"I've discovered I feel something I never expected to feel," he told her. "I've discovered that you're not just my colleague, not just the avatar of Nimue Alban, not just a *seijin,* and sure as hell not just my *friend*."

"Don't, Koryn," she said softly, almost pleadingly. "Don't."

"Don't what? Tell you I love you?" She flinched, but he only shook his head. "I hate to say it, but I can be a bit slow sometimes, so it surprised me, too, when I realized. It's true, though. I *do* love you, Nimue Chwaeriau. I'm sorry if that upsets you, but there's not much I can do about it."

His smile was whimsical, but his eyes were dark, dark as they bored into hers.

"Koryn, you don't know what you're saying. You don't know what you're saying it *to*!"

"Yes, I do. Maybe better than you do."

"You think so?" she asked harshly.

She activated a PICA function she hadn't used since the moment she first awoke in Nimue's Cave, then reached up with her free hand and peeled away her entire face. A skull looked out at him, the planes of its structure shimmering with the bronze tone of Federation synthetics, not the white of human bone, and her gleaming sapphire eyes made it look even more inhuman as they looked back at him from it.

"*This* is what I am, Koryn!" the lipless mouth below those eyes said.

"And your point is . . . what?" he asked, never looking away, never flinching.

She stared at him, and he met that stare levelly.

"Do you really think I could have spent the last three years learning about the Federation and its technology without understanding that the woman across the table from me—the woman I've realized I *love*—wouldn't exist without it? That if it hadn't been possible for Owl to build the body you live inside, I never even would've met you? Of course I understand that, Nimue! And how could I possibly think that whatever it took for me to meet you is anything but a miracle? That *you're* anything but a miracle? Good God, woman! Do I *look* like an idiot?!"

She stared at him, still holding her face in her hand, then shook her head. A tear glimmered at the corner of one of those eyes as her PICA's autonomous programming responded to her emotions.

"Koryn," she said, "there are any number of women—real women, *flesh and blood* women—who would love to love you. But I'm not them."

"Are you telling me you don't feel anything for me?" he asked levelly. "Because I think I may not have been the only slow learner in this room, and I think you do. I think you may not have let yourself think about it, but I think you do."

She sat motionless, the perfect electronic memory of a PICA spinning through five-days, months—*years*—of conversations over this very table. Of planning sessions for the Royal Guard even before he knew the truth of what she was. Of jokes and laughter. Of the way she'd found herself turning towards the door when her more than human hearing recognized his stride coming down the hall. Of the . . . happiness she'd come to relax into when she was with him.

"I—" she began, then stopped. Shook her head.

"You're my friend," she said finally, and her voice sounded uncertain somehow, almost tentative, even to herself.

"Among other things," he said. Then he gave her a smile that was more lopsided than his scarred cheek could have accounted for. "Do you think you could put your face back on?" His smile grew a little broader. "It's hard to read your expression when you don't have one."

"Which?" She astonished herself with a spurt of laughter. "An expression? Or a face?"

"Both. It's sort of hard to have the former without the latter," he pointed out, and she realized he truly was totally relaxed, comfortable with the gleaming synthetic skull she'd just showed him.

"All right," she said, and used both hands to replace the artificial skin and muscles she'd peeled away. She smoothed the seam with her fingertips, triggered another command, and the hairline join vanished as the nanotech fused "skin" and "muscle" once more. Then she crossed her arms and looked across the table at him.

"Koryn, maybe I do feel something more than just friendship. But it's not what you need. I can't give you what you need."

"So Merlin can't give Nynian what she needs?" He leaned back, folding his own arms. "Strange. They seem very happy together!"

"But—"

She stopped again, with no idea what she'd started to say, and his eyes were warm and gentle. She felt herself falling into them and dug in her heels. He didn't understand. Not really. He *couldn't,* and—

"Nimue," he said, "stop being afraid."

"*Afraid?!*" she said sharply.

"Afraid," he repeated.

"Of what?" She felt almost angry now. "Of *you?*"

"Of the Gbaba," he said, and she twitched fully erect in her chair in complete surprise.

"What do the *Gbaba* have to do with this conversation?" she demanded.

"They have a lot to do with the reasons Nimue Alban never let herself love someone," he said unflinchingly. "Not the way I love you. Not the way I think you may have let yourself love me without realizing it."

She stared at him and realized her lips had begun to tremble.

"Nimue Alban was going to die," he told her. "She was going to *die,* and so was her entire world and anyone she let herself love, so she *didn't* let herself. Not the way she could have. The way a person as special as she was *should* have. Do you think I wouldn't realize it had to be that way? I can't begin to truly understand how terrible that knowledge, that decision, must've been, the kind of emotional and spiritual scars they had to leave, but I know it was terrible and I know there *are* scars. I only have to watch you and Merlin, see how deeply you feel, how incredibly, fiercely protective you are, to understand that much. You knew you'd be dead before you were forty, and so would anyone you'd let yourself love. Tell me you didn't build barriers. Tell me you didn't wall away part of yourself just so you could continue to function, kill a few more Gbaba, before they murdered your entire species!"

Another single tear trickled down her synthetic cheek, and he reached across the table to wipe it with a spotless linen napkin.

"I can't begin to imagine what that was like. Maybe I see a shadow of it in the possibility of the 'Archangels'" return, but not the reality. But even though you're still Nimue Alban in every way that counts, you don't live in her world. You live in mine—in *ours*. This world doesn't have to end. It may, as far as we're concerned, if the 'Archangels' come back and undo everything we've accomplished, but it doesn't *have* to. This isn't a threat we can't possibly defeat, and we sure as hell don't *know* we're doomed! And even if we were, it wouldn't matter. I love you, and *that's* what matters. Not how long we have, not whether or not your body's synthetic. And not whether or not you *deserve* to be loved when you're still alive and all the people Nimue Alban did love are dead."

She twitched as if he'd struck her. And, in a way, he had, because she'd never thought about it that way.

Never realized he was right.

"I talked to Nahrmahn a few weeks ago," Koryn told her. "We were talking about the first Siddarmark campaign, when Merlin came up with his insane, brilliant plan to send ironclads fifteen hundred miles inland on the canals. That was so out-of-the-box the Temple boys never saw it coming. How could they have?! But has Merlin ever discussed that winter with you?"

"No . . . ," she said slowly. "He gave me a download, a summary, of it. We've never really *discussed* it, though." She tilted her head. "Why?"

"Because we almost lost him," Koryn said softly. Her eyes widened, and he shrugged. "I don't know if even

Merlin realizes that, but it's true. He blamed himself for this—for *all* of this—and he hated himself because of all of the people he'd personally killed. The people who never had a chance of surviving against him. He wouldn't talk about it, wouldn't admit it to anyone else, but the guilt and the pain inside were *consuming* him, Nimue."

Her nostrils flared as she remembered all the times Merlin had shouldered her aside, the way he'd taken the burden of bloodshed out of her hands so often. She'd realized from the start that he was protecting her from the kind of blood guilt he felt, but she hadn't realized that guilt had burned as deeply and with as much power as Koryn was describing.

"He just . . . shut down," Koryn continued. "He wouldn't talk to Cayleb or Sharleyan, or even Maikel, about it. He wouldn't talk to *anyone* . . . except Nahrmahn. And from a couple of things Nahrmahn *didn't* say, I'm pretty sure he wouldn't have talked to Nahrmahn, either, if Nahrmahn hadn't pretty much taken it out of his hands. But you're making the same mistake he did, Nimue. Probably because you used to be the same person. You aren't in that dark a place, but it's still the same mistake.

"He felt *responsible* for all of us, and because he's a good person, a moral person, it was his job to protect us, not our job to shoulder some of his responsibility for what happened. But isn't that another way of saying he thought we were all children? That we weren't adults? But we *are* adults, you know. We've made our choices, every one of us, and we know exactly what we face because you and he have explained it to us, every step of the way. You haven't deceived us, you haven't misled us, you haven't duped us, and you sure as hell haven't forced us! We're standing beside you because we *want* to. Because you gave us the chance, as well as the choice. Because we're *proud* to be here. And if we're all going to die in the end, then we'll do *that* beside you, too, and never look back. Not because some existential, unstoppable force like the Gbaba didn't give us any choice, but because we *had* a choice. Because unlike the Federation, we have a chance to win, and you and Merlin and Pei Shan-wei and Pei Kau-yung and all of the other men and women who died to put you here *gave* us that chance."

His own eyes gleamed with unshed tears, and he shook his head at her.

"Maybe there never were any real *seijins*, not the way the Church teaches about them. But you and Merlin are what *seijins* ought to have been. What *seijins* like Khody may actually have been, *despite* the Church. And if you're going to march through my life like some mythic heroine brought to life by magic pretending to be technology, then don't you *dare* not let me walk through it beside you! You may be a thousand years older than me, looked at one way, but I'm thirteen years—*standard* years, not Safehold—older than *you* were when you transferred to *Excalibur,* and I'm damned straight not a child. I have the right to stand beside you and look the future in the eye just like you do. I have the right to die for what I believe in, for the truth you and Merlin have taught me, if that's what happens, just like Nimue Alban *did.* But most of all, I know what I'm saying, and I have the right to say it and have you look me in the eye and tell me you don't love me if that happens to be the truth."

Their eyes locked across the breakfast table, and she felt her mouth quiver as the intensity of that demand burned through her.

"So tell me," he said softly. "Tell me you can look me in the eye and tell me that."

The palace seemed to hold its breath around them as his face blurred beyond the veil of tears her artificial eyes produced. And then, slowly, she shook her head.

"No," she heard herself say, and those tears were in her voice, not just her eyes, as her hand reached out across the table. "No, I can't."

"So we can consider this finally confirmed?"

Lord Protector Greyghor Stohnar looked across his desk at Samyl Gahdarhd, the Republic of Siddarmark's Keeper of the Seal, and Gahdarhd shrugged.

"It's not going to be *really* confirmed for a long time to come," he said. "Not with the entire damned Empire apparently going up in flames. But having said that, I think it has to be true. If he'd gotten out, Yu-kwau would have been trumpeting it to Langhorne's Throne by now."

"And if he didn't get out, given what we know did happen in Shang-mi, it was probably just as ugly as the reports say it was," Daryus Parkair, the Republic's Seneschal, said bluntly, his expression grim. "If they got their hands on him, the best thing he could hope for was that it was quick . . . and I doubt to Shan-wei that it was."

Stohnar nodded slowly and ran one hand through his hair. He was only fifty-one, but that hair had gone completely white and the fingers of his hand had developed an irritating, almost continuous tremor.

At the moment, his brown eyes were dark as he tried to imagine what it must have been like. Like Parkair, but unlike Gahdarhd or Henrai Maidyn, the Chancellor of the Exchequer, Stohnar had been a soldier in his time. He'd seen the ugliness of combat. And despite that, he was grimly certain nothing he'd seen could have compared to the streets of Shang-mi as the screaming rioters overran Emperor Waisu's guardsmen and stormed the coach. The gentlest version they'd heard said Waisu had been beaten to death. The uglier version said he'd been literally ripped apart alive, using his own carriage horses to inflict the same punishment his Spears had inflicted on so many serfs over the years.

Stohnar suspected the ugly version was also the accurate one.

"I really don't like myself very much for saying this," he said, "but there's part of me that can't help feeling a certain satisfaction about what happened to him." He shook his head. "What does it say about me that I could want *anyone* to die that way?"

"It says you're a human being who saw millions of your own citizens murdered in an invasion that Waisu's army helped lead, My Lord," Dahnyld Fardhym, the Archbishop of Siddarmark, replied gently. "And the fact that you don't *like* feeling that way says you're a human being whose moral compass still works."

"I'd like to think you're right, Dahnyld," Stohnar said. "I'd like to think you're right."

He turned to gaze out his upper-story office's window across Protector Palace's wall at the roofs of Siddar City. He looked at them for several seconds, then turned back to the men gathered in his office.

"I don't see a thing we can do about what's happening in Harchong," he said then. "And, to be honest, we've got enough problems of our own. Speaking of which, how bad is it, Daryus?"

"It isn't good," Parkair replied frankly. "It's not a total disaster, though. Not yet, at least. And we're one hell of a way short of Sword of Schueler levels."

"So far, anyway," Gahdarhd amended in a sour tone. Parkair cocked an eyebrow at him, and he shook his head.

"Oh, your estimate's accurate as far as it goes, Daryus. The problem is I'm not sure it's going to stay that way. And to be honest, that's mostly because we lost Archbishop Zhasyn. If *anybody* had the moral authority to sit on those idiots, it was him. But he just . . . used himself up during the Jihad. He and Archbishop Arthyn got the reconciliation courts set up, but we needed more time and we didn't get it."

Stohnar nodded heavily. Arthyn Zagyrsk, the Archbishop of Tarikah, and Zhasyn Cahnyr, the Archbishop of Glacierheart, had indeed created the reconciliation courts that both Stohnar and Rhobair II had signed off upon. That provided at least a legal framework for the return of some of the millions of Siddarmarkian Temple Loyalists who'd fled to the Temple Lands during and after the Jihad. The courts had offered a means to adjudicate legal claims and property ownership as an essential part of rebuilding a stable society. What they hadn't provided was a *moral* framework, a basis for genuine reconciliation between one-time neighbors who hated one another with a bitter, burning passion because of the atrocities and bloodshed which had turned the Republic's western provinces into a corpse-littered wasteland dotted with the mass graves of the Inquisition's death camps.

Maybe Gahdarhd was right. Maybe Zhasyn Cahnyr's moral authority as the fearless wartime archbishop of Glacierheart could have made a difference. Unfortunately, they'd never know. And not just because he'd "used himself up during the Jihad," either. Oh, there was plenty of truth to that, but in a just world, he would have been given the final years of peace he'd so richly deserved. Instead, he'd literally worked himself to death as the passionate spokesman for compassion, godly charity, and reconciliation.

And in that final monumental task of his life, he'd failed.

"I don't think it's going to get anywhere near as bad as it was during the Sword, Samyl," Parkair disagreed. "What I think you're probably right about, though, is that it's going to be with us for a long, long time. And, frankly, all the speculators pouring in are making it a hell of a lot worse. They're pissing off *both* sides, because both of them see them for what they are: carrion-eaters."

Stohnar winced, but Parkair—as always—had cut to the heart of the matter with all the tact of a pike charge.

"Unfortunately, we can't keep them out," Maidyn said. "Not unless we want to issue a decree or pass a law which makes it illegal for our own citizens to move from one province to another. Or to offer to buy up land that's lying fallow and untenanted. Even if the price they're offering is maybe as much as fifteen percent of its pre-Jihad value."

His expression was disgusted, and Stohnar snorted.

"I'd love to restrict migration. For that matter, I'd love to declare martial law and prohibit *any* land sales, if that's what it took to get a handle on all this profiteering! But I don't have the constitutional authority. Neither does the Chamber, under existing law, and the noble and high-minded delegates from Tarikah and Westmarch would fight us tooth and nail if we tried to get the kind of legislation to change that passed."

"Old Tymyns might not," Parkair said.

"I'll give you that Tymyns would at least recognize an honest thought if it crossed his mind." Stohnar's tone was caustic. "But Ohlsyn and Zhoelsyn have him convinced *they're* honest. And don't get me started on Trumyn or Ohraily! And all the rest of them are right in the speculators' pocketbook, too. Besides, if I take them on over this, I'll alienate a lot of the other delegates, and we can't afford that. Not when we're coming up on the vote on Thesmar or *your* proposals, Henrai. Thesmar we could probably get through anyway, but not your bank. So you people tell me—where do I make my fight? On trying to control the speculators or on trying to get your bank chartered?"

"Langhorne, I wish Tymahn was still alive," Maidyn sighed. "Even *I'm* not sure 'my' bank is the right answer, Greyghor, but we've got to do something! And Braisyn's worse than useless."

Stohnar ran his hand back through his hair. He'd been doing that a lot lately.

Tymahn Qwentyn had thrown the full resources of his family's banking dynasty behind the Republic in its fight for survival. The Republic had survived; the House of Qwentyn hadn't. It could have. It should have, and that only made its collapse hurt even worse. Maidyn and Stohnar both knew the Duke of Delthak had stood ready to pour support into the House of Qwentyn. But then Tymahn had died—and at least he'd done that peacefully, in his own bed—and his older son Mahrtyn, the obvious heir apparent, had gotten himself murdered by another banker who'd blamed the Qwentyns for his own family's ruin. And that had left Braisyn, the younger brother, who'd never expected to inherit control of the house and who'd been far more interested in freezing out his nephew Owain, Mahrtyn's son, than anything else. The instant Owain recommended accepting Delthak's offer to buy into the House of Qwentyn in order to save it, Braisyn had come out in full-fledged resistance and killed the entire deal.

That was what had truly wiped out the banking house. And, in the process, wiped out what had been effectively the central bank of the entire Republic of Siddarmark. Stohnar hadn't thought of it in those terms—the concept of a "central bank" wasn't one which had been clearly enunciated on Safehold—but that was what the House of Qwentyn had been. It was the entity which had exercised a curbing effect on unsecured lines of credit or undercapitalized enterprises, whose own loan portfolio had been so vast it effectively controlled the Republic's interest rates. It was the entity whose officers and agents had managed the currency flow. It hadn't done any of those things as an official agent of the Republic, but because someone had to regulate the banking system if it was to be kept stable and the House of Qwentyn had gradually assumed that role out of what amounted to enlightened self-interest.

Now it was gone. Owain Qwentyn and his wife and children had left the Republic, immigrating to Charis where Stohnar had no doubt he would soon find himself in a new partnership with Duke Delthak, given Delthak's wyvern's eye for talent. The rest of the House lay in ruins, with Braisyn and a dozen of his cousins bickering over the skeleton. And in its absence, an economy which would have been in serious trouble anyway, in the wake of the Jihad and the deaths of so many millions of its citizens, was on the brink of outright, catastrophic failure.

The Exchequer was already deeply in debt from the

ruinous expenses of the Jihad, but at least it knew how big that debt was. No one—least of all Henrai Maidyn and the Exchequer—had any idea how many totally unsecured loans and letters of credit had been issued to fuel the speculation in land. More of them had been issued to support the importation of Charisian manufactory methods, or to fund the privatization of the Republic's foundries in the wake of the Jihad. What they *did* know was that those notes and loans were trading at less than half their face value and that the value of the Siddarmarkian mark was plummeting, and not just in comparison to the *Charisian* mark.

"We've *got* to get the Bank—or something like it—up and running," Maidyn said now. "The Church's insistence on redeeming all those notes Grand Vicar Rhobair issued when he was Treasurer and paying them off at par is only making *our* situation worse. The Church had a lot more notes out there than we did, but despite everything, it still has the depth of holdings—and the cash flow, thanks to the tithe—to retire all its debt eventually. More than that, everyone's realized Rhobair intends to do just that, which means the *Church's* paper is still good for something besides lighting fires and wiping arses. And everybody knows Charisian notes are—literally—as good as gold. For all intents and purposes, both the Charisians and the Church are now using what amounts to paper money, and people are willing to accept it from both of them because they know both Charis and the Church can redeem their paper in specie if they have to.

"With Tymahn and Mahrtyn gone, Shan-wei only knows how much paper's been issued—or by who—here in the Republic. That's why no one's willing to accept *our* 'paper money.' It's also why my people estimate that close to a third of all our manufactories—and that includes the new ones—are about to collapse. And that's going to throw thousands or hundreds of thousands of manufactory workers out of work. And that's going to cause ripple effects all through the rest of the Republic. So we have to at the very least do what Charis has done and establish controls on future issues of credit. If we can figure out how to do it, we really need to do what the Church is doing, too, and retire all the notes we issued during the Jihad at their face value. Even if we can do all that, we're still looking at all the notes *other* people have issued here in the Republic, so we're still heading into a serious . . . call it a recession. If we *can't* do it, we're probably looking at a general collapse, and I have no idea how long it will last or how bad it will be. Except to say it will probably be worse than anything any of us have ever seen before."

"We still need to get some kind of handle on what's going on in the western provinces, too, though, Henrai," Parkair said. "There's got to be some way we can pour a little water on the coals before they flame up all over again!"

"Daryus, if it's a choice between getting the Bank approved and seeing everything from Icewind to the South March border go up in flames, I have to vote for the Bank," Maidyn said flatly. "Civil unrest, insurrection— hell, even outright civil war!—you and the Army can fight. If the bottom falls out of our economy, that's something *no* army can fight. It may not get as many people killed outright, but it'll do even more damage to the Republic as a whole. And if it gets bad enough?"

The chancellor looked around at the other faces, his expression grim.

"If it gets bad enough, you could see the Army fighting right here in the streets of Siddar City."

His tone was flat, and when he finished speaking, it was very, very quiet in the lord protector's office.

"I want that fool *dead*."

His Celestial and Consecrated Highness Zhyou-Zhwo Hantai's voice was iron-hard and colder than Bedard ice as he glared after the withdrawing prelate.

"Your Celestial Highness," Grand Duke North Wind Blowing began, "I understand your feelings, but Archbishop Bau—"

"I want him *dead*," Zhyou-Zhwo repeated even more flatly, glaring at his father's first councilor. "See to it. Unless you want to *join* him, Your Grace."

North Wind Blowing had been a courtier for over fifty years. Despite that, his face tightened as he heard the utter sincerity in the crown prince's voice.

"If that's what Your Celestial Highness wishes, then of course it will be done," he said, forcing his voice to remain level despite the ice water suddenly flowing through his veins. "I would, however, be derelict in my responsibility to Your Celestial Highness if I did not point out that he *is* an archbishop of Mother Church. Executing someone who wears the orange is likely to precipitate a conflict with the Church—with the *Church*, not simply The Temple—at a time when Your Celestial Highness can ill afford to . . . fight on additional fronts."

He met Zhyou-Zhwo's furious eyes steadily.

"I point this out," he continued, "because I wish to know if Your Celestial Highness could be content with his assassination rather than his official execution."

The crown prince's expression relaxed ever so slightly. He looked at the grand duke for several breathless seconds. Then he nodded.

"How he dies is unimportant, so long as he dies *soon*," he said. "He and those like him who abandoned their posts at the first sign of danger—who allowed this to happen in the first place—will pay. And however he dies, I think those who we wish to understand will recognize whose hand struck the blow."

"As Your Celestial Highness says," North Wind Blowing murmured, and bowed deeply as Zhyou-Zhwo rose from the throne and stalked out of the Audience Chamber. The first councilor remained bowing until the boot heels of the crown prince's personal guards had accompanied him and the door had closed behind them. Then he straightened slowly, conscious of the increasing stiffness of his spine, and drew a deep breath.

Zhyou-Zhwo was forty-one years old, and he'd never been noted for his gentle temper. Nor had it been much of a secret in Shang-mi that he'd been impatient for his own time upon the throne. But now—

North Wind Blowing shook his head, profoundly grateful no one else had been present. It was unfortunate that Zhyou-Zhwo was probably right that everyone would realize who'd ordered Baudang Zhynchi's murder, but no one would be able to *prove* it unless the grand duke's assassins were far clumsier than usual. And at least Zhynchi was probably the most expendable of the Harchongese prelates. For that matter, it was at least possible his death might encourage even greater dedication to the Crown's needs among the Empire's archbishops, which could scarcely be a bad thing. That was, after all, one reason North Wind Blowing had encouraged the crown prince's fury to focus on Zhynchi in the first place. The fact that focusing it there had helped divert it from *North Wind Blowing* had been an even more important factor, of course.

The first councilor crossed to the Audience Chamber's window, looking out across the tropical color of Yu-kwau and the sparkling water of the Bay of Alexov. They really should have moved the imperial capital here long ago, he thought, and not just because of the climate. There were fewer serfs in the South, and those that existed were less . . . refractory. There was little chance—so far, at least—of seeing the sort of madness that was spreading from Shang-mi all across Tiegelkamp. Still, these Southerners were an arrogant and presumptuous lot, too conscious of their own wealth and insufficiently aware of the deference they owed their betters. That could prove . . . regrettable down the road, if North Wind Blowing failed to keep their influence in Zhyou-Zhwo's court trimmed back. Fortunately, few understood that game better than he.

And they'd be here for a while, he admitted grimly, eyes tracking the white sails of a schooner as it headed towards the open bay. The crown prince had so far refused to officially accept his father's death. It was only a matter of time until he had to, and North Wind Blowing wasn't entirely certain why he'd resisted so long. Despite his rage and his fear—however fiercely he might refuse to admit it—of the spreading violence in the North, the first councilor never doubted Zhyou-Zhwo wanted the Crown just as ferociously as he ever had. Perhaps he simply didn't want to appear overly eager? Didn't want to create the impression that he'd scarcely been able to wait for Emperor Waisu's death? That could be a particularly unfortunate conclusion for people to draw, given how much truth it contained.

His reasons scarcely mattered. There was ample confirmation Waisu was dead, although the exact details of that death might remain unclear. Within the next few days—the next few five-days, at the latest—Zhyou-Zhwo would be forced to "accept" the Crown, if only to maintain continuity of the imperial authority. If he continued to be coy about it, North Wind Blowing would have to insist upon that himself. Which, now that the first councilor thought about it, might be exactly why Zhyou-Zhwo had refused to make the suggestion himself. If he could place the first councilor in the role of suppliant rather than mentor and guide. . . .

That was a thought, and not necessarily a happy one.

If that was what was happening, it indicated that the crown prince was capable of greater political subtlety than North Wind Blowing had assumed he was. The first few years of any new emperor's reign were always the most . . . problematical. Too many emperors had come to the Crown with the mistaken intent of exercising personal rule. Sometimes it took longer than others for the professional ministers and the imperial bureaucracy to reassert the proper flow of the Crown's business. Under the present circumstances, when so many of those bureaucrats had failed to escape the sack of Shang-mi, that process could be even more extended than usual, and the Empire could ill afford a power struggle between the Crown and its ministers.

No, best to keep a king wyvern's eye upon the situation. And, in the meantime, it would be wise to watch his own flanks, as well. For that matter, it would be equally wise to redirect Zhyou-Zhwo's anger and hatred onto someone or something *external* to the Empire.

Anything that focused His Celestial and Consecrated Highness' ire at non-Harchongese enemies would simultaneously direct it *away* from the imperial ministers who'd failed to prevent the fall of Shang-mi.

. X .
Imperial Palace,
Desnair the City,
The Crown Lands,
Desnairian Empire.

"So that's the size of it, I'm afraid, Sire," Symyn Gahrnet said. "Unless we improve the Osalk-Sherkal Canal and extend it into Hankey—which would require significant improvements on the Sherkal River, as well—we just don't have the transportation access we need. I'm sorry. I know that's not what you wanted to hear, but—"

Gahrnet raised his hands shoulder high, palms uppermost, and Mahrys Ahldarm, Emperor Mahrys IV of Desnair, scowled.

That was all he did, however, which owed a great deal to the fact that Gahrnet was his cousin. It might also indicate an awareness of pragmatic reality, the Duke of Traykhos thought, which would be good. At fifty-nine, Mahrys was in the prime of his life. With only reasonable good fortune he could look forward to at least two more decades on the throne, and he'd learned some hard lessons as a younger man during the Jihad.

"Symyn's right, Sire," Traykhos said now, and the Emperor transferred his unhappy expression to his first councilor . . . who was also his uncle. In Desnair, even more than most mainland realms, government was very much a family affair.

"We didn't make sufficient allowance for how much heavy transport this will require," Traykhos continued. He shrugged. "We should have, if only from our experience during the Jihad, but it's not really Symyn's fault we didn't. None of the rest of us did any better." It was his turn to scowl. "It's not the sort of thing a gentleman spends a lot of time thinking about."

"Then we damned well better *start* thinking about it," Mahrys growled.

He looked around the council table at his most trusted advisors—Traykhos; Anzhelo Styvyns, the Duke of Pearlmann and Desnair's Chancellor of the Exchequer; Zhules Estayben, the Duke of Sherach, the Army Minister (whose responsibilities included the Navy once more); Sir Rhobair Gahrnet, the Duke of Harless and Symyn's older brother, who'd become the imperial Foreign Minister; and Symyn himself, who held no official council position but was nonetheless one of its more influential members. They looked back at him with remarkable aplomb, given what had happened to some of their predecessors. Some might have thought it was due to the inexperience and overconfidence of youth—at sixty, Traykhos was the oldest councilor present by almost twenty years—but Mahrys knew that wasn't the reason.

"I'd like it if we never made any mistakes," the Emperor continued, "but we all know that's not going to happen. So instead we'll just have to learn from them and do better next time. Having said that, do we have any suggestions about how to do better? Symyn?"

"Improving the canals would be the simplest solution," Gahrnet replied after a moment's consideration. "It wouldn't be the fastest, we can't build them everywhere I'd really like to, and I'm not sure it would be the cheapest approach, but it's something our engineers already understand how to do. Having said that, there could be . . . other options."

Mahrys cocked his head, eyebrows knitting ever so slightly, at the words "other options." He clearly suspected he knew where his cousin was headed, and equally clearly he wasn't enthralled by the thought.

Gahrnet kept his own expression firmly under control. It wasn't that he disagreed with what he knew the Emperor was unhappy about, but despite their close relationship and despite the lessons both of them had learned in the Jihad, Mahrys IV remained a man of passions even more than one of judgment.

Although he wasn't about to say so, Gahrnet knew he was considerably smarter than the Emperor. For that matter, he was considerably smarter than his older brother, as well. On the other hand, much as he loved Rhobair, that was a lower bar to clear than many, he acknowledged. And whatever their relative intellectual attainments might be, all three of them—indeed, every man in this council chamber—were united in their unwavering hatred for the Empire of Charis and all things Charisian.

Which was the real problem with what he needed to suggest.

"As I say, the canals are something we understand how to do." He chose his words carefully. "From the viewpoint of efficiency and, probably, cost-effectiveness, though, I don't think it's the *best* solution. Much as we all detest Charis, no form of land transportation currently available can compete with the efficiency and scale of transport by water. Or, at least, that's been the case until very recently."

"You're thinking about those . . . 'steam automotive' things, aren't you?" Traykhos observed sourly.

"I am," Gahrnet acknowledged. What he'd really have liked to suggest was that they needed to hire some of the Charisian experts who genuinely understood the new manufactory processes. That, unfortunately, would have been going too far. As Traykhos had pointed out, that wasn't the sort of thing a gentleman thought about. The implied corollary, however, was that anyone who did think about it *wasn't* a gentleman, and the last thing in the world Mahrys IV was prepared to contemplate was the sort of mobocracy so disgustingly on display in Charis.

Which left the automotives as a sort of halfway step. Possibly.

"I don't like that thought." The Emperor's tone was a lot sourer than his first councilor's had been, but at least it fell short of the blast of outrage the notion of recruiting Charisian advisors would have provoked. "It opens the door to Cayleb and Sharleyan and all those other Shan-wei–damned Charisian notions!"

"I understand that, Sire," Gahrnet said, "and I don't make the suggestion lightly. But you've charged me to acquire the capability to match Siddarmark's and Charis' manufacturing ability, and I'm afraid that means adopting at least some of their innovations."

"The guilds would scream bloody murder," Pearlmann put in.

"They're *already* screaming bloody murder," Traykhos pointed out in grudging support of his nephew.

"Yes, they are," Gahrnet agreed, "and no wonder! If we adopted the Charisian model as it stands, it would destroy them. That's why I've stressed how important it is to involve them in the process. Obviously, we have to find our own way, and I'd never suggest just jumping into the cesspool with Cayleb and Sharleyan, Sire. But whatever we think of their methods, we need at least some of their *tools*."

Mahrys scowled some more, but then he nodded, however grudgingly.

His uncle Ahlvyn, Gahrnet and Harless' father, had died in the Kyplyngyr Forest disaster which had destroyed the flower of the Imperial Desnairian Army. If there were any two people in the entire Empire who hated both Siddarmark and Charis more than they did,

Mahrys had never met them, and he knew how utterly both of them detested anything that smacked of the Church of Charis or Charisian attitudes in general.

Despite their father's death, both of Sir Ahlvyn Gahrnet's sons had been part of the faction urging Desnairian . . . disengagement from the Jihad after the Kyplyngyr, but not because they didn't want revenge. They'd urged that policy because they'd understood—as Mahrys himself had—that once the Church had been defeated, Siddarmark would be free to turn its new-model army upon its traditional Desnairian enemies. Only Mother Church's intervention had saved Desnair after the last war between it and the Republic. With her defeat there would be no check on Siddarmark's actions, and the consequences of a new-model invasion would have been dire, to say the very least. So it had clearly been time to husband Desnair's resources and rebuild as powerful a defensive army as possible in hopes that Lord Protector Greyghor would decide he'd lost enough lives and decline to spend more of them in a war of vengeance.

The strategy had worked. Or, at least, Siddarmark hadn't invaded Desnair after the Church's military collapse, although the reasons for that were debatable. What wasn't debatable was that Desnair and its poverty-stricken neighbor Delferahk hadn't even been invited to the negotiating table where the Jihad was ended. Technically, both of them were still at war with the Charisian Empire, although no one on either side had been crude enough to say so. The recognition of the Grand Duchy of Silkiah as a sovereign realm, paying tribute to no one, was an extra fishbone to stick in Mahrys' craw, but being simply *ignored* by the victors had been far more infuriating.

And it had left Desnair—and Delferahk—in an unenviable position in terms of the new manufactory techniques. They were outside the tidy, comfortable Charisian-Siddarmarkian system and nobody inside it was interested in inviting them aboard. Mother Church hadn't exactly strained herself coming to the Empire's assistance, either. In his fairer moments, of which he had as few as possible, Mahrys acknowledged that Desnair's effective desertion of the Jihad at the moment of Mother Church's greatest need made that pretty much inevitable. Rhobair II had more than enough slash lizards chasing his sleigh, and he clearly felt a greater sense of obligation to those who hadn't abandoned the Jihad, like the two million men of the Mighty Host of God and the Archangels marooned in the Temple Lands, than he did to anyone in Desnair.

Understanding the reasons didn't make Mahrys a bit happier with the consequences, however. Nor was he going to overlook the debt he owed Charis. But if he meant to collect that debt, he needed the military wherewithal to face Charis and its allies, and that meant he needed to hugely increase the capacity of his own manufactories and acquire the same sort of new-model weapons.

And he had to do it without eroding the authority of the Crown and without permitting baseborn men to replace the men of blood who made Desnair what it was.

"Symyn has a point, Sire," Harless said, speaking up at last. Mahrys glanced at him, and the duke shrugged. "We're not the only ones trying to improve our manufacturing ability, Sire," he pointed out. "The good news is that Siddarmark's in so much trouble. Its currency is effectively close to worthless now, and the ongoing situation in their western provinces is getting worse, according to my sources."

Mahrys nodded. In addition to his responsibility for the Empire's diplomacy, Harless ran its spy networks. They'd taken horrendous losses during the Jihad. It had almost been as if the Charisians, or at least that accursed *seijin,* Athrawes, had actually been able to peer inside men's minds and know when they were spying for someone else. But Harless had rebuilt steadily over the last five or six years.

"From what we're seeing so far, Siddarmark's efforts to 'industrialize'—" Harless used the Charisian-coined word with an expression of distaste "—have hit a major roadblock. Whether it's a long-term setback or only temporary is impossible to say at this point, but it does give us an opportunity to at least make up some ground on them.

"As I say, that's the good news. The *bad* news is Dohlar."

Mahrys' expression turned thunderous. The Kingdom of Dohlar had been Mother Church's most effective champion during the Jihad, at least until the Mighty Host had fully engaged the combined forces of Siddarmark and Charis. One might have expected that to have post-Jihad repercussions for the traitorous Earl Thirsk and the even more despicable Sir Rainos Ahlverez, who'd betrayed the Army of Justice in the South March. Unfortunately, it hadn't. In fact, Dohlar was enthusiastically embracing the Charisian mode of "industrialization," despite the social unrest it must provoke. Nor was Charis, in the person of the insufferable Duke of Delthak, unaware of the openings that decision provided. The Gorath Bay Railroad, a joint Dohlaran-*Charisian* venture, had broken ground on its first automotive works barely two months ago.

"I can't speak to the economic consequences of Thirsk's arse-kissing with Charis," Harless went on. "Diplomatically, though, they're drawing closer and closer together, and Silkiah is actively licking Charis' hand. I think they'd rather be beholden to somebody who's hundreds of miles away by sea than to Siddarmark, which is only just on the other side of their northern border. And Charis has a bigger bowl of gravy to dip their spoon into, at least at the moment. So we're in danger of finding ourselves frozen out, and unless we're able to build our own manufactories up, we'll find ourselves dependent on our potential enemies. We'll actually have to buy our weapons from Charis or one of its lackeys, and only fools—which, unfortunately, neither Cayleb nor Sharleyan are—would sell us weapons that could actually threaten them."

"I'm aware of that," Mahrys said, his tone rather icier than the one he normally addressed to his cousin.

"We know that, Sire," Gahrnet said, drawing the Emperor's potential ire back away from his brother. "I think Rhobair's point—and mine, too—is that time isn't working for us, except, perhaps, in the case of Siddarmark. We need to rethink our approach to this, and we need to be willing to adopt Charisian tools. We damned well don't need the mind-set that comes with them, but we need the tools themselves."

"How would you like to proceed?" Mahrys asked, sitting back in his chair.

"I think we need to organize ourselves better, Sire," Gahrnet told him. "You need to sit down with your Council, or at least with us, and define exactly what you want to accomplish. I know we've discussed it many times, but those discussions have been a bit . . . amorphous. I'm thinking we need to set specific goals, and specific mileposts to accomplish in pursuit of those goals. I suppose what I'm talking about is a sort of ongoing, coordinated process. What I'd really like to see is a plan that covers, say, the next five years and will be periodically reviewed and modified as events make necessary. At the end of every year, we'd extend our planning period for another year, sort of a . . . a rolling horizon."

Mahrys nodded thoughtfully, and Gahrnet hid his satisfaction. He was a loyal servant of the Crown, but he wasn't blind to the opportunities which would fall his way if he was made the official custodian of any such plan. The pecuniary possibilities alone were enormous. Although what was even more important, he told himself virtuously, was that that sort of centralized control would leave him far better placed to produce the "industrialization" Desnair required.

"In the short-term," he went on more confidently, "I believe we need to look very closely at adopting the concept of these 'railroads' of the Charisians, Sire. As I understand it, no individual rail wagon can carry as much cargo as a large barge, but each automotive can pull scores of wagons and we can build the damned things anywhere. We don't need rivers, and if we made them a Crown monopoly, I imagine they'd bring in enormous amounts of revenue to help fuel our other efforts."

Mahrys nodded again, far more enthusiastically. The *Holy Writ* prohibited secular rulers from charging for the use of the canals it was the godly's responsibility to build and maintain. That didn't mean it didn't happen.

The Canal Service cut across all national boundaries, at least in theory, and was responsible for levying the service fees which helped pay for the canals' maintenance. Those fees were supposedly earmarked solely for canal maintenance, but they had a persistent way of hemorrhaging into the local authorities' coffers. It was all very sub rosa, however, and discretion required that the pilferage be reasonably modest lest Mother Church's auditors be forced to take notice.

But the *Holy Writ* didn't cover "railroads." *Their* revenues belonged to whoever owned them, and if every Desnairian railway belonged to the Crown. . . .

"For now," Gahrnet said, "we'd have to buy our automotives, and probably our rails, direct from Charis. The good news is that those moneygrubbing bastards would cheerfully sell us the rope to hang their own grandmothers if the price was right, so I don't see any problem with the purchase itself. Once we have an automotive or two of our own, we can take them apart and see if our mechanics can figure out how to build more of our own. I don't see why that should be impossible, Sire, especially if we insist that our mechanics have to be trained in Charis to keep them in service once we get them home."

"That will cost a lot of marks," Pearlmann pointed out. His tone was more that of a man making an observation than someone raising an objection, and Gahrnet nodded.

"It will, but we still have the gold mines. And," he turned to face the Emperor more squarely, "once we begin building our own railroads and demonstrate how useful they are—for farmers, not just manufactory owners—and start charging to transport freight and passengers, I expect it would turn quickly into a net profit maker, not an ongoing charge on the Exchequer."

"Anzhelo?" Mahrys looked at the chancellor, one eyebrow raised.

"I can't guarantee that, Sire," Pearlmann said. "I'd be extraordinarily surprised if Symyn isn't right, though. It's one of the reasons those frigging Charisians like Delthak are dragging in marks hand over fist!" He glowered at the thought. "Frankly, it's about time somebody else in-vaded their trough."

"There's something to that," Mahrys agreed. "On the other hand—"

The Emperor broke off, looking up with a frown as the door to the council chamber opened.

"I beg your pardon, Your Majesty," the uniformed footman said, bowing deeply. "A messenger has just ar-rived for Duke Harless. He says the matter is urgent."

"Urgent enough to interrupt this meeting?" Mahrys asked coldly.

"So he says, Your Majesty," the footman replied, still bowing.

The Emperor cocked a rather fulminating eyebrow at Harless, then grimaced.

"Very well," he said. "Send him in."

"Of course, Your Majesty!"

The footman disappeared, to be replaced a moment later by a tallish, dark-haired man in the expensive but sober tailoring of an upper-level government bureaucrat.

"A thousand apologies, Your Majesty," he began, "but—"

"Yes, yes!" Mahrys waved an impatient hand. "I know—it's urgent. And," he relented slightly, "you don't normally waste our time, Sir Hyrmyn. But get to it, please."

"Thank you, Your Majesty," Sir Hyrmyn Khaldwyl, who was effectively Harless' senior deputy, bowed al-most as deeply as the footman had. Then he reached into his tunic, withdrew a large envelope, and passed it to the duke.

"This just arrived from our embassy in Yu-kwau, Your Grace," he said. "I took the liberty of reading it as soon as it was delivered."

"Yu-kwau?" the Emperor repeated sharply, and Khal-dwyl nodded.

"Yes, Your Majesty." His expression was grave. "I'm afraid it's been confirmed. Emperor Waisu is dead."

Someone inhaled sharply. Not in surprise, but in consternation, and Mahrys' jaw tightened. He'd never much cared for Waisu, or for Harchongians in general, for that matter. But he'd always recognized a certain commonality of interest between his own crown and that of Harchong, because both had been bastions of stability against the steadily encroaching madness out of Charis, Siddarmark, and the Reformists. In fact, Mahrys and Harless had tried for the last couple of years, with a uniform lack of success, to inveigle Waisu into a post-Jihad alliance, or at least into an agreement to coordinate policy with Desnair.

But if events in North Harchong were as bad as preliminary reports suggested—and as this one seemed to confirm—the situation was even worse than Mahrys had believed. If Harchong went down, Desnair truly would be alone against all of the "progressive" forces seeking to destroy the order and stability God and the Archangels themselves had established here on Safehold.

Waisu never listened to us, the Emperor thought grimly, *and look what* that *got him!*

In reality, Mahrys knew, it had been Waisu's ministers, like Grand Duke North Wind Blowing, who'd refused to listen with all the traditional—and invincible—arrogance which made Harchongians so universally detested. Although, to be honest, North Wind Blowing had probably been more concerned about getting too close to someone whose social policies were as "liberal" as Desnair's. Now, though—

"Has Zhyou-Zhwo taken the Crown yet?" he asked.

"Not as of yesterday, Sire," Harless replied, looking up from the dispatch he'd been rapidly scanning. "And while Hyrmyn's right that the Emperor's death has been confirmed, it hasn't been officially *announced* yet. The confirmation is solid, Sire, but it was made unofficially to our ambassador. Probably by someone in Yu-kwau but not in the Crown Prince's inner circle, if you take my meaning."

Mahrys grunted in understanding. No doubt a lot of South Harchongians were less than enthralled by what the imperial family's abrupt arrival entailed for local power arrangements, especially if the Hantais' exodus ended up being more prolonged than anyone had initially predicted.

"I wonder what he's waiting for?" Pearlmann murmured, and Traykhos shrugged.

"I don't have any idea, but he can't wait too long. Not without risking a serious threat to the continuity of the Crown's power. They can't afford anything remotely like an interregnum with things going as badly in the North as they appear to be going."

"Agreed," Mahrys said, sitting farther back in his chair and stroking his mustache in thought. He stayed that way for several seconds, then leaned forward and planted his hands on the conference table.

"Agreed, and given what's happening in the North, he may be more amenable to our diplomatic viewpoint than his father was."

"Forgive me, Sire," Gahrnet said dryly, "but is Zhyou-Zhwo likely to be any freer to ignore his ministers than his father was?"

"That *is* an interesting question," Mahrys acknowledged with a bleak smile. "On the other hand, our earlier reports indicate that quite a few of those ministers didn't make it out of Shang-mi, either."

"No, they didn't," Harless agreed. "They have to be doing a lot of . . . reorganization, and according to my agents in Shang-mi, Zhyou-Zhwo's been resentful of the bureaucrats' influence for a long time."

"So he may see this as an opportunity to 'reorganize' things on a basis more to his liking." Mahrys nodded. "And even if he doesn't, even Harchongese bureaucrats have to be shaken by what's happened to them and their families. And who are they going to blame for it?" The Emperor smiled coldly. "I'll tell you who they're going to blame. They're going to blame Charis and the Reformists for provoking the Jihad and they're going to blame the Grand Vicar for *ending* the Jihad. And they're especially going to blame him—and Maigwair—for what happened to the Mighty Host."

His smile turned even thinner and colder as he met his advisors' eyes.

"I believe it might be time for a personal message of condolence from one Emperor to another," he said.

MARCH YEAR OF GOD 904

·✦·

. I .
Shan-Zhi Forest
and
Pauton Cathedral,
City of Pauton,
Boisseau Province,
Harchong Empire.

Bairahn Mahgynys peered through the eyepiece and turned the adjusting screw with finicky precision. The marker on the graduated rod came into sharp focus and he nodded in satisfaction. He straightened, checking the numbers on the survey transit's graduated base ring, then carefully recorded them on his log sheet.

He stowed the logbook in his rucksack and looked up, listening to the work crews widening the muddy cut through the fringe of the unconsecrated Shan-Zhi Forest. The sharp, crisp sounds of axes and the steady rasping of long, two-man crosscut saws were overlaid by shouting voices, whistling dragons, the occasional crack of a drover's whip, and the crashing sound as trees toppled to the ground. It was a far, far cry from what Mahgynys had witnessed upon his arrival here in Boisseau, just over a month ago.

"Time to move," he said. "How are the trail-breaking crews coming?"

"You're catching up to them," Hauzhu Shozu told him with a crooked grin. "You're only a couple of miles behind now. Your part seems to go a lot faster than their part."

"Why His Grace pays them so much," Mahgynys replied with a broader smile.

"He does, really," Shozu said more soberly, and it was true. Oh, by the standards of someone like Mahgynys—a trained and highly skilled professional—the peasants and escaped serfs swinging those axes and saws weren't paid very much at all. By the standards of the Empire of Harchong, however, Duke Delthak's wages were scandalously high. In less than two months, every man in one of those crews would earn better than a year and a half of anything he'd ever earned before. That was why attitudes had changed so much over the past six five-days. What had been sullen, half-unwilling wariness—the sort of wariness serfs and peasants always showed someone who promised something good in their lives—had transformed itself into enthusiasm. The thought of money in a man's pocket, of the promise that *they*—peasants, even *serfs*—would be trained to operate and maintain the steam automotives which would someday snort their way through the forest along the roadway they were clearing. . . .

Shozu shook his head mentally, still unable to fully process it himself.

"We get this project finished," Mahgynys went on, collapsing the legs of the transit's tripod while one of Shozu's assistants began rolling up the surveyor's chain, "and the pay's getting better all around." He looked at Shozu steadily. "Of course, getting it finished's going to depend on a lot of things the Duke can't control."

"We're doing our best." Shozu shrugged rather more philosophically than he actually felt. "It helps that so many people trust Bishop Yaupang. And Baron Star Rising's always been fairer with the common folk than a lot of nobles. I'd be lying if I said I was positive they could make it work, though."

"Going to depend a lot on people like you," Mahgynys said quietly, and Shozu nodded.

Unlike two-thirds of the Harchongians Duke Delthak had hired for his survey crews, Shozu was a free peasant. In fact, by the standards of a Harchongese commoner, he was a significant landowner, with over twelve hundred acres under the plow. It had taken his family the better part of two centuries to put together a parcel that size through marriages, purchases, and land swaps, but it had made Hauzhu Shozu a man of influence in the community around Rwanzhi. He was also fully literate and remarkably well-educated for a Harchongese peasant . . . and his third eldest son had actually been accepted by one of the small, secular academies in Shang-mi.

Which was why he had no idea whether or not Zhyqwo was still alive.

"Like I say, we're doing our best. And, to be honest, having you people here surveying the right-of-way is the best argument in favor I could give any of my neighbors!"

It was Mahgynys' turn to nod and hope his expression concealed his own doubts. Not as to whether or not this was a good idea, but whether or not it was going to work. It was just like Duke Delthak to jump in before anyone could have guessed either way about that. Overall, the duke had a pretty fair record of guessing right, but there'd been a few disasters, like the bath his investments had taken in Siddarmark following the collapse of the House of Qwentyn. Mahgynys didn't have access to the actual numbers on that, but if the ones he'd heard bruited about were anywhere near accurate, they would have wiped out many a lesser individual's fortune. Of course, no one else on Safehold, aside from the emperor and empress, had ever amassed a fortune remotely as vast as the duke's. If anyone could afford to back a hunch, it had to be him, and his investment partners were generally willing to follow his lead. It might have taken a little more argument this time to bring them around. Then again, it might not have. When Their Majesties politely suggested to one of their most loyal cronies that an investment would be welcome, it would have taken a board member with balls of steel to argue with the duke's decision to make that investment.

It was just that at the moment the jury was very much

out on whether Baron Star Rising and his ramshackle coalition of aristocrats, rogue clerics, townsmen, peasants, and—God help them all—serfs was going to pull it off. The anathemas being thundered at Bishop Yaupang and the churchmen who dared to support him from Yukwau and the bloodthirsty threats of wholesale executions for any secular "traitors" following in their wake did not bode well.

On the other hand, he reminded himself, *Their Majesties—and the Duke—have a habit of succeeding however bad the odds look, don't they? It's only that just* looking *at this place makes me cringe inside.*

He shrugged, shouldered the tripod, and started hiking along the muddy trough being carved through the forest. Someday soon—if Duke Delthak's current gamble paid off the way his gambles had a habit of paying off—that trough would be the roadbed for the Rwanzhi-Zhynkau railroad, connecting the Bay of Pauton to the Yalu Inlet. That was over four hundred miles as the wyvern flew, and it didn't count the other lines which would tie the major towns of Boisseau together in a way which had never been possible before.

He wondered if even Shozu began to understand what that would mean for West Harchong's economy and people.

Assuming they could keep the wrong people's fingers out of the pie, at least.

▼ ▼ ▼

"My Lord, My Lord Bishop, I *understand* how important this is," Mayor Yingcho said, looking back and forth between Baron Star Rising and Bishop Yaupang Lyauyan. "And I know how important the Charisians' offer is. Don't think I don't, and don't think I'm not in favor. But we all need to be aware of how His Majesty's bound to react when *he* hears about it."

The mayor had a point, Baron Star Rising reflected. In fact, he had a very good one. The problem was that this was a classic case of damned-if-they-did-and-damned-if-they-didn't. And the pressure wasn't getting any lighter.

"You're right, Faizhwan," he said, turning away to gaze out the office window across the square at Bishop Yaupang Lyauyan's palace on the other side of Cathedral Square. It was a very modest palace for one of Safehold's oldest dioceses. For that matter, even the cathedral was decidedly "modest" by the Harchongese Church's standards.

"We do need to be aware of that," he continued, "especially because the best word for how he reacts is going to be 'poorly.'"

"Ever the master of understatement, my son," Lyauyan observed in a dry tone. The bishop was six years younger than Star Rising, but the baron felt no patronization in the younger man's choice of address. Yaupang Lyauyan was one of the unfortunately few Harchongese clerics in whom personal piety always trumped political considerations. In fact, he regarded politics, and especially political expediency, secular or temporal, with unmitigated loathing. What *he* cared about were people and souls . . . which was how he found himself up to his neck in the bitterest political struggle to wrack Harchong since the Creation.

"Well, that's how he and the Court have reacted to everything *else* we've done, My Lord," Star Rising pointed out, "and none of the rest of it approaches this."

"It's an act of open rebellion," Tahnshwun Zheng-chi, Baron Crystal Fountain, said. The other three looked at him, and he shrugged. "I didn't say I'm against it. I only said it's an act of open rebellion, and let's be honest—it is."

"Trying to prevent the complete collapse of central authority in His Supreme and Most Puissant Majesty's western provinces is scarcely an act of rebellion, My Lord," Bishop Yaupang retorted. "Only the most benighted and shortsighted of individuals could think it was!"

"Forgive me, My Lord," Crystal Fountain said, cocking his head, "but don't you think that rather describes the people around His Majesty at this moment?"

"Of course I do," the bishop replied, although all of them were perfectly well aware it was actually a more accurate description of Emperor Zhyou-Zhwo himself than of most of his councilors. There were some things they weren't yet quite prepared to say even to one another. That didn't keep them from thinking those things quite loudly, however.

"We've explained as clearly as we can why we've taken the actions we have," Star Rising said mildly.

Crystal Fountain nodded, but he also sat back in his chair at the long, polished table with a worried expression. His barony lay between Zhynkau and Ti-Shan, only a few score miles from Star Rising, and he and Star Rising knew one another well. For that matter, they were related by blood. Star Rising's wife, Fengzhou, was Crystal Fountain's first cousin, and Star Rising had no doubt of the other baron's commitment. Crystal Fountain was, however, understandably anxious at the not-so-veiled threats coming out of Yu-kwau.

"I know we have, Runzheng," Crystal Fountain said, "and I know we don't have a choice about what we *do*. I'm only suggesting we might want to consider very carefully how we *describe* what we're doing."

"Forgive me, my son," Lyauyan's tone was almost compassionate, "but I very much doubt that will matter in the end. Not where anyone in Yu-kwau is concerned, at any rate. And whether it does or not is really beside the point when it comes to doing our duty before God and our own consciences. What matters is preserving our people's lives, and when it comes to accomplishing that, what our people here in Boisseau and Cheshire think is far more important than what the Emperor thinks. They have to *believe* in us if we're going to expect them—*ask* them—to risk their own and their families' safety by taking our word for what's going to happen. And if they don't—"

He shrugged, and Crystal Fountain's expression tightened a bit more.

"The Bishop's right, My Lord," Sai-hwahn Tsaiyu said, entering the conversation for the first time. Socially speaking, he was junior to everyone else present, and he'd been hesitant to speak his mind at first. But he'd grown more confident as the crisis and his understanding of it deepened, and in the process, he'd demonstrated he had common sense by the dragon load. Now all the others looked at him, and he grimaced.

"I won't pretend I'm happy about any of this, My Lords," he said, "and all of you know why. But we've put our hands to the hammer because Baron Star Rising and the Bishop are right. None of us knows where this is going to end, but we all know where it'll go if nobody gets a bridle on it damned fast. Pardon my language, My Lord," he added with a nod in the bishop's direction.

As usual, when Tsaiyu opened his mouth, he had a point, Star Rising thought. A blacksmith by trade, with the burly shoulders and massive arms of his craft, he was a senior member of the Blacksmith's Guild in Boisseau. As such, at least a quarter and more likely a third of his fellow guild members considered his willingness to serve on the Emergency Council an act of treason, although probably not for the same reasons Emperor Zhyou-Zhwo did. None of them—including Tsaiyu—had much doubt what would happen to the privileged position of their guild if Charisian-style manufactories moved into Harchong. The difference between those other guild members and Sai-hwahn Tsaiyu was that he could look beyond the personal costs, recognize the inevitable when he saw it, and at least try to mitigate the oncoming shipwreck.

"I've never worried my head over politics outside the guild right here in Boisseau," he continued. "Not until the entire world went to crap, anyway. But it's only the peasants' faith in the Bishop and, to be honest, in Baron Star Rising that's kept a lid on things so far. We're less than six hundred miles from Shang-mi as the wyvern flies, and there's no sign the Army—or anybody else—can do a damned thing to tamp down the bloodshed in Tiegelkamp and Chiang-wu. It doesn't sound to me like the fighting's going to stop magically at the border, either. So if we want to keep it out of Boisseau, if we want to keep our families alive—*my* family, not just yours and the Baron's, My Lord—then we have to convince the people right here that we know what we're doing and our answer offers them something a hell of a lot better than just burning things down and getting their own back. Because the truth is, a lot of them would *rather* burn everything down to get their own back, and it's hard to blame 'em. Couple that with how often they've been lied to in the past, and we've got a pretty steep hill to climb if we expect them to take *our* word for anything."

Tsaiyu was not a great admirer of peasants or serfs. He'd looked down on them most of his life from his position as a well-paid artisan, Star Rising knew. He was scarcely alone in that, however. *Star Rising* had looked down on them, despite what he knew had been an unusual sense of obligation to impose as little misery as possible upon them. In fact, the only man in this room who probably hadn't looked down upon them was the bishop. But whether or not he *liked* peasants and serfs, Sai-hwahn Tsaiyu understood resentment and he understood hatred. Just as he understood that while there might be less of those emotions in Boisseau and Cheshire than there were in provinces like Tiegelkamp, that wasn't the same as saying there was none of them.

"Agreed," Crystal Fountain said after a long, still moment. "Agreed. I'll vote in favor. I just hope that if worse comes to worst your friends in Charis will get us out of the Empire before His Majesty comes to collect our heads, Runzheng!"

"I'm sure they'll at least try," Star Rising told him with a lopsided smile. Then he looked around the bishop's office one more time. The five of them represented just under a quarter of the Emergency Council's total membership, but they were its acknowledged leaders. If they presented a united front, the motion would pass. Probably not without a lot of noise and shouting, and at least four other council members were sure to vote against it, if only to cover their arses with the Emperor. Not that that particular bit of cover would do them any good in the end if, as Crystal Fountain said, "worse comes to worst."

Despite that, there was no doubt in his own mind about what they had to do. The Bishop—and Tsaiyu—were right. They had to secure the support of their own people—a support willing enough and strong enough to defy even the Emperor, at least passively—and half measures simply couldn't do that. Boldness, on the other hand, might, and he was more than a little surprised to realize that for the first time in the five months since the sack of Shang-mi, what he actually felt was optimism or something very like it.

He'd been stunned when the offer from Cayleb and Sharleyan Ahrmahk arrived. He'd hoped at best for troops to help maintain something like order along Boisseau's coast and, perhaps, some of the same sort of relief effort which the Charisian crown had poured into Siddarmark in that horrible first winter after the Sword of Schueler. And, he acknowledged, he and Lyauyan had both possessed far more faith in the godly charity of the Church of Charis than either of them did in the Church of Harchong's.

What they'd gotten back had gone so far beyond their expectations—their hopes—that he'd found it difficult to take in, initially at least. In fact, if not for the envoy they'd chosen to extend the offer, he probably wouldn't have believed it. But when Merlin Athrawes said he spoke for the Emperor and Empress of Charis, that was pretty much that.

The offer still hadn't been made public, for a lot of reasons, including the inevitable reaction of Emperor Zhyou-Zhwo and his court the instant any open provision of Charisian aid became known. Given the Hantai dynasty's burning hatred for all things Charisian, there was no conceivable way the Emperor would accept or even tolerate Charisian assistance. After all, they were the ones responsible for this mess in the first place, weren't they? And the only reason for their "generosity" was as part of Charis' ongoing campaign to totally destroy the order God and the Archangels had decreed. And to get their hands on even more of the marks Charisians worshiped with far greater fervency than they'd ever shown God! What else could be expected out of an entire empire of lunatic, moneygrubbing Reformists?

And the truth was that if what Athrawes had dubbed "the Ahrmahk Plan" worked, the long-term advantages for Charis would be incalculable. If it succeeded, the people of Boisseau and Cheshire would never forget the way Charis had come to their aid. And Charisian manufactory owners and their newfangled "corporations" *would* make a dragon load of marks in the end. In fact, a part of Star Rising was tempted to see it all as a cynical act of doing well out of doing good, but he knew better. No one could look into Merlin Athrawes' *seijin*-blue eyes and doubt the sincerity behind them.

But before the Ahrmahks were prepared to guarantee such enormous sums out of their privy purse, they needed at least some return guarantees. At the very least, they needed to know the Emergency Council was capable of maintaining order, and until the Council shook off the shackles of its obedience to the imperial court, it couldn't do that. The very thing which made the peasantry—and even serfs—trust the Council was the fact that it was local. Bitter experience had taught those peasants and serfs the truth in the ancient maxim that "Only two things come out of Shang-mi: death and taxes." They might not be any too fond of some of their own landlords, but they had enough faith in local aristocrats like Crystal Fountain or Star Rising himself—and, especially, in clerics like Bishop Yaupang—to take a chance on trusting *them*.

They would never trust the Imperial Crown—not really—and the village broadsheets had posted the tirades coming out of Yu-kwau. In a way, the Crown's furious denunciations only made the peasants and serfs trust the Council even more, but that couldn't last. Not if the Council persisted in attempting to walk the tightrope between doing what was necessary for the people who trusted it to survive and openly defying Zhyou-Zhwo. They'd done their best to convince Yu-kwau that they'd had no choice but to take every step they'd taken if they meant to maintain order in Boisseau and Cheshire, and the Emperor didn't care. Either he didn't believe them or else he truly rather would see his empire's western provinces go down in blood and ruin rather than accept serious reforms, far less outright Charisian assistance. Anything that might conceivably convince him the Emergency Council had no intention of defying his authority could only convince the peasants and the serfs that the Council had no intention of *making* those reforms.

There were a lot of council members who didn't want to make them. Sai-hwahn Tsaiyu was a case in point. But only a handful of them believed they or their families could survive if they *didn't* make them. And so they'd come to this.

"What do we want to call ourselves?" Crystal Fountain asked after a moment. "'Rebels United in Madness'?"

"Probably not the best choice, my son," the bishop said with a deep chuckle.

"Well, we have to call ourselves *something* if we're going to make this permanent, My Lord," the baron pointed out. "Something with a little more . . . heft to it than 'Emergency Council,' at any rate."

"Agreed," Star Rising said. "And I don't know about any of the rest of you, but I genuinely don't want to try to set myself up as some kind of warlord, like some of those murderous bastards in Tiegelkamp! If this is going to work, we need something with a genuine, functional parliament—like the ones they have in Charis."

Crystal Fountain's eyes widened, and Star Rising snorted.

"I'm not proposing we hold elections and turn everything over to the serfs tomorrow, Tahnshwun! We're going to need that level of reform in the end, though, and you know it. So I suppose I *am* proposing we transition to it as rapidly as we can. The temptation's going to be to hang on to control because we obviously know best, and that temptation will be even stronger because I suspect we do, at least for now. But as the Bishop says, we *have* to convince the commons they'll have a genuine voice going forward if we expect them to risk listening to us."

"Agreed . . . I suppose," Crystal Fountain said with manifest reluctance.

"For now, what about calling ourselves a 'self-governing region'?" Yingcho suggested. The others looked at the mayor, and he shrugged. "That way we're still not bidding open, deliberate defiance to the Emperor but we are making it clear we're going to make our own decisions."

"You don't expect His Majesty to view it that way, do you, Your Honor?" Tsaiyu asked almost gently, and Yingcho barked a laugh.

"I look like I arrived on the morning's turnip wagon?" He laughed again. "No, but I suspect at least a few of our fellow council members will assuage themselves with the hope that he *might*."

"I hate to think anyone in the Council's that stupid," Star Rising sighed, "but you probably have a point, Faizhwan. So how does the 'Western Self-Governing Region' sound?"

"I'd vote for it in a heartbeat," Crystal Fountain said, "if Rainbow Waters hadn't already cribbed it for himself."

Star Rising grimaced, but his fellow baron had a point. If the Emperor was livid with the Emergency Council, he was apoplectic over Earl Rainbow Waters' decision to "invade" eastern Harchong from the Temple Lands. The earl had been scrupulous about proclaiming that his only intent was to secure public order and protect the imperial authority, but Star Rising doubted he'd expected Zhyou-Zhwo to believe it for a moment. For that matter, *Star Rising* didn't believe it. He couldn't when he found himself in such an analogous position in the west. But Rainbow Waters had proclaimed the provinces of Langhorne, Maddox, and Stene a "self-governing region" in the Emperor's name. Whether or not he'd be able to make that stand up in the end, even backed by two or three hundred thousand veterans of the Mighty Host of God and the Archangels, remained to be seen, but his effort looked like it was succeeding, at least in the eastern halves of those three provinces. His name was one to conjure where the peasantry was concerned, and his troops' loyalty had so far been sufficient to prevent or at least severely limit the sorts of merciless atrocities wracking Tiegelkamp, Thomas, and de Castro Provinces.

Still, Crystal Fountain had a point about how Zhyou-Zhwo would react to a second "self-governing region"! On the other hand, they couldn't allow themselves to be stymied by worries over the emperor's probable reactions, since they knew he'd denounce them and sentence them all to death in absentia no matter what they called themselves. Selling it to the more delicate flowers on the Council suggested a modicum of tact at this point, however.

"So, what about just calling ourselves the 'Provincial Council'?" he asked. "We stay away from terms like 'self-governing' entirely that way. But we also get rid of the 'Emergency' to suggest we're something more permanent than that."

"I don't know if that would carry a *sufficient* connotation of permanence, my son," Lyauyan mused. "That's what we need to convince everyone we're talking about, after all. If it's a choice between that and . . . further irritating His Majesty, I'm afraid my vote would be to go ahead and irritate him."

"Then suppose we call ourselves 'the Provisional Council of the United Provinces of Boisseau and Cheshire'?" Star Rising said. All of them looked at him, and the bishop chuckled.

"Well, it does have the wordiness we Harchongians prize, but it doesn't have enough *adjectives*, my son! Why not 'The Ineffable and Celestial Provisional Council of the United Provinces of Boisseau and Cheshire'?"

The baron chuckled back, but he also shook his head.

"I'm serious, My Lord," he said. "The 'provisional' bit is our cloak of respectability and loyalty to the Crown, but the whole thing's so long you know everyone will shorten it. That's what Harchongians do. And what they'll shorten it *to* is 'the United Provinces.'" His smile disappeared. "That's the important bit, my friends. That's what all of our people here in the provinces themselves will remember, what they'll think about. The truth is Tahnshwun's right when he calls this an act of open rebellion. It has to be if we're going to survive, given that His Majesty won't let us do what we *need* to do to survive. I don't know if Rainbow Waters sees it the same way, but let's be honest among ourselves. For us and the people we know and care about to live through this, we have to cut the chain between us and Yu-kwau. I don't like it, and the thought of becoming actual rebels scares the hell out of me, but that's where we are, and the truth is that it's the Emperor himself, and his councilors, who've brought us to this point. Is anyone in this office really prepared to dispute that?"

He let his eyes circle the room. No one spoke, but no one looked away, either, and he nodded slowly.

"So if this is treason, let them make the most of it! We've just become the United Provinces of Boisseau and Cheshire, whether we wanted to or not. For that matter, I'd say there's a damned good chance we'll end up adding Omar and Bedard—maybe even the half-dozen caribou herders in Pasquale!—before we're done. We almost have to, assuming we survive at all. And when we start that transition to a genuine parliament of our own and drop the 'provisional,' no one in the United Provinces will even notice, because they'll already be thinking of themselves as an independent realm."

He looked around the bishop's office again, and this time—one by one—every head nodded back.

. II .
Sai-kau-Jai-hu High Road,
Tiegelkamp Province,
and
Emperor Zhyou-Zhwo's Palace,
City of Yu-kwau,
and
St. Lerys Foundry,
Kyznetzou Province,
Empire of Harchong.

"No! Please—*no!*" the richly dressed young woman screamed as the door was torn from her frantic hands and the snarling mob dragged her through it. "Poppa! *Poppa!*"

"*Syuhwei!*" Her mother clung to her, frantically trying to pull her back into the coach. "Syuhwei! *Do* something, Manzhwo!"

Her husband's eyes were wide, desperate. His head twisted around as he somehow managed to hold the opposite coach door closed, but it was clearly only a matter of time—and not much of it—before that door, too, was wrenched from its hinges.

"*Poppa!*" His daughter's scream filled his ears as she was ripped from her mother's grasp, vanished into the surging tide of bodies crashing about the coach. He heard the matching shrieks from the coachload of servants behind them, but they meant nothing compared to that beloved voice. He cursed the cowardly coachmen and outriders who'd abandoned them, taken to their heels the instant the howling mob boiled out of the scrub wood to either side. If the bastards had stood and fought instead of running—! Not that it had done them any good, in the end.

He darted one last look back out the window on his side, then whipped the dagger from his belt.

"*Manzhwo!*" his wife screamed, looking after her daughter, bracing herself against the frame of the door as more hands reached through it for *her*.

She never saw him coming, never realized what was happening until his dagger slashed across her throat, severing her jugular. Her blood sprayed her assailants, soaking them. One or two paused, pawing at their eyes—to clear their vision, not in horror—and her husband threw her dying body from the door. She hit the hard-paved roadway, gurgling and choking as she died, and he flung himself into the brief opening her twitching corpse had forced in the mob of howling savages. He landed on her back and lunged forward, not letting himself think about the horrible softness under his feet, not letting himself think about *anything* but his need to reach his daughter. Not to *save* her, because he couldn't—not any more than he'd been able to save his wife. But if he could just reach her side before they pulled him down—

"*Poppa!*" the seventeen-year-old girl shrieked as her winter cloak was ripped away, her gown was torn to shreds. Her chemise followed and her captors bellowed in triumph as her naked body twisted and fought.

Her father's only weapon was his dagger. He managed to wound two of the attackers, but then someone tackled him from behind and he crashed to the paving. He fought frantically, and they laughed at him. He lurched back to his feet somehow, but someone wrestled the dagger from his hand. A peasant's rough boot kicked him in the belly. He went down, coughing and gagging, and they wrenched him up again.

"*Poppa!*"

Hard calloused hands twisted his arms up behind him, arching his spine, and another hand tangled in his elegantly groomed hair. It wrenched his head back, and they turned him, facing him towards his daughter as she was flung to the icy ground, her limbs pinned, her legs spread wide.

"*Please!*" he begged. "Sweet Langhorne, *please!* Do whatever you want with *me,* but *please*—!"

The fist smashed into his mouth, hard enough to knock out teeth.

"Shut up and enjoy the show," an ugly voice snarled. "*We* sure as hell will!"

And they laughed at him while his daughter's screams filled his ears.

▼ ▼ ▼

"Shit," Zhouhan Husan said softly as he and Tangwyn Syngpu drew rein. He gazed down at the naked, brutalized body. From the looks of things, she'd taken a long time dying, but at least someone had simply cut her throat when they were done raping her. The man impaled on the carriage's wagon tongue—husband or father, it was impossible to judge his age from the state of his savagely mutilated body—had been less fortunate. Almost a dozen other stiff, broken bodies, two-thirds of them women, lay twisted and already frozen around the second coach.

"Stupid bastard," Syngpu growled, glaring fire-eyed at the dead man. "You stupid, *stupid* bastard! Trying to outrun them in a Shan-wei–damned *coach*?"

He had a point, Husan acknowledged. The two passenger coaches were—or had been, before they were looted, overturned, and burned—huge, lumbering vehicles. The lead coach, especially, had been a luxurious vehicle, designed for comfort and opulence, not speed, and they'd used a third one to haul *furniture* and what looked like tapestries with them! They'd had horses in the traces, not dragons, probably in an effort to get at least a little more speed out of the things, but what kind of idiot—?

They'd have had a much better chance of escaping if they'd put *saddles* on the damned horses, instead of harness. Not a *good* chance, but a better one. Even a noble should have been able to figure that out!

Husan glanced sidelong at his friend. He knew who Syngpu was truly angry with, and it wasn't the slaughtered nobleman and his family. It wasn't even the vengeance-maddened serfs and peasants who'd descended into a viciousness worse than any rabid animal's.

Not really.

"Not our fault," he said quietly. "Not *your* fault."

"No?" Syngpu looked at him. "It was somebody else set those woods on fire? Put all this—" he jabbed a thumb over his shoulder at the long column of rifle-armed men marching down the high road behind them "—together?"

"It was *going* to happen," Husan said. "It was only a matter of time. And if you hadn't—if *we* hadn't—started it when we did, all those rifles and anything else they had time to build would've been on the other side. And then more of our people would've gotten killed and it wouldn't have changed a thing."

"Whoever did this aren't 'our people,' Zhouhan!" Syngpu snapped. "And if I catch up with them, I'll make that point what you might call clear."

Husan only nodded. The chance of their catching up with the marauders responsible for the trail of carnage they'd been following for the last day or so were no more than even. They had to try, but even if they did catch them, even if they shot or hanged every single one of them, it wouldn't really change anything. Not in central North Harchong, anyway.

Damned well might make us feel *a little better, though,* he acknowledged, and reached across to squeeze Syngpu's shoulder. He couldn't be sure, but he doubted the butchered young woman sprawled like so much discarded meat on the high road's shoulder was more than a year older—if that—than Syngpu's daughter Pauyin. And some of the violated bodies they'd passed had been much younger than that.

"Sergeant Tsau!" he said, still looking down at her, his hand still on Syngpu's shoulder.

"Yes, Sir?"

It still felt unnatural to be addressed as if he were an officer, but Husan supposed that was what he was now.

"Burial detail," he said. "I know the ground's frozen. See if there's enough left of the carriages to burn 'em. If not—"

He waved a hand at the scrubby evergreens fringing the right-of-way, and Tsau nodded.

"And if anyone wants to say a few words, probably wouldn't hurt," Husan added quietly.

▼ ▼ ▼

It was very quiet in the council chamber. Not a restful quiet, but a tense, singing silence in which eyes were careful not to make contact with one another. It lingered, growing ever more intense ... then shattered as Emperor Zhyou-Zhwo's palm slammed down on the polished tabletop.

"Do *none* of you have anything to say, My Lords?" the emperor snarled. Unlike every other set of eyes, his swept the table, hot with anger, and more than one of his councilors looked away from that fiery glare.

"I see you don't." The emperor sat back in his ornate near-throne of a chair, gripping the armrests hard enough his knuckles whitened. "The Empire—*Our* Empire—is disintegrating, and not one of Our 'councilors' has any 'counsel' to offer!"

Grand Duke North Wind Blowing's jaw tightened as he heard the imperial "*Our*" in that contemptuous sentence. The crown prince had "unwillingly accepted" his father's death and "reluctantly permitted" the Council's "earnest plea" that he take up the Crown in his own right to overpower the natural resistance of a grieving son, and his ascension to the throne bade fair to be the most tumultuous in generations, and not just because of the violence wracking the northern half of his empire. Too many of the Imperial Council's members had died in Shang-mi, and now North Wind Blowing understood the real reason Zhyou-Zhwo had postponed his coronation. It hadn't been simply to force the Council to beg him to take up the throne. That *had* been part of it, assenting to his elevation to Emperor only reluctantly ... and making the point that *they'd* had to come to *him* if they wanted to hold their own positions.

But there'd been another reason, too. It had given him time to sound out the available pool of nobles before he had to formally fill the vacant Council seats. Time to make sure the men put into them knew they were beholden to him, not their colleagues.

"Highest," Mangzhin Tyan, Earl Snow Peak, said finally, "we have no counsel to offer because we—as you—know there can be only one response to such defiance of the Imperial authority. Unfortunately, at this time, that response remains temporarily beyond our capabilities. That won't be true forever, however. That much I swear!"

Zhyou-Zhwo glowered at him, but at least some of the heat leached out of those dark eyes, and North Wind Blowing tried to feel grateful. It was difficult. As Snow Peak's choice of honorifics indicated, he spoke not simply as a member of the Council, but as the new senior ranking officer of the Imperial Army, and he had never been a member of North Wind Blowing's faction even before his recent promotion.

"Earl Snow Peak is correct, Your Supreme Majesty," Zhwunzhyng Rwan, Earl Golden Sunrise, added a bit cautiously. "In the fullness of time, the authority of your Crown must inevitably be reestablished throughout the northern provinces, but at this instant, our ability to do that remains sadly limited."

At least Golden Sunrise was one of North Wind Blowing's most loyal allies, not one of the toadies Zhyou-Zhwo had named to replace those who'd died. There was barely enough of the old guard left to form a scant majority, and the first councilor allowed himself to nod in sage agreement with his colleague.

"Perhaps We are not presently in a position to take effective action," Zhyou-Zhwo said after a moment. "But We must still respond to this shameful proclamation." He tapped the sheet of parchment on the tabletop with an angry fingertip. "If We allow this to stand unchallenged, then We endorse a dangerous precedent. At the very least, We must make it crystal clear We do not and never will accept this sort of attack on Our legitimate prerogatives!"

Golden Sunrise glanced at North Wind Blowing from the corner of one eye, then looked back at the emperor.

"Ultimately, you are, of course, correct, Your Supreme Majesty," he said. "At this moment, however, might we not consider the advisability of simply not responding at all?" The emperor's face tightened, and the earl went on quickly. "If we say nothing—if the *Council* says nothing in your name—then you, in your person as Emperor, will have *conceded* nothing. It will always be within the scope of your prerogative to make the reassertion of your authority in those provinces crystal clear. In the meantime, we avoid any appearance of ineffectuality and may concentrate on more serious and immediate threats to the Crown's authority."

"Indeed?" Zhyou-Zhwo's tone was icy, but without its previous core of fury, and North Wind Blowing allowed himself a cautious trickle of hope.

The situation in central Harchong had gone from one horror to another over the past months. According to the rumors and counter-rumors flowing to them, Shangmi was largely in ruins after an orgy of arson and rapine. Virtually the whole of Tiegelkamp and most of Chiangwu Province were wrapped in flames, and the carnage continued to spread despite the bitter winter cold. There was scarcely a man in that council chamber who hadn't lost family, and every one of the northern nobles present had lost immense amounts of his personal wealth, as well, with no end in sight.

"Do you truly feel that is our best course, My Lord?" another voice, this one with a southern accent, asked. Zungju Byngzhi, the Duke of Summer Flowers, was another newcomer. He was also one of the very few nobles of South Harchong whose pedigree compared favorably with most of the Northerners on Zhyou-Zhwo's reconstructed council, and his expression was intent, thoughtful, as he cocked his head at Golden Sunrise.

"In the absence of a good option, My Lord, one must choose the least bad of the ones available to one," Golden Sunrise replied. "I would never suggest His Supreme Majesty should suffer such an insult to his prerogative in silence if I believed we could effectively punish these arrogant upstarts at the present time."

"Yet will not prolonged silence be seen as acquiescence?" Snow Peak asked in the tone of one who was simply musing aloud.

"It might," Golden Sunrise conceded, keeping the corner of one wary eye on the emperor's expression. "I fear, though, that we must advise His Supreme Majesty to . . . choose his fights at this perilous moment in his Empire's history. As impertinent as Star Rising and the others may be, they've always taken care to be meticulous in proclaiming their ultimate loyalty to His Supreme Majesty and to the Crown."

Zhyou-Zhwo's face tightened ever so slightly, and Golden Sunrise continued smoothly.

"Ultimately, of course, such pretensions as theirs must be brought to heel, yet surely at this moment the situation in the eastern provinces constitutes a far greater immediate threat to both His Supreme Majesty's prerogatives and the territorial integrity of his realm!"

Oh, shrewdly done, Zhwunzhyng! North Wind Blowing mentally congratulated his ally as Zhyou-Zhwo's eyes flashed.

The first councilor watched Snow Peak's expression. The army commander was an experienced courtier, so that expression showed very little, but it was there for eyes which knew what to look for, and North Wind Blowing knew exactly why.

Earl Rainbow Waters had crossed the frontier into Maddox from the Episcopate of St. Bahrnabai at the head of almost a quarter million men two months earlier. Like Star Rising and his fellows, the disgraced earl had been very careful to proclaim that his sole purpose was to restore public order. And he'd been amazingly successful at it. Two hundred and fifty thousand men wasn't a huge number when spread over so vast an area, but the earl's name carried enormous weight among the serfs and peasant farmers. Despite the Spears' best efforts, rumors about the Mighty Host and tales of how Rainbow Waters had fought for his troops' return and at least kept them fed and clothed in their involuntary exile had trickled into the eastern provinces for years.

In the process, the earl had been transformed into some sort of icon, a combination of Langhorne and the *seijins* of old returned to the world! He was undoubtedly the only great noble of Harchong—and such he remained, despite the confiscation of his lands—even rebellious serfs were prepared to follow.

Many of the eastern towns appeared to have succumbed to his reputation, as well, with one city council after another petitioning him to take their citizens under his protection. And there were persistent rumors—rumors North Wind Blowing's agents had confirmed, although he had not yet passed the information to the emperor or the rest of the council—that another quarter million of the Mighty Host's veterans were flowing into eastern Langhorne and Stene under Rainbow Waters' nephew, the Baron of Wind Song, with similar results.

Not even Rainbow Waters' reputation—or his well-disciplined troops—were sufficient to prevent outbursts of rapine and all the hideous violence that went with them, but compared to the areas outside his control, they were incredibly few and far between. Which meant, of course, that even the local members of the minor aristocracy were undoubtedly grateful for his presence, although they were keeping their mouths shut about it, for the most part.

Snow Peak was as aware of that as anyone. Indeed, the reason he'd been promoted to his present post after his predecessor's death in Shang-mi was his bitter rejection of the Church's demands where the equipping and—especially—training of the Mighty Host of God and the Archangels were concerned. He'd resigned his position as one of the Mighty Host's senior commanders the day Rainbow Waters caved in to those outrageous conditions, and his hatred for the banished earl was almost as great as the emperor's own. Perhaps it was even greater, as the area under Rainbow Waters' sway continued to expand, because the "army" under his own command could never have matched that accomplishment even if the peasants and serfs had been prepared to embrace it. He had more men than Rainbow

Waters, but very few of them were equipped with new-model weapons.

Yet all of that paled beside the true threat of Rainbow Waters' success. Unlike Star Rising or any of the minor nobles who backed this "Provisional Council" of his, Rainbow Waters sprang from one of the empire's greatest aristocratic dynasties. He was a great noble who commanded an army fanatically loyal to *him*, not to Emperor Zhyou-Zhwo.

Many an independent kingdom had been sprung out of less promising soil than that. Zhyou-Zhwo knew that, and Snow Peak was the man who was supposed to be building an army capable of making certain that didn't happen this time.

"As I say, Your Supreme Majesty," Golden Sunrise continued, "when our resources are so limited, surely the path of wisdom is to husband them where we can and expend them only where it is most useful . . . and vital."

Zhyou-Zhwo nodded ever so slightly, but his expression was manifestly unhappy.

"Your Supreme Majesty, we must all recognize Earl Golden Sunrise's greater personal familiarity with those seeking to create this 'Provisional Council,'" Duke Summer Flowers said, and North Wind Blowing's jaw tightened at his judicious, reasonable tone. "And clearly the situation in the East is an intolerable one. There is, however, a significant difference between Baron Star Rising's actions and those of Earl Rainbow Waters, I believe."

Zhyou-Zhwo's expression had darkened further at the Southerner's none-too-oblique reminder that Golden Sunrise's earldom lay in western Tiegelkamp. That it was, in fact, within or directly bordered by the area over which the "Provisional Council" sought to extend its authority. That was nothing compared to the murderous fire in his eyes as someone dared to mention the outlawed earl's name in his presence, however.

"And that difference is what, My Lord?" North Wind Blowing's tone carried a carefully metered frigidity.

"Why, only this, My Lord Grand Duke," Summer

Flowers replied mildly. "Earl Rainbow Waters is clearly in a state of rebellion, whatever he may profess. Simply crossing our frontier by himself would have constituted an act of profound disobedience to His Supreme Majesty's will and expressed decree, yet he's dared to bring armed *serfs* at his heels! That creates a clear and unmistakable—unimpeachable—basis for His Supreme Majesty's forces to crush him and his supporters in the field, as they inevitably will under My Lord Snow Peak's able command once the manufactories here in the South have suitably equipped his forces. The threat of this 'Provisional Council' is far more subtle than that. It has no armies in the field, it hasn't crossed His Supreme Majesty's frontiers, and it's careful to present an appearance of loyalty to the Crown. If its pretensions and ambition aren't openly and strongly rebuked, does His Supreme Majesty not risk the appearance of *endorsing* its actions and, by extension, granting it an authority it does not and cannot possess?"

Fortunately, North Wind Blowing was looking at Summer Flowers, not the emperor, as the first councilor's eyes widened, despite his decades of political experience. Summer Flowers was a Southerner, and the southern provinces had chafed under the political domination of the northern nobility for centuries. The last thing North Wind Blowing had anticipated was that Summer Flowers would frame an argument in terms that undercut that southern drive for greater autonomy!

"What you say is true and well taken, My Lord," Golden Sunrise said. "Indeed, as I've argued myself, ultimately this sort of intolerable usurpation of His Supreme Majesty's prerogatives *must* be dealt with. I merely seek to most effectively . . . prioritize the threats with which he and we, as his councilors, must deal. And, as you say, the 'Provisional Council' has no troops and has crossed no borders. I do not and never have counseled that it would be recognized in any way by His Supreme Majesty, or that there should be even a hint of a suggestion that it will be tolerated in the end. For now, however, it would seem to me that—"

"Forgive me, My Lord Earl," Summer Flowers interrupted, "but there are armies in the field, on Harchongese soil, which most assuredly have crossed our frontiers. I refer to the Charisian Marines who have landed in the Bay of Pauton and the Gulf of Boisseau."

Golden Sunrise's mouth snapped shut. His eyes darted to Zhyou-Zhwo's face, and North Wind Blowing cursed silently. If Summer Flowers had surprised him earlier, that was nothing compared to this! South Harchong had tried long and hard to cultivate Charisian investment in its own manufactories, less for the financial support, however welcome that might have been, than as a means to acquire Charisian techniques. The last thing Summer Flowers should have wanted was to tread upon the emperor's instant, instinctive, ineradicable hatred for Charis and all things Charisian!

"My Lord Duke," Golden Sunrise said after a second, "the Charisian presence in Boisseau and Cheshire is totally unauthorized by His Supreme Majesty! Nor is it mentioned at any point in the proclamation of the 'Provisional Council'! If—"

"No," Summer Flowers interrupted yet again, "it isn't. But everyone knows about it, My Lord. And whether it's Star Rising's intention or not—I am, of course, in no position to comment upon that—this proposed council will inevitably be *perceived* by His Supreme Majesty's foes as a threadbare mask for Charisian penetration of his territory. Especially if these rumors about the so-called 'Ahrmahk Plan' are true."

North Wind Blowing watched Zhyou-Zhwo's expression and body language from the corner of his eye and saw Summer Flowers' final sentence go home with deadly effect. The emperor's face darkened, seemed to swell, and he leaned forward in his chair.

"Perhaps you're correct, My Lord Duke," Golden Sunrise said, careful to keep his tone mild and respectful, "but—"

"That will be enough, My Lord," North Wind Blowing said sharply. Golden Sunrise looked at him in surprise, and the first councilor glared at him. "My Lord Summer

Flowers has made an excellent point. One, I confess, I had not considered deeply enough." He made himself nod courteously and gratefully to the Southerner. "Had I done so, I no doubt would have made the same point to His Supreme Majesty, because it's a valid one."

Golden Sunrise sat back in his chair, eyes turning into shutters, as he realized North Wind Blowing had just thrown him to the krakens.

"And well you should have, My Lord!" Zhyou-Zhwo snapped, glaring at North Wind Blowing before turning even more fiery eyes upon Golden Sunrise. "It's the Charisian poison we have to blame for every misfortune which has befallen our entire world in the last twenty years! And now these traitors, these treachers, these . . . these lackeys of Shan-wei, want to allow that bastard Cayleb and his harlot into Our realm?!"

Golden Sunrise seemed to sink in upon himself, and North Wind Blowing glared at him just as furiously as the emperor, wondering if he'd distanced himself quickly enough.

"We thank you, My Lord Summer Flowers," Zhyou-Zhwo said in more temperate tones, turning his eyes from the hapless Golden Sunrise to the southern duke. "Yours is indeed a welcome voice of reason in this council chamber!"

"If I may serve in any way, that is my greatest honor, Your Supreme Majesty," Summer Flowers said, half-rising from his chair so that he might bow deeply across the table to the emperor. "And, in fairness to My Lord North Wind Blowing, had he even a few less crises weighing upon his heart and mind, I'm sure the same point would have occurred to him."

"That's most gracious of you, My Lord," North Wind Blowing said as the Southerner seated himself once more.

"Indeed it is," the emperor confirmed in rather chillier tones. "And I think, perhaps, it would be as well, My Lord North Wind Blowing, if you were to prepare a proper condemnation of this proclamation for Our perusal by midday tomorrow."

"Of course, Your Supreme Majesty." North Wind Blowing inclined his head, his expression hiding his dismay.

"And that brings Us to another point We wish to consider," Zhyou-Zhwo continued. "The state of Our arms is most unsatisfactory." His gaze shifted to Snow Peak. "We understand it will be some time before Our army may take the field against the rebel Rainbow Waters and Our other foes, both domestic and foreign. It is, however, Our wish that the deficiency in Our troops' weapons and equipment be made good as rapidly as possible."

Which would be much easier to accomplish if we had greater access to Charisian manufacturing techniques. Which, of course, is the last *thing you want,* North Wind Blowing thought with a sinking sensation.

"At the same time," Zhyou-Zhwo went on, as if he'd read his first councilor's mind, "it is obviously necessary to minimize Charisian pollution of Our realm. Nor will We tolerate any enrichment of our enemies! It is Our belief Our friend and brother emperor in Desnair has much good counsel to offer us in that regard, and so We commend his letters to that effect to the Council's study. It is Our will that our lords Snow Peak and Summer Flowers give their especial attention to this matter and present Us with options for pursuing a strategy similar to the one Emperor Mahrys has embraced in his own realm."

"Of course, Your Supreme Majesty," North Wind Blowing murmured.

He bent his head once more, cursing viciously behind the serene expression while he wondered if Snow Peak and Summer Flowers had orchestrated this outcome beforehand. Whether they had or not, the moment was about to make them close allies . . . and formidable foes.

And the fact that it would make accomplishing the emperor's goals so much more difficult was completely beside the point.

▼ ▼ ▼

"After you make sure all our machine tools are accounted for, start thinking about the best way to crate them up for shipment." Zhaspahr Mahklyn's expression was unhappy, but his tone was calm.

"Yes, sir." Tymythy Khasgrayv didn't look a lot happier than Mahklyn felt. "Nengkwan's people aren't going to be very pleased about that, though," he added.

"Not our problem." This time Mahklyn's voice was flat. "*We're* not the ones whose emperor can't pour piss out of a—"

Someone knocked on the frame of Mahklyn's office door and he looked up.

"Yes?"

"Master Nengkwan is here, sir." It was one of St. Lerys Foundry's Harchongese supervisors, and his expression was substantially less happy than Mahklyn's or Khasgrayv's.

"I see." Mahklyn glanced at Khasgrayv, then back at the Harchongian. "Ask him to join us, please, Zhyngchi."

"Yes, sir." The Harchongian disappeared, and Khasgrayv shook his head.

"Speak of Shan-wei and you'll hear the rustle of her wings, sir," he said in a tone that couldn't decide whether it was wry or disgusted.

"Not his fault, Tym," Mahklyn said. "Matter of fact, if he had his druthers—"

"Master Nengkwan, sir," the Harchongese supervisor interrupted, and both the Charisians stood to greet the newcomer.

Zhwyfeng Nengkwan was fifty-two, nine years older than Mahklyn and twenty-two years older than Khasgrayv. He was also very richly dressed, portly, and darkhaired. That hair was turning white at the temples and there were matching white streaks in the dagger beard that always made him remind Mahklyn somehow of an overweight, dark-eyed Merlin Athrawes, although the *seijin* was a good eight inches taller than Nengkwan.

"Master Nengkwan," he said, reaching across his desk to clasp forearms. The Harchongian's grip was firm, but his eyes were worried.

"Master Mahklyn," he responded, and nodded courteously to Khasgrayv, as well. "I apologize for arriving on such short notice."

"I'm at your disposal, sir," Mahklyn responded, forbearing to mention that no notice at all was even briefer than "short notice."

"I'm afraid I bear unhappy tidings," Nengkwan told him, coming to the point with un-Harchongese brevity. "The Emperor's Council met in the Palace earlier today."

"I see." Mahklyn glanced at Khasgrayv, then back at Nengkwan. "Should I assume from your presence and what you've just said that the meeting concerned Saint Lerys?"

"Not specifically." Nengkwan shook his head. "It will, however, have what I very much fear will be . . . significant repercussions for not only Saint Lerys but all of our other joint ventures with Duke Delthak."

"I see," Mahklyn repeated more slowly, then gestured for his visitor to take the chair in front of his desk. After Nengkwan was seated, Mahklyn and Khasgrayv resumed their own chairs.

"Please continue, Master Nengkwan," Mahklyn invited.

"To put the matter as briefly as possible, His Supreme Majesty has instructed Grand Duke North Wind Blowing to prepare a proclamation condemning Baron Star Rising's initiative in Boisseau," Nengkwan said, and Mahklyn nodded. The odds of Zhyou-Zhwo's accepting anything that even hinted at local autonomy had always been minute. Stupid of him, but that seemed to be what Harchongese emperors—and aristocrats in general, for that matter—specialized in being.

"At the same meeting," Nengkwan continued, "the Emperor discussed his intentions and plans for the rearming of the Imperial Army. Which led to a discussion of our 'industrialization' efforts in general."

Mahklyn could actually hear the quotation marks around the newfangled word, and he really didn't blame the Harchongian. Mahklyn hadn't understood—not at first, anyway—why Duke Delthak had started using that term instead of the original "manufactoryization" which had seemed so much more natural to most people, but he'd come to realize it made sense. It was an obvious play on the adjective "industrious" as a description of someone who worked hard and effectively, but the real reason the duke had begun referring to "industry" and "industrialization" was because in his grand vision—well, his and Their Majesties'—the ultimate objective was something which would extend far beyond simple manufactories.

"And that discussion was the source of the 'repercussions' you mentioned earlier?" he asked, and Nengkwan nodded.

"His Supreme Majesty wishes for the Empire's industrialization to be more . . . organic. He made his feelings on the matter quite clear."

"I see," Mahklyn said yet again. He tipped back in his chair, elbows propped on the armrests, and steepled his fingers under his chin. No doubt Zhyou-Zhwo had used rather stronger terms to describe his anti-Charisian agenda.

"His Supreme Majesty hasn't said so in so many words," Nengkwan continued, and Mahklyn heard the unspoken "yet" in the portly banker's tone, "but my sources strongly suggest he'll shortly move to begin rescinding Charisian charters."

He met Mahklyn's eyes steadily, and the Charisian nodded. He had to respect Nengkwan's fundamental integrity in warning him, giving him additional time to make his own plans. Of course, he'd been making them anyway, even before Duke Delthak's last directives arrived, because it had been unpleasantly obvious which way the Yu-kwau wind was setting.

"I hope his advisors will point out the possible . . . unfortunate consequences of any such move," he said after a moment.

"As do I, although I'm less confident of that than I was."

There was a bitter edge in Nengkwan's reply, Mahklyn noted. Interesting. One of Nengkwan's silent partners in his extensive partnerships with Delthak and two or three other Charisian enterprises was the Duke of Summer Flowers, who happened to sit on the reconstituted Imperial Council. Imperial advisors didn't come a lot more senior than that, and Summer Flowers stood to lose heavily—more in terms of future profits than in out-of-pocket costs, admittedly—if Nengkwan's ventures failed. So if the banker was no longer confident of Summer Flowers' backing, did that indicate the duke had lost favor with the emperor? Or might it indicate that Summer Flowers had smelled a political opportunity that outweighed mere money?

One never knew what might happen in Harchongese politics, he reminded himself, so it might well be both!

"His Majesty knows his own mind best, of course," he said after another thoughtful pause. "But that step would be very hard to un-take. As I know you understand, Charisian investors take the sanctity of charters and articles of partnership—" *and the rule of law,* he added silently "—very seriously. If His Majesty and his Councilors decide to unilaterally dissolve those charters, Harchongese investors will find it difficult to attract future Charisian investment and participation here in the Empire."

"Trust me, Master Mahklyn," the bitterness in Nengkwan's voice was much stronger, "I'm well aware of that. And I'm also aware that—"

He cut himself off, and Mahklyn hid a thin, bitterly amused smile. Of course Nengkwan was aware that Charisian *financial* investment was the least of Harchong's needs.

Silence lingered in the office. Then Nengkwan stirred in his chair.

"As I said, nothing's been officially decided or announced at this time, but I very much fear it's only a matter of time, and not a great deal of it. My sources within the Council remain effective enough to give me at least some warning before it is announced, however. And I felt it was my duty to . . . alert you to these developments immediately. I'm sure there are preparations you would wish to make."

"I'm deeply grateful, Master Nengkwan," Mahklyn said with complete sincerity.

If word of Nengkwan's warning to his Charisian partners reached the emperor, the consequences for the banker might be severe. Which didn't even consider the financial side of things. If the Charisians pulled out their equipment and their technical manuals—if they had the *time* to pull those things out—in addition to their personnel, the consequences would be devastating. And as one of the consortium's heaviest investors, Nengkwan's losses would be heavy.

Too bad I can't tell the poor bastard we've already been planning for something exactly like this, Mahklyn thought. *On the other hand, maybe he already knew. Maybe he knows he's not really telling us anything we didn't already guess so he might as well bank as much Charisian goodwill as he can for the future.*

He looked at Nengkwan's expression and decided that last thought had been unfair. No, Nengkwan was that rarest of creatures: an honest man. One who was unhappy not simply because of his potential losses, nor even because of the consequences for his empire, which he foresaw, but because he, too, understood the importance of the rule of law. And the moral responsibility of keeping his own word.

"You and Duke Delthak and all of our other Charisian investors have always been honest and forthright in our dealings, despite the lingering enmity the Jihad engenders in far too many hearts and souls," Nengkwan said, still meeting Mahklyn's gaze steadily. "I can be no less in return."

And there's the proof of it, Mahklyn thought, *because he means every word of that.*

"If I may, I'll say precisely the same thing about you in the Duke's stead," he said out loud, and rose to offer his hand across the desk again and smiled crookedly.

"Under the circumstances, sir," he said, "I think we're in agreement that the three of us all have better things to do than sit around talking." *Especially where word of it might get back to Zhyou-Zhwo and his toadies.*

"I'm sure we do," Nengkwan replied, clasping his forearm firmly. "May Langhorne bless you until we meet again."

"And you."

Mahklyn inclined his head courteously and waited until Nengkwan had left the office, then turned back to Khasgrayv.

"Adds a little point to our earlier conversation, doesn't it, sir?" Khasgrayv observed. "But if Zhyou-Zhwo's serious about unilaterally abrogating our charters, is he likely to *let* us pull out our machine tools?"

"Hard to say." Mahklyn shrugged. "The articles are very specific about the fact that Delthak Enterprises owns the machine tools—all the heavy equipment we've been using to upgrade and expand the existing facilities—at least until the *new* foundry goes on line. But if he's going to shitcan the entire consortium, who knows? I'd think even he would think two or three times about offending Their Majesties too blatantly at this point, given what he already has on his plate, but he's Harchongese. So he might be fully capable of cutting off his nose and one ear to spite his face! We'll proceed on the theory that he isn't, though, and cross that bridge when we get to it if it turns out he is."

"Yes, sir. In that case, I'd probably better get on it, hadn't I?"

"I think that would be an excellent idea," Mahklyn agreed, and settled back into his chair, his expression pensive, as Khasgrayv closed the office door behind him.

In the short term, losing the machine tools and other heavy equipment would be a significant blow to Duke Delthak's Harchongese associates. In the longer term, however, that loss would pale beside the loss of the technical manuals and plans Mahklyn and his corps of Charisian experts had brought with them, and manuals and plans that couldn't be removed could always be burned. Especially in a foundry, with all those puddling hearths so conveniently to hand.

Except. . . .

I wonder how Nengkwan's going to react when he finds out I'm leaving all of that behind? Zhaspahr Mahklyn mused. *For that matter, I wonder* why *I'm leaving it behind?*

It didn't make a great deal of sense to him, but Duke Delthak's contingency instructions had been abundantly clear, and the truth was that it didn't break Mahklyn's heart.

Nengkwan tried to do right by us. The least we can do is return a little of the favor, he decided, and that was good enough for him.

. III .
Selyk,
Westmarch Province,
Republic of Siddarmark.

"What the—?!"

Shormyn Mahkluskee jerked upright on the freight wagon's driver's seat as the dragon in the traces squealed, crow-hopped with four of its six feet completely off the ground, and lunged sideways.

He had no idea what could have startled the creature that badly. Draft dragons were noted for placidity, not flightiness, and he and Grygory had made this trip often since his return from the Temple Lands. Certainly the dragon had grown accustomed to the normal noises and distractions of street traffic! Besides, Selyk wasn't a huge metropolis. It had suffered heavily in the Jihad's fighting—for that matter, most of its population had scattered. Some, like Mahkluskee himself, had sought refuge with Mother Church in the Border States and Temple Lands while others had fled eastward to escape the Sword of Schueler's carnage. Many of those refugees had trickled home again and they'd been rebuilding ever since, but Selyk's population was still only about half its pre-Jihad size. There wasn't all that much street traffic, and especially not on a late winter's morning.

In the end, it didn't matter what had frightened the dragon, though.

▼ ▼ ▼

"And remind me to tell your father when he gets back here—*if* he gets back here—that Orsyn Hylmyn wants another wagonload of grain," Madlyn Tompsyn said, and her son Sheltyn grinned at her tone.

The Tompsyns had been through a lot during the Jihad, but his mother had never lost her sense of humor. It might have been strained more than once, and it had disappeared entirely on some of the worst days, but it had always reemerged. That and her love for his father had been the lifeline which kept them together during the nightmare trek after Zhaspahr Clyntahn's Sword of Schueler swept through their hometown like fire and pestilence. His younger brother, Tohmys, had died of pneumonia during that trek, and they'd almost lost his sister Ellyn, the baby of the family. They had lost Sheltyn's fiancé, Mohraiah, to the same pneumonia which had killed Tohmys. She'd died in his arms, the sound of her fading breath wet and laboring in his ear, and a part of him had died with her. But they'd survived as a family, they'd returned to their homes after the Republic's victory, and his mother—his indomitable, unbreakable, magnificent mother—was the reason they'd been able to.

"I'm sure Dad's out there making all sorts of deals, Mother," he said now, his own tone soothing, and she snorted.

"And sealing the bargains with beer, I suppose?" she asked tartly.

"That's how it's done," Sheltyn pointed out, and looked to his surviving brother for support. "Isn't it, Styvyn?"

"Don't get *me* involved in this!" Styvyn said. "I don't have the least idea how that works. And I'm sure not going to admit it if I do in front of witnesses!"

"Coward!"

"Prudent," Styvyn replied, bending to toss fresh coal into the rudimentary fireplace.

Unlike towns blessed with milder climates, Selyk's market square boasted permanent booths for its licensed vendors. They were about as bare-bones as a structure came, but they had steep, snow-shedding roofs, weathertight walls, and chimneys. They also had windows in three of their four walls, although light came in only through those facing on the square at the moment. The others were tightly shuttered, given the cutting wind coming out of the south.

"The last thing I'm going to do is get crossways of Mom," Styvyn continued as he straightened. "You know how *that* always ends up!"

▼ ▼ ▼

"Mom's going to smell it on your breath, you know, Daddy," Ellyn Tompsyn observed, tucking a hand into her father's elbow.

"Smell what?" Tobys Tompsyn asked innocently.

"Beer, Daddy. Beer." Ellyn shook her head. "It's only ten minutes back to our booth, so I don't think the smell's going away before we get there. And when *she* smells it, she's going to have your cars."

"Nonsense." Tobys pulled his arm free to give her a hug as they left the pastry-maker's booth and headed down the aisle towards their own. His other hand raised the parcel he'd just paid for. "I have my secret weapon."

"Oh, Daddy," Ellyn said in a tone of profound disappointment. "You'd actually use Mom's *sweet tooth* against her?" She shook her head. "I can't believe you'd stoop that low."

"In a skinny Siddar City second," Tobys replied complacently, and Ellyn laughed.

In fact, her father had concluded several profitable transactions this morning, he'd had only two steins of beer in the process, and her mother knew exactly what he'd been doing. Just as she also knew Tobys hadn't touched a drop of anything stronger than beer since their return to Selyk. That was a good thing, and an edge of grief that somehow made her present happiness only greater went through Ellyn as she remembered darker, grimmer days. She'd been only eight when the Sword of Schueler crashed over Selyk and people who'd been family friends all her life suddenly wanted to kill them. Her memories of their flight were horrible but much less distinct than those of the older members of her family. She remembered how bitterly she'd wept for her brother when he died, though, and she remembered her father after he'd gotten his wife and surviving children into something approaching safety. Remembered how his iron strength had failed him and—as he himself put it—he'd "crawled into a bottle" and stayed there for almost five months.

It had taken all her mother's love and strength to pull him back out of it, but she had. And he'd stayed there, even when the Army told him he was too old to enlist.

That was eight years ago, and Ellyn sometimes thought it was a miracle—one named Madlyn—that her father hadn't become one of the "Siddar Loyalists." That was the self-identifying label for the exiles who'd returned home from the eastern Republic filled with searing hatred for the Temple Loyalists' "treachery." But he hadn't, and the dark days which might have turned him into that were long enough ago now that her mother could tease him about his beer once again. In fact, it had become even more of a treasured joke between them, a reaffirmation that they both knew he would never return to that dark place again. That was what made their chaffering about it so comforting.

"I don't know, Daddy," she said now, thoughtfully. "I think the Blessed Bedard might say it was my duty as a loving daughter to protect you from your baser instincts."

"You are *not* getting your mom's mountainberry tarts, young woman!" Tobys shook his head in profound disappointment. "And you accused *me* of stooping?"

"I never said I didn't have a sweet tooth, too," Ellyn pointed out with dignity, and he laughed in a cloud of breath-steam, shimmering in the icy sunlight, and hugged her more tightly.

"No," he acknowledged. "No, you didn't."

"Of course I didn't, and that doesn't change—" Ellyn broke off, her head tilting. "What's all that racket?"

▼ ▼ ▼

"*Settle down!*" Mahkluskee shouted, coming halfway to his feet as he threw his weight against the reins. "Settle down, Grygory!"

The dragon's head flew up as the check rein to the ring in its sensitive nostrils came tight. But this time, not even that was enough. It twisted and lunged again, squealing frantically, and the twenty-ton freight wagon jumped the curb and went swinging through the market. Pedestrians scattered to avoid it. Voices cried out in alarm and warning, and the shouts only added to the dragon's agitation. Its squeals turned into a whistling scream of panic, and it lunged even harder against the traces.

▼ ▼ ▼

"What in the world—?"

Madlyn Tompsyn shook her head at the sudden uproar and started towards the booth's unshuttered front windows.

"I don't know." Styvyn was closer to the front of the booth than his brother or his mother, and he reached it first. "It sounds like—*oh my God!*"

▼ ▼ ▼

"*Daddy!*" Ellyn cried as she and her father hurried around the corner and turned into their booth's aisle, and Tobys Tompsyn's heart froze.

The package of hot mountainberry tarts hit the paving and crushed under his boot as he and his daughter sprinted towards the wreckage.

▼ ▼ ▼

Shormyn Mahkluskee crawled out of the remains of his shattered freight wagon. A pair of experienced drovers had leapt in to assist, grabbing the dragon's nose ring, wrestling it into trembling submission. Mahkluskee was deeply grateful, but he had no attention to spare for Grygory as the horror of the accident filled him.

He stumbled, nearly falling, as he hit the ground, vaguely aware that there was something wrong with his left arm, but he forced himself upright and staggered towards the booth the plunging wagon had demolished.

▼ ▼ ▼

"Madlyn!" Tobys shouted. "Sheltyn—Styvyn!"

Braisyn Klymynt, whose family owned the booth next to the Tompsyns', turned at the sound of his voice. He'd been heaving wreckage aside. Now he saw Tobys and Ellyn running towards him and his face tightened. Tobys charged straight for the booth, then staggered, spinning around, as Braisyn tackled him.

"*Madlyn!*" he half screamed, and Klymynt shook his head.

"Don't—" He stopped and swallowed hard, tears streaking his weathered face. "Don't go in there, Tobys," he said brokenly. "Let . . . let us get them out."

Tobys looked at him. For a moment, only incomprehension looked out of his eyes at his friend. Then something crumpled inside him.

"*Madlyn,*" he whispered.

"I don't . . . I don't think she felt much," Klymynt said. "Never even saw it coming. Her . . . her or the boys."

Tobys staggered, his knees buckling. He would have gone down if Ellyn hadn't turned into him, burrowing into his warm, solid body, burying her face against his chest. She needed him. His daughter needed him, and somehow he got his arms around her, hugging her fiercely, while the market square disappeared behind a shimmering curtain.

"How?" he asked numbly.

His wasn't the only booth that had been wrecked. Klymynt's had been half demolished, two others showed massive damage, and at least a half-dozen other people were down, many with broken bones.

"That idiot lost control of his dragon!" someone else

threw in, and Tobys turned his head. It took him a moment to find the speaker, then follow his pointing gesture to see the battered-looking man standing there with a dazed expression. There was something familiar about him, but Tobys couldn't quite—

"The fucking Temple Loyalist couldn't even manage his own Shan-wei–damned dragon!" the man who'd pointed him out snarled, and Tobys Tompsyn's universe vanished into a terrible, driving fury.

. IU .
Siddar City,
Old Province,
Republic of Siddarmark.

"Langhorne, Daryus! What the hell *happened*?" Greyghor Stohnar asked.

"We're still trying to put that together." The seneschal's voice was harsh. "So far—*so far*—it sounds like something that . . . just happened." He shook his head sharply, manifestly unhappy with his own choice of words. "I mean, it doesn't look like this was preplanned, not the result of anything anyone saw coming. It sounds like it was an honest accident and the reaction just got out of hand."

"'Got out of hand,'" Samyl Gahdarhd repeated. "I guess that's one way to describe it."

"I'm not trying to minimize this, Samyl!" Daryus Parkair snapped. "I'm only trying to explain how it started, not saying a word about how it *ended*!"

"I know that." Stohnar laid a hand on Parkair's arm. "We all know that. But that doesn't make it any better."

"I know." Parkair shook his head again. "And my people are trying to get to the bottom of it. As soon as they know anything more, so will you. So will all of us."

"Greyghor's right," Gahdarhd said, his tone apologetic.

"I'm just still trying to wrap my mind around it myself, I suppose. My people didn't see this coming, either. Not on this scale, at any rate. And not in Selyk."

"No one did," Stohnar pointed out, "but it's not like this is the first incident like it. I doubt it'll be the last, either." It was the lord protector's turn to shake his head. "I know tensions run higher during the winter months when 'cabin fever' gets added to everything else, but I don't know if this is going to get any better after the thaw."

"At least Daryus had troops available to restore calm," Henrai Maidyn pointed out.

"This time. And after a quarter of the town went up in flames," Parkair growled.

"Surely it's not as bad as the early reports suggest," Maidyn countered. "It never is, Daryus!"

"You're probably right," Stohnar said before Parkair could respond. "That doesn't mean it's good, though. And I especially don't like what we're hearing about lynchings."

"It's going to get worse before it gets better," Gahdarhd cautioned. The others looked at him, and he shrugged. "I'm not trying to borrow any trouble, but the truth is that we're likely to see more incidents like this one, especially as the news spreads. For that matter, Selyk wasn't anywhere near as volatile a situation as some of the larger towns in Westmarch and Cliff Peak. Tensions are high in all the western provinces, but especially in places like Alyksberg and Aivahnstyn."

"I know what you're about to say, Samyl," Stohnar interrupted. "And we still can't. Not yet."

"Greyghor, my boys may've managed to put a lid on Selyk—for now, at least—but Samyl's got a point," Parkair said. "They may've put out the actual house fires, but they couldn't put out the one that *started* all this, not really. I understand why we had to let the bastards come home, but the resentment—the *hatred*—our people who stayed loyal to the Republic feel for Temple Loyalists would be awful hard to overstate."

"And my agents tell me some of the speculators are deliberately turning up the heat," Gahdarhd said. "The more hatred they generate, the more Temple Loyalists they can get to accept bargain prices, trying to get out with what they can salvage."

"I know. I know!" Stohnar's expression was grim. "And I'm hoping, come spring, we'll finally be able to do something about that. But we still can't. Not yet," he repeated. "Not until Fyguera has Thesmar up and running."

His most trusted subordinates glanced at one another, then looked back at him and nodded, although Gahdarhd's nod was rather grudging.

Stohnar didn't blame the keeper of the seal, but he couldn't afford to fight all the battles he wished he could. The death toll from Selyk would trouble his dreams, and he knew Gahdarhd and Parkair were right; there *would* be more incidents, and some of them might well be even worse.

But at least we're turning the corner, he told himself. *Or getting close, at any rate. If we can just hang on a little longer. . . .*

The newly organized Province of Thesmar, created out of the southern half of the old South March Lands, had been granted its official provincial charter last month. Its first Chamber delegates were en route to Siddar City even now, and the immensely popular Kydryc Fyguera, who'd held the city of Thesmar against everything the Sword of Schueler could throw at it, had been elected as its first governor. That had accomplished one of Stohnar's major post-Jihad objectives, and he expected it to have a calming effect—ultimately—on the western provinces' festering animosities. And, for that matter, in Shiloh Province, farther east. It wasn't going to magically cure all ills, but it ought to be a significant step in the right direction, and he knew Thesmar's new delegates would be a welcome reinforcement for his supporters in the Chamber. It was unfortunate that securing its creation and the approval of Maidyn's central bank had required so much dragon-trading with the land speculators' political spokesman. There'd been no other way, however, and he still wasn't out of the woods on the Central Bank.

The speculators didn't like the thought of being reined in by official credit laws. Neither did manufactory owners who feared they'd be shut down if the new laws went into effect, or bankers who feared the consequences of government interference in their traditional modes of doing business . . . or who'd been doing well—personally, at least—by exploiting the current situation. For that matter, it would have been impossible to estimate the number of people, including those still trying to rebuild shattered farms and small businesses, who feared the tightening of credit, often with good reason. And then there were the senior members of the guilds, who hated the very notion of Charisian-style manufactories. One would have expected them to favor anything which would dry up money and handicap the "industrialization" of Siddarmark. Instead, they'd become so invested in resisting *anything* Stohnar and his cabinet proposed that their vociferous opposition to the bank had come as no surprise. It was fortunate they, at least, had so much less influence than they'd once possessed. That wasn't remotely the same as *no* influence, however, and perhaps their resistance to it wasn't quite as blind as Stohnar preferred to assume it was. Perhaps they were actively hoping for an economic collapse because they thought it would allow them to reassert the pre-Jihad model which had favored them so strongly.

If they believed anything of the sort was possible, they were even bigger idiots than he'd thought they were, impossible as that seemed.

"I need another five or six months," he said now, looking at the others but focused on Parkair. "At *least* another five or six months. Can you give them to me?"

"Probably," the seneschal said after a long moment. "It's likely to get messy, though. And I'll be honest, not all of my boys are as impartial as we'd all like to think they are. Some of them are going to have a pretty hefty thumb on the scales when it comes time to decide whose head gets broken."

"I know, and I'll give you all the support I can through the civil government, but I need to keep as many western delegates in my pocket in the Chamber as I can until they give me Henrai's bank. After that, you can break all the heads you need to, and Samyl and I will be able to really turn the screws on the provincial governors and *their* chambers. But until then—"

He shrugged, and Parkair grimaced.

"I understand," the seneschal half sighed, "and I'll do my best. But—I hope you won't take this wrongly, Henrai—I suggest you get that done as soon as you can, because I don't see the situation getting a lot better anytime soon."

. V .
Tellesberg Palace,
City of Tellesberg,
Kingdom of Old Charis,
Empire of Charis.

"Stefyny!" Her Highness Alahnah Zhanayt Naimu Ahrmahk, Crown Princess of Charis, crowed exuberantly.

"And good morning to you, too, Your Highness," Nynian Athrawes observed mildly as the crown princess dashed past her to half tackle the dark-haired, gray-eyed young woman who'd accompanied her.

"Oh, hi, Aunt Nynian!" Alahnah said over her shoulder without interrupting her happy dance with Stefyny.

"I see your priorities are nicely developed," Nynian said dryly.

"She gets that from her father," Empress Sharleyan offered.

"With no input at all from the maternal side of her family?" Nynian nodded. "I see. Thank you for explaining that to me."

Sharleyan laughed and opened her arms to embrace the older woman.

"It's good to see you. We've missed you."

"Some more than others, apparently," Nynian said, turning to smile at Alahnah and Stefyny.

"Outside her immediate relatives—and the Breygart kids, of course—she doesn't really have any close friends," Sharleyan said a bit wistfully. "Not like Mairah and I were, anyway. I realize 'Aunt Stefyny' is family, too, but you know what I mean."

"Yes, I do," Nynian said more gently, although she knew Stefyny was secretly amused at being "Aunt Stefyny" to someone a whole seven years younger than she was. Still, that was beginning to fade a bit. She was much closer to *Cousin* Stefyny these days, and there were times she must still wonder if she'd followed the white fox-lizard through the looking glass. Or the white rabbit, for that matter, since unlike anyone else her age on Safehold, Stefyny had read the original version of *Ahlys in Wonderland*.

Nynian felt her smile fade at that thought as she watched her daughter hugging the Crown Princess of Charis and thought about what it had cost Stefyny to become who she was. She remembered the waif whose iron courage—and love—had challenged the certain death of crossing the "kill line" in a Church's concentration camp to find food for her sick father. Who'd survived and escaped the even more hideous rigors of the Punishment only because of Merlin Athrawes' direct intervention. She remembered the little girl who'd waked up in Nimue's Cave, and wondered if Nynian Rychtair was an angel. She remembered that little girl and her brother, and their father, learning the truth about how they'd been saved, about "Mother Church." And she remembered the day she'd held that same sobbing girl in her arms. The day even Stefyny's indomitable strength had almost broken forever.

The day Greyghor Mahlard, who'd become an auxiliary volunteer in the Tellesberg Fire Brigade, charged back into a burning apartment house in an effort to save one more life.

Nynian had adopted that little girl and her brother Sebahstean even before she'd married Merlin Athrawes in that very quiet ceremony in Maikel Staynair's private chapel. She'd adopted them because they'd needed her, and because she'd needed them. They'd been her chance to fill the inevitable childless void left by her avocation as the Sisters of Saint Kohdy's mother superior and the leader of Helm Cleaver. And they'd been her chance to help rebuild the lives of two youngsters who'd paid far too high a price.

A chance, she knew, which was perhaps even more important to Merlin than it was to her.

And it didn't hurt that you were—that you both *were—members of the inner circle, did it?* she asked herself, feeling her smile return and quirk with amusement. *Both of them "knew too much" to run around with parents who* weren't *members of the circle! And, God, aren't you grateful to Him for giving you both of them? And Merlin! Maikel's right. Sometimes, He really does reward us more deeply than anyone could deserve, doesn't He?*

"May I go show Stefyny the new colt, Mother?" Alahnah asked now, and Sharleyan shook her head.

"After you hug Aunt Nynian, I suppose that could be arranged," she said, and Alahnah laughed.

"Sorry, Aunt Nynian!" she said, bestowing a tighter than usual embrace by way of apology. "I just haven't seen Stefyny in *forever*!"

"Forever," Nynian reflected, had rather a different meaning for someone who would turn ten—the Terran equivalent of nine—next month.

Alahnah had returned to Tellesberg with her parents while Nynian and Stefyny and Sebahstean had awaited Merlin's return from Boisseau before following. In many ways, none of them had wanted to insert Merlin into a situation as delicate as the one in the new "United Provinces," but Cayleb and Sharleyan had needed someone whose authority to speak on their behalf could not be questioned. That had made Merlin the inevitable spokesman to present the "Ahrmahk Plan" to Baron Star Rising and Bishop Yaupang. He'd maintained a very low profile during his time in Pauton, and so far it seemed they'd kept anyone in Yu-kwau from realizing he'd been there. Not that it looked like it made a lot of difference to Zhyou-Zhwo and his council in the end.

"I quite understand that two months is an intolerable length of time to be apart," she said now, very seriously, cocking her head at Merlin's goddaughter. Alahnah looked back up at her, equally seriously . . . only to dissolve in giggles when Nynian slowly arched one eyebrow in an expression she'd learned from Merlin.

"Well, it seemed like that to *me*," the princess said.

"And I really do understand," Nynian assured her. "On the other hand, neither Stefyny nor I have seen your sister in two months, either."

"She's not much to look at yet," Alahnah said. Her mother clucked her tongue, and Alahnah smiled. "At least she doesn't cry *all* the time anymore, though. That's better."

"Do you really want to go there, young lady?" Sharleyan asked. "I can always start reminiscing with Aunt Nynian about someone else and voyages. Now, let me see. Who *could* I be thinking of?"

"I'm sure *I* don't know." Alahnah's immense dignity was sadly undercut by the twinkle in her eye, but then she grabbed Nynian's hand and started tugging in the general direction of the nursery.

"Come on! Mother has her in my old cradle—the one they made for me on *Destiny*. The *boys* didn't get to use it!"

She lifted her nose with an audible sniff, and her mother shook her head.

"Only because they were twins and wouldn't both fit, and you know it," she said.

"That's not what Poppa said," Alahnah said smugly. "*He* said you were saving it for your next daughter."

"Oh, he *did*, did he?" Sharleyan glanced sideways at Nynian, then back at her older daughter. "Well, I think he and I are going to have to have a little talk, aren't we?"

"Really?" Alahnah looked up over her shoulder with

a gap-toothed grin. "Should Uncle Merlin bring the potato slices?"

▼ ▼ ▼

"She *is* a handful, isn't she?" Merlin observed in a deep, amused voice as he stood on the palace balcony and watched Alahnah half-leading and half-dragging Stefyny towards the royal stables.

"Gets it from her mother," Cayleb replied with a lurking smile. Then he turned to the *seijin* and grinned much more broadly. "I expect to be hearing from Sharley about that shortly, but she had it coming."

"Don't try to get me involved in this," Merlin said mildly. "I'm only the godfather and unofficial uncle around here."

"Nonsense. You are, by any measure, the senior member of the inner circle and, for that matter, of the entire human race. So, obviously, you have to be on *my* side."

"You *so* do not want to go there," Merlin told him. "Remember, bcfore I was Merlin I was Nimue. Lurking gender loyalties, and all that."

He smiled as he spoke, and his obviously genuine amusement warmed Cayleb's heart. There'd been far too many dark places behind those sapphire eyes—still were, really—but thanks to Nynian, to Stefyny and Sebahstean, and to Alahnah and his other godchildren, Merlin Athrawes had finally learned to forgive himself. And how to be who he'd become, however he'd gotten there.

"I'm sure your essential fairmindedness and honesty will range you on the side of truth and justice—which is to say, *my* side—eventually, despite any lingering biases you may cherish," the emperor said now, and Merlin laughed.

"I think I feel a bout of neutrality coming on."

"In that case, I shall swallow my disappointment and sad disillusionment and suggest we get started," he said. "It's not getting any earlier."

"No, it isn't," a female voice observed over Cayleb's

earplug. "In fact, some of us have supper coming up in a couple of hours," Nimue Chwaeriau added.

"What you get for living in inconvenient time zones," Cayleb retorted as he and Merlin left the balcony and entered the large library. He and Sharleyan each had individual working offices which connected to that library, and he led Merlin into his and pointed at one of the comfortable chairs.

Merlin settled into it with a nod, and Cayleb took his own seat behind the desk.

"All right, Nimue," he said in a much more serious voice. "You said you have something important to tell us before we get everyone on the circuit."

"Yes, I did," the young woman who'd also once been Nimue Alban said from her chamber in far distant Manchyr. Her voice was . . . odd, Cayleb thought, and looked across the office at his guest. Merlin had obviously heard it, too, but he only shrugged.

"We're here," Cayleb said, and the others knew what he meant. The only people presently on the circuit were Nimue, Merlin, Cayleb, Sharleyan, Nynian, and Maikel Staynair. In a very real sense, this was the inner circle of the inner circle.

He waited, but she said nothing for several seconds. That sort of silence was very unlike her, and Cayleb wondered what was going on. Then Nynian, sitting in the nursery with Nynian Zhorzhet Ahrmahk in her lap, cleared her throat gently.

"Is there a reason Koryn isn't part of this conversation, Nimue?"

More silence lingered, and then—

"Yes." The oddness in Nimue's voice was more pronounced. It sounded almost like . . . tears, Cayleb thought, and saw Merlin sit suddenly straighter in his chair.

"Why isn't he?" Nynian asked with that same gentleness.

Gahrvai had become a member of the inner circle shortly after Zhaspahr Clyntahn's execution. He'd made a lot of valuable contributions over the years since, but that didn't explain the strange note in Nimue's voice.

Or, Cayleb thought suddenly, why Owl wasn't providing visual imagery of her. That could only be at her request.

"Because . . . because he's asked me to marry him," Nimue said finally.

"What?" Cayleb twitched upright. "That's wonderful!" Then he looked at Merlin, saw the sudden thoughtfulness in his expression. "Isn't it?" he finished a bit lamely.

"Speaking as someone who had the lamentable misjudgment to fall in love with another PICA—another iteration of *you,* now that I think about it—can I ask why that's making you sit alone in your chamber and cry instead of dancing on the battlements?" Nynian asked. "Surely you have to know nothing in the world could make Koryn happier!"

"Of course I know that . . . for now, anyway," Nimue half snapped. "But what about ten years from now? *Fifteen?*"

"If you're thinking about his mortality, do you think that's something that hasn't crossed *my* mind?" Nynian riposted. "Don't forget, I'm twenty years older than he is!"

"And even if you are," Staynair said gently, "Owl's almost ready to begin installing the new implants."

Cayleb nodded. Aside from Merlin and Nimue—and Nahrmahn Baytz, who was a special case in every conceivable way—all of the inner circle relied upon contact lenses and earplugs for access to the SNARCs, the network of heavily stealthed orbital platforms which connected them to one another and to Nimue's Cave. The PICAs had built-in coms, although Merlin's high-speed interface was nonfunctional, as a consequence of the hacked software which had allowed Nimue Alban's original PICA to remain online indefinitely. Nimue Chwaeriau had been built with different software, designed by Owl, and her high-speed interface worked just fine.

None of the circle's organic members could match that capability, because none of them had the "wetware" implants which had been standard for citizens of the Terran Federation. They could have had them, but any Safeholdian healer who saw them would instantly recognize them as neither natural nor explicable. Undoubtedly, they'd be put down as the work of more than mortal hands, and that was something none of them could risk when the jury about whether or not they really did worship Shan-wei, not God, was still out in so many Safeholdian minds.

But it had occurred to Nahrmahn Baytz that perhaps there was a way around that. He'd discussed it with Owl, the artificial intelligence with whom he shared his virtual reality. And as tended to happen when Nahrmahn got involved, everyone *else's* reality had suddenly shifted.

Federation wetware would have been impossible to disguise, but only because the Federation had never seen any reason why it should "disguise" it, any more than earlier centuries of humanity had seen any reason to disguise eyeglasses or fillings in teeth. Conceal the implants cosmetically, perhaps, but everyone had them, everyone knew what they were, and no one worried about it.

Would it be possible, Nahrmahn had asked, to design a set of implants that *could* be disguised, even from the examination of a skilled healer or an autopsy?

Owl's answer had been no. On the other hand, it might be possible to design implants that would be *difficult* for a healer to detect . . . and wouldn't be available for an autopsy to discover. It had taken him longer than he'd originally projected, but he'd succeeded in designing an organic-based implant. One whose components would be completely internal, woven into its recipient's nervous system and hidden by skin and muscle, and would dissolve completely within twenty minutes of its recipient's biological death. It was remotely possible an alert healer might spot them in someone who'd suffered an injury sufficiently traumatic to actually expose his or her central nervous system, and Safeholdian surgeons *did* do brain surgery upon occasion. So the risk of discovery under extreme conditions would remain. But aside from a small number of "ganglia," they would be nearly microscopic. It was unlikely a physician dealing with such a severe injury would have any time to spare to notice them, and no one who'd received Federation self-repairing nanotech would ever need brain surgery.

Owl had completed his final simulated evaluation of the new system two five-days ago and it had passed with flying colors. Not entirely to Merlin's delight, Nynian had volunteered to be the initial human guinea pig and the two of them would be flying to Nimue's Cave in a few days.

"I know about the implants, Maikel," Nimue replied now. "In fact, I think that's the main reason Koryn asked me now. I've been . . . I've been putting him off by reminding him about Nahrmahn and Ohlyvya, Merlin and Nynian. But if the new implants work as well as everything else Owl's come up with, there's no reason he can't record his personality, as well, which means he can be just as 'immortal' as I am."

"Then where's the problem?" Nynian asked gently.

"He needs an *heir*," Nimue said, her voice suddenly harsh and bitter. "And I can't give him one."

The new silence was intense, and Merlin found himself wondering if anyone else—except perhaps Nynian—heard the true, grinding sorrow in that voice. Nimue Alban had lived her entire life—and died—knowing she would never be a mother. That she would never conceive or bear a child who could only be killed by the Gbaba before she was out of adolescence. That no responsible human being would ever do that again.

Now Nimue *Chwaeriau*, the person who was Nimue Alban's true heir, even more than Merlin Athrawes, found herself on a world where babies, children, were the most joyous treasure imaginable . . . and living in a body which *couldn't* conceive.

"Nimue, he *knows* that," Sharleyan said finally. "If he's asked you anyway. . . ."

"He's an only child, Sharley," Nimue said. "He's his

father's sole heir. He says that's not important to him, but I know it's important to Rysel. And not just because Koryn's his son. The Earl *despises* most of the alternative heirs. And even if Koryn says it isn't important to him, even if he means it, what will he feel like in twenty or thirty years?"

"I think he'll feel exactly the way he feels now, honestly," Sharleyan said. "He's not a fickle man, Nimue. He knows his own mind . . . and his own heart. And he's not going to lie to you about what he thinks and feels."

"No, he's not," Nimue acknowledged, and Cayleb heard the almost forlorn pride in her voice. "But I won't . . . close off that avenue. He may not care about heirs, but I've seen him with kids, Sharley. This is a man who wants, needs, to be a father, and who'd be a damned *good* one. I'll be his lover, but I can never marry him, take that away from him. I just . . . can't."

"Oh, don't be silly!"

More than one of the people on the circuit twitched at the bubble—the *amusement*—in Nynian Athrawes' voice.

"I'm not being silly!" Nimue snapped. "This is *important* to me!"

"Yes, it is," Nynian replied. "In fact, in some ways, I think it may be more important to you *for* him than it is to him. For that matter, there are some . . . issues here for *you*, too, whether you've faced them all or not. And before you bite my head off, let me point out two or three things to you if I may?"

"Go ahead," Nimue said after a few fulminating seconds.

"Thank you," Nynian said rather more gently. "First point. I'm married to another version of you. I *know* why Nimue Alban knew she'd never be a mother, and I know what kind of scar that leaves. Trust me when I say that, because I truly do.

"Second point. Whatever ignorant people who haven't tried it may think, there's no difference between a parent's love for a biological child and her love for an adoptive child. I've never had a baby of my own, either, but I do have a daughter and I do have a son, and no one could possibly love anyone more than Merlin and I love them. I never thought I'd have children any more than Nimue Alban did, Nimue, and for a lot of the same reasons, really. I wasn't worried about the Gbaba, but I wasn't going to offer them up as hostages to Zhaspahr Clyntahn's Inquisition. Now you and Merlin have made it possible for me to change my mind about that, and I'm not going to sit here and watch you throw away the same opportunity you brought me. I can't. I'm sorry if that pisses you off, but you're going to need a better reason than *that* to tell the man who loves you you won't marry him."

Unlike Nimue, all of them could see Nynian's face, and Merlin felt his eyes soften as he looked into his wife's gaze and remembered a long-ago conversation with Ohlyvya Baytz. A conversation Nynian Rychtair had forced him to confront in ways he would never have imagined were possible.

And now she was doing it all over again for a different iteration of Nimue Alban.

"I . . . hadn't thought of that," Nimue said after a long stillness, her voice soft.

"Of course you hadn't," Nynian told her simply. "Nimue, you've had a lot of reasons to hold that door closed, including the fact of his mortality. But you've come far enough to admit you love him and to share his bed, sweetheart. So what about opening the door a little wider? Sharing his entire life—openly, at his side—as well?"

"I still don't know how that would work for the succession," Nimue said.

"Probably not very well," Cayleb said a bit unwillingly. "Corisandian inheritance law's not quite as bad as it was with Hektor when I adopted him, but I'm not at all sure the Corisandian peerage would accept an adoptive heir when there are legitimate heirs of the blood available. And this is one issue Daivyn couldn't overrule them on. He could create new titles for your child— and I'm sure he'd insist on doing just that, given how he feels about both of you!—but unless the 'legitimate heir' is attainted for treason, he can't arbitrarily hand an existing title to someone else. On the other hand, I think you might be wronging Rysel a bit. I think he'd care a lot more about his son's being happy than he would about who's going to inherit any titles after both of them are dead."

"I think Cayleb's right, Nimue," Nynian said, "but it doesn't really matter, because that brings me to my third point. Which is that the question doesn't have to arise at all."

"I beg your pardon?" Nimue asked a bit skeptically.

"You're a *PICA*!" Nynian laughed. "I'm *married* to a PICA, so I'm what you might call intimately—in more than one sense of the word—familiar with his ability to reconfigure himself physically. If you can transform yourself into a man, like Dagyr Cudd, do you expect me to believe you couldn't pretty perfectly simulate a pregnant *seijin*? Without the minor disadvantages of things like morning sickness, I mean."

"*Minor?*" Sharleyan snorted. "Now there speaks an *adoptive* mother!"

"Details, details!" Nynian waved one hand in a graceful dismissal, then bent and planted a kiss on the top of her namesake's head. "Don't distract her."

"Well, yes," Nimue said. "I could simulate a pregnancy, but the endpoint of the process is supposed to be a *child*, Nynian, and simulating a *delivery* would be just a tad more difficult!"

"More details," Nynian told her, but her tone was far less airy. She straightened, wrapping both arms around the baby in her lap, and her expression was focused and intent.

"Listen to me, Nimue. There are quite a few women in the inner circle now, the majority of them of childbearing age. I'm not anymore, I'm afraid, but any one of those other women would happily—*lovingly*—donate ova to you and Koryn. Surely you don't doubt that! And have you actually forgotten what 'Doctor Owl' has already done for Zhain Howsmyn? Trust me, he has everything he needs in the Cave to fertilize those ova with Koryn's sperm and bring the baby to term in an artificial womb. So the two of you *can* have children, and that child *will* be Rysel's biological grandchild and heir . . . and every inch as much yours as she is Koryn's. Nimue, love, the two of you can have as many children as you want!"

"We . . . we could, couldn't we?" Nimue's voice was soft, tears floating within it. "This . . . this never even occurred to me!"

"That's because Nimue Alban would never have been cruel enough to create a child only because she wanted one so badly," Maikel Staynair told her, his voice as gentle as Nynian's had been. "But it's also because you were so focused on protecting Koryn and Rysel. That's *always* your first instinct, just like it is Merlin's—to protect others, not yourself. You're too busy creating possibilities for *us* to think about how desperately we wish we could create them for *you*. But Nynian's right. I'm positive of that."

"Of course she is!" There were tears on Sharleyan's cheeks, as well, and she reached out to grip one of Nynian's hands. "Of course she is! In fact, I'll volunteer *my* ova right now, Nimue. And I'm sure Elayn or Irys—or any of us—will do exactly the same thing."

"You would?" Nimue's tone sounded wondering, and Sharleyan laughed through her tears.

"Oh, Maikel is *so* right about you and Merlin!" she said. "After everything the two of you have done for us, for our *world*, for everyone and everything that matters to us, we finally have the opportunity to do something for *you*! How could you think for an instant we wouldn't take it?"

APRIL YEAR OF GOD 904

·✦·

. I .
Nimue's Cave,
The Mountains of Light,
Episcopate of St. Ehrnesteen,
The Temple Lands.

<Wake up, love.>

Nynian Athrawes opened her eyes as the beloved voice flowed through her.

<Welcome back, sleepyhead!> that same voice said.

The smooth stone ceiling above her had become a familiar, almost comforting sight over the years, but not as comforting as the face smiling down at her. She smiled back, then stiffened as she realized Merlin's lips hadn't moved.

"Is this—?" she began, only to pause as another face appeared beside Merlin's.

<Just a moment,> a second voice said somewhere in the depths of her mind, and the air above her was suddenly spangled with a series of glowing icons. There were twenty of them, arranged in five neat rows of four.

<That's better,> the second voice said, and Owl's disembodied head smiled at her. <It will take you a while to master the fully interactive interface, Nynian. I'll take you through a tutorial when you're ready, but until you're familiar with it, the more intuitive aspects of it are locked out. For now, you can visualize the proper icon to cue your implant's CPU to bring up the appropriate function. Later, after you've become fully familiar

with the interface, all that will be required is the decision on your part to activate the function you desire.>

"I . . . I see," she told the AI, then looked back at Merlin. "This is going to take some getting used to," she said. "Especially for an old woman like me!"

<*Old!*> his voice snorted in her brain. <Are you sure you want to throw adjectives like that around with *me*, young lady?>

Nynian laughed, reassured by the familiar tartness of the exchange. It was true that she was sixty-four years old, her dark hair lightly threaded with the first strands of silver, but sixty-four was only fifty-eight in the years of long-dead Terra, and she'd received the enhanced basic medical nanotech Merlin and Owl had made available to all of the inner circle. It wasn't remotely the same as the antigerone therapies which had allowed the original "Adams" and "Eves" to live as much as two or two and a half centuries, even without the booster treatments still available to the "Archangels" in Eric Langhorne's command crew. It did, however, assure she would be disease-free, immune to Alzheimer's or any form of cancer, that any injuries would heal with near-miraculous speed, and that she could expect to live to at least a hundred and fifty years. If they hadn't managed to overthrow the Church of God Awaiting by then, her longevity would undoubtedly raise a few eyebrows. On the other hand, if they *hadn't* overthrown the Church by then, raised eyebrows would be the least of their problems.

Then there was always the minor fact that while *Nimue Alban* might have been born over a millennium ago, Merlin had been in existence for less than fifteen years. So which of them did *that* make a cradle robber?

"So how do I talk back to you?" she asked.

<*The same way you always do, I'm sure!*> Merlin's sapphire eyes laughed at her. <You've never been shy about giving me grief before!>

"You only thought I was giving you grief before," she warned him, then looked past him to Owl's head. "Owl? How does this work?"

<As I said, you need only visualize the appropriate icon.> One of the floating icons, a pair of stylized lips, glowed more brightly than the others and flashed slowly.

Nynian frowned as she focused her attention on the flashing image. It felt a little odd, because she discovered she wasn't actually "seeing" it with her eyes at all. The image was projected into her field of vision, much as Owl had projected data and video onto her contact lenses for years, but there was still a subtle difference, although it took her a moment to realize what that difference was. *This* image was projected directly into her *mind,* with a sharpness and clarity that bypassed the actual optic nerve. It had a . . . solidity, although that wasn't really the word, greater than anything she'd ever actually "seen."

And yet, sharp as it was, it snapped into even greater sharpness as she concentrated on it.

<Visualize it like this?> she asked, and her own eyes widened as she realized the mental commands which should have gone to her vocal cords, her tongue and her lips, had gone somewhere else entirely.

<*Exactly* like that, love!> Merlin told her, reaching down to lay one strong, long-fingered hand against her cheek. <I always knew you were a clever one!>

<I know we've all said this way too many times by now, but this really is like magic,> she "said." <Like the telepathy in those old pre-space novels Nahrmahn found.>

<I suppose it is, in most ways.> Merlin extended a hand and lifted her into a sitting position. He was very gentle about it, and she felt only a minor twinge of discomfort as a reminder that she'd just undergone the most intrusive neurosurgery any native Safeholdian had ever experienced. <I can't say for sure what the authors had in mind, of course,> his voice continued somewhere inside her brain, completely bypassing her eardrums and yet "sounding" exactly like himself, <but I expect it's close to what they were reaching for. And I had Owl modify your software just a bit. For the Federation, with the planetary datanets available on a

wireless basis everywhere, things like range and security were approached rather differently. No one needed very much transmission or reception range, because data nodes were so frequent and so widespread they were always tied into the net, pretty much anywhere. And "security" consisted of encryption and other ways to safeguard data flows and prevent hacks. No one ever worried about whether or not an implant's signal might be *detected* because no one saw any reason to hide it.

<Our situation's just a little different, however, so your implants have more transmission and reception range—not a lot more: there's a limit to the power of any EM transmitter I want anywhere near your cerebral cortex, but enough that we can talk to each other from one side of a baseball field to the other, let's say, even without a SNARC. And while you've got all the standard protections against hacking, *our* main security concern's making sure any transmissions between us stay covert, which is another reason to keep them low powered enough they're pretty severely range-limited. You'll be able to tie your implants into the SNARCs, but you'll have to route them through your existing exterior com to get the range you'll need and its stealth features will go on covering you when you do.>

She nodded slowly, her eyes intent.

<But I'll be able to talk to you like this whenever I want? Wherever you are?> It was his turn to nod, and she snorted in amusement. <Well, that sure sounds like "telepathy" to *me*!>

<I don't disagree, although there are some big differences. For example, we can't exchange emotions the way "telepaths" could in the books. Information flow's something else, but even there, there are hard limits to what we can exchange in real time. That's more of a matter of bandwidth, but once you're fully acclimated to your CPU, you'll be able to drop files directly to anyone else who's received the implants. Not just data files, either. Experiential files, too. Not just accounts of things you've seen or experienced but the actual memories of them. And, now that I think about it, there is some emo-

tional exchange involved there. It's just not a direct exchange between individuals and it can't be done in real time, only in uploaded files. There's no way for "two to become one," but that doesn't mean you won't be able to share files that allow you to . . . understand one another in ways you never could before. Although I won't be able to do as much of that as you and the others will.>

<Why not?> she demanded as she heard the bittersweet edge in his mental tone.

<Bandwidth again,> he said simply. She raised an eyebrow, and he shook his head. <My high-speed port's still down, Nynian, and there are a lot of databytes in an exchange like that. Too many for the human nervous system to transmit to another human nervous system in real time. That's one of the big reasons I did so much damage to Nahrmahn's brain when I recorded him with the EMS headset. Instead, you'll have to "zip" the memory in your CPU, then send it across to the intended recipient. But even compressed, it'll still be a huge file, and unlike your new "wetware," I still can't process high-speed data transfers on that scale. That's why Nahrmahn has to slow the internal clock on his VR down to match the real world whenever I visit. I can't process—no, scratch that, I can't access the datastream at a high enough baud rate. You have a far higher rate than I do, so he'll be able to maintain a higher compression ratio with you. I just won't be able to do the same thing.>

Disappointment darkened her eyes, and he bent to kiss her gently.

<Didn't say it can never be fixed,> he told her. <In fact, Owl and Nahrmahn have been quietly at work on building me an entirely new "brain" for quite a while now. One that does have a high-speed port.>

<Oh? And why is this the first *I've* heard about that?>

<Because none of us were sure it was going to be possible and there was no point mentioning it if it wasn't,> he said reasonably. <It's actually been a more complicated challenge than the one they faced when they built Nimue, because they started from scratch for her. They

had to figure out how to build her and they did it all with their own "proprietary" hardware and software. My problem's "only" a software glitch, but the software's also hardware because it's hardwired into my existing brain. Nimue's PICA was never emancipated; she always used it as a remote, which is why the system was designed to dump every ten days whether she wanted it to or not. The whole idea was to build a PICA with features that meant it couldn't "go rogue," no matter what happened, and the people who built me wanted to make damned sure no one screwed around with those safeguards. Doc Proctor did anyway, but not even he could get around all the protections without a few . . . side effects, and Owl's decided that trying to fix me the way I am would only run the risk of creating additional, unanticipated problems farther downstream. So he's had to figure out how to build a mollycirc brain—using his and Nahrmahn's "proprietary" design—that will permit permanent, long-term independent operation. In essence, they have to build an emancipated PICA's brain that they can drop into a PICA *chassis* which was specifically designed to prevent anyone from doing that. He tells me they're getting close, and we've been working on recording my post-Nimue memories for a while now. We're still a couple of years behind the curve, but we're getting there. So by the time they have my new brain ready, we should have a complete record of me to download into it. Hopefully.>

<As long as no one goes fooling around with your brain until we're sure we have a *complete* record,> she said, leaning her head upon his shoulder.

<Trust me,> he kissed the top of her head, <I'm not taking any chances on forgetting about you.>

<Good.> She tilted her face up to kiss him, then sighed and leaned back into his shoulder. <And now, suppose you walk me through what the rest of Owl's icons do? The sooner I get this mastered, the sooner we'll be able to clear it for the others!>

"I want every member of their families here in the South arrested!" Emperor Zhyou-Zhwo snarled. "Every *one* of them, do you hear?!"

"Of course, Your Supreme Majesty!" Grand Duke North Wind Blowing said quickly, bending his head in desperate, disgusted obsequiousness. *This* was what came of an emperor trying to exercise direct rule, he thought furiously. Policies as stupid as Zhaspahr Clyntahn's "collective security"! They *might* work—against some of the families involved—but most of them would have seen this possibility coming from the beginning and taken whatever steps they could against it. As anyone but a fool should have realized from the start. Not that he didn't understand the basis for Zhyou-Zhwo's rage perfectly. But if the emperor had simply been willing to let the professionals do their jobs—!

"Your pardon, Your Supreme Majesty," Duke Summer Flowers said, "but what do you wish us to do with them after they're taken into custody?"

A very good question, North Wind Blowing thought. And another sign of the southern duke's growing stature on the Imperial Council that he dared to ask it. The first councilor tried to feel more grateful that someone had asked than resentful that the someone involved was Summer Flowers.

It was difficult.

"An excellent question, My Lord Duke," Zhyou-Zhwo said. He'd hesitated a moment or two before responding, and he offered no immediate expansion when he did. North Wind Blowing hid his sour amusement behind an attentive expression. Of course he hadn't thought it through before he issued his demand!

"If I might suggest, Your Supreme Majesty," Summer Flowers murmured into the awkward pause, "none of these people have themselves personally offended against your prerogatives or authority. Nonetheless, their relatives in these 'United Provinces' most certainly have. I would suggest they be treated as prisoners of state and confined in reasonable comfort—for now, at least—as a pointed reminder to those treachery-minded relatives of theirs that your patience is not unlimited. Your Supreme Majesty need not enumerate any specific charges against them in order for them to be held indefinitely at your pleasure. None of their families could miss your message, but your forbearance in not charging them at this time may inspire those treachery-minded relatives to recognize your mercy and patience and forsake their treason."

"An excellent formulation of what I had in mind, My Lord," Zhyou-Zhwo said warmly. "In fact, I believe it would be appropriate, since you've understood me so well, for you to assume responsibility for seeing that it's done in Our name."

"You honor me with the responsibility, Your Supreme Majesty," Summer Flowers said, inclining his head in a gracious bow, and North Wind Blowing masked a silent curse behind an approving smile.

The emperor smiled, as well. But then he allowed his smile to fade and his face hardened once again.

"We wish Our Council in general to consider this matter in depth now that we have confirmation of this 'Ahrmahk Plan,'" he said, and his tone made the last two words an obscenity. "We are well aware that this . . . this bribe will make it exceedingly difficult for even Our loyal subjects to resist Cayleb's foul blandishments. We fear we will be unable to prevent those *less* loyal to Us from swilling at the trough Cayleb and his harlot have spread before them. We believe, however, that it is essential to expose this 'generosity' for what it truly is—a bait offered in the name and service of Shan-wei!"

North Wind Blowing's heart sank. The last thing they needed was to re-inflame the Jihad in the midst of such widespread insurrection. Especially since the serfs had always regarded Mother Church as their landlords' handmaid, as complicit in all the things for which they blamed the aristocracy as the aristocracy itself! If they—

"Truer words were never spoken, Your Supreme Majesty," another voice said strongly, and North Wind Blowing bit his tongue as he turned his gaze to the youngest—and one of the newest—members of the Imperial Council.

Bishop Kangsya Tung-zhi, the former Bishop of Mai-kau, Chiang-wu Province's largest and richest bishopric, had been elevated to replace Baudang Zhynchi as the Archbishop of Boisseau at the emperor's personal insistence. In many ways it didn't matter, since Tung-zhi could be only the archbishop-in-exile until the authority of Crown and Church were restored in the restive provinces. For that matter, he'd been a *bishop*-in-exile since Mai-kau was overrun shortly after the fall of Shang-mi! But North Wind Blowing didn't trust the ambitious hardliner as far as he could spit.

Tung-zhi, who was less than half Zhynchi's age, was a cousin of the former Archbishop of Chiang-wu, Wyllym Rayno. He was also a member of the Order of Schueler who'd vehemently rejected the official story of how Rayno had died as a Charisian lie which Rhobair Duchairn had embraced as part of his campaign to destroy Zhaspahr Clyntahn's authority as Grand Inquisitor. The first councilor had never been able to prove it, but his agents' reports strongly suggested that Tung-zhi had kept the Inquisition's full repressive rigor clandestinely alive in his former bishopric with secret tribunals whose sentences had been carried out in equal secrecy.

And, of course, the young idiot was totally blind to how his own policies might have contributed to the current disaster. North Wind Blowing would shed no tears for illiterate serfs or the opportunists who now sought to profit from their rage, but at least he understood it *was* rage . . . and that it had come from somewhere.

"This poison *must* be stamped out, Your Supreme

Majesty," Tung-zhi continued. "There can be no compromise with it. Indeed, our current circumstances—the state of Your Supreme Majesty's realm—are directly attributable to those . . . ill-advised Church leaders who did just that and sought compromise with Shan-wei's servants in the world. Surely all of us can now see where that sort of accommodation must inevitably lead!"

North Wind Blowing's heart sank still farther as the emperor nodded in grave agreement.

"As a son of Mother Church, I thank you for those words of wisdom, Your Eminence," he said to the man whose predecessor he'd had assassinated. "And as Emperor, We intend to act upon it. The proof of your wise counsel is there for all to see in Our northern provinces, and this further confirms Us in Our determination to see to it that Our *southern* provinces are no longer similarly contaminated. Cayleb and Sharleyan have donned the mask of private charity in the West, but does anyone seated around this council chamber truly believe that?"

In fact, all of North Wind Blowing's agents suggested that was precisely what Cayleb and Sharleyan had done, and he experienced a moment of pure and bitter envy as he considered the reportedly bottomless gold and silver mines they'd discovered on Silverlode Island to make that possible. The thought of *anyone* having that much money in their private purses was enough to make him nauseous, but all the evidence suggested this was, indeed, the act of private charity the two of them had proclaimed, without any formal obligations to the Charisian Crown on the part of its recipients.

That didn't mean there weren't any, of course. North Wind Blowing doubted anyone would miss the Charisian hook hidden inside that generous gift. Which made the gift no less generous . . . or less politically explosive.

"No, Your Supreme Majesty," he said. "Obviously their true plans run far deeper than that."

It was the only answer he could have given.

"Then now is the time to purge the South of at least one of the poisons consuming the North," the emperor said. "It is Our will that all of these pernicious commercial agreements between Our subjects and any Charisian entity be immediately dissolved. We decree the seizure of all Charisian assets and property anywhere situate within Our Realm. And We wish for this to be accomplished within the next five-day and without alerting Our enemies to Our intent before it is accomplished."

North Wind Blowing's stomach tied itself into a knot as Emperor Zhyou-Zhwo looked around his council chamber with cold, steely eyes.

"We trust We have been sufficiently clear about this," he said.

. III .

Protector's Palace,
Siddar City,
Old Province,
Republic of Siddarmark.

"You know this isn't going to help our situation, don't you, My Lord?" Henrai Maidyn said sourly. "Not one little bit. I'm already hearing a lot of unhappy comments about it, even from those who understand why we need the Bank."

"Why am I not surprised?"

Greyghor Stohnar turned away from the chancellor of the exchequer, folding his arms across his chest as he looked out into the snowy dawn. The fresh snow covering the roofs of Siddar City was already streaked with chimney soot, and the cold radiating through the glass seemed to sink to his bones. The tremor in his hands was more pronounced these days, too. He would have liked to blame that on the cold, but he couldn't. Which was one reason he spent so much time with his arms folded this way to hide it, he reflected.

"I'm assuming their unhappiness stems from more than just pique?" he said.

"In too many cases, it stems from something more like *desperation*," Maidyn replied. He came to stand at the lord protector's shoulder, looking out the window with him. "And it's hard to blame them. We don't have all the details yet on exactly how Cayleb and Sharleyan are handling this, but what we do know suggests they're practically giving money away. And *they're* doing it, not the Empire."

"It's their money," Stohnar said mildly, although even his personal friendship for the Ahrmahks had been tested when he'd first heard about the "Ahrmahk Plan." He didn't like admitting that to himself, but it was true. "They can loan it—or give it away—to anyone they want, and we're not really in the best position to complain about that." He turned his head and looked down at the shorter Maidyn. "If they hadn't been exactly that generous when the Sword of Schueler hit us, God knows how many more of our people would have starved to death."

"I understand that, My Lord. I truly do." Maidyn returned his gaze levelly, then looked back out the window. "But as the Holy Bédard observed, 'Gratitude is a garment that chafes.' I'm afraid quite a few of our financial interests are doing a lot of chafing right now. They know what kind of trouble we're in, but instead of bailing us out, Cayleb and Sharleyan are pouring millions into *Harchong*. The way a lot of our people see it, that's almost economic treason!"

"*Almost?*" Stohnar arched a sardonic eyebrow. "Somehow I doubt the people who feel that way are attaching any qualifiers."

"No, they aren't," Maidyn conceded. "And there are times I find it difficult to disagree with them. Unfortunately, I also understand what Cayleb and Sharleyan are doing . . . and why they can't do it for us as well."

"Really?" Stohnar turned his back to the window and cocked his head. "I wonder if we're seeing the same reasons?"

"I can think of at least four right off the top of my head," Maidyn replied.

"First, the situation in West Harchong is a hell of a lot worse than anything we're looking at here, and as you say, we both know how Cayleb and Sharleyan react to starvation and atrocities. But their tools to do anything about it are limited, to say the least. They can't intervene militarily because they don't have as many troops to commit as Rainbow Waters has in the East. Even if they did, the minute they landed more than the handful of Marines they've got in Boisseau and Cheshire—or the 'civilian volunteers' helping Staynair and the Grand Vicar maintain order in those coastal enclaves in southern Tiegelkamp and Stene—everyone would scream about 'Charisian invasions.' For that matter, despite the good job Rainbow Waters is doing in the East, he doesn't have enough manpower to pacify anything further west than Maddox, either. So if they want to keep West Harchong from descending into the sort of chaos and anarchy that's turning Central Harchong into a wasteland, they have to find a different tool. That's what the 'Ahrmahk Plan' is.

"Second, though, not even Cayleb and Sharleyan have a bottomless purse. Frankly, I'm astounded they're dipping as deeply into it as they are, and I'm not at all sure how long they can keep it up before people start speculating about the soundness of the *Charisian* mark. But if they have limited resources—and they do—they have to commit them where the need is worst. Fortunately, that's not us. Yet, at least.

"Third, it sounds as though these United Provinces are enacting across-the-board reforms on the Charisian model. Reforms a lot more sweeping than anything we're contemplating, really. That's probably because the Harchongians' situation is so much more dire that they don't have any choice, but it's still true. And when they're finished, those provinces will be tied directly into the Charisian economic system. I don't know if we could adopt that level of reform even if all our people were willing to try, frankly. For that matter, some of the people who *are* willing to try—some of our strongest supporters in the Chamber—would be afraid the 'Ahrmahk Plan' would turn us into—or, in their eyes, *keep* us as—another Charisian appendage rather than allowing us to grow our own manufactories and control our own economy. I'm not sure that wouldn't happen myself; the difference is that I'm fairly sure that would be better in the end than where we're headed 'going it alone.' But whatever I may think, the fact is that we're still a long way short of the United Provinces' situation. As much trouble as we're in, we have an existing infrastructure we can't just torch and burn to the ground. We can probably make substantial strides in the direction of those reforms once the Central Bank's up and running, but until then—?" He shrugged. "Not so much.

"And, finally, as generous as we both know they are, they aren't doing this solely out of philanthropic motives." He waved one hand. "I'm not saying they don't have those motives, because you and I both know them and we've seen that they do. But they were always frank with us about the political—and military—upside for them in helping to feed our people, too. It helped prop us up, kept the Army in the field, and provided them with the Mainland ally they needed so desperately. And it bought them one hell of a lot of goodwill, too. No one as smart as the two of them could fail to see the opportunity to do the same thing in West Harchong. If the Ahrmahk Plan succeeds, the United Provinces will be so fully integrated into the Charisian system that Charis will be not simply their natural trading partner, but their *inevitable* trading partner. Assuming they do manage to prevent a complete collapse—and I think they have a good chance of that, the way things sound—Charisians will make money hand over fist once the United Provinces' internal economy really takes off. I'm not saying that's the only—or even the main—reason Cayleb and Sharleyan are doing this, mind you, but they can't be blind to that outcome. I'm sure they'll lose at least some of the loans they're making. In fact, I won't be surprised if they have to write off as many as fifteen or even twenty percent of them in the end. But if they've got the money to spend, and it looks like they do, there couldn't be a better long-term investment anywhere in the world."

"Succinct," Stohnar said with a slight, tired smile. "The question is how we make ourselves equally attractive to them."

"I know I sound like a stuck echo, but the way we do that is to get the Bank in place and our own financial house in order. I do know—*we* do know—Cayleb and Sharleyan Ahrmahk. For that matter, we both know Ehdwyrd Howsmyn! They'd love to invest in our success, but they're not about to pour even more money into an economy that's already . . . overheated, chaotic, and out-of-control. They *can't* without making it even worse! If we can manage to get all those factors under some kind of control, then I know some of that Ahrmahk Plan money will start flowing our way. Whether or not even they have deep enough pockets to make a difference in something the size of the Republic—after all, we've got ten or eleven times the United Provinces' population—may be another question, but if we can just straighten out our mess, the two of them will sure as Shan-wei *try*!"

. IV .
Desnair the City,
Empire of Desnair.

"Bastards," Symyn Gahrnet growled, tossing the report back onto the Duke of Harless' desk. "The frigging bastards."

Harless smiled crookedly at his younger brother and leaned back in his chair.

"Approximately what Sir Hyrmyn said, in rather more diplomatic language," he said, and Symyn snorted. Sir Hyrmyn Khaldwyl wasn't particularly wellborn, but he wasn't exactly a commoner, either, and he was a senior-level career diplomat. Officially, he was one more of Harless' advisers; in fact, he was the duke's primary tutor, with a tendency to ask "teaching questions."

"Really?" Symyn asked now, and Harless shrugged.

"Brilliant move on their part, really, assuming they've actually got the gold and silver. How often does the possibility to buy half a continent come someone's way? And who else could do it?"

The second question came out more than a little bitterly, and with good reason, Symyn thought sourly. For as long as anyone could remember, the "bottomless gold mines of Desnair" had been one of the Empire's most effective political and diplomatic tools. They hadn't really been bottomless, of course, but they'd provided a succession of emperors the leverage to buy the support of the Church and other realms when it was most needed.

The fact that it seemed Cayleb and Sharleyan Ahrmahk's gold mines—their *personally owned* gold mines—actually *were* bottomless was a particularly bitter gall for the man responsible for Desnair's current diplomacy.

"Irritating, isn't it?" Symyn asked out loud, then chuckled with an edge of apology as his brother shot him a baleful glare.

"Sorry!" He raised both hands in a pacifying gesture. "I mean, I know it really is, and I don't doubt the Emperor's being pretty damned unpleasant about it. But I think I may be able to calm him down a little."

"Really?" Harless said skeptically.

"Really." Symyn nodded. "Look, I know His Majesty has to be truly pissed off by the notion of Charis fishing in troubled waters and landing a doomwhale like these 'United Provinces.' He won't like their additional influence on the Mainland, and he *really* won't like the fact that ultimately they're going to suck an effectively independent West Harchong into their clutches . . . and make a boatload of money in the process. Hell, they're going to make a whole *bunch* of boatloads of money down the road. So, yes, I understand why he's a bit, um, choleric, these days."

"I could think of a few stronger words," Harless observed.

"I'm sure you could. But what we need to point out to him is how this will drive Zhyou-Zhwo even deeper into our arms. And the timing may be in our favor, too. We're starting to get our own feet under us, and that gives us what that bastard Delthak calls a 'technology demonstrator' all our own to show off to Harchong."

Harless frowned, rubbing his upper lip thoughtfully. His brother had a tendency to be overly optimistic, but he probably had a point this time. A very good one, actually.

The empire had just taken delivery of three Charisian-built steam automotives. They'd been delivered to Desnair the City by an enormous Charisian steamer whose steam-powered cranes had hoisted them to the dock with easy efficiency. Perhaps even more importantly, though, they'd been accompanied by a pair of Charisian-built steamers which had been purchased by the Crown at the same time as the automotives. And those other steamers had been packed with the machinery needed to create a modern, Charis-style foundry that would produce—among other things—the rails those automotives required.

All of that had cost a fortune, but the emperor had made that fortune available out of his only-*almost*-bottomless gold mines, and it meant there was no Charisian ownership stake in any of it. Every bit of it belonged to the Crown, to be bestowed where Emperor Mahrys chose and on whatever terms he dictated. More than that, the idiots had agreed to provide experts to set up Desnair's new purchases and be sure everything was operational, and they actually seemed to believe His Majesty considered himself bound by their stupid "patent" and "licensing" laws. They didn't even seem to realize that, for all intents and purposes, they were *giving away* their vaunted "industrialization" for free.

"You know, you're right, Symyn," he said after a moment. "Oh, the timing's not *perfect,* but if I point out to

His Majesty that he can offer the Harchongians access to *our* new manufactories. . . ."

"Exactly." Symyn nodded. "Nobody in his right mind thinks we're going to be as productive as the Charisians. Not right off the bat, anyway. It'll take time. But once we've got our foothold, once we've started the process, we'll build our own manufactories on our own terms, and that'll give us a carrot of our own. We may not be able to match the 'Ahrmahk Plan,' but give me ten or fifteen years to build, and I'll guarantee Zhyou-Zhwo won't be the only ruler who'd rather deal with us than find themselves attached to Cayleb and Sharleyan's apron strings!"

MAY YEAR OF GOD 905

⋆

. I .
Boisseau Province,
United Provinces,
West Harchong.

"And so, Almighty God, we thank you and all your Blessed Archangels and ask your continued blessings upon this, our effort to provide for Your children as we know You would have us do. Amen."

Bishop Yaupang lowered his hands and stepped back on the slightly raised platform with a benevolent smile, and Runzheng Zhou, rebellious Baron of Star Rising and formally attainted traitor, watched his guests from the corner of one eye. He'd been afraid they might take offense, despite their disclaimers, but if they had, there was no sign of it in their expressions or their body language. He drew a slight breath of relief, then froze as one of those guests turned and raised an eyebrow at him.

"You were concerned about something, My Lord?" Merlin Athrawes asked mildly.

"Ah, no. Not really," Star Rising said, although that wasn't strictly true. Athrawes' other eyebrow rose, and the baron shrugged ever so slightly.

"All right, I was a tiny bit concerned that the Archbishop might be offended when he wasn't asked to . . . say a few words."

"My Lord, I doubt Maikel Staynair's said a *few* words on a formal occasion since he was first ordained," Athrawes replied with a chuckle. "Mind you, they're usually *good* words, but they do tend to flow on. And on. And, now that I think of it, *on*."

"There is a special penance laid up for those who mock their elders," Maikel Staynair said serenely from the *seijin*'s other side. Star Rising was a little surprised the white-haired archbishop had been able to hear him over the sharp, rippling wind-pop of the flags strung around the platform, but the old man's brown eyes twinkled when he looked at him.

"Forgive me, my son," he said, "but so many decades of listening to confessions has made my ear exceptionally keen. And, no, I wasn't in the least offended." His expression sobered. "In fact, I think it was wise of you and Bishop Yaupang to avoid piling yet another log on the fire. We all know how Emperor Zhyou-Zhwo would react to this at the best of times. I would truly prefer not to make that even worse by adding an extra religious component to it. Especially not when Bishop Yaupang is so obviously a good and compassionate servant of God." He shook his head. "I couldn't have said it any better, and this is his flock, not mine. Let them hear their shepherd's voice, not me, especially on a day like this."

Star Rising nodded in sober agreement . . . and gratitude. He'd never met Staynair before this five-day, and it was an enormous relief to discover Merlin Athrawes had been nothing but accurate in describing the archbishop's spiritual integrity and—yes—humility. It was impossible for him to imagine a Harchongese archbishop of the Church of God Awaiting allowing *anyone* to "upstage" him at a public appearance.

And God knew Staynair was right. Star Rising was fortunate in that he'd had very few relatives in South Harchong, and those he had had were no longer there. Or not most of them, anyway. One of his cousins had been too stubborn—and too furious at him—to heed his advice and get himself and his immediate family out of Zhyou-Zhwo's reach. No doubt Cousin Enbau was busy blaming Star Rising for what had happened to him since, but it was a little difficult for the baron to work up much sympathy for him.

Unfortunately, he wasn't the only person whose relatives had been taken into custody by the Emperor's

Spears. So far, only a handful of nobles had renounced their participation in the United Provinces, but others would no doubt be tempted if the emperor and his cronies got around to leveling specific threats against family members. In the end, it wouldn't matter—not if he had time to get enough of the town burghers, free peasants, guildsmen, and serfs fully engaged before it happened.

And it was very possible Staynair's visit would push that process along. It had taken less than five minutes in his presence for Star Rising to feel the aura of compassion the archbishop carried with him everywhere he went. A more eloquent spokesman for the Church of Charis was impossible to imagine, and none of the Harchongians in the United Provinces were likely to miss the fact that he was the Church of Charis' *archbishop*, the equivalent of its grand vicar. No Grand Vicar—and damned few archbishops—had ever visited West Harchong. Certainly not outside Shang-mi or the other great cities. Maikel Staynair intended to tour *all* of Boisseau and Cheshire. He couldn't visit every town and hamlet, but his route had been planned so that at least two-thirds and more probably three-quarters of the United Provinces' people would be able to reach at least one of his stops, hear at least one of his sermons. Some of them might spend a few days on the road to get there, but Star Rising had no doubt thousands—*hundreds* of thousands—of them would do just that.

And even a very few minutes of one of Maikel Staynair's sermons would knock any lingering fear of Shan-wei worship out of anyone but the most bigoted. In a lot of ways, the baron wished they had been able to start that process right here, today, but this was the day of all days that would be reported in detail to Zhyou-Zhwo. Best to keep it as non-enraging as possible.

Not that it was going to do much good.

He snorted sourly at that thought, then turned his head as the second-most prominent Charisian present this day stepped down from the platform towards the huge oblong marked off by the wooden stakes and strings.

The Duke of Delthak was, by any measure, the wealthiest man in the world, outside Cayleb and Sharleyan Ahrmahk, and their wealth exceeded his solely because of their personal ownership of Silverlode Island. Delthak had *built* his fortune, from the ground up, and he was growing wealthier—a lot wealthier—every single day. He didn't look much like the Harchongese ideal of a great noble, however, which was probably as well. He was a bit on the portly side, with hair just beginning to silver, and he wore the sort of clothing any prosperous businessman might, not the resplendent finery Harchongians were accustomed to seeing their great nobles don on public occasions. And the mind boggled at the thought of any Harchongese duke carrying a *shovel* over his shoulder.

Of course, it wasn't just any shovel, and Star Rising squinted as the brilliant sunlight reflected from its silver-plated blade.

"I confess, I never would have thought of something like this," he said to Athrawes and Staynair. "I see the symbolism, though, and I like it. I wonder why no one else ever did it?"

"Actually, the process began with Empress Sharleyan," Athrawes replied. "She and the Emperor realized they needed something more than just behind-the-scenes financing and policy decisions to convince their subjects the Crown truly supported the improved Charisian manufactory techniques. It was what you might call a . . . dicey situation at the time. Clyntahn was already thundering anathemas, but we *needed* those manufactories if we were going to survive. So Her Majesty decided to make the Crown's position unmistakably clear by turning the first few shovels of dirt for as many of the new manufactories as she could get to." He smiled. "Hard to miss the symbolism—as you say—of having a crowned head of state dig the first hole."

"Or the symbolism in having a crowned head of state *not* dig the first hole, in this case," Staynair put in. "It's another way to emphasize the fact that this isn't a Charisian manufactory, however much private Charisian subjects may have invested in it."

"I admit that would be a good message to communicate," Star Rising said. "I doubt anyone in Yu-kwau's going to pay much attention to that part, though."

"It never hurts to try, my son," Staynair said serenely, and Star Rising chuckled.

"You truly *are* a man of faith, aren't you, Your Eminence?"

"It's a requirement for the job, my son. In Charis, at least."

"Ouch!" Star Rising shook his head with a louder chuckle. "I suppose I had that coming."

"Oh, His Eminence is never shy about giving us an elbow when we need one," Athrawes told him wryly.

"That's a requirement for the job, too," Staynair observed mildly.

"If you'll pardon me for pointing this out, Your Eminence, I would think staying alive is also an important part of doing your 'job,'" Star Rising said in a far more serious tone. "And in that respect, I'd feel more comfortable if—"

"I'm afraid hanging onto Merlin is out of the question," Staynair interrupted him in a courteous tone. "But I'm quite comfortable with the arrangements that have been made for my security in his absence."

"Your Eminence, I hope this won't sound too mercenary of me, but I'm really happy our relationship with Charis seems to be working as well as it is right now. I suspect there are likely to be . . . unfortunate repercussions if we allow something unpleasant to happen to you on Harchongese soil."

"Which is why nothing's going to happen to him, My Lord." Athrawes smiled reassuringly. "I don't think it was the honeymoon she would have preferred, but *Seijin* Nimue will do just fine watching the Archbishop's back."

"I beg your pardon?" Star Rising felt both of his eyebrows rise.

"Well, the truth is that Their Majesties' decision to

ask General Gahrvai to assume direction of our security detachments here in the United Provinces had a little something to do with it," Athrawes agreed with another, stronger smile. "Nimue really didn't like the thought of her new husband being sent that far away from her, so Prince Daivyn insisted she go with him. And since she just happens to be in the vicinity—"

He shrugged, and Star Rising nodded slowly, although he strongly suspected that the circumstances which had made *Seijin* Nimue available were less fortuitous than Athrawes chose to imply. But maybe, he thought, that was another part of the "low-profile" approach to Staynair's visit? *Seijin* Nimue was less well known outside the Charisian Empire itself than the infamous, terrible—and terrifying—*Seijin* Merlin. For that matter, Merlin was so inextricably tied to Cayleb and Sharleyan in the public mind that no one could possibly have seen his presence as anything but an example of imperial Charisian involvement. Nimue Gahrvai was a known *seijin*, but she was far less infamous than Merlin and associated much more in people's minds with Prince Daivyn and Princess Irys. It was unlikely the United Provinces' enemies would construe Staynair's visit as anything but proof of the Charisian Empire's "meddling" in Harchong, but it was at least possible some who were still on the fence about supporting Star Rising and his colleagues might. Especially if Athrawes ostentatiously turned around and went home after the groundbreaking ceremony for the United Provinces' first modern foundry and manufactory complex.

The odds might not be high, but as Staynair had said, it never hurt to try.

"Consider any concerns on my part withdrawn," he said now, looking past the other dignitaries to the red-haired young woman in the uniform of the Charisian Imperial Guard standing at Sir Koryn Gahrvai's side. "From everything I've ever heard, *Seijin* Nimue should be more than capable of keeping you alive, Your Eminence."

"Indeed." Staynair smiled and reached up and out to

lay one hand briefly on Athrawes mailed shoulder. "*Seijin* Nimue is just as capable as *Seijin* Merlin. In fact, I've always said she's the only person on Safehold who's fully his equal in every way.

"Except, of course," his smile turned downright sly, "for the fact that she's *far* better looking than he is."

. II .
Southland Drilling Well No. 1,
Sairahston,
Oil Springs Valley,
Barony of Southland,
Princedom of Emerald,
Empire of Charis.

"I hope you're right about this, Ahmbrohs," Ehdwyrd Howsmyn said over the com from his cabin aboard the steamer bearing him rapidly homeward from the United Provinces. "I mean, a gusher would be more exciting, but I'd really rather not lose the rig or any of our people."

"Not to mention the bad PR," Merlin Athrawes added dryly from Boisseau. "Especially if we did lose people as well as equipment. 'Extra, extra! Archangel Hastings Punishes Impious Shan-Wei Worshipers!'" He shook his head. "I agree it would probably be spectacular, but the last thing we need is another Lakeview gusher on our very first hole."

"If I continued to believe in the patron of my order," Father Ahmbrohs Makfadyn replied in a slightly repressive tone, "I'd probably take offense at your levity, Merlin. As it is, I can only concur. But everything—including Owl's sampling—suggests this should be . . . reasonably sedate."

"'Reasonably,'" the Duke of Delthak repeated. "Why,

oh why, does that not fill me with unbounded confidence?"

"With all due respect, Your Grace—and Your *Seijin*ship—would you please stop picking on my geologist?" a fourth voice said, and Makfadyn turned to smile reassuringly at the younger, taller man standing beside him.

Doctor Zhansyn Wyllys, fellow of the Royal College, and member of the inner circle for the last three years, was black-haired, with deep-set brown eyes. At the moment, those eyes were locked on the wood-and-steel gantry four hundred yards from their current position. They were rather more anxious than Makfadyn's, but that was understandable in the President of Southland Drilling and Refining.

"I am *not* 'picking on' him, Zhansyn." Merlin could almost hear the twinkle in Delthak's voice. "I'm just saying that as one of the investors in your project, I'm hoping Ahmbrohs called it right when he suggested drilling here."

"Oh, so now it's *my* suggestion? I see!" Makfadyn's smile broadened. "I would've sworn there was something about terraforming crews' surveys involved in the selection process, wasn't there? Let me see, let me see. . . ."

"*Officially*, it's your suggestion," Merlin said. "And for damned good reasons!"

"I know. I know!" Makfadyn replied, his expression sobering at least a little.

The Archangel Hastings, as the patron of geography, was also the patron of ge*ology*. And geology was another of those areas in which the *Holy Writ* provided Safehold with far more insight than one might have thought judging from the planet's pre-Merlin technology levels. Apparently it had occurred to Eric Langhorne and Adorée Bédard that human beings were going to dig holes, some of them pretty deep, even on Safehold. As such they'd taken the opportunity to both further buttress the *Writ's* demonstrated authority and to nip any potential conflicts in the bud. Makfadyn—an ardent Reformist even before the Jihad—had been the closest thing to a trained geologist Safehold had boasted. That combination had brought him into close contact with the Royal College long before he learned of the inner circle's existence, and he'd been quietly rewriting Safehold's understanding of geology since Owl and the library in Nimue's Cave had become available.

In truth, though, it had been more a matter of expanding the *Book of Hastings* than rewriting it. Langhorne and Bédard hadn't worried too much about molten metallic planetary cores or anything that went on deeper into the planet than its mantle, since only a civilization which had already broken free of the Strictures could have dug deep enough to learn much about those areas. But they'd been careful to avoid anything that would conflict with observational data, which meant most of *Hastings* was completely accurate . . . however far it went.

For geology near the surface, and bearing in mind the strata which had been revealed by little things like the Holy Langhorne Canal's deep mountain cuts, there was a lot of information. That information had proved very useful for coal miners, iron mines, water drilling, etc., and it proffered even a rudimentary theory of tectonics, but it was strangely silent about things like oil sands and oil shale. Nothing in the *Writ* said those things couldn't exist; it simply didn't discuss them the same way it did aquifers and the sorts of methane pockets coal mines could turn up.

Actually, it did discuss oil sands in passing, at least as the pathway by which petroleum leaked to the surface, which had offered the window into the Strictures Southland D&R needed once Doctor Wyllys cracked the secret of petroleum distillation. The people of Safehold had known about petroleum—only it was called black gum on their planet—since the Creation. Thanks to the *Book of Pasquale*, petroleum had featured in topical preparations in Safeholdian pharmacology, and Safeholdians had made limited use of it for things like natural asphalt. Its potential as fuel, however, had been overshadowed by oil tree, oil vine, and kraken oil. Despite the poisonous nature of oil vine's products, both it and oil tree pods grew almost everywhere on Safehold, whereas black gum was available only in those areas where it oozed to the surface. Oil tree oil also burned far more cleanly than black gum, although even it produced more smoke than—and burned more dimly than—kraken oil . . . which actually came from doomwhales, not krakens, these days.

Long before he was ever recruited for the inner circle, however, Zhansyn Wyllys had been intrigued by petroleum. Initially because his family's fortune had been made in doomwhaling and he'd come to the conclusion that the doomwhaling industry would never be able to provide the sheer quantity of oil Charisian manufactories, especially, would require. Partly because demand for oil was climbing so steeply, on an ever-sharpening curve, and partly because both oil tree and oil vine were scarcer in Old Charis than on the Mainland, which reduced those options' ability to meet that demand. And as a student at the Royal College, he'd been introduced to—and become fascinated by—the techniques of distillation and refining. What would happen, he'd asked himself, if he applied those techniques to black gum?

There wasn't a lot of black gum in Old Charis. There'd been more than enough for his experiments, yet far too little for any sort of volume production. But the Barony of Southland in the Princedom of Emerald was a different story. Black gum seeps were fairly common in Southland, although they were concentrated in only a few areas, mostly along the foot of the Slywkyl Hills, which formed the heart of the barony. The most productive of those in western Southland were found outside the appropriately named town of Black Sand, one of Southland's larger towns, where the hills disappeared into the coastal flat twenty miles inland. But the most spectacular seeps were located in Oil Springs Valley. The valley, which ran deep into the hills from the east, above Sheryls Port, the barony's major harbor, had literally dozens of seeps. In fact, they'd given their name to one of the two modest rivers—the Black Gum—which flowed into Sheryl Bay through the port.

Despite the Archangel Hastings' book, no one had ever realized that the reason the Oil Springs Valley seeps were so spectacular and widespread was that the valley sat directly on top of a deep strata of oil sands trapped between two layers of shale. The upper layer was fractured in several locations, and there was sufficient pressure to force the oil to the surface.

Wyllys had found his way to Oil Springs Valley well before his recruitment by the inner circle, and vastly to the irritation of his father. Styvyn Wyllys was of the opinion that his son should have been concentrating on better ways to refine and use kraken oil, not looking for new approaches which would inevitably challenge Wyllys & Sons' thriving and lucrative sales. He'd turned a deaf ear to Zhansyn's pleas that this was an opportunity for Wyllys & Sons to expand into a totally new market, and the furious row which had ensued—in the course of which Styvyn had cut his errant son off without a hundredth-mark for his "disloyalty"—was a major reason Zhansyn was no longer invited to celebrate God's Day of Thanksgiving with the rest of the Wyllys family.

His success in distilling "black gum" into a number of more useful compounds, especially the one he'd dubbed "white oil," and which had been called "kerosene" on a planet called Earth, had pretty much finished off that relationship. His father's fury had grown only greater as "white oil" began nibbling into the kraken oil market, especially in Old Charis, where the traditional Safeholdian aversion to innovation had turned into fascination with anything new. And, unfortunately for Styvyn Wyllys, he'd been able to tell himself that while white oil might steal some of his sales, black gum seeps were far too limited to pose a significant challenge. He'd been unable to see the writing upon the wall and had rejected his son's last-ditch effort to repair their relationship by offering him a partnership in petroleum development.

Because of that, Southland Drilling and Refining—Styvyn had apparently missed the "drilling" implications of that name—had been capitalized by Delthak Enterprises, the Ahrmahk dynasty, and Prince Nahrmahn Garyet of Emerald, instead. Wyllys retained fifty-one percent of the voting stock. He'd been a little surprised by that generosity on Duke Delthak's part at the time SD&R was chartered, but that was because he hadn't yet known about the inner circle, the Terran Federation, or the truth of the Church of God Awaiting. Archbishop Maikel had taken an interest in the project, as well, and had formally assigned Makfadyn to assist Doctor Wyllys' efforts.

With funding in hand, over the next couple of years Wyllys had scaled up his initial refinery into something much larger, capable of handling far more crude than he'd been able to collect and transport from the surface seeps. No doubt his father had taken that as yet more evidence that his lunatic son was chasing the white fox-lizard, but Zhansyn hadn't minded. He'd had his eye on bigger game, and Southland had begun drilling just over two five-days ago, using the new and vastly improved rig Delthak Enterprises had developed from existing water drilling technology.

The drilling industry had already begun adopting steam engines instead of the dragons which had been used to power the drills before, but Delthak had made a lot of other improvements, including significantly stronger and more durable gantries and a much more sophisticated system for casing the drill bore as the well proceeded. Now—

"Excuse me, Father."

Makfadyn and Wyllys turned as a tall, brown-haired man approached them. His expression was a curious blend of apprehension and anticipation.

"Yes, Zhoelsyn?"

"Father, there's a lot more black gum showing in the cuttings, and the pipe's starting to shake."

"Excellent!" Makfadyn said.

"I'm a little anxious about that vibration, Father."

Zhoelsyn Abykrahmbi was SD&R's chief engineer. He had quite a lot of experience in drilling for *water*, and he'd brought in more than one artesian well in his career. One or two of them had been spectacular.

"I'm sure we're in good hands, my son," Makfadyn said benignly. He signed Langhorne's Scepter and smiled at the engineer. "And in addition to faith in God, I have every confidence in your preparations."

"Thank you, Father." Abykrahmbi sounded more than a bit dubious, but he nodded and headed back to his drilling crew, and Wyllys shook his head at the priest.

"I think he wanted just a little more reassurance than that, Ahmbrohs," he said.

"I *do* have confidence in him," Makfadyn replied in a mild tone. "Or as much as I *can* have, at the current stage of our technology."

And that, Merlin reflected, was a good point. Safeholdians had been drilling for water for a long time, although with only dragon-powered drills, their power budget had been limited, to say the least. They'd developed some fairly sophisticated techniques even before steam—and Delthak Enterprises—had gotten involved. As usually happened when Ehdwyrd Howsmyn was anywhere near, those existing capabilities had been adapted and improved upon in some truly novel ways, which meant Southland Drilling's beginning point was decades in advance of anything James Miller Williams or Edwin Drake had possessed back on Old Terra.

On the other hand, they were notably deficient in things like blowout preventers and the other esoteric safety technologies the petroleum industry had developed on humankind's birth planet. Still, Makfadyn had raised another sound point earlier in the conversation. Owl and his remotes had indeed surreptitiously sampled the Oil Springs Valley geology, and there was little chance of Abykrahmbi's rig hitting one of the gas pockets which usually propelled oil gushers . . . and provided the deadly explosive component which often accompanied them. So—

"*Yes!*"

A single shout went up from the wellhead, echoed a moment later by the entire drilling crew, as a thick tide of what would have been called "light sweet crude" by an Old Terran oilman welled up out of the casing around the central drilling pipe. It surged several feet above the casing lip in a squat, brown-black fountain that spilled down into the preventive levee which had been built around the gantry to channel it away from the wellhead and keep it out of the nearby river.

"Get the drill out!" Abykrahmbi shouted, and the bit stopped turning immediately.

One of the many reasons Oil Springs Valley had been selected for the first drilled oil well in Safeholdian history was that the target strata of sand was barely six hundred feet down. That was still a lot of drill shaft, though, and the oil continued to bubble up, waist high or better on a tall man, as the shaft was extracted, section by section. It took quite a while, but finally the drill head itself came up, and the oil fountain danced even more strongly now that the flow path was no longer obstructed.

But even as the drill head was swung out of the way, another snorting, steam-powered crane lowered the valve assembly into place. It was big enough and heavy enough to settle onto the waiting collar at the top of the casing despite the slow, powerful upward current of oil, and brawny roughnecks with huge wrenches began tightening the bolts to hold it in place. The assembly was almost eight feet tall, and all of the valves were open, providing a path for the oil as the assembly sank into place. The internal piping was narrower than the drill pipe had been, however, which increased the stream's pressure significantly. A geyser of oil spurted out its top, pounding down from above even as more forced its way in a circular fan through the gap between collar and casing, battering their legs and lower torsos as they worked. But as the bolts tightened, the horizontal flow gradually eased until, finally, it ceased. Oil continued to gush from the top of the valve assembly for several more minutes before the valves were cautiously tightened and the flow stopped completely.

Silence lingered for a moment as the panting, battered, oil-coated work crew stood calf-deep in a broad pond of crude around the valve, watching the last trickles run down the outside of the assembly.

Then the cheers began.

"I *told* you it wouldn't be a gusher!" Makfadyn told Wyllys . . . and all of their distant audience. "See? Next time maybe you'll trust me!"

"And maybe we would have trusted you more *this* time if you'd had more of a track record," Duke Delthak replied in a deflating tone. "I seem to recall someone who kept leaving qualifiers strewn about just in case."

"I have no idea who you could be talking about," Makfadyn said severely. "In fact, I'm sure—"

He broke off as Zhoelsyn Abykrahmbi charged back up to his employer. Wyllys had always known the engineer believed in being hands-on, and Abykrahmbi was coated in oil from head to toe, his teeth an almost shocking flash of white as he beamed triumphantly.

"I told you I was confident about your preparations!" Makfadyn greeted him, and Abykrahmbi's smile turned still wider.

"Yes, Father, you did!" he said. Then he looked at Wyllys. "Timed the flow through the central valve before we closed it down, too, sir. Assuming the flow rate holds steady, looks like about four hundred to four hundred fifty barrels a day!"

"Outstanding!" Wyllys said, punching the engineer on an oil-soaked shoulder, and Merlin nodded.

The official "barrel" used by the petroleum industry back on Old Earth had been just under a hundred and sixty liters, courtesy of Richard III of England who had set the size of a tierce of wine at forty-two gallons. No one had ever changed it, and when Old Terra's early oil industry had needed a standard measure—not to mention leak-proof barrels in which to ship product—they'd turned to the most readily supplied size of wine barrel. It had also happened to weigh about a hundred and forty kilos when filled, which was about the largest size a workman could wrestle around unassisted.

The equivalent Safeholdian wine barrel was only forty gallons, and Safeholdian oil producers had adopted it as their standard measure for much the same reason it had been adopted back on Old Earth. So if Abykrahmbi's numbers were accurate, the well would be producing somewhere around sixteen to seventeen thousand gallons a day. As the pressure dropped, so would the production rate, but that was a very respectable initial flow. Indeed, it was seven times the rate Williams had gotten out of his first Canadian well fifteen hundred Standard Years ago. Of course, they'd started with a lot of advantages he hadn't had . . . including Pei Shan-wei's meticulous geological surveys.

"We'll have the well connected to the pipeline by day after tomorrow," Abykrahmbi continued, and Wyllys nodded.

He'd built his refinery just outside Sheryls Port to take advantage of the harbor. It was close enough to the black gum seeps which had supplied his initial oil flow, although only at the rate of a hundred barrels or so a day, for him to freight it to the port by dragon-drawn wagons. Shipping it, barrel by barrel, over the roads between the seeps and his facility was a pain in the arse, however, given the nature of Emeraldian roads in general. That was why the new Southland Drilling Railroad would finish laying track between the port and the valley in the next month or two. But Wyllys had taken it a step farther in anticipation that the well would succeed. Sairahston was less than twenty miles from Sheryls Port, and he'd constructed a pipeline to connect the new oil fields directly to the refinery. For the present, even with Well Number One's highly satisfactory production rate, that pipeline would be hugely underutilized. But—

"That's wonderful news, Zhoelsyn," he said now. "And since you seem to have done *reasonably* well with Number One," he grinned hugely, "I suppose you should go ahead and get started on the rest of them now, don't you?"

"Just as soon as Duke Delthak's people can get the rigs shipped to us, sir!" Abykrahmbi promised, still grinning hugely. "If we come in at the same depth, and assuming no dry holes, I'll have four more wells producing for you by the middle of next month!"

AUGUST YEAR OF GOD 905

·✦·

. I .
Lake City,
Tarikah Province,
Republic of Siddarmark.

"You be careful out there, Rychyrd."

Rychyrd Tohmys paused in the act of picking up his latest purchase and looked up in apparent surprise.

"Careful, Master Hahraimahn?" The young man looked over his shoulder and out the shop window. The sun had set and the sky was cloudy, heavy with the promise of rain, but while the streetlights were few and far between, it wasn't exactly stygian. "It's only four blocks, and it hasn't even started sprinkling yet. If it does—" he grinned suddenly "—I promise I'll keep them nice and dry inside my tunic!"

"I'm not talking about the *books,* boy." Stywyrt Hahraimahn's tone was sharper than it had been, and Rychyrd's smile disappeared. "I know you're one who takes care of his books," the bookseller continued, "but the mood out there's not what I'd call warm and gentle right now."

Rychyrd glanced back out at the dimly lit street then turned back to Hahraimahn.

"You really think something might . . . happen?" The thought clearly troubled him. Hahraimahn only wished he felt confident that it troubled the youngster for the right reason.

"I think plenty of 'somethings' have *already* happened," he said grimly. "And I think your family're known Temple Loyalists. You think what happened last five-day doesn't have the idiots' tempers running high?"

Rychyrd frowned. He couldn't pretend he didn't know what Hahraimahn was talking about, and the incident had been ugly. But still—

"I'm not saying Feldyrmyn wasn't completely justified," the shop owner said. "I happen to think he was, and it doesn't matter whose army he served in, either. Langhorne only knows what would've happened to his wife and that girl of his if he hadn't done it! But two of them are still in the hospital, and their pride hasn't taken it well, either. Thugs like that, they're likely to think they need to 'square accounts,' and they won't give a single damn who they use to do it. So you be careful!"

"I will," Rychyrd promised. "But, like I say, it's only four blocks."

"Four *long* blocks," Hahraimahn pointed out.

"I'll be careful," Rychyrd said more soberly. "I promise."

"Good. I'd just as soon not be scraping you up off the sidewalk. You spend too much money in here for that!"

Rychyrd chuckled at the joke, picked up the paper-wrapped parcel, and headed for the door. The bell above it jingled musically as it closed behind him, and Stywyrt Hahraimahn shook his head, his expression more worried than he'd allowed Rychyrd to see.

The boy was considerably less than half Hahraimahn's age, and despite the printer's ink that ran in his own veins, the shopkeeper sometimes thought the lad had his head too far into his books and not far enough into reality. There wasn't a malicious bone in young Rychyrd's body, and he couldn't seem to truly get it through his head that other people had *lots* of malicious bones.

Or why anyone could possibly want to exercise that malice against *him*.

His father, Clyntahn Tohmys, had taken his entire family over the border to the Barony of Charlz in the Border States when the Sword of Schueler swept through Tarikah. He hadn't fled because of any rabid loyalty to the Temple. Although he'd had no patience with the Reformists and he'd believed quite a lot of the anti-Charisian propaganda of Zhaspahr Clyntahn's Inquisition, the reason he'd fled was that he was a man of peace. He was loyal to the Republic, but he was also loyal to Mother Church, and he abhorred violence. So when the Sword brought fire and death to Tarikah, he'd taken his family to a place of stability, moving in with his wife's distant cousins to ride out the Jihad.

As a loyal Siddarmarkian, he'd been among the first to return from voluntary exile when the Reconciliation Courts were announced. He'd taken the family strongbox to Charlz with him, so reestablishing ownership of his extensive farm outside Lake City had been relatively straightforward. But he hadn't counted on how deep and implacable the hatred left in the Jihad's wake truly ran.

Too many of his neighbors had died during the Church's invasion, and too many others had been murdered by the Sword or subjected to the Punishment in the Inquisition's camps. Few of his pre-Jihad family friends remained, and the Siddar Loyalists returning from their own exile in the Republic's eastern provinces were too filled with dark and hateful memories.

Hahraimahn didn't like what he saw coming, but he knew Clyntahn had seen it as clearly as he did. There was no home left for the Tohmys family here in Tarikah. Not anymore. Clyntahn had moved his family into the city after the third time one of his barns had been burned as a warning, and as soon as he could arrange the sale of his farm for something remotely like its actual value, he would be returning sorrowfully to Charlz or even to the Temple Lands themselves. It was a sad, sad story which Hahraimahn had already seen play out too many times.

And that was why he was worried about Rychyrd. The boy loved books and poetry and lived inside his head more than he did in the world outside it. Possibly even worse, he'd spent the years of his family's sojourn in Charlz listening to his parents speak of the home and friends they'd left behind with wistful nostalgia. His vision of the Republic had been formed out of those conversations—built on his parents' *good* memories, not the bad—and he wasn't as pragmatic as his older brother, Aryn.

You keep your eyes open out there, boy, the bookseller thought as the first raindrops pattered against the shop's windows. *Not everybody's as goodhearted as you are.*

▼ ▼ ▼

"*Crap,*" Rychyrd Tohmys muttered as the first cold drop hit him on top of the head. He really hadn't expected the rain to begin before he got home, but his father had always twitted him about his tendency to take counsel of his hopes rather than experience.

He looked up in time to catch three or four more drops squarely in the face. Despite the darkness, there was enough street traffic for the grating of iron-shod wheel rims on stone paving to drown any sound the rain might make, but the breeze picked up, fluttering the flames in the oil-fueled streetlamps, swinging the hanging signboards.

It wasn't just going to rain sooner than he'd expected; it was going to rain far harder than he'd anticipated, as well.

He paused, looking around, holding the precious package in his arms. It was heavy, but it was far lighter than what it contained: the world. The printed page. Poetry, history, four of the playwright Ahntahn Shropsky's most famous plays. He'd been stocking up for months, ever since he'd realized his father was serious about returning to the Barony of Charlz. Lake City had a lot of rural flavor, but it was still a provincial capital of the Republic of Siddarmark and it had been rebuilding apace ever since the Jihad. Compared to the hills of Charlz, its bookstores were a treasure trove for any scholar. They were, in fact, the one thing about the Tohmys family's return to Siddarmark which had actually exceeded Rychyrd's dreams.

And he was about to lose them. His mother and father were going to drag him back to Symberg, the tiny town ninety miles from nowhere (otherwise known as

Mhartynsberg), where his mother's fourth cousin would greet their return with mixed emotions. Wyllym Styrges had welcomed them with open arms when they'd fled the chaos of western Siddarmark. He was a dutiful son of Mother Church, and he'd found room on his farm for all of them. His visitors had repaid his generosity by pitching in on the unending chores of a successful farmer and nearly doubled his pre-Jihad production. But he was only in his forties, with a rapidly expanding family of his own, and the farm simply wasn't that huge. His relief when Clyntahn Tohmys took his family back to Siddarmark had been palpable, and it was hard to blame him for wishing the Tohmyses could have stayed there.

Rychyrd wished the same thing.

The rain began to patter across his shoulders, leaving dark blotches on the brown wrapping paper of his books, and he opened his tunic, shoving the three volumes into it and hunching forward to protect them with his body. He had over three blocks to go, if he followed the main avenues, and he'd promised his mother he would. But he didn't see how he could keep his books dry for that long a walk, especially in lighting conditions this poor. Lake City's sidewalks were well-maintained, but this far north, there were always flagstones which had been heaved up by the alternating freeze and thaw of winter. If he tried to pick up his pace, he was bound to hang a toe on one of them in the semi-dark.

But there was an alternate route. . . .

Rychyrd hesitated for another moment, then turned and headed for a nearby alley mouth. The buildings on either side were so close together their upper-story balconies overhung the alley, turning it into a tunnel of sorts. There were plenty of gaps in its "roof," but between the gaps, he would actually be out of the rain, and it would let him cut one entire block from the walk.

The lighting was even more problematic, unfortunately. Occasional pools of brightness where someone's windows looked out onto the alley were interspersed with much wider chasms of inky blackness where there were no windows and the balconies overhead choked off whatever light might have trickled in.

Those patches of darkness were favored by citizens of Lake City who preferred not to bother the city guard with their business transactions. Rychyrd was young, and small for his age, but not young enough to prevent a few of those citizens from calling out sultry invitations as he hurried past, and he shook his head with a smile. His actual experience with the "fairer sex," as his father had always put it, was nonexistent, aside from a handful of clumsy kisses. Given some of the books he'd read, however, he had a very shrewd notion of what those inviting voices were suggesting, and a part of him—*not* the most cerebral one—was tempted to accept the invitations. They'd probably want more than he could afford, but it wasn't like he was going to have *books* to spend the marks on much longer. And his older brother Aryn had always insisted that real life experience was more important than anything he could glean out of a book!

Rychyrd's smile turned into a chuckle at that thought. Aryn was only five years older than him, but sometimes those years seemed like a lifetime. Aryn had never wanted to return to the Republic; in fact, he'd fought his parents' decision. The difference in their ages meant he'd been twelve when the Tohmys family fled to Charlz. Rychyrd had been only seven—he'd turned eight later that same year, in Charlz—and his memories of the Republic and of the chaos which had enveloped Tarikah, even before their departure, were very different from Aryn's. For that matter, he'd come to realize that "his" memories were really echoes of his parents' stories about a Republic which had never known the Sword of Schueler. About a Republic which had died forever when the Reformists and the Inquisition's madness had ripped the world apart. He'd built his own vision of Siddarmark out of those tales . . . only to discover how far short of the vision its reality fell in far too many ways.

He stopped chuckling, bending his head as the rain picked up. Away from the main streets, there was practically no traffic noise—the rumble from beyond the solid blocks of buildings which walled in the alley was more like the sound of a distant sea, not remotely loud enough to drown out the pattering rush as the rain pelted the balconies above him. He found himself dodging from dark patch to dark patch, sheltering under the island overheads to stay out of the downpour as much as he could.

It was the Siddar Loyalists, he thought. They didn't care that Clyntahn Tohmys had always considered himself a loyal Siddarmarkian, that he'd refused to enlist in the Barony of Charlz's militia or army even at the height of the Jihad. They didn't care that he'd fled from the huge farm his family had worked for over two centuries only because he had a wife and two young sons he was determined to keep safe from the madness swirling about him. He'd returned from one of the Border States, not even the Temple Lands, but it didn't matter. He'd left "in the hour of the Republic's need," and that made him a traitor.

It hadn't been all that bad at first, not while Archbishop Zhasyn was alive. But since his death there'd been no one with the stature to stare the Siddar Loyalists down. Archbishop Arthyn did his best, and Archbishop Olyvyr, the Reformist-minded Archbishop of Cliff Peak, who'd replaced Archbishop Zhasyn on the Reconciliation Courts was a decent, fair-minded man. But the two of them were like the ancient bishop who'd stood on the shore of the Wind Gulf Sea and forbidden the tide to come in.

Old Master Hahraimahn hadn't been far wrong to call the Siddar Loyalists "thugs." In fact, *Rychyrd* didn't think he'd been wrong at all, although his father—with dogged fair-mindedness—had insisted not all the Siddar Loyalists were street toughs with nothing better to do than harass decent people. It was a point upon which he and his wife were not in agreement, however, and Rychyrd—and Aryn—both sided with Danyel Tohmys in this case.

But—

"Well, what *do* we have here?" a voice said suddenly. It was very different from the voices which had offered Rychyrd "a good time." It was harsh, deep, male, and it came from the heart of the dark patch in front of him.

The young man froze, standing in a shaft of wan illumination spilling from a lantern on the balcony ahead of him. Then he swallowed hard and took a step backwards as four or five figures swaggered out of the darkness.

"It's that book-loving bastard, that's what it is," another voice said, and Rychyrd's stomach clenched as he recognized it. Before the Jihad, Byrt Tyzdail's family had worked side by side with the Tohmyses. Their farms had lain right next to each other, and for generations, Tyzdails and Tohmyses had helped plow and sow one another's fields, gather one another's harvests, build one another's barns, drill one another's wells.

But there were no Tyzdails now. Only Byrt. His parents and two of his brothers had died that first horrible winter of the Sword. His older sister, her husband, and three of her children had disappeared into one of the Inquisition's camps . . . and never been seen again. His younger brother had joined the Republic of Siddarmark Army . . . and died somewhere in Cliff Peak.

Only Byrt remained, and perhaps it was inevitable that his hatred for Temple Loyalists should burn with a white hot, searing heat. But it burned hottest where those who had once been friends—friends whose actions had betrayed his own dead family—were concerned.

Friends like Clyntahn Tohmys and *his* family.

"Oh! It's the *book-loving* bastard," the first voice said mockingly. "That mean we should treat him any different from all the *other* bastards?"

"Sure we should," Tyzdail said flatly. "We let some of *them* go."

Rychyrd backed away, sweat beading his forehead. He was probably younger than any of the Siddar Loyalists—he was a good ten years younger than Byrt, for example—and that meant he was probably faster. Running down the alley, with its occasional piles of refuse

hiding in the dark, would be an excellent way to fall and break bones. But *not* running—

"Going someplace, shitass?" another voice said from behind him, and he froze. He darted a look over his shoulder and his heart plunged as two more men emerged from the darkness.

"Oh, look!" the first voice taunted. "The wittle wabbit doesn't have any place to wun now. Oh, boo-hoo!"

"Look," Rychyrd said, though he knew it was unlikely to do any good, "I just want to go home. And my entire family's going to leave as soon as my dad can sell the farm. We'll be *gone,* and we'll never bother any of you again."

"But we don't *want* you to go and leave us," Tyzdail said. "We want you right where we can reach you, any time we like."

"Byrt, I never hurt you. Neither did my *family,*" Rychyrd said, turning and managing to get his back against the alley wall. "We weren't even here!"

"No, but your fucking friends were," the first voice grated. "Already dealt with a lot of them, but you pick your friends, you pick sides. And you picked the wrong one, friend."

"I was *seven years* old!" Rychyrd protested. "Nobody asked me to pick anything!"

"Then I guess you're just stuck with your old man's choices," Tyzdail said. "Maybe he'll get the message." The older man's laugh was ugly. "*You* sure as Shan-wei will!"

There were seven of them, Rychyrd realized sinkingly. Seven—every one of them older and most of them a lot bigger than he was. He tried to sink into the wall behind him, feeling his knees begin to shake, bitterly shamed by the icy torrent of fear pouring through him.

Then one of the thugs raised his hand, opened the slide of a bull's-eye lantern, and the dim shaft of light— blinding in the alley's darkness—hit him in the eyes. He didn't understand. They'd already identified him, so why—

The shaft of light moved, swinging away from him,

and he sucked in a deep breath. They hadn't opened the slide to get a better look at him; they'd opened it because they wanted him to get a better look at the ready clubs and knuckledusters. They wanted him to *see* what was coming.

He opened his mouth for a final plea he knew would be useless.

▼ ▼ ▼

Aryn Tohmys swore under his breath as the rain pounded down. At least he'd seen it coming and grabbed his oilcloth poncho and his father's hammer-islander before he headed out into it, but the poncho leaked and the rain had turned into a downpour, interspersed with rumbles of thunder. He hadn't seen any lightning yet, but it was coming, and Rychyrd was about due a piece of his mind when he finally found him.

Doesn't have any business worrying Mom this way, he thought balefully. *Him and his* books! *I know he doesn't want to leave them behind, and Langhorne knows he works hard to buy the things. But he's got to start getting home earlier. If he doesn't—*

He swallowed the thought. Rychyrd's job as an assistant cook—a cook who spent more time washing dishes than cooking—in a downtown restaurant demanded long hours. It was always late when he got done, and by the time he went by his favorite bookstores, it was even later by the time he got home. But this was a new record. He should have been home at least an hour and a half before Aryn set out to find him. Personally, Aryn suspected he'd found someplace along the way where he could find cover from the rain and protect his precious books. But his mother had been so worried that Aryn had volunteered to go find the reprobate and drag him home by the ear.

So far, he hadn't done much finding.

He stepped from the open sidewalk to the cover of a shop awning and opened the door. He pulled the hammer-islander off his head, careful to keep it—or his poncho—from dripping on the merchandise, and stepped into the interior's mellow lamplight.

"Aryn!" Stywyrt Hahraimahn sounded surprised. "What are you doing here? I'm just about to lock up for the night."

"Looking for Rychyrd," Aryn sighed. "Mom's about to have a wyvern because he's not home yet. You wouldn't happen to have seen him, would you?"

"Yes, I did." Hahraimahn crossed the shop to Aryn, his expression suddenly taut. "He came to pick up those books he'd put on layaway. But that was three *hours* ago! You're telling me he's not home yet?!"

Aryn felt a sudden chill which had nothing to do with leaking ponchos. Three hours? To walk four blocks? And he'd walked those same blocks to get here without seeing a single sign of Rychyrd along the way.

"No, he's not. Or wasn't when I left, anyway." Aryn ran his right hand through his unruly hair. "Now *I'm* starting to worry!"

"I told him to be careful." Hahraimahn sounded torn between concern for a young man of whom he was deeply fond and irritation—fear, really—at the thought that he might not have been listened to. "I told him after what happened with Feldyrmyn there were some really stupid, really pissed people out there."

"Yeah." Aryn ran his hand through his hair again.

Hairklys Feldyrmyn was another native of Tarikah who'd come home after the Jihad. In his case, he'd come home from the Episcopate of St. Hailyn in the Temple Lands, however, because he truly had been a Temple Loyalist. In fact, he'd enlisted in the Army of God and seen some of the Jihad's toughest fighting. The experience hadn't made him any fonder of Reformists, either, and while he'd come home with his wife and daughter after the peace treaties were signed, it hadn't been to stay. All he'd wanted was to reclaim his family farm and sell it to provide a nest egg for a new life back in the Temple Lands. He'd made no secret of his plans—or of his contempt for the "traitors to Mother Church" who'd made the Temple's defeat possible, for that matter—and seven or eight Siddar Loyalists had decided to make an example out of him and his family.

Unfortunately for them, the tough-minded, cantankerous veteran had been armed with a dagger and knew how to use one. The thugs had been street brawlers, not soldiers, and from everything Aryn had heard, he'd deliberately not killed anyone when he could have. But if he hadn't killed them, he had put five of them into the local Pasqualate hospital, two of them in critical condition.

"All right," he said after a moment. "I know he was here, I know he left, and I know I didn't pass him on the way."

"So where—?" Hahraimahn began, then stopped. "No," he said.

"That's what I'm afraid of," Aryn said. "Especially if it had already started to rain?" He raised one eyebrow at the bookseller, and Hahraimahn nodded unhappily. "You know how he is about his books. I'll bet you he *did* take the shortcut."

"Let me get my coat and a lantern," Hahraimahn said grimly. "I'm coming with you."

▼ ▼ ▼

"Oh, Rychyrd!"

Rychyrd Tohmys floated up out of the depths as he recognized that voice. It was Aryn, but why did he sound that way? So . . . broken? He started to reach out, then jerked in agony as his arm tried to move.

"*Lie still!*" Aryn snapped. "Master Hahraimahn's gone to find the Guard . . . and . . . and a healer."

Healer? For who? Rychyrd blinked in puzzlement. Or, rather, he tried to blink. His right eye seemed glued shut—the eyelid refused to move at all—and a stab of panic went through his haziness as he realized he couldn't see a thing through the left eye, either.

It's only the dark, he told himself, feeling the rain pound down on him. *It's just because it's dark. That's all.*

"I—" he began, then broke off, coughing to clear his throat. He realized he was spitting out blood, but that was nothing beside the tearing agony in his ribs when he coughed. He tried to curl into a ball around the pain, but he couldn't. Partly because his brother's hands were on his shoulders, holding him down, but mostly because it hurt too much.

And then the memory of the bull's-eye lantern, the clubs and the iron knuckles, went back through him again, and he moaned in anguish.

"How . . . how bad?" he got out.

"I don't know," Aryn told him. "There's not enough light. We'll have to wait for the healer. But I know your right arm's broken, and so is your nose."

"Not . . . not me," Rychyrd whispered. "Books. How . . . how bad . . . my books?"

Aryn's jaw clenched. He'd lied when he said there wasn't enough light. Hahraimahn had left his lantern, and the fact that Rychyrd didn't even know that was terrifying. But his eyes burned—with tears, as much as rage—as he saw the shredded, torn pages scattered on the filthy, sodden alley's floor. Knew whoever had done this had taken a special, sadistic delight in destroying his little brother's most treasured possession.

"They're fine, Rychyrd," he said, his voice serene, his hands gentle on his brother's shoulders. "They're fine."

. II .

Grand Vicar Rhobair's Office,
The Temple,
City of Zion,
The Temple Lands.

"I'm sure the Lord Protector wishes he hadn't had to do quite so much dragon-trading, Your Holiness," Vicar Bryahn Ohcahnyr said, "but from our initial reports, it looks like he and Chancellor Maidyn got pretty much everything they asked for."

"Demanded, you mean, Bryahn," Grand Vicar Rhobair corrected wryly, smiling across his enormous desk at the Treasurer of the Church of God Awaiting. That job had been Rhobair's for far longer than he really cared to remember, and the tall, fair-haired and brown-eyed Ohcahnyr had been one of his senior subordinates during the Jihad.

"I don't think anything as gentle as 'asking' could have produced *this*," the Grand Vicar continued, his expression turning more somber. "Not with how quickly it's going to start biting credit."

"No," Ohcahnyr agreed. "But we both know that's exactly what the Republic needs to do, Holiness." The treasurer shrugged. "The Pasqualates can make some medicines taste better than others, but it's been my experience that the stronger the medicine, the worse it tastes."

"And the more it's needed," Tymythy Symkyn added. The Grand Vicar glanced at him, and the chancellor twitched his head in Ohcahnyr's direction. "You and Bryahn are right about how bad it's going to taste, but maybe it will finally pull Siddarmark back from the brink. And there's a limit to how long they can stagger along before they fall over the cliff if it doesn't pull them back at least a bit."

Rhobair nodded soberly, because his subordinates were right. As the man who'd been Mother Church's treasurer, he was far from blind to the size and strength of the revenue stream available to even a vastly reduced Church of God Awaiting or of how that revenue's reliability had helped the Church recover from her disastrous, overextended position at the end of the Jihad. The Republic's revenues would have been less reliable and robust under any circumstances. Given the circumstances Greyghor Stohnar and Henrai Maidyn had actually faced, it was a not so minor miracle the entire Siddarmarkian banking system hadn't simply collapsed.

"They're not out of the woods yet," he said, leaning

back in his chair and linking the fingers of his hands behind his head.

He gazed at the mystic, ever-changing wall of his office with its panoramic view of the Zion waterfront. Unlike many similar walls here in the Temple, this one showed what was actually happening at the lakeside quays and wharves. Indeed, if he'd touched one of the god lights on his desk, he could actually have *heard* what was happening there. Another of the god lights would have caused the panorama to shift on a regular basis, sweeping through over two dozen other living, breathing murals, but the waterfront was his favorite. The ever-changing panorama of ships and small craft, the cargos being swayed over the sides of the ships, the living, breathing, endlessly stirring water. . . . All of those were parts of what drew him repeatedly to that particular view. But the real reason, what brought him back here whenever his soul most sorely needed refreshment, was the huge, new complex of shelters and hospitals he'd had built and named in loving memory of Father Zytan Kwill.

In another month or two, as Zion headed into fall and winter, those shelters would spread Mother Church's protective arms about hundreds, even thousands, of her most vulnerable children. Last winter, less than two hundred Zionites had perished of cold and privation, despite the ferocity of its far northern climate. That was still two hundred too many, yet it was enormously better than the thousands in which those deaths had once been reckoned. He'd accomplished many things since ascending to the Throne of Langhorne, including ending the Jihad which had killed so many millions of God's children. Yet the Zytan Kwill Center and the other, smaller shelters dotted strategically about the city were the single achievement that gave him the most simple pleasure and joy.

I'm sorry you didn't live to see it, Father Zytan, he reflected now. *On the other hand, I expect the name gave you a good laugh in Heaven.*

His lips twitched in fond memory at the thought, and

he turned his chair to face Ohcahnyr and Symkyn without bringing it upright.

"They're not out of the woods yet," he repeated, "and I'm not going to make any rash predictions. But I really do think that with only a little luck, they've actually turned the corner. And thank God and Langhorne! The last thing we needed was for Siddarmark to turn into its own version of Harchong."

"Truer words were never spoken, Your Holiness," Ohcahnyr replied. "Although this 'Ahrmahk Plan' does seem to be working in West Harchong."

"Despite Zhyou-Zhwo's best effort to drown it at birth," Symkyn agreed grimly. "I don't know what that man uses for a brain, and I don't *want* to know what he uses for a soul!"

"As Grand Vicar, I shouldn't say it, but I don't know, either." Rhobair grimaced. "And I don't like the anti-Charis strand in his invective." He shook his head and let his chairback come fully vertical. "It's as if no one ever told him the Jihad was over."

"Because for some people it isn't, Holiness." Symkyn's voice was gentle, and he raised one placating hand when Rhobair glanced at him. "I see more of the routine diplomatic correspondence than you do, Holiness. It's my job to deal with it instead of just dumping it on your desk. And I'm not saying anyone wants to restart the Jihad tomorrow. But there are way too many people out there in positions of power who resent the Shan-wei out of the way it ended." He shook his head. "I could wish more of them were at least like those of our less happy colleagues here in Zion who're genuinely concerned over the state of humans' souls. For most of them, though—?" He shrugged. "Most of them are like Zhyou-Zhwo or Emperor Mahrys. They don't like the post-Jihad political and—especially—*economic* world, and they're far more eager to use the Church of Charis as a pretext than they are driven by their deep and burning dedication to restore Mother Church."

"You mean they're just biding their time." Rhobair's tone was unhappy; it wasn't surprised.

"Your Holiness," Ohcahnyr said, "there's a certain species of ruler who's *always* 'just biding his time.' I admit Tymythy has to deal more directly with them than I do, but you know as well as we do that that particular species can always find a pretext when it decides the time has come." He gave the Grand Vicar an almost gentle smile. "It's not your fault, it's not *our* fault, and God and the Archangels only expect us to do the best we poor mortals can, not to accomplish miracles."

"You're right, of course," Rhobair sighed, then he brightened. "And despite the situation in Central Harchong, things are looking up overall. Not just in the 'United Provinces,' either. It looks like Rainbow Waters is going to make his protectorate stand up in East Harchong, too."

"I could wish he was in a little better health, but, yes, it does, Your Holiness," Symkyn agreed. "And while I hope the Earl will be with us for many years yet, I have to say Baron Wind Song seems every bit as capable. I don't think he's quite as intelligent as his uncle, but, then, who is?" He smiled quickly, fleetingly. "And every man who ever served in the Mighty Host seems as devoted to the Baron as to the Earl. And the Baron, Langhorne bless him, is even more devoted to him."

"To quote Bryahn, 'truer words were never spoken,'" Rhobair said, then snorted in amusement. Symkyn looked a question at him, and he shrugged. "I was just thinking that marrying Wind Song off to Gustyv Walkyr's daughter would have been a master stroke on my part during the Jihad. I wish I could claim credit for it even now, but it never even would have occurred to me!"

"You're not alone, Holiness," Symkyn assured him. "It would have seemed too much like cradle robbing for most of us, even in an arranged dynastic marriage. She's—what? Sixteen years younger than him?"

"More like fifteen years and one month," Ohcahnyr said with the precision of a man who spent his life working with numbers. "I think that discrepancy bothered her mother more than it did her father, but Madam

Walkyr's come around since. Something to do with the grandchildren, I understand."

"It sure wasn't the title!" Rhobair retorted with a chuckle. "Wind Song's estates had already been confiscated by then." He gazed at the view of the harbor again for several seconds, then back at his vicars. "And the remarkable thing is how little that bothered him compared to the confidence he and his uncle were doing the right thing. I think that had a lot to do with Lady Sahmantha's decision to marry him despite her mother's reservations."

"Probably," Symkyn agreed. "But that same attitude is why I'm confident he'll be not only able but willing to continue his uncle's work if something happens to Rainbow Waters."

Rhobair nodded. Rainbow Waters had always been a physically robust, active man, but the responsibilities of fighting the Jihad against the combined forces of Charis and Siddarmark had taken their toll even before he was exiled, his lands confiscated. His hair was entirely silver now, he moved more cautiously than he had, and he'd looked undeniably frail the last time he and Rhobair had spoken face-to-face.

Well, of course he did! You're no spring wyvern yourself these days, especially after the Jihad, and he's eight years older than you are. The man's got a right to look a little worn, and whatever may be true physically, mentally he's just as sharp as he ever was. Hopefully at least some of your subordinates think the same thing about you!

He chuckled again at the thought, and both the vicars looked at him.

"Just a thought about how well people wear . . . or don't," he told them, waving it away.

Then he pushed up out of his chair. Both of his guests stood, and he walked around the desk to escort them to the door.

"Your Holiness—" Symkyn started in a semi-scolding tone, then stopped as Rhobair cocked his head. "Never mind," he said instead, and Rhobair smiled in gentle triumph.

He didn't need Symkyn to remind him that none of his last half-dozen or so predecessors would have dreamed of escorting visitors from their offices. That was one precedent—one of many, really—Rhobair Duchairn had refused to continue. The Grand Vicar was God's servant and, in a very real sense, the servant of his fellow vicars, as well. They'd forgotten that, and it was one of the many things God had used the Jihad to remind him of.

"You know, Holiness," Ohcahnyr said as they crossed the enormous office, "Earl Rainbow Waters has saved a lot of lives, but he never could have done it without the backing and political support you and Vicar Allayn gave him. At the risk of sounding like I'm sucking up to you," he smiled at Rhobair's involuntary spurt of laughter, but his expression sobered quickly, "the only reason those people are still alive is because you insisted we support the Mighty Host in exile and then acted so quickly to provide the backing the Earl needed."

"*Mother Church* did that—well, she and God. Not me," Rhobair demurred. "And anything I may have done was only possible because of the kind of support you and Tymythy have given me. None of it would've happened or even been possible without you at Treasury, Allayn running the Army, and Tymythy keeping me as far away as possible from the diplomatic correspondence."

"That's all true enough, Holiness," Ohcahnyr said, "but I think it's fair to say you did have a *tiny* bit to do with it."

"Well, maybe a tiny bit," Rhobair allowed with a smile.

"I have to agree with Bryahn, Holiness," Symkyn said. "Oh, and I just remembered something else I meant to tell you. And I hope you won't think *it's* 'sucking up' to you."

"What?" Rhobair asked, cocking a suspicious eyebrow.

"Tifny asked me to tell you it's official. We're naming the baby Rhobair. Actually," he rolled his eyes "we're naming him Rhobair Tymythy Ahntahn Zhak Symkyn."

"*Langhorne!*" Rhobair said with a far louder crack of laughter. "The poor boy's less than a month *old*, Tymythy! That name's longer than *he* is!"

"But he'll grow into it, Holiness," Symkyn said as they reached the office door and stepped out into the spacious antechamber. The bishop who served as Rhobair's secretary rose, inclining his head respectfully but without the deep bow previous grand vicars would have received—and demanded. "Most of those names are from Tifny's side of the family, anyway."

"Except for the one you chose to flatter me, you mean?" Rhobair said.

"Well, of course, Your Holiness!" Symkyn said, and Rhobair reached out to rest his right hand on his shoulder, laughing even harder.

"Well, consider it a mat—"

He broke off in mid-word. His hand tightened on Symkyn's shoulder like a claw. His left rose to his chest, clutching at his cassock as his eyes widened in shock. Then those eyes rolled up, his knees buckled, and the hand on Symkyn's shoulder relaxed suddenly, its fingers completely flaccid, even as the vicar cried out in denial and reached out to catch him.

. III .
Uicar Tymythy Symkyn's Office,
The Temple,
City of Zion,
The Temple Lands.

"And so we charge you, Brothers in God, to gather here in Zion—"

Symkyn had to stop and clear his throat. It wasn't the first time he'd done that in the last hour. He didn't expect it to be the last before he was finished with this day's crushing responsibilities, either, and Father Zhon

Fyrdnand, his secretary, wept openly, dashing the tears away almost angrily with his left hand while his pen scratched obediently as he took down the dictated summons.

Symkyn wanted to tell Father Zhon it was all right. That this could wait. But it wasn't all right, and it couldn't wait. As Chancellor of the Church of God Awaiting, it was Symkyn's responsibility to serve as caretaker in the Grand Vicar's name until the Council of Vicars could assemble to nominate and elect Rhobair II's successor.

And who could we possibly elect to truly *succeed him?* Symkyn closed his eyes briefly. *He was only* sixty-one, *for Langhorne's sake! We should have had him for at least another* twenty years—*maybe even long enough to get through Harchong and whatever's happening in Siddarmark. And what's happening right here in the Vicarate, for that matter! He was the glue holding the Reformists and the Moderates and the Conservatives together, God. Where are You going to find us someone else who could have done that? Someone who can complete the reconciliation—even right here in Mother Church, much less throughout Your world—that You'd called him to?*

God didn't answer, and Symkyn inhaled deeply. The *Writ* said God would always find the right man, but there were times he found that more difficult to believe than others. After all, God had permitted Zhaspahr Clyntahn's reign as Grand Inquisitor.

But He hadn't allowed it to continue forever, the vicar reminded himself fiercely. He'd found Rhobair Duchairn, touched his heart, transformed a man who'd been as much a part of the system as anyone and more so than most into the genuine Good Shepherd Mother Church had needed. Surely He could do that again! And in the meantime—

"Our brother Rhobair will lie in state in The Temple for a full five-day," he resumed after a moment, his voice husky. "We charge you in his name, and in the name of Mother Church, to join us here with all haste for his funeral mass and for the Convocation to select his successor. To this end—"

OCTOBER YEAR OF GOD 905

·◆·

.I.

CMS *Sea Wyvern*,
Temple Wharf,
and
The Temple,
City of Zion,
The Temple Lands.

"I wish I was more confident this was one of your *good* ideas, Your Eminence."

Bishop Bryahn Ushyr's voice had been trained since seminary to carry to the distant corners of even a large cathedral, but it was pitched low enough no one else could have heard it through the tumult and crowd noise as the high-sided steamship nuzzled the wharf's massive fenders. CMS *Sea Wyvern*, flying the standard of the Empire of Charis below the golden scepter of Langhorne which denoted her present service to the *Church* of Charis, was the pride of the Charisian merchant marine: six hundred feet long and forty-five feet from waterline to boat deck. That made her the largest steampowered vessel ever built on Safehold, for the moment at least, and she towered over every other ship in the vicinity. Her sheer presence almost concealed the presence of the half-dozen steam-powered tugboats, all flying the gold-on-green scepter banner of the Temple Lands.

The sibilant roar of *Sea Wyvern*'s venting steam, the jet of white startlingly dramatic as it blasted through the coal smoke from her funnels, contributed quite a bit to that tumult, but it was only an addition, almost an afterthought compared to the noise of the crowd which had assembled to await her arrival. The city waterfront had grown accustomed to the fire-and-smoke-breathing tugs and lesser craft which had become increasingly prevalent, even here in Zion, but the sheer size of the leviathans Charis had introduced to the seas of Safehold, each seemingly larger than the last, was another matter. The big oceangoing freighters normally docked at Port Harbor on Temple Bay, almost a hundred and forty miles from the Temple precincts, and passenger steamers remained a rarity almost everywhere. *Sea Wyvern*'s size alone would have turned her arrival into an event, yet there was far more to it. This was the first Charisian passenger ship—for that matter, the first Charisian-flagged ship of *any* type—to dock at Temple Wharf in almost fifteen years . . . and she carried the first prelate of the breakaway Church of Charis ever to visit the Temple.

It was impossible to parse the sound coming from the throats of that enormous crowd with any degree of precision, but at the moment it seemed to contain less jeers than cheers, and the Temple Guard and Army of God were both out in force for crowd control.

"Nonsense! Of course it's a good idea, Bryahn," Maikel Staynair told his most trusted aide serenely as he waved to the crowd. "And even if it isn't," his expression sobered for a moment as he glanced sideways at Ushyr, "Rhobair Duchairn deserves it of us."

Ushyr looked as if he would have liked to argue the point, but he had even more experience than most with the iron beneath the archbishop's gentle surface. The gentleness was genuine; the stubbornness was elemental.

"Cheer up," Staynair told him, turning back to the quayside, "Captain Karstayrs wouldn't have let me come if *he* thought it was a bad idea."

The bishop gave his superior a moderately smoldering look, then glanced over his shoulder at the remarkably tall, fair-haired captain in the orange-and-white uniform of the Archbishop's Guard. Aside from his height, Captain Karstayrs' appearance had nothing in common with Merlin Athrawes, which struck Bishop Bryahn as a good thing. The one thing he was certain of was that bringing *Seijin* Merlin or *Seijin* Nimue—or any known *seijin*—to Zion would have been a very *bad* idea. He rather doubted Karstayrs was remotely as blasé about all of this as the archbishop's attitude might have suggested, either. The captain had been scanning the dockside crowd through narrow eyes, but he seemed to sense Ushyr's look and those brown eyes looked away— briefly—from the wharf to meet the bishop's.

"You might as well give up, Bryahn," a deep, resonant—and resigned—voice said over the plug in his right ear. "He's got the bit in his teeth, and he's the only person I know who's even stubborner than Sharleyan. All we can do is hang on for the ride."

Staynair snorted inelegantly but never looked away from the tide of humanity crowding against the cordon of Temple Guardsmen and Army of God infantry. For the moment, at least, the crowd seemed well mannered, despite the strands of protest threaded through its noise, and the truly strident were a distinct minority. There was a sense of excitement and curiosity in the air, but the overriding emotions seemed to be solemnity . . . and sorrow.

The archbishop nodded to himself. The passing of a Grand Vicar was always traumatic for the entire Church, but Rhobair II had been truly beloved by the citizens of Zion. Much of the rest of the Temple Lands might have had mixed, or at least conflicted, feelings about Rhobair's decision to seek rapprochement with the Church of Charis. The people of Zion hadn't. They'd known the worth of the man they called the Good Shepherd, they'd been prepared to follow his example and embrace his passionate quest for reconciliation, and their grief at his death had been deep and profound.

Which wasn't to say there weren't plenty of people in Zion who would have seen laying the heretic Archbishop of Charis dead on the paving of God's city as their highest duty to God and the Archangels. And if they truly believed in the Archangels' divinity and the words of the *Holy Writ*, they'd be right.

His bearded lips quirked at the thought and he glanced at the younger bishop beside him with a familiar pang. He never had gotten Bryahn Ushyr the parish he needed. Not for long enough, at any rate. The bishop was only forty, barely thirty-six in the years of long-dead Terra, and he'd had no more than two years as the priest of his own congregation before his elevation to the episcopate. Staynair regretted that. In some ways, he supposed, it didn't really matter, because Bryahn had been recruited by the inner circle even before the end of the Jihad. He knew what a perversion the *Holy Writ* truly was, and looked at one way, all he'd really missed was five or six more years of living a lie.

Staynair still wished he'd had those years, though, because that wasn't at all the way the archbishop looked at it. There was no question in his mind that Ushyr's priestly calling was as genuine as his own—that both of them had truly heard the voice of God, *despite* the Church of God Awaiting. And, like Staynair himself, Ushyr had spent years perusing all of the religious history and texts stored in the computers in Nimue's Cave. Both of them had attacked those files, those documents, with the ferocity of men finally free to seek God beyond the lie, and as both of them had learned how much of humanity's great religions Eric Langhorne and Adorée Bédard had stolen to create their *Writ*, Ushyr had concluded that his archbishop was right. Safeholdians' faith was no less strong, no less genuine, despite the lies, and God *would* know His own, wherever they might be or however they might know Him. And He could *reclaim* them as His own by ripping away the mask of the Church of God Awaiting in His own good time, using the hands of whomever He chose . . . even those of a woman who'd been dead for a thousand years. Not everyone who'd learned the truth had been able to retain their faith in any God. Indeed, not all of them had even wanted to. But Ushyr had, and so Staynair had no concerns about the state of his aide's soul. No, his concern

was that his protégé had been denied the opportunity—
the sheer joy—of ministering to the souls in his charge
on an individual basis.

And the reason he had was that Staynair had never
been able to spare him. First as his secretary, then as his
aide, and now as the head of his vastly enlarged staff,
Ushyr had simply been too invaluable for anything else.

The archbishop smiled at the thought, then raised
one hand in a gesture of benediction and blessing as
the mooring hawsers went ashore and dropped over the
waiting bollards.

▼ ▼ ▼

"Now behave yourself, Your Grace," the tallish man in
Temple Guard uniform said quietly as the enormous
steamship finished tying up. Vicar Zherohmy Awstyn
looked at him, his expression less than amused, but
Bishop Militant Khanstahnzo Phandys only gazed back
with one eyebrow raised.

"I fully intend to 'behave myself,' Khanstahnzo." Awstyn's tone was frosty. "I'm not exactly a teenager who
needs to be reminded to clean his fingernails before he
appears in public!"

In fact, he was nine years younger than Phandys,
which made him one of the youngest members of the
vicarate Rhobair Duchairn had been forced to rebuild
almost from scratch, and he'd recently been elevated to
a post on the new Grand Vicar's staff. Phandys, on the
other hand, was the commander of the Temple Guard,
answerable only to Vicar Allayn and the Grand Vicar,
and he'd been Rhobair II's most trusted and most loyal
confidant for over ten years. His lingering grief over
Rhobair's passing was there in his eyes for anyone to
see, but there was a spark of humor, as well.

"I know that, Your Grace," he said now. "And I suppose it's not well done of me to tease you over it. On
the other hand, reminding you is one of my jobs, since
I'm the fellow in charge of all of the ceremonial hoopla
as well as security. Besides," he touched the vicar's elbow lightly, "you looked like you could use the chance

to give someone a nifty little set down, and being the someone who helps you get that out of your system is one of my jobs, too."

Despite himself, Awstyn snorted in amusement.

"You were probably right about that," he acknowledged. "I will behave myself—I promised His Grace I would—but I can't pretend I'm not in two minds about this."

"Of course you are," Phandys said. "You're a man of faith, which is one of the reasons Grand Vicar Rhobair supported your elevation to the Vicarate. And you're not afraid to voice your opinions, which is one of the reasons he treasured you so much after you got there. And it's why Vicar Tymythy sent you to greet our guests, because he knew how well you'd represent him and Mother Church, whatever personal reservations you might have."

"I'm glad you think so," Awstyn said, more than a little touched by the bishop militant's insight. Then he drew a deep breath as the brightly varnished gangplank, with its spotless white hand ropes, was run out and up to the steamer's entry port.

"And now," he said with a crooked smile, "I suppose it's time for me to go start behaving myself."

▼ ▼ ▼

"I am Vicar Zherohmy Awstyn, and the Grand Vicar designate has charged me to welcome you to Zion in his own name, that of the Vicarate, and of Mother Church, Your Eminence."

The sandy-haired young man in the orange cassock—well, he seemed young to Maikel Staynair, anyway, although he and Ushyr were very much of an age—bowed deeply, but not *too* deeply, as the archbishop stepped from the end of the gangway onto the marble-faced quay. Despite the enormous crowd, the Temple Guard had actually created an island of semi-privacy, where normal speaking voices could be heard but not *over*-heard by others, the archbishop noticed.

"I thank you for the welcome, Your Grace," he replied, returning the bow with one of his own that was no deeper . . . but no shallower, either. They both straightened, and the archbishop smiled. "Allow me to present Bishop Bryahn Ushyr, the head of my staff, and Captain Samyl Karstayrs, of the Archbishop's Guard. I'm sure he and Bishop Militant Khanstahnzo have a great deal to discuss, and I apologize—" his smile grew broader, almost impish "—for making so many complications for them. And for you, of course."

His smile vanished and his eyes were suddenly dark.

"And I deeply regret what's brought me to Zion." He shook his head sadly. "I will always treasure the opportunity I had to meet Grand Vicar Rhobair at the peace conference, however much all of us may regret the bloodshed which led us to that meeting. I can't tell you how saddened I was to learn of his death when so many of the great tasks to which he'd set hand and heart were yet undone. But I was saddened for us, not for him. If there was ever a man in all this world whose soul deserved its reward more than Rhobair Duchairn's, I've never met him. He truly was the Good Shepherd Zion called him."

Awstyn stood for a moment, looking into Staynair's eyes, then inhaled deeply.

"Your Eminence, I was recently reminded to behave myself today," he said. "I'm sure that one as well informed as you've always proved yourself must be aware from your sources here in Zion that I'm one of the vicars who continue to have . . . reservations about the Church of Charis, however."

He paused, one eyebrow raised, and Staynair chuckled.

"I believe you might take that as a given, Your Grace," he replied. "On the other hand, I would add that those same sources have always stressed your integrity and compassion," he added more seriously. "I'm sure the tension between our churches must be difficult for you."

"It is," Awstyn acknowledged, "but that was never because I doubted the sincerity or the depth of your own faith and that of your flock, Your Eminence. And now that I've met you, I realize it's even deeper than I'd thought it was. And whatever our other differences may be, I agree with every word you just said about Grand Vicar Rhobair. I was honored—and deeply blessed—to have known him, and the world is a poorer place today."

"In that case, Your Grace," Staynair laid a hand lightly on Awstyn's forearm, "why don't you and I join the rest of the Vicarate to see what we can do about making this visit and this celebration something that would have pleased him?"

"I think that would be a very good idea, Your Eminence." Awstyn smiled at him. "And, with that in mind, allow me to escort you to The Temple. The Grand Vicar designate charged me to tell you he's eager to meet you face-to-face at last."

▼ ▼ ▼

Captain Karstayrs tried not to feel undressed as he followed Maikel Staynair towards the box which had been set aside for the Temple's Charisian visitors. It was difficult, for a lot of reasons.

The fact that he was unarmed was one of them. The Archbishop's Guard had never carried the katana that remained part of Merlin Athrawes' various *seijin* personas, so Karstayrs had never carried one either, during his so-far brief existence. He didn't really miss the blade, but he *was* acutely conscious of the emptiness where his pistol holster should have been. It wasn't that he distrusted Khanstahnzo Phandys' competence or the men he'd handpicked for this assignment. It was just that it was *his* job, not Phandys', to see to it that Maikel Staynair returned to Charis intact.

But the absence of his revolver was actually a minor component of his uneasiness. For one thing, there were at least a half-dozen Temple Guard revolvers in his vicinity. If he should happen to require a weapon, he was confident he could . . . acquire one of them, whatever its current owner thought about the transaction. Then there was the fact that Staynair and Ushyr both wore what Cayleb persisted in referring to as their "antiballistic undies." As Sharleyan had discovered in Corisande, they couldn't prevent bruising or even broken bones, but they were impenetrable by anything less powerful than a new-model rifle round at close range, and they'd stop any blade short of his own battle steel katana with ludicrous ease.

No, the real reason he felt undressed was because he'd been forced to shut down every one of his PICA's active sensors and his com, as well.

Maikel Staynair and his party had been lodged outside the Temple precincts in a luxurious mansion three blocks away from the Plaza of Martyrs. No doubt the decision to house them there had been a ticklish one. Technically, he was a mere archbishop—and of a schismatic church, at that—which meant he should have been exiled to the outer edges of the mansions and apartment buildings available to Mother Church, given all the vicars and senior archbishops crowded into the city. On the other hand, he was also the head of that schismatic church, with a flock far larger than any single prelate of the Church of God Awaiting except the Grand Vicar himself, which meant he should have been given a place of honor within the Annex itself.

The Church had split the difference with what Karstayrs personally felt was excellent judgment. Staynair's party had the entire mansion to itself, it was closer to the Temple than any of the housing assigned to any other archbishop, and he'd been not simply invited but encouraged to bring his own Guardsmen with him to assure his security. The Temple Guard had been scrupulous about liasing with Karstayrs, as well. Indeed, Bishop Militant Khanstahnzo had discussed all of his needs with him personally, although Karstayrs wondered how he would have reacted if he'd known who he was really discussing them with! But best of all, from Karstayrs' viewpoint, the mansion was just outside the hard limit he and Nimue had drawn around the Temple. He could use his PICA's systems, including his active sensors and internal com, from the mansion's grounds if he needed them . . . and as long as he did so with excruciating caution.

He couldn't now, and that bothered him. It bothered him a lot, and not simply because he felt half blind without them.

He knew the true basis for Bryahn Ushyr's doubts about this visit's wisdom had less to do with concerns over Maikel Staynair's physical safety than it did with the thought of introducing a PICA into the Temple itself. Oh, Staynair's safety was a definite factor in Ushyr's thinking, but the possibility of . . . awakening something best left undisturbed was an even greater one. It was also one Karstayrs shared, which was why Merlin Athrawes had flatly refused to allow Nimue Gahrvai or one of *her* personas to make the trip with them. If something unfortunate were to happen, the inner circle would need at least one surviving PICA to deal with the consequences.

The temptation to simply send the stealthiest possible passive array along with Staynair had been almost overwhelming. In fact, that was exactly what Cayleb, Sharleyan, Nahrmahn Baytz, and Owl had all argued they should do. And they'd had a point. But Merlin Athrawes had no intention of entrusting Staynair's safety to anyone else, and a sensor array came in a piss-poor second to a PICA where that was concerned. There were some people whose lives he was prepared to risk in the service of Nimue Alban's great task. Maikel Staynair wasn't one of them, although he'd given up on getting *Staynair* to see things that way, and if it came to it, he would go fully active inside the Temple itself if that was what it took to get Staynair out of it alive.

He'd been careful to not mention that particular resolve where the archbishop might hear it.

Staynair's protection was the counterargument he'd unscrupulously deployed to swing Sharleyan into actively supporting his decision, but he'd admitted—if only to himself and Nynian—that it was only a part of his own reasons. It was the weightiest part, by far, but *only* a part. Because even though it might not be entirely rational, the opportunity to come onto the grounds of the Temple itself, to enter the very heart of the abomination Eric Langhorne had created here on Safehold, had been too much for him to resist. He'd *had* to come, had to be here, had to see this and feel this for himself.

And it was probably a good thing he had, because no remote small enough for them to infiltrate under someone's clothing or disguise as a piece of jewelry without anyone's noticing could have pulled in everything the much more sensitive ones hidden inside *him* had already gathered. And were still gathering, for that matter. And that smaller, less capable sensor wouldn't have had the flexibility to look in all the directions he was looking as he followed individual power runs and placed them—and the devices they served—on the map he was creating. It would be partial and woefully incomplete when he finished it, that map, but it would be incomparably better than anything they'd had before.

And it would bear some serious thinking on once he got it home, too, because what he'd already picked up only emphasized how right Nahrmahn was to worry about the possibility of whatever had gone wrong with Chihiro's master plan fixing itself.

The Temple was riddled with even more—*far* more—power sources than they'd been able to detect and track from outside its walls. They'd blazed up on his passives the instant he and the rest of Staynair's party had been ushered across the Plaza of Martyrs and into the Temple proper.

He'd always thought Chihiro's decision to plate the Temple's silver dome in eight centimeters of armorplast had been ridiculous, even for a lunatic like him. There'd been far less . . . exorbitant ways to keep that dome mystically mirror bright for centuries on end. It certainly hadn't been required for any conceivable structural reason! Indeed, when Nimue Alban first observed the Temple, she'd thought she'd seen flimsier planetary-defense command bunkers.

It hadn't occurred to her—and it damned well should have—that the reason she'd thought that was that she *had* seen flimsier PDC bunkers. Because even though the people living and working in the Temple and its

"Archangel-built" Annex didn't know it, a planetary-defense bunker was precisely what Chihiro and the surviving "Archangels" had set out to build.

The Temple's exterior walls might look as if they were faced with seventy-five centimeters of fine de Castro marble, but that "marble" was actually solid ceramacrete, carefully disguised to look like marble, and it was sandwiched around battle-steel bulkheads that were themselves twenty centimeters thick. The central dome was a hemisphere of "marble-faced" battle steel almost as thick as the walls' bulkheads, and the skylights which pierced it were ten-centimeter slabs of armorplast, all of that *under* the eight centimeters of the exterior armorplast. The "stained glass" of its spectacular windows was equally formidable, and while its interior walls were rather less impenetrable, even they would have sneered at any conceivable muscle-powered—or, for that matter, gunpowder-powered—assault. They were also riddled with molecular circuitry controlling power, light, air conditioning and heat, powered doors, fire suppression systems, information terminals, surveillance systems which obviously reported to *something*, and the smart walls in the endless offices and living quarters. He'd detected over two dozen separate wireless nets, spreading beyond even the walls' mollycircs, tying together literally hundreds or even thousands of high-tech devices and artifacts the Church and its servants either never knew were there or else took totally for granted as part of the all-encompassing proof of the Temple's divine nature.

He had no idea, even now, how deep the complex went, but he'd come to the conclusion that it must go deeper than they'd believed. Nimue's Cave was actually a complex of artificial caverns, each bigger than most of the Terran Federation Navy's shuttle hangers, hollowed out to house and conceal the tech base Pei Shanwei and her terraforming crews had left for her. It was big enough to provide a formidable support base and fabrication facilities which could easily have springboarded modern technology on a planetary scale, if only they'd been able to operate openly. But it couldn't have supported and maintained anything on this scale, and he'd already detected a half-dozen concealed doors—concealed from the current Church hierarchy, not just interlopers such as himself, he suspected. Two of them, including one which opened directly into the Plaza of Martyrs, were big enough full-scale assault shuttles could have passed through them with ease when they were open. There were clearly ramps behind those concealed doors, diving deep into the earth, and he found himself wondering just how big a hole Chihiro had dug when he built the place . . . and what those ramps might lead to. Since there was no other high-tech presence on the planet, they'd always known any support base for the Temple had to be under it, but they'd never suspected how big it must be or how deep it might go.

Which was stupid of us, he thought now. *Chihiro built this place after the Commodore turned Langhorne and Bédard into plasma, but not as the exercise in megalomania I'd thought it was. Or not just as an exercise in megalomania, at least. This was his HQ, the command center he and Schueler used in their fight against the "Fallen." Of course he built it like a damned bunker! And of course the SNARCs couldn't pick all this up from the outside. Just the thickness and damping effect of the fortifications would have made that difficult, and whether it was before or after the War Against the Fallen, he obviously took a lot of additional steps to harden this place against passive sensors, as well as active ones. Be interesting to know whether that was because he was more worried about the Fallen or about hiding from any Gbaba probe that happened by.*

He'd never know the answer to that question, but at least he understood now why he'd been able to see so little from the outside. What he still didn't know—and what not even this visit could tell him—was what Chihiro might have hidden away in his cellar.

They reached the designated box. It was located in a place of high honor, to one side of the box set aside for the Grand Vicar himself, on the occasions when he attended a mass celebrated by someone else here in what was, after all, his church. At the moment, the Grand Vicar's box was unoccupied, which meant Staynair had been assigned the most prestigious seat in the entire Temple, and Karstayrs wondered how *that* decision had sat with the more conservative vicars.

Now Father Zhon, the Langhornite upper-priest who'd been assigned as Maikel Staynair's guide and personal liaison to the Grand Vicar designate, waved courteously for Staynair and Ushyr to seat themselves in one of the box's luxurious pews. Like every other aspect of the Temple, those pews and the box about them had been built at the same time the enormous circular cathedral was first constructed. No one would have dreamed of altering the Archangels' handiwork, and the Temple's inhabitants took the occasional "holy servitor" which appeared whenever repairs were necessary for granted as one more of the everyday miracles that "proved" the Temple's divinity.

Karstayrs shook his head, politely declining a seat of his own, and took up a parade rest position just inside the box's door. Father Zhon glanced at him quizzically, then smiled, gave a small bow, and disappeared.

As he did, the voices of the magnificently trained choir which kept the Temple perpetually awash with sacred music so that God's house might always be filled with His praise, faded into silence.

▼ ▼ ▼

As a bishop militant, Tymythy Symkyn had seen more than his share of combat. Much of it had been ugly. He'd been certain he was going to die at least three times in the campaign of 897. He'd thought he knew then what terror was.

He'd been wrong.

The cheers thundered about him, louder and stronger than ever as he neared the end of the traditional five-mile procession route from the Borough of Langhorne's Church of the Holy Langhorne to the foot of Temple Hill and the shining silver-and-bronze gates of the Plaza of Martyrs rose before him. Those cheers had been with him from the moment he emerged from the church's doors to begin his final journey as a vicar. Every yard of sidewalk, every cross street and intersection, had been packed by the children of God, and every cheering voice, every shouted benediction, every banner and every drape of bunting, had only told him how unworthy he, of all men, was to walk in the footsteps of giants this day.

He drew the crisp air deep into his lungs and tried to order his pulse rate to slow. His pulse didn't listen to him, and a voice which sounded remarkably like that of Rhobair II reminded him that he was only mortal, not an angel or an archangel with the power to command the physical universe to obey him.

His lips twitched at the reminder . . . and at the memory of the Grand Vicar he'd served and the mentor he'd learned to love. If anyone in all of the Creation would have understood his nervousness, his sense of profound unworthiness, and his determination to be worthy anyway, it would have been Rhobair Duchairn.

He straightened his shoulders . . . again. From personal experience, he knew his ceremonial vestments really did weigh more than old-fashioned chain mail, which shouldn't have surprised him, given their thickly encrustated bullion embroidery and the number of gems and pearls which adorned them. And it was going to get worse when he was vested with the full formal regalia of his new office.

At least they protected him from the chill.

Actually, he thought, glancing up as the solid phalanx of vicars escorted him solemnly into the Plaza of Martyrs and across it towards the Temple's soaring majesty, God and the Archangels had provided a beautiful day for his consecration. He remembered the weather on the day of Rhobair II's consecration. It, too, had fallen in October, but the heavens had been heavy, gray clouds swirling low above the City of God, rain sifting down to contribute a raw, wet edge to the bone-chilling wind. Today's temperature was merely cool, not even brisk for

Zion in October, the gusty breeze was a laughing, cheerful thing, and the sky was a brilliant blue vault, just burnished around the edges with wispy white clouds. The breeze blew a scattering of dried, colorful leaves across the plaza before him—not even the Temple's gardeners could keep all of them raked, this time of year—and the morning sun turned the Temple's silver dome into a brilliant mirror.

It had seemed wrong to him, when he rose with the dawn, realized what sort of weather the day had brought. Wrong that he should have sunlight and a wind that laughed with the joy of Creation while Rhobair, the man who'd done so much, risked so much, to break Zhaspahr Clyntahn's iron tyranny had gone to *his* consecration through blowing billows of icy rain. He'd found himself taking God to task for that as he knelt in his normal morning meditation . . . then been shocked to realize he was *scolding* God on this of all days! It was fortunate that He who had created humans understood their frailties so well, he'd thought—not for the first time. That was another thing Rhobair Duchairn had helped him realize. That God *understood*. That He wasn't just the stern Lawgiver or the pitilessly just Judge of the *Book of Schueler*. That He was also the compassionate Father of the *Book of Bédard,* Who accepted human beings for who and what they were, frailties included, and wanted them to bring their problems and their doubts and, yes, even their *anger* to Him. If they didn't bring those things to Him, how could they let Him help them deal with them?

And as he'd thought about that lesson, as he'd bent his head in apology to God and his mind and heart heard not the thundering anathemas of Zhaspahr Clyntahn's God but rather the laughing sympathy of Rhobair Duchairn's, he'd realized the Good Shepherd hadn't needed clear skies. That it had been fitting, somehow, for him to go to his consecration through God's rain and wind, washing away the filth which fallible mankind had allowed to encrust His world and His Church. Despite the cold and the wet, the Plaza of Martyrs and every street and boulevard leading to the Temple's high, green hill had been packed by the people of Zion, by every child of God who could possibly reach the city, standing shoulder-to-shoulder, holding up children so they could see the man who'd brought down the Inquisition as he walked through that rain, bareheaded, to receive Langhorne's crown, and they hadn't cared. They hadn't *cared* that they were cold and wet, because they'd understood what they were seeing, realized what they'd become part of as they watched the procession pass.

So, no, Rhobair II hadn't needed sunlight and blue skies. He'd had something vastly more important than that.

Not that Tymythy Symkyn didn't appreciate them to the full, and he suspected the watching crowds didn't mind them one bit, either.

He actually chuckled at that thought, grateful for it. And then he drew another, still deeper breath, and felt the presence of God pour through his soul as he stepped through those silver-and-bronze gates into the enormous Plaza of Martyrs.

The sweeping, majestically proportioned steps ascended from the Plaza to the Temple itself, where graceful columns rose more than sixty feet to support the gleaming dome and the eighteen-foot solid gold icon of the Archangel Langhorne which topped it. The six-acre Plaza was large enough for scores of thousands of the faithful to gather on God's Day to hear the Grand Vicar's annual sermon, and, like the streets leading to it, today it was a solid ocean of humanity on either side of the central avenue cordoned by the Temple Guard for the procession to pass through. Their cheers faded into abrupt, reverent silence as the procession crossed the broad band of gold inlaid into the Plaza's marble at the foot of the Temple stairs and protected from centuries of foot traffic just as the floor of the Temple was. That band marked the formal boundary between the Plaza and the Temple proper, and he murmured a brief, familiar, heartfelt prayer of thanks that the Plaza had been restored to its pre-Jihad beauty and sanctity. His memory of the charred stakes, the grim pyres which had consumed so many of the Inquisition's victims, was only too clear, and he understood precisely why Rhobair Duchairn had made the Plaza's cleansing and restoration one of his most urgent priorities. Symkyn had been here, standing less than fifty yards from where he was at this moment, with sixty thousand other of the Faithful, as the newly consecrated Grand Vicar Rhobair II had conducted the open-air mass of contrition, formally acknowledging Mother Church's guilt for the atrocities committed here. And he'd been here when the plaque acknowledging those atrocities, memorializing their victims and beseeching God's forgiveness for the way in which they'd died, had been set into the façade of the central Fountain of Langhorne . . . and when Rhobair had rededicated and reconsecrated the Plaza to its original purpose.

But now Rhobair was gone, and Tymythy Symkyn felt very small, very frail, and more mortal than he'd felt in years as the procession started up those sweeping stairs through the ringing, reverent silence—burnished and perfected, not broken, by the laughter of the breeze and the pop of banners—and the moment roared towards him.

▼ ▼ ▼

The mighty doors of the Temple swept open. Not the smaller doors, set into those enormous bronze—only they weren't really bronze, Captain Karstayrs reflected—portals. These were the Doors of Langhorne themselves, forty feet high and covered from top to bottom with bas-relief representations of the Archangels in glory, which were opened only once each year, on God's Day, when the open air of God's world swept into every corner of the stupendous cathedral dedicated to His worship.

But they were also opened on one other occasion—the investiture and consecration of a new Grand Vicar. They were opened so that God might enter His house to witness as the newest heir of the Archangel Langhorne took up his Scepter in God's name.

No mere mortal could have opened those stupendous slabs of battle steel. Instead, they swept apart with ponderous, majestic grace as the Door Wardens pressed their hands to the glowing god lights, and a wordless sigh of renewed wonder and awe swept through the packed cathedral at the fresh evidence of God's finger moving in the world.

Samyl Karstayrs' face was impassive, but his built-in sensors detected the activation of additional electronics buried in the Temple's vaulted ceiling. And then, just below that ceiling, the air itself began to glow with a soft, golden radiance, a halo floating like a crown eighty feet above the crystoplast floor. Then the seals of the "Archangels" set into the lapis three inches below the crystoplast's surface began to glow, as well. The skylights in the dome, soaring to almost a hundred and sixty feet above the floor, were designed so that shafts of sunlight illuminated those seals, and powered mirrors made certain those columns of light stayed where they were supposed to be whenever the sun was in the heavens, despite its motion. But today, they were lit not with simple sunlight but with an inner illumination that glowed with all the colors of the seals themselves.

Those in the pews nearest the seals bowed their heads, signing themselves with Langhorne's Scepter, and it was harder for Karstayrs to maintain his impassivity as he watched them. No wonder these people had never doubted the truth of the *Holy Writ*! And no wonder that *Writ* mandated that every true child of God make the pilgrimage to the Temple at least once in his or her life. How else could they be properly indoctrinated with the physical *proof* that Mother Church did proclaim the will of God?

In many ways, that proof made it even more remarkable that Rhobair Duchairn's heart had rebelled against Zhaspahr Clyntahn's lunacy. Even at the height of the Jihad, the Temple itself—the god lights, the mystic walls, the perpetually maintained internal temperature—had never repudiated Clyntahn. They'd continued to function without so much as a flicker, and surely that had proved God approved of Clyntahn's war!

Yet Duchairn had rejected it because he'd decided the truth in his heart was more important, more valid, than any external validation. Perhaps he had been a member of the Group of Four. Perhaps he had played his own role in enabling the Jihad which had killed so many millions. And perhaps he *had* given all that devotion and faith to a religion built on the greatest single lie in human history. But Merlin Athrawes had been forced to accept that for all its lies, all the obscenity of its purpose, the men and women who embraced that religion truly did embrace God, however He'd been twisted by its creators. And Nimue Alban had been raised in a faith far older than that of Safehold. One that believed in true contrition, in redemption. One that validated Rhobair Duchairn far more brightly than any mirrored sunlight or glowing "angelic" seals ever could have.

And God we're going to miss him, Karstayrs thought now as that phalanx of vicars moved slowly, reverently, through those enormous opened doors. There were over three hundred vicars and half again that many archbishops in that column, and the Temple's opened doors were so vast they admitted the procession with ease. It moved down the central nave towards the altar at the heart of the circular cathedral, preceded by scepter-bearers and candle-bearers, by thurifers with their censers of fragrant incense, and by a hundred choristers whose voices rose in majestic, harmonious beauty the instant they crossed the threshold.

And at the heart of that procession, moving in a hollow open space, was a single man in magnificently embroidered vestments. Every vicar, every archbishop and bishop, in that procession wore the crowns and coronets of their priestly rank . . . except him. The bishops' coronets were simple golden circles. The archbishops' were more elaborate, crowns set with cut rubies whose facets caught the golden glow that coated the ceiling above them. The vicars' crowns were more elaborate still, set with sapphires, like the rings of office upon their fingers. But that one man's head bore not even a simple priest's cap, and as *he* passed over the threshold, a single brilliant circle of pure white light fell about him, turning the embroidery and gems of his vestments to glittering glory and moving as he moved, accompanying him along the aisle.

I wonder what would happen if they deviated from the choreography? The question passed through Karstayrs' mind. *The ceremony for the investiture of a Grand Vicar's never changed since the day Chihiro himself instituted it. How completely are the Temple's computers locked into observing it? Would that spotlight even be able to* find *the new Grand Vicar if he wasn't exactly where the ceremony laid down by Chihiro puts him?*

It was an intriguing thought. And if it were to happen, how would Safeholdians react? If the very things which made this so effective at maintaining their faith and their awareness of the sanctity of Mother Church and the Grand Vicar were suddenly out of sequence—if that circle of light followed someone else, instead of the Council of Vicars' chosen successor to Langhorne— how would *that* set with Safehold?

Too bad we won't have the chance to find out, he reflected. *Talk about the* Nahrmahn Plan! *If I thought Owl could hack the Temple, break into the system and reprogram all this . . . pageantry and turn it around on them. . . .*

He put the temptation behind him and focused on the ceremony unfolding all around him.

. II .
Grand Vicar's Apartment,
The Temple,
City of Zion,
The Temple Lands.

"Thank you, Father," the broad-shouldered, red-haired man in the simple cassock said, rising as his guests were escorted into the spacious office. His cassock was a dark, sapphire blue, almost the color of Merlin Athrawes' eyes, and he was the only man in the ranks of Mother Church's clerics permitted to wear it. The office itself was only one of several which had just become officially his, and it was furnished far more comfortably than some of those other, more formal offices.

"That will be all," he continued, and the upper-priest who'd served as guide paused as he straightened from his bow. He looked very much like a man whose eyebrows wanted to rise, but he controlled them with the ease of long practice, despite any unhappiness he might have felt.

"Of course, Your Holiness," he said instead, bending to kiss the ring extended to him. Its set was neither the single ruby of a bishop or an archbishop nor the single sapphire of a vicar. It was a massive sapphire circled in a band of tiny rubies and etched with the Scepter of Langhorne. Only one man in all the world was permitted to wear that ring, and it had been made and consecrated especially for him before it was slipped onto his finger the day before. On the day of his mortal death, it would be ceremoniously destroyed so that no one else might ever wear it.

The upper-priest withdrew with a courteous nod to the guests he'd escorted into the Grand Vicar's presence, and the red-haired man behind the desk smiled after him, then shook his head.

"I'm afraid Father Vyncyt has a few doubts about leaving me alone in your presence, Your Eminence," Grand Vicar Tymythy Rhobair said, and Maikel Staynair smiled back at him.

"I trust you don't think I'm surprised by that, Your Holiness?"

"No. No, it was quite obvious you weren't. Please, sit!"

Tymythy Rhobair waved the hand which bore that glittering ring—the ring he hadn't extended for Maikel Staynair or Bryahn Ushyr to kiss—at the chairs facing his desk. The Charisians obeyed the invitation, and Ushyr twitched as the surface of his chair shifted to conform perfectly to the contours of his body.

Staynair took the movement in stride without any outward sign of surprise, as befitted someone twice the age of anyone else in the office. He also suppressed a flicker of amusement as he watched Ushyr. The bishop's reaction was perfect, despite the fact that he'd sat in chairs exactly like these in Nimue's Cave on more than one occasion.

"Forgive me, Bishop Bryahn," the Grand Vicar said with genuine apology. "It's been a . . . stressful day or two, and I'm afraid I forgot this is your first visit to the Temple. Normally we try to warn people about things like that."

"That's perfectly all right, Your Holiness," Ushyr replied. "Actually, it's not my first visit, although it is the first time I've visited Zion since my ordination. And I'm afraid I'm one of those priests who went to one of the more provincial, shall we say, seminaries." He smiled briefly. "So aside from my pilgrimage mass, this is the first time I've been inside the Temple proper. It's certainly the first time I ever expected to be sitting in one of the Temple's chairs! I *was* warned, of course. There seems to be a bit of a difference between being warned and actually experiencing it, however."

"There is, indeed, My Lord," Tymythy Rhobair said dryly. "I remember the first time I experienced it for myself quite well." He smiled back, but then he settled into his own chair and the smile faded. "In fact, one of the reasons I invited you—invited you both—to this meeting was to apologize for the fact that you weren't quartered in 'the Temple proper.'"

"I assure you, Your Holiness, that we took no affront," Staynair said. "We are, after all, schismatics. I'm sure it would've been very upsetting to many of the faithful laity—and quite a few of your Vicars, for that matter—if we'd been assigned an apartment inside the Temple, and we couldn't have been more comfortable in the quarters you did make available to us."

"I appreciate your understanding, Your Eminence," Tymythy Rhobair said. "And it's nothing less than I would've expected of you, given your reputation and the correspondence I was privileged to maintain with you as Mother Church's Chancellor. Despite that, the apology was in order. The initial housing assignments were made by Bishop Rahzhyr in the Office of Protocol. He's a good man, and I truly believe that in his own heart and mind, he fully embraces the belief that all of God's children simply have to learn to get along once more. But he had to deal with some . . . interesting constraints, and as a mere Grand Vicar *designate*, I hesitated to overrule him. All of which is true, but leaves out the minor fact that I think my nerve failed just a bit. I know what the Grand Vicar—Grand Vicar Rhobair, I mean—would have done, and I regret beginning my own Grand Vicarate with a moment of weakness."

"You may call it a moment of weakness if you wish, Your Holiness, but I think the term is too harsh." Staynair's tone was serene as he gently corrected the head of Langhorne's Church on earth. "The *Writ* may tell us the Grand Vicar speaks with the infallible word of God from Langhorne's throne, but any perusal of *The Commentaries* reassures us that in other settings, he's allowed to make mistakes or even, as in this case, an accommodation with the pragmatic aspects of our unprecedented situation. Frankly, I think Bishop Rahzhyr was wise. I'm sure you created quite enough uproar within the Vicarate when you invited me to attend your elevation at all!"

"No doubt I did." Tymythy Rhobair tipped back in his chair, blue eyes intent. "On the other hand, Grand Vicar Rhobair told me several times that one of his regrets was that he'd been unable to invite you to *his* elevation. I decided that was one regret I wasn't going to entertain. And even more importantly, I was indeed thinking about those 'pragmatic aspects of our unprecedented situation.' I'm afraid I used your invitation to send a message."

"Of course you did." Staynair chuckled gently. "Your Holiness, I haven't corresponded with you for so many years without realizing why Rhobair Duchairn picked a 'simple soldier' as his Chancellor. And while I'm certain you felt more than a few qualms when your name was placed in nomination as his successor, I genuinely can't imagine anyone he'd be more satisfied to see sitting in your chair."

"I hope you're right about that," Tymythy Rhobair said seriously. "And I hope God will speak as clearly and unambiguously to me as He did to Grand Vicar Rhobair. And that I'll *listen* as well as he did, for that matter. His death left a huge hole. Trying to fill it is a . . . daunting task."

"I'm sure." Staynair nodded. He also refrained from pointing out that Tymythy Rhobair's choice of names upon his acceptance of the Scepter had sent a message in its own right. He was only the third Grand Vicar in the Church of God Awaiting's history to assume Langhorne's Throne with more than a single name, and like both of those other Grand Vicars, he'd done it to underscore his determination to continue his immediate predecessor's policies.

"I won't lie to you, Your Eminence," Tymythy Rhobair continued. "There are many vicars who continue to cherish reservations about the status of the Church of Charis and its relationship to Mother Church. Vicar Zherohmy, one of my most valued aides, is one of them, although his reservations are substantially weaker than those of some of the other vicars. For that matter, even I have some reservations. I'm sure you'll understand when I say that schism among the children of God can never be a good thing, no matter how sincere those on either side of that schism may be."

"Schism may be regrettable, Your Holiness," Staynair replied calmly, "but it may also sometimes be *necessary*. Without the schism between Charis and Zion, Zhaspahr Clyntahn's perversion of all Mother Church was created to be would have continued unabated." He met Tymythy Rhobair's eyes levelly. "And the ferocity of the Jihad and especially the . . . excesses of Clyntahn's Inquisition made it impossible to heal that schism by the time the guns fell silent again at last. We may regret that. We may *weep* over that, and there are times I do just that. Yet despite any regret we all may feel, I fail to see any way to heal it at this time, no matter how sincere the faith on either side of it may be."

"Nor do I," Tymythy Rhobair admitted. "Having corresponded with you and now met you in person, I find it easier to understand the degree of moral authority you wield in the Church of Charis. If anyone *could* heal the schism, it would probably be you, but that would exceed even your power in Charis. And I greatly fear that if I were to proclaim the schism healed from Langhorne's Throne it would prove a point you've made more than once. The *Writ* tells us the Grand Vicar speaks infallibly only when he speaks in accordance with the word of the *Writ* and when touched by the spirit of God. So far, I've found nothing in the *Writ* that condones schism, yet I find nothing in the spirit of God that would condone any effort on my part to force Charis back into the fold. Surely the outcome of the Jihad seems to indicate that wasn't what *He* had in mind, and who am I to argue with Him?"

The Grand Vicar's tone was whimsical, but those blue eyes were very steady.

"He does seem to have set us an interesting puzzle, doesn't He?" Staynair smiled quizzically.

"I'm sure that in the fullness of time He'll get around to un-puzzling us," Tymythy Rhobair said. "In the meantime, I'm equally sure He doesn't want us killing each other in His name. I think that's one of the things the Jihad made fairly clear, as well. And, speaking of not killing each other, I'd like to take this opportunity to thank you in person for the Church of Charis' efforts in Harchong." His expression darkened. "I can't tell you how much I hate and regret the reasons Mother Church *needed* your assistance, but you personally and all of your priests and lay missionaries have done far more than we could have expected from you. And I know from the reports of Mother Church's clergy and laity who've worked with you that your people have refrained from actively proselytizing. I know that must've been very difficult, and that the only way it could've happened was for you to have made it a part of your instructions. Of course," his lips twitched in a brief smile, "I also know example is the strongest form of proselytization. Langhorne knows Mother Church's orders have been using it against each other for centuries, and none of them ever had this sort of horrible opportunity. For that matter," his expression was very serious once more, "Mother Church herself, or at least the Church of Harchong, was instrumental in creating that 'opportunity.' I will thank God for every life you saved, every soul you convinced to believe God truly cares about even the poorest of His children, whichever Church they embrace. Would I prefer Mother Church had done that? Infinitely! But I can only rejoice if you've been able to do it where she can't."

"Your Holiness, you're right to call that opportunity 'horrible,' and I know the Church of Rhobair Duchairn—or of Grand Vicar Tymythy Rhobair—played no part in creating it. This is an echo—pray God, the *last* echo—of the poisons which created Zhaspahr Clyntahn and allowed him to do so much damage. Grand Vicar Rhobair made draining those poisons the great task of his life, and it seems to me he's found a worthy successor, at least in that regard. I thought that from the moment I heard of your nomination. I can't possibly tell you how deeply and devoutly grateful I am to see and hear it confirmed."

"I don't know if I'll prove a worthy successor in the end, Your Eminence, but I intend to try. I've had too many examples to settle for anything less. And not just Grand Vicar Rhobair. I had the honor of serving my first two years in the Temple Guard under Hauwerd Wylsynn's command. I had the even greater honor of calling him my *friend* for years after that." Tymythy Rhobair shook his head. "When Zhaspahr Clyntahn purged him and Vicar Samyl and all their friends, I was one of many who truly realized—who could no longer deny to ourselves—that Clyntahn's God had far more in common with Shan-wei than with Langhorne. Like too many of us, I saw nothing I could do about it. For that matter, and to be completely honest, I had no idea *what* to do about it. I was too deeply caught between my faith in God and the Archangels, my loyalty to Mother Church, the Inquisition's distortion of what the Church of Charis was truly saying, and my own physical and moral fear to find a way to oppose Clyntahn. I couldn't see as clearly as Grand Vicar Rhobair did."

"Very few people could," Staynair said. "And fewer still were in a position to act. I never knew Rhobair Duchairn before the Jihad, but the depth and the scope of that man's spiritual journey are breathtaking."

"A judgment which means even more coming from you," Tymythy Rhobair replied. "However, even if my journey hasn't been quite as breathtaking as his, the work's fallen into my hands. Vicar Haarahld is assuming my old position as Chancellor, at least for now. He has sufficient reservations about the schism himself for me to doubt he'll find it a comfortable position, but he understands God never promised to make us comfortable, and I believe his reservations will only make him even more attentive to his responsibilities. And among those responsibilities will be to facilitate communication between you and myself. What we've accomplished jointly in Harchong leads me to hope we can find other opportunities to work together to build trust and acceptance. In the short term, that will probably only . . . solidify the schism, I'm afraid, by making it more acceptable from both sides. Unfortunately, I believe that before we can become brothers again we must at least stop seeing one another as enemies and rivals, and serving God together is the best way I can think of to accomplish that."

"Truer words were never spoken, Your Holiness," Staynair said sincerely. "And I believe we've made a substantial start in that direction. Not just in Harchong, but here in this office. In the courtesy which has been shown to me, to Bishop Bryahn, to every member of my staff here in Zion in a situation I know has been extremely difficult for a great many of Mother Church's sons and daughters."

"It has. I doubt it was any less difficult for the Church

of Charis, however. And, in that regard, may I ask a personal question?"

"Of course."

"How is Bishop Paityr? I'd hoped he might accompany you to Zion, but I can't say I was honestly surprised when he didn't."

"Bishop Paityr is well," Staynair replied. "What happened to his father and his uncle and so many of his friends and relatives in the Temple Lands left scars, of course. The fact that his stepmother and his brothers and sisters all escaped to Charis helps in that regard, but what's helped even more are the opportunities God's given him to serve Him in Charis. I can tell you of my own certain knowledge that his faith is unshaken and that he's come through this ordeal even stronger than he went into it. And as I'm sure you know better than most, his strength and integrity have always been greater than most."

"I'm glad—very glad," Tymythy Rhobair told him. "Tell him that for me, please. I wish I'd been able to say it to him in person."

"Your Holiness, he's not quite ready to return to Zion, but that has less to do with unhealed wounds—although, in all honesty, not all those wounds *are* healed, even yet—than with his fear of the reaction the return of a Wylsynn to Zion might provoke. Especially the return of a Wylsynn who's served the Church of Charis so long and so well. There are some situations he thinks need not be tested just yet, and I find myself in agreement with him." The archbishop smiled suddenly. "You ran risk enough inviting an *Out Islander* who broke with Mother Church. God only knows how your clergy would react if you'd invited a scion of one of the Temple Lands' great 'dynasties' who'd done the same thing!"

"You're probably right. *He* was probably right." Tymythy Rhobair nodded. "But please tell him for me that if the day ever comes when he does feel ready to revisit Zion, he has a permanent invitation. He remains my brother in God and the son and nephew of two men I will always deeply respect. Tell him that."

"I will," Staynair assured him. "Just as I'll tell him I believe God's blessed us with someone who I'm confident—whatever *his* doubts may be—will indeed prove a worthy successor to the Good Shepherd of Zion."

. III .
Sochal,
Tiegelkamp Province,
North Harchong.

"—don't like the sound of that, Your Grace. I don't like it at all. And another thing that bothers me is that—"

Lord of Foot Laurahn broke off and looked up as Hwadai Pyangzhow entered her husband's office. Hwadai would have liked to think that represented courtesy on his part. It didn't. Zhailau Laurahn was capable of courtesy, although it didn't come naturally to him, but it was Kaihwei Pyangzhow's quick gesture which had stopped him.

"Yes, my dear? What can I do for you? I'm afraid the Lord of Foot and I are rather busy just now."

"Yes, I see that," she replied. "Actually, I was looking for Pozhi. We need to go over those storehouse accounts. I checked his office, but he wasn't there."

"Well, he's not here, either," her husband said. "If he isn't in his office, try the winter store. If he's not there, he's probably out with the harvest masters. If he is, send one of the stableboys out with a note to tell them you need to see him."

He looked at her, one eyebrow raised, obviously impatient to return to his conversation with Laurahn, and she bit her lip against a sharp retort.

"Of course," she said coolly, then gave the lord of foot a graceful nod and withdrew, closing the door behind her.

She stood with her hand on the latch for a moment,

then straightened her spine, drew herself up to her full five feet three, and turned away. Her rich, elegant skirts made a gentle rustling sound as she walked down the carpeted hallway, and paintings looked down upon her as she passed. She didn't know any of the people in those paintings, just as she had no idea—and was pretty sure she *wanted* no idea—where the expensive plates and solid silver flatware which graced her dining table had come from. She was reasonably confident the golden candelabras in her bedchamber had once belonged to a church somewhere, although she couldn't prove it, and the light coronet her husband insisted she wear everywhere looked suspiciously like something a bishop might have worn on an occasion which was only semiformal.

She hated it. She hated this house—which wasn't hers; God only knew what had happened to the people who'd once owned it—and she hated the rich clothing. She hated those paintings, not one of which was of anyone remotely related to her or her husband. She hated hearing someone call her "Your Grace" and she hated what she knew her husband had done to gain her that honorific.

She paused, looking out a window over manicured lawns and autumn-colorful shrubbery, clenched hands concealed in the folds of her skirt, and her eyes were bleak. Two years ago she'd been a simple "My Lady," and she'd thought she was unhappy then. She'd learned better since.

She drew a deep breath, squaring her shoulders, commanding herself not to weep, and remembered the despair she'd felt the day her father told her who she would marry. She hadn't known Kaihwei Pyangzhow, Baron Spring Flower, very well—they'd met less than half a dozen times—but his reputation had preceded him. Gently reared maidens weren't supposed to know about what happened with comely young serf women. They especially weren't supposed to know about what happened if the comely young serf women in question were unwilling. That didn't mean they didn't.

But he'd been a baron. Not much of a baron, perhaps,

with only a small estate, but still a baron, and her father had been a simple country squire. A relatively wealthy one, without any sons to pass his wealth to, yet merely a squire, with no hint of a connection to the aristocracy, when he longed to be so much more. But he *had* had daughters, her father. And so he'd sold one of them so that he could talk about his son-in-law the baron . . . and Pyangzhow had bought her with his title to gain her father's wealth.

It hadn't been all that bad a marriage. Not by the standards of many arranged Harchongese marriages, at any rate. She knew women who'd been far unhappier than she, and aside from an occasional conjugal visit to beget heirs, he'd left her to design her own life within the constraints of their marriage. He'd even treated her with relative courtesy, at least in front of others.

But then the whole world had gone insane, and he—

She bit that thought off, shook her head once, angrily, and set off once more in pursuit of Kangdyng Pozhi, her husband's chief bailiff.

▼ ▼ ▼

"I see no reason to disturb Her Grace with any . . . unpleasant details," Duke Spring Flower said as the door closed behind the duchess.

"Of course not, Your Grace," Zhailau Laurahn murmured, bending his head briefly.

"And from what you've been telling me, I'm afraid some of those details are going to be *quite* unpleasant," Spring Flower continued, frowning down at the map unrolled on the large, beautifully carved desk between them. "We can't have these . . . people bidding defiance to my authority. And to the Emperor's express commands, of course."

"As you say, Your Grace." Laurahn looked down at the map, then tapped it with a fingertip. "It looks as if the real problem is coming out of the mountains, here."

"Fucking mountain rats," Spring Flower muttered, and Laurahn nodded.

The lord of foot's finger rested between the city of

Zhyndow, on the eastern flank of the Chiang-wu Mountains, and the village of Ranlai, on the road between Sochal and Zhyndow. It would have been inaccurate to call it a high road, but it was better than most Harchongese secondary roads because Zhyndow had been more prosperous—and larger—than most mountain towns. The operative word was "had," however. Today it was a sea of burned-out, deserted, scavenger-haunted ruins.

Ranlai was far smaller than Zhyndow had once been—Laurahn doubted its population had ever exceeded four or five hundred—but with Zhyndow's demise, it had become the closest town to the Chynduk Valley, which twisted its way for over four hundred and fifty miles along the sinuous trace of the Chynduk River, from Ky-su, in the north, to Zhyndow, in the south. It was also the marketplace to which the mountaineers from the Valley brought their produce, now that Zhyndow was gone.

There were at least half a dozen towns considerably larger than Ranlai inside the Valley, however, threaded along the Chynduk and Haishyng, its eastern tributary. There were also dozens of smaller farming villages and hamlets tucked away in the mountains' steep-sided coves, because for all its isolation the Chynduk Valley had always been more prosperous than many another swath of Harchong. That prosperity made the people living in those towns and villages and hamlets a potentially lucrative source of taxes and "emergency levies" to help quell the rebellions and brigandage convulsing the Empire, yet they seemed disinclined to place themselves under Duke Spring Flower's benevolent protection.

Which, Laurahn conceded with cynical amusement, was understandable enough. Unfortunately, it was his job to teach them to be more reasonable. Or, at the very least, to keep their lack of reasonableness from contaminating the more tractable towns—like Ranlai—closer to Sochal and Fangkau by example.

"I ought to send you in there to clear them out once and for all," Spring Flower growled.

"Nothing would give me greater pleasure Your Grace," Laurahn lied, controlling a shudder at the thought. "But you're right when you call them 'mountain rats,' and that valley is Shan-wei's own rathole. They'd only scurry up into the mountains and wait until we left, I'm afraid."

"Maybe during the summer." Spring Flower frowned, fingers caressing the heavy links of the golden chain around his neck. "But what about *winter*, Zhailau?"

"A winter campaign in the Chiang-wus would be brutal, Your Grace," Laurahn said with considerable understatement. "I'd probably lose more men to weather than to enemy action."

"Yes, yes, yes!" The duke waved his hand impatiently. "I *understand* that. But these bastards have to have barns somewhere, don't they? Winter pastures?"

"Well, yes, Your Grace," Laurahn said slowly.

"Then suppose they were to 'scurry up' the slopes . . . and looked down to see you burning all their food just at the start of winter." Spring Flower smiled unpleasantly. "Suppose you did that to a town or two—like Zhutiyan—and the farms around them, say. Don't you think that might . . . inspire the rest of the whoreson bastards to be more reasonable?"

"Yes, I believe it would," the lord of foot agreed.

"And if it didn't, you could always burn the rest of them out, one farm at a time," Spring Flower added coldly, and Laurahn nodded.

Of course, most of the people living along the Chynduk would starve if he burned their barns. But Shan-wei knew enough other peasants had starved over the last winter and more would follow them this winter. A few thousand—or a few *score* thousand—more would make little difference, and their desperation would let Spring Flower pick and choose who among them he might decide to feed in return for their submission.

And it *would* get the duke's point across to the towns he already controlled.

"There are a few steps we should probably take in the next five-day or two if that's what you wish me to do, Your Grace," he said after a moment. "In particular, I'll have to stage my own supplies up into the Valley. I could probably forage off those barns before we burn them, but I can't count on that, and it's almost a hundred and fifty miles from here to Zhutiyan. Without Zyhndow as a forward supply point, I'll need a base closer to the Valley, especially for a winter campaign in the mountains. And, to be honest, the sooner we start making preparations the better." He looked up, meeting the duke's eyes. "There won't be much time to get this arranged between now and first snowfall, I'm afraid."

"Well, since Ranlai's still buying their wheat despite my orders to the contrary, why don't you use that for your base?" Spring Flower smiled unpleasantly. "I warned the mayor and his precious town council about that. You can go arrest the lot of them and send them back to Sochal to discuss that with me in person—briefly." His smile turned even colder. "And it wouldn't do to warn the rats we plan to put a ferret down their rathole once the harvest is in. So you could take along a few hundred of your men to take the offenders into custody and then leave them there—purely as a 'show of force'—and establish patrols between there and Zhyndow to keep anyone from sneaking up into the mountains to tell them when your supplies begin arriving at your new base."

"That . . . should work, Your Grace," Laurahn said after a moment, carefully concealing his unhappiness.

It was possible the duke's plan would work; it was more likely it wouldn't, although he had no intention of telling Spring Flower that. The duke had no military background or experience, and that meant he had no idea what sending troops into the mountains on the eve of a high northern winter would be like. Even if he had known, he wouldn't have cared any more than he—or Laurahn himself, the lord of foot acknowledged—cared about what would happen to the mountain peasants if it succeeded. If it *didn't* succeed, however, Laurahn knew who'd be blamed for it, and it wouldn't be the winter weather.

"With your permission, Your Grace, I need to go discuss this with Chaiyang," he said. "Off the top of my head, I don't see any insurmountable difficulties," which didn't mean he couldn't manufacture some if Hanbai Chaiyang and he were sufficiently inventive, "but we'll have to do some reorganizing to free up the strikeforce we'll need. Frankly, the Sergeant Major has a better feel for how our more effective troops are distributed at the moment."

. IV .
Zhutiyan,
Chynduk Valley,
Tiegelkamp Province,
North Harchong.

Tangwyn Syngpu kept his face impassive as he followed Baisung Tsungshai up the steps into the Zhutiyan town hall. As town halls went, Zhutiyan's wasn't all that impressive. Certainly he'd seen far grander ones, not only in Siddarmark with the Mighty Host but even here in Harchong. The Zhutiyan town hall had one advantage over most of those he'd seen recently, however.

It hadn't been burned down.

A small group of four people, one of them a woman, waited for them at the head of the stairs. He reached the top, and one of the men stepped forward.

"Commander Syngpu?" he asked, and Syngpu nodded. A lot of his followers thought he should embrace what seemed to be the current trend and proclaim himself "Lord of Foot Syngpu," or even "Lord of *Horse* Syngpu," but he was a *sergeant,* not a damned general! "Commander" seemed a workable compromise.

"Yes," he said simply, returning the other man's slight bow with what he knew was a less polished one of his own.

"I am Zaipau Ou-zhang, Mayor of Zhutiyan. I bid you welcome on behalf of the city."

"Thank you," Syngpu replied, and he meant it.

Ou-zhang was tall but rather frail looking, with silvering hair and a deeply lined face. The man standing at his right shoulder was perhaps an inch shorter, but he was also at least ten years younger, with broad shoulders, and there wasn't a trace of white in his black hair. The third man was a white-haired, rather worn-looking fellow in the blue cassock of an under-priest of the Order of Chihiro of the Quill. The woman was the shortest of the four, a good eight inches shorter than Syngpu, with a slight build, the delicate bone structure of a wind hummer, and a face which was attractive but far from beautiful. Her head barely topped her male companions' shoulders and she couldn't have weighed much over a hundred pounds—if that—but there was nothing *fragile* about her.

"This is Squire Gyngdau," Ou-zhang continued, indicating the broad-shouldered man, "and his sister-in-law, Madam Gyngdau." The woman inclined her head briefly. "And this is Father Yngshwan, our senior parish priest." The mayor smiled thinly. "He's been sort of our acting bishop since his more senior fellows followed Archbishop Zhau south a year or so ago. I'm sure they'll be back any day now."

Syngpu felt his eyes widen slightly, despite his determination to let his face give nothing away, at the caustic bite in Ou-zhang's last sentence, but Father Yngshwan only shook his head and clicked his tongue at the mayor.

"I welcome you in the name of Mother Church's true sons, Commander," he said, looking at Syngpu. "And I should point out that my good friend the Mayor neglected to mention that almost everyone *junior* to my humble self is still at his post, right here in the Valley."

"And every one of you excommunicated by that bastard Zhau before he hightailed it," Ou-zhang grated.

"Which has no effect unless validated by the Grand Vicar," Father Yngshwan pointed out serenely. "Under the circumstances, I fail to feel hell's breath on the back of my neck, Zaipau. If Shan-wei is breathing anywhere, I suspect it's upon more highly placed necks than my own, and I wouldn't care to own one of *those* necks at the end of the day." He laid a hand on the mayor's shoulder and squeezed lightly. "We have rather weightier matters to consider now that the Commander is here, however."

"Truer words were never spoken, Father," Gyngdau said, speaking for the first time. His voice was deep and the hand he extended to Syngpu was well manicured but strong, the hand of a man who'd been known to work his own fields at need. "I hope this is going to work out, Commander," he said frankly. "For a lot of reasons."

"We'll just have to see what we can do about making that happen, then, Squire," Syngpu replied, clasping forearms with him, and Ou-zhang waved for him and Tsungshai to accompany them into the town hall.

▼ ▼ ▼

Syngpu felt out of place in the mayor's office.

The view through its windows was spectacular, looking northwest up the steep slopes which trended steadily upward towards the distant blue majesty of Mount Kydyn's towering peak. Kydyn stood more than sixty miles west of the town, rising like a seventy-mile-wide giant as part of the Chynduk Valley's God-created parapet.

Zhutiyan itself sat on a small rise, high enough to be above the inevitable spring floods, in a bend of the deep, fast-flowing Chynduk River from which the valley took its name. The river's floodplain was about thirty miles wide at this point, dotted with patches of forest painted with fall's bright colors and wide rectangles of wheat fields and cornfields enclosed by moss-grown stone walls which must have taken centuries to pile in place. The corn was long gone, as were most of the farmers' other crops as winter drew steadily closer, and teams of men and women with rythmically swinging scythes were harvesting the wheat as he watched.

And that was the true reason he felt so out of place. It wasn't the shelved books, the whiskey bottle and glasses, the curtains on either side of that double-paned window, the ceramic-tiled stove in one corner, waiting for winter. It wasn't even the painting on the wall facing the mayor's desk—a painting of a much younger Ou-zhang and a slim, smiling woman in a traditional Harchongese wedding gown. Syngpu was a peasant, and he'd never owned anything nearly so fine as what he saw about him in this provincial mayor's office. But the scene out that window—the peacefulness, the order, the sense of something almost like tranquility as those people gathered their crops. That was what made him feel so out of place, because it was something he hadn't seen in far too long.

"I'm sure you can understand that there's a certain . . . uneasiness on the part of many of our friends and neighbors, Commander," Squire Gyngdau said, after the whiskey had been poured and they'd sat back in their chairs.

"Be surprised if there wasn't," Syngpu said frankly. "That," he waved his glass at the view from the window, "is hard to believe, after what I've seen over the last year." He shook his head, letting the grimness flow into his eyes, the set of his mouth. "After what I've seen for a long time, now. First with the Mighty Host, and now right here."

Madam Gyngdau sat behind the mayor's desk, quill pen poised to take notes, but she cocked her head, looking up at his words, and her expression was thoughtful.

"Did I have *that*," Syngpu waved his glass again, "I'd be thinking three or four times—more like a score, really—before I was inviting a lot of men with guns into the midst of it."

"Well, that's rather the crux of the problem, isn't it?" The squire's smile was small, tart, but genuine. "From what we're hearing, quite a lot of other men with guns are thinking about inviting *themselves* 'into the midst of it.'"

"Not 'a lot' of other men, Miyang," Mayor Ou-zhang growled. "That unmitigated bastard Spring Flower!" He grimaced, glancing at Madam Gyngdau. "Pardon the language, Yanshwyn."

"I am shocked—*shocked*—that you should use such language to describe the Duke not merely in the presence of a lady but of a sanctified servant of the Archangels such as myself, as well!" Father Yngshwan scolded, and Ou-zhang snorted.

"Forgive me, Father. I meant to describe him as 'that Shan-wei–damned, mother-loving, carrion-eating, slime maggot's bastard Spring Flower.'"

"*Much* better, my son," the priest said, signing a benevolent Scepter, and Madam Gyngdau's lips twitched.

"I can't argue with that characterization," her brother-in-law said, and cocked his head at Syngpu. "Can I ask how much Master Tsungshai's already told you about our situation, Commander?"

It was interesting, Syngpu thought. The squire had attached the honorific "master" to young Baisung as if a mere peasant actually deserved it. It hadn't sounded like a concession on his part, either, and he filed that away beside what he'd already learned about Gyngdau from other sources.

"He's told me a lot about the Valley," Syngpu replied after a moment. "Not so much about Spring Flower and the rest. He's been away for a while."

Gyngdau nodded at the generous understatement.

In fact, Baisung Tsungshai had found himself employed as an artificer in the Jai-hu manufactory when Syngpu ambushed Captain of Horse Nyangzhi's column and captured the rifles which had made the fall of Shang-mi possible. In fact, almost a quarter of those rifles had borne Tsungshai's inspection stamp. Jai-hu was a long way from home for a peasant—well over four hundred miles as a wyvern might fly; at least twice or three times that far as mere humans traveled—but he hadn't been given a choice about relocating. The Chynduk Foundry, where he'd learned his trade, had been shut down shortly after the Jihad when there'd been no more orders for Chynduk's rifles. The reason those orders had dried up when the Imperial Army so desperately needed new, modern weapons had been obvious, of course. Its owners hadn't been aristocrats—not even lowly *barons*—and no one could waste such an opportunity for graft on mere commoners.

Technically, Tsungshai, like virtually everyone born in the Chynduk Valley, was a freeborn peasant, not a serf, but that hadn't mattered when the Crown ordered him to Jai-hu to ply his trade in the gun-making manufactory there, instead.

That manufactory no longer existed. Like most of the rest of Jai-hu, it had burned to the ground, much to Syngpu's regret. There was no way he could have kept it in production for very long, given how the Rebellion had interrupted deliveries of steel and coal, but he wished with all his heart that he'd gotten his hands on it before the tooling—and several thousand barrel blanks and rifle stocks—were destroyed.

Tsungshai had made a worthwhile addition even without the manufactory, however. Not only was he the perfect choice to teach a horde of barely literate serfs and peasants how to maintain their weapons, but he was also smart and well-educated for a peasant. In fact, he was considerably better educated than a shepherd boy from Thomas Province named Tangwyn Syngpu. If Syngpu had been tempted to promote himself to lord of foot, Tsungshai would have to be at least a captain of foot—more probably a captain of horse—and the boy was loyal, too. That counted.

"I'll be honest," Syngpu said now. "What young Baisung had to say's the real reason we've come to this side of the Chiang-wus." He shook his head slowly. "Last winter . . . last winter was bad. Lost a good third of my men, and not more than half of 'em because they just decided to go home."

The ghosts of the men he'd lost to frostbite and starvation flittered through his eyes, and Madam Gyngdau looked up at him again. He didn't notice.

"Over the summer, we got our numbers back up. Not as much as we could've if we'd recruited hard, but I won't take a man as doesn't have someone I trust to vouch for him. And we've attracted Langhorne's own camp followers! Not just whores, either." He glanced apologetically at Madam Gyngdau as he used the noun, but she only waved her left hand dismissively while her right kept scratching notes. "These're good women, for the most part. Most of 'em're mothers, really. And more'n a couple of them are a right sight 'better born' than they want to admit these days, I'm thinking. We've looked after 'em. Not going to pretend it's all been out of the goodness of my boys' hearts, Father." He looked at the priest. "Been some 'arrangements' made, and some of the women haven't earned their keep cooking or washing, if you know what I mean. But we've looked after them. Long as they're with us, they're *safe,* and they know it."

"My son, if they are, it's because you and your men have made them that way," Father Yngshwan said quietly. "I'll worry about *venial* sins when this is all over."

Syngpu nodded in acknowledgment, then looked back at Squire Gyngdau and the mayor.

"It's those women—them and their kids—have me worried, really," he said. "They're my responsibility now, and I'm not sure I could get 'em through another winter like the last on my own." He paused, then shook his head. "No, that's not true. I *know* I can't. So when Baisung told me about the Valley, suggested you might need someone like us, I had to find out. That's when I sent my first messenger. Didn't have any idea about this Spring Flower of yours. I was just looking for a way to keep those kids alive."

His burly, powerful shoulders started to sag, but he squared them stubbornly as he faced the three far better-dressed, far better-educated men in that office and admitted his need. Silence hung as all four of his hosts looked at one another. Then, almost as one, they nodded. Yet Syngpu noticed that it was neither the squire nor the mayor, nor even Father Yngshwan, who nodded first; it was *Madam* Gyngdau, nodding to the priest.

"How many men do you have under your command?" the squire asked.

"Baisung?" Syngpu looked at the younger man, and Tsungshai pulled a battered notebook out of his tunic.

"As of the first of the five-day, we counted just over forty-two hundred effectives," he said, consulting the pages. "We have half again that many rifles with no one to carry them." His eyes, too, were dark as he recalled the grim winter which had created that imbalance. "And currently we've got seven hundred and three women . . . and one thousand seven hundred and twelve children." He cleared his throat. "Over two hundred of them are orphans," he added quietly.

Madam Gyngdau's pen faltered for a moment as he read off the numbers. She bent more deeply over her own notes, and Syngpu thought she might be biting her lip before the quill started scratching again.

"That's a lot of mouths to add right on the brink of winter." The squire held Syngpu's eyes levelly, but the ex-sergeant refused to look away. A second passed, then two, and then Gyngdau nodded with what might almost have been approval.

"We'll work our way," Syngpu said then. "I think you know what we're really bringing to the dance, but every one of my boys was a farmer or a shepherd or a miner before he found a rifle in his hands, too. Give 'em work to do, *honest* work, and you won't regret it."

"You know, I believe you're right," Gyngdau said. He smiled slightly, but then his expression turned grim. "I believe you're right, but the truth is, we've got enough farmers, and enough shepherds. I won't say we can't use more, but right this minute what we really need is something else."

"Figured you might when I sent that first message."

"But I doubt you realized how *badly* we'd need that something else," the mayor said.

"Or that your reputation preceded you," Father Yngshwan put in. Syngpu looked at him, and the priest shrugged. "I won't say anyone was putting you and your men up for *seijin*hood, Commander. But young Baisung's not the only Valley boy to make his way back to us since the Rebellion started. From what some of the others have had to say, it sounds like you've spent as much time hanging *peasant* rapists as aristocrats."

"A rapist's a rapist, Father," Pauyin Syngpu's father said grimly, his eyes like fire-cored ice. "Same thing's true for any man who's what the Bédardists call a 'sadist.' Didn't really know that word 'fore I joined the Mighty Host. Learned it in Tarikah. Didn't really need a label for it, though, and it doesn't much matter what you call him. Don't care how he's dressed; don't care how he talks, either. Langhorne didn't die and make me God, but there's some things a man's got to face when they fall in his way."

"I'll pray to the Archangel Bédard to ease that burden on your soul, my son," Father Yngshwan said quietly, his worn face serene and his voice calm. "For now, though, what matters is that a man with your reputation, and fighters with the reputation your men have, aren't going to suddenly turn into rapists themselves if someone offers them a winter roof and food in their bellies."

"No, Father." Syngpu faced him unflinchingly. "No, they aren't."

"That's good," Gyngdau said, "because we need experienced fighters, and we really need fighters with *rifles,* not just bows and slings."

"So I understand." Syngpu sat back in his chair, his expression still grim but his heart soaring as he realized he'd just been told his men *would* be offered "a winter roof and food in their bellies" for themselves and, even more importantly, the women and children for whom they'd made themselves responsible. "I take it that's where this Spring Flower comes in?"

"You take it correctly, Commander," Mayor Ou-zhang said. "*'Duke'* Spring Flower doesn't share your view of rapists and sadists."

"In fairness—and, believe me, my son, it pains me to be fair in this case—Spring Flower was no worse than most other petty nobles before the Rebellion," Father Yngshwan said.

"Well, he's made up for it since, Yngshwan!" Ou-zhang said tartly, and the priest nodded.

"Duke Spring Flower was *Baron* Spring Flower before the Rebellion," he continued, turning back to Syngpu.

"Not much of a baron, either, when you come down to it."

"What he means, Commander, is that Miyang here—" the mayor twitched his head in the squire's direction "—held more land than the entire 'Barony of Spring Flower.' And he had more people working it, too. Every damned one of them a freeman or freewoman."

"Be that as it may," Gyngdau said, making a waving away gesture, "he was only a tiny fish. He's turned into a kraken with dreams of being a doomwhale since. And if the documents he's presented are to be believed, he's on his way to accomplishing that. It's been impossible for him to go south to swear fealty for his newly enlarged titles, of course, but it's pretty clear the Emperor truly has elevated him to a dukedom."

"And the offal lizard figures that dukedom should include everything he can steal while the stealing's good," Ou-zhang said. "Bastard started out with a coin-sized barony just outside Fangkau. That's a town a matter of two hundred miles from here by road. By now, he controls everything west of Fangkau and east of Ranlai, almost as far north as Daimyng, and as far south as the Zhauchyan River, above Kwailan. That's damn near fifty miles each direction from where he started out and Ranlai's barely thirty miles from Zhyndow. And Zhyndow is only seventy miles from Zhutiyan."

Syngpu pursed his lips in a silent whistle. That was a larger area than he'd expected. If Spring Flower could control that many square miles, given the bands of marauders ranging Tiegelkamp and the rival warlords trying to carve out their own tunic-pocket kingdoms, he had to have more manpower than Syngpu had assumed.

"We've managed to keep things relatively peaceful here in the Valley," Squire Gyngdau said. "Mostly, to be honest, that's because we've never had any barons up here in the mountains. The closest we came were a few landowners—like me—with bigger parcels than most. Theoretically, we owed fealty to Grand Duke Snow Wind, but as long as we paid our rents, he wasn't all that interested in us, and we liked that just fine. He didn't do anything for us, but he didn't do very much *to* us, either, if you take my meaning."

Syngpu nodded, and the squire shrugged.

"But because we didn't have any serfs," he continued, "the Crown let us organize our own militia . . . after a fashion, anyway. No matchlocks or crossbows, of course. And God forbid we even *think* about rifles! But we were able to train with pikes and slings, and the Valley's barely twenty miles across east of Zhyndow. It's a lot narrower than that south of Ky-su at the northern end, and there aren't more than half a dozen cliff lizard paths through the mountains on either side, so with corks at Zhyndow and Ky-su, our militia bands were enough to keep any bandit out of the Valley."

"But you're thinking this 'Duke's' likely to be more stubborn than that," Syngpu said.

"That's *exactly* what we're thinking," the squire confirmed. "And if he is—"

He broke off as someone knocked on the office door. They all looked in that direction, and the mayor raised his voice.

"What?" he asked testily, and the door opened.

"I'm sorry, Your Honor," the man who'd opened it said. "I know you said not to disturb you, but a runner's just come in with a message for you and the Squire. And another for the Father."

"A runner?" Gyngdau's voice was considerably sharper than Ou-zhang's had been. "A runner from where?"

"Ranlai, sir," the man in the doorway said, then looked back at the mayor. "And it doesn't sound good."

Ranlai,
Duchy of Spring Flower,
Tiegelcamp Province,
North Harchong.

"So I told him to take it easy, Sir," Sergeant Major Hanbai Chaiyang growled, shaking his head in disgust. "The girl's got three more brothers, and don't figure His Grace'll be any too happy if he kills all three of *them,* too!"

"Probably not," Lord of Foot Laurahn agreed, his own eyes bleak.

"I swear to Langhorne, Sir, there's times I'd shoot the bastard myself for a tenth-mark!" The sergeant turned his head and spat a jet of chewleaf juice onto the frosty ground. "Hell! Half the time, I'd do it for a *hundredth.* He's as much trouble as any three of the other men."

"I know. And, frankly, I'm getting close to *having* you shoot him. If he wasn't one of the originals, I'd have already done it."

Chaiyang nodded, although there was more acknowledgment than agreement in the nod, and Laurahn didn't really blame him.

He stood outside the house of Ranlai's mayor. Or, rather, of Ranlai's *former* mayor. If the man was unreasonably lucky, he might get to continue breathing, but his term of office had just been cut short. The fact that his older daughter was a ripe and attractive nineteen might work in his favor, once Duke Spring Flower laid eyes on her. Of course, it might not, too, the lord of foot reflected. Dead daddies were so much easier to deal with.

Laurahn folded his arms, watching as the lanterns he'd ordered distributed to light the town's streets were lit and hung to cast what radiance they could. It wouldn't be much, but he had no intention of letting the townsfolk skulk around through dark alleys they knew so much better than his troopers did. Mostly because he didn't trust them not to sneak away, but also because even a rabbit might turn on the fox-lizard if it was desperate enough, had too little to lose. It would be terminally stupid, but it could happen. More than that, dark alleys lent themselves to planting anonymous daggers in some drunk trooper's back, and if some hothead thought he could get away with it unnoticed. . . .

"Seriously, Sir," the sergeant major said. "It's getting to where that might not be s' bad an idea. Matter of fact, there's three or four others I could add to that list. Probably help discipline a lot, but just culling 'em for stupid'd be reason enough. True enough for all of 'em, but *especially* Fenghai!"

Laurahn chuckled sourly, but, damn it, Chaiyang had a point. A good one, really. But there were possible downsides to it, as well.

He looked away from the sergeant major while he considered it.

Corporal Gwun Fenghai was one of the reasons they needed those streetlamps. He was big, strong, brutal, and none too bright or he would have attained more than junior noncommissioned rank in the fifteen years he'd spent as one of the Emperor's Spears. The man was effectively illiterate and he spent his off-duty time sleeping, drinking, or fornicating, with emphasis on the latter. When he combined *both* of the latter, he had a tendency to rape any female who crossed his path. Sometimes the females in question had fathers or brothers who were foolish enough to take exception, at which point he demonstrated his one true talent.

He was very, very good at killing people. Probably because he enjoyed it so much.

That made him valuable, in the same way a vicious guard dog was valuable. And the truth was that his taste for rape and brutality had been a net positive as a Spear, despite all the disciplinary issues. It was the Spears' job to *be* brutal, to make peasants and serfs so terrified the thought of rebellion would never enter their heads.

Zhailau Laurahn had been a Spear in his previous

life, as well. In his case, he'd been a somewhat over-age captain of bows, commanding a single platoon in the town garrison of Qwaisun, with Hanbai Chaiyang as his platoon sergeant and Gwun Fenghai as one of his corporals. That was before they'd discovered that even with Fenghai's contribution, the Spears hadn't been brutal *enough*—or that there hadn't been enough of them, at any rate. When the Rebellion exploded, with hordes of enraged serfs and free peasants overrunning garrisons right and left, Captain of Bows Laurahn had decided he had no desire to be overrun when they got around to him. He'd deserted, and Chaiyang had quietly picked out his more trusted cronies to invite along. Over a hundred men had joined them, and they'd gotten out only a couple of five-days before several thousand rebels stormed Qwaisun and massacred the garrison, Spears and regular Army alike.

That was before they took their time sending every aristocrat or suspected sympathizer sheltering in the small, overcrowded city after its butchered protectors.

Laurahn had envisioned finding a quiet, defensible spot and setting himself up as the local warlord, and he'd settled on Qwaidu, a smallish town sixteen miles or so northwest of Sochal. The town was nowhere near as defensible as he might have liked, but it was where he'd washed up as winter set in, and he'd managed to surprise it before the local citizens and surrounding farmers could disappear. More importantly, before the farmers could make the contents of their barns and granaries disappear.

Despite that success, though, that first winter had been hard. Even his troopers had grown gaunt as the icy five-days dragged by, and probably a quarter of Qwaidu's pre-Rebellion population had perished of hunger and cold. He and Chaiyang had held the men together somehow—part of the current problem with Fenghai stemmed from the fact that they'd had to turn their heads and look away from some of the troopers' more egregious conduct—but he'd doubted they could survive another winter at Qwaidu. If for no other reason because so much of the labor force had managed to creep away, despite his vigilance, or simply died. For men who had spent their entire careers repressing farmers, his deserters seemed remarkably unaware of the fact that farms with no farmers produced no food.

Despite that, his total manpower had grown to over a thousand over the course of the winter months. Half the new recruits were deserters, like his core force, but the other half were ex-serfs and ex-peasants. On the face of it, they made odd companions for his ex-Spears, except that they didn't. The important thing was that all of them were "ex" whatever they might once have been, and most of the rebels who'd wanted to join him had made themselves outcast among their erstwhile fellows by their actions. For that matter, at least two-thirds of them had been brigands, not rebels, even before the Rebellion.

But in many ways, the augmented manpower had been as much of an embarrassment as a reinforcement, and he'd realized he couldn't over-winter at Qwaidu a second time. His "regiment" was too large for the depleted farmers to support, yet if he found it another home, it might well be too small to hold that home against the other carrion-eaters tearing at the Empire's corpse. No doubt quite a few other Qwaidus had been used up over the winter by other Laurahns and their men, so the list of possible havens had shrunk . . . and the competition for those that remained would be fierce.

He'd cast longing eyes on the Chynduk Valley, especially when tales of the stuffed barns and larders of the Valley's peasants—tales which, he was sure, had grown in the telling over the hungry winter months—flowed around his improvised barracks. But the one tentative move he'd made in that direction the previous fall had been soundly trounced by Valleyer militia. He was confident he could have beaten the defenders—his men had been better armed, although not *that* much better, and more numerous at the point of contact—but he'd have lost too many to hold any sizable chunk of the Valley afterward. In fact, not even his entire "regiment" would have been equal to that task, even with no casualties at all, given how many Valleyers there were.

No, he'd decided he had no choice but to move on,

hope for greener pastures somewhere else. Possibly even bargain his way into a better-established warlord's service. That might be the safest way to get through the upcoming winter, and a quiet assassination could always change who sat in the warlord's chair, when all was said.

And that was when he'd been approached by Duke Spring Flower.

It was only *Baron* Spring Flower in those days, but Kaihwei Pyangzhow aspired to greater heights, and he'd been scaling them steadily. Laurahn had seen quite a bit of his correspondence with Yu-kwau over the months since then, including his passionate proclamation of loyalty to the Emperor. All he was doing was acting in the Emperor's name to restore the imperial authority in His Majesty's realm. He was beset and surrounded by traitors, thieves, outlaws—rebels!—yet he would persevere in His Majesty's name to the very end!

The baron had been busy stealing his neighbors' estates at the time he and Laurahn met. Two other local barons and their families had been mysteriously murdered—no doubt by their rebellious serfs—leaving him no choice but to merge their fiefs with his own, although he craved the Crown's forgiveness for the expedients to which the desperate emergency had driven him. There'd been the small matter of Fangkau's charter as a free town which he'd been forced to abrogate, as well, when the burghers of the town council refused to subsidize his operations against the rest of countryside, although he begged His Majesty's ministers to understand that only the imperatives of sustaining the Crown's authority could possibly have driven him to such a move. Or to make such demands upon the town in the first place! Unlike the other petty—and not so petty—nobles seeking their own aggrandizement, his only and earnest desire was to see the day His Majesty returned to his realm in triumph.

Laurahn didn't know if anyone in Yu-kwau bought any of that, but they couldn't change what was happening on the ground anyway, and the Emperor was clearly desperate to hear such protestations of loyalty. He'd been pleased to elevate Spring Flower's barony first to an earldom and then to a dukedom, and the terms of his grant strongly suggested that the boundaries of that dukedom would be whatever borders the new duke could create.

All in the name of the Crown, of course.

In the process, Spring Flower had assembled a small army of men very like Laurahn's, but the baron—or earl, or duke—had no military experience of his own. Then he'd heard about the interlopers at Qwaidu, which he viewed as part of his new duchy. Faced with the possibility of moving against them with his own, far more numerous force, he'd chosen to parley, instead. As he'd pointed out, both forces would be badly hurt if they clashed, and neither he nor Laurahn could afford that. So, instead, acting as the Emperor's liegeman, he'd offered Laurahn a new imperial commission, with no embarrassing questions about where he'd been for the past year or so. In place of Laurahn's self-awarded rank of captain of foot, the equivalent of a major in other armies, he'd offered direct promotion—recognized by crown warrant—to *lord* of foot, the equivalent of brigadier's rank, with promises of more to come. And just to sweeten the pot, he'd offered to subenfeoff Laurahn as one of his own vassals, the new Baron of Qwaidu, with the confidence that the Emperor would confirm his new title.

Which was how the brand new Baron of Qwaidu to be—the Crown had not yet assented to the ennoblement—came to be standing here in the breezy autumn chill thinking about a campaign he really didn't want to fight.

Oh, he would enjoy the hell out of humbling the arrogant Valleyers in the end. It was just that getting *to* the end was likely to prove . . . unpleasant.

"I'm turning in," he told Chaiyang abruptly. "I've got the day's dispatch to write up still. Fenghai's on one of the pickets right now?"

"Yes, Sir."

"Well, why don't you just go have a word with him. You tell him to keep it in his trousers for the next few five-days, or else I'll cut it off with a dull blade before I string him up."

"Yes, Sir." The sergeant major grinned. "And about those brothers of hers?"

"Tell him—" Laurahn paused, then grimaced. "Tell him he'd better have at least three witnesses, and not just those drinking buddies of his, that it was self-defense or the same thing goes. Except I'll heat the blade first."

"Yes, Sir." The sergeant major's grin broadened. "I'll make sure he gets that message directly. Maybe with just a couple of bruises t' help it through his skull t' be sure he takes it t' heart?"

"With a *lot* of bruises, as far as I'm concerned, Hanbai," Laurahn replied, then nodded brusquely and headed for the ex-mayor's office. The sooner he got his daily dispatch to the Duke written, the sooner he could move on to more enjoyable pursuits.

▼ ▼ ▼

"—an' after *that*, I'm gonna find the son-of-a-bitch who squealed, an' I'm gonna rip his fucking arm off an' beat him to death with it before I shove it up his arse! An' *then*—"

Private Gaidwo Mai-ku nodded sagely while doing his best to let the words in one ear and out the other. It was difficult, because Gwun Fenghai had been rambling on about it for the last solid hour and showed no sign of tiring anytime soon. The corporal had a way of chewing any thought to death . . . probably because he had so few of them. At the same time, it was risky to not at least appear to listen to him. He had a tendency to take out his frustrations on anyone who seemed to ignore him.

And the thumping the Sergeant Major gave the stupid bastard's not making him any damned easier to live with!

Mai-ku kept *that* thought to himself, as well.

"—not like the stupid little bitch didn't have it coming, either! Swishin' her little arse around, wavin' it under ever'body's nose, an' then lookin' down *her* nose at me like she was some kinda nun or somethin' and—"

"What was that?" Mai-ku said suddenly, straightening from his slouch and reaching for the rifle leaned against the tree beside him.

"What was *what?*" Fenghai growled, obviously pissed off at the interruption of his monologue. "I didn't hear noth—"

The corporal started to turn in the direction Mai-ku was looking just in time to see a blur of motion as the double-edged fourteen-inch bayonet slammed through his throat and interrupted that monologue rather more emphatically.

Mai-ku was still fumbling to get his rifle into position when a second bayonet sent him after the corporal.

▼ ▼ ▼

"Long-winded bastard, wasn't he?" Private Yonduk Kwo grunted, withdrawing his bayonet from the ruins of Fenghai's throat. "Least he *died* quiet!"

"And unless you want to talk to the Commander, be a good idea to keep it quiet yourself," Sergeant Yuhnzhi Taiyang whispered back ferociously, clouting the private none too lightly across the back of his head.

Kwo looked at him, then rubbed the back of his head and grinned. No one would have confused the discipline among Tangwyn Syngpu's men with spit and polish, but it was effective. Besides, even though Kwo might be almost ten years older than Taiyang he was also six inches shorter. Only an idiot took liberties with the tall, burly runaway serf, and there was a reason the sergeant had taken charge of the platoon's first two sections personally tonight.

"'Pears to me you've got a point, Sarge," he whispered back.

"Good." Taiyang looked around. The other seventeen men of his two slightly understrength sections drifted out of the darkness to join them, and he nodded.

"In that case, let's get to it," he told them, and pointed at the strings of lanterns glowing like lost blink-lizards along the lanes and alleys of Ranlai.

▼ ▼ ▼

It was, perhaps, unfortunate for the Baron of Qwaidu (designate)'s men that no one had warned him about the Chynduk Valley's latest immigrants. Zhailau Laurahn had heard of Syngpu's band, although their paths had never previously crossed. And if he'd had any idea Syngpu was in the vicinity, their paths wouldn't have crossed now, either. Although he'd taken the precaution of putting out sentries, it had been largely pro forma, a matter of avoiding bad habits rather than out of any sense of urgency, because he'd "known" he faced only timid townsmen and well-cowed serfs.

Even more unfortunately for his men, they—even Sergeant Major Chaiyang—had taken their cue from him. Not one of them even suspected what was sweeping through the chilly autumn night in their direction, and very few of their sentries lived long enough to find out.

▼ ▼ ▼

Taizhang Yanzhi stepped out of the tavern, wiping his mouth with the back of his wrist. He'd have liked something stronger than beer, but he had the duty in a couple of hours. If he was late relieving Fenghai's post, the other corporal was likely to knock him on his arse . . . for starters. And if Sergeant Major Chaiyang smelled anything stronger than beer on his breath, the beating wouldn't stop there.

Yanzhi didn't like beatings. He'd gotten enough of them as a boy on his local baron's estate, and administered far more of them than he'd ever received by the time his beard sprouted. He'd never been a particularly large man, but he'd been quick, strong, cunning, and vicious, and the small gang of fellow toughs he'd recruited had taught their fellow serfs to be just as afraid of them as they were of the Spears. It was much easier to steal what they needed than to work for it, and life had actually been pretty good . . . before the Shan-wei–damned Rebellion came along and fucked everything up.

Yanzhi scowled at that familiar thought as he started down the town's central street towards the closer of Ranlai's two inns. His platoon was quartered in its stables, and while he didn't much care for the smell of manure—it reminded him of his father, who'd taught him the art of beating others by practicing on him—he'd had worse. Especially over the last winter. He and four of his gang had fled their home estate once it became evident the Rebellion was headed their way and that the same people who were hanging aristocrats would be just as delighted to hang them, too. It was unfortunate none of the others had made it through the winter, although he was sure Myngzhung Mau, the last of them, wouldn't have minded sharing his extra coat with him.

Especially after Yanzhi misplaced a dagger in Mau's ribs while he was sleeping.

He'd regretted that, because he and Mau had grown up together. But a man had to do what a man had to do, and they'd been running low on food, anyway.

At least that wasn't likely to happen this winter. He might not care for Chaiyang's discipline, and he sure as Shan-wei didn't like sharing the same platoon as Feng-hai, but at least there was a roof overhead—even if it was a stable's roof, at the moment. And Duke Spring Flower understood the importance of keeping the men he relied on to break heads for him well fed. It could've been worse, he reminded himself. Could've been a *lot* worse, in fact, and—

He paused in midstride, eyes narrowing as something stirred in the dimly lit inn yard. The inn's lanterns were brighter than most of the ones the detachment had scrounged to illuminate the town, but that wasn't saying much. And there were any number of reasons someone might be crossing that inn yard. Yanzhi wasn't the only man out and about, despite the hour, after all. But something about that movement, the way its path had seemed to curve, almost as if it was deliberately seeking out the darkest patches—

The eyes which had narrowed went wide as the chilly breeze carried a sound to him. It wasn't much of a sound. In fact, it was almost lost in the sigh of the wind itself, but he'd heard too many wet, gasping gurgles like it.

He spun on his heel, suddenly grateful he'd had only beer, and went racing back along the street's uneven cobblestones. He even remembered the right thing to say, despite the relative briefness of his military career.

▼ ▼ ▼

"Corporal of the guard! *Corporal of the guard!*"

"Oh, *shit,*" Sergeant Taiyang grated. Private Kwo had taken care of the lone sentry standing at the inn yard's gate quickly and efficiently. The man hadn't died silently enough, however . . . as the screaming lunatic who'd turned to race back the way he'd come demonstrated. This was no time to waste breath cursing the luck, though, and he jabbed his right hand at the stable ahead of his double section, instead.

"Get in there *now!*" he barked.

The forty-three members of Taizhang Yanzhi's platoon inside that stable outnumbered Taiyang's men by better than two-to-one, but that wasn't nearly good enough against men who'd been trained by Tangwyn Syngpu and Zhouhan Husan. And since the alarm had been so thoroughly raised, there was no longer any need to be quiet about it, either.

The attackers erupted through the stable's doors while the men inside it had barely begun to rouse. Most of them had been bedded down already, with only the eight men of Yanzhi's own section up and about as they grumpily prepared to relieve the pickets around Ranlai. Now they looked up as the first half-dozen riders stormed into the stable, and three of them made the mistake of diving for their weapons.

In fairness to their instincts, it probably wouldn't have made a lot of difference in the end. Their movement, however, *guaranteed* it wouldn't.

Six rifles fired as one, and then Taiyang's men charged with the bayonet.

▼ ▼ ▼

Lord of Foot Laurahn had just started to unlace his tunic, smiling at the timid-looking young woman waiting for him in the mayor's bed. She was a bit on the young side for him, but at least she didn't seem terrified. That was good. Unlike many of the Spears, he really preferred to bed someone who was neither kicking and screaming at the time nor rigid with fear.

He froze in mid-motion as he heard a voice yelling something he couldn't quite make out, and then his shoulders stiffened as he heard the unmistakable crackle of gunfire.

Zhailau Laurahn possessed many less than admirable qualities. Abject stupidity wasn't one of them, though. He grabbed the sword belt hanging over the back of the bedroom's single chair, made sure the double-barreled pistol was securely in the attached holster, snatched up his boots in his free hand, and went charging for the stairs in his bare feet.

"*Sergeant Major!*" His bellow rattled the windows. "Sergeant Major—*stand to!*"

▼ ▼ ▼

"So much for surprise," Tangwyn Syngpu muttered as rifle fire began to sputter and flash.

"What's that saying of Duke Serabor's? The one Captain of Foot Giaupan took such a liking to after he heard it?" Zhouhan Husan responded.

"The one about no plan surviving contact with the other bastards?" Syngpu snorted. "Doesn't mean I can't wish that once—just *once*, Zhouhan—it would actually damned happen."

"Reckon there's no end to what a man can *hope* for. Don't mean he's gonna get it, though."

Syngpu grunted in acknowledgment, then grimaced and beckoned to Baisung Tsungshai.

"No point being sneaky now," he said, and pointed. "Go."

"Yes, Commander!"

Syngpu knew the youngster just *itched* to call him "Sir." Fortunately, he was smart enough to know better.

The thought actually made the older man smile as Tsungshai waved once and two hundred men surged forward at his heels howling the long, quavering warcry Syngpu had learned from the Charisians and their Siddarmarkian allies. Some of his men had seemed a bit hesitant about that, at first, but Syngpu figured anything which had scared the shit out of *him* so thoroughly would probably have the same effect on someone else. For that matter, he really wished he had one of the Siddarmarkians' bagpipers. He knew what *that* would've done to the other side's morale!

If wishes were horses, you'd never wear out your boots, he reminded himself, and nodded to his headquarters group.

"Best we keep up fairly close," he said.

▼ ▼ ▼

"How many?" Lord of Foot Laurahn demanded harshly as the sun eased up across the eastern horizon. The morning was already cold; the wind was rising; the temperature was clearly headed farther down, despite the rising sun; and he hadn't found time to grab a coat.

Which was the *least* bad thing about the nightmare night just past, he reflected grimly.

"Don't have a hard count, Sir," Sergeant Major Chaiyang—and thank Langhorne that at least Chaiyang was still with him!—said. The sergeant major had just returned from a visit to the two cobbled-together infantry sections that constituted their rearguard. "Best I can make out, right on sixty-five."

The Lord of Foot's jaw clenched. He'd taken two hundred and seventy men, an almost full strength infantry company, into Ranlai.

"Lot of 'em probably got out on their own, Sir," Chaiyang pointed out. Laurahn looked at him, and the sergeant major shrugged. "Surprised in the dark? Most of 'em bedded down for the night?" He shook his head. "A bunch of 'em took to their heels, and hard to blame 'em, really, Sir."

He held the lord of foot's eyes steadily in the gathering light, and, after a heartbeat or two, Laurahn nodded. Chaiyang had a point. He didn't want to admit it, because part of him insisted that if he'd only been able to rally more men they'd still be in Ranlai and their attackers wouldn't. But the truth was that he and Chaiyang had done amazingly well to get as many as sixty of their men out intact. He didn't want to think about the nightmare fighting withdrawal it had taken before they finally broke contact with their pursuers, but every man he had with him had stuck it out, and every one of them had brought his rifle out with him.

Under the circumstances, they had nothing to be ashamed of.

It was unfortunate that Duke Spring Flower probably wouldn't see it that way.

"All right, Sergeant Major," he sighed finally. "You're right. But we're still a good fifteen miles from home. Best we get back on the road again. I'll take the lead sections; I want you back there watching our arses in case any of those bastards—whoever the hell they were—decide to keep following us after all. If they do, I want you to *discourage* them, got it?"

"Oh, yes, Sir. I'll do that little thing," Chaiyang promised him.

▼ ▼ ▼

"How's it going, Zhouhan?" Syngpu asked.

"Slower than we'd expected," Husan admitted. "And looks like we'll be leaving more of the food behind. A *lot* more." Syngpu looked at him, and the other sergeant shrugged. "According to the townsfolk, that bastard Laurahn swept up two-thirds of their wagons and draft animals to haul in food from the farms closer to Sochal."

"Should've thought of that." Syngpu scowled, disgusted with himself. "Sort of thing a bastard like this Spring Flower *would* do, isn't it?"

"Can't think of everything." Husan shrugged again. "And we brought all the wagons the Squire and the Mayor could find in time, anyway."

Syngpu grunted in acknowledgment, but the fact that his second in command was right didn't make him any happier.

"How much *are* we going to get out?" he asked.

"I make it a third, maybe a bit more, but not much."

"Shit."

"Third's a hell of a lot better than none," Husan pointed out, and Syngpu grunted again, no more happily than before.

He would have loved to hold Ranlai, but he couldn't. Not permanently, anyway. By Miyang Gyngdau's and Mayor Ou-zhang's best estimate, Spring Flower's total troop strength was probably in the vicinity of eight or nine thousand but might run as high as eleven or even twelve. Syngpu doubted they were either as well armed or as well trained as his own men, but that was twice his own current troop strength. In fact, it would outnumber his properly armed strength even after he'd distributed all of his "spare" rifles to new recruits, and his ammunition supply was anything but copious.

Young Tsungshai was confident he could get a powder mill into operation. There was no great secret to what went into gunpowder, anymore. Even many of the Empire's peasant farmers knew the ingredients by now. The trick was combining them without blowing themselves up. Well, that and the fact that the Crown which had outlawed the possession of *sling bullets* would have looked even less kindly upon anyone stupid enough to make gunpowder.

So the odds favored Tsungshai's managing it, which would at least give them gunpowder. But they were also critically short of the percussion caps their Saint Kylmahns required, and there was no way they could produce more of *them*. Tsungshai could probably get the abandoned rifle works back into operation well enough to convert caplocks into flintlocks, much as Syngpu hated the thought, but they were going to be short on ammunition for at least the next month or two no matter what.

All those factors together meant it would be stupid—or worse—to try to hold the town, especially since Spring Flower and Laurahn must know they had to retake it if they were going to sustain their authority in the territory they already held.

"So, do we burn the rest of it, or not?" Husan asked now, and Syngpu fought an urge to glare at him.

"All the townsfolk decided to come with us?" he asked instead, and Husan nodded.

"Won't say they're all happy about it, but none of 'em're dumb enough to hang around. One or two, at least, are right pissed at us about that, to be honest, but even the ones who're maddest know they'll get turned into examples if they don't."

"Not like they could've done anything to stop us," Syngpu pointed out. "But you're right. That's exactly what'll happen to them. Got to punish somebody for it, don't they? Can't just admit they screwed up and we kicked their arses."

The peasants looked at each other with matching disgust, and then Syngpu shrugged.

"Part of me—a big part, come to that—says burn it all," he admitted. "But that's stupid. Only people we could be damn sure *wouldn't* starve would be Spring Flower and his bully boys. At least if we leave it it'll be a little more food they don't have to steal from some other poor set of bastards. Besides," he grimaced, "after last winter, the thought of burning *anybody's* food doesn't really set well."

"Not with me, either," Husan agreed. "I do wish we could've gotten more of it back to the Valley with us, though."

"The Squire and Father Yngshwan say they've got enough to get all the townsfolk through, as well as us. Don't expect they'd be saying that if there was any question in their minds. So let's just get the wagons we've got loaded up and on the road before we end up in a 'fighting retreat' our own damn selves! Don't figure they can get themselves collected to come after us with more'n a thousand men or so, which'd be kinda dumb of them. Can't be sure they don't have more men handy, though, and with all these civilians along, I'd rather not find out I was wrong about that someplace twixt here and Zhyndow."

He shook his head, but then he smiled thinly.

"Course, if they want to come try to get these wagons back once we're *past* Zhyndow, why, I'll be just happy as a pig in shit to argue the point with 'em."

NOVEMBER YEAR OF GOD 905

·✦·

. I .
The Delthak Works,
Barony of High Rock,
Kingdom of Old Charis,
Empire of Charis.

"I'm impressed, Stahlman. Again, I mean," Ehdwyrd Howsmyn said.

The Duke of Delthak reached out to pat the small, well-dressed, weathered-looking man standing beside him on the shoulder, and Stahlman Praigyr grinned. When he did, it exposed the gap where his two front teeth should have been. In that moment it was very easy for Delthak to forget the tailored tunic and remember the grimy, oil-smeared, hands-on artificer who'd mid-wifed Safehold's very first steam engine. The fact that there was a noticeable oil stain on the sleeve of that tunic made it even easier, and the very end of an oily rag hung out of Praigyr's right back pocket.

It hadn't been all that hard to take the artificer off the shop floor. Taking the artificer out of the shop manager was a little tougher. No, it was a *lot* tougher.

"Does seem to be working right handy, doesn't it, Your Grace?" Praigyr agreed. "And should be interesting to see if Doctor Vyrnyr and Doctor Windcastle's numbers're as good as usual."

"I have every faith in them," Delthak assured him, and he did.

Both Dahnel Vyrnyr and her longtime partner Sahmantha Windcastle had been members of the inner circle for over two years. Recruiting them had been Rahzhyr Mahklyn's idea, and it had worked out extraordinarily well.

Vyrnyr had virtually created the science of hydraulics and pneumatics even before she'd ever heard of an AI named Owl. Hydraulics had been a part of Safehold from the very beginning, but like so much of Safehold's technology, it had consisted of the rote application of the rules and provisions of the *Holy Writ* without much real understanding of the underlying principles. Vyrnyr hadn't been prepared to settle for that, and the Royal College of Charis had given her someplace to do that not-settling.

Windcastle, on the other hand, was more . . . pragmatic. She was the engineer of the pair, focused on applying Vyrnyr's new theoretical understanding to solve real-world problems. The combination had inevitably involved them deeply in Delthak Enterprises' myriad of new technologies, and Windcastle had worked especially closely with Praigyr, who had been promoted—not without resisting manfully—to Vice President for Steam Development.

"I have every faith in them, too," a voice said rather tartly in Delthak's earplug. "So now that we're all sure it's going to work, could you possibly convince my boss to come back to the office? There are a few dozen documents he needs to sign."

Delthak snorted, then turned the involuntary laugh into a hasty cough, but Zhanayt Fahrmahn had a point.

It was almost impossible to keep Praigyr out of the workshops under his supervision, although, to be fair, that was true for several of Delthak's senior executives. Taigys Mahldyn, President of Delthak Firearms, one of Delthak Enterprises' subsidiaries, was a case in point. Praigyr was better at finding excuses to disappear into his playroom than most, however. He was fully capable of handling what would have been called the "white-collar" aspects of Steam Development, despite the fact that he looked remarkably like a monkey lizard. It was true that his literacy skills had been rudimentary when he first entered Ehdwyrd Howsmyn's employ twenty years earlier, but the man who was now the Duke of Delthak had possessed a sharp eye for talent long before he met a *seijin* named Merlin Athrawes, and he'd believed in pushing those who had it to achieve all they could.

And he *still* couldn't keep Praigyr from going to play with his wrenches at the drop of anything that remotely resembled an excuse. That was why he'd assigned Zhanayt Fahrmahn as Praigyr's executive assistant. One of the women Delthak had groomed as the first female manufactory supervisors of Safehold, she'd been a member of the inner circle since shortly after Zhaspahr Clyntahn's execution. She was an accomplished artificer in her own right, which made her the perfect foil for Praigyr when his eyes went big and round and he started brainstorming yet another new idea. She also made sure her boss dealt with all of the truly critical paperwork that went with his job while she dealt with the rest of it. That was what she was doing at this very moment, in fact, working alone in her office while Praigyr escaped to personally oversee the demonstration of Steam Development's newest brainchild.

I wish I had the new wetware, Delthak thought now, as he finished coughing and straightened. *Unfortunately—or perhaps fortunately, for Zhanayt—I'll have to postpone the appropriate response. For now, anyway.*

"Well, Stahlman," he said out loud, instead, "I don't want to rush you or anything, but I have several other things I have to deal with still today. And I'm sure—" he added a bit repressively "—that *you* need to get back to the office, too. So why don't you and I get that check ride out of the way?"

Praigyr had drooped noticeably at the mention of offices, but he brightened at the words "check ride."

"Let's do that little thing," he said. "Now that we know it's not going to blow up," he added, chuckling at the phrase which had become a tradition for Steam Development's prototypes.

He and Delthak walked across to the peculiar-looking

vehicle, rather less than half the size of a standard dragon-drawn freight wagon, which sat quietly on the shoulder of the paved oval track. It was peculiar for several reasons. One was the steel tube, heavily wrapped in stone wool—what an Old Terran would have called white asbestos—which emerged from its rear. Another was its wheels. They would have been slightly undersized for a conventional wagon its size, but they were also made of steel with wire spokes and fitted with much larger versions of the inflatable rubber tires Delthak Enterprises had perfected for the bicycles it had introduced to Safehold years earlier. There was something else odd about its front wheels, though. Or, rather, what was odd about them was that there was no wagon tongue affixed to them. Instead, a vertical shaft rose through its decking just in front of a driver's seat which had been moved back three feet or so from its position on a normal freight wagon. The end of that shaft supported a control wheel, mounted horizontally, and a framework to the shaft's left bore a pair of levers while a heavy foot pedal rose through the decking to its right.

The two men clambered up onto the bench seat. It was broad enough that Delthak could sit to Praigyr's right without crowding him as the artificer settled directly behind the wheel and flashed that enormous gap-tooth grin again.

"Time t' see if we got all the 'fiddly bits' right this time, Sir!" he announced, and reached for one of the levers and pulled it perhaps a third of its full throw.

Nothing happened for a moment, but then the vehicle began to roll silently forward. It moved very slowly, initially, but it accelerated quickly to a brisk walking pace. Praigyr turned the horizontal wheel, and his grin threatened to split his head as the vehicle's front wheels turned in obedient response, following the test track's course. He opened the throttle a little wider and the vehicle sped up, still silent but for the sound of its tires on the paving, and Delthak slapped the smaller man on the back.

"It looks like you did get them right for a change,

Stahlman!" His grin was as broad as Praigyr's. "I know we're both busy, but why don't you open her up a little more and take us around the track four or five times before we let someone else play with her?"

"Why, sounds like a pretty fair idea to me!" Praigyr replied. "Except, of course, that after *I've* taken her around it'll probably be time for *you* to try your hand at the wheel here before we go do all those other things."

"I know you're only trying to keep your arse out of your office as long as possible," Delthak said repressively, then chuckled. "And in this case, it worked. Come on! Let's see this thing move a little faster."

▼ ▼ ▼

"Looks like you've come up with another game changer, Ehdwyrd," Merlin Athrawes said much later that evening.

The Duke of Delthak sat beside the Duchess of Delthak, leaning back in his armchair while a tiny infant girl drowsed on his shoulder. Her name was Sharleyan Elayn, and for all her tiny size she was as much a miracle as her twin brother, Maikah Rhaiyan, who slumbered more deeply in his mother's arms.

Zhain Howsmyn had been born the daughter of an earl, but Sir Maikah Traivyr was a *Charisian* earl. That meant he'd been blissfully immune to the sorts of prejudice aristocrats and other realms felt for those "of no blood." She was ten full years younger than her husband, but the Earl of Sharphill, had approved wholeheartedly of her marriage, and not simply because he'd already realized Ehdwyrd Howsmyn was going to wind up far wealthier than most mere aristocrats. That *had* been a factor in his thinking, although even his wildest imagination had fallen immeasurably short of the wealth Howsmyn had actually attained. Far more importantly, however, his daughter—his only child—had clearly adored the short, stout young commoner who'd won her heart.

Over the years, his common-born son-in-law had become the son he'd never had and Sharphill had never regretted approving the marriage. Indeed, his only regret had been that it was a childless marriage and that the Sharphill title must pass to one of his nephews or one of their children upon Zhain's death. It wasn't that he hated any of those nephews; it was just that they were *nephews*, not children or grandchildren. Even more than that, though, what he regretted was that as much as his daughter loved children, she clearly wasn't going to have any of her own. She and her husband had sponsored over a hundred and fifty Siddarmarkian orphans as their foster children, and she had filled her life by pouring her motherhood into those kids, and into the dozen orphanages the Duke of Delthak's privy purse financed all over the Charisian Empire. Yet her father had always mourned for those biological grandchildren he would never know.

But Sir Maikel hadn't known about Nimue's Cave or an electronic person named Owl, either. And he hadn't known about the medical science of the Terran Federation or ever heard of something called polycystic ovary syndrome. Zhain Howsmyn was fifty-three years old, but those were Safeholdian years, not Standard Years. By the calendar of Old Terra, she'd been "only" forty-seven when Owl's medical unit diagnosed the problem, corrected the hormone imbalance, and injected the medical nanobots to correct the long-term damage to her ovaries which had prevented her from conceiving.

Her father had been eighty-four Safeholdian years old when he'd held the tiny, fragile, infinitely precious grandchild bearing his name, and his twin sister, named for her long dead grandmother. Of all the miracles Merlin Athrawes and Owl had made possible, Sharleyan and Maikel were the two for which Ehdwyrd Howsmyn was most grateful.

"Not me," he said now, keeping his voice low and shaking his head gently to avoid disturbing his daughter. "That was all Stahlman's idea. Oh, Owl and I—and don't forget Zhanayt!—helped with the mechanics, but the idea was all his. You're right about its being a game changer, though."

"In *so* many ways," Merlin agreed.

Steam had already been applied to several different vehicles, but all of them were huge and bulky, like the steam shovels and agricultural tractors the Delthak Works had been turning out for several years now. That was because boilers, feedwater tanks, and coal took up a lot of space. They'd used oil in some of their designs, but that hadn't brought down the size of the boilers and oil was substantially more expensive than coal. So if the vehicle had to be big enough for the boiler, it might as well be big enough for at least some coal stowage. And it wasn't as if construction equipment or farm tractors needed a lot of range before they refueled.

But Stahlman Praigyr's new brainchild was different. In fact, it was very similar to a steam engine designed back on Old Terra by brothers named Doble. Instead of a conventional boiler, it used a single coiled spiral tube which contained only about a gallon of water—a minuscule amount, compared to a conventional boiler. It was heated to an extraordinarily high temperature and pressure, however, which was only made possible by combining its concept with Zhansyn Wylsynn's new "white oil." Kerosene forced through nozzles under high pressure burned as a vapor, at intensely high temperature, and the high-pressure steam from the spiral boiler fed a two-cylinder uni-flow engine. The prototype installed in the vehicle he and Delthak had tested that afternoon produced twenty dragonpower, or about forty-five Old Terran horsepower, but he was already designing engines that would be ten or fifteen times as powerful. And compared to any other boiler and engine, they were *tiny*.

Delthak's contribution to the project, courtesy of Owl and the library computer in Nimue's Cave, was the duplication of Doble's closed condenser, which captured and recondensed the water any steam engine vented *as* steam. Praigyr had practically salivated at the notion, since it cured the greatest weakness of steam as a mobile system: the need to refill any vehicle's feed water tank at frequent intervals. His current estimate, which Owl's analysis suggested was low, was that he ought to be able to achieve something on the order of a thousand miles on Mainland high roads on twenty-five gallons of water and twenty-five gallons of kerosene. And given the exposed area of the boiler coil and the combustion temperature of the kerosene, his new engine should be able to raise steam in under a minute even in sub-zero temperatures. Alcohol would have to be added to the water supply to keep it from freezing, but Safehold's average temperature was substantially cooler than Old Terra's had been, which meant antifreeze had always been a staple of its hydraulic systems.

"It's going to be interesting to see how this shakes out in combination with the railways," Merlin continued. "I don't see any way for it to supplant them. Even back on Old Terra, highway trucking could never challenge railroads' ability to haul thousands of tons of cargo over long distances. Not before counter-grav made surface lorries and trains obsolete, anyway! Over shorter distances, and as the final distributive stage, though, they had a tremendous effect on the transportation industry. And we're about to introduce vehicles that can move tons of cargo under their own power on a planet with high roads as good as most superhighways back on Old Terra *at the same time* we're building the first railroads." He shook his head. "I don't have any idea how *that's* going to play out!"

"As you say," Duchess Delthak said with a chuckle, "it will be interesting to see." She smiled at her husband. "Between the pair of you, you've made sure we'd be living in interesting times even without the Jihad!"

"Well, I know how you hate being bored, love," Delthak teased, and she snorted.

"Of course, that diesel you and Sahmantha Windcastle have been working on could shake things up even more, if the Old Terran history I've scanned is anything to go by," she said more seriously.

"I'm just as happy we've all agreed to hold that one in reserve," Merlin replied, shaking his head. "Steam we've pretty much established is acceptable under the Proscriptions. Internal combustion, even without electricity, might be a little more iffy. Besides, if this works out as well as Owl is projecting, we may not need diesels."

"No, not immediately, anyway," Delthak agreed. "They will be more compact, though."

"Yeah, but they'll also need *transmissions*," Merlin pointed out. "Stahlman's brainchild—and if I have anything to do with it, these things will end up being called 'Praigyrs'—is direct-coupled to the drive wheels. Can't do that with a diesel."

"True," Delthak acknowledged. Power-for-power, a properly designed diesel would weigh somewhere around half as much as the new "Praigyr"—and, he admitted, the name was probably inevitable, even without Merlin getting behind it and pushing—but it would also have to operate at a far higher number of revolutions per minute. Some form of a geared transmission to step the rpm down would be essential, and that would eat up most of the diesel's weight advantage over a Praigyr.

"Speaking of transmissions—" he went on.

"Not going to happen," Merlin said.

"But it makes so much sense someone else is likely to think of it before we get it introduced," Delthak argued.

"No," Merlin said again. "I don't know that I fully agree with Cayleb and Sharleyan—and Domynyk and Dunkyn, for that matter, let's not forget them—on this one, but they're pretty insistent. And if I don't *fully* agree with them, that doesn't mean I don't think they have a point. That's one reason I'm so pleased to see the Praigyr as an alternative to diesels. For now, at least. Besides, you have enough new toys coming off the Delthak idea train to keep you busy without it."

"I know," Delthak acknowledged. "I just want to get the conceptual foundation in place as early as I can. That way it'll be less of a leap when the time comes. Maikel and Paityr may have made sure the Church of Charis is a lot more relaxed where the Proscriptions are concerned, but we still can't just kick them over. The more prep work I can do on anything new, the less likely the conservatives are to start muttering about 'demonically inspired abominations' all over again! Trust me, that's something I still hear a *lot*."

"I understand your point, Ehdwyrd." Merlin frowned. "And you're right; we do have too many examples of new hardware springing forth like Athena from the brow of Zeus." Delthak chuckled at the analogy no one outside the inner circle could possibly have understood. "On the other hand, Domynyk and Dunkyn have a point. If we put the 'conceptual foundation in place,' one of your people is going to grab it and run with it sooner than any of us really want to roll it out. That's your fault."

"My *fault*?" Delthak arched both eyebrows, and his wife chuckled again.

"I didn't say it was a bad problem to have," Merlin told him, "but in this case it *is* a problem. We *have* gotten everyone accustomed to the way those infernal Charisians keep kicking over the applecart, and the job you've done in recruiting innovators and then pushing them even harder to innovate is a big part of that. I'll admit, you had a head start, given how Charisian attitudes towards innovation already differed from those of the rest of Safehold, but the way you've gotten behind that is truly remarkable." Merlin's expression was sober, now, his tone serious. "I know I tease you about it sometimes, but the truth is that you've probably done at least as much in that direction as Cayleb and Sharleyan or Maikel. So as soon as you started musing about the concept, one of those innovators of yours would grab it and start turning it into hardware."

"Would that really be such a terrible thing in this case, Merlin?" Zhain Howsmyn asked. "We've done just that with a lot of ideas that were far more of a challenge to the Proscriptions than this would be!"

"I agree. In fact, that's part of where Domynyk and Dunkyn are coming from on this one. There's not a single new theoretical concept involved, only a matter of engineering and design, so it's unlikely anyone would condemn it as a Proscription violation. Their concerns are based more in terms of military strategy than industrial or religious strategy."

"Excuse me?" The duchess looked puzzled.

"I understand their thinking, sweetheart," Delthak said. "They want to keep an extra ace tucked up our sleeve."

"What you talking about now?" she asked. "I'm sure it's something devious. You were such a *straightforward* person before you fell in with Merlin."

"Evil companions," he told her, leaning across to kiss her cheek. Then he settled back as Sharleyan stirred sleepily. He put a gentle hand on the back of the baby's head, nestling her into his shoulder.

"Right this minute," he said, "Charis is the shipbuilder to the world even more than we ever were before. Every steamship in existence was built in a Charisian yard, and we've got a backlog of orders that's big enough to keep us expanding our shipyards for the next five years even if no one ever orders a single additional ship. But we won't be the only shipbuilders forever, and that's good, a big part of the Nahrmahn Plan to drive other realms into actively fostering their own industrial development." He shrugged—very gently, mindful of his sleeping daughter. "One of the reasons Cayleb and Sharleyan have officially proscribed any foreign *warship* construction is to push other rulers to build their own yards because the only way they'll get modern warships of their own is to build them themselves."

"Oh, that much I understand," Zhain told him. "I even understand why you're building all those 'joint-venture' shipyards in places like Dohlar and South Harchong."

"It's a pity that idiot Zhyou-Zhwo shot himself in the foot before we got the Yu-shai yard off the ground for him," Delthak sighed. "If the stupid bastard had just waited one more year—just *one*—he could've expropriated an entire operational shipyard of his very own. And he would have felt so *clever* at having ripped us off that way!"

"Stupidity and bigotry are their own worst enemies," Merlin agreed.

Outside the inner circle, no one on Safehold could possibly have guessed just how hard Delthak Enterprises and the Charisian crown were working to lose their current generation of "industrial secrets" to any competitor they could find. They might not have been so eager to do that, despite their need to spread industrialization as widely and deeply—and quickly—as possible if they hadn't had so many centuries of technological advantage banked in Nimue's Cave, though. That advantage wasn't infinite, however, especially since it had to be filtered through the limitations imposed by the Proscriptions. Which was rather the crux of Domynyk Staynair and Dunkyn Yairley's argument in this case.

"Assuming your husband is his usual efficient self, there'll be shipyards in every major Mainland realm in the next few years, Zhain," he continued. "Zhyou-Zhwo may not have thought about that before he kicked Charis out of South Harchong, but Symyn Gahrnet in Desnair is certainly thinking about it right now. The Desnairian approach to industrialization sucks wind in a lot of ways, but that doesn't mean it can't ultimately succeed. After a fashion, at least. In fact, I'm sure Gahrnet *will* succeed in building a Desnairian industrial sector; it just won't be as large or as efficient as it might have been if Mahrys were willing to adopt the Charisian model."

"He can't," Howsmyn interjected with an edge of satisfaction. "Not unless he's prepared to overturn the fundamental basis of Desnair's social order."

"No, he can't," Merlin acknowledged. "Bottom line, that's Zhyou-Zhwo's problem, too, although it's going to be interesting to see how that ultimately works out now that he's lost the entire northern half of his empire. *South* Harchong was always a lot closer to the Charisian—or at least the Siddarmarkian—model than North Harchong. Now he's trying to force-feed the South on the North's way of doing things. It's entirely possible he's going to find himself facing another revolt if he's not careful. But unless he does, I think it's inevitable he and Mahrys will find themselves drawn closer and closer together. Desnair and South Harchong might be uncomfortable partners, but Mahrys and Zhyou-Zhwo are definitely birds of a feather."

"One way or another, though, I'm sure Ehdwyrd will still get those shipyards built!" the duchess said loyally.

"Oh, indeed I will!" Her husband smiled evilly.

"Now what are you up to?" Merlin sounded suspicious.

"Well, it just happens that Stywyrt Showail's about to hire one of Delthak Shipbuilding's top people right out from under Nahrmahn Tidewater," Howsmyn told him.

"Shallys?" Merlin's eyes narrowed.

"Shallys," Howsmyn confirmed, and Merlin chuckled.

Dymytree Shallys had been one of the talented artificers Nahrmahn Tidewater had recruited for Delthak's original canal building yard on Lake Ithmyn. He'd gone with Tidewater to the larger Larek Yard, where the new Delthak Shipbuilding subsidiary of Delthak Enterprises built its deepwater steamships, including over half the Imperial Charisian Navy's growing number of steam-powered warships. He'd risen to assistant yard manager and been assigned as Delthak's primary liaison with the Navy, because he'd proven almost equally talented as an administrator.

He was also ambitious and unscrupulous. Those were two traits Master Shallys had gone to some lengths to conceal, but Nahrmahn Baytz had become aware over two years ago of his plans to steal his current employers blind. What Shallys hadn't suspected was that those current employers were just fine with that.

"So Showail's ready to make his move?" Merlin shook his head. "I hadn't realized he was getting so close. On the other hand, that's more up your and Nahrmahn's alley than it is mine right now."

"Yes, he is," Delthak said with a nod of understanding. "And Shallys will be relocating to Desnair the City with him. I'm sure they'll both make buckets of money helping Mahrys 'steal' our technology. Although Show-ail probably won't be able to figure out which makes him happier—the money or putting one over on me."

The duke chuckled, and his wife laughed out loud, then shushed a sleepily stirring Maikel Rhaiyan.

"*Such* a straightforward person when I met you," she said then, mournfully, a twinkle in her eye. "That poor man has no idea you've been playing him like a fiddle for years, Ehdwyrd."

"And if that 'poor man' wasn't such an unmitigated prick, I wouldn't have been able to, either," Delthak riposted. "The only thing I really regret about it is that there aren't any child labor laws in Desnair and I know damned well that that son-of-a-bitch will have kids in his manufactories and his shipyards." The duke's round, cheerful face turned grim. "That's another thing he'll do to spite me, and some of those kids are going to get killed and some of them are going to get crippled and just . . . thrown away."

"Mahrys and Gahrnet would be doing that anyway, even without Showail," Merlin told him. "And I'm afraid that's going to happen other places, as well. Siddarmark, for one, like those idiots in Mantorath, for example. Not in your joint ventures, maybe, but we all know it's going to happen."

"I know that," the duke growled. "Doesn't mean I have to like it, though."

"No, you don't." Zhain laid her free hand on his knee. "But the example of your success despite your *refusal* to use children is already part of the debate in the Temple Lands and Dohlar!"

"And anywhere Delthak Enterprises is involved," Merlin added.

"Stop trying to make me feel better!"

"Oh, we don't have to make you feel better!" Merlin shook his head. "You're too pleased with yourself about having played Showail and Shallys to feel depressed for long!"

"True, too true, if I do say so myself with becoming modesty," Delthak acknowledged, perking up visibly.

"I don't think that word—'modesty'—means what you think it means," Merlin said. "On the other hand," he conceded with a grin as he pictured Shallys and Showail congratulating themselves on having stolen so much information and so many industrial techniques without ever realizing how badly the inner circle had *wanted* them stolen, "it *was* pretty smooth. Almost Nahrmahn-esque, one might say."

"Oh, no! I'm not in that stratospheric company . . . yet," Delthak demurred.

"Maybe not. But Showail and Shallys' defection does sort of underscore why Domynyk and Dunkyn really, really don't want the notion of geared turbines suggested to anyone else just yet. I doubt anyone else would be able to actually cut the gears for a long time to come even if someone did suggest the possibility to them, but you may recall that the Temple surprised us a time or two during the Jihad."

"Agreed. Agreed!" Delthak sighed.

And, he acknowledged, the admirals had a point. At the moment, no one else on Safehold could challenge the Imperial Charisian Navy's steam-powered warships, but that was bound to change. As Merlin had pointed out, Charisian shipyards weren't allowed to sell modern warships to anyone else as an "obvious" ploy to maintain the Charisian monopoly upon them. In fact, it was a "ploy" to put additional pressure on anyone who might wish to challenge Charis' absolute maritime supremacy to build shipyards of their own. And, sooner or later, there *would* be non-Charisian steam-powered ships in other people's navies.

Should the "angels" actually return in the next decade or so, that probably wouldn't matter. No one could build a fleet capable of facing the ICN in that short a time; it was more important that they make the *effort* to, spreading technology ever wider. If, however, Safehold was lucky enough to have eight or nine more decades before any "angelic" return, then other people certainly would be able to build significant fleets. And given their inability to introduce electricity without drawing a celestial bombardment, there was an upper limit to the inner circle's ability to keep introducing superior technologies to stay ahead of the opposition. So the trick was to keep the pressure on everyone else to adopt Charisian innovations without pushing them into letting their own innovators, like Dynnys Zhwaigair or Lynkyn Fultyn, jump too far ahead. And, the duke conceded, that truly did make geared turbines something they should hold in reserve.

At the moment, even Charisian-built ships were restricted to a top speed of around twenty-six knots, or about twenty-three Old Terran knots, and they couldn't maintain that speed for very long before their triple-expansion reciprocating engines began tearing themselves apart. Forced lubrication helped—indeed, it was the only thing which made that possible—but the vibration problem was a more intractable one. Replacing those reciprocating engines with steam turbines would allow significant increases in speed and eliminate the vibration problems that prevented reciprocating engines from running at high rpm for extended periods, and designing and building turbines that size wouldn't be an insurmountable obstacle, especially since every single assembly line on Charis would have plenty of turbines around to reverse engineer. They were the heart of the pneumatic machine tools Howsmyn and his artificers had developed.

Unfortunately, to be efficient, a turbine had to run at higher revolutions per minute than a reciprocating engine, and turbines directly coupled to propeller shafts couldn't. Their rpm had to be stepped down to something a ship's propellers could actually use, and that forced them out of their efficiency envelope and drove fuel requirements up sharply. The monetary cost of the fuel might not have been a problem; the volume and tonnage costs definitely were. There was a limit to how much coal could be crammed into a ship, and that limit and the efficiency of its engines determined its maximum operational range. Put most simply, existing expansion engines were slow and fragile at high speeds but burned far less fuel per mile steamed; turbines were fast and robust, but came with a voracious appetite for fuel. So to obtain the speed and the mechanical reliability of turbines required significant sacrifices in endurance and range.

Unless, of course, someone produced a geared transmission that could be inserted between the turbine and the propeller shaft. If someone did *that*, the turbines could run at their most efficient rate, which would then be geared down to something a propeller could actually use.

"All right," the Duke of Delthak said, smiling crookedly at his wife. "I'll be good. I'll just sit in the corner and stifle myself where this whole transmission thing is concerned and I won't even pout about it.

"For now."

FEBRUARY YEAR OF GOD 906

· ✦ ·

. I .
Tellesberg Palace,
City of Tellesberg,
Kingdom of Old Charis,
Empire of Charis.

"I think I hate you," Sharleyan Ahrmahk said with a smile as Nimue Gahrvai entered the sitting room, her husband at her heels.

"Why?" Nimue cocked her head. "What have I done now?"

"Not had morning sickness," Cayleb told her with a chuckle, stepping forward to embrace her, then extending a hand to General Gahrvai. "She's been harping on that for the last couple of five-days."

"Why?" Nimue repeated as Sharleyan opened her arms to hug her in turn. "It's not as if—" She paused, then looked back and forth between the emperor and empress. "You're joking, right?"

"No, I am *not* joking," Sharleyan said. "Owl confirmed it last Wednesday."

"You two are like *rabbits!*" Nimue said with a laugh, hugging Sharleyan even tighter. "What? Four heirs weren't enough?"

"Never enough heirs . . . as long as they don't get into dynastic wars," Cayleb replied. "More importantly, you can't have too many sibs to *support* the heir."

"And I still hate you," Sharleyan told Nimue with a laugh of her own. "And I think I hate Irys, too. *She's* never morning sick, either."

"That's true," Nimue said, standing back and laying one hand on her own "baby bump."

She was officially seven months pregnant now, but those were Safeholdian months, which worked out to about six and a half Old Terran months. At her request, Owl had run computer projections based on Nimue Alban's genetic profile to determine how a normal pregnancy would have affected the original Nimue, and her PICA had faithfully simulated the results of those projections. One difference between her and Sharleyan—aside from the fact that Sharleyan truly was pregnant—was that Owl had determined that Nimue would probably have "carried high," which gave her rather a different profile.

"That's true," she repeated, and smiled just a bit wistfully. "On the other hand, I won't get to feel them kick, either."

"I know you won't," Sharleyan said with a gentler smile, then chuckled. "On the other hand, you won't have the pair of them taking turns to sit on your bladder, either! I know it's not the same, Nimue, but trust me, there are some advantages to doing this your way. Especially with yet another set of Corisandian twins! Did the two of you absolutely *have* to do that?"

"Of course we did, Your Majesty," Sir Koryn Gahrvai said, taking her hand and bending to kiss her cheek. "It's a Corisandian tradition."

"Showoffs!" Sharleyan shook her head at him.

"At least ours are fraternal, not identical, like certain other people's I could mention," Nimue pointed out.

"And this way we have one we can name for both of our fathers and one we can name for both of our mothers," Gahrvai said. He put an arm around Nimue and she leaned her head against his shoulder.

"I never expected to have the chance to do that," she said softly.

"That's us Corisandians," Gahrvai said, kissing the top of her head. "Always ready to help out a lady."

"There are times I am awed by your selflessness," she told him dryly, and it was his turn to chuckle.

"I have to say this is one outcome I never would have visualized that first morning when I found 'Captain Chwaeriau' standing post outside Hektor and Irys' chamber," he said. "Should have, I suppose, given how pissed off I was. Always seems to be the people you love who can *really* make you mad, so it's no wonder you started right off that way!"

"Speaking of making people mad—or scandalizing them, at least—are noses still out of joint about 'cradle robbing'?" Cayleb asked.

"Probably," Gahrvai said. "Of course, no one really knows how old the mysterious *Seijin* Nimue truly is, although it's painfully obvious she's much younger than my ancient and decrepit self."

At forty-six, he was the oldest person in the room. But that was only the equivalent of forty-two Standard Years old, and he was dauntingly fit for his age. It was true he did look rather older than that, however. His dark hair was graying prematurely, and the right cheek which had been severely scarred in the course of the all-too-nearly-successful attempt to assassinate Hektor and Irys on their wedding day gave him a grim warrior's mien. Nimue Gahrvai, on the other hand, looked preposterously young. That was part of her *seijin* persona's mystique, and the obvious age differential between her and Merlin Athrawes had been deliberate. In truth, combining Nimue Alban's pre-Safehold lifetime with Nimue Chwaeriau's years of existence, she was barely three Standard Years younger than he.

"You should've gotten all this marriage stuff out of the way sooner," Sharleyan said as she waved their guests towards the table under the open skylight. "Then you'd have been close enough to Alyk and Sharyl that no one would even have noticed the difference between *your* ages!"

"I had to bring her around to it gradually," Gahrvai said, pulling out Nimue's chair and seating her before he took the chair beside hers. "Besides, Alyk was a bad enough shock to Manchyr's system without adding us to it."

"*Manchyr's* system?" Sharleyan snorted magnificently as Cayleb seated her, then settled into the chair facing Gahrvai's. "You should've seen what happened in Cherayth! I know you weren't a member of the circle at the time, but go back and ask Owl to play some of the surveillance video for you. His reputation had preceded him, and Elahnah was ready to whisk Sharyl back to Halbrook Hollow and keep her there as long as he was in the kingdom. Heavens! She was ready to send her to a *convent* for however long it took!"

"Oh, believe me, Alyk's told me all about it." Gahrvai grinned. "And I don't blame Her Grace one bit. If she'd been my daughter, I'd have sat up nights with a loaded revolver until he sailed for Manchyr again!"

"Stop it, both of you!" Nimue scolded, although her grin was almost as broad as Gahrvai's. "He's totally devoted to her, and you know it!"

"Of course I do," Gahrvai acknowledged. "Wouldn't be half as much fun to twit him if he wasn't. All those years as Corisande's most notorious bachelor, and he falls for a schoolgirl!"

"Not quite a *schoolgirl*," Sharleyan disagreed. "She was twenty-five, for goodness sakes!"

"And he was *thirty-nine*," Gahrvai riposted. "There are times when I wish I could point out to certain individuals in Manchyr that *my* wife is actually the odd thousand years or so older than I am, because I do get the occasional 'wyverns of a feather' comment. Especially from Taryl. Fortunately, he's had less opportunity to pick on me since he resigned from the Royal Council and went back on active duty with the Navy. Charlz has taken to substituting for him, though."

"Ah, yes! The joys of old family friends!" Cayleb said. "With emphasis on the 'old' in this case."

"Seriously, that's a marriage I completely approve of," Sharleyan said. "Sharyl is one of the smartest people I know, and stubborn. And, to be honest, I'm not unhappy to no longer have to worry about the dashing Earl of Windshare's ability to ruffle feathers and get himself challenged to duels."

"It *is* more restful," Gahrvai acknowledged. "Especially for those of us who kept finding ourselves acting as his second." His expression turned more serious. "I was always afraid that one day he'd either get himself killed or else find himself forced to kill someone else. Either one would've been . . . bad."

"That's true," Cayleb agreed. "But having him married to Sharleyan's cousin was a serious political coup, too. The fact that it was another of those gooey-hearted love matches may have made the romantics among us—and, by the way, I count myself in that number—go all weepy eyed, but from a political perspective I'm in favor of every marriage between the Empire's princedoms and kingdoms we can get."

"Always the cynical politician," Nimue said, but her tone was one of distinct approval.

"I wouldn't have pushed it just because of the political advantages, but that doesn't mean I'm blind to them after the fact," Cayleb said a bit tartly.

"And speaking as someone who's been Alyk's closest friend for thirty-plus years, she's been incredibly good for him," Gahrvai said. "As you say, Sharleyan, she is one of the smartest people you're going to meet. The truth is, she was smart enough to realize a lot of his reputation was a cover."

"A cover?" Sharleyan arched an eyebrow at him.

"A lot of people assume Alyk's new, more . . . measured and thought out approach to life is due to the fact that he knows she's smarter than him and he's willing to let her steer. And there's truth to that, to be honest. But what's also true is that his principles always ran deep—deep enough he hid them under that whole 'rake' façade. I don't know for certain how many of those duels of his involved an actual seduction, but I'm willing to bet it couldn't have been more than three—four, at the outside. He liked to project the image that he was nipping in and out of bed at every opportunity, but he wasn't, really. Oh, he did love to flirt! Don't get me wrong about that! But the half-dozen serious affairs he had that I know of were all with . . . experienced ladies who were as free as he was. I think that when Sharyl figured out what had really been going on, it amused her more than anything else. Intrigued her, too, I suspect. She's the one who took the initiative, you know. Trust me, nothing would ever have happened between them if she hadn't! He probably wouldn't even have flirted with her, given that she was only about two-thirds his age. The fact that he gravitated towards her despite the age difference was what convinced me, at least, that he was absolutely serious."

"You mean she carries his heart around in her pocket," Sharleyan said with a fond smile.

"That's exactly what I mean," Gahrvai agreed, taking Nimue's hand in his. "There seems to be a lot of that going around in Corisande."

"I hope you two aren't going to get all gooey before we've even had lunch," Cayleb said sternly.

"Wouldn't dream of it," Gahrvai said . . . and leaned over to kiss Nimue's cheek.

. II .
Tellesberg Palace,
City of Tellesberg,
Kingdom of Old Charis,
and
The Delthak Works,
Barony of High Rock,
Empire of Charis.

"Going to be a beautiful sunset," Koryn Gahrvai murmured, two days later, as he and Nimue joined Cayleb and Sharleyan on their private balcony.

"We *do* do that well here in Tellesberg, don't we?" Cayleb allowed. "Takes years of practice to get it just right, you understand. Of course, it's just one of many things we Old Charisians do well, now that I think about it."

"And so modest about it, too," a deep voice observed. In Cayleb and Sharleyan's case, it spoke over their earplugs. Gahrvai was one of the slowly increasing number of the inner circle who'd found an excuse to disappear for the five-day and a half it took to install Owl's new wetware and no longer needed earplugs or contact lenses.

"Well, when you're an Old Charisian, you have so much to be modest *about*!" Cayleb told him, then "oofed" as his loving wife poked him in the ribs.

"Thank you, my daughter," Maikel Staynair said.

"You're welcome, Your Eminence."

"Actually, at the risk of reigniting Cayleb's ego, Charisians in general do have a lot of things to be modest about," Nimue said. "I have to say, I've really been looking forward to seeing your and Stahlman's latest venture, Ehdwyrd!"

"We'll try not to disappoint," the Duke of Delthak replied. "And we're running just a bit ahead of schedule, actually."

"We're not going to wait for Nahrmahn?" Sharleyan asked.

"He and Owl are sorting through the daily take from the SNARCs," Delthak replied. "He says we should go ahead without him, and I don't want to lose the light to that Old Charisian sunset your husband was just bragging about when we launch. Besides, he said something insufferably Nahrmahn-ish."

"Like what?"

"Something about SNARCs and electronic personalities who can watch it as many times as they want from as many angles as they like."

"That *does* sound like him," Sharleyan acknowledged. "And I have to admit, I'm definitely in favor of not missing our window on this one."

"There are arguments in favor of delaying till tomorrow so we can launch even earlier in the day, when we'd have plenty of time to make adjustments," Delthak pointed out, but it was obvious from his tone that he was only teasing her.

"Any more thoughts about using hydrogen in the production ships instead of kerosene?" Merlin asked before Sharleyan could respond in kind. At the moment, he and Nynian were in their comfortable cabin aboard the steamer returning them from a quick trip to Boisseau.

"We're putting it on hold for now, at least in the experimental ships." Delthak shrugged. He stood on an observation platform outside an enormous wooden shed at one of the Delthak Works' several test tracks while a dozen blast furnaces produced their own fiery iteration of a sunset and the SNARC parked directly above Charis looked down upon him. "There's a lot to be said for it, and we've had a lot of experience with gas jets and burners now, but the ducting could pose some problems. Increases the chances of a hydrogen leak, for one thing—not to mention providing a pathway for an unfortunate spark. At least for the moment we've decided it's more important to keep the power plants completely separated from the gasbags as a precaution." He shrugged again. "This *is* an experiment, after all. There are plenty of other ways we can wreck it if we really try, without adding any additional risk factors. If we do go to series production, we'll look at the notion again, but for right now, safety's our main concern.

"Probably not a bad idea," Merlin conceded after a moment. "And it's going to be a spectacular enough achievement even without that particular bell or whistle."

"Yes, it is," Admiral Rock Point put in across the com.

"As long as it works." Delthak sounded like a man putting out a sheet anchor he didn't really expect to need. "And, speaking of working. . . ."

His voice trailed off, and there was silence on the com. It was a tense, waiting, anticipatory silence, and then the huge shed's enormous doors rolled fully open and a chuff of smoke went up from the steam-powered tractor which had been waiting for this moment. The tractor moved forward, pulling a thick towing hawser behind it, and a blunt, gray bullet of a nose poked itself through the doors.

It moved slowly but steadily, almost majestically, under the tractor's urging, and as it emerged into the slanting late afternoon sunlight the watchers saw the scores of Delthak workmen coming with it, clinging to dozens of tethers as they guided it carefully forward.

As the nose completely cleared the doors they could see the rest of the vehicle coming along behind it. It was enormous—ten feet longer than the original *River*-class ironclads—and shaped like some huge version of the tethered observation balloons the Imperial Charisian Navy had deployed for the final campaigns of the Jihad. Not surprisingly, because that was precisely what it was, but with a few added features.

The most obvious of those added features were the cruciform stabilizers at the tail of the gasbag and the pair of podded engine nacelles thrusting out on either side of the thirty-foot-long control cabin nestled under the gasbag's midpoint. The twin-bladed propellers were locked in the upright position; even so, they barely cleared the frame of the shed's—no, the *hangar's*—gaping doors.

It took the better part of fifteen minutes to tow it totally out of the hangar, and no one said a word as they watched its progress in rapt silence. Once it was completely clear, the workmen on the tethers moved carefully, using their weight as they allowed it to pivot until its rounded nose pointed into the gentle wind coming out of the west. The tractor's massive weight provided a solid anchor as it pivoted, and they adjusted its position with finicky precision. Obviously, it was a task they had rehearsed carefully.

"It looks even bigger than I expected," Sharleyan murmured finally.

"*She,* Sharley," Delthak corrected. "She, not *it,* please!"

"Sexist!" Nimue shot back with something very like a giggle.

"Simply a traditionalist," Delthak replied. "This is a ship, so she's a she."

"Well, *she* looks even bigger than I expected."

"She's thirty feet shorter than *Sword of Charis*-class was," Cayleb pointed out. "That should have given you some kind of scale to prepare yourself."

"If you'll recall, galleons spend most of their time *floating*," his wife replied tartly.

"Well, this is floating, too!" Cayleb told her with a chuckle.

"But not in *water*, clown!" She clouted him across the head and he laughed.

Still, she had a point, Merlin reflected. True, the airship turning to point its—*her*—nose into the wind was actually shorter than the shuttles squirreled away in Nimue's Cave. But while Sharleyan had seen those shuttles, even walked under the shadow of their wings, she'd never seen them actually fly. And what they were looking at, at this moment, was something totally new in Safehold's experience.

The airship stopped, bobbing ever so gently, tugging against its tethers. Shouted commands rang out, too distant for Delthak's com to pick up and relay. And then the workmen released the tethers. They disappeared, reeled up into the structure under the long, stretched oval of the gasbag, and the locked propellers began to turn. Slowly, at first, then with gathering speed, until they vanished into a blur of motion and the entire craft moved slowly forward. It drifted towards the tractor, and the towing hawser drooped as the tension came off it.

And then the moment they'd been awaiting came. The airship released the towing hawser. It fell away, ballast bags thudded down from the airship's keel, it bobbed as its buoyancy increased with the lost weight, and then the nose tilted upward. It climbed into the wind, propeller blades a throbbing blur, curving into the west as it climbed in obedience to the rudder and elevators on its stabilizers. It swept upward with majestic grace, its haze-gray envelope, the same color as the Navy's warships, gleaming in the mellow light of the westering sun. They'd chosen to make the maiden flight largely in darkness because no one really knew how even Charisians would respond to the sight of something half the length of a soccer pitch soaring overhead.

"God, that's *beautiful*," a momentarily subdued Cayleb murmured as the airship swept steadily higher, shrinking as it went.

"Hear, hear," Rock Point said, his voice almost equally soft. "I only wish Ahlfryd was here to see it."

"So do I—so do *all* of us, Domynyk," Sharleyan said with a sad smile. "At least he got to learn the truth before we lost him, though."

"I know," Maikel Staynair's brother said. "And God knows he died doing what he loved to do. I always teased him about that. I told him anybody who played with explosives as much as he did was bound to blow himself up eventually." He shook his head sadly. "I just wish I'd been wrong."

"It wasn't the explosives, it was the breech failure," Delthak said, never looking away from the ascending airship. "And, no, I'm not going to beat myself up over it again. It looked good on every inspection—including Owl's. Just one of those things we all wish to hell had never happened."

"Yes, it was, and I didn't mean to be a wet blanket," Rock Point said. "He really would have loved this, though!"

"If we hadn't already named the *Ahlfryd* for him, I'd've named this one in his honor, female pronouns or not," Delthak said. "Because you're right. If he were still here, he'd be dancing on top of the gasbag!"

Fond, bittersweet laughter muttered across the com, because Delthak had a point, Merlin reflected, and not just about Sir Ahlfryd Hyndryk or how much they all missed him. Baron Seamount really would have been ready to dance at the mere thought of the Delthak Works' newest brainchild. Although he probably would have disapproved of the notion of naming it after him. In fact, he *probably* would have disapproved of Sharleyan's determination to name the imperial yacht after him.

Fortunately for his sense of propriety, assuming he was keeping an eye on them from wherever he was now (and rather to Zhain Howsmyn's chagrin), the first powered airship in Safeholdian history had been christened *Duchess of Delthak*, instead. Despite her size, she was actually on the small size for a powered airship. And, as Delthak had said, she was a purely experimental vessel, but that made her no less impressive as an achievement. And in time, if all went well, she would serve as the official inspiration for much more substantial designs farther down the line.

Unlike a dirigible like the ill-fated *Hindenburg*, with its aerodynamic external aluminum shell, or a simple blimp, with no true support structure for its gasbag, *Duchess of Delthak* was a semi-rigid design. Her keel of high-tensile steel and blue spruce—a native Safeholdian tree very similar in many respects to its Old Terran namesake—stabilized and supported the lower half of her gasbag, which otherwise held its aerodynamic shape only when its gas cells were inflated. It also provided more structural strength than a blimp would have had, as well as anchorage for her control cabin and the nacelles for her Praigyr steam engines, but at a far lower weight penalty than a rigid design.

To the best of Owl's knowledge, no one had ever powered an Old Terran dirigible with steam. Then again, no one on Old Terra had ever had to worry about a cosmic bombardment for fooling about with electricity. And, Merlin acknowledged, watching *Duchess of Delthak* dwindle with altitude and distance, most people would have had the odd qualm or three about hanging a boiler on a bag full of hydrogen. By far the most common source of disaster for Old Terra's airships had been fire or explosion.

But while the Praigyr's operating temperature might be well above seven hundred degrees, those were *Fahrenheit* degrees, another legacy of Eric Langhorne's deliberate suppression of the metric system, and seven hundred degrees was actually only about eighty percent of the compression temperature of the air in a diesel. And it wasn't as if the Praigyr had an exposed firebox. The combustion chamber was sealed and heavily insulated, and its kerosene fuel burned at such a high temperature that the exhaust was little more than water vapor. Coupled with the fact that any hydrogen which escaped the gasbag would be enthusiastically racing towards the edge of space and *away* from the engines, the likelihood of an engine-induced catastrophe was minute.

Duchess of Delthak was unbelievably light for something her size. Her gasbag was 18 percent as long (and 83 percent as wide) as *Hindenburg*'s had been, yet her gross weight came to just over 4,800 pounds, only about 3 percent that of the ancient dirigible. The 123,000 cubic feet of hydrogen in her gas cells produced 8,360 pounds of lift . . . which, after allowing a ton and a half for fuel, feed water, and ballast would let her lift her three-man crew to her designed altitude of 9,000 feet with a 500-pound safety margin for cargo.

Producing all that hydrogen presented its own challenges. During the Jihad, all of the Balloon Corps' hydrogen had been generated by reacting zinc in hydrochloric acid, which had been possible only because the Lizard Range in eastern Old Charis contained large deposits of what had once been known as calamine (or, more properly, zinc silicate) on Old Terra. It had been mined, in rather smaller quantities, for over a hundred years to support the production of brass, although demand had risen sharply as the scale of Charisian manufactories skyrocketed. On the other hand, the miners had never before had the tools and explosives Delthak Enterprises had made available, so it had been relatively straightforward to mine and smelt the zinc in the needed quantities. But transporting that much hydrochloric acid and controlling the reaction had been logistically difficult. It had also been dangerous. Delthak's personnel had gained a great deal of expertise in the management of explosive gases from handling the coal gas his blast furnaces had been producing for years now, but "safe" was an elastic term when applied to producing hydrogen in such quantities, and transporting liquid acid in bulk was always risky.

Since the Jihad, however, Sahndrah Lywys had "discovered" that hydrogen could also be liberated, albeit at a small loss in efficiency, from ferrosilicon dissolved in a heated sodium hydroxide solution made with old-fashioned lye. Safehold was well accustomed to producing lye in large quantities, given its many uses in textiles and cleaning generally, and ramping it up further had presented little problem. Well, little in the way of technical problems; producing it with a pre-electric tech base significantly increased the environmental impact, but that was true of a lot of the workarounds the inner circle had been forced to adopt. All they could do was hold those impacts to the minimum possible and adopt less destructive techniques the instant they could.

The good thing about ferrosilicon was that the Delthak Works' blast furnaces could produce it in industrial quantities by firing charges of crushed quartz and iron ore, which had led to its Safeholdian name: ironquartz. The highest silicon concentration Duke Delthak could achieve with a coke-fired blast furnace was only about fifteen percent, but that was workable, and he'd developed a more efficient—well, safer, anyway—portable hydrogen generator for the Balloon Corps. It consisted primarily of a sealed steel vessel, small enough to load into a dragon-drawn freight wagon, in which ironquartz and the sodium hydroxide solution were combined. The reaction was exothermic and heated the solution to about two hundred degrees, starting the process, but the vessel could be heated externally to jumpstart gas production. Every pound of ironquartz yielded about 3.4 cubic feet of the gas, and Delthak Aircraft, the newest subsidiary of Delthak Enterprises, was in the process of designing a permanent, high-capacity ironquartz hydrogen generation plant which would be safely located underground to minimize explosion risks and generate somewhere around 840,000 cubic feet of hydrogen a day.

Despite her diminutive size compared to the *Hindenburg*, Delthak's new brainchild was still far larger than the *Wyvern*-class observation balloons of the Jihad. The *Duchess*' gas cells held over four times as much as a *Wyvern*'s, and she could carry enough fuel for an endurance of seventeen and a half hours, which gave her a range of seven hundred miles at her forty-mile-per-hour cruising speed. In theory, at any rate; headwinds or tailwinds could change that number drastically. During that time, her Praigyrs would burn off enough kerosene (and lose enough feedwater, despite their closed condensers) to reduce her gross weight by three thousand pounds, so to maintain her altitude, her crew would be forced to vent sufficient hydrogen to compensate for the weight loss.

That hydrogen—all 44,000 cubic feet of it—would have to be replaced before *Duchess Delthak* could take to the air once again. Delthak's portable generators made replacement reasonably practical, so that wasn't a huge problem. But if they could burn that gas as fuel, instead of kerosene, they'd quadruple their cargo capacity—or gain a significant increase in range—using hydrogen they'd only have thrown away anyway.

Not even an unlimited supply of hydrogen could have overcome the explosive nature of the gas itself, however. Airships were undeniably fragile and hydrogen *was* dangerous, which was why it had been used on Old Terra only until helium became available in sufficient quantities. But while helium was far safer, it was also far rarer and impossible to refine in industrial quantities without electricity. It also offered less lift—only about half as much, given the practical design and operational differences between hydrogen- and helium-filled airships—so even if they could have obtained it in sufficient volumes, using it would curtail both weight and range significantly.

Airships would be another of the inner circle's "technology demonstrators"—and damned impressive ones—and their enormous range and endurance would be extremely valuable, but the future almost certainly lay with fixed-wing aircraft, just as it had back on Old Terra.

The proscription of electricity created problems even there, since it ruled out spark plugs or even glow plugs for gasoline-powered engines. The current generation Praigyr produced about 0.13 Old Terran horsepower per pound, whereas *Hindenburg*'s diesels had produced 0.3 horsepower per pound. Despite that, Owl had already produced a Praigyr-engined biplane design that was well within Safehold's capabilities. But while there was ample room for Owl's design to be tweaked as Praigyr improved the engines named for him, they would never really be able to get past the unfortunate fact that a steam engine—even a Praigyr—had to weigh about twice as much as any internal combustion engine of comparable output built with the same technology.

On the other hand, *diesel* aircraft engines were a distinct possibility. Even they would have a poorer power-to-weight ratio than a gasoline-powered engine could have attained. They would, however, be lighter than Praigyrs and fully capable of powering practical aircraft.

"Too bad she doesn't have the range to overfly Desnair or South Harchong," Merlin said out loud after a moment or two. "Assuming Zhyou-Zhwo didn't drop dead of a heart attack—admittedly, the best outcome—he and Mahrys would both at least froth at the mouth nicely."

"They would, wouldn't they?" Delthak said wistfully. "And I'd love to see Showail explaining to Mahrys why he couldn't build one of his own."

"You're a bad man, Ehdwyrd," Sharleyan chuckled. "Besides, much as I may dislike Showail, we need him doing what he's doing. For that matter, I like Mahrys even less, but we really don't want to lose *him* at this point, either."

"True, unfortunately," Merlin conceded.

Symyn Gahrnet's first "five-year plan" was actually going rather better than the inner circle had hoped. Which wasn't to say it was going as well as they might have liked. Or remotely as well as industrialization was proceeding in some of the other Mainland realms, like Silkiah and Dohlar, for that matter. The Kingdom of Dohlar, especially, with little more than half Desnair's population, was streaking ahead of the empire in terms of infrastructure.

Probably because Desnair had no Earl Thirsk, he reflected.

Never had a conversation that worked out better, he thought, remembering a long-ago stormy night in the earl's library. *Except, possibly, that first one with Haarahld!*

King Rahnyld V had attained his majority under Dohlaran law in 902, but he was a levelheaded young man who'd been strongly shaped by witnessing his father's failures during the Jihad . . . and by Thirsk's tutelage after it. He'd also been both smart enough—and *stubborn* enough—to retain Thirsk as his first councilor, refusing to allow his ex-admiral regent to retire as he'd longed to do, and he and Thirsk had made a point of keeping the crown's fingers as far out of the Dohlaran economy as possible. They'd shaped Dohlar's tax policy to favor investment, abolished Rahnyld IV's punitive import and export duties, and adopted Charisian patent and licensing law, all of which had turned the Kingdom of Dohlar into a natural magnet for Charisian investors and strongly encouraged domestic Dohlaran innovation. Delthak Enterprises was far from the only Charisian corporation partnering with native Dohlarans, and the results were impressive. Whereas Desnair had just purchased six more automotives from Delthak Automotives, Dohlar was now building its own . . . and had just sold three to the Temple Lands.

In fairness to Showail, Gahrnet was about to announce the start of production—*limited* production—at the first of four imperial automotive works being built by the Desnairian crown, although none of them would be as efficient as Delthak's current manufactories. Desnarian automotives would all be effectively hand-built "one-offs" for quite some time, whereas Delthak Automotives had them in assembly-line production. Worse, the Desnarian manufactories were about to hit a painful bottleneck in steel production ... unless they swallowed their pride and imported it from Charis. But there would still be *four* of them, and they'd soon be producing more automotives than Desnair's slowly growing rail net could really use. That strongly suggested Gahrnet had his eye on the export market, and given what had happened to automotive production in South Harchong following Zhyou-Zhwo's exile of all things Charisian, it was pretty clear which export market he had in mind.

No doubt all of the ills of a "planned economy" would present themselves in Desnair in due time, but that didn't mean Mahrys wouldn't be able to build an industrial sector of his own. It would be neither as robust nor—certainly—as rapidly expanding as Dohlar's, but it would be there. And in all honesty, without Mahrys getting behind that and pushing, it might well not have been. It was entirely possible, even likely, that Desnair would have remained as industrially moribund as Delferahk and Sodar. There wasn't much in Sodar to attract investment, even by Charisians, and Delferahk was ... well, it was *Delferahk,* with a nobility stubbornly dedicated to protecting the status quo that favored them so heavily rather than embracing economic change. Which was precisely what somewhere around eighty or ninety percent of Desnairian "men of the blood" would have been doing without Mahrys and Gahrnet to kick their arses. Desnair had managed to produce at least a narrow middle class which *might* have been able to sustain a Desnairian industrial revolution, but that assumed the aristocracy wouldn't have drowned the baby at birth. Which, given what industrialization would inevitably do to the traditional agriculture-based aristocratic society that had produced their status and their wealth, would have been only too probable, Merlin reflected.

"There are times I wish Henrai Maidyn had the kind of authority Mahrys has given Gahrnet," he said out loud. "Although given the state of the Siddarmarkian economy, I don't know if even that would let Henrai sort out the mess."

"It's getting better," Delthak argued. His tone, Merlin noticed, was more hopeful than confident. "The central bank is officially up and running now and the credit situation is bound to get better."

"Only after getting worse first," Cayleb pointed out. "I'm surprised we didn't hear the screams from the Siddar City banks and those frigging speculators out west right here in Tellesberg—without SNARCs!—when he announced the new regulations."

"It *is* going to be ugly," Delthak conceded, turning away from where *Duchess of Delthak*'s gray shape had disappeared into the darkening sky. He started down the steps of the viewing platform towards his waiting bicycle. "But the Republic's a huge market, Cayleb. And before the Jihad, it was the most . . . business-friendly Mainland realm by a long chalk."

"But a lot of that was because of the Charisian expatriates in the Charisian Quarter in Siddar and the other big eastern cities," Sharleyan said, and her voice had gone as grim as her expression. "I don't know if Henrai and Greyghor fully realize even now how much the Sword of Schueler's massacres hurt them in that regard. It wiped out an unholy percentage of the Republic's bankers, importers, and manufactory owners."

"And the carrion-eaters who rushed to seize the opportunities that presented in places like Mantorath are among the worst offenders when it comes to overextending themselves," Delthak agreed. He mounted his geared bicycle, and began pedaling his way home, and his expression couldn't decide whether it was more disgusted or apprehensive. Or possibly just resigned. "When those notes start coming due and they can't renew them on the same ridiculous terms thanks to Henrai's new bank, they're going to be at least as pissed as the land speculators."

"And it's going to have a more immediate effect on industrialization, too," Merlin said glumly.

"Greyghor and Henrai both know that," Nynian put in. "I think they're hoping that if they can just get a tourniquet on the bleeding, Charis will swoop in and snap up as many 'distressed bargains' as possible. It won't make the man-in-the-street love Charis when we start buying out 'good Siddarmarkians' just because they didn't have the sense God gave a wyvern when it came to managing their business affairs, but it would buoy up their industrial sector . . . such as it is."

"That's exactly what they're hoping," Nimue agreed. "And if they really can stabilize things, convince the markets in Tellesberg they've actually turned the Republic into a safe place to invest, it'll probably happen."

"For that matter, Sharley and I have been thinking about dropping Greyghor a note about a possible Ahrmahk Plan for Siddarmark," Cayleb said, nodding his head. "Proportionately, it would have to be on a smaller scale, given how much bigger the Republic is than the United Provinces. The same amount of loans simply wouldn't cover as big a percentage of the need, but it would have to help. And loans to Siddarmarkians that could be paid back would be a lot less likely than outright Charisian ownership to rile those 'good Siddarmarkians' you're talking about, Nynian."

"That's true," Delthak said more cheerfully. "And even though Greyghor and Henrai both understand why we haven't been able to do that already, getting quietly started on planning for it now would be a huge help when the time comes."

"Exactly what we were thinking," Sharleyan agreed. "The two of them have been having an awful time of it, but they're both good men. I think we can count on them to keep the offer under wraps until the situation does settle down enough to make it practical."

MAY YEAR OF GOD 906

·◆·

. I .
Nimue's Cave,
The Mountains of Light,
Episcopate of St. Ehrnesteen,
The Temple Lands.

"Does this officially make me an uncle?" Nahrmahn Baytz asked, leaning back in a virtual chair and nursing an equally virtual glass of wine. "Now that I think about it, *can* somebody who's dead be an uncle? Official or not, I mean."

"As long as the job calls for somebody who's annoying, you're a natural," Nimue Gahrvai replied without looking over her shoulder.

She and her husband stood in a sealed chamber at the heart of Nimue's Cave. Koryn Gahrvai wore booties, scrubs, and a surgical mask, as well, even if none of them looked very much like the gear pre-space surgeons had worn back on Old Terra. Nimue didn't need a mask, since she wasn't planning on any breathing. For that matter, she didn't really need the scrubs she, too, was wearing, since her entire chassis had been subjected to the kind of sterilization organic flesh didn't take to well.

"I don't think 'annoying' is the right word," Nahrmahn said in affronted tones. "I think of myself as . . . intellectually challenging."

"Really? *I* think of you more as intellectually challeng*ed*," Nimue shot back, still watching the readouts.

The large, smooth-sided apparatus in front of her was about six feet long, four feet wide, and four feet tall, not counting its domed, obviously removable lid. There were no visible electrical feeds, no tubes or piping, no nutrient tubes anyone could see. There were only the vertical sides, the bronze color of so many of the Federation's artifacts, rising from a polished stone floor, and the simple panel of readouts atop its lid.

They showed temperature information, heartbeat rhythms, and half a dozen other critical data components, but at this moment the most important one was the digital clock counting down at the center of the instrument cluster.

She didn't really need to watch those readouts with her eyes, since she was tied directly into Owl as the AI oversaw events, but it was one of those psychologically comforting things someone who lived inside an artificial body craved from time to time. Especially at moments like this, she thought, reaching out to take her husband's gloved hand in hers.

There were still times when that thought—*her husband*—took her totally by surprise. It was a possibility Nimue Alban had spent all of her twenty-seven years avoiding even thinking about. She remembered when she'd realized her parents' marriage had collapsed in such bitterness because her mother had become pregnant with her against her father's wishes. It wasn't that her father hadn't loved her—too much, she thought sometimes—after she was born; it was the fact that she'd been born at all into a world he'd known was doomed even before most of the rest of the human race had begun figuring it out. She'd loved her mother, too, but the very thought of repeating Elisabeth Ludvigsen Alban's error had been the stuff of nightmares for her. She hadn't realized—or possibly hadn't *allowed* herself to realize—how much her refusal to even contemplate any kind of serious romantic interest had owed to those nightmares. Even when she'd been so desperately trying to convince Koryn he'd made a dreadful mistake, she hadn't realized that. Nor had she grasped how right

Nynian had been about the reason she'd turned her inability to conceive into an insurmountable barrier to marriage in her own mind.

Marriage, the ability to admit she loved a man, and the very thought of children were concepts from which she'd fled for her entire life, and her subconscious had turned them into mutually reinforcing arguments against doing the two things which had terrified her more than the thought of her inevitable death had ever terrified Nimue Alban.

I wonder if Merlin worked that all out, too? she thought now. *Nynian already had Stefyny and Sebahstean before he got around to proposing to her, so was the possibility of creating a child even on his mental radar? And would it have stopped him for a moment if it had been? Once he realized how he felt about her?* She shook her head mentally. *Probably not. It's funny, for two people who started out the* same *person, but in a lot of ways, he's a lot braver than I am. At least where personal relationships are concerned. I wonder if that's because by the time I came along, he'd already established most of those relationships and I didn't have to. I sort of just . . . slotted into a lot of them, almost as an extension of him. Or as the "little sister" he calls me. And I guess that's what I am. But Koryn wasn't part of the inner circle when I was "born," so I didn't really have that kind of pre-engineered slot where he was concerned. And the sneaky bastard snuck up on me shamelessly!*

She squeezed Koryn's hand gently, and he looked down at her. That was something else that had taken getting used to, and not just with Koryn. Her husband was tall for a Safeholdian, but he was four inches shorter than Nimue Alban had been . . . and still seven inches taller than Nimue Gahrvai was. She'd had to grow accustomed to being surrounded by towering giants, and it had been harder than she'd expected.

And a lot harder than that airily overconfident "big brother" of mine assumed it would be!

She snorted at the thought, and Koryn quirked an eyebrow at her.

"Something amusing?" he asked. "Aside from Nahrmahn, of course," he added, twitching his head in the direction of the corner occupied by Nahrmahn's image. Or, rather, in the direction of the corner over which Owl had superimposed Nahrmahn's normal hologram using Nimue's broadband receiver and Koryn's neural implants.

"I resemble that remark!" Nahrmahn's voice called in the backs of their heads, and Nimue chuckled.

"Just thinking about what it took to get me here," she said, and her smile smoothed into a more serious expression as she shook her head. "Not just *here* here," she added, waving at the spotless chamber about them. "I mean 'into existence' here. I think the term 'unlikely' describes it pretty nicely, actually."

"I'm a simple man raised in a theocratic society that predisposes its members to expect divine intervention," Koryn replied, tucking an arm around her and pulling her in against his side as the digital timer counted down. "As such, I don't have any problem with it." He squeezed tighter. "I said it was a miracle, and that's what it was. And in about—" he checked the timer "—twenty-eight seconds, we'll have a couple of more miracles to keep you company. Not just in the world, either." He pressed his cheek against the top of her head. "Have to build a couple of new rooms in my heart, too, I think."

"I think it's big enough already," she said softly, hugging him back. "Mind you, I don't mind if you give each of them their own room, too."

"That's the good thing about hearts," he told her. "Expansion's no problem. Sort of like someone else's virtual reality, only better."

Nahrmahn made a loud raspberry sound, and Nynian smiled.

"Can't fool us, Nahrmahn!" she said loudly. "You're as soft and gooey inside as an old-fashioned marshmallow, and we all know it."

"Am not!" he protested in an affronted tone.

"Are, too!" she shot back.

"Am—"

"Forgive the intrusion," Owl's tenor voice interrupted, "but I believe the moment is at hand. Are you ready?"

Nimue cocked an eyebrow up at her husband, and chuckled again as his nostrils flared and he nodded.

"Judging by the male parenting unit's somewhat glassy eyes, I would say we're ready . . . but nervous," she said wickedly.

"Tell me you're not taking sadistic glee in a PICA's ability to override physical cues whenever she wants to," Koryn muttered, and she laughed. Then she looked up at the central video head at the center of the chamber's high ceiling.

"Seriously, Owl, we're ready," she said.

"In that case, let us proceed," the AI replied softly, as the timer ticked down to zero, and there was the quiet, sibilant sound of a breaking pressure seal as that domed lid rose smoothly upward in the invisible grasp of a tractor beam.

Nimue heard Koryn inhale deeply beside her, saw him square his shoulders, and then they stepped forward.

"Conditions are optimal," Owl informed them. "Both babies are in excellent health. Would you prefer to begin with Lyzbyt Sahmantha or Daffyd Rysel?"

"I left that one up to Koryn," Nimue said, smiling warmly up at Koryn.

"Ladies first, always," Koryn replied, smiling back down at her, and another, internal lid swung up on its hinges to reveal a thick, fibrous-looking mat.

"Very well," Owl said, and Nimue realized she'd just drawn one of those deep breaths she no longer truly needed, as well.

She picked up a scalpel from the tray of sterile instruments at her elbow. She looked down at it for a moment, turning it in her slender, strong, sterilized fingers. Then she handed it to Koryn.

"Are you sure, sweetheart?" he asked taking it in his right hand.

"I'm sure," she replied, blinking synthetic eyes which persisted in tearing, and he looked down at her for a moment. Then he touched her cheek gently with his free hand before that same hand caught her right wrist.

He stepped closer to the open lid, still holding her wrist in his left hand. Then he set her hand on his own right wrist.

"Not doing this alone, love," he told her. "Not any of it. So, what say we start out the way we're going to proceed—together?"

"That—" She cleared her throat. "That works for me."

"Good."

Koryn reached out, her hand going with his, and the scalpel blade, sharp as Nimue's own katana, touched that fibrous surface. He drew it slowly, slowly down the line Owl projected, cutting the mat cleanly, exposing the amniotic fluid beneath. The placenta curled down from the underside of the mat to the amniotic sac drifting in that fluid, and his breath caught as he beheld his infant, unborn daughter with his own eyes for the first time.

There'd been video from inside, and audio as he listened along with the slowly maturing babies to the sound of a human heartbeat, of human lungs breathing. Their mother couldn't produce those sounds for them, but there were hours of her voice reading to them, talking to them, singing lullabies. His eyes had softened as he listened to her, heard the welcome and the longing, all the greater because she'd never allowed herself to admit how much she'd yearned for this moment. He'd asked her to marry him knowing it could never come to her, and it hadn't mattered to him at all. Nor would he have loved her one bit less if it hadn't. He would have been content, and he knew it. But now they had this magical moment, as well, and despite the truth he knew now, a passage from the *Book of Bédard* flowed through his mind. "The two shall be as one, and they will conceive and bear children together, yet the creation of a child is but a beginning. The creation of a *life* is their true task, and their solemn joy, and their greatest gift. Remember that always, both of you, for that child's nurture is in your hands. Be certain that you do not fail of your charge."

He felt that task, that journey, stretching out before

them. Knew he was as eager to begin it as he was frightened he might prove inadequate to it. But she was strong, so strong, the woman he loved. She'd never faltered before any task. She would neither fail at this one nor let *him* fail. He knew that with every fiber of his being. Yet now it was time for him to introduce her children to her, and he realized in some ways he'd been less frightened facing Cayleb Ahrmahk's Marines in the mountains of Corisande than he was now.

He looked at Nimue, and she nodded. She plucked the scalpel from his fingers and pushed his hand gently.

"Go on," she said. "Daddies always spoil their daughters. You might as well start now. Because *I'm* going to start spoiling Daffyd Rysel in about five minutes."

"Deal," he said softly, and slid his gloved hands down into the thick, warm fluid, cradling that tiny, infinitely precious body.

He lifted her gently, gently, out of the only world she'd ever known, and she stirred like a sleepy kitten inside the glistening envelope of the sac. He turned to Nimue, and she slit the membrane with infinite care.

It was warm in the delivery room, but it was still cooler than Lyzbyt Sahmantha had been in her watery world, and she squirmed unhappily, her tiny face screwed up in a ferocious frown. Nimue dried her quickly, then wrapped her in the sterile, self-heating blanket. Its smart fabric would maintain a perfect body warmth for the baby, and Nimue lifted her, holding her against her shoulder, one hand massaging her back.

Lyzbyt Sahmantha had been born without undergoing the labor contractions which would have helped clear her lungs in a normal delivery, but Owl had monitored the hormonal balance of the placenta, encouraging the reabsorption of the amniotic fluid from them in order to clear them for this moment. Indeed, that was what the timer had been counting down to. Those lungs had practiced breathing movements for months, preparing them for this moment, but they'd never truly breathed before this moment, and nothing happened now for several seconds, despite the stimulating movement. But then Nimue's eyes rose to Koryn's, glistening with tears, as they both heard that first, shallow, priceless breath. As those tiny lungs inhaled their very first sip of oxygen.

Her breathing was unsteady, at first. It was obviously difficult for her, but her breaths gathered strength, steadied down into a regular rhythm, and Nimue pressed her cheek against that tiny blanketed form as she looked up into Koryn's eyes. They waited another three minutes, until the umbilical stopped pulsing, then unwrapped the little girl far enough to clamp and cut the cord. Then Nimue gathered her back up, rewrapping her warmly and tenderly, before she turned to Koryn.

"Meet our daughter," she whispered, and tears trickled down his scarred face as he took back the fragile weight and held her to his chest. Nimue put an arm around him—or as close to around him as she could reach—and pressed her cheek into his shoulder as they both smiled down at those tightly shut eyes, that rosebud mouth.

They stood that way for several seconds, and then Nimue stirred.

"Let me put her in the bassinet," she said. "Ladies may come first, but you should never keep a gentleman waiting, either."

▼ ▼ ▼

"At the risk of sounding just a tad unoriginal," Cayleb Ahrmahk said over the com a few hours later, "God, they're beautiful!"

"For squinchy-eyed, miniature lobsters, of course!" Nahrmahn put in, and laughed as Koryn made a rude hand gesture in the direction of his personal computer. "They're *all* squinchy-eyed, miniature lobsters at this stage, Koryn! Even my own beautiful daughters were. And, trust me," his voice gentled, "they *are* beautiful."

"I don't believe you ever mentioned that particular metaphor to Mahrya or Felayz, dear," Ohlyvva Baytz said from the dowager princess' suite in Manchyr Palace. "Probably just an oversight, I'm sure, given how *delighted* they would have been to hear it."

"The truth is the truth," her deceased husband replied. "Besides, by now Mahrya's figured it out for herself. And, she's also figured out it doesn't keep them from being beautiful."

"You're right, they are." Nimue smiled down into the double bassinet between her and Koryn's chairs. "I can't thank you all enough. Especially you for thinking of it—and hitting me over the head with a big enough clue stick—Nynian. And you, Elayn."

"You're entirely welcome," Elayn Clareyk told her with a smile.

Nynian had been right; every woman of childbearing age in the inner circle had volunteered as their egg donor. But Nimue and Koryn had accepted Elayn's offer in the end. Her golden hair and green eyes weren't a perfect match for Nimue's red hair and sapphire eyes, but they offered more "northern genes" than Sharleyan's or Irys' would have. Well, Irys' chestnut hair probably would have come close enough, but the Daikyn chin had a tendency to breed true and they'd decided against risking any "family resemblances," despite the fact that she and Koryn were cousins.

They'd also taken shameless advantage of the fact that Nimue was a *seijin*. She'd insisted that she had to return to the *seijins'* hidden, mystic home as the time of her children's birth drew near. No one had wanted to argue with a *seijin*, and no one had quite dared to ask any questions—openly, at least—when General Gahrvai and his wife quietly disappeared a month or so before her time. No one saw them board ship to leave Corisande, but, then again, it was well known that no one had seen *Seijin* Nimue *arrive* aboard ship in Corisande, either.

As Merlin had observed at the time, "Sometimes it's good to be the *seijin*."

That had neatly disposed of the need for any obstetricians, midwives, official birth records, or any of the other impedimenta which might have been awkward, under the circumstances. And it would also allow Nimue and Koryn a few blissful five-days of privacy to settle down with their offspring before they returned to Manchyr as mysteriously as they'd departed.

"Are you two still planning on another two full five-days before you head home?" Merlin asked now. Nimue raised an eyebrow, and his holograph shrugged.

"No reason you shouldn't!" he assured her. "I'm just remembering how . . . hands-on Koryn is where the Guard's concerned. And you, too, now that I think about it. For that matter, Tymahn would probably appreciate a bit of a heads-up before you turn up on the palace doorstep. I'm planning on slipping a 'seijin's mysterious note' under his door to give him a couple of days' notice. I'm sure he'll appreciate it."

"Oh, I'm sure," Koryn agreed with a chuckle. Major Tymahn Maiyrs was his second in command in the Corisandian Royal Guard. Now he looked across at Nimue and raised an eyebrow. She looked back for a moment, then sighed.

"You're right about that hands-on stuff, Merlin," she said a bit glumly. "And I know it's going to suck us both in, unless I decide to give up seijin-ing in favor of motherhood, and I don't think we can afford that. I don't know how you and Cayleb have managed it, Sharley. I mean, I know physically how you've done it; I just can't figure out how you manage to carve out family time from everything else! If I'm going to be honest, that's probably what worries me the most."

"You'll manage, too." Sharleyan smiled encouragingly. "It's not easy, and sometimes you just have to put your foot down and tell all those people who want you to figure things out for them that they'll have to deal for the afternoon while you spend some quality time getting a baby fix." She chuckled. "It's surprising how understanding your staff can be if you just drop a few casual hints about headsmen."

"I don't own any headsmen," Nimue pointed out.

"No, and you don't need them. You have your own katana, last time I looked. And then there's that whole seijin business. Do you really think anyone's going to argue with you?"

"Probably not," Nimue conceded.

"Well, there you are." Sharleyan elevated her nose

with an audible sniff. "There are some people the world knows better than to piss off. Any mother falls into that category. Throw in a crown—or a katana—and people get out of the way in a hurry."

"And at least your nanny will understand what's going on," Merlin pointed out.

"And get to lord it over the entire palace staff," another voice said. "God, I am so looking forward to that! A miller's daughter from Tarikah getting to run an entire aristocratic establishment!"

"Easy there, slash lizard!" Kynt Clareyk laughed. "You don't want to make too many waves."

"I'm not going to make any waves at all," Hairyet Trumyn said firmly. "I won't have to ... as long as they're reasonable and do things my way."

Nimue laughed, but there was more than a kernel of truth in that.

Hairyet Trumyn had grown up in the same Siddarmarkian town as Elayn Ahdyms, although they hadn't actually known one another ... before the Sword of Schueler. They'd met only after the Sword had killed every other member of their immediate families, when they'd each found herself alone, aside from Elayn's younger sister. Loss and grief, terror and despair, hunger and cold, and the desperate need for someone they could *trust* in the midst of such overwhelming darkness had brought them together—*driven* them together—as they fought to somehow survive. The expedients to which they'd been driven had left dark spots in their souls, but through it all, they'd comforted one another, wept with one another, guarded one another, *protected* one another, and they'd clung to the bond that had forged between them.

After the Jihad, when Elayn had met and married Kynt Clareyk—and, just incidentally, become a duchess in the process—Hairyet had found her own suite in their home. Along with Elayn, she'd begun to heal emotionally and spiritually ... only to discover she'd developed ovarian cancer. Siddarmarkian surgeons were remarkably sophisticated for a pre-electricity culture, but the cancer had already metastasized far beyond anything they might have treated.

She'd known she was dying, and she'd done her best to make peace with that, but it had been hard after surviving so much. And in some ways, it had been even harder for Elayn. But unknown to her, the Brethern of Saint Zhernau had already been considering her own nomination to the inner circle. Hairyet's prognosis had been handed down barely a five-day before Elayn's nomination was confirmed, and the circle had readily agreed to consider Hairyet for membership, as well, on an accelerated basis. In a worst-case situation, she could always be placed in cryo sleep until the confrontation with the Church was resolved, one way or another. They'd already been forced to do that more than once, and Owl's expanded medical facilities had ample room for her, as well. But that hadn't been necessary. Her personality had survived not only the Sword, the Jihad, and being miraculously cured of cancer, but also learning the truth about the Archangels and the Church of God Awaiting, unbowed.

As Manchyr Palace was about to discover.

When Nimue and Koryn returned to Manchyr, they would be accompanied by *Seijin* Krystin Nylsyn. The tales of the *seijins* during the War Against the Fallen abounded with *seijins* who'd been teachers or scholars, as well as warriors. Some of them had been healers, and that was what Hairyet—Krystin—had become. Despite her brash personality, the laughter she used as her window to the world, she'd seen too much, *lost* too much. She had to give back, and her own miraculous survival courtesy of Federation medical science had told her how she had to do it. So, yes, she would be the autocratic empress of the Gahrvai family's nursery, and as such would cover for any little . . . irregularities about Nimue's version of motherhood. But she would also come to Manchyr with complete neural wetware and a direct connection to Owl and his medical database.

At the moment, she was in Chisholm with Duke and Duchess Serabor, although her naturally blond hair would become permanently black, her complexion would turn several shades darker, and she would acquire a small, rather attractive mole high on one cheekbone—all courtesy of Owl's nanites—to go with her new name when she stepped into her own *seijin* persona. The combination of dark skin, hair as dark as Sharleyan's or Nynian's, and "Krystin's" naturally ice-blue eyes would be sufficiently esoteric in Corisande to underline her *seijin* status. And, hopefully, the relatively few people who'd met her in Chisholm would fail to recognize her if they happened to meet *Seijin* Krystin at some later point, as well.

"If you can stand it, Krystin," Nimue said now, "Koryn and I would really appreciate it if you could get Merlin to run you out to the Cave in his recon skimmer sometime next five-day. It probably wouldn't be a bad idea to start . . . I don't know, shaking down in our new relationship. And Owl and I are still tinkering on how a PICA's system can process nutrients well enough to lactate convincingly. We could probably use your insight on that, too." She smiled. "Owl's wonderful, but there are certain elements of this whole physiology thing that he understands a lot better intellectually than he does experientially."

"In my defense, I'm not equipped to experience them," Owl pointed out against a background mutter of laughter. "And I might also suggest that if you were not possessed of a super-abundant quantity of that quality which in myself I should describe as maintenance of aim, you wouldn't insist on breast-feeding."

Cayleb laughed as he recognized the line from his own long-ago midshipman's efficiency report, and Nimue made the same rude gesture at Owl's video head.

"If you can't see it any other way, think of it as additional cover for the fact that I don't have an organic body," she said. "And I don't see why everyone thinks I'm being stubborn about it!"

"Of course not," Merlin said soothingly. "Why, you're hardly stubborn at all compared to a couple of other women I know. Who," he added hastily, as Nynian glowered at him, "shall remain nameless!"

"Good," Nynian told him, then looked at Nimue. "You be just as stubborn as you want, Nimue! Trust me, if you give these people an inch, they'll take a mile."

"Darn right," Sharleyan said firmly.

"As I said, 'nameless,'" Merlin put in with a smile.

"I'll be delighted to come on out," Krystin said. "And Merlin doesn't have to drive. Owl and I are perfectly capable of getting me from Chisholm to the Cave on our own. Next Thursday be good?"

"Perfect," Nimue said gratefully. "I really do want a little longer to just enjoy the babies—and Koryn, of course," she added, eyes twinkling as she glanced across at him. "But we do have to be getting back. There's a lot going on, and the one thing we can all count on is that something we've never seen coming is about to bite us on the arse. Koryn and I probably need to be home to help deal with whatever it is when it happens."

.II.

Protector's Palace,
Siddar City,
Republic of Siddarmark,
and
Tellesberg Palace,
City of Tellesberg,
Kingdom of Old Charis,
Empire of Charis.

"We're going to be late," Daryus Parkair said, closing his watch with a snap.

"No, we're going to be exactly on time," Henrai Maidyn corrected rather more tranquilly. "They can't start until we get there. So, by definition, everyone else is *early*."

"There speaks a bachelor," Parkair said sourly. "Zhanaiah's going to be a lot less amused when I come stumbling in a half hour late. She's also going to insist on sniffing my breath, given the low company I normally keep!"

Archbishop Dahnyld Fardhym laughed.

"I promise I'll stand as your witness that you didn't touch a drop before the after-dinner toasts," he offered.

"Fat lot of good that'll do," Parkair grumbled. "She thinks you're one of the worst offenders, Your Eminence!"

"Possibly because he is?" Zhasyn Brygs suggested with an innocent expression, and Fardhym laughed again, harder.

"Only because Greyghor keeps such good whiskey in his liquor cabinet, my son," he said, and it was Brygs' turn to laugh.

They all needed something to laugh about, but his need might well be the greatest of all, because he was the newly appointed Governor of the Central Bank of Siddarmark, an institution few had been eager to see and many longed to throttle as promptly as possible. A longtime assistant to Henrai Maidyn at the Exchequer, Brygs had been an excellent choice for a job no one in his right mind would have wanted. Although he was two years older than Maidyn, he looked at least five years younger . . . for the moment. Everyone in Greyghor Stohnar's office suspected that was going to change.

"I can't argue about the quality of his whiskey," Parkair said after a moment, "but we really are going to be late if he doesn't get a move on. And Zhanaiah isn't the only one who's going to be pissed if we keep everyone sitting around."

"That's true," Maidyn conceded.

He pulled out his own watch, glanced at it, then grimaced. He crossed to Stohnar's enormous desk and reached up to the embroidered bell pull above it. He tugged, and a moment later the office door opened in response to admit a tall, fair-haired man who walked with a pronounced limp.

"Yes, My Lord?" the newcomer said.

"As the Seneschal has just pointed out—*I*, of course,

would never have mentioned it—" Maidyn said, ignoring a snort from Parkair's direction "—we're going to be late if we don't get a move on, Brawdys. Would you happen to have any idea what's holding up our esteemed Lord Protector?"

"Nothing, as far as I know, My Lord," Brawdys Samsyn, Greyghor Stohnar's personal secretary said. Although he'd been with Stohnar less than five years, Samsyn didn't seem particularly awed by his august audience. His limp was a memento of the Jihad, when Brigadier Samsyn had been severely wounded in the final fighting in Tarikah Province. A man who'd faced dug-in riflemen of the Mighty Host of God and the Archangels was unlikely to be fazed by a mere Chancellor of the Exchequer.

"Then where is he?" Maidyn asked. "It's not like him to run this late without a good reason."

"I'm not sure," Samsyn replied, frowning slightly, because Maidyn was right about that. "He and I finished all the day's paperwork over two hours ago, and Ahdym finished fussing over his appearance no more than forty-five minutes after that. It's his wife's birthday, so the Lord Protector wanted to get ready and let him go early." The secretary's frown flashed into a smile. "She doesn't know about the seats at the theater the Lord Protector arranged for them as a birthday present. They're presenting Shropsky's *Protector Zhaikyb* tonight. As far as I know, the Lord Protector's just sitting there—probably reading—to be sure he doesn't undo any of Ahdym's handiwork. You know what Ahdym would have to say if he did *that*!"

Maidyn shook his head with an answering smile. Ahdym Manyx had been Greyghor Stohnar's personal valet for over twenty years. Their mutual attachment ran deep, and it was like Stohnar to prepare so early expressly so he could turn Manyx loose early tonight. Maidyn knew how touched Behverlee Manyx would be by both the gift and the thoughtfulness, but Samsyn was only too right about Ahdym's reaction if he heard about

Stohnar turning up with so much as a hair out of place because he'd left early.

"Well, somebody better go roust out his exalted posterior," the Chancellor said, "and as the junior member of our company, I'd say you've just been chosen to go beard the dragon."

"Oh, *thank* you, My Lord!" Samsyn said.

The secretary walked across the office to a rather more plebeian door opposite the official entrance. It opened onto a short hallway, and he walked down it to the closed door of the lord protector's private library, shaking his head fondly as he went. He knocked gently.

"My Lord?" he called through the door. "The masses are getting impatient!"

There was no answer, and he frowned and knocked again, harder.

"My Lord!" he said more loudly.

Still no one answered, and he opened the door. Greyghor Stohnar sat in his favorite reading chair, the history of the Republic he'd been reading recently open in his lap. One hand was on the page, holding the flat magnifying glass he'd found increasingly useful for reading small type over the last few years, and his head was deeply bent over the glass.

He didn't look up, which was unlike him, and Samsyn's frown deepened as he crossed the library towards him, his feet silent on the expensive carpet.

"My Lord?" he said in a softer tone.

He reached out, laying a hand gently on the lord protector's shoulder . . . and Greyghor Stohnar slumped sideways in his chair, head lolling laxly, as the expensive volume in his lap thudded to the floor.

▼ ▼ ▼

"His personal healer's calling it a heart attack," Nahrmahn Baytz said from his computer habitat in Nimue's Cave, his expression grave. "Owl's preliminary analysis concurs. Not too surprising, I suppose, after the way the Jihad aged him."

"No, not a surprise," Cayleb said softly, after a moment. "God, I'm going to miss him, though. We all are."

"In *so* many ways," Merlin concurred, reaching out to squeeze Nynian's hand as they looked at one another and remembered the grim days of the Jihad and Greyghor Stohnar's equally grim, unbreakable determination. How ferociously he, like too many others, had used himself up in his nation's hour of need. They'd reached Tellesberg only the day before, and this wasn't the sort of news they'd wanted to celebrate their homecoming.

"Any head of state's death has to have a significant impact," he continued, "but *Greyghor*?" He shook his head. "There hasn't been a Mainland head of state to match his stature in decades—except Duchairn, possibly, and he was on the other side during the Jihad. And losing him now, when the Bank is still in the process of spinning up—!"

"And so close behind losing Rhobair," Maikel Staynair said quietly. "That's going to have an impact, too."

"Agreed, but it could have been a lot worse," Sharleyan said. All of them looked at her, and she shrugged. "Oh, on the personal level, I'm going to miss him as much as any of us. In terms of policy continuation, though, the consequences are likely to be a lot less severe than they could've been."

"That's true." Nynian nodded. "Under the Republic's constitution, Henrai takes over as acting Protector until the next scheduled election, and that's not for another two years. So we may have lost Greyghor, but his replacement will probably be even more focused than he was on dealing with the Republic's economy."

"That's an excellent point," Delthak agreed, brightening noticeably. "Do we know who's going to replace Henrai at the Exchequer?"

"Not yet." Nahrmahn shook his head. "If I were a betting man, though, I'd put my virtual marks on Klymynt Myllyr."

"Um." Cayleb frowned and scratched his chin. "Good points and bad points to that, I suppose."

"That's one way to put it," Trahvys Ohlsyn put in,

tipping back in his office and gazing out his window at the Tellesberg harbor. The Earl of Pine Hollow looked like a leaner and—although he was only about five and a half feet tall—taller version of his deceased cousin, and their expressions were very similar as he considered the information. "Myllyr's not what I'd call a financial genius," the first councilor continued, "but he did get a lot of experience as Parkair's senior staff quartermaster. I'm pretty sure he'll understand at least the basics of what's going on. And," he brightened slightly, "he should be fairly acceptable in their western provinces."

Several heads nodded at that. Klymynt Myllyr was a native son of Tarikah Province, and he'd been a junior officer in one of the regiments in the Republic of Siddarmark Army's desperate fighting retreat on Serabor. He'd fought with enormous tenacity until he was severely wounded and invalided back to Siddar City just before the newly arrived Imperial Charisian Army relieved Serabor. While he was recuperating, he'd been tapped as one of the seneschal's assistants, and he'd done well. The fact that he was a Westerner would go down reasonably well in Tarikah and Westmarch, and his record in the Stylmyn Gap would win him points in the eastern provinces, as well.

"I can see the pluses, politically," Pine Hollow said. "But he's not the most brilliant person Henrai could turn to, and I'm not talking just about his experience in high finance!"

"He's not an idiot, either, though," Nynian countered. "He understands the mess the Republic's in, and I can't think of anyone who would be more loyal to Henrai."

"Agreed," Nahrmahn said firmly. "To your point, Trahvys, I suspect political concerns are the primary driver in choosing him, but Nynian's right about how loyal he is. And I suspect everyone involved, including Myllyr—maybe even especially Myllyr—figures that, in practical terms, Henrai will be his own Chancellor. Everybody in Siddar City knows no one has a better understanding of what's going on or worked harder at standing up the Central Bank then Henrai did. My guess is that he'll go right on setting policy and making the critical strategic decisions for the Exchequer and that Myllyr will concentrate on carrying out those decisions. More like a chief of staff than a minister in his own right. And he and Brygs do get along well, so I doubt they'd have any problems working in harness."

"I could wish Henrai would have someone who could take more of the burden off of him," Merlin mused. "Being Lord Protector at a moment like this will be about the farthest thing from a cakewalk I could imagine. But I think you're right about how he—and Myllyr—would see Myllyr's appointment to the Exchequer, Nahrmahn. And that only makes your point about policy continuation even more valid, Sharley."

"And it's pretty traditional for a chancellor who succeeds a protector to win at least one term in his own right," Nynian agreed with a nod. "That would give him *seven* years to push his reforms, not just two."

"*If* they follow tradition," Nahrmahn pointed out. "A lot'll depend on how well his reforms work out in those first two years. Greyghor could probably have weathered just about any storm and been reelected in 908. His stature as the Republic's wartime leader was towering enough to overcome almost anything short of an outright economic collapse or some major escalation of the violence in the western provinces. Henrai doesn't have that going for him, and the fact that he's the public face of the banking reforms ties him to them. If they look like they're succeeding, he probably sails to election in his own right. If the perception is that they're only making things worse, God only knows who'll become protector!"

"This habit of shooting holes in my more hopeful analyses is really irritating, Nahrmahn," Nynian said. "Valuable, possibly, but definitely irritating."

"It's why you keep me around," the virtual personality told her with a chuckle. Then his expression sobered again. "Despite my pessimism, I really do hope you're right, though. We all knew Greyghor was fading, but none of us expected to lose him this soon and with so little warning. If that's true for us, it's going to hit the vast majority of Siddarmarkian citizens even harder. I doubt anyone outside Siddar City itself really understood how fragile his health was growing. God knows he tried hard enough to keep people from guessing! It'll be interesting to see if they rally around Henrai as his successor or if his death only contributes to the . . . general restiveness."

Heads nodded all around, and as Merlin Athrawes looked into his wife's eyes, he saw the same thought: "interesting" was putting it mildly.

<I'd really like a chance to stop living in "interesting times," at least for a few years,> he told her over her implants, and she grimaced, then laid her head on his shoulder.

<So would I, sweetheart,> she replied. <So would I.>

OCTOBER YEAR OF GOD 906

·✦·

. I .
Lake City,
Tarikah Province,
Republic of Siddarmark.

"You see?" Lord Protector Henrai Maidyn said as the carriage rolled down the broad avenue. "I told you this would work out just fine."

"My Lord, there's a tiny difference between 'hasn't been a disaster yet' and 'work out just fine,'" Archbishop Arthyn Zagyrsk replied. The archbishop looked at the lord protector over the top of his wire-rimmed spectacles, his eyes serious. "I'll admit your visit's been less . . . stressful than I'd anticipated—so far—but there's still plenty of anger simmering out there, too."

"I know." Maidyn's more sober tone acknowledged the archbishop's point. "But Greyghor or I should've been out here at least two years ago. There are a lot of reasons we weren't, including the fact that his health was worse than he or his healer were admitting to us for a long time." The current lord protector's eyes turned sad for a moment. "A lot of reasons," he repeated, "but that doesn't change the fact that we *should* have been out here. Even the people who support us have a right to wonder where the Shanwei we've been while their neighbors kept killing each other." He shook his head. "I had to make the trip, especially if we're going to tackle the speculators next. And we've *got* to get a handle on that situation—for a lot more reasons than just its effect on the economy."

Zagyrsk nodded, and looked out the carriage window,

listening to the icy sleet rattle against it, then begin oozing down the glass.

It was a sign of Maidyn's seriousness that he'd made the trip this late in the autumn, given typical Tarikah weather, the archbishop thought. Lake City was over two thousand miles from Siddar City even for a wyvern; for mere mortals, it was much, much farther. Maidyn had made the journey by water, taking one of the fast Charisian steamers up the Republic's east coast, then through Hsing-wu's Passage to the rebuilt town of Salyk and up the Hildermoss River by steam barge. The journey had taken him more than two five-days, and even with the semaphore—which was far less reliable this time of year, given northern East Haven weather—to stay in touch with the capital city, he had to be worried about what might be happening *there* while he was *here*.

And despite all of that, he was right.

"I wish I had a better feel for how this meeting's likely to go," Zagyrsk said after a moment, looking back at the lord protector. "Avry's given me his best estimate, but I'm afraid he's still a little less sensitive than I'd like to what a Bédardist would call 'interpersonal relationships.'" He smiled briefly. "I know he's got the *numbers* right; I'm just a bit less confident about his read on some of the motivations."

"I think he's probably fairly close to right about those, too," Maidyn replied. "Of course, that may be because what he's saying matches what I've been thinking so well. We do have a tendency to trust the judgment of people who agree with us!"

Zagyrsk chuckled, despite his manifest worry. He'd held the Archbishopric of Tarikah since well before the Jihad, and Auxiliary Bishop Avry Pygain had been his personal secretary throughout the war. He'd been *Father* Avry at the time, but when Rhobair II abolished the office of bishop executor, decreeing that it was no longer needed, since archbishops would henceforth spend their time in their archbishoprics seeing to their flocks' spiritual needs rather than in Zion playing politics, Pygain had been elevated to Auxiliary Bishop of Tarikah. The auxiliary bishops filled some of the same functions of the old bishop executors, but today they served mainly as chiefs of staff to their archbishops. It was a role to which Pygain was eminently suited, and Zagyrsk had come to the conclusion that his auxiliary bishop was destined to remain one of Mother Church's bureaucrats, not one of her pastors. That happened to a lot of Chihirites of the Quill—God gave those He called to His service different talents, however genuine their vocation to serve Him might be—and it was a natural and comfortable fit for Pygain.

"I do wish Tymyns was here instead of Siddar City, though," the lord protector continued. "I invited him to come with me, but he turned me down—politely, of course—and that's a real pity. I think Draifys and I have made some real progress with the provincial chamber, but I'm a mere lord protector. The people they send to the Chamber of Delegates carry a lot bigger stick back here in Tarikah, and they keep pounding away at exactly the wrong narrative. If we could just pry Tymyns loose from Ohlsyn and Zhoelsyn, break up that united front of theirs, it might be a real game changer."

"I agree, but I don't think it's going to happen," Zagyrsk said gloomily, looking back out the icy window. "Old Ohrvyl has a lot of supporters here in Tarikah. They look at him as one of their own, and he's always had a reputation for honesty. Deservedly, in my opinion. Emotionally, I think he's a little too close to the Siddar Loyalists, but I don't think he'd ever let that control his decisions. It may *reinforce* them, but it doesn't control them, if you take my meaning. The problem is that he's not well-educated, and he knows it. He's . . . overly impressed by people who are, and Zhoelsyn and Ohlsyn both have a lot more formal schooling than he does."

"And they're younger, and they're smoother," Maidyn acknowledged equally glumly. "They've got him convinced they're as honest as he is . . . and that I have ulterior motives. That my policies favor the eastern commercial interests at his constituents' expense, despite the fact that so many Easterners are screaming about the

Bank even louder than you Westerners! And I hate to say it, Your Eminence, but part of the reason they can convince him of that is because he *is* close to the Siddar Loyalists and they play on that."

"I know." Zagyrsk nodded. "And they're not the only ones. I don't envy Ahndrai Draifys at the best of times, but I come closer to that than I do to envying Mhardyr, down in Cliff Peak!"

Maidyn made a disgusted sound of agreement.

Ahndrai Draifys had been appointed Governor of Tarikah by Greyghor Stohnar in 896, when Dairyn Trumbyl, the pre-Jihad governor, basically handed his key of office over to the Army of God as soon as it crossed the frontier. His appointment had been confirmed by a special election in 900, and he'd won reelection for a second term less than three months ago. Tairayl Mhardyr, the Governor of Cliff Peak had been the provincial lieutenant governor when the Sword of Schueler struck. *His* predecessor had been murdered in his own office by pro-Temple fanatics, and Mhardyr—who'd been out of the provincial capital at the time—had succeeded him. Like Draifys, he'd been unable to return to his province until the Army of God and the Mighty Host of God and the Archangels had been driven out, but he'd been reelected twice since then, including this past June's elections.

They were rather different men.

Mhardyr was a career politician, someone who'd achieved success by carefully noting the direction the wind set. Which, Maidyn conceded, could be said of anyone who worried about his constituents' desires and made achieving them his primary duty. He was regarded with mixed feelings by some of those constituents, however. For his supporters, his rejection of Zhaspahr Clyntahn's Inquisition from Siddar City was the public face of the province's loyalty to the Republic, and he'd done an efficient job of looking after his displaced citizens in the refugee camps in eastern Siddarmark. His detractors, on the other hand, pointed out that he'd done all of that from the safety of Siddar City and tended to compare him unfavorably to Zhasyn Cahnyr's decision to return to his archbishopric. It wasn't really fair, perhaps. Cliff Peak had been totally overrun before any resistance could be organized, whereas Cahnyr's archbishopric had fought off all attacks under its beloved archbishop's leadership. There'd been no place in "his" province from which Mhardyr could have exerted any sort of control, and he'd undoubtedly accomplished more for the displaced Cliff Peakers in the East than he could ever have accomplished back home.

Besides, Maidyn thought dryly, it was patently unfair to compare any mere mortal to Zhasyn Cahnyr! But still—

"At the moment, my sympathy for Governor Mhardyr is distinctly limited, Your Eminence," the lord protector said sourly. "I understand he has problems, but we could use at least a little of his support! And I know damned well—pardon my language—that he understands the problem!"

Zagyrsk nodded, his expression no happier than it had been.

Tairayl Mhardyr was a basically honest man—or he had been, at any rate. Maidyn knew that, because the two of them had worked closely together, arranging support for displaced Cliff Peakers during the Jihad. There were times, however, when the man who'd succeeded Greyghor Stohnar as Lord Protector had to wonder what had happened to that honesty. Probably it had run up against political pragmatism, given that no one could have won a governor's election in Cliff Peak without the support of the political machine that belonged to Styvyns Trumyn and Vyncyt Ohraily. They were Cliff Peak's senior delegates to the Chamber of Delegates . . . and about as *dis*honest as even corrupt politicians came.

Unlike Mhardyr, Ahndrai Draifys had been a successful Lake City law master, who'd only dabbled in politics on the side. They'd been more of a hobby than a vocation, before the Sword of Schueler, but because of that interest in politics, he'd had a better notion than many of what might be coming. He'd gotten his family out over two months before the Sword struck, and Stohnar had selected him as Tarikah's governor-in-exile mostly because he'd been the first member of the provincial government to make it to Siddar City.

It was probable that no one had been more surprised than Draifys by how well he'd performed in that position, and unlike Mhardyr, he tried to be as evenhanded as he could in his administration now that he'd returned home. It was evident that his personal sympathies lay with those who had remained loyal to the Republic, especially to those who'd stood their ground and fought, but he understood why Greyghor Stohnar had insisted the government of the Republic must be the government of *all* Siddarmarkians, whatever their stance during the Jihad might have been.

Unfortunately, Stohnar had been unable to prevent passage of the Disenfranchisement Act which had stripped the franchise from anyone who'd fled the Republic's borders during the Jihad. He'd protested strongly—as had Maidyn—but the Chamber of Deputies had passed it by more than a sufficient margin to override Stohnar's veto. Stohnar's (and Maidyn's) primary objection had been to the DA's sweeping overreach. Under the DA, it didn't matter why someone had fled the Republic; it applied to families who had refugeed out to Charis just as much as it did to Temple Loyalists who'd sought refuge in Zion itself or even taken active service in the Army of God. *Anyone* who'd left the Republic during the Jihad had lost his franchise and couldn't get it back before swearing an oath of personal loyalty before a magistrate. In the western provinces—including both Tarikah and Cliff Peak—the Act went even further, however. In those provinces, the loyalty oaths had to be "verified" by the provincial governments and notarized and attested to before the Reconciliation Courts.

Maidyn knew damned well that the provincial legislatures were deliberately dragging their heels when it came to verifying loyalty oaths for anyone who'd gone west, instead of east. As a consequence, voting was strongly skewed towards the Siddar Loyalist element, which held clear majorities in both provincial legislatures. That limited Draifys' options in far too many ways.

But at least, unlike Mhardyr, he was *trying!*

"I didn't say Tairayl Mhardyr was a sterling example of rectitude and moral courage, My Lord," the archbishop said. "I don't see as much of him as Archbishop Olyvyr, because—thank Langhorne!—I have to deal directly primarily with Governor *Draifys.* I have exchanged quite a lot of correspondence with Governor Mhardyr because of the Reconciliation Courts, of course. On the basis of that correspondence, I think that left to his own devices he'd steer a more . . . disinterested course. I do know he's well aware of the resentment Trumyn and Ohraily's policies are feeding, at any rate. And I don't doubt he understands how much that's hamstringing your and the Seneschal's efforts to get a handle on this ongoing cycle of violence."

Zagyrsk's eyes were sad behind their spectacles, and for just a moment he looked utterly exhausted. Almost as worn-out as Zhasyn Cahnyr had looked at the end, Maidyn thought with a sudden flicker of anxiety, and for too many of the same reasons. Zagyrsk had fought hard to protect the people of Tarikah, and even the hapless inmates of the Inquisition's concentration camps. He'd run a serious risk of being denounced by Clyntahn and consigned to the Punishment himself more than once, and between them he and his intendant, Ignaz Aimaiyr, had saved thousands of lives. But they'd lost *millions,* and Maidyn knew Zagyrsk would never forgive himself for that. Which could only make the current unrest even harder for him. What he was seeing now was only a pale shadow of what the Sword of Schueler had wrought, but this time he enjoyed the full support of Mother Church and the federal government . . . and still couldn't stop it.

"I know Mother Church says human nature is basically good, Your Eminence," the lord protector said. "There are times I find that hard to believe. And, to be honest, I've never understood how someone who hears confessions so regularly as her priests do could really believe that. I know both God and the Archangel Bédard say that's what we *ought* to believe, but—"

He shrugged, and Zagyrsk summoned a smile.

"Don't forget that the Blessed Bédard wrote her book before Shan-wei's Rebellion, My Lord. What Mother Church actually teaches is that human nature is *more* good than bad, but in these fallen days, the margin's gotten far thinner. As the gentleman we've just been discussing demonstrates."

"I guess that's one way to put it," Maidyn said. "But that's why I hope this meeting goes as well as Bishop Avry appears to hope it can. And your support's nothing to sneeze at, either. I don't expect miracles. I'm just hoping we can at least slow the bleeding a little."

As a physician, the Pasqualate archbishop understood the lord protector's analogy perfectly. There were more than sufficient people with completely legitimate reasons to hate anyone who'd sided with the Church during the Jihad. Zagyrsk might regret that, but he understood human nature too well to expect anything else. Those legitimate reasons would have created a lot of anger, a lot of unrest, no matter what. But he and Governor Draifys had become aware long ago that someone was organizing and directing much of that hatred—focusing it, strengthening it. At first, they'd thought the instigators were some of those people with legitimate, personal reasons for their anger. More recently, however, they'd begun turning up evidence—not just suspicion, but evidence—of who was actually behind it. Evidence that mashed entirely too well with what Henrai Maidyn and Samyl Gahdarhd had long suspected from Siddar City.

The land speculators whose predation had already done so much to stoke the unrest had found their opportunities to strike cut-rate bargains dwindling as the Siddarmarkian expatriates who'd returned only to reestablish ownership and get what cash they could out of their pre-Jihad property sold out and went back to the Temple Lands. Those who'd come to stay, or who wanted something close to what their property was actually worth, were disinclined to take offers that were sometimes as much as ten whole percent of a farm's or a gristmill's pre-Jihad value. So the speculators had decided to apply a little psychological pressure to induce them to be more "reasonable," and if a few dozen—or a few hundred—people were beaten or killed in the process, that was just fine with them.

Zagyrsk wasn't prepared to present his evidence in a court of law, because much of it was circumstantial and more of it depended on the testimony of witnesses whose lives would be endangered if the more strident Siddar Loyalists heard what they planned to say to the magistrates. But he *was* prepared to state his personal certainty that the Siddar Loyalists themselves were being manipulated by calculating, cynical offal lizards, and throw his moral authority—and Mother Church's—into the scales on the other side.

"We'll do what we can, My Lord," he assured the other man.

▼ ▼ ▼

It was chilly in The Church of the Holy Martyr Saint Grygory.

The church, affectionately known to generations of Lake City citizens as Saint Gryg's, was the oldest church in town by over fifty years, since the original Lake City Cathedral had been demolished and the new, larger cathedral built forty-seven years ago. It was also placed on a hilltop—a *windy* hilltop—that provided a magnificent view of East Wing Lake, which explained why it was so chilly, despite the flues running through the sanctuary's walls and floor from the basement hypocaust. Father Grygory Abykrahmbi, the parish priest—who strongly encouraged his flock to use the affectionate diminutive, explaining (with a straight face) that he didn't want anyone confused into thinking the church had been named after *him*—had instructed the sexton to be sure the hypocaust was fired up early, and it radiated a comforting warmth from walls and floor alike. Unfortunately, most of that warmth dissipated before it got to the pews in which the participants in the morning's meeting were gathered.

Lord Protector Henrai's Army security detail had inspected the church carefully, and a pair of cavalry troopers—without their carbines but with their revolvers prominently on display—stood just inside the vestibule. The major commanding the detail had wanted a stronger presence inside the church, but Maidyn had turned him down. The last thing they needed was to hand their opponents the opportunity to accuse them of "profaning God's house" with a massive invasion force. And it would have set the wrong tone for what was supposed to be a meeting of reconciliation.

Given how its participants had segregated themselves—Siddar Loyalists to the right of the central aisle and returning Temple Loyalists to the left—it didn't look very reconciled to Maidyn at the moment.

Well, it's your job to change that, he told himself. *Probably be a good idea if you got started on it.*

He sat behind the large table just outside the church's sanctuary, looking at those pews, with Archbishop Arthyn to his left and Father Grygory to his right. Auxiliary Bishop Avry sat at a rather smaller table to one side, poised to take notes. Governor Draifys had offered to come, and in many ways his support would have been welcome. But he'd already made his position clear enough, and Maidyn had decided not to involve him just yet in his own meetings with the locals. It was important that he and they understand one another's unfiltered positions. That meant a direct dialogue, and there was at least a chance that keeping the governor out of it during its opening stages, would help prevent local politicians and business leaders from digging in to established positions and antagonisms. The possibility might not be very great, but at this point, he was prepared to pursue any advantage he could beg, buy, or steal. And he fully intended to involve Draifys in later meetings.

Assuming there *were* any later meetings. At the moment, he was none too sure there would be.

"Your Eminence," he said, turning to Zagyrsk, "I think it would be a good idea if you opened our meeting in prayer."

"With Father Grygory's permission?" Zagyrsk replied, raising his eyebrows at the priest, who chuckled.

"I'm far too craven to tell my archbishop no, Your Eminence!" His tone was so droll some of the hard faces in the pews on both sides of the nave smiled and a few even laughed outright. "Seriously," Abykrahmbi went on, his own broad smile easing into something milder, "I would be honored."

"Thank you, Father," Zagyrsk said. He stood, looking at those pews, and squared his shoulders.

"My sons—and daughters," he added, looking at the half-dozen women who were present, "I promise I'll keep this brief. After all, it's not Wednesday!" That won a few more chuckles, and he smiled. Then he raised his hands.

"God," he said, "we beseech You to be with us at this meeting and to remind us that whatever mortal men and women may think, *You* love all of Your children. Amen."

He sat back down, and a stir went through the seated men and women. Archbishop Arthyn was well known for his succinct, to-the-point sermons and prayers, but that had been unusually . . . economical, even for him.

Maidyn let the stir settle, then cleared his throat.

"I wish Archbishop Dahnyld could be that brief Wednesdays in the capital, Your Eminence," he said with a wry smile, and saw several faces grin in appreciation. "However," he continued, "brief as you were, you also spoke directly to the reason for this meeting. We're here—all of us—because we seem to've forgotten the point you just made. I hope that by the time we leave Saint Gryg's today we'll have remembered it and proposed some concrete steps to remind the rest of Tarikah's citizens of the same point."

The smiles had vanished, and two or three people glowered across the aisle at one another.

"I believe in laying my cards on the table face up

from the beginning," Maidyn told those glowers, "so let me begin by explaining my position and my responsibilities, and how I understand them, as clearly as possible.

"I've already discussed the reasons for my journey to Lake City with Governor Draifys and the leaders of your Legislature, and we'll be meeting again very shortly, undoubtedly many times, to discuss what can be accomplished legislatively and through new policies to improve the situation here. But in my view, a commission such as the Archbishop proposes to set up would be able to address those same problems with more effectiveness than any solution we might attempt to impose upon them. Those of you gathered here represent the business community of your city. You are farmers, ranchers, bankers, merchants, healers, and law masters. You *are* your community—its leaders and those most intimately involved in making it prosper . . . or fail."

He paused, his gaze sweeping the pews, and in the quiet, they could hear wind roar softly around the eaves and sleet rattle against the church's stained glass.

"I told the Archbishop on the way here this morning that I don't expect miracles," he resumed after a moment, "and I don't. But whatever our past positions, whatever our past actions, we're all Siddarmarkians. Not one of us would be here if we didn't think of the Republic as our home. That means all of you are neighbors, and the Archbishop and I have invited you here today, invited you to accept seats on his commission, because we have to restore that sense of neighborhood and community and *you* are the only people who can do that. Without that sense of community, there can be no peace, and without peace there can be no stability, and without stability there can be neither safety nor prosperity.

"I wasn't Chancellor of the Exchequer for so many years without understanding how important vital, healthy provincial economies are to the Exchequer as a whole. Or without understanding that they can't be healthy if the society they serve isn't equally healthy. And it's true that from the perspective of Protector's Palace, Tarikah's contribution to the Exchequer is of critical importance, especially given the current state of the Republic's economy as a whole. All of you understand that cold, hard fiscal reality.

"But from the perspective of the *Lord Protector*—from *my* perspective, the perspective of my responsibilities to the *people* of Siddarmark, not its economy, and from my own heart—bringing an end to this bloodshed and violence without ordering the Seneschal to send in his troops . . . that's far more important than any contribution Lake City or Tarikah might make to the federal budget. As Chancellor of the Exchequer, it was my overriding responsibility to balance the books, to find the marks to pay for the federal government's operations, for the Army, for the dozens of public services for which it's responsible. As Lord Protector, my overriding responsibility is to see to the safety of our citizens. That includes their financial and economic safety, but their physical safety supersedes any other responsibility or duty of my office.

"It wasn't so very long ago that your province and your community were torn apart by the Sword of Schueler and the Jihad. I know—believe me, I *know*—how grievous the death toll was. I also know how hard it's been—how hard you've *worked*—to rebuild something approaching Tarikah's pre-Jihad prosperity for your returning citizens. I want to see that rebuilding to continue, and I want—I don't think any of you can fully understand how *much* I want—to see it continue with no federal troops patrolling your streets, no cavalry detachments supporting your local city guard. This is *your* province, *your* home, and you are the proper custodians of it. But I very much fear that if we can't find a way for you to restore—and maintain—local order and tranquility, I'll have no choice but to increase the Army's presence. I don't want to do that any more than I think you want me to do it, but my oath of office will leave me no choice."

He paused again, letting that sink in, watching his final sentence hit home. Then he straightened in his chair, squaring his shoulders.

"So now that you understand why I'm here, does anyone want to suggest where he—or she—thinks we should begin?"

▼ ▼ ▼

"My dad says he thinks Maidyn means it," Ahndru Ahrdmor said, sitting back with a mug of hot cherrybean and listening to the heavy pounding of the rain which had replaced the day's earlier sleet. "Says he made a lot of sense."

"Um." Ahryn Tohmys' expression was as noncommittal as his tone, but his eyes were flinty, and Ahrdmor sighed. Then he sipped cherrybean, lowered the mug, and shook his head.

"Nobody's asking you to pretend what happened to Rychyrd never happened," he said quietly. "I'm just saying Dad thinks he really wants to get the troops out of the streets and let us get back to normal."

"'Normal,'" Ahryn growled. "Tell me, Ahndru, just what is this 'normal' everyone wants to get back to? Don't believe I've ever seen it."

"Me neither," Ahrdmor conceded. He was a year younger—and four inches taller—than his friend. "And I'd really like a piece of the bastards who caught Rychyrd, myself. Don't think I wouldn't! But where's it *stop*, Ahryn? They send one of ours to the hospital, so we send one of theirs to the hospital, and all it does—just like the Archbishop and Father Grygory say—is keep the cycle going, and this is where we *live*. You want to catch that son-of-a-bitch Tyzdail? Fine! Let's go find him, whatever hole he's hiding in, and drag his sorry, cowardly arse out of it. I'll hold him down while you break both his kneecaps with a hammer. Won't lose a wink of sleep over it, either. But you think that's going to accomplish anything except making both of us feel better?"

Ahryn shoved himself angrily back in his own chair, looking out the tavern's windows into the sodden night's bone-gnawing chill. He knew Ahndru was right. For that matter, he knew Archbishop Arthyn was right. If the cycle of violence and reprisal continued, the community around him would never heal.

But what Ahndru didn't seem to grasp was that Ahryn didn't care. This wasn't "his" community anymore . . . assuming it ever had been. He was still in Lake City for one reason, and one reason only: to sell the Tohmys family farm for something remotely approaching a fair price. His parents would need that money in Charlz—or in the Temple Lands, if they chose to continue farther west, put more distance between themselves and the Republic they'd once called home. They'd need it to care for a son who would never walk again without crutches, who would never again read one of his beloved books.

Familiar rage bubbled in the pit of his belly as he thought about that. Thought about Rychyrd's vain attempt to hide his despair when the healers told him his right eye was permanently blind and that even with the best spectacles anyone could grind for him, he would never again see anything but blurry images out of the left. It hadn't been enough for Tyzdail and the other bastards to *cripple* his baby brother, they'd taken away the one thing that might have made his shattered life bearable.

That had been the final straw for Clyntahn and Danyel Tohmys. As soon as they could safely move Rychyrd, they'd taken him away from the hateful city in which their son's life had been broken. They hadn't cared about selling the farm anymore. In fact, Clyntahn had blamed himself for having stayed too long, for trying to get a better price for the land his family had owned for so many years, so many generations. If he'd only taken what the speculators had offered, gotten his family out of Tarikah sooner. . . .

Ahryn understood, but he was grimly determined his parents were going to have what they needed to care for his brother. He knew how much that farm was truly worth, and he'd promised his father he'd get it. Both his mother and father had argued with him at first. They'd wanted him safely out of Lake City, as well. Danyel had looked at him, eyes wet with tears, and begged him to come with them. Begged him not to let Lake City take her other son from her.

But Ahryn had been adamant, and eventually, they'd relented. His mother had demanded that he promise to be careful, to avoid trouble, and he'd given her that promise because until he did, his father had refused to deed the farm over to him. But Clyntahn Tohmys had registered the new deed in the end, given Ahryn authority to negotiate its sale, and for the last two months, that was what he'd been doing.

He'd helped his family pack, delivered the crates of books Rychyrd would never read again to the Lake City Public Library. There'd been tears in his own eyes as he loaded those crates into the cart but he'd managed to keep them out of his voice because the last thing Rychyrd had needed was proof of his own grief, his own anger. Rychyrd was right, of course. If he couldn't read them anymore himself, he could at least pass them on to a home where other booklovers *could* read them, and it had seemed to ease his pain, at least a little. Nothing would ever truly take it away, though. Ahryn knew that as well as Rychyrd did.

And then he'd ridden the freight wagon down to the canal station with his parents, helped them stow everything aboard the barge his father had chartered, hugged and kissed everyone, waved goodbye, returned the freight wagon . . . and gone hunting.

His friend Ahndru didn't know the real reason no one had seen Byrt Tyzdail for the last eight or nine five-days. No one did, although the fish at the bottom of East Wing Lake might have given them a clue.

Ahryn intended to keep it that way, however he might long to tell Tyzdail's cronies what had become of him. Or, for that matter, however he might long to send them along to keep him company. But Tyzdail had been only one of the two tasks he'd assigned himself. The more important of them, he admitted, but still only one, and he had yet to accomplish the second. Somehow he had to find a buyer, provide his parents with the nest egg they needed.

"Anything more from Ovyrtyn?" Ahrdmor asked, and Ahryn stiffened as the question unintentionally flicked his raw emotions.

"No." He managed to bring the single word out almost normally, not in the snarl he'd wanted to unleash.

Taigys Ovyrtyn and Grygory Hahlys were currently the two biggest "investors" in Tarikah real estate. Hahlys was a native of Old Province, not Tarikah. He'd been part of the original "land rush" after the Jihad, and he'd arrived with a purse full of ready marks. His reputation for driving hard bargains had been well earned in those early days. It had also made him even more bitterly disliked than most of his ilk, but he'd had the wit to partner with Ovyrtyn, a native of Tarikah whose family had stayed fiercely loyal to the Republic. More than a third of that family had died, and Ovyrtyn stood high in the local community's esteem because of their sacrifice. He'd become Hahlys' entry port for many of his land deals and permitted the interloper to continue buying up distressed properties.

"You know, my dad says Ovyrtyn drives harder bargains with people like us," Ahrdmor said, and Ahryn grunted.

He'd heard the same thing himself, and seen evidence enough to prove it. And, probably, it wasn't too surprising that someone who'd lost as many cousins as Taigys Ovyrtyn had would feel especially satisfied screwing bargain prices out of "Temple Loyalists." Unfortunately, there were few other avenues available to Ahryn. The Tohmys farm was too big a purchase for anyone besides Hahlys and Ovyrtyn's purse. Unless he wanted to break it up into smaller parcels, at least. And if he did that, he wouldn't find a buyer for all of them—not under current circumstances.

"I'm sure he does," he growled after a moment. "I know the best price he's offered me so far is maybe a quarter of what the place's really worth."

"Only a quarter?" Ahrdmor looked distressed. He knew why Ahryn was selling. More to the point, he knew how much the farm was truly worth.

"That's what he says," Ahryn replied. He started to add something else, then stopped himself and sipped cherrybean, instead.

Ahrdmor looked at him curiously for a moment, but decided not to press the point. Instead, he leaned back and began describing the attractive—and available—young lady with whom he intended to spend the evening. Ahryn listened, chuckling appreciatively at all the proper spots, but his mind wasn't really on his friend's amatory adventures.

He was remembering that last conversation with Ovyrtyn. The one in which Ovyrtyn had cut his offering price. Ahryn hadn't been completely truthful with Ahrdmor, because Ovyrtyn's current "take-it-or-leave-it" offer was actually only about twenty percent of the farm's appraised tax value, and appraised tax values were almost always lower than actual values. He'd pointed that out to Ovyrtyn, and the land buyer had shrugged.

"Best I can do," he'd said. "In fact, you'd probably better jump now, really. It's only going to go down."

"Why?" Ahryn had asked tightly.

"Because we're running out of money," Ovyrtyn had said frankly, and grimaced. "I'm not saying I'd offer you any more than I thought I had to. No point either of us pretending I would. But the way things are headed now that Maidyn's Shan-wei–damned 'Central Bank' is mucking around, nobody knows what the credit market's going to be like next month. Hell, nobody knows what it's going to be like next *five-day*! All we do know is that it's going to get tighter, and, the truth is, Grygory and I are overexposed as it is. Eventually, all this land's going to come back to its pre-Jihad values, but for right now, we're land-rich and money-poor, and that's just the way it is."

Ahryn had looked at him, jaw clenched, and Ovyrtyn had shrugged.

"Look," he'd said, "I heard what happened to your brother. I'm not going to pretend I don't have . . . issues of my own with people who ran for the hills instead of standing and fighting, but you and he were only kids.

Wasn't your idea, and it's not right. Beating the hell out of a kid his age, it's not *right*."

To his credit, he'd sounded as if he actually meant it, and Ahryn's jaw muscles had relaxed just a bit.

"A good businessman doesn't let sympathy interfere with business," Ovyrtyn had continued, "and I'm not going to tell you I'd pay you what your family's place will be worth in a few years, no matter what. That's not my job, and I'd be lying if I suggested I'd do anything of the kind. But I'm not the senior partner; Grygory is, and he's the one setting policy. Under other circumstances, I might have been able to buy at my previous offer if you'd taken me up on it then. Now, I don't have a choice. Your family's already left, and I know you want the cash out of the farm for them. I understand that. But you're a young man with no family of your own to support, and I'll be honest. In your place, I think I'd find myself a job here in the city to make ends meet and wait a while. If you think you're in a position to hold onto the farm for another—I don't know, three or four years?—land prices will probably recover to a point that will let you drive more of a seller's bargain. You can't now. And if this 'Central Bank' does what a lot of people are afraid it'll do, it's going to be a hell of a lot longer before land prices start going up again. If you do decide to sell now, I can pay you in cash, money on the barrel head. It's not what your property's worth, son, it's just all you can get for it right now."

Ahryn had sat there in the quiet warmth of his office for several minutes. Then he'd stood and held out his hand across the desk.

"Let me think about it," he'd said. "I understand what you're saying. And I think you mean it." He'd been a little surprised to hear himself say that, and even more to realize it was true. "But I just can't sign it away for that price. Not without thinking about it long and hard, first."

"Understood." Ovyrtyn had clasped forearms with him. "And my current offer's good till the end of next five-day. After that, I'm afraid it may drop again. Not saying that to twist your arm, although I might anyway, but because it's true."

"I understand," Ahryn had repeated, and left.

Now, as he listened to Ahrdmor's glowing description of his lady friend's athleticism, he remembered that conversation and felt the slow, steady burn of despair-fueled anger smoldering in the pit of his belly.

▼ ▼ ▼

"I think we may actually be making some genuine progress," Henrai Maidyn said as he and Arthyn Zagyrsk rolled towards Saint Gryg's once more.

It wasn't raining today, and the two of them were heavily bundled against the cold wind humming in off the lake. It was going to be even colder inside the church than for their previous meetings, but that was fine with Maidyn. He'd been cold before in his life, and the sense that both sides of the commission the archbishop had impaneled genuinely wanted to find ways to decrease the tension was far more important than mere physical warmth ever could have been.

"I believe you may be right, My Lord," Zagyrsk conceded. "And I'm certainly enheartened that almost everyone we asked to serve has agreed to take a seat on the commission. Nothing we've come up with so far is going to just knock all this hostility on the head, though. And as soon as the commission openly sets up business, people on both sides are going to start trying to tear it apart." He smiled sadly. "That whole human nature thing you and I were talking about before the first meeting."

"But that was over a five-day ago," Maidyn replied with a lurking twinkle. "Surely human nature's evolved to a new pinnacle of greatness in *that* much time!"

"I see you are a man of extraordinarily deep faith, my son," Zagyrsk said.

"Either that or extraordinarily deep desperation." Maidyn's tone was more sober. "On the other hand, I think they really do want to do something about the problem."

"I'm sure you're right about at least that much," Zagyrsk said with matching seriousness. "My concern is that there are too many people with a vested interest in *not* doing something about it."

"People like Ohraily and Trumyn, you mean."

"Certainly, but, to be honest, I'm more concerned about people closer to home. Like Grygory Hahlys. The last thing he wants is for the situation to stabilize and let land prices do the same thing! If I could, I'd emulate *Seijin* Brahntly and drive the speculators out of Lake City with a whip."

From his tone, he wasn't even half-joking, Maidyn reflected.

"Well, since neither of us are *seijins,* Your Eminence, I'm afraid we'll just have to do our best. And at least I may be a *little* less unpopular in the West when I go home." He smiled whimsically, looking out the window on his side of the carriage. "I'd like that," he said. "I'd like that a lot."

▼ ▼ ▼

Ahryn Tohmys stood in the cold wind, huddled deep inside the warmth of his thick coat, and watched the street through empty eyes.

The frigid day was far, far warmer than his heart, and the hand in his left coat pocket clenched around the crumpled letter. The letter from Wyllym Styrges, telling him what his mother had not yet found the strength to write herself.

Telling him what his brother Rychyrd had decided.

They took it all away from you, Rychie, he thought bleakly. *Everything. And I'm not really surprised. But, oh, how could you do this to Mom? How?*

But he knew the answer, of course. There was a limit to the pain someone could bear, and Ahryn hadn't been there to help him bear it. Hadn't been there to *make* Rychyrd talk to him about the things their mother wouldn't have pushed him on because it would have hurt him so much. Hadn't been there to see the warning signs, to watch him, to keep him from hobbling off into that barn with that length of rope.

And now he was gone, and Ahryn hadn't been there because he'd been *here,* too focused on selling the family farm to keep his kid brother alive.

The pain went through him once again, colder and far sharper edged than any wind that had ever blown, and he felt the tears on his half-frozen cheeks.

He should have taken Ovyrtyn's offer before the land buyer had to prune it back. He shouldn't have delayed after Ovyrtyn expressly warned him he could only go down, not up. He should have taken it and sent a letter by semaphore to his parents, told them—and Rychyrd—he was coming to join them, that he'd be there within the five-day. Maybe that would have been enough to keep his brother going until he'd gotten there. But he'd gone on hoping, lying to himself, *delaying* himself from accepting the inevitable when he should have known it *was* inevitable in the face of so much uncertainty about credit and banking laws. Ahryn didn't understand those esoteric details himself, but he understood enough. He understood who'd destabilized them all. Who'd created the conditions which had kept him here instead of in Charlz where his brother had *needed* him to be.

A part of him knew he was focusing his own self-anger on others. That he hurt so much, the pain was so deep, he had to find someone else to bear the weight of his fury. But it was a tiny part of him, and he wasn't listening to it. He didn't care. His family had suffered enough, been broken too terribly, for him to feel anything but the rage, the volcanic lava seething just under the surface.

The world had crushed his brother, his parents, under its uncaring heel, and Ahryn Tohmys would find a way to *punish* the world for that.

He heard the sound of approaching hooves and grating wheels and looked up.

▼ ▼ ▼

The carriage drew up before The Church of the Holy Martyr Saint Grygory and one of the escort's cavalry troopers dismounted to open the door.

Henrai Maidyn nodded his thanks as he started down the carriage's steps to the pavement. Then he heard a shout. His head turned in its direction.

The last thing he ever saw was the muzzle flash of the revolver in a brokenhearted older brother's right hand.

. II .
Protector's Palace,
Siddar City,
Old Province,
Republic of Siddarmark.

"Mister Ambassador."

Chancellor of the Exchequer Klymynt Myllyr stood, extending his hand in greeting, as his secretary escorted Mahlkym Preskyt into his office.

It was the Chancellor's working office, not the one he reserved for more formal occasions, Preskyt noted. Then again, he and Preskyt were old friends.

The day was cold and blustery, but Preskyt didn't mind that as much as some of his colleagues in the Charisian diplomatic service might have, because he'd grown up facing far worse. A native Chisholmian who'd been born and raised in the foothills of the Snow Crest Mountains, he stood almost six feet tall, with blond hair and blue eyes. Indeed, he looked considerably more like the stereotypical idea of a Siddarmarkian than his host did. Myllyr was two inches shorter than he was, with dark hair, dark eyes, and a badly scarred left cheek only partially concealed behind his full beard.

"Thank you for agreeing to see me, My Lord," Preskyt said formally, mindful of his official office as he clasped forearms with the Chancellor.

"I'd rather talk to you than pore over another column of figures any day!" Myllyr said feelingly, releasing the ambassador's forearm and waving him into the comfortable armchair on the other side of his desk. He waited until his guest had sat, then seated himself again and folded his hands on his blotter.

"But the fact that I'd rather talk to you than deal with more numbers doesn't mean I don't have a pretty shrewd—and unhappy—idea about why you wanted to see me, Mahlkym," he continued, and Preskyt nodded. Myllyr might not be in Henrai Maidyn's league when it came to the finer points of the Republic's economy, but he was no fool.

"I'm afraid you probably do, My Lord," he conceded. "First, though, Their Majesties have specifically instructed me to assure you of their continued faith in Lord Protector Henrai and the ultimate outcome of his reforms."

"But you're here because we haven't been able to meet our obligations under the treaty," Myllyr said, grasping the horns of the dilemma with all the subtlety of someone who'd been a colonel, not a diplomat.

Something to be said for colonels, Preskyt thought dryly.

"Something along those lines, I'm afraid," he acknowledged out loud. "Their Majesties are fully aware of the difficulties involved, and they've assured the Grand Duke of their ultimate confidence in the Republic."

"But he's getting impatient," Myllyr said, and snorted. "Don't blame him—not one bit! His people have all their pigs and wyverns in place, and we don't. To be honest, I'm surprised—grateful, but surprised—he's been patient this long." The Chancellor fixed the Charisian with a sharp eye. "Wouldn't happen that's because the Emperor and Empress have been sitting on him just a bit, would it?"

Definitely *something to be said for colonels*!

"I wouldn't put it in precisely those terms," Preskyt allowed with a slight smile. "I believe, however, that you may have captured the essence of the situation."

"Not surprised." Myllyr leaned back in his chair, his expression much more serious. "Cayleb and Sharleyan have always been good friends to the Republic," he said.

"And I want you to know how much both the Lord Protector and I appreciate what you've already passed on for them about extending their 'Ahrmahk Plan' to the Republic. I think it'll have a beneficial effect, ultimately, although chucking it into the midst of our local bankers before they've adjusted to the new reality might only make things worse. God knows half of them'd be fighting like krakens in a feeding frenzy to get any loans funneled into their own greedy hands! And it'd create all kinds of problems if the Exchequer started doling out loans as Cayleb and Sharleyan's agent. Change it from something coming out of their privy purse to official 'Charisian interference' in our economy in a heartbeat. Or into a 'Charisian plot' to buy control of the canal! God help us if some of our real idiots got hold of *that* notion! Shan-wei to pay and no pitch hot."

Preskyt nodded, although he cherished his own doubts on that head. Personally, he thought the Siddarmarkian economy was in enough trouble that the possibility of the kind of loans the United Provinces had received— were still receiving—from the Charisian monarchs could only have helped. His instructions from Tellesberg suggested Cayleb and Sharleyan thought the same thing, but they'd also been very clear that the decision about any announcements was up to the lord protector. He knew his own country best, he was the one fighting the forest fire on the ground, and it was essential they maintain their cordial relationship with Maidyn, especially with such a nasty backlash against Charis beginning to emerge in certain sectors of Siddarmark.

Of course, offering up a Siddarmarkian "Ahrmahk Plan" might do a little something about that backlash, too, he reflected. *But it's not your call, Mahlkym. And the truth is, there probably isn't a* good *way to handle it right now*.

Unfortunately, until someone did find a way to handle it, good or bad, one of the most important post-jihad projects was completely stalled.

For hundreds of years, the four-hundred-and-fifty-mile-long Salthar Canal linking Silkiah Bay in the east and Salthar Bay in the west, had barged cargoes across Silkiah, eliminating the long voyage around South Cape and bringing the grand duchy a rich revenue stream. The reason wasn't hard to understand, especially for a Charisian. Even for a steamship, able to maintain a steady fifteen knots and not dependent on wind and canvas, the voyage from Tellesberg to Gorath Bay going west took over two months—sixty-six days, to be precise—despite the fact that the two capital cities were less than seven thousand miles apart on a straight line. Unfortunately, the continent of Howard got in the way. In fact, that same steamship could have reached Gorath two five-days sooner if it sailed *east,* clear around the circumference of the planet, to get there.

It wasn't surprising the Salthar Canal had always been regarded as a critical waterway, but the canal's builders had never visualized the explosive growth of maritime commerce over the last fifty or sixty years. It had become impossible for the canal to handle the necessary volume of cargo years before the Jihad ever began, and the situation had grown only worse since. The situation would be helped enormously when the Salthar-Silk Town Railway, paralleling the canal, opened for traffic early next summer. Yet not even the SSTR would be able to handle the tonnages people eager to shorten the weary, arduous voyage between Tellesberg or Manchyr and Gorath Bay—or in the other direction, to Siddar City, for that matter—already wanted to ship, and those tonnages could only increase.

The notion of building a canal almost five hundred miles long capable of handling seagoing freighters would have been considered lunacy less than ten years earlier. The introduction of Lywysite during the Jihad and the steam-powered earthmoving machines springing from the ever-fertile minds of the Delthak Works' artificers and engineers *since* the Jihad had changed that, however. No one could have broken ground on such a project in the immediate aftermath of the Jihad, because Delthak's "steam shovels" and "dragondozers" had been only conceptual drawings, not even prototypes, at the time. Given the Duke of Delthak's record for achieving what he set out to accomplish, however, everyone had realized it was only a matter of when, not if. And that was why the Treaty of Silk Town had been written in 902.

It was painfully evident that something like a Silkiah Canal would be an irresistible prize for any greedy potentate. Everyone had been much too polite to mention names like Mahrys or Waisu, but it had seemed only prudent to ensure any grasping fingers stayed as far away from it as possible. That meant making the owners of those fingers aware of how sharply they'd be swatted if they reached in its direction, and the best way to do that was to make its construction a multinational project. The final canal would be operated by an independent governing board, but it would belong to all of the nations involved in its construction and they would be represented on the board—and share in its revenues—in proportion to their investment in building it. More to the point, their joint ownership would serve as a pointed warning to those greedier souls that they would face more than one foe if they attempted to seize the canal.

The Treaty of Silk Town had called for precisely that: a three-nation project financed—and protected—by the three realms with the most vital strategic interest in it: the Grand Duchy of Silkiah, the Empire of Charis . . . and the Republic of Siddarmark.

At the moment, two of those three partners were ready to proceed. The third wasn't. The Siddarmarkian Exchequer was stretched entirely too thin covering just the Republic's essential core expenses. It certainly didn't have the cash to pay its share of the canal construction budget, and the chaos of its credit markets meant it couldn't float a bond issue to cover those costs, either. That was one reason Preskyt thought it might be wiser for Lord Protector Henrai to go ahead and publicly announce the Ahrmahk Plan. Cayleb and Sharleyan could have covered as much as a third of the Republic share of the budget out of the Mohryah Lode's current production. It would have strained even their cash flow, but they could have done it, and that massive an infusion of capital might have done the Republic a world of good.

But Maidyn was afraid of the potential negative consequences of, as Myllyr had rather inelegantly put it, "chucking" the Ahrmahk Plan into the Republic's credit markets. No one could predict the exact consequences, and the lord protector's new Central Bank was still an untried institution, just getting its feet under it. Until he was certain of its stability, better able to gauge its ability to manage interest rates and eliminate under-funded liabilities, a sudden huge influx of outside capital might actually make matters worse. And that didn't even consider what one of Preskyt's colleagues had taken to calling "the optics" of it. There was already that nasty, gathering swell of resentment against Charis. If Cayleb and Sharleyan swooped in, bought up the necessary Siddarmarkian bond issues, a lot of people—especially any would-be financiers who got frozen out—would scream that Charis was trying to buy ownership of the canal and deprive Siddarmark of its fair representation on the governing board . . . or in the canal's future revenues. It wouldn't have been logical, and it certainly wouldn't have been reasonable. In fact, Cayleb and Sharleyan would have been loaning the Republic the money it needed to buy *its* share of the canal instead of simply paying the same money to increase their own share.

That wasn't how their opponents and detractors would present the case, however. Preskyt knew that. So Maidyn was probably right to sit on the news of the Ahrmahk Plan, and especially how it might relate to the Silkiah Canal, until he'd be able to sell at least the majority of his bonds to Siddarmarkians, not those "greedy Charisian" foreigners.

The problem was that no one knew how long he'd need to accomplish that.

"I understand your point, My Lord," the ambassador said. "For that matter, I'm pretty sure Grand Duke Silkiah understands it, as well. And I *know* Their Majesties do. Unfortunately, Kahnrad is facing mounting internal pressure to begin construction."

"I'm sure he is," Myllyr said glumly. He swiveled his chair to look out the window. "Silkiah's met its financial obligations, or will have shortly. I know they're not quite all the way there yet. And Charis's met its obligations in full. We're the anchor lumbering along behind."

"I'm sure the Grand Duke would never put it that way, My Lord."

"Only because he's polite and diplomatic. I'm an ex-colonel, and I can be more honest about it. We *are* the anchor, Mahlkym."

"Well, I suppose that would be one way to put it," Preskyt conceded. "But while Their Majesties promised Grand Duke Kahnrad they'd raise your concerns with him, they also assured him of their confidence in your leadership at the Exchequer and the Republic's determination—and ability—to meet its obligations under the treaty."

Myllyr looked back at him, then snorted.

"Good of them to say so, anyway," he said. "In more ways than one. But I'd say they're probably right to have confidence in *Lord Protector Henrai's* leadership." He shook his head. "I doubt it's much of a secret who's really running the Exchequer in addition to the rest of the Republic!"

"I think you're underestimating your own role, My Lord," Preskyt said gently. "I have my own sources in your government, you know. They tell me a lot about who's running what."

"On a day-to-day basis, that's probably fair," Myllyr said after a moment, then quirked a sudden smile. "I *do* make a pretty fair adjutant, if I say so myself! But the truth is, the Lord Protector makes his own economic policies and everyone knows it. Damn good thing, too! Even the people who hate him most over his Central Bank realize he understands our economy better than anyone else. They may not like the medicine he's feeding them, and some of them may figure he's out to pluck their personal wyverns right down to the bone. But so far, it's pretty clear they expect him to bring the Republic as a whole out the other side in one piece. Hard to think of anyone else who could make that claim just now."

"I tend to agree, My Lord. I'm only saying you're more than an inked stamp. Everyone who knows anything at all about federal policies knows that, and I'd venture to say that there's not a soul in the City who doesn't trust your honesty. Believe me, that's not a minor factor when it comes to stabilizing the banks!"

"Maybe not, but we're getting a little afield from the reason you dropped by. Did Their Majesties give you any estimate of the Grand Duke's patience to share with me?"

"Not any specific estimates, My Lord. They did charge me to tell you that, given the projected time span on the construction, *they* don't feel anywhere close to desperate. Obviously, they'd like to begin as soon as possible, but it'll still be at least a year and more likely two before the Delthak Works could deliver the steam shovels and dragondozers to make a real start. And Duke Delthak's engineers estimate it will take at least fifteen years to finish construction once they begin. So it's not as if another year or two will make that huge a difference."

"Understood." Myllyr nodded. "On the other hand, I noticed during the war that you Charisians always seem to get done sooner than scheduled!"

"We do try to not let the grass grow under our feet, My Lord. That's true. And the SSTR will help a lot in the meantime."

"Yes, and Mahrys is still pissed about that for oh, so *many* reasons!" Myllyr observed, brightening in obvious satisfaction.

"I believe one might reasonably say that. If one were an ex-colonel, and not a suave and polished diplomat, of course."

The two of them smiled at one another.

One of the things Mahrys IV had most resented about the pre-Jihad treaty the Church had brokered to prevent Silkiah from sparking yet another war between Desnair and Siddarmark had been the fact that the Salthar Canal was a bare, tantalizing hundred miles beyond the border of the Duchy of North Watch. It had been a case of "so near, and yet so far away" which he had found particularly hard to bear. The fact that the Mersayr Mountains had made it impossible to cut a canal between the Gulf of Jahras and Salthar Bay had only poured salt into the wound.

In the wake of Charis' invention of the steam automotive, he'd obviously hoped to build a railway of his own across the two-hundred-mile-wide Mersayr Neck, south of the Silkiah border, to suck away some of the Salthar Canal's lucrative revenues, and he'd started looking for investment partners well before Duke Delthak announced his partnership with half a dozen Silkiahan investors to build the Salthar-Silk Town Railway. The SSTR's route was better than twice as long as Mahrys' proposed rail line, but only in straight-line terms. It crossed the level, almost flat plain between the Mersayr Mountains to the south and the Salthar Mountains to the north, within sight of the existing canal, whereas Mahrys' route would have to snake its tortuous way through the Mersayrs. The mountainous switchbacks would add at least fifty percent to the straight-line distance for any Desnairian railroad, and building it through such rugged terrain would hugely increase its cost.

And, of course, the proposed Desnairian consortium wouldn't have had Duke Delthak or the Delthak Works behind it.

Needless to say, Mahrys' plans had died at birth, or possibly even a little earlier, which was a source of unalloyed pleasure for them both.

"The important thing is that we get the canal built in the end," Preskyt said now. "We'd all like to get to it as soon as possible, but Their Majesties are perfectly ready to wait until the Lord Protector feels comfortable that he has his own house in order. Their dispatches to me make it abundantly clear that their first desire is to make sure you have the time you need to get to that point. They weren't so inelegant to put it in quite these terms, but what they're really saying is that they're prepared to sit on Kahnrad a while longer and even a bit harder, if they have to."

"We appreciate that," Myllyr said sincerely, but Preskyt shrugged his thanks away.

"They haven't forgotten the Jihad, My Lord." The ambassador's expression had turned very serious. "They haven't forgotten what it cost the Republic, and they haven't forgotten who stood at their shoulder at the time it mattered most. I can't begin to tell you how Lord Protector Greyghor's death grieved them. I know you spoke to them at the funeral, but that was in a formal setting. They spoke to me about their feelings rather more informally on my last visit back to Tellesberg. Trust me, they miss him deeply and I think they see the canal as a final legacy to him. And they spoke very warmly of Lord Protector Henrai. They like him, they trust him, and they're prepared to do everything they can to help him succeed in the task he's undertaken."

"That's good to hear," Myllyr said simply. "That's very good to hear."

They sat in silence for several moments, then the Chancellor inhaled deeply and slapped both palms on his blotter.

"Thank you for coming by to tell me that, Mahlkym," he said. "Especially the last bit. It means a lot to me. Not simply that Their Majesties are prepared to support us, but why. The Lord Protector's always spoken very fondly of them, too, and I know how much he'll value what you've just said. That and knowing we can rely on Charis to stand with us will be an enormous relief for him. For all of us, really. Won't help too much when the idiots start yelling again, but at least those of us who have to put up with the yelping can feel a *little* serenity!"

He smiled, and Preskyt chuckled. He climbed out of his own chair and Myllyr stood, once more extending his arm across his desk.

"You're entirely welcome, My Lord. It was my pleasure, as well as my duty to Their Majesties. I'll be—"

The office door opened abruptly, interrupting him in midsentence, and he turned his head as Myllyr's secretary stepped into the room. The Chancellor did the same thing, but his expression was far more irritated than his guest's. He opened his mouth, but the secretary spoke first.

"I'm—"

The man stopped and cleared his throat. He blinked several times, and Preskyt felt his eyebrows rising as he realized the young man was fighting back tears.

"What is it?" From Myllyr's tone, he'd realized the same thing, and his irritation had turned into concern.

"I'm—I apologize for . . . for interrupting, My Lord." The secretary's voice was husky, wavering around the edges, and he held out a folded sheet of paper.

"We've just received a semaphore message from Archbishop Arthyn, My Lord," he said.

MAY YEAR OF GOD 907

◆

. I .

Tellesberg,
City of Tellesberg.
Kingdom of Old Charis,
Charisian Empire.

The steam automotive snorted into Tellesberg's Central Station on the Tellesberg-Uramyr Line under a dense canopy of steam-shot smoke.

The triangular red and white checkerboard shields displayed on either side of the dragon-catcher marked it as a Delthak Railways' special. If anyone had missed that indication, however, the fact that the entire train consisted of just six cars—two passenger cars, both bearing a red shield with a green wyvern, sandwiched between four cars carrying the badge of the Imperial Guard of Charis and something over a hundred Guardsmen, between them—might have been another.

Another thirty Guardsmen, headed by an extraordinarily tall major whose black hair was just beginning to show threads of white, waited on the covered platform.

The automotive continued forward until its smoke-gushing stack—and attendant scatter of cinders—was well clear of the platform roof, then halted in a sibilant hiss of air brakes. The doors of the four passenger cars in Charisian colors opened, disgorging *their* Guardsmen, who fanned out alertly. They found positions facing away from the passenger cars, weapons ready although not overtly brandished at the small crowd of spectators.

The thirty-man detail on the platform came to attention as a liveried porter rolled the short boarding steps up to the forward door of the lead passenger car and the trumpeters in the colors of the House of Ahrmahk raised their instruments. The porter climbed the steps, rapped once on the door, then opened it and stepped back down to the platform. Nothing happened for a moment, but then a slender, slightly built young man—he looked to be twenty-five or twenty-six years old—appeared in the open door and the ready trumpets sounded a fanfare which had never before been heard in Tellesberg.

The youngster looked around, his brown eyes frankly curious, then said something over his shoulder and started down the boarding steps. A considerably shorter man with white hair came after him, shaking his head and saying something no one else could hear over the trumpets, the stamp of feet and slap of weapons as the waiting Guardsmen presented arms, and the automotive's venting steam. The young man obviously heard it, however, and shook his own head with a grin his bushy beard and full mustache couldn't hide.

Emperor Cayleb stepped forward as the visitor stepped fully down onto the station platform, followed by half a dozen armsmen in the same green-and-red livery as the shields mounted on the passenger cars. He and the young man bowed to one another, and then the emperor extended his hand.

"Welcome to Tellesberg, Your Majesty," he said.

"Thank you." They clasped arms, and the young man shook his head. "I'm deeply honored that you came to meet me in person, Your Majesty."

"Well, Her Majesty insists that every once in a while we actually pretend we have something approaching manners," Cayleb replied with an absolutely straight face. "Especially for visiting heads of state who drop by to celebrate our sons' birthday."

King Rahnyld V of Dohlar looked at him for a moment, then chuckled. It was true that the ostensible purpose for the first state visit by any Dohlaran monarch to Charis was to celebrate the birthday of the royal twins.

It was even possible a particularly credulous hermit living somewhere among the summits of the Mountains of Light might actually believe that.

"In that case, it probably behooves me to pretend the same thing," the younger man said. "That we have something approaching manners in Gorath, too, I mean. Fortunately, you've already met my First Councilor, so that's one introduction we can skip without my appearing in the least impolite."

"True," Cayleb said, extending his hand in turn to Lywys Gardynyr. The Earl of Thirsk would be seventy next year, and stiffness of his crippled left shoulder seemed more pronounced than the last time they'd met, but his eye was bright, and he shook his head at his monarch.

"I doubt you'll fool anyone about how well behaved you are—or *aren't*—Your Majesty," he told Rahnyld. "Not after they've had the opportunity to spend a few hours in your company."

Rahnyld only smiled with obvious affection and touched the man who'd been his regent on the shoulder.

"I'll try not to embarrass you, Lywys," he promised. "Of course, there aren't any guarantees."

"I'll take what I can get," Thirsk said philosophically as a much younger girl with fair hair and gray eyes came a bit more timidly down the stairs. Her coloring was quite different from Rahnyld's, but her features were very similar, and Rahnyld reached out to take her hand as she stopped and curtsied to Cayleb.

"Your Majesty, may I present my younger sister, Rahnyldah?" he said, drawing her forward.

"Welcome to Tellesberg, Your Highness," Cayleb said with a much gentler smile.

"Rahnyldah was too young to attend the peace conference," Rahnyld continued, "so she pestered me unmercifully to accompany me on this trip." Rahnyldah's blush—she was at least ten years younger than her brother—was painfully evident given her coloring, and Cayleb shook his head reprovingly at Rahnyld.

"I feel certain no princess this fair could possibly pester anyone 'unmercifully,' Your Majesty," he said severely. "If she's anything like my daughter—who, by the way, Your Highness, is only about a year older than you—she was simply . . . emphatic."

Rahnyldah looked at him for a moment, then smiled at him and visibly relaxed.

"Better," Cayleb said. He held out his hand, and she glanced up at Thirsk from the corner of one eye before she reached back. The emperor raised it gracefully, kissed its back, and held it for a moment before he released it, and she smiled even more broadly at him.

"Actually," Rahnyld said a bit more seriously, "my sister Stefyny is the one whose nose is out of joint. She really wanted to come, too, but unlike Rahnyldah, she did get to attend the peace conference, and someone had to stay home."

Cayleb nodded in understanding. Princess Stefyny was actually four years older than Rahnyld, and he had no brothers. If anything unfortunate happened to him, the crown would pass to her, and her presence at home in Gorath insured the succession against accidents.

"Well, I'm delighted Princess Rahnyldah *was* able to come, and Alahnah and the twins are waiting to show her around the Palace. For that matter, Archbishop Maikel's invited them all on a tour of the city tomorrow or the next day, followed by lunch at the Archbishop's Palace, as part of the boys' birthday festivities. The *tour* may turn out to be boring," Cayleb smiled at the princess, "but Alahnah informs me that Mistress Maizur, His Eminence's cook, produces the best briar berry cobbler in the world."

"I'd like that, Your Majesty," Rahnyldah said, without even glancing at Thirsk, which told Cayleb quite a lot about how she'd been briefed before the trip. And even more about her brother's and his first councilor's attitude toward the Church of Charis.

"In that case, why don't we all head over to the Palace?" he said, and waved for his guests to proceed him down the lane between the ruler-straight lines of Guardsmen.

The trio of vehicles waiting for them outside the station had neither dragons nor horses in the traces. In fact, there *were* no traces, and Rahnyld's eyes widened a bit as he took in the wire-spoked wheels with their fat rubber tires.

"After you, Your Majesty."

Cayleb beckoned for the visitors to climb into the lead carriage first, and they obeyed the polite command. The vehicles were lower to the ground than conventional carriages, and King Rahnyld handed his sister into the indicated carriage as she stepped straight across from the curb. He followed, but Thirsk only shook his head with a smile and waved for Cayleb to precede him. The emperor smiled back, clearly contemplating out-stubborning his guest, then accepted defeat and followed the king. Thirsk came last, while Major Athrawes climbed into the separate compartment at the front of the vehicle and settled in behind the glass windshield beside the driver.

The driver waited while the other members of the Dohlaran party climbed into the other two carriages and Merlin's second in command gave him the sign. Then he opened the throttle mounted on the steering column, where an Old Terran vehicle might have mounted a gearshift, and they rolled away from Tellesberg Central Station in almost total silence.

"I've heard a lot about your 'steam dragons,'" Rahnyld said as the superbly sprung carriage moved along the cobblestone street.

Tellesberg's cobbles were smoother than most, but *any* cobblestones were uneven, by the very nature of things. They were designed to be that way to insure secure footing despite the odiferous gifts draft and riding animals were known to leave in their wake. Despite that, the combination of springs, shock absorbers, and pneumatic tires prevented the kind of bouncing and jarring they might otherwise have experienced, especially at such a rapid speed. The streets between Central Station and Tellesberg Palace had been cleared of all other traffic for the Dohlarans' arrival, and Imperial Guardsmen and infantry from the Imperial Charisian Army lined the sidewalks. With no other traffic, the driver could open the throttle wider than he might have under other circumstances, and Princess Rahnyldah, especially, looked suitably impressed as they moved forward at well over thirty miles an hour.

"I'll admit we're showing off," Cayleb said cheerfully. "For what I think are probably obvious reasons, Her Majesty and I snabbled up the first luxury steam passenger carriages." He grinned, obviously enjoying himself. "We thought it was our imperial duty to run the risk of such a newfangled mode of transportation in order to support Duke Delthak's efforts. Needless to say," he widened his eyes at Rahnyldah, "our advisors and *Seijin* Merlin were aghast at our taking such a chance!"

"I'm sure, Your Majesty," Thirsk said dryly as Rahnyldah suppressed another giggle.

"Actually, there's at least a modicum of truth in that," Cayleb said more seriously. "We've made it our business to support the Duke's efforts in every way we can."

"And very successfully, too." Thirsk nodded. "His Majesty has adopted much the same policy in Gorath."

"So I've understood." It was Cayleb's turn to nod. "The problem, of course, is that eventually something's sure to go wrong. After all, things have 'gone wrong' with conventional draft dragons more times than anyone could count, so it's only a matter of time until something goes wrong with a *steam* dragon. And when 'something goes wrong' with something new and different—"

He shrugged.

"We've had that same thought," Rahnyld said. "In fact, we've already had something 'go wrong.'" His eyes darkened for a moment. "It's not like piles of coal haven't spontaneously caught fire before, but when it happened to *Arbalest* there were plenty of voices to proclaim it was 'a sign from the Archangels'!"

His tone made it abundantly clear what he thought about any such claim, but he had a point, Cayleb reflected. The wet coal in one of HMS *Arbalest*'s forward bunkers had ignited spontaneously, and her crew had suffered over thirty casualties, six of them fatal, fighting the blaze. More, the ship's wooden hull had suffered significant structural damage. They'd gotten it under control—and saved the ship in the process—eventually, but the Royal Dohlaran Navy's first homebuilt steam-powered warship had emerged with a reputation as a jinxed ship.

"We had plenty of problems with new concepts during the Jihad, Your Majesty." Thirsk's tone was rather more serene than his monarch's. "And a lot of people said a lot of the same things when we did. Trust me, Admiral Hahlynd knows how to deal with it."

"Oh, I know that, Lywys," Rahnyld assured him. "It just pisses me off."

"Crowned heads of state aren't 'pissed off,'" Thirsk told him with a smile. "They may be 'extremely irritated' or they may progress from there to a 'towering rage.' But 'pissed off' is what their underlings are. Don't you agree, Your Majesty?" He raised an eyebrow at Cayleb, who snorted.

"We Charisians are simple, uncultured Out Islanders, My Lord," he replied. "I could not begin to *count* the number of times I've been 'pissed off.' In fact, quite a lot of them had to do with you and Admiral Hahlynd during the Jihad. I can't tell you how much I prefer having you as friendly neighbors."

"Trust me, Your Majesty," Rahnyld said, his expression much less that of a young man seeing wonders and much more that of a crowned king, "you can't possibly prefer that more than we do."

▼ ▼ ▼

Tellesberg Palace's front gate was a tight squeeze for the caravan of steam-powered carriages, and it would have been impossible to fit them through the gate tunnel of the central keep. In an era of breech-loading artillery and high explosive shells, stone walls offered far less protection than they once had, however, and a new and much broader gate had been cut through the center of one curtainwall. It was provided with a stout steel-barred portcullis and the sides of the cut were pierced by loopholes for riflemen—Cayleb Ahrmahk was an innovator, not an idiot—but it provided ample room for the vehicles to pull up to the foot of the broad flight of stairs at the foot of the grandly carved portico of the newest portion of the palace.

They'd outdistanced the mounted Guardsmen, both Charisian and Dohlaran, but there was an ample supply of Imperial Guardsmen on hand and Major Hayzu Delakorht, the commanding officer of Rahnyld's personal armsmen, and Captain Lynkyn Nuhnyez, third in command of Rahnyld's armsmen and specifically responsible for Princess Rahnyldah, had accompanied their principals in the second carriage. As the line of armsmen in the black, gold, blue, and white of the House of Ahrmahk came to attention, Delakorht and Nuhnyez fell in on the heels of their royal charges. It was obvious they would have preferred to have more of their own men present, but both of them had come to know Major Athrawes at the peace conference which had ended the Jihad and it was equally clear they had no qualms about Rahnyld and Rahnyldah's physical safety.

A very pregnant Empress Sharleyan waited for them at the head of the stairs, and Rahnyld bowed deeply to her. Then it was Rahnyldah's turn. The girl went down in a deep, perfectly executed curtsy, and Sharleyan reached down to catch her hand and pull her back upright.

"Very nicely done, Your Highness," she told Rahnyldah with a smile. "As someone who used to be a princess herself, I'm sure you were nervous about facing an ogress of an empress, but you are most welcome in this house. You and your brother."

"Oh, no, Your Majesty!" Rahnyldah protested. Then she blushed. "I mean . . . I mean *thank you* for welcoming us, and I *was* nervous, but not because I thought you were an . . . an—"

"My dear," Sharleyan said, "I'm old enough to be your mother, so there's not much point trying to bamboozle me. Yes, you were nervous. And, yes, you were afraid I'd be an ogress. But I'm not, so you aren't anymore. Right?"

"Right, Your Majesty," Rahnyldah said finally, and dimpled as she smiled up at the empress.

"Good." Sharleyan patted her hand, then touched her own swollen abdomen. "And, as I'm sure you can tell, I'm just a tiny bit pregnant right now. So my ankles are swollen, my feet ache, my back hurts, and I am incredibly grouchy." Her smile was broader than ever. "Since all of that's true, I'm going to let Cayleb be the host and handle all the details of greeting your brother while I go find a comfortable chair and get off my feet. Why don't you come with me? I'm sure you'd rather meet Alahnah and Gwylym and Braiahn than listen to an hour or two of formal greetings. Of course, the boys are only seven—and boys—but Alahnah's a year older than you are, and this is *Seijin* Merlin's daughter, Stefyny." She indicated the slender young woman standing beside her. "Lady Stefyny has very kindly volunteered to keep the boys occupied and out of your and Alahnah's hair."

"Oh, that would be wonderful!" Rahnyldah said, then paused and looked up at Earl Thirsk and her brother. "May I, Rahnyld?"

"Of course you can, Rahnee." The king gave her a hug, then pushed her gently in Sharleyan's direction. "Now scoot! Go let Her Majesty get off those feet of hers."

"Thank you!" Rahnyldah said, and the king watched Sharleyan and Stefyny sweep his sister away. She was already chattering enthusiastically, and Captain Nuhnyez looked back at his monarch with a grin as he followed his charge.

"Thank you for making her feel so welcome, Your Majesty," Rahnyld said, turning back to Cayleb.

"Given the fact that relations between our realms are much warmer than they were, and bearing in mind that deplorable Out Islander informality I believe I've already mentioned, I think we might dispense with all the 'Majesties' and use a simple 'Rahnyld' and 'Cayleb,' at least in private," Cayleb suggested.

"Thank you . . . Cayleb," Rahnyld said after a moment. He clearly hadn't expected one of the two most powerful monarchs in the world to invite a youngster twelve years his junior to address him by his given name, even if the youngster in question *was* a king.

"Good! Because now, I'm afraid, we have to go handle some of those details Sharley just shuffled off on me. If you'd accompany me?"

"Of course," Rahnyld murmured, and followed the emperor's brisk stride down a hall of polished marble towards an airy, breezy council chamber which overlooked the palace's central garden.

▼ ▼ ▼

"May I come in, My Lord?" Merlin Athrawes asked much later that evening, and Lywys Gardynyr turned from the window where he'd been admiring the embers of sunset as they settled into the waters of Howell Bay.

"Of course you may!" the Earl of Thirsk said warmly, holding out his working hand.

Merlin clasped forearms with him, then moved to stand looking out the window at his side. The *seijin* was the next best thing to a foot taller than the diminutive earl, and despite the proliferation of modern firearms, the Imperial Guard retained its blackened breastplates. They might have dispensed with the chain mail hauberks which had once accompanied those breastplates, but the armor added even more to the *seijin*'s undeniable air of . . . solidity.

"Much nicer weather than the first time you dropped in on me. In a *lot* of ways," Thirsk said softly after a moment, and Merlin shrugged.

"I'm just glad it worked out as well as it did," he said after a moment.

"So am I." Thirsk's tone was fervent and he turned to look up at the taller *seijin*. "You know, there are times I still find it difficult to believe you didn't use the girls' safety to hold a pistol to my head."

"Well," Merlin looked back down with a lurking smile, "honesty compels me to admit that if we hadn't been pretty damned sure it was what you already wanted to do, the temptation to . . . turn up the wick probably would've been more difficult to resist." His smile vanished. "On the other hand, I'm confident Cayleb and Sharleyan *would* have resisted, even so."

"So am I," Thirsk repeated. "It's amazing what deadly weapons compassion and morality are when they're deployed in the service of diplomacy."

"As long as they're deployed against people who have a sense of morality of their own," Merlin conceded. "I don't think they'd have much effect on a Zhaspahr Clyntahn."

"No," Thirsk's smile turned cold and thin. "You found the right argument to get through to him. But you did show compassion, you know. It had to be tempting as hell to hand him over to the Punishment instead of just hanging him."

"I can honestly say it wasn't," Merlin replied. Thirsk's eyebrows arched in polite skepticism, and Merlin stroked one of his mustachios. "I'm not pretending I didn't want that son-of-a-bitch to suffer," he admitted. "But personally, speaking for myself, I think the spectacle when he faced the noose and realized no one was riding to his rescue was a more effective rejoinder to his style of extremism than the Punishment ever could have been. Someone who snivels and begs and practically pisses himself on the gallows stairs doesn't make the best martyr fodder."

"No, he doesn't," Thirsk said softly. He looked out the window again, remembering how the admiral for whom Prince Gwylym had been named had died.

"I can't begin to tell you how happy I am to see Rahnyld here in Tellesberg as a visitor and honored guest," Merlin continued after a moment. "Or how happy I am to see you still at his side."

"I wouldn't be, if I had my druthers," Thirsk said frankly. "I turned *seventy* this year, Merlin. I'd much rather be sitting in a vineyard playing with my grandchildren!"

"I'm sure you would." Merlin allowed one hand to rest lightly on the earl's shoulder. "But young Rahnyld needs a steady hand to support him a while longer, I think. And not every young king's wise enough to retain the man who was his regent as his first councilor once he attains his majority. God knows the world's seen more than enough newly crowned kings who only wanted to cut the 'apron strings'!"

"Like that idiot Zhyou-Zhwo in Harchong?" Thirsk grimaced, and Merlin nodded.

"You don't *have* to be stupid to make that mistake, but it does help. Of course, Zhyou-Zhwo does have the minor excuse that he's trying to squirm out from under the thumb of the professional bureaucrats. You and Duke Dragon Island did a pretty fair job of pruning back the bureaucrats in Gorath before Rahnyld assumed personal rule."

"We tried, anyway." Thirsk's grimace turned into a crooked smile. "I never thought I'd think of an Ahlverez as a personal friend," he admitted. "Not after Armageddon Reef and Crag Reach, anyway! But Rainos has surprised me a lot of times over the years."

"And Rahnyld's lucky to have had both of you," Merlin said seriously.

"I'm glad you think so. There are still people in Gorath who think we're too pro-Charis, though, you know."

"I don't doubt it. But from here, it looks like the obstructionists are losing ground steadily."

"That's probably fair." Thirsk nodded. "They aren't going to give up without a fight, but Charis' generosity—especially Duke Delthak's willingness to invest so heavily in the Kingdom—makes it difficult for them. Although," the earl looked at Merlin shrewdly, "I do have to wonder at times why Cayleb and Sharleyan are going so far out of their way to actively discourage Dohlaran economic dependency on Charis."

"I beg your pardon?" Merlin asked politely.

"Oh, don't look so innocent, Merlin!"

Thirsk turned to face him fully and tucked the thumb of his right hand into his belt in the gesture which had replaced folding his arms after his left arm was crippled. His expression made it abundantly clear that he realized he was speaking to one of Cayleb and Sharleyan Ahrmahk's most trusted councilors.

"It's as obvious as the nose on your face—Shan-wei! As the nose on *my* face!" he continued. "You Charisians could completely control all these new innovations, make us come to you to buy your products at your price. And instead, you're busy investing in manufactories in other countries, which can only ultimately compete with your *own* manufactories. I'm reasonably confident Cayleb and Sharleyan don't cherish some deep-seated nefarious plan to absorb Dohlar, and from an economic perspective, I can't really see what Rainos calls a 'downside' for Dohlar even if they did, frankly. Not if it's going to build shipyards and automotive foundries and steel mills in Dohlar. But I do have to admit that I don't really understand it."

"At the moment, Duke Delthak's making a lot of marks, My Lord," Merlin pointed out. "The manufactories and foundries may be in Dohlar, but a third of the ownership is Charisian, and so is a third of the profit. In some ways, it's just a matter of producing what we sell you close enough to home that we don't have to ship it in!"

"Of course it is," Thirsk said dryly.

"Maybe it's as simple as their wanting to tie the world together with shared common interests, then," Merlin suggested. "With the schism formalized, the Church is a weaker glue than she used to be. Especially after the Jihad. Grand Vicar Rhobair was—and Grand Vicar Tymythy Rhobair *is*—worlds away from that bastard Clyntahn, but both of them have demonstrated the wisdom to stay away from Church-imposed diplomacy. Trust me, we thank God for it on a regular basis, but it does leave a certain vacuum on the diplomatic front."

"Given how preoccupied Zion is with what's going on in Harchong, Tymythy Rhobair doesn't have much time and energy to devote to imposing diplomacy on anyone else even if that was what he wanted to do," Thirsk observed, and Merlin nodded.

"Fair," he acknowledged. "But even if that were the only reason they've abandoned the Church's tradition of imposing international solutions—it's not, but even if it were—I think Cayleb and Sharleyan could still make a valid case for finding common interests, common ventures—*cooperative* ventures—anywhere they can. The object's to encourage all realms to decide it's smarter to profit from peaceful commerce than shoot at each other again, My Lord. Mind you, human nature being human nature, the odds may not be in their favor. Still, if someone can make out better without going back to war with his neighbors the chances that he *won't* go back to war have to be at least a little better."

"There's something to be said for that," Thirsk allowed. "Just the trip here was remarkable. Five years ago—Langhorne! *Three* years ago—that trip would've taken months. Today, it took us just over two *five-days*, and most of that was crossing from Silk Town to Uramyr!"

He shook his head, his expression bemused, and Merlin hid a smile of triumph behind a gravely thoughtful expression.

Rahnyld and his party had left Gorath for Salthar, at the western terminus of the Salthar Canal, aboard one of the fast, steel-hulled twenty-knot steamers Dohlar had purchased from Charis. The journey to Salthar had taken less than two days; a sailing vessel, even with favorable winds, would have taken at least five.

They'd crossed the full breadth of Silkiah by train in less than twelve hours, then boarded another steamer—this one a chartered Delthak Shipping passenger liner escorted by a pair of fast cruisers of the Imperial Charisian Navy—in Silk Town and sailed for Uramyr on the western flank of the mountainous isthmus which separated Howell Bay from Westrock Reach. As Thirsk had said, that leg had been the lengthiest, at almost ten days, but it had also been the next best thing to six thousand miles. And from Uramyr, they'd made the last leg of their trip to Tellesberg by rail by way of Chermyn's Town, covering the next best thing to three hundred straight-line miles in just under ten hours, despite the rugged terrain which had forced the track-laying crews to snake their way through the mountains.

"I have to say all the new applications have caught Rahnyld's imagination," Thirsk continued after a moment. "To be honest, though, I'd also have to admit there are still times when the pace of all this change makes me nervous." He shook his head. "We went for so many centuries without anything like this . . . this *burst* of innovation. Now it's here and, in some ways, it's only been gathering speed ever since the shooting stopped. I don't even recognize the world anymore, in a lot of ways, Merlin, and there are times I'm afraid we may be pressing too closely on the Proscriptions. When that happens, I remind myself Zhaspahr Clyntahn opposed it, which automatically means God and the Archangels almost certainly approve of it! But there are still times. . . ."

"I'm sure there are, My Lord," Merlin said. "I can only point out that all of those 'innovations' are actually the product of a fairly small number of fundamentally new concepts. We're seeing scads of variations rung on the theme, but they're all based on little more than a handful or two of new *concepts*. I know Zhaspahr Clyntahn was prepared to approve anything if it was likely to give him an edge in the Jihad, no matter what that meant for the Proscriptions. But for all Clyntahn's vilification, I think most people understand Bishop Paityr had a rather different view of God's mind, and Grand Vicar Rhobair and Grand Vicar Tymythy Rhobair have both endorsed Bishop Paityr's conclusions on those new concepts. I'll confess the number of ways in which they've affected Safehold is pretty staggering, but it's mostly been a matter of working out the logical implications of the processes which have been attested by the Inquisition."

"I know. I know!" Thirsk pulled his thumb out of his belt to wave his hand. "I really do understand that, Merlin. But do you know what Rahnyld had to say to me while we were steaming across the Gulf of Tarot?"

"No, My Lord," Merlin said, somewhat less than truthfully.

"He pointed out that assuming the numbers we've heard in Gorath are accurate, we could've made the entire trip from Gorath direct to Tellesberg in only *seven* days by 'airship.'" The earl shook his head again, his expression more bemused than ever. "*Seven days,* Merlin! Langhorne! What are you people going to come up with *next*?"

"I'm sure I have no idea what Duke Delthak and his 'brain trust' are going to propose tomorrow, My Lord," Merlin said even less truthfully. "On the other hand, I don't think Their Majesties *or* His Grace are going to let Rahnyld or any other crowned head of state anywhere near one of Delthak's airships for quite a while yet. Especially not for any sort of long over-water flights!"

"And praise Langhorne fasting for it!" Thirsk said in heartfelt tones. "If they weren't prepared to put their foot down pretty firmly on that, Rahnyld would be nagging away at them this very moment! In fact, he probably *is* going to try his damnedest to finagle at least a short flight while we're here."

"A *short* flight might be worked out, My Lord. But so far we've only made the actual crossing between Charis and Silk Town four times, and our pilots went by way of Tarot each time. It's going to be a while before anyone's talking about regular round-trip, over-water schedules!"

Thirsk nodded, but Merlin wondered if the earl suspected just how quickly that was actually likely to change. The *Duchess of Delthak* was completely unsuited to that kind of service, but the follow-on *Duchairn*-class airships were another matter entirely. The *Duchairn*'s gasbag was almost twice the length of the *Duchess*-class', with four times the volume and almost ten times the useful lift. Its Praigyr-2 engines had fifty percent more dragonpower than the *Duchess*' Praigyr-1s, and its endurance at cruising speed was eleven and a half days. The 6,800-mile straight voyage from Gorath to Tellesberg, heading east against the southern tradewinds, would take a *Duchairn* the seven days Rahnyld had cited. The voyage from Tellesberg to Gorath, on the other hand, with the trades pushing her along rather than slowing her, would require less than four and a half.

Of course, it's never going to be as safe as a steamship, he acknowledged. *Airships are just too fragile for it to be any other way. But it's actually less death-defying than the voyage Thirsk and his galleys made the long way around in the Armageddon Reef campaign!*

"We do live in interesting times, My Lord," he acknowledged out loud after a moment.

"More so for some of us than for others." Thirsk was looking out the window again, watching the last of the blood-red light fading from the western sky, and he shook his head somberly. "I don't envy Lord Protector Klymynt one bit right now."

"I don't think anyone does," Merlin said. "Losing Lord Protector Henrai that way, and at that particular time. . . ." It was his turn to shake his head. "I'm sure Cayleb and Sharleyan will have more to say to you about this, but we really needed Henrai to oversee his reforms. And the way the violence's spiraled back up again out West after the assassination. It's at least as bad as it ever was, and every sign is that it's going to get even worse before it starts getting better again. The way things are looking now, the Republic's going to be in serious trouble—probably even more trouble than it's in now—for a long time to come."

"That's our reading from Gorath," Thirsk agreed.

Then he paused long enough to raise one of Merlin's eyebrows before he turned back from the window and looked up in the bright glow of his chamber's gas-jet lighting.

"As we were crossing Silkiah, I couldn't help noticing how the rail line parallels the Salthar Canal. And I also couldn't help noticing that ground still hasn't been broken on the *Silkiah* Canal."

"No, it hasn't," Merlin agreed, studying the earl's expression.

"Well, I realize it behooves Dohlar to tread lightly where Charis' relationship with Siddarmark is concerned, since we *were* on the other side during the Jihad. Lord Protector Greyghor and Lord Protector Henrai were remarkably civil about it, but even they had trouble forgetting we invaded them without bothering with any formal declarations of war. Most of the other Siddarmarkians I've encountered since the peace conference have been rather less inclined to let bygones be bygones."

The small Dohlaran shrugged.

"The truth is, they *shouldn't* forget it. Yes, we were obeying Mother Church's commands, but my God, how many *million* Siddarmarkians died because we did?" He shook his head, eyes haunted. "*I* have trouble forgiving us for that some days. I don't think any reasonable human being could blame Siddarmark for harboring a grudge."

"I wish I could argue with that," Merlin said somberly.

"Well, as I say, I have no desire to . . . complicate your relationship with Siddarmark, and we both know there's an element in the Republic that's not a lot happier with the 'moneygrubbing Charisians' right now than it is with Dohlar. The last thing either of us need is to mobilize that unhappiness against the two of us by feeding it. But Grand Duke Kahnrad met Rahnyld in Silk Town before we went aboard ship. It was a pleasant visit, but I couldn't avoid the suspicion that he was sounding us out."

"Sounding you out about . . . ?"

"About the canal," Thirsk said. "He pointed out—just in passing, you understand—that in many ways, Dohlar has a considerably stronger natural interest in the new canal than Siddarmark. We're more of a maritime power; the border we share with the Grand Duchy is actually two hundred miles longer than its land border with Siddarmark; and the mouth of Gorath Bay is less than six hundred miles from Salthar by sea while Bedard Bay is over *three thousand* miles from Silk Town for one of your airships. It's well over twice that by sea."

The earl paused, looking up at the towering *seijin,* and Merlin gazed back down without speaking for several seconds. Then he shrugged.

"I can't argue with any of that, My Lord," he acknowledged. "We do, however, have a treaty with Silkiah and Siddarmark."

"I know you do, and that's one reason I have no intention of addressing this matter publicly. I had to point out to Rahnyld why it would be a bad idea for us to do that, though. He *is* young, and he's a lot more . . . enthusiastic about his duties as king than his father was. And as his fascination with airships suggests, he's *really* enthusiastic about all the new possibilities Charis is opening up. I'm afraid Kahnrad didn't hesitate to fire up his imagination . . . not that it *needed* much 'firing' from anyone else!"

"It may be time for Their Majesties to have a word or two with the Grand Duke," Merlin observed.

"It may. At the same time, though, and doing my honest best to leave the purely Dohlaran elements out of consideration, he has a point, Merlin." Thirsk waved his hand again. "The canal's not going to get itself built in a day, even with Charis getting behind it and pushing. Hell, even with *Duke Delthak* getting behind it and pushing! Kahnrad would be more than human if he wasn't counting the days until you can actually break ground on it, and it doesn't look like Siddarmark will be able to provide its share of the financing anytime soon. Not with the spate of bankruptcies and collapsing cartels we're hearing about in Gorath, anyway. We have every reason to see that canal built, especially given what it's going to mean for our maritime commerce. I understand the diplomatic aspects of your existing treaties and your existing relationships, but I think it's unreasonable to expect Kahnrad to not be getting . . . impatient."

Merlin nodded unhappily. Thirsk had an excellent point, and the situation seemed unlikely to improve anytime soon.

"As I say, I can't argue with anything you've just said,"

he said after a moment. "And I think it would be completely reasonable for you to mention your conversation with Kahnrad when you meet with Cayleb and Sharleyan. He's a clever fellow, of course. I'd say it's most likely the real reason he was talking to you was to put a little more pressure on *them*. And, as you say, it's hard to blame him for any impatience he may be feeling."

OCTOBER YEAR OF GOD 907

✦

. I .
Pauton-Quijang High Road
and
City of Zhynkau,
Boisseau Province,
United Provinces,
North Harchong.

Lieutenant Yausung Ryndau, United Provinces Provisional Militia, stood on the hilltop and watched with cautious satisfaction as his platoon's lead squads moved forward through the chilly autumn afternoon.

Most of the crops were in, but the wind rattled the dry cornstalks still standing in the fields that lined the narrow farm track and sighed in the scrub conifers around his hilltop. In the distance, he heard the high-pitched wail of an automotive's whistle as it thundered along the Rwanzhi-Pauton Line behind him, but the sound was no longer startling. The United Provinces' steadily expanding rail net reached as far north as Chalfor in Cheshire and as far east as Tiangshi. There was even talk of expanding the United Provinces protection as far as the ruins of Shang-mi and extending the Tiangshi Line the additional hundred miles or so to the capital. Indeed, there was even some talk about reaching beyond Shang-mi all the way to the far side of the Chiang-wu Mountains, another eight hundred miles— for a wyvern, not a landbound mortal; it was a hell of a lot farther by high road—beyond the old capital. There were a lot of theoretical arguments in favor, given the mountains' defensive strength. Ryndau understood that, but personally, he thought that would be reaching a bit too far.

Of course, the decision wasn't up to him.

He ignored the whistle and raised the Charisian-manufactured double-glass. He peered through it, adjusting the focusing wheel with one forefinger, and concentrated on his platoon as its squads leapfrogged along the farm track. His vantage point was high enough to look down on the sunken lane over the dry corn tassels, and the double-glass brought Sergeant Zheng's squad into razor-sharp focus. The lieutenant had had the double-glass long enough now that it had become merely marvelous, no longer an outright miracle, and he swung his gaze back to Platoon Sergeant Yingkan Fuzhow, then nodded approval as Fuzhow waved for Zheng's squad to halt in place while Sergeant Chwaiyn's squad took over the lead. Visibility down on the road bed was limited, but Fuzhow was aware of that and Chwaiyn's squad filtered forward while Zheng's held position in what their Charisian instructors called "overwatch."

The western side of the dirt road was bordered by a wall of piled, dry-laid stone that was slightly better than waist high, but there was only a well-weathered split rail fence on the east. Some of the rails were badly warped—Ryndau doubted it would actually have been up to the task of keeping the occasional wandering cow out of the corn—but it defined the farm road's borders. Unlike the stone wall, however, it was no barrier to the human eye and the visibility was far better to the east. The stone wall limited what could be seen in the other direction, especially if someone had chosen to hide behind it. In fact, the platoon sergeant had one of 4th Platoon's sections sweeping up the far side of the stone wall just in case someone had decided to do exactly that. It was hard going through the dried corn, and although he couldn't hear it from his own position, Ryndau knew

they were making Shan-wei's own racket as they forced
their way through the brittle stalks.

Sergeant Chwaiyn's lead section paused as they approached a bend where the road turned sharply west.
They spread a bit wider, positioning themselves so that
the man at the eastern end of their line could see around
the bend. He dropped and crawled under the lowest rail
of the fence to get a better angle and his gaze swept the
next stretch carefully. Then he raised his left hand to
signal the all-clear and Corporal Naiow started forward
with his section. They turned the corner and—

CRAAAACK!

Ryndau twitched. In fact, he barely managed to avoid
jumping in astonishment as the rifle shot crashed across
the afternoon's chill. His head whipped around, and he
swore as two or three dozen more rifles thundered from
the cornfield to the east. An instant later, fifty men came
charging out of the corn behind the high, piercing howl
of the battle cry the Imperial Charisian Army had appropriated from the old Royal Charisian Marines.

Platoon Sergeant Fuzhow's head snapped around in
the same direction. He was too far away for Ryndau to
hear what he was shouting, but despite the totality of
the surprise, his astounded squads wheeled towards the
oncoming Charisians. Chwaiyn's men tried to scramble
into a firing line of some sort, but Zheng's vaulted over
the stone wall and spread out on the farther side, leveling their rifles across the improvised parapet.

The Charisians went to ground, flattening among
the skeletal cornstalks rather than charge into Zheng's
rifles. As they did, one of the Charisian noncoms distributed among the UPPM's squads began whacking
Chwaiyn's men with his baton, designating casualties.
Virtually Naiow's entire section sat down in disgust as
the baton thwacked the backs of their helmets. The rest
of Chwaiyn's men went prone in whatever cover they
could find and began firing back.

More blank cartridges began to crackle as Zheng's
riflemen fired back at the Charisians, as well. The
attackers—like Chwaiyn's survivors—had the advantage

of being prone in excellent concealment, but cornstalks wouldn't have stopped real bullets whereas Zheng's men had the advantage of the stone wall's solid protection, and Ryndau stopped swearing. If Zheng and what was left of Chwaiyn's squad could hold the Charisians in play until Fuzhow swung his other two squads out on their flank, they might still—

KABOOM!

An entire chain of thunderous explosions roared from the *western* side of the stone wall, directly behind Sergeant Zheng's men, and Ryndau's jaw clamped as whistles began to shrill. They were loud enough to cut through the crackle of rifles, and Ryndau managed—somehow—not to start swearing all over again as the umpires signaled the ignominious end of the training exercise. Instead, he drew a deep, deep breath and turned to the brown-haired man standing beside him.

"You even warned me it was an ambush exercise," he said in a tone of profound self-disgust.

"Well, yes," Lieutenant Bhradfyrd agreed in a pronounced Tarotisian accent, and shrugged. "I think the problem is that Yingkan thought he had better visibility to the east than he really did."

Ryndau nodded glumly, watching as the Charisian ambushers stood and waded out of the cornfield and clambered over the rail fence. They mingled with the Harchongians, laughing and smacking their discomfited students on the back like the winning team in a baseball game. Their camouflage-pattern uniforms would have blended into the dense rows of dead corn anyway, but they'd taken a page from the ICA's scout snipers and fastened additional foliage to their helmets, breaking up any betraying outlines.

A petulant part of the lieutenant tried to convince himself that that was the only reason they'd gotten away with it.

The rest of him knew better.

"You're right," he sighed. "And your people counted on that, didn't they?"

"To some extent." Bhradfyrd shrugged. "Visibility

was better to the east than trying to look directly over the stone wall, after all. But 'better' isn't the same thing as 'good,' and we counted on your people being preoccupied with the worse blind spots on their left. And—" he allowed himself a grin "—we also figured you'd do exactly what Zheng did and go over the wall to use it for cover when we hit you from the right."

Ryndau nodded again, glumly.

"I suppose I need to have a little talk with Platoon Sergeant Fuzhow and Sergeant Zheng about following doctrine," he growled.

"Probably." Bhradfyrd nodded. "But I wouldn't go too hard on them, Yausung." Ryndau raised an eyebrow, and Bhradfyrd shrugged again. "Yes, standard doctrine in an ambush scenario is to go to ground and return fire in place while you assess, because the other fellows are likely to have thought three or four steps ahead of you. In this case, Fuzhow—or maybe Zheng, on his own initiative—let himself be rushed into jumping the fence without thinking about the possibility that we'd done just that and planted Kau-yungs on the other side of it. And that got Zheng's entire squad 'killed.' But it's like General Gahrvai and Duke Serabor always say— 'doctrine is a guide, not a shackle.'" Ryndau grimaced as the Charisian quoted the training manual to him. "In this case, Fuzhow—or Zheng—made the wrong choice, and you need to point that out to both of them. But you don't want to kill their willingness to improvise. They'd have done better to follow doctrine this time, and that will *usually* be the case, but you want your noncoms to think for themselves, especially when they get dropped into the shitter. So the trick is to find a way to kick them in the arse for screwing up while simultaneously patting them on the back for how quickly they responded. And they *did* respond quickly, Yausung. Quite a bit more quickly than we'd anticipated, really."

Ryndau nodded, then inhaled deeply.

"I suppose I'd better get down there and get my licks in while the lesson's still fresh. Care to come along and help kick?"

▼ ▼ ▼

"Overall, your men are doing a lot better, Hauzhwo," Sir Koryn Gahrvai said as he settled into the armchair in front of the crackling hearth. He and Brigadier Zhanma—the United Provinces had adopted Charisian ranks for its militia officers—had discussed Lieutenant Bhradfyrd's report of the latest training exercises over a comfortable dinner, and he listened appreciatively to the wind roaring softly around the eaves as Zhanma took the armchair facing him. October nights in West Harchong made the roaring fire more than merely welcome to a boy from Corisande even without the wind-roar, and Gahrvai stretched out his booted ankles to enjoy the warmth.

"For a bunch of peasants and serfs with manure still caking their boots and 'officers' who are still reading the rulebook as we go along, I guess we are, Sir." Hauzhwo Zhanma sounded a bit sour.

"Actually, there's some truth to that," Gahrvai said with a smile. "Especially that bit about still reading the rulebook. Your people haven't been doing this very long, and it takes time to get *really* sneaky. Or to be ready for the other side to pull sneaky shit on you. I don't even want to talk about what Emperor Cayleb and his Marines did to *us* when they invaded Corisande!" He shook his head. "Your boys' learning curve isn't quite as sharp as ours was, but that's because the ones who screw up aren't actually getting killed. Trust me, it makes a difference!"

Zhanma snorted in sour amusement.

"I imagine that's true, Sir," he conceded. "And better to be handed our heads in training exercises by people who are on our own side."

"Absolutely." Gahrvai's tone was much more serious than it had been.

"And the truth is, I've got at least as much to learn as lieutenants like Ryndau," Zhanma added. He shook his head. "If you'd told me four years ago what I'd be doing today, I'd have told you you were crazy!"

"Been a lot of that going around for the last ten,

twenty years," Gahrvai said, and Zhanma snorted again, harder.

Gahrvai smiled, then raised his beer stein and sipped. In Corisande, they would have been treating themselves to brandy about now, but Harchong made amazingly good beer and he'd never really been that fond of brandy. *Whiskey,* now—

He suppressed a chuckle he didn't really want to explain to his host and gazed into the fire's incandescent heart while he contemplated how his own life had changed over the last couple of decades. And the truth was, that Zhanma and his Harchongian peasant-troopers and shopkeeper-officers were doing at least as well as the professional Royal Corisandian Army had managed when Cayleb Ahrmahk and his Marines swept through it like a hurricane.

Zhanma himself was a case in point. No one would have described the pre-Rebellion captain of horse as an intellectual, but he was no fool, either. And he had a surprising amount of moral integrity. He'd enjoyed his own pecuniary arrangements with the port authorities in Zhynkau, but for a typical Harchongese officer in his position, he'd been a paragon of incorruptible honesty. More than that, he'd had the courage to accept Baron Star Rising's leadership and take command of the provisional militia the United Provinces had raised after the Rebellion despite the fact that he knew exactly how the Emperor would reward his actions if and when the imperial authority was restored in West Harchong. Some of Star Rising's supporters had signed on because they expected to do very well for themselves out of it. Gahrvai knew that, and as his wife had pointed out when he grumbled about that point with her, expecting anything else out of human beings would have been both unrealistic and unreasonable. But that wasn't why Zhanma had given the baron not just his support but his loyalty. Oh, he *was* going to do well out of it, assuming everyone involved got to keep his or her head, but that wasn't his primary motivator. Gahrvai couldn't work as closely with him as he had without realizing that.

"To be honest," he said now, lowering his stein, "I think it's probably time to start considering that expansion we've talked about." He waved the stein. "Most of your people are making the mistakes *trained* troops make now, not the kind mobs of civilians make. Between my people and the training cadre we can stand up out of the Militia, I think we've got the capacity to handle the expansion now. And with winter coming up, we can take more men out of the fields and give them some intensive drill over the next few months."

"Do you really think we're ready for that?"

It was a serious question, and Gahrvai frowned into the fire as he considered how best to respond.

"No," he said finally. "But the thing is, nobody's ever truly 'ready' for something like this. Or, to put it another way, if you wait until you're completely confident you *are* 'ready,' you've usually waited too long."

Zhanma looked at him for a long, silent moment, then nodded.

"You're thinking about that last imperial proclamation, aren't you?"

"I think you could safely assume it's one of the factors in my opinion."

Gahrvai's tone was dry, and Zhanma chuckled with very little amusement.

Zhyou-Zhwo's attitude towards the United Provinces had not grown noticeably warmer. In fact, his most recent proclamation had declared Boisseau, Cheshire, and the newly affiliated Omar in open rebellion, which could mean only one thing for Star Rising, the members of his Parliament, and anyone who supported them. That was unlikely to come as a surprise to any of those supporters, but the fact that he'd made it official suggested several unpleasant possibilities. The most likely was that he'd been moved by Bedard's decision to become the third of the United Provinces and reports that Omar was very seriously considering becoming the fourth. It *could* simply reflect an effort to frighten Omar and Pasquale into staying the hell out of any association with Zhynkau. Another, more worrisome possibility, however was that his timing reflected a growing confidence in his ability to do something about the situation.

"Do you think he's actually ready to move against us?" the brigadier asked now, and Gahrvai made a rude noise.

"I think he may *think* he's ready to move against you, but he isn't," the Charisian said. "Oh, I'm sure he's got a lot more men than we do here in the United Provinces, but they're not as well-equipped, they don't have as much training, and they're on the wrong damned side of the Gulf of Dohlar . . . with the Imperial Charisian Navy between them and here. I don't think he could be wildly enthusiastic about venturing out to sea against Earl Sarmouth's cruisers. And even if he is, Earl Snow Peak *definitely* isn't."

Zhanma considered that for a moment, then cocked his head.

"It would be nice of them to be that stupid, wouldn't it?" he said almost wistfully.

"Personally, I'd prefer for them to be smart enough to just stay home," Gahrvai replied a bit more grimly. "Failing that, then, yes. It would be nice for them to be stupid enough to piss away their army while it tried to learn how to breathe water.

"That's not going to happen, though, so I'm not worried about what we're hearing out of him. I'm thinking more about what we're hearing from your own Parliament. If it's serious about backing Crystal Fountain's proposal, you'll need more warm bodies come spring. And what I'm saying is that I think between your own people and my people we're in a position to start training those warm bodies now." Gahrvai shrugged. "If you don't need them, we can release them come planting time. If you do need them, waiting until spring to start training them could be . . . a less than ideal option, shall we say?"

Zhanma nodded as he chewed on the truth of that observation.

So far, Baron Crystal Fountain's proposal was *only* a proposal, but support for it was growing steadily. As the man who would be ultimately responsible for the military aspects of it, Zhanma was decidedly of two minds about the entire idea. It made sense to expand the United Provinces' authority at least to the eastern boundaries of the provinces in question. At the moment, they controlled virtually all of Cheshire, all of Bedard, and all of Omar west of the de Castro Mountains, but only about the western two-thirds of Boisseau. Crystal Fountain was right that they needed to secure control of the rest of Boisseau at a minimum. Omar's population was sparse enough that occupying the rest of its territory was secondary, but Boisseau was the most populous of the United Provinces, and a lot of those living under Parliament's protection had fled from homes and farms in the eastern part of the province.

Their new government owed those refugees the security to return home. In fact, they really needed to extend their grasp into Tiegelkamp and secure the western edge of that province. The Chiang-wu Mountains would form a formidable rampart against any attack from the east, and there were rumors that the warlords in Central Harchong were growing stronger. Some of them had proclaimed their intention of restoring the Emperor's authority, although everyone knew that was no more than an effort to legitimize the power they were busy seizing for themselves. But if they continued to grow, they'd pose a genuine threat to the United Provinces. And the ruins of Shang-mi would exert a natural attraction. Shang-mi had been the capital of Harchong since the Creation. Control of the city, even in its ruined state, would bolster any warlord's authority significantly.

And controlling those ruins wouldn't hurt the *United Provinces'* authority, either, Zhanma reflected.

But coming up with the trained and armed troop strength to make that stand up would be a challenge, and Gahrvai was right. If there was a realistic chance the Provisional Militia would be called upon to implement what its proponents were calling the Crystal Fountain Plan, they'd best get started training the men now.

"I don't have any formal direction to start expanding

our roster," he said after several thoughtful minutes. "I think you and I probably need to seek what they call 'clarification' about that. But, frankly, I'll be surprised if Baron Star Rising and the rest of the Council don't agree with you. Arming them might be a bit of a stretch, though."

He arched both eyebrows at Gahrvai, and the Charisian raised his beer stein in acknowledgment of the implied question.

"I think we can take care of that," he said. "I don't have any formal direction about that, either." That was technically true, at least as far as the official position of the Charisian Empire was concerned. The inner circle was another matter, of course. "I'll be extraordinarily surprised if Their Majesties don't support the proposal, though, and the truth is that the United Provinces are in far better shape economically than they were even a year ago, Hauzhwo! I'm pretty sure Parliament can come up with the money to buy enough rifles and ammunition. Frankly, at the moment, you don't need much in the way of field artillery. Mortars would be plenty to deal with anything you might run into, and I've got enough of those to support you right now. So rifles are really all you'd need, and we could probably come up with more than enough of those just out of the Mahndrayn-97s in storage at Maikelberg. I'm sure Their Majesties would be happy to lend them to you."

"I'm pretty sure the Emperor would construe that as an 'unfriendly act,'" Zhanma observed.

"Somehow, I think Their Majesties could live with that," Gahrvai said dryly.

A Hill above the Saint Lerys Canal, Kyznetzov Province, South Harchong.

It was unusually hot, even for October, as the sun beat down on the hillside. The same sunlight gleamed from helmets, rifle barrels, and bayonets as the next best thing to five thousand men maneuvered against one another on the plain between the hill and the Saint Lerys Canal. The Kyznetzov Mountains loomed behind Bauzhyn Nyang-chi, the Baron of Dawn Sky, blue and misty looking with false promises of cool breezes, and he found himself wishing he was somewhere among their highest peaks. And not just because of the heat.

"I am *not* telling His Majesty you don't think we can get the job done, My Lord!" Mangzhin Tyan snapped. The Earl of Snow Peak reined his horse a little closer to his chief of staff and farther away from his aides-de-camp, swept one arm in a furious gesture at the men deploying below their hilltop perch, and lowered his voice . . . a bit. "We can't just spin out our time in 'training maneuvers' like this forever! Those bastards need seeing to, and if *you* can't get the job done, then tell me now so I can find someone who can!"

Dawn Sky's jaw clenched. As a mere baron, he was at the very bottom of the food chain among Harchongese nobles, and his estates in Central Harchong had been among the first to be overrun. Indeed, he was alive to be excoriated by Snow Peak only because he'd been a minor functionary in Shang-mi and he and his family had accompanied the then-crown prince to Yu-kwau before the sack of the capital. But without a more highly placed patron, he'd be doomed to obscurity and grinding poverty, and he had a wife and four children. He'd come to the conclusion that his chance of reclaiming his barony ranged from very poor to nonexistent, which meant finding a new path by which to make his way in the world.

But why, oh why, did it have to be *this* path?

"My Lord," he said once he was sure he had control of his own voice, "I didn't say I don't think we can get the job done. I said we're not yet ready. It grieves me as much as I know it grieves you, but it's the truth. We lack sufficient arms for the men and the men are not yet fully proficient in the use of the arms they have."

Which, he did not add aloud, didn't even touch on the minor difficulties inherent in transporting an invasion army across the Gulf of Dohlar in the face of an Imperial Charisian Navy that would probably disapprove. Or the fact that the best weapons they could provide their men still used black powder, with all the issues of smoke and fouling that brought with it, rather than the smokeless powder—the "cordite"—the accursed Charisians had introduced in the closing months of the Jihad.

Snow Peak glared at him, but at least he didn't bark out an instant condemnation of Dawn Sky's point. That was an unexpected mercy. Dawn Sky had come to the conclusion that however good Snow Peak's political instincts might be, and however much like a soldier that hawk-like face and strong nose might make him *look,* he was at best marginally competent in his new role. Worse, he seemed to know it (however little he chose to admit it), and he had a pronounced tendency to take out his frustrations on his subordinates.

That no doubt explained why his aides and mounted messengers were so busy keeping their eyes anywhere but upon him.

The earl glared at Dawn Sky for a moment longer, then made himself draw a deep breath and look away. He let his eyes sweep the men marching across the hot, dry flatlands southwest of his present position, instead. They looked impressive, and the dust clouds raised by so many booted feet only added to the martial menace they projected.

"We may be short of weapons, but I'll put these men up against anyone in the world," he growled.

"Of course, My Lord," Dawn Sky agreed with fervent promptness. Unlike Snow Peak, however, Dawn Sky had actually served with the Mighty Host of God and the Archangels for over half a year after Earl Rainbow Waters had assumed command. Snow Peak had stormed back home to his estates in protest the instant Rainbow Waters embraced the Temple's demand that he turn a rabble of serfs and peasants into an actual army. Dawn Sky would have stayed with the Mighty Host—and, despite the casualty totals, there were times he wished he had—if his father's death hadn't forced him to resign his post and return home to put his inheritance in order.

However little Snow Peak wanted to admit it, those almost seven months made Dawn Sky invaluable to him. Unfortunately, they also meant the baron had a much better idea of what was involved in modern infantry tactics. And because he did, he had all too vivid an appreciation for what would happen to the old-fashioned columns and densely packed squares maneuvering through those trampled fields of grain. They moved smoothly, with polished efficiency, almost as if they were treading the measures of some intricate dance.

And if they tried maneuvering like that in the face of modern rifle fire, far less what Charisian-style angle-guns could do to them, none of them would ever come home again.

"My Lord," the baron continued, "there's nothing at all wrong with our troops' spirit and martial ardor! In those terms, I agree with you fully. And I don't doubt that they're easily a match for any of the peasant scum we'd be likely to meet. Formed troops are always superior to mobs."

Snow Peak nodded, his face losing some of its rage, as Dawn Sky repeated one of his own favorite aphorisms to him. And, as far as it went, that aphorism was entirely accurate. What the earl seemed unable—or unwilling—to grasp was that the "United Provinces'" new militia was a far cry from a mob of rebellious serfs and peasants fresh off the farm with their boots still caked with manure.

"What does concern me," Dawn Sky went on, watching the earl's expression carefully, "is the proficiency they've gained with their new weapons. Or, rather, the *lack* of proficiency. It's not their fault, or their officers' fault," he added quickly as Snow Peak's eyes narrowed. "The difficulty is that we haven't had sufficient weapons—or sufficient *ammunition*—for realistic training. Maneuvers like these—" he waved his own hand at the columns of dust rising from the flatlands nearer the canal "—are vital. They teach unity, they give our officers confidence and teach our men to be confident *in* them, and that's essential for discipline and to maintain cohesion when the fighting actually begins. But we need to develop *fire* discipline and accuracy, as well. Not even the militia units we've called up for service have any real experience with new-model weapons. They received none of the modern weapons during the Jihad, and we'd concentrated on arming the Spears in the North before the Rebellion."

Which, he added silently, *is why all of those new-model rifles are now in the hands of the rebels.*

"No doubt that's true of the damned rebels, too!" Snow Peak half snarled. "They don't have all of that 'fire discipline,' either. And they're damned mud-eating serfs! Show them cold steel coming at them and they'll take to their heels soon enough!"

"You're probably right about most of them, My Lord. Especially in Tiegelkamp and Maddox. But the Shan-wei–damned Charisians have been supporting the bastards in the 'United Provinces' from the beginning, and the Temple Lands have been supporting Rainbow Waters."

The eyes which had narrowed before turned into fiery slits as Snow Peak reacted to that last, accursed name, but Dawn Sky made himself continue in a calm, measured tone.

"The truth is, My Lord, whether we like it or not, that in both the East and the West, our adversaries are probably at least as well equipped as our men. Worse, they have foreign troops in support, and those foreign troops have access to modern artillery. Like you, I would put our men up against anyone in the world on a man-for-man basis with complete confidence." He uttered the lie with deep sincerity. "But if we can't support them with the same sorts of weapons the traitors on the other side have, we'll be sending them into combat at a huge disadvantage. I'd be prepared to do that, despite the casualties they'd suffer, if I believed they could carry through to victory. I'm just not convinced they can."

The baron held his breath as he watched Snow Peak's taut features. It was possible he'd gone too far, been too frank, but someone had to save the earl from his own enthusiasm. Dawn Sky understood exactly why Snow Peak needed to show the emperor progress, but if he promised more than he could deliver, the consequences for him would be disastrous. And if the consequences to Dawn Sky's *patron* were disastrous. . . .

"You don't think I can go to His Majesty and tell him we're afraid to fight, do you?" the earl demanded after a lengthy pause. His tone was caustic, but at least he wasn't screaming.

"My Lord, it's not that we're *afraid* to fight," Dawn Sky protested. "It's that we can't fight and *win* without more preparation. And that's not our fault, either!" The baron allowed a little outrage into his own expression. "It's the mark-pinchers' fault, My Lord! If they can't find the marks to buy the weapons and ammunition we need to carry out His Majesty's will, then *they* should be the ones explaining to him why that's true!"

Snow Peak snarled, but at least this time it was a snarl of agreement.

"You're right," he growled, "and I told that bastard Sunset Peak exactly that after our last Council meeting! All he could do was whine about that useless prick Ywahn and tax receipts."

"With all due respect, My Lord, he has to do better than that if we're going to accomplish His Majesty's instructions."

Snow Peak said something as inaudible as it was unprintable and glared out at the marching troops, and Dawn Sky drew an unobtrusive breath of relief. Zhyngyu Ywahn was no aristocrat. He was as commonly born as many of the Empire's traditional bureaucrats, and he'd been first permanent under clerk of the exchequer under Duke Silver Meadow before the Rebellion. He filled the same role for Earl Sunset Peak, who had inherited Silver Meadow's office, and at the moment, in the way of all Harchongese bureaucrats, Ywahn was more concerned about guarding his own rice bowl than he was about accomplishing Zhyou-Zhwo's demands. He was even more willing to do that because of the emperor's determination to rule in his own right, which undercut Sunset Peak's ability to ignore the royal displeasure or shunt it off onto another as the Crown's ministers had done for centuries.

And, better still from Snow Peak's perspective, *Sunset* Peak was a member of Grand Duke North Wind Blowing's faction, and he and Snow Peak loathed one another cordially. The duke's tenure as first councilor was seriously in doubt, given Zhyou-Zhwo's attitude, so diverting the imperial ire onto one of North Wind Blowing's key supporters really had no downside for the earl.

"You're right," Snow Peak said again, turning back to Dawn Sky. "You're absolutely right." He shook his head, his expression grim, his jaw set in steely determination. "Obviously, no one wants to disappoint His Majesty, but I'd be derelict in my duty if I didn't keep him fully and accurately informed about the comparative state of our arms . . . and the reason for it. Including the fact that our enemies are actively supporting the damned rebels in both the eastern and western provinces."

Dawn Sky nodded gravely and reflected that pointing Zhyou-Zhwo's anger at Charis couldn't hurt . . . and wouldn't take much effort, for that matter.

"Write up a report I can submit to His Majesty," the earl continued. "Give me your best estimate for how long it will take at the present rate of investment to adequately equip our troops. Start with small arms, but estimate how long it will take and how much it will cost to provide at least portable angle-guns for them, as well."

Dawn Sky nodded again, with considerably less enthusiasm. Drafting the report to aim the emperor in the right direction probably wouldn't be very difficult. After all, he wouldn't even have to lie, which would be a novel experience. Unfortunately, it would be his name at the end of the report, so if the emperor decided to shoot the messenger. . . .

"Make sure to reference all our correspondence with Earl Sunset Peak. I want the fact that we've been telling him about these problems documented."

"Of course, My Lord!" Dawn Sky agreed much more cheerfully.

"And in the meantime," Snow Peak said, turning his horse's head towards the downhill slope, "I think it's time you and I got out into the middle of that." He twitched his head at the dusty plain and smiled a crooked smile. "It never hurts for the officers, at least, to know we're keeping an eye on them."

"No, My Lord, it doesn't," Dawn Sky replied, for once in full agreement with his superior.

"Then let's be going."

Snow Peak touched his horse with his heels and started down the hill, his aides and messengers flowing in his wake. Dawn Sky let them get a bit of a head start, then followed them, frowning as he started considering the most effective way to lay all the fault at Sunset Peak's feet.

. III .
HMS *Thunderbolt*,
Lace Passage,
Hankey Sound;
Warrior Quay,
Queen Zhakleen Harbor;
and
Royal Palace,
City of Gorath,
Kingdom of Dohlar.

Clouds of seagulls and wyverns wheeled and dipped as HMS *Thunderbolt,* the name ship of the Imperial Charisian Navy's newest and most powerful class of armored cruisers, made her stately way through Lace Passage towards the Zhulyet Channel at a steady twelve knots. The *Falcon*-class scout cruiser HMS *Fox-Lizard* led her through the channel; two more *Falcons* trailed her watchfully; and Cayleb Ahrmahk stood on the armored cruiser's flag bridge, gazing across the water at Cape Toe, three or four miles to the west.

It was just past low water, but the tide was making, coming in with *Thunderbolt,* and choppy waves broke white across the huge shoal Dohlarans called the Dangerous Ground on the cruiser's larboard side. *Thunderbolt* was still almost twenty hours from the City of Gorath at her present speed, which should put them there sometime around midday tomorrow, and it was hard to imagine better weather for the journey. They'd been lucky in that way since they'd left Salthar, and Owl's weather satellites promised tomorrow would be just as fine.

The breeze was brisk, blowing the cruisers' smoke to leeward of their ruler-straight wakes, the sky was a brilliant blue dome stranded with high, narrow bands of cloud, and the emperor's expression was somber as he raised his double-glass and studied the fortifications which crowned Cape Toe. They were newly built—or rebuilt, at least—with low earthen berms for the concrete-roofed casemates in which the new twelve-inch guns crouched. In fact, they'd been completed less than six months ago as the Kingdom of Dohlar finished the massive fortification project upon which it had embarked in the aftermath of the Battle of Gorath.

They were impressive, those defenses, but his gaze was drawn to the banner above the earthen ramparts. It flew at half-mast, and he didn't like thinking about why. The reason for it had much to do with his present mood, but he had more than one reason to feel somber this beautiful early autumn afternoon as he recalled the time another Charisian cruiser had passed that cape. The fortifications which had topped it had been Hell's own furnace that day, wrapped in smoke and wreathed in fire, crowned in jagged explosions as HMS *Gwylym Manthyr* and her consorts poured fire into it, and the surface of Lace Passage had been torn by shot and shell.

"Bit of a difference from the first time I was this way," a voice said from beside him, and he turned his head with a lopsided smile.

"I was just thinking the same thing," he acknowledged.

"I prefer it this way," the Earl of Sarmouth said. His eyes were fixed on those fortifications, his expression distant. Cayleb had watched HMS *Gwylym Manthyr* and the *Town*-class ironclads force the channel into Gorath Bay, but only through the SNARCs' remotes. Sir Dunkyn Yairley had stood on a flag bridge very like this one in the midst of that shrieking vortex. "I do have somewhat . . . mixed emotions," he confessed. "And I always worry about how happy the Dohlarans are likely to be to see me again whenever I drop in on them."

"Dunkyn, it's been almost ten years, and you've made this trip—what? A dozen times since then?"

"More like ten."

"All right, *ten* times since the battle. And you've had dinner with Kaudzhu and a bevy of his officers each time, then sat around the table drinking good whiskey, smoking those terrible cigars of yours, and telling each other your side of the Jihad. You know how warmly Thirsk talked about you when he was in Tellesberg, too." A flicker of regret passed through Cayleb's brown eyes as he spoke Thirsk's name. "Trust me, nobody in Gorath's likely to rake up the past while we're here!"

"Which doesn't mean there aren't still plenty of people who'd *like* to rake up the past," Sarmouth pointed out. Cayleb shook his head in exasperation, and the earl smiled. "I do have access to the SNARCs, too, you know," he said. "And I know there are still a few grudges being nursed over there." He tilted his head in the direction of Cape Toe. "And in the city, for that matter. Little hard to blame them when I'm the one who blew their original fortifications into 'dust bunnies,' to use Merlin's charming phrase. Oh, and the one who leveled the city walls, while I was at it!" He chuckled a bit sourly. "If I were them, *I'd* still be pissed at me!"

"All right, it's true you aren't universally beloved in Dohlar," Cayleb allowed. "You're a long way from universally *hated*, though, and you know *that*, too. For that matter, the people who love you least are the ones who never personally crossed swords with you. You know, the sort who're always perfectly willing to send someone *else* out to get killed? Personally, I've never had much of a problem with the notion that I'm not hugely popular with people like that, myself. What matters a hell of a lot more is that most Gorathians understand how careful you were to avoid civilian casualties. I've taken a look at those SNARC reports, too, Dunkyn. Most of the people who're truly pissed off at you are the manufactory owners whose establishments you turned into rubble and the Church hangers-on who lost their leverage when Thirsk and Dragon Island kicked the Inquisition the hell out of Dohlar. It's not the average citizens of Gorath, at any rate. And it's certainly not their *navy*!"

Sarmouth considered that for a moment, lips pursed in thought, then nodded, because Cayleb was right. He'd devastated the Royal Dohlaran Navy at places like Saram Bay and the Trosan Channel, as well as right here in Gorath. He didn't like to think about how many Dohlaran seamen he'd killed in those battles. But he and his opponents had emerged from the crucible of combat with a sense of mutual respect. The Dohlarans had been outgunned and outclassed in every quality but courage and discipline, facing the finest, most powerful fleet in the world, yet they'd fought every step of the way, every weary mile from Claw Island to Gorath Bay. They'd done that without ever simply giving up the way the Navy of God had . . . and not all of those battles had been Charisian victories. The ICN had been a long time forgiving the Kingdom of Dohlar for what had happened to Gwylym Manthyr and his men when they were surrendered to the Inquisition, but very few Charisian seamen had blamed the Dohlaran *Navy* for it.

It was odd. Who would have guessed, at the start of the Jihad, in the initial campaign that culminated off Armageddon Reef and in Cayleb Ahrmahk's night attack on Crag Reach, that *Dohlar* would emerge as Charis' only true peer on the seas of Safehold? Or that in a war marked by atrocity and massacre the Royal Dohlaran Navy would win the ICN's grudging admiration not just for its courage but for its integrity and honor, as well?

And that was Thirsk's doing, Sarmouth thought, gazing at that half-masted flag above the modern breech-loading guns. *His and Caitahno Raisahndo's and Pawal Hahlynd's. And now Pawal's the only one left.*

"You're right, Cayleb," the admiral said. "I know you are, too. It's just—"

"It's just that you hate the reason we're here," Cayleb finished for him, quietly, when he paused, and Sarmouth nodded.

"I guess I do," he admitted, and shook his head. "Who would've thought it, all those years ago?"

"Only someone who knows you, Dunkyn," the emperor said, patting him on the shoulder. "Only someone who knows you."

▼ ▼ ▼

"Damn, that's a *big* boat," Sir Rainos Ahlverez, Duke Dragon Island and commanding officer of the Royal Dohlaran Army, observed as *Thunderbolt* glided smoothly across Queen Zhakleen Harbor towards the Gorath waterfront. "It's *lots* bigger than anything *you've* got, Pawal!

"It's not a '*boat*,' damn it!" Pawal Hahlynd, Earl of Kaudzhu, commanding officer of the Royal Dohlaran Navy, hissed back at him. "*She* is a *ship*, you cretin!"

"A boat's a boat." Dragon Island grinned unrepentantly. "Although that one's big enough even someone like me probably wouldn't get seasick if I went aboard it."

"I know you're only an ignorant, landlubber general, Rainos," Kaudzhu growled, "but if you embarrass me in front of Cayleb and Sarmouth, I swear to Langhorne I'll bring in ringers from the Gorath Gulls for the next Army-Navy baseball game." Dragon Island looked at him, and Kaudzhu shook a finger under his nose. "I mean it! Their manager's my cousin, and I'll swear his entire starting lineup into temporary service!"

"Lywys probably would've appreciated my behaving myself, too, wouldn't he?" the duke said after a moment, and shook his head with a fond smile. "Who would've expected that to matter a damned thing to me?"

"He had that effect." Kaudzhu's smile was sadder than Dragon Island's. "He always had that effect, even on bastards like Rohsail. And Rohsail was a much harder case than *you* were!"

"So I've heard. Not as hard as my dear cousin Aibram, though."

"I wouldn't want to speak disrespectfully about a member of your family, especially one who's deceased, but if Duke Thorast's brains had been Lywysite, they wouldn't have been enough to blow a gnat's nose. On a good day."

"That's not the way a mere earl should describe the man who held one of the Kingdom's most ancient and venerable duchies," Dragon Island said severely. "Especially not since it's overly generous."

Kaudzhu snorted and shook his head at the man

who'd once been one of his bitterest enemies simply because of his family's hatred for Lywys Gardynyr. No one outside his immediate family had missed Aibram Zaivyair, the previous Duke of Thorast, when overindulgence, too much wine, and pure bile carried him off. His son was only a minor improvement, but at least the current duke had learned not to challenge the united front of Thirsk and Dragon Island. Or, Kaudzhu acknowledged, his own contribution to that team.

There were days—many of them—on which he deeply regretted Caitahno Raisahndo's death, and not just on a personal level. Not only had Raisahndo been both a friend and a trusted colleague, he'd had a far better head for politics than even he himself had realized he did. A lot better one than Pawal Hahlynd had ever had, at any rate. He'd been the only real choice to command the Navy when Thirsk became First Councilor, and he and Rainos Ahlverez had been pillars of strength for Thirsk and Bishop Staiphan Maik as the earl withdrew Dohlar from the Jihad and fought just as hard for peace as he ever had against Charis. And it was Raisahndo who had overseen the organization of the rebuilt royal Dohlaran Navy's command structure on the model of the Charisian admiralty. And then they'd lost him in that stupid, stupid boating accident. The admiral who'd survived the loss of his flagship in the Battle of Shipworm Shoal had *drowned* when a sudden summer squall capsized the longboat transporting him across Gorath Bay for a routine meeting that any of his subordinates could have chaired. His loss had been at least as severe a loss to *his* navy as Baron Seamount's death had been to the Imperial Charisian Navy.

But naval officers had a long tradition of stepping into dead men's shoes. This wasn't the first time Pawal Hahlynd had been forced to step into a friend's place, and he'd done his best to fill Raisahndo's. He wasn't Raisahndo's equal. He knew that, whatever other people might tell him. But he didn't think he'd done *too* terrible a job, and he hoped Caitahno approved of his efforts.

And the truth is, you're probably too hard on your-

self, Pawal, he thought now, watching the huge Charisian warship follow the harbormaster's cutter towards her assigned anchorage. *You and the whole damned Navy don't have anything to be ashamed of! Lywys never thought so, anyway, and he was probably a lot better judge of it than you are. And thank God he and Rainos patched up their differences!*

Thunder began to roll along the harbor fortification as the batteries rumbled out a twenty-four-gun salute, and Kaudzhu nodded in satisfaction as he noted the perfect, metronome-steady timing.

▼ ▼ ▼

"I think Thirsk was wise to finish demolishing the walls," Sharleyan Ahrmahk said over the smoky thunder of the salute. She and Cayleb had both joined Sarmouth on *Thunderbolt*'s flag bridge to watch the cruiser's final approach to Gorath.

"I do miss them, in a way, though," Cayleb said. She looked up at him, one eyebrow raised, and he shrugged. "I've watched every stage of the changes over the SNARCs, but my mental image of Gorath's always been the one that imprinted on me back when I was merely Midshipman Ahrmahk." He shook his head. "'The Golden Walls of Gorath' were really pretty spectacular, especially when the sun hit them in the afternoon. And I hate to think how long it took to build them in the first place."

"A lot longer than it took to knock them down, anyway." Sharleyan's tone expressed grim satisfaction.

"With all due respect, Your Majesty," Sarmouth observed, "it might be just a tiny bit more tactful not to mention that to our hosts."

"I have no intention of creating a fresh war with Dohlar, Dunkyn," Sharleyan said dryly. "But we promised they'd come down, and you and your people damned well made sure they *did*." She patted his arm approvingly, and it was his turn to shrug.

"Actually, we just more or less blew holes in them," he said. "Lots of holes, I'll grant you, but we didn't have the time—or ammunition—to do a proper job of *demolishing* them. I hate to think how much of Sandrah's Lywysite the Dohlarans used completing the job! And if you'll look over there where every damned citizen of Gorath appears to be standing, you can see what they did with the rubble."

He pointed to the west, where a vastly expanded quay extended well out into the harbor, built out of the golden stone which had once walled the Kingdom of Dohlar's capital. He might have been wrong about *every* Gorathian's being present, but not by much, Cayleb reflected.

"Thirsk was the one who insisted on calling it the Warrior Quay," Sarmouth went on, "but no one argued with him. Took them damned near three years to get it built, too! I'd say they had quite a lot of demolition to do even after our best efforts."

"Maybe, but I'll guarantee you it was cheaper and faster to finish taking those walls down, after what you and your boys did to them, than it would have been to try to repair them!" Cayleb said.

"That's probably fair," the admiral acknowledged.

An officer on the cutter's tiny quarterdeck raised a signal flag. He held it poised motionless for perhaps fifteen seconds while another seaman crouched over the pelorus, reading off the changing bearings to him until they reached exactly the right spot. Then he waved his flag sharply, and chain roared out of *Thunderbolt*'s hawsehole as her anchor plunged into the water.

"Steam does take a lot of the challenge out of it," Sarmouth observed.

"Oh, *please* don't climb back up on the 'steam is killing seamanship' wagon!" Sharleyan groaned.

"Well, to some extent it is," Sarmouth replied. His tone was dead serious, despite what looked suspiciously like a lip twitch. "Mind you, I don't think that's a bad thing, and Lock Island's still careful to teach the basics. I know no one's ever going to have to control a line of galleons again, but knowing the difference between a tack and a buntline's probably still a good thing."

Cayleb laughed out loud and Sharleyan shook her head in disgust.

The Imperial Charisian Navy had established Safehold's first formal naval academy on Lock Island, the island in the center of The Throat, the passage between the Charis Sea and Howell Bay. Its full official name was the Bryahn Lock Island Academy, named for Cayleb's cousin, who'd died in the Gulf of Tarot. It no longer hurt whenever Cayleb thought about Bryahn, and he was sure his cousin would have approved of the Academy's curriculum, including even—no, *especially*—the time the midshipmen spent learning to handle schooners and old-fashioned square-riggers. For that matter, it would be a few years yet before the last of the ICN's sail-powered warships were retired. The Navy's fast schooners—armed now with modern, breechloading five-inch guns—were adequate for almost any routine patrolling or pirate suppression mission, and they had far greater endurance than any steam-powered vessel their size. Despite that, though, they were clearly the navy of the past, and Sarmouth was right that the skills required to command sailing vessels were no longer *essential* in a navy of steel, steam, and coal. But he was also right that the training in teamwork and sail-powered seamanship taught an appreciation of wind and weather—and the need to work together to survive the sea—that a fifteen- or sixteen-thousand-ton cruiser wouldn't.

Or not until it was too late to do any good, at any rate.

"Well, whether or not Captain Pruhyt knows the difference between a tack and a buntline, that was as neat a job of anchoring as I've ever seen," the emperor said now. "Remind me to compliment him on it."

"As opposed to ripping him a new arsehole if he'd screwed it up, you mean?" Sarmouth said with an innocent expression, and Sharleyan smacked him lightly across the back of his head.

"I will have you know that *my husband* would not have ripped anyone 'a new arsehole' just because he mortally embarrassed the Imperial Charisian Navy, not to mention the House of Ahrmahk, in front of the Royal Dohlaran Navy and the entire population of Gorath. Please! He is neither small minded, petty, nor vindictive."

"Really, Your Majesty?" Sarmouth frowned gravely. "Forgive me, but that didn't seem to be your position when he set that nil bid of yours in Tuesday night's spades game. Am I missing something?"

"You don't want to go there, Dunkyn," Cayleb said. "Believe me, you *don't* want to go there."

"My, look at the time!" Sharleyan said. "Why don't I just nip down below decks to get Merlin and Alahnah before one of you says something we'll all regret?"

▼ ▼ ▼

Earl Kaudzhu watched the smaller escorting cruisers drop their anchors. The evolution wasn't executed quite simultaneously—the smallest of the visitors displaced almost seven thousand tons, nearly four times as much as the largest galleon he'd ever commanded, and there were limits to how precisely ships that size could synchronize a maneuver like that—but they came damned close. As he looked at those rakish stems, flaring bows, and bristling gun turrets, he realized the new Imperial Charisian Navy was just as professional and even more deadly than the old one had been.

"How many of those smaller ones do they have, Pawal?" Dragon Island asked him in a more serious tone. He had to raise his voice to be heard over the cheers rippling along the crowded waterfront. This was the first time any Charisian monarch—or Chisholmian monarch, for that matter—had ever visited Gorath, and the Gorathians seemed to have decided to take it as a compliment. Kaudzhu considered the question for a moment, then shrugged.

"Our current reports are that they have five of the *Thunderbolt*-class—that's the big one out there in the middle—and nine of the *Falcon*-class. For right now, that is. We're pretty sure they're building at least six more *Falcons,* but we don't think they've laid down any more *Thunderbolts* yet." He smiled a bit crookedly. "Of course, *our* spies have never been as good as *their* spies. As far as I'm aware, that hasn't changed."

"We haven't seen any sign that their spies are getting suddenly clumsy over at Clearwater, either," Dragon Island agreed dryly.

Clearwater Palace, just down the broad thoroughfare of Trumyn Avenue from what had been the Schuelerite Convent of Saint Tairysa, had been built two hundred years ago for the mistress (and half-dozen illegitimate children) of the current monarch's seven- or eight-times grandfather. Its pedigree had always made it something of an embarrassment to the House of Bahrns, and Rahnyld V had handed it over as the Royal Army's formal headquarters when Dragon Island—who'd been simple Sir Rainos Ahlverez at the time—was named to the Army's command. After the Jihad—and Grand Vicar Rhobair's decision to divest the Order of Schueler of much of its real estate—Saint Tairysa's had been acquired by the Crown as the Royal Dohlaran Navy's new headquarters, which put Dragon Island's and Kaudzhu's offices conveniently close together.

"No, they *haven't* gotten clumsy," Kaudzhu said. "It does seem just a bit unfair that Charis is still the only realm with *seijins* working for it, though."

"Lywys got the odd letter from them," Dragon Island pointed out. "Mostly to tell him about things I'm sure Cayleb and Sharleyan *wanted* us to know about, but I think it's pretty obvious they wish us well. A lot more than they wish us *ill,* at any rate."

"'They' being Cayleb and Sharleyan or the *seijins*?" Kaudzhu raised an eyebrow at him, and Dragon Island snorted.

"Both, at least for now. And just between you and me, I'd like to keep it that way!"

"I believe you'll find general agreement with that at Saint Tairysa's," the earl said dryly, as the visiting warships' banners came down from their mainmast gaffs.

Thunderbolt's banner showed a pair of interlinked crowns above its kraken, one gold and one silver, which indicated that both Cayleb and Sharleyan were personally embarked. As the colors descended from the mainmasts, slightly smaller flags ran simultaneously up the stern-mounted staffs aboard each ship, marking the formal transition from a ship underway to one at anchor.

"And that—" Kaudzhu continued, twitching his head at the anchored ships "—is one of the best arguments in favor of staying on their good side that I know of. The Charisian Navy's a hell of a lot smaller than it was at the height of the Jihad, Rainos, but any one of those ships could sink our entire navy in an afternoon."

"I know." Dragon Island's expression was completely serious now as the initial wave of cheers began to fade and the Royal Army band began to serenade the crowds with traditional Dohlaran airs while they awaited the imperial visitors. "I didn't call it a 'big boat' for nothing, Pawal! How big are those damned guns?"

"The *Thunderbolts* have ten-inch main batteries," Kaudzhu replied. "Same size as the *Manthyr,* but the barrels are a little longer and they're mounted in turrets." Dragon Island frowned, and the earl raised one hand to point. "*Manthyr*'s main guns were in barbettes, like some of your coast defense guns, but without the overhead protection. They were pretty much out in the open, with only armored bulkheads that were just over head-high on the gun crews for protection."

Dragon Island stopped frowning and nodded.

"Since the Jihad, Charis has adopted full turrets. They're heavier, and the machinery needed to rotate them has to be bigger and more powerful, but it puts the entire gun crew behind armor. And the other thing it does is let them mount more guns on the center line."

"How?" Dragon Island asked.

"You should really ask Ahlfryd Makyntyr what it feels like to stand anywhere near the muzzle of a ten- or twelve-inch gun when it's fired," Kaudzhu said wryly. "Trust me, the experience is . . . unpleasant. It was bad enough with muzzleloaders, but breechloaders tend to fire heavier charges, and that makes it even worse! If they're close together, guns in open barbettes suffer from the kind of blast interference that can cripple or kill your gunners. But the gunhouse—the turret—protects the crews, so you can do what Charis has done with the *Thunderbolts*."

"Stack them that way, you mean?"

"You really are an ignorant layabout of an Army officer, aren't you? Stack them. You actually said *'stack them'?!*" Dragon Island made a rude gesture with the second finger of his right hand, and Kaudzhu laughed. "The Navy, which is obviously far more sophisticated than you semi-literate Army types, calls that 'superfiring,'" the earl continued. "Or, at least, that's what Captain Zhwaigair calls them, though I think he stole the term from Charis. Basically, the turret protects the gun crews and that lets them mount another turret to fire across the first one. So where *Manthyr* had four ten-inch guns, the *Thunderbolts* have six. They could have had eight if they'd wanted to add an additional turret aft, as well, but they didn't. Probably because they didn't want to drive up the tonnage still farther."

"Six ten-inch guns," Dragon Island repeated softly. "My God. They fire—what? Three-hundred-pound shells? Four hundred?"

"Right on four hundred for the high explosive," Kaudzhu agreed. "Over five hundred for the armor piercing."

"Our six-inch shells weigh less than a quarter of that. And they've got *six* of them aboard each ship?"

"Exactly. And our reports are that they have a maximum rate of fire of just over two rounds a minute." Dragon Island looked at him, and Kaudzhu shrugged. "They've got hydraulic power available on their mounts, unlike your gunners in the field, Rainos. So, yes, they *can* fire that rapidly. And each *Thunderbolt* has twelve six-inch in those casemate mounts you can see. Their rate of fire's about twice that of the ten-inch. The *Falcons* are a *lot* less dangerous, of course. They only mount ten six-inch each."

"Oh, *far* less dangerous!" Dragon Island rolled his eyes.

"Like I say, an excellent argument in favor of staying on good terms with Charis."

"I think you could say that," Dragon Island concurred, watching the flag-bedecked steam launches putting out from Warrior Quay to collect their illustrious guests and move them ashore.

▼ ▼ ▼

Merlin Athrawes climbed the stone stair that rose out of the harbor's water.

The lower half-dozen steps or so were clearly submerged at high water, but someone had carefully scraped them free of the weed—and anything else which might have caused an imperial foot to slip—which normally encrusted them. The iron handrail had been freshly painted, as well, and as his head cleared the top of Warrior Quay, the massed Army band struck up "Sunset Throne," the official anthem of the Charisian Empire.

He stepped fully up onto the quay to find himself facing an honor guard of picked men from the Royal Dohlaran Army. The major at its head saluted him sharply, and the honor guard snapped to attention behind him.

"Major Klairwatyr!" the Dohlaran identified himself, voice raised to be heard through the music. "Welcome to Gorath, *Seijin* Merlin!"

"Thank you, Major," Merlin replied as half a dozen more Imperial Guardsmen followed him up the steps and fell into position behind him.

"I trust you'll find everything in order," Klairwatyr continued, and Merlin smiled.

"I'm sure we will," he agreed. In fact, the SNARCs had every inch from dockside to the royal palace under close surveillance. That wasn't exactly something he could explain to Major Klairwatyr, of course. On the other hand, those invisible, unseen spies had amply confirmed how vigilantly Dohlar intended to protect its Charisian visitors.

Earl Thirsk would have approved, he thought.

"I'm sure you'll want to walk the formation before

Their Majesties join us," the Dohlaran continued, and Merlin nodded.

"As I say, Major, Their Majesties—and I—have every confidence in you and your men. But I am ultimately responsible for them, and I've always been in favor of the belt-and-suspenders approach when it comes to keeping the two of them alive." He allowed his smile to broaden slightly. "That's kept one or both of them that way a time or two, actually, over the years."

"So I've heard," the major agreed with answering smile, and beckoned for Merlin to join him. "My men will be honored, *Seijin*."

▼ ▼ ▼

Twenty minutes later, Cayleb Ahrmahk climbed the same steps. The band segued instantly into the strains of "God Save the King," and he paused at the top of the stairs as a roar of welcome went up from the crowd beyond the cordon of troops which sealed off the end of the quay. He raised one arm in acknowledgment, then turned and extended his hand to steady Sharleyan up the last few steps. The crowd had cheered at his appearance; it went wild at Sharleyan's, and his eyes laughed into hers as she stepped fully onto the quay and tucked her arm through his.

They moved forward steadily towards Archbishop Staiphan Maik and Samyl Cahkrayn, the Duke of Fern. Maik and Fern bowed deeply as they approached and they returned the courtesy.

"Welcome to Gorath, Your Majesties!" Fern had to shout to make himself heard through the tumult.

"Thank you!" Cayleb shouted back for both of them. "It's a very . . . exuberant greeting!"

"It should be!" Archbishop Staiphan replied. "I wish you could have seen the reaction here in Gorath when the semaphore message that you were coming—that *both* of you were coming—reached us!" He shook his head, his expression grave. "I don't think anyone expected it!"

"It was the least we could do for Earl Thirsk," Cayleb said, stepping closer and pitching his voice lower. "I only wish we could've gotten here in time to tell him that ourselves."

"He knew you wanted to, Your Majesty," Fern said. The white-haired Chancellor of Dohlar smiled sadly. "Not even a Charisian ship could have made the trip quickly enough for that, though, I'm afraid."

"No." Cayleb shook his head. "In fact, the only reason we were able to get here this quickly is that we'd expedited our return to Tellesberg from Cherayth to be home for the birth of Duke and Duchess Thesmar's daughter."

"It was another daughter, then?" the archbishop said with a huge smile. "That makes—what? Nine?"

"Four boys and five girls," Cayleb confirmed with a smile of his own. "I told Hauwerd he could stop anytime now."

"And he said—?" Maik replied with a chuckle. He and Hauwerd Breygart had gotten to know one another well as the then bishop helped him and Lywys Gahrdynyr hammer out the terms of the cease-fire between Dohlar and Charis.

"He said something about 'inevitable consequences,' Your Eminence," Sharleyan said with a laugh of her own. "I do think he was happy to have another girl, though."

"I don't doubt it," Maik said fondly. Then his expression sobered and he squared his shoulders and looked at Fern.

"I think we should be getting you to the Palace," the duke said, responding to the unspoken cue. "His Majesty's eager to see you both again, and Lywys' daughters will be joining us there." He looked at Sharleyan a bit apologetically. "I know your semaphore messages emphasized that you preferred to go to them, Your Majesty, but the security issues—"

He shrugged, and Sharleyan nodded.

"I understand, Your Grace," she said. "I'd much rather have visited them in their own homes than drag them out into some sort of formal dog-and-dragon show. But I never really thought we'd be able to." She smiled a bit sadly.

"In that case, Your Majesties," Fern bowed once again, flourishing an arm in the direction of the coaches waiting at the end of the quay, surrounded by their own security detail, "please permit me to convey you to His Majesty."

▼ ▼ ▼

"It's good to see you both again," Rahnyld V said, turning from the window as Fern and Maik followed Cayleb and Sharleyan into the simply but comfortably furnished library. Merlin followed at their heels and stationed himself quietly to one side. "I only wish I wasn't seeing you so quickly ... or that it was for a different reason, at least."

His eyes were dark, and his right hand rose to touch the mourning band around his left arm.

"We wish the same, Rahnyld," Sharleyan replied. She crossed the carpet to him, holding out both hands. He looked at her for a moment, then took them in his own hands, and she squeezed firmly. "We got underway as soon as we realized how ill he was, although we never really expected to make it before you lost him. We're so glad that at least we had the visit in Tellesberg first. I know you have to miss him dreadfully."

"I do," Rahnyld half whispered. He squeezed her hands back, then released them and extended his right arm to Cayleb. They clasped forearms, and the youthful king drew a deep breath.

"I do miss him," he said, "but we were lucky to have him as long as we did. And in the end, he went gently, with Lady Stefyny holding his hand and young Zhosifyn reading the *Writ* to him." The king smiled at the archbishop, then looked back at the Charisians. "The *Book of Bédard,* as it happens. He said he'd had enough of *Chihiro* and the martyrs in his life."

"I think all of us who lived through the Jihad can say that, Your Majesty," Maik said.

"Amen to that, Your Eminence," Cayleb said with quiet sincerity.

He was deeply grateful Thirsk had been granted the gift of dying in his own bed, surrounded by the family he loved so much and whom he'd fought so long and so hard to protect. But, like Rahnyld, he was going to miss the earl, and not just for personal reasons. Thirsk's sudden illness had surprised all of them, even Nahrmahn, and he'd been gone before the inner circle could do anything about it. The good news was that he'd had over ten years to put his stamp upon Dohlar, its foreign policy, and—above all—its youthful monarch. That was something all of Safehold would be grateful for in the years to come, whether the rest of the planet knew it yet or not.

"I can't tell you how honored we are by your decision to come," Rahnyld continued soberly. "I know it must've been difficult, and—"

"Nowhere near as difficult as it would've been a few years ago, Your Majesty," Sharleyan interrupted. "As, I think, you know from personal experience. Not that Earl Pine Hollow or the rest of the Council were delighted with our decision." She smiled crookedly. "To be honest, if Admiral Sarmouth hadn't been conducting that exercise out of White Rock Island, they probably would've pitched a tantrum!"

Rahnyld chuckled and Fern snorted in obvious amusement, although there might have been just a touch of sourness in the sound. Dohlar had ceded White Rock Island, the largest and most populous island on the Dohlar Bank and less than fifteen hundred sea miles from Gorath Bay, to the Empire of Charis as part of the peace settlement. The Imperial Charisian Navy had turned St. Haarahld's Harbor, barely a hundred and forty miles from Fern's own duchy across the Fern Narrows, into a major naval base and coaling station. That just happened to put the ICN in easy striking distance of Dohlar, positioned to dominate both the Gulf of Tanshar and Hankey Sound, and there were those in Dohlar who resented a Charisian presence that close to the kingdom.

King Rahnyld could have been one of them, if not

for Lywys Gardynyr. Thirsk had understood why the navy was, and would always be, the senior service for the Empire of Charis. Because that empire was spread across almost half the planet, its scattered islands united only by the seas of Safehold, Charis *had* to retain control of its sea lanes, and for that it needed strategically located bases, especially since the introduction of steam. Steam-powered ships were faster and far more powerful than any galleon, but their voracious appetite for coal made them much shorter-legged than those same galleons. Refueling stations were critical, and in White Rock's case there was the added incentive to maintain a forward naval force to keep an eye on the Desnairians at the southern end of Hankey Sound. And, for that matter, on the Border States, to the north.

Charis could easily have pressed far more ambitious territorial demands on Dohlar after its withdrawal from the Jihad, but Cayleb and Sharleyan had settled for White Rock in the west, Claw Island in the east, and tiny Talisman Island in between. And Charisian possession of Talisman more than made up for any resentment Rahnyld—or, for that matter, Duke Fern—might have felt over White Rock. It was less than a hundred miles off the coast of Shwei Province, and the Harchong Empire had never recognized Charis' possession of it. Which didn't bother Cayleb or Sharleyan a bit ... and had to do interesting things to Emperor Zhyou-Zhwo's blood pressure.

Samyl Cahkrayn, for one, could put up with quite a lot as long as that was true.

In this instance, though, the fact that Sir Dunkyn Yairley and *Thunderbolt* had been participating in a scheduled joint exercise with the Royal Dohlaran Navy had provided secure transport for Cayleb and Sharleyan after the Salthar-Silk Town Railway transported them to Salthar Bay.

"I'm glad the Earl was available," the king said now. "And not just because of how important to me personally it is that you've come to Gorath for Earl Thirsk's burial." He didn't mention, Merlin noticed, that Dohlar had set the schedule for Thirsk's formal interment in the vaults of Gorath Cathedral only after the Charisian ambassador had informed Fern that Cayleb and Sharleyan were coming and when they would arrive. "No one in Dohlar's missed the fact that this is your first visit ever to any mainland realm outside Siddarmark or Silkiah. Or the fact that you came together *and* that you brought Alahnah with you." He looked into his guests' eyes, his own steady and much older in that moment than his calendar age. "As Lywys always told me, symbolism matters. It matters a lot."

"Fair's fair, Rahnyld," Cayleb told him with a slight smile. "You did come to visit us in Tellesberg first, you know!"

"And if that helped set this up, I'm even happier I did," Rahnyld said, refusing to be diverted. "There are still people here in Dohlar who cling to their resentment of what happened in the Jihad and how it ended. The fact that you're here, that from the very beginning Charis has offered a hand to help us back to our feet, means a lot. Thank you for making that possible."

"Friendship beats the hell out of shooting at each other," Cayleb replied after a moment, letting his eyes move to Maik and Fern as well. "Earl Sarmouth and I were talking about that just yesterday. Sharleyan and I would have come anyway, but if our visit can help ensure that Dohlar and Charis never shoot at each other again, I think that would be the most fitting gift to honor Lywys Gardynyr's life and his death."

"Make God and all the Archangels send that you're right, Your Majesty," Archbishop Staiphan said after a moment. "And if you are, I know somewhere Lywys will be as happy and as grateful as I am."

▼ ▼ ▼

"I've been looking forward to meeting you, Your Highness," Hailyn Whytmyn said, smiling at Alahnah Ahrmahk as she approached the crown princess in the ballroom King Rahnyld had made available for the evening's reception.

Music played in the background, but the gathering

was actually quite small. Earl Thirsk's three daughters, his two sons-in-law, and his seven grandchildren, accompanied by King Rahnyld and his sisters, on one side, and Alahnah, her twin brothers and her parents, Stefyny and Nynian Athrawes—and, of course, *Seijin* Merlin himself, standing alertly just inside the ballroom doors—on the other.

"Princess Rahnyldah couldn't stop chattering about you, but my father was quite impressed with you, as well. And believe me, impressing him wasn't the easiest thing in the world to do."

"Well, I'm pleased to hear that, of course," Alahnah replied, taking the older woman's proffered hand. "I know *he* impressed *me*. I was scared to death before Father introduced us to each other."

"Really?" Lady Whytmyn looked surprised, and Alahnah laughed.

"My Lady, Father always said there was only one admiral on the other side of the Jihad who really frightened him. Guess who he was talking about?"

"Oh, Father would've loved to hear that!" Lady Whytmyn said with a delighted laugh of her own. "Because *he* said the only admiral who ever personally scared him because of the way 'he kicked my arse,' if you'll pardon the language, was named Ahrmahk."

"Then I guess they were well matched," Alahnah said with a grin.

"Yes, I think they were," Lady Whytmyn agreed, then reached out and drew the tall young man at her side forward.

"Princess Alahnah, may I present my son, Lywys? I'm afraid his sister, Zhudyth, is over there with her father, speaking to *your* father at the moment. I understand twins run in your family, as well?"

"Yes, they do, My Lady," Alahnah agreed. "And in my brother Hektor's family, too, for that matter."

"So I understand." Lady Whytmyn shook her head. "I can't imagine how your mother manages five children in addition to all her other duties. Just two were enough to drive me to distraction!"

"Nannies, My Lady," Alahnah told her. "*Lots* of nannies."

Lady Whytmyn chuckled, and Alahnah smiled at her before she turned to greet the older woman's son.

"Your Highness," Earl Thirsk's grandson murmured, bending over her offered hand to kiss it.

At thirteen, Alahnah's height had shot upward—she was going to be very tall for a Charisian woman—but despite his grandfather's small size, Lywys Whytmyn was already approaching six feet in height. Of course, he was also almost seventeen.

He also had an engaging smile, dark brown eyes, and broad shoulders, she noticed. And the hand which had taken hers wasn't the soft, manicured hand of a courtier, either.

"Master Whytmyn," she said, smiling up at him as he straightened. But her smile faded and she squeezed his hand gently. "I'm so sorry about your grandfather. I liked him very much and I'll always be glad I had the chance to meet him."

He gazed down at her for a moment, his head slightly cocked, then smiled much more broadly back down at her.

"I'm glad you liked him, Your Highness, because I'm pretty sure he liked you, too," he said, and glanced at his mother. "I think your seamanship impressed him. Grandfather always did say you can tell a lot about someone by the way he—or she—handles herself at sea. And he said you handled yourself very well. In fact, he said you had a seaman's eye, didn't he, Mother?"

"Yes, he did." Lady Whytmyn's smile was sadder than her son's as she looked at Alahnah and nodded. "He laughed himself sick over the way you and *Seijin* Merlin stole his wind in that last race across King's Harbor, Your Highness."

"Well, I *am* Charisian," she pointed out with a twinkle. "As Father's fond of pointing out, that means brine flows in our veins, not mere blood. And having *Seijin* Merlin for a godfather didn't hurt! Besides, we knew the tide set better than he did. If we hadn't, I'm pretty sure he'd've pinned our ears back."

"He certainly would have *tried*," Lady Whytmyn told her with a chuckle. "If there was anything in the world my father hated more than losing, I never figured out what it was."

"That's what *my* father—Merlin, I mean—most admired about the Earl, I think, My Lady," Stefyny Athrawes said. She'd accompanied Alahnah as both lady-in-waiting and chaperone, and although she was only twenty years old, her level gray eyes were sharp and observant. "He said to me once that anyone with a single ounce of quit in him would have just rolled over and died in the Earl's place. But your father?" She shook her head, those gray eyes dark. "Not him. Not in a thousand years, Father said. Not in a thousand years."

"That's—" Lady Whytmyn paused and cleared her throat, then smiled mistily at Stefyny. "That's very good of the *Seijin*. And I think he's right. But until that awful night aboard *Saint Frydhelm,* there was nothing Father could do. Not as long as Clyntahn had me and Stefyny and Zhoahna and the kids to hold over his head. *Seijin* Gwyliwr and *Seijin* Cleddyf changed that, and I'll be forever grateful to them—and to *Seijin* Merlin—for that. Charis—"

Her voice broke again, and she reached out to lay a hand on her son's shoulder, then looked at Alahnah again.

"Charis has been far kinder to my family than I would have imagined was possible, Your Highness," she said. "We're alive today—all of us—only because of what your mother and father and the *seijins* did for us. Don't think we'll ever forget that."

"Having met your father, My Lady," Alahnah said, looking into her eyes, "the honor was ours. As Father's always said, 'Here I Stand,' and he told me once that he could never have stood beside a man he admired more than he did your father."

"Then his and your mother's hearts are as generous as they are wise," Lady Whytmyn told her. "And sometimes—sometimes, Your Highness—something wonderful can come out of all of the grief and the pain and the loss."

▼ ▼ ▼

"What do you think of Stefyny and Hailyn's proposal?" Cayleb Ahrmahk asked, much later that evening over the SNARC-linked coms.

"I think it's a really good idea," Nahrmahn Baytz said promptly from Nimue's Cave. "In fact, I can't find a downside however hard I look!"

"I can," the Duke of Serabor disagreed. He sat in his Maikelberg office, tipped back and nursing a cup of cherrybean while he gazed out at a bleaker, far colder morning. Like Nynian, Koryn Gahrvai, and a growing number of the inner circle's members, he'd received Owl's new wetware. That was a point which tended to irritate Cayleb, since so far it had been impossible for him or Sharleyan to disappear long enough for the same treatment.

"What?" Nahrmahn's image blinked at Serabor and his tone was slightly affronted. "What downside?"

"Oh, come on, Nahrmahn!" Serabor replied without ever moving his lips. He sipped more cherrybean. "I'll admit I think the upsides outnumber the down, but just exactly how do you think the folks in Siddarmark who're already less than delighted with Charis will react when they find out *Earl Thirsk*'s grandchildren are going to be educated in Charis?"

"There's not much we can do about anyone bigoted enough against Dohlar to be worried about that, Kynt," Domynyk Staynair pointed out from Tellesberg.

"Probably not," Serabor acknowledged. "Doesn't mean it's not going to happen, though. Especially with Rahnyld's brainstorm."

"*Which* of his brainstorms?" Sharleyan asked.

"Either of them!" Serabor said. "The notion of sending Rahnyldah to Charis along with the Mahkzwails and the Whytmyns will put more than a few noses out of joint back home in Dohlar, too. Some of 'em will resent the implication that Dohlaran schools aren't good enough and some of 'em will see it as one more sign we've already got way too much influence in Gorath, but I'm not too worried about that. What I *am* concerned about is the anti-Charis crowd in Siddarmark, because a lot of that bunch will see this as one more example of our letting Rahnyld 'suck up to us' at the Republic's expense. You *know* none of them will believe for a minute it was her idea, not his, don't you, Sharley?"

"Probably not," Sharleyan sighed, remembering the glow in Rahnyldah's eyes when she found out where Thirsk's grandchildren would be completing their education.

It was obvious Rahnyldah had enjoyed her visit to Tellesberg even more than any of them had suspected at the time, and it seemed likely that had more to do with her reaction than any logical comparison of the merits of the schools involved. By the same token, though, Stefyny Mahkzwail and Hailyn Whytmyn and their husbands had a point. Charisian schools—not just those affiliated with the Royal College, but those administered by the Church of Charis, as well—*were* the best in the world . . . and getting better steadily. They weren't the only parents who wanted to avail their children of that opportunity, although it helped in their case that they'd quietly converted to the Church of Charis during their time in hiding with the Sisters of Saint Kohdy. Rahnyldah just as obviously wanted the same opportunity, although Sharleyan suspected at least part of that was because of how much she and Alahnah had liked one another.

Queen Mother Mathylda had been more than a little doubtful about the notion. Unlike Thirsk's daughters and their families, she remained firmly attached to the Church of God Awaiting, and she was uncomfortable at the notion of exposing her youngest child to the allure of the Church of Charis. She'd made that clear, although she'd been very tactful about it, and Sharleyan wondered if she'd been surprised when her son overruled her. For her part, Sharleyan couldn't decide how much of Rahnyld's decision came from his obviously deep love for his baby sister and how much came from the cold calculation that granting her wish would weave yet another strand into the growing net of common interests binding Charis and Dohlar. Personally, Sharleyan was perfectly content with both possibilities, but it would be interesting to know just how Rahnyld had seen it.

"Of course some of them are going to think exactly that," she said finally. "And the reason they are is that, while I wouldn't use the phrase 'sucking up,' that's clearly part of his thinking. He's a smart young man; he's had good teachers who taught him to look forward, not back, when it comes to his kingdom's best interests; and he knows perfectly well how well Rahnyldah and Alahnah have hit it off. Of course he recognizes the advantages of sending us his sister . . . and of 'encouraging' that friendship with Alahnah at the same time."

"I don't see a downside there," Nahrmahn put in. "It's not like Alahnah's going to let friendship for Rahnyldah influence any decisions she makes on the far distant day when she inherits the crown. I mean, if you and Cayleb were doddering old wrecks likely to be joining me here in the Cave anytime soon, that might be worth worrying about. But now? Pffft! In the meantime, though, having *her* in *our* corner, bending Rahnyld's ear in our favor if we need it, isn't likely to be a bad thing, now is it?"

"Probably not, Your Highness," a much younger voice put in. "And I know Alahnah would be delighted to see her in Tellesberg. Of course, she might not be the *only* person Alahnah would be happy to see in Tellesberg."

"Excuse me?" Sharleyan glanced at Cayleb, then at the fair-haired, gray-eyed image projected onto her contacts. "That sounded sufficiently . . . mysterious, Stefyny!"

"Oh, it's probably not anything to worry about, Your Majesty," Stefyny Athrawes told her. "It's just that she said something to me before she headed off to bed."

"Like what?" Sharleyan looked at Cayleb again. "She didn't say anything to *me* when she kissed me good night."

"Well, like I say, it's probably not real important," Stefyny said, smiling slightly. "She did mention, though, that she thought Lywys Whytmyn was 'really cute.' In fact, now that I think of it, I believe what she actually said was 'really, really cute.'"

"Oh, Lord!" Sharleyan leaned forward, covering her eyes with one hand and shaking her head as Cayleb laughed.

"Don't worry, Sharleyan," Nynian Athrawes said over her implants. She sat before the mirror in her bedchamber, brushing her long lustrous hair, and smiled. "She's thirteen. By the time she's an old lady like Stefyny—" she grinned as her adopted daughter's image stuck out its tongue at her "—she's going to've thought a *dozen* young men were 'really, really cute'!"

"You are *not* making this any better, Nynian," Sharleyan told her without ever uncovering her eyes. She sat that way for several seconds, then drew a deep breath and shook her head.

"Thank you ever so much for that bit of information, Stefyny," she said. "Not that it changes the overall calculus, because Kynt's still right that the 'never-Charis' element in Siddarmark's bound to see it as an effort by Rahnyld to curry favor with us."

"Exactly. And then there was that other little matter," Serabor said.

"I'm afraid Kynt has a point about that, too," Maikel Staynair put in.

"I'm sure he does," Cayleb said. "I just wish he didn't make so damned much sense."

"Well, we knew it was coming," Duke Delthak pointed out. "We got enough SNARC imagery of Thirsk discussing it with him, not to mention with Fern and Dragon Island. And like Sharleyan says, he's smart. I do wish I knew how much of this is part of Thirsk's ongoing policy of rapprochement with Charis and how much of it's a deliberate attempt to drive the wedge between us and Siddarmark deeper, though."

"I'm pretty sure there's a lot of both of those involved," Cayleb acknowledged. "I don't think he's so much trying to cut Siddarmark out of the equation as it is that he's trying to cut Dohlar *into* it, though." He waved one hand impatiently as his wife raised her eyebrows at him. "What I'm trying to say is that I don't think he's looking at *hurting* Siddarmark; I think he's only looking at *helping* Dohlar and that happens to come at Siddarmark's expense. And let's be honest here. It's not like Siddarmark wasn't already walking wounded!"

A soft sound of agreement flowed over the com from more than one person, and Merlin Athrawes looked across the bedchamber at Nynian. She saw him in the mirror, stopped brushing her hair, and looked over her shoulder at him. Then she sighed.

"No, it's not," she agreed over her wetware. "And I see a lot of possible advantages in taking Rahnyld up on his offer. But the timing would be really bad."

"He hasn't made an actual 'offer,'" Merlin pointed out. "So far, he's only speculating about possibilities. Obviously, he'd like *us* to make an offer, but he's too smart to push it if we don't, I think."

"I agree," Cayleb said. "But he's right, just like Thirsk was. Dohlar does have a greater natural interest in the canal, and Dohlar's economy is in a hell of a lot better shape than Siddarmark's. I think he's a little optimistic about how quickly he could get the bonds out and sold, but the money's there."

"But if word gets out that we're seriously contemplating replacing Siddarmark with Dohlar, you can pretty much write off Lord Protector Klymynt's reelection in August," Serabor said. "To be honest, that's what I'm most afraid of here—the downside I was talking about, Nahrmahn. As long as all anyone knows about is the proposal to educate a bunch of kids in Charis, I don't see a problem. But if someone suggests we're planning on 'selling out' the Republic while Myllyr's running for reelection, he's toast, and you know it."

"We're not contemplating anything of the sort," Sharleyan objected.

"We're not contemplating it *yet*, love," Cayleb sighed. "But as Nahrmahn is overly fond of pointing out upon occasion, the clock's ticking. Under our worst-case assumption, we've only got another seven years or so before the 'Archangels' turn up again." More than one face tightened as he reminded them of that unpalatable fact. "I know the Canal's more of a cherry on top than a critical component of our strategy, but it's a pretty important cherry, I think. It would be a huge boost to the spread of technology, if only because of the new construction techniques we'd be introducing. The timing won't be all that significant either way, if it turns out Schueler's clock did start with the end of the War Against the Fallen, not the 'Creation,' and we've got another seventy or eighty years to work with. But even if that's the case, the sooner we get started the better in a lot of ways."

"You're right," Sharleyan agreed, "but so are Nynian and Kynt. I think we almost have to agree to Thirsk's family's suggestion about his grandchildren, and I don't think we can do that without inviting Rahnyldah along, too. There are too many strategic and diplomatic positives on that side of the balance, even without looking at our moral responsibilities. But I think we need to make it quietly clear, not just to Rahnyld, but also to Fern, Archbishop Staiphan, and certainly Dragon Island that it's essential there be no public discussion about Dohlaran involvement in the canal at least until after the August elections. Does anyone disagree with that?"

. IV .
Zhyndow–Sochal Road,
Grand Duchy of Spring Flower,
Tiegelkamp Province,
North Harchong.

"No, the bastards *aren't* getting away this time!" Captain of Foot Rung snapped. "Lord of Foot Qwaidu will have my arse if that happens, but before he does, *I'll* have yours. Is that *clear* enough for you, Captain of Swords?"

Captain of Swords Mahngzhwun Cheng looked back

at his company commander and for a moment something unfortunate hovered near the tip of his tongue. He managed to restrain it without too much difficulty by reminding himself of what had happened to others who had expressed themselves too forcefully to Zhungdau Rung.

"It's clear, Sir," the captain of swords said instead. "But I don't know if we can catch them. They're moving fast, and I've only got two of my platoons up." He grimaced in disgust. "I'd like to know who warned them about which way we were coming!"

Rung glared at him, but the captain of swords had a point. Someone had tipped off the band of refugees, and it had to have been one of Grand Duke Spring Flower's other serfs. Whoever it was, he needed to be roasted head-down over a slow fire, preferably after watching the rest of his family enjoy the same experience. Especially since the grand duke was going to be more than a little unhappy if so many fugitives slipped through his troops' fingers.

"Look," he said now, jabbing a finger at the map spread on the tree stump between them. "They ran from Maichi, and they must've known the Grand Duke's shifted the court back to Fangkau, because all the evidence suggests they were following the main road from there to Sochal. They had to've figured they could sneak around the town down some of those damned farm tracks without anyone noticing them with so many of our people pulled to Fangkau . . . until some fucking wyvern whistled in their ear. I wish we knew exactly when they realized they'd been reported and we were already on the hunt, but we don't. We *do* know they decided to go by way of Shanglau, but the messenger wyverns from Third Company say they aren't on the Shanglau-Sochal road. So they have to have turned south at Shanglau and taken the long way around, towards Sung-tai. They may have turned north again, tried to move through Ranlai, but we're right in their path if they come that way. So that means the only way they could give us the slip would be to head up *this* way—" his fingertip traced the brown line of a road . . . of sorts "—between Half-Moon Wood and the Wyvern. Right?"

Cheng nodded. There was no other way the band of fugitives could go. Oh, they might head off cross-country, but it was unlikely. They had women and children along, and half their carts were probably being pulled by men, not mules or dragons.

"All right. We're here—" Rung jabbed again, this time at the square that marked the Fynghau Farm, just under six miles southeast of Ranlai "—and you've got *horses,* Captain of Bows! Get them on the damned road to the Yang-zhi Farm now. And I don't want to hear that a bunch of shit-footed farmers and their bitches and brats carrying everything but their outhouses with them can cover thirty miles before my *cavalry* can cover fifteen! Is that clear?"

Cheng nodded again, although both of them knew Rung's description of the challenge fell a bit short of reality. It was closer to twenty-eight miles by road from the Sung-tai Farm to the Yang-zhi Farm, and it was almost sixteen miles from the Fynghau Farm to the Yang-zhi Farm. More to the point, his horses were already badly worn and there was no telling how long the runaway serfs had been on the road. If they'd been warned soon enough and they'd been prepared to march in the dark, they could be halfway to the Ranlai-Zhyndow Road by now, in which case they were actually closer to it than he was.

He didn't like to think about the state of his mounts. He'd been hoping to rest them for at least a few days, and now this! If he pushed them the way Rung obviously had in mind in their present condition, he'd lose some of them, and Baron Qwaidu would be livid if he foundered very many. In the baron's opinion, cavalry horses were worth more than serfs, and Cheng couldn't disagree. On the other hand, if he didn't founder at least some of them, Rung would conclude he hadn't tried hard enough. And if the runaway serfs got past him in the end, Baron Qwaidu was likely to agree with Rung, with unpleasant consequences for one Mahngzhwun Cheng.

"Yes, Sir," he said. "It's clear, and we'll do our damnedest."

"I don't want to hear about any 'damnedest,'" Rung said coldly. "What I want to hear is 'We caught them, Sir.'"

Cheng's jaw clenched. He truly hadn't been trying to cover his arse with that remark. Or he thought he hadn't. What he'd intended obviously didn't matter, however. So instead of speaking, he only nodded again, curtly, slapped his breastplate in salute and headed across the stubbled field, shouting for his platoon commanders.

Shit, he reminded himself, flowed downhill. It was time to make sure it was in the right channel.

▼ ▼ ▼

"Sir, I'm a little worried about Hautai's section. Don't like the look of their horses," Platoon Sergeant Saiyang said.

Captain of Bows Maizhai Rwan-tai looked at him with a frown. He'd watched Saiyang cantering back towards him in a splatter of mud. Like everyone else in 3rd Platoon, the platoon sergeant looked more like a vagabond than a cavalry trooper. He was mud to the eyebrows, his even muddier horse looked ready to collapse, and Rwan-tai had strongly suspected what Saiyang was going to tell him. The problem was that none of his other three sections were in much better shape than Corporal Hautai's.

"How bad is it?" he growled.

"Not so bad I'm worried about losing any of 'em . . . yet, Sir," Saiyang replied. "Think they need a rest stop pretty damn soon, though."

"We can't be more than four or five miles short of the farm," Rwan-tai said. "They're not good for another hour?"

"More like an hour and a half, given the going," Saiyang pointed out, glowering down at the muddy, rutted surface of the road. The last couple of five-days' constant rain hadn't made anyone any happier. It also hadn't done a thing for the roadbed. This section had seen precious little traffic over the last year or so, so there'd been little incentive to maintain it, and it had never aspired to the status of the high road in the first place.

"All right, for another hour and a *half*," Rwan-tai growled.

"Depends on whether or not you want 'em to be able to catch anything once we get there, Sir," the platoon sergeant said with a shrug. "Not much spring in any of 'em, no matter what we do, and a scared man runs pretty fast. If the mounts're already blown when we start chasing—"

He broke off with another shrug. After twenty-three years as a Spear of the Emperor, Lyungpwo Saiyang figured he'd seen just about everything. That included officers who sent their men out on harebrained, useless, Shan-wei–damned *stupid* excursions, and at least Rwan-tai was smart enough to listen to his noncoms.

Usually, at least.

Rwan-tai glowered at his phlegmatic platoon sergeant, but Saiyang was probably right, damn him. Not that Rwan-tai expected Captain of Swords Cheng to sympathize with him if he said so.

Fifteen miles didn't look like much, especially by road . . . on the map. But that supposed the "road" in question deserved the name, and it also supposed the horses traveling along it hadn't already been ridden hard for the last couple of five-days. They needed *rest,* damn it, and he simply couldn't push them above an alternating trot-walk unless he wanted them to start breaking down. On this miserable, mucky road, the best he could manage was no more than five miles an hour, little better than a man on foot, and it had taken almost half an hour to roust his weary platoon out of its sodden bivouac and get it on the road in the first place. The rest of Captain of Swords Cheng's squadron was at least half an hour—and probably more—behind that, and Rwan-tai didn't doubt that Captain of Foot Rung had been riding the captain of sword's back the entire time he was trying to get his men into their saddles.

A cavalry squadron was an impressive force—close to two hundred and fifty men at full strength, though it was seldom *at* full strength in the field—but horses were more fragile than most people realized. It was far easier to ruin a good cavalry mount than to keep it sound, and given the Rebellion's chaos, finding remounts was a serious challenge. And Rwan-tai reminded himself to be less efficient about looking after his own horses in the future. If he and Saiyang hadn't run the tightest platoon in 2nd Squadron, someone else would have been sent off to play point.

"All right," he sighed finally. "Fifteen minutes. Then we're back on the road." He glowered some more. "If the other platoons catch up with us before we get to the farm, there'll be hell to pay."

"Know that, Sir." Saiyang slapped his breastplate in salute, then urged his own horse back to a weary, un-enthusiastic trot as he headed up the road after the platoon's lead section.

Rwan-tai watched him go with mixed feelings. On the one hand, the platoon sergeant was right—horses as worn as theirs would have a hard time catching a terrified serf across country at the best of times. If they'd been ridden into near exhaustion before the pursuit even started, that "hard time" would turn into an exercise in futility, at which point he'd be ripped a new arsehole for having worn them out on the road. But if he *didn't* wear them out on the road and the rest of the squadron overtook him despite its more laggardly start, Captain of Swords Cheng would rip him a new one for *that*. And the truth was that they'd probably already missed their prey, and if they had there wouldn't be any pursuits. In which case, whether or not Corporal Hautai's mounts were fit to catch nonexistent serfs wouldn't matter, and Cheng would ream him up one side and down the other for resting his horses and not getting there in time for the pursuit they wouldn't have been capable of sustaining in the first place.

The world, Maizhai Rwan-tai reflected, not for the first time, wasn't exactly running over with fairness.

▼ ▼ ▼

"Oh, crap," Sergeant Taiyang growled, gazing up the road from his position behind the tumbledown stone wall. He was rather fond of that wall, and he and his platoon had spent quite a bit of effort making it look even more tumbledown—and useless for cover or concealment—than it really was. "And here I thought I was gonna have time for lunch."

"Doesn't look like more'n a section or so," Corporal Ma-zhin pointed out. He was six years older than his youthful platoon sergeant, although he looked younger. Yuhnzhi Taiyang was a huge, powerfully built man whose life had been hard enough even before the Rebellion to make him look far older than his age. He was also just as tough as he looked. "Doesn't seem like more'n we can handle."

"Unless there's more behind them," Taiyang grunted. He raised his head a bit higher above the wall, shading his eyes with one hand and wishing he had one of the rare double-glasses or even an old-fashioned spyglass. He didn't, but from the looks of things, Ma-zhin's estimate wasn't far off. But it wasn't like Qwaidu's bully boys to ride around in single sections anymore. Especially not this close to the Valley.

"There probably *are* more coming on behind," he said, dropping back. "Bet you these bastards're out looking for that lot headed in from Kaisun. If they are, they know damned well they'll need more'n one miserable section to haul 'em in."

"Can't argue with that," Ma-zhin acknowledged. "So, what do we do?"

"Thinking," Taiyang said.

"Might want to think faster," Ma-zhin suggested. "Be crossing in front of Chaiyang's squad in another ten minutes."

Taiyang grunted again and squinted his eyes while he considered. Assuming that cavalry section was by itself, he should have at least as many men as the Spears. He was down half a dozen men, but units in the field were always understrength, whichever side they were on. If, however, there was an entire squadron behind what they'd already seen, the numbers would get a lot dicier.

He was tempted to just lie here behind these nice stone walls and let the bastards ride past, if that was what they wanted to do. The refugees whose flight his platoon was stationed to cover were well down the road by now. They should be passing Zhyndow within another couple of hours. From there, Commander Syngpu would have them under his own eye, and after that, they'd be as safe as if Langhorne himself had them cupped in his hands.

Taiyang was one of Syngpu's original recruits. He'd been barely nineteen at the time, although he'd always been big and strong for his age. After the last four years, he would have followed Tangwyn Syngpu in an invasion of Hell itself, and he knew damned well no Spear ever born was going to ride down a column of refugees under Syngpu's protection.

But he only knew where the refugees were *supposed* to be. Any number of things could have put them behind schedule, and if something had, and if he let these bastards by him. . . .

"Oh, the hell with it," he growled, and Ma-zhin looked at him with a knowing smile.

"Wipe that fucking grin off your face!" Taiyang snarled. He *hated* being so predictable, but the truth was there'd never been any chance he'd just sit here.

"Didn't say a *thing*," Ma-zhin protested.

"Oh, shut up!" Taiyang snapped and reached for the whistle hanging from the lanyard around his neck.

▼ ▼ ▼

"Deserted, of course," Captain of Bows Rwan-tai growled in disgust as the dilapidated outbuildings drew into sight. The gutted main farmhouse still stood, more or less intact, but most of the barns and outbuildings had either burned or been torn down so the scavenged lumber could be used for other purposes. It looked like even some of the stone walls separating the empty fields from the road had been scavenged, as well.

"Not that big a surprise, Sir," his platoon sergeant replied philosophically. "No reason for 'em to stop if they are ahead of us. And those Valley bastards don't usually come this far west."

Rwan-tai nodded. The Valley rebels were entirely too well armed and led for his taste, but there wasn't much out here, beyond the Valley, to attract them. They did venture out from time to time, though. Usually only for some specific purpose. In fact, unlike Platoon Sergeant Saiyang, he'd half expected at least a picket somewhere along the road short of the ruined farm, given the incoming gaggle of fleeing serfs.

He wished the stubborn bastards would just leave well enough alone. It wasn't as if Baron Qwaidu or Grand Duke Spring Flower had made any recent attempts to invade their frigging Valley. Not since the previous winter, anyway. Rwan-tai was just as happy to have missed that fiasco, but neither the grand duke nor the baron had realized then how substantially the Valleyers had been reinforced. They still didn't have a clue who their new commander might be, but whoever he was, he obviously knew his business. And he was damned well armed, too. In fact, if he hadn't been content to sit there behind the mountains, if he'd wanted to come into the open, he could probably have—

A whistle shrilled from behind a stone wall that looked completely deserted.

Captain of Bows Rwan-tai turned towards the sound in surprise . . . and discovered that one thing the Valleyers clearly understood was the need to take out the other side's officers as quickly as possible. The bullet slammed straight through his breastplate and hurled him from the saddle. He hit the muddy road in an explosion of anguish and heard dozens of other rifles crackling like hellish thunder.

. V .
Sochal,
Grand Duchy of Spring Flower,
Tiegelkamp Province,
North Harchong.

"Shan-wei damn it!" Grand Duke Spring Flower snapped. "What the *hell* happened out there?"

"It was the damned Valleyers, Your Grace," the Baron of Qwaidu replied. "They came out of the mountains and they ambushed Captain of Foot Rung. From the sound of things, there must have been at least a couple of hundred of them, dug in on both sides of the road." He shrugged. "I have to admit that it sounds like his lead section wasn't as alert as it might have been, but in their defense, they'd been in the saddle pretty much constantly for at least two five-days before they got the word about the runaways."

"That's not much of an excuse, My Lord," Spring Flower said coldly.

"It wasn't meant as an excuse, Your Grace. It was only an *explanation*."

Zhailau Laurahn met Spring Flower's glare levelly. In his opinion, Spring Flower didn't look much like a grand duke, despite his looted finery. Or possibly *because* of his looted finery. On the other hand, he supposed a lot of people would've said that about him as a baron. And whatever he looked like, Kaihwei Pyangzhow *was* a grand duke; the confirmation of his most recent elevation had arrived from Yu-kwau four months ago. For that matter, the same dispatch had recognized Laurahn's title. That made him formally Spring Flower's vassal, subject to the grand duke's power of high, middle, and low justice, but Yu-kwau was a long way from Fangkau and Spring Flower had discovered how badly he needed a military man like the newly ennobled Baron Qwaidu.

The last year or so had been . . . busy. Spring Flower had pushed his borders steadily outward from Fangkau to the north and to the east. He'd decided against pushing equally hard in the south for several reasons. One was the warlords fighting it out for control of the Mynzhu River between Dosahl and Kengshai. At the moment, they were keeping one another occupied quite nicely, and the last thing he wanted was to provide an outside threat they might come together to resist. That would have been reason enough to expand his own territories elsewhere for the moment, but the enclave the Army of God had established at Zhyahngdu on Zhyahng Bay—with *Charisian* support, of all damned things—was another one.

Zhyahngdu had become a major relief center, administered jointly by Mother Church and the Church of Charis, which struck Qwaidu as more unnatural than anything else that had happened in the last four years. The combined effort had built entire refugee villages, complete with schools and hospitals. By now, somewhere around a quarter million Harchongians had fled to Zhyahngdu, where the combined churches had poured mountains of supplies ashore, but the AOG garrison amounted to little more than a couple of brigades. They had to be stretched thin covering the enclave's perimeter, which had turned Zhyahngdu into a tempting prize for any raiding brigand, and three of the southern warlords had patched up their quarrels long enough to mount an attack on it.

It hadn't worked out well. Stretched thin or not, dug in Army of God infantry fighting from prepared positions with modern rifles and artillery would have been bad enough, but in order to attack them, the warlords' troops had been forced to come within artillery range of Zhyahang Bay, as well. The timing had been unfortunate, since one of the Imperial Charisian Navy's armored cruisers had just arrived, escorting a supply convoy to the enclave. The massive weight of *its* artillery had turned a failed attack into a total disaster, eliminating three-quarters of the warlords' troops, and their fellows farther from Zhyahang Bay—and wise enough to stay there—had divided their territories among themselves.

Zhyahngdu was almost eight hundred miles from Fangkau for a wyvern, and Qwaidu was just as happy Spring Flower had no intention of pushing his borders in its direction. Besides, there was plenty of hunting elsewhere.

Prior to the Rebellion, North Harchong's thirteen provinces had been home to over twenty-five million Harchongians, with the majority concentrated in Boisseau, Tiegelkamp, Stene, and the southern half of Chiang-wu and Maddox. Somewhere around a quarter of the total had lived in Tiegelkamp, although Langhorne only knew how many of those six or seven million people had fled—or died—over the last four years. The total had to be high though, given the staggering number of deserted towns and abandoned farms. Despite the total numbers, even Tiegelcamp had always been sparsely populated, once one got away from the scattered towns. Now the entire province was in the process of reverting to wilderness, and Qwaidu had organized sweeps of territories surrounding the new grand duchy to "recruit" tenants for his and Spring Flower's new estates.

Several of those estates had once been independent towns. Now they were simply manors, owned outright by Spring Flower and his handful of favorites, like Qwaidu, and the grand duke didn't much care if the serfs he bound to his estates had once been free peasants, or even citizens of one of the chartered towns. They were ready hands and strong backs; that was all he cared about. In fairness, many of the involuntary serfs had decided the survival of their families under his protection was more important than any niggling questions about whether or not they'd been bound to the land legally. The ones who disagreed learned quickly that it was wiser not to argue the point, whatever they might feel about it. The smarter ones learned by example. The slower ones *became* the example.

By now, Spring Flower's grand duchy had swollen

to almost a hundred thousand square miles, stretching well over two hundred miles east of Fangkau—farther than the city of Shaiki—and as far south as Kaisun. That was a staggering amount of territory, more than enough to merit its designation as a grand duchy. It took a large army to protect that vast a domain, too, and Spring Flower's originally modest force had grown accordingly. By now, Qwaidu had over seventy thousand men under his command, with a solid core of ex-Spears fleshed out by new recruits. Quite a lot of those onetime civilians had been caught up in his sweeps outside the grand duchy and decided they'd rather serve in the army than break their backs on someone else's acres. Besides, Qwaidu's men got first call on food, clothing . . . and women. For those who were married, the army provided their families with security and at least some luxuries. For those who weren't, there was a ready supply of comely wenches, and those who didn't come willingly could always be . . . convinced.

But there was one annoying fly in Spring Flower's ointment. The Chynduk Valley had defied every attempt to bring it under his protection. He'd even offered the Valleyers generous terms, only to have them rejected. And the two expeditions Qwaidu had mounted against them had been disasters. It was probably as well that none of Spring Flower's potential rivals realized how badly his troops had been hurt after the second invasion attempt. Qwaidu might not know who the Valley's new military commander was, but he knew he wanted the bastard dead.

Not as badly as Spring Flower wanted him dead, however. It was bad enough that the Valley's prosperous farms, grist mills, and labor force remained out of reach, but the grand duke could have lived with that. It was the Valley's *example* he couldn't tolerate. Despite all efforts to suppress it, the word had spread that the Valley continued to defy him, and every few months some clutch of serfs would flee the land, trying to reach the Chynduk's promised freedom.

Most never made it, but the need to make examples of

those who'd made the attempt was a constant, niggling waste of useful labor. Worse, some of them did evade pursuit, like the six or seven hundred serfs who'd just escaped Captain of Foot Rung. And, even worse, Rung's lead squadron had lost over a hundred men in a bickering, running fight with Valleyer infantry. According to Rung, they'd killed twenty or thirty Valleyers in return. Personally, Qwaidu doubted they'd gotten even a dozen of them. He'd fought those bastards himself, and he knew the terrain between Ranlai and the Valley. Besides, Rung had captured only a handful of weapons.

"Your Grace," he said finally, looking up from the map on the table between them, "chasing serfs after they've already run for it is . . . not the best approach. Most of the time, they get a head start before we even know they've run. If they've planned it properly, they can be halfway to the damned Valley before we find out about it! And we're using up horses we can't afford to lose, especially with winter coming on. Now, winter also means we should see a drop in things like this—nobody wants to be caught without a roof when the snows hit— but they'll start up again as soon as the ice melts. And as long as the Shan-wei–damned Valley's out there, we'll keep right on seeing this kind of crap."

"Well, so far your attempts to deal with the Valley haven't been very successful, have they?" Spring Flower observed in an unpleasant tone.

"No, Your Grace, they haven't. And they won't be, at least until sometime next year. We've got the manpower. What we don't have are the weapons. In fact, the damned Valleyers have better weapons than *we* do. I have to wonder if they've gotten that rifle manufactory back into operation."

Spring Flower's teeth grated almost audibly. The Chynduk foundry was another reason he wanted the Valley. The thought that a mob of commoners and outright serfs might have put it back into production and be using that production against him was enough to make anyone's blood boil. On the other hand—

"So you think you'll be able to do something about the situation 'sometime next year'?"

"We *may* be able to, if His Majesty and Earl Snow Peak really can get a few thousand new-model rifles through to us," Qwaidu said. "We can't unless they do, so a lot depends on how likely that is."

He paused, arching one eyebrow, and Spring Flower shook his head irritably.

"I can't say for sure. I believe they'll make every effort—all my sources in Yu-Kwau agree on that. Whether or not they'll be able to get them past the damned Charisians and that miserable son-of-a-bitch Rainbow Waters is another question. I think the odds are at least fair, especially if they grease the right palms between Zhyahngdu and Dosahl. And—" he shot the baron a level look "—a lot will also depend on how ominously you can loom down on the southern border to keep those bastards' fingers out of the pie when the time comes."

"That's essentially how I read the probabilities, as well, Your Grace. And if we can get modern arms into the men's hands in any sort of numbers, the situation in the Valley will change radically. In the meantime, though, I think we need to focus on sealing it off from the outside. I don't like the idea of tying down permanent garrisons out in the middle of nowhere, but Captain of Foot Rung has a point. Fifteen hundred men permanently based between the Yang-zhi Farm and Zhyndow would make it impossible for anyone to get in—or *out*—of the frigging Valley that way. And the other end's already closed. Or can be, easily enough."

Spring Flower nodded slowly. The town of Ky-su, at the northern end of the Chynduk Valley, was far beyond his own current frontier, but Zhynzhou Syang, once a mere captain of swords in the Emperor's Spears, had become yet another of Harchong's warlords and made Ky-su his stronghold. His "Barony of Cliffwall" was tiny and had yet to be recognized by Yu-kwau, but so far he'd made it stand up against all comers.

"I knew Syang before the Rebellion," Qwaidu continued. "I know damned well he wants the Valley even worse than we do, but he also knows he doesn't have a hope in hell of taking it out of his own resources. On the other hand, he knows how much influence *you* have in Yu-kwau, Your Grace. I think there's the possibility of a . . . cooperative effort that would help all of us."

. VI .
Merlin Athrawes' Suite,
Royal Palace,
City of Gorath,
Kingdom of Dohlar.

Merlin Athrawes sat on the balcony, gazing out across the roofs and walls of Gorath as the Dohlaran capital drowsed under the warm afternoon sun. The city walls weren't the only part of Gorath which had been built out of the famous "golden stone," and the light poured down like honey on the city streets and the broad, slow-moving ribbon of the Gorath River and the parkland which followed much of the river's course. Gorath—especially its architecture—reminded him a lot of cities Nimue Alban had seen in northwestern Spain or on the plains of Italy back on Old Earth.

It was actually quite beautiful. He understood why Dohlaran painters loved the light so much. And it was enough to make him feel even more homesick than usual for the murdered world of Nimue's birth.

He was alone on the balcony, parked in a comfortable lounge chair with a mug in his hand and a pot of cherrybean on a small spirit burner at his elbow. It was very quiet with both Nynian and Stefyny absent, and the suite felt empty without them. Sebahstean hadn't been able to accompany them to Gorath at all; midshipmen and junior lieutenants in the Imperial Charisian Navy went where their ships went, not where their *families* went. But his sister and Nynian had abandoned Merlin today, as well, accompanying Alahnah to an afternoon tea with the women of the Mahkzwail and Whytmyn clans. Sharleyan had been invited, but she and Cayleb were deep in meetings with Fern, Dragon Island, and Rahnyld and had been forced to decline.

Merlin, as a mere male, had been pointedly—although *politely,* he conceded—excluded from the invitation.

He'd wondered if Hailyn Whytmyn and Stefyny Mahkzwail might have made an exception in his case if they'd known about Nimue Alban.

Probably not, he'd concluded. And just as well, really, when he thought about it.

And so he sat on the balcony, drinking his cherrybean, soaking up the sun, and generally consoling himself in the absence of the women in his life. Whatever it might have looked like to a casual observer, however, he wasn't looking at the city at all, at the moment. He was watching something very different, and he exhaled noisily as the take from the SNARC above the Chiang-wu valley came to an end.

"Impressive," he said out loud, since there was no one to hear him. He took another sip of cherrybean. "That man's impressed me from the very beginning."

"Syngpu?" Nahrmahn's voice said in the back of his brain.

"No, Helmuth von Moltke," Merlin growled. "Of *course* Syngpu!"

"I fail to grasp why you so persistently rise to his baiting, Merlin," another voice said. Owl had finally become accustomed to addressing Merlin by first name rather than his rank, at least on informal occasions. It had only taken the AI ten or twelve years.

"Surely you are aware that he knew precisely who you referred to?"

"Of course he is!" Nahrmahn chuckled. "That was the entire point of his comeback. And a nicely ironic one it was, too, considering von Moltke's birth class. Although, actually, now that I think about it, he has shown much of the same talent, hasn't he? And despite the . . . geographical limits of the Chynduk Valley, he's probably had even more impact on West Haven than even von Moltke—the elder, I mean—had on Europe."

"Tell me you already knew who I was talking about and didn't dive into the library base for a little fast research!" Merlin shot back with a grin.

"Unfortunately, in this case he did," Owl said before Nahrmahn could reply. "He and I came across von Moltke—both uncle and nephew, actually—while performing research for Duke Serabor."

"Really he's more like the elder than the younger, though," Nahrmahn said thoughtfully. "I'm not comparing their situations, although as I say, his impact on North Harchong's got to be at least as significant for West Haven as the unification of Germany was for Europe. And the one thing Syngpu's never going to do is waver back and forth between options like von Moltke's nephew did. Once he makes up his mind, he's pretty damned . . . formidable about sticking with it."

"You're right about his impact, but I wonder how many people realize how big a part he played in launching the entire Rebellion?" Merlin mused.

"Not a lot, and a lot of those who did know are dead now." The rotund little prince's avatar shook his head sadly. "There's been a lot of that going around."

"And there'll be a lot more if that bastard Spring Flower and his pet Qwaidu ever break into the Valley," Merlin said more grimly.

"They're not going to do that tomorrow or even the day after tomorrow," Nahrmahn pointed out. "In fact, Owl and I estimate it'll be at least a couple of years—minimum—before someone like Spring Flower or Qwaidu could seriously threaten them, barring anything neither of us can foresee at the moment."

"Granted. But if Spring Flower ever does get his support base built up enough, he's going to have to try. It's the way his mind works. He can't afford to have the Valley sitting up there on his flank like some sort of promised land for escaped serfs."

"This notion of just sealing both ends of the Valley would defang a lot of that."

"Nahrmahn, you used to be a prince. Tell me just locking the door is going to make someone like this bastard decide to let sleeping Valleys lie!"

"No, not so much," Nahrmahn conceded, and Merlin snorted.

"The good news is that Syngpu and the others have such a robust support base in the Valley," he said after a moment. "And the fact that Syngpu is probably about two thousand percent better as a commander than Qwaidu or anyone else on Spring Flower's payroll. The bad news is that the Valley's on its own and Spring Flower's power base just keeps growing, Nahrmahn."

Merlin shook his head, blue eyes darker even than usual. The warlordism in Central Harchong was as bad as ever, just different. The small fry were being choked out as the big fish swallowed up the little ones. It was a slow process that chewed up and spat out a lot of human beings, and the chaos of every-man-for-himself wasn't coming to an end anytime soon. Indeed, it was likely to continue for years, yet. It was, however, becoming apparent which players were most likely to survive at the end of the day, and Spring Flower, unfortunately, placed high on that list. Which meant that, eventually, he and Qwaidu *would* try to press home a campaign up the Chynduk.

"The terrain's on their side, and their weapons are at least as good—better, actually." Nahrmahn, Merlin thought, sounded like a man trying to cheer him up. "In fact, if Spring Flower's impatient enough to push Qwaidu into a premature invasion attempt, the losses might just open the door for some of his own competition to hit him from behind with hopefully fatal consequences."

"Which is exactly why they're coming up with this strategy, instead," Merlin said glumly. "I wish Star Rising and the others would get more aggressive about pushing on to Cliffwall Pass!"

"There's no question that that's where they're headed eventually," Nahrmahn pointed out.

"No, and I understand all the reasons to be cautious, just like I understand why staking a formal claim to Shang-mi's likely to have . . . significant diplomatic repercussions, let's say. I don't really have a problem with methodical advances. In fact, I'm all in favor of not biting off more than they can chew! I just wish they were biting off those mouthfuls a little closer together. What I'm afraid of is that if they wait too long, they'll have to settle for the western end of the pass. I hate the very thought of what Spring Flower and Qwaidu will do if they break into the Valley, but the long-term implications for the United Provinces are just as bad, in a lot of ways. They need the *eastern* end of the pass if they really want to use the Chiang-wus as a defensive bulwark. The high road through the pass is almost eight hundred miles long, Nahrmahn! Think of all of the defensive positions that would give them. But if they wait too long, Spring Flower's going to have exactly the same advantages against anyone going the other way."

"I know." Nahrmahn nodded again. "And Koryn's training cadre's bringing them along pretty well, I think, with exactly those points in mind, whether he's fully discussed them with Star Rising or not. A lot depends on timing, of course. First because I don't think the UPPM's up to campaigning across that much distance, if only because of how much area they'd have to hold after they got there. They need at least another couple of years to train more men just to have the warm bodies, let alone find them weapons! And, second, because moving troops over that kind of distance is so time-consuming. Their ability to respond quickly to any aid request from the Valley—or any suggestion from us that they ought to be making contact with the Valleyers—is likely to be pretty arthritic."

"Exactly the reason I'm fretting," Merlin agreed. "Just getting the lines open as far as Shang-mi, so they could ship the troops by rail at least that far, would be an enormous help, and I know you're right. They can't go a lot faster than they are. It's just that. . . ."

He fell silent for a long moment, then shook his head sharply.

"Damn, I don't want to see those people go down, Nahrmahn! I know no one in the circle does, but they're such *decent* people, and I've seen way too many decent people get ground up in the gears."

"I know," Nahrmahn repeated, smiling sadly at his friend. "I know."

"What we need," Merlin said slowly, "is some sort of . . . rapid response plan to have waiting if the Valley's situation changes suddenly. Something that could buy the Valleyers the time the UP needed to advance to them—assuming we can talk them into it."

"I believe that's called 'magic,'" Nahrmahn said dryly, and Merlin chuckled humorlessly.

"I'll give you that. But 'magic' is what we Charisians do on a routine basis, isn't it?"

He took another swig of cherrybean and leaned back, cup in his right hand, tapping the tip of his nose with his left index finger while he pondered. Then, gradually, his eyes narrowed and the finger-tapping slowed. It stopped, and Nahrmahn's avatar cocked his head.

"Since Nynian isn't here, I'll take it," he said.

Merlin blinked at him, eyebrows arched, and the Emeraldian grinned.

"To quote her favorite question, 'What have you thought up *this* time?'"

"Well, I wouldn't call it a fully formed plan just yet," Merlin said, with a slight answering smile and a pronounced glint in his eye, "and to make it work—if we *can* make it work—we'll need to . . . point some things in another direction. Have to get started on it pretty quick, too, actually. Not that that wouldn't be worthwhile in its own right, now that I think about. . . ."

His voice trailed off and Nahrmahn glared at him.

"It's *my* job to infuriate people with tantalizing hints, not yours!" he growled. "I don't appreciate your stealing my small amusements, Merlin!"

"What?" Merlin blinked, then grinned at him. "Sorry!

Not that you don't deserve to get a little of your own back, from time to time. But I wasn't really trying to be mysterious. It's just that it's occurred to me that sometimes when there's an obstacle in the way, it makes more sense to go over it than through it."

. VII .
Ky-su,
Cliffwall Pass,
Tiegelkamp Province,
North Harchong.

Zhynzhou Syang tipped back in his chair, propping his heels on the hearth before the quietly seething flames, and considered the exquisite calligraphy of the letter in his hand. He was a simple man, and the elaborate, illuminated capitals were too showy for his taste. In fact, they made it difficult for him to puzzle out some of the words.

But underneath all of the fanciness, the letter was as simple as he was.

He read through it again—not easy, given the quality of lamp oil available in the Chiang-wu Mountains with autumn coming on—then stood, dropped it on the battered table which served him for a desk, and crossed to the window.

Darkness fell swiftly in the Chiang-wus' deep passes as the year aged, and the night beyond the window's cloudy glass was dark, shot through with the first windy flakes of a snow that was early, even for northern Tiegelkamp. He wondered if any of it would stick. Probably not much, this early, and any that did accumulate would melt quickly. But it wouldn't be very many more five-days before snow that didn't melt began to pile high in Ky-su's narrow streets.

He'd managed to accumulate enough supplies to get them through the winter . . . he thought. He'd never really considered the administratiye responsibilities of even a minor nobleman, but it seemed he had a knack for it. The right combination of ruthlessness and organization. That was the real reason he'd survived as long as he had. The disintegration and chaos of the Rebellion might offer opportunities, but the risks were just as great, and he knew he was no military genius. Yet his ability to keep his followers fed through a Tiegelkamp winter had been all the "genius" they'd needed. Now they expected him to do it again, and unless the winter lasted longer than usual or it turned out he'd miscalculated somewhere, he should be able to.

Probably.

He sighed, looking out into the night, feeling the future grind towards him, and thought about that letter.

The Chynduk Valley's farmers had made the difference for Ky-su last winter. Their willingness to trade with him, to sell him the food he'd needed, was all that had gotten him through, and he'd bought a lot of grain—much of which their gristmills had ground into flour—this year, as well. But there was a bottom to his purse, and he lacked the strength to expand his territory. Indeed, he was hard-pressed to hold what he already held. He'd eked out a barter-level economy largely by raiding outside his own borders, but plunder was growing more scarce. All the easy pickings were gone, and he was too small a fish to compete with the krakens emerging from the Rebellion's chaotic womb. He had too little land and too few farmers to feed his followers out of his own resources, and as more and more refugees streamed into the Valley, the Valleyers had less and less surplus food to trade, even if he'd had the wherewithal to buy it.

He leaned closer to the window, bracing his hands on the sill, and closed his eyes as he felt the night's chill radiating from the glass, a gentler promise of the bitter cold to come.

Yes, he thought. He'd make it through *this* winter. But he couldn't keep it up forever, and he'd seen what happened to other would-be warlords when that happened.

He drew a deep breath and opened his eyes again,

looking out into the cold, windy dark, and faced the truth. He didn't much care for the inevitable decision, but that was what it was: inevitable. He had increasingly less to trade; the Valleyers wouldn't feed his men for free out of the goodness of their hearts; and he lacked the strength to *compel* them to feed him. Even if he could have broken into the Valley successfully, he could never have held it. And that meant he really had no choice, didn't it?

He didn't like a lot of what he'd heard about this Spring Flower, and Zhailau Laurahn had been a pain in the arse even when Syang outranked him. The thought of acknowledging him as his superior was less than pleasant. But unless an even more efficient predator unexpectedly sprang up, Spring Flower's steady expansion would reach the Cliffwall Pass eventually. Staying on his good side had to be a good thing, especially if that "regularized" Syang's status as Baron Cliffwall. He doubted much would come of Spring Flower's hints about *sharing* the Valley with him, but Zhynzhou Syang had learned a lot over the last four years. He'd learned that power and wealth might be wonderful things to have, but that something else was even more important.

It was called "survival."

. VIII .
Zhutiyan,
Chynduk Valley,
Tiegelkamp Province,
North Harchong.

"And *bow* to your partners!"

The caller had a deep, resonant baritone that boomed out over the fiddles, flutes, and drums as the dance reached its conclusion. A cheer went up from the spectators as the dancers obeyed the call, bowing deeply to one another across the square, then reached out to one another, laughing while men thumped each other on the back and women embraced.

"Ten minutes!" the caller announced as Father Yngshwan ceremoniously turned the big sand glass mounted on the wall behind him. "Ten minutes! You boys—" he smiled at the musicians "—better take the chance to wet your whistles! Next set's a wind dance, and I've not been run out of wind once in the last twelve years! Won't happen tonight, either!"

A loud, laughing groan—and not a few catcalls—greeted his announcement. The traditional Harchongese wind dance continued until either every one of the dancers—or the caller—"ran out of wind" and acknowledged defeat, and the competition for bragging rights was ferocious. Exactly when to announce one was always a nice tactical decision for the caller, based upon the competing fatigue levels of his dancers and his voice. Only a supremely confident caller actually offered the dancers a rest break before the dance, but if the burly, white-haired farmer calling tonight's dance felt a single qualm, there was no sign of it.

"Might's well wet *my* whistle, too!" He wiped his forehead—the weather was unseasonably warm for the Chiang-wu Mountains in October and he'd worked up a sweat—and his smile turned broader. "Setting up for my best work, you might say. None of you sissies're gonna outlast me, anyway!"

More laughing catcalls answered, then he jumped down from his wagon-top perch and headed for the kegs himself. At least a dozen men were waiting to buy him his beer, and he deserved it. He'd worked hard already this boisterous evening, and the wind dance, especially the version of it performed in the Chynduk Valley, could last a long, long time.

Tangwyn Syngpu stood with his own beer mug, watching with a smile of his own. He'd found a quiet, private little pocket between two walls of baled hay from which to enjoy the festivities. Those hay bales were purely decorative, but that was hardly surprising. Technically, the enormous structure around him was a barn, and there was even a loft filled with hay, but its floor was not only planked but varnished, and the wagon of the caller's traditional perch was brightly painted, its metalwork polished. He was reasonably sure it had been parked exactly where it was since the day it had been built. Since the day the entire *barn* had been built. Langhorne, they'd probably built the barn *around* it!

There'd been nothing like it in Thomas Province, where he'd grown to manhood. Thanksgiving barn dances there had been held in far more modest structures, or even in the open—weather permitting, which it had seldom done, at this time of year. The fact that Zhutiyan had built its dance barn on such a scale, with such permanence, only underscored the Valley's relative prosperity. Looking around it—or out the enormous open doors at the long tables on the roofed veranda, laden with roast wyverns, huge kettles of corn and lima beans, tub-sized bowls of mashed potatoes, squash, and green beans, and platters of corn bread and rolls—made him truly realize what he and his men had accomplished here. They hadn't built this place, but they'd certainly helped preserve the prosperity—and the people—it represented.

"He hasn't, you know," a voice said beside him, and he turned to discover Yanshwyn Gyngdau at his elbow. He hadn't seen her approaching his quiet—although "quiet" was a purely relative term, under the circumstances—vantage point. Of course, that wasn't too surprising, given her diminutive size and the dance barn's crowded state.

"What?" Syngpu shook his head.

"He hasn't," she repeated, smiling up at him. "Run out of wind in the last twelve years, I mean." She pointed at the caller with her chin. "I don't imagine he will tonight, either."

"Oh, I don't know." Syngpu cocked his head, his expression thoughtful. "Suppose that depends on who's doing the dancing."

"Is that a *challenge* I hear?" another voice asked as Miyang Gyngdau appeared in his sister-in-law's wake, with his wife, Rouchun on his arm.

"Evening, Squire. Madame Gyngdau," Syngpu greeted them, raising his mug in salute.

"Don't you think it could be Miyang and Tangwyn tonight?" Gyngdau quirked an eyebrow. "It *is* Thanksgiving. Sondheim says we're all family today."

"I guess he does . . . Miyang," Syngpu acknowledged.

"See? That wasn't so difficult, was it, Tangwyn?" Rouchun said teasingly. She was a tall, sturdy woman, barely an inch shorter than her husband, who was only a couple of inches shorter than Syngpu himself. She would have made two of her sister-in-law, Syngpu thought.

"No," he agreed. "It's just we're in public."

"I know." Gyngdau nodded.

Syngpu was always careful to address him and Mayor Ou-zhang—for that matter, all of the Valley Assembly's members—formally in any public venue. As a general rule, Gyngdau approved of that, and it was like Syngpu to emphasize the point that he respected the Assembly's authority. Too many men in his position would have been looking for the chance to increase his own power at the civilians' expense.

In fact, that was exactly what far too many men *were* doing outside the Valley.

"I know," Gyngdau repeated. "But you and your men are the real reason all of this—" he waved at the laughing, jubilant crowd around them "—is still here."

"Like to think we've earned our keep," Syngpu acknowledged. As always, he felt vaguely uncomfortable at the praise.

"You've done more than that," Yanshwyn said so quietly he had to strain to hear her through the background sound. "A *lot* more."

Syngpu looked down at her, automatically shaking his head. He opened his mouth to rebut her comment, although he wasn't sure why he wanted to.

"She's right," Gyngdau said before he could speak. His eyes swiveled to the squire, and Gyngdau chuckled.

"You told us that first day that we wouldn't regret giving your men 'honest work' to do, and you were right. Without you, and the rifles you brought with you, and the militia you've trained, Spring Flower and Qwaidu would have forced this Valley months ago, and you know it. *We* know it. But that's not all you've done for us. I can think of at least a dozen other things—bringing back Baisung to get the manufactory back up and running, to name just one—and Langhorne knows nobody else in the Valley knew how to make gunpowder!"

"Might be you're right about that," Syngpu said after a moment. "To tell the truth, though, I'd as soon be back in Thomas watching my sheep. Nothing personal," he added hastily. "Not saying your folk haven't made my boys right at home here in the Valley. It's just—" He paused. "It's just that it was so much . . . simpler then."

"For all of us," Gyngdau said quietly. "And I suppose I wish you could be there still, too. But since you can't, I hope you won't mind my being thankful you're here, instead."

Syngpu felt his face heat and bobbed his head in acknowledgment without speaking. Gyngdau looked at him for a second or two, then smiled and shook his own head.

"Well, Rouchun and I are supposed to lead out the wind dance," he said. "I think I'd better get over there and see how much beer I can pour down old Fyngzhow before he climbs back up on that wagon!"

"And how much good do you think that's going to do?" his wife demanded. "He's been doing this for over thirty years, Miyang! And the man can drink more beer than any three other men I know. You're certainly not going to get him drunk in only ten minutes!"

"No, but if I can get enough beer into him he may run out of bladder before he runs out of wind!"

Rouchun shook her head with a laugh, nodded to Syngpu, and followed her husband off through the crowd, and Syngpu smiled after them. He was a bit surprised by the warmth of his own smile.

"It's not going to work, but it's probably worth a try," Yanshwyn said.

"Anything's worth trying at least once," Syngpu replied.

"Anything?" she repeated. There was something a bit odd about her tone, and he looked back down at her.

"Just about," he said slowly. "Why shouldn't it be?"

"I haven't seen Pauyin tonight," she said, instead of replying directly.

"She's over at the nursery."

Syngpu twitched his head out of the open doors to the schoolhouse on the far side of the square. Its unshuttered windows blazed with lamplight, and a temporary waist-high fence had been constructed around it to help the dozen or so women riding herd on the gaggle of young children inside it. At the moment, the volunteer nannies had organized some sort of game that seemed to involve lots of squealing as the competing teams streamed in and out of the schoolhouse door doing something Syngpu couldn't quite figure out.

"I hope someone's going to spell her before the evening's over!" Yanshwyn said with a laugh.

"Oh, she and Baisung stood up for the first three dances," Syngpu replied. "She said she'd rather spend the rest of the evening with the babies and the other kids."

"Good for her." Yanshwyn smiled fondly . . . and possibly a little wistfully. "They're lovely babies."

"They are," Syngpu agreed, his eyes still on the schoolhouse windows. "Both of them."

Yanshwyn looked up at his profile, wondering if he heard the softness in his own voice. His granddaughter, Saiwanzhen, had been born only two months after her mother's seventeenth birthday. He'd never discussed that birth with Yanshwyn, despite how closely she'd worked with him as the Valley Assembly's general secretary, but Pauyin had.

Yanshwyn had been teaching Syngpu's daughter to read and write for almost two years now, and Pauyin had become a valuable assistant. She'd also become a friend. More than that, she'd become the daughter Yanshwyn Gyngdau had never had, and in many ways Yanshwyn had become the mother Pauyin had lost. And because of that, Yanshwyn knew—because Pauyin had told her—how much Tangwyn Syngpu loved the toddler. Saiwanzhen might be the child of rape—and, although Syngpu had never told her, Yanshwyn knew how the child's biological father had died—but no man had ever loved a grandchild more fiercely. It didn't matter how she'd been conceived; all that mattered to him was whose daughter she was.

And it was the same way with his grandson, Yanshwyn thought, watching that profile, seeing the way the expressionless face Syngpu presented to the world softened as he gazed at that schoolhouse. She remembered the way that mask-like face had softened another day, the unshed tears which had glittered at the corners of those dark eyes, when Pauyin and Baisung Tsungshai stood before Father Yngshwan and he pronounced them man and wife. And she remembered the tears he *had* shed the day Pauyin's son was born and his son-in-law told him they'd named the boy Tangwyn.

He doesn't think we know, she thought. *He truly thinks we don't know how deeply he feels. Don't realize how good a man he is.*

"Is young Tangwyn over that cold of his?" she asked.

"Seems to be." Syngpu looked down at her. "Was ugly for a five-day or so, though. Pauyin took it better'n I expected, really."

"Oh, *she* did?" Yanshwyn said, and he chuckled.

"All right," he acknowledged. "Took it more calmly than *I* did. Satisfied?"

"Well, you did seem a little distracted at Thursday's meeting," she pointed out.

"Sorry." His expression turned back into an iron mask, his eyes shutters in a wall, as she watched. "Fengwa, her sister. She always had hard colds."

Yanshwyn's face softened and she reached out, touching his arm. She knew how Fengwa Syngpu and her brother Tsungzau had died, but Syngpu never spoke about them. There was a locked room in his heart, she thought. One he allowed no one into.

He felt her hand and his eyes refocused on her face.

"Sorry," he said again, his voice rougher around the edges. "You don't need to be hearing my problems."

"Why not?" She squeezed his arm gently. "You always seem to have time to listen to mine."

"That's different," he said.

"How?" she challenged.

"It's just . . . *different,*" he insisted, and she shook her head.

"You know, generally you don't remind me much of Zhyungkwan. Except in one way, that is."

"What way?" he asked warily.

She seldom mentioned her dead husband to him, although he'd picked up quite a few details about him from others, especially her brother-in-law. From Miyang's description, Zhyungkwan Gyngdau and Tangwyn Syngpu couldn't have been much more unalike, physically, and Zhyungkwan had been a man of letters. Even now, Syngpu dreaded the very thought of the correspondence he couldn't entirely avoid as the commander of the Valley's militia.

"He'd fall back on that same male tactic whenever logic failed."

"What 'male tactic'?"

"Just repeating the same thing over and over again as if he was actually explaining something." She shook her head. "It's like you all think that if you just say the same word enough times your meaning will suddenly become clear to us poor, befuddled females. Or—" her eyes softened "—as if there's something you don't really want to *be* clear about."

She really did have beautiful eyes, Syngpu noticed, not for the first time, but something about them made him uneasy.

"No reason not to be clear," he said.

"Oh?" She cocked her head. "I think there are quite a lot of things you don't want to be clear about, Tangwyn."

"Like what?" he asked defensively, and bit his own tongue as those eyes of hers narrowed.

"Like why you always change the subject if somebody points out all the things you've done for everyone here in the Valley," she said. "Like why you're always willing to listen to someone else's problems and never want to talk about your own. Like why you're so angry at yourself."

He stared at her, feeling as if someone had just punched him in the belly.

"I don't—I'm not—"

He felt himself floundering and tried to pull his arm away from her, but she wouldn't let go. And somehow, despite the fact that he was nine inches taller than she and weighed twice as much, he couldn't pull that arm out of her grasp.

"I've known you for two years now, Tangwyn," she said. "And there's one thing I still don't understand. That I may understand even less now than I did the day we met. She looked at him very levelly. "Why can't you let go of whatever it is that makes you so *angry* at yourself?"

"I've more than enough to be 'angry' over!" His voice was harder than it had been. He felt a different sort of anger—anger at *her*—rising and stamped on it hard. "Most people do, these days."

"Bédard knows you do," she said, her voice so quiet he could barely hear it against the dance barn's noisy background. "Your family, what happened to Pauyin, everything you've seen. My God, Tangwyn! It would take a *saint* to not be angry about that! But that's not what I'm talking about. Why are you so angry at *you*?"

"I'm not," he said . . . and heard the lie in his own voice.

She only looked up at him, waiting. He stared back down at her, astounded by the depth of those eyes, trying to understand how the conversation had turned so suddenly.

"Maybe I am," he admitted finally, defensively. "Maybe I've seen things—done things—these last nine years I'm not so very proud of. A man puts his hand to the plow, he's answerable for what he sows behind it, come harvest time."

"Surely you don't think that makes you unique?" she demanded, and a strange thought went through him. Before they'd met, he wouldn't have been all that sure what "unique" meant. Now he was. His brain started to follow the implications of that, but she went right on, giving him no opportunity for side excursions.

"Zhyungkwan was part of the Mighty Host, too," she told him. "From the beginning—as long as you were, from the first levy through the fighting on the Sair River. And he wrote me letters, Tangwyn. Long letters. He was my best friend, not just my husband, and I knew him well enough to read even more out of those letters than he told me. He *hated* the Jihad." Her voice was still soft, but it quivered with passion. "He hated what he had to do and he hated what *that* did to *him*. He wrote me about how the 'Sword of Schueler' had devastated Siddarmark, about how the people who'd survived it hated Mother Church . . . and why. He even wrote me about those horrible concentration camps, about the men and women—the *children*—he knew were dying there every day. It wasn't him. There wasn't anything he could have done about it. But he felt so *dirty*, so fouled, just *being* there. He was a *good* man, Tangwyn—just like you are—and that only made it so much worse."

There were tears in her eyes now, and he realized he'd covered the hand on his arm with his own hand.

"And then you came home to *this*." She waved her free hand to indicate not the dance barn around them, but the world outside the Valley. "Of *course* you've seen and done things you wish you hadn't had to!"

"It's not—" He paused. "It's not that simple, that easy." His voice had deepened. "I didn't 'come home to this.' I *started* this."

He stared down into her eyes, astonished to hear himself admit that bitter truth to her, to anyone. He tried to stop himself. He knew he *had* to stop, yet he couldn't.

"You don't know," he told her, the words pouring

out of him. "*I* started this. Zhouhan and me—we came home against orders. We found men who'd had a bellyful of lords and ladies, of the Church helping grind the heel into their faces. We found them, and we trained them. And we're the ones—Zhouhan and me, *we're* the ones—who stole the rifles they used to take Shang-mi. We were there for that, too, and I'm the butcher who started it all!"

He felt the tears, wet on his cheeks, felt himself leaning towards her.

"That's what I've done. What I've done on top of anything I ever did in the Jihad. You think I'm angry at myself? Well that's why!"

"Oh, Tangwyn," she half whispered. That free hand reached up, touched the side of his face. "Oh, Tangwyn! You didn't start this, you only *led* it. It would have happened anyway—it *had* to happen, after the Jihad, after the Emperor refused to let the Host even come home. Believe me, if he'd lived, Zhyungkwan would have been *proud* to stand beside you when you took those rifles! He came from the Valley, Tangwyn. He knew serfs were just as much the children of God as anyone else even before he joined the Host. And he saw how they changed, how they grew, how they learned to think of themselves when Earl Rainbow Waters and his officers treated them as *men*, not animals! He wrote me about how proud he was to serve someone like the Earl . . . and about how the Empire was going to have to change when the Host came home again!"

Her voice quivered with a passion he'd never heard from her, but her hand was moth wing gentle on his face.

"What happened to your family's happened to God only knows how many other families over the years," she said, "and nobody outside those families ever spoke for them, ever tried to stop it. But you did something about it. You said it had to stop, not just for your family, but for every family. You said it had to end. And there was no way it was ever going to end unless someone *made* it stop, whatever it cost. Nothing that vast, that evil, that had lasted so long, could have been stopped without violence. And all the bloodshed, and all the atrocities, and all the horror are because of *that*. Because it was the only way to stop it and because when men and women are treated like animals for their entire lives, some of them will believe it. When the chance comes, they'll *strike back* like animals. They'll do every hideous thing that was ever done to them to someone— *anyone*—else. And while they do, other men will see only the opportunity to be sure they're the ones with a heel on someone else's neck when the smoke clears.

"But you're not an animal, Tangwyn Syngpu. You don't want your heel on anyone's neck, and you'll die to keep anyone's heel off the people you care about. You didn't come home just for vengeance for what happened to your family. You came home to rescue Pauyin, and then you turned around to rescue *everyone else* in the Empire!" Her tone was fierce, her eyes shining with tears. "Don't you *dare* call yourself a 'butcher' to me! *Don't you dare!*"

She stopped, quivering, her eyes like wet fire, and he stared at her. Stared at her and realized he'd never truly seen her before this moment. That he hadn't *let* himself see her.

He wiped tears from her cheek with his thumb and smiled crookedly at her.

"Well, all right then," he said softly, "I won't."

"*Good!*" she said fiercely, shaking his arm. "Good."

"Might be some other things I should be saying to you," he went on, his smile more crooked even than before.

"There might," she agreed with an answering smile.

"Got a temper for such a little bitty thing," he observed. "Might get dangerous."

"It might," she agreed again.

"Not much in life worth having as is and just a little dangerous," he said softly.

They stood for what seemed a very long time, looking at each other, alone in their hay-bale corner of the world. They stood there until fiddles scraped and the band struck up a warning tune.

Syngpu raised his head, glanced over his shoulder, saw the couples beginning to form, and looked back down at Yanshwyn.

"Well, then!" he said more briskly.

"Well? What's 'well'?" she challenged.

"Well, they're getting ready to dance," he told her with a grin. "So I'm thinking it's time somebody finally danced that old windbag out of wind, and I'm thinking that tonight, it might just be us!"

"It might," she agreed for a third time, and laughed as they started for the dance floor.

AUGUST YEAR OF GOD 908

· ✦ ·

. I .
Siddar City,
Republic of Siddarmark, and
City of Cherayth,
Kingdom of Chisholm,
Empire of Charis.

"You're crazy!" The burly man's tunic bore the shoulder badge of the Weaver's Guild. "He's ruining the Republic!"

"And you're an idiot if you think that's what he's doing!" The taller young man's hands were calloused, obviously from hard work, but his tunic showed no guild affiliation. "He's just trying to make some *progress* possible. Yeah, and to look out for the people doing the *real* work! It's people like *you* who're 'ruining' the Republic."

"The Shan-wei–damned bankers, you mean!" another man growled. His clothing was more finely cut than that of the other two, but it was shabby. Obviously, both he and it had seen better days.

"Well?" the first man demanded. "If the banks are the ones doing it, who the hell else am I supposed to blame for it? He was in charge of the treasury before they made him Lord Protector, wasn't he? And he's gone right on doing the same stupid shit since they did!"

"No one *made* him Lord Protector," yet a fourth man joined in. "Well, maybe the bastard who assassinated Lord Protector Henrai did."

"More power to him," the third man, who hated bankers, growled.

"That's enough of that!" The younger man turned on him. "I don't care how much you disagreed with Lord Protector Henrai, that's enough!"

"I only meant—"

"Don't apologize!" the guildsman snapped. "Man was probably only trying to save the Republic! Might not be such a bad idea for his successor!"

The younger man wheeled to face him, his expression dangerous.

"That kind of talk can get a man in trouble," he said ominously.

"Why?" the guildsman jeered. "Never encouraged anyone to do it. Just expressing an opinion. One of those 'hypothetical thoughts' the Bédardists talk about! Everybody's got a right to an *opinion*, don't they? You going to do something about it if you don't like mine?"

"For half a counterfeit copper mark, I *will*!"

The younger man took a step towards the guildsman, then stopped as a heavy hand fell on his shoulder.

"None of that!" the city guardsman said warningly.

"But he said—"

"I heard what he said." The guardsman turned to consider the guildsman. "Didn't sound like just an 'opinion,' to me. Course I could be mistaken . . . or not. And if I'm not, I do believe that constitutes incitement to murder," he added coldly, and the guildsman flushed. "Heard this other fellow, too." The guardsman jerked a thumb at the shabbily dressed man. "And I didn't much like his opinion either, myself. I'm not allowed to express my personal opinion on duty on election day, though. If I were, I imagine I'd have a word or two for both of 'em." He gave them both a glare, then turned back to the younger man. "But you don't want to be raising your hand to them, especially here." He jabbed his nightstick at the polling sign over the tavern's entrance. "That kind of thing on election day'll get you at least a month turning big rocks into little ones."

"Might be worth it," the young man muttered.

"Maybe it would," the guardsman agreed. "I'm not supposed to have an opinion on *that* on election day, either. But if you're determined to do it, at least wait until all three of you've voted. Don't want to be arrested before you've cast your ballot, do you?"

"No," the youngster acknowledged.

"Good. So don't you—don't *any* of you—" he swept his nightstick in a gesture which included all of them "—make me talk to you again before you do. Because if you do, you'll be talking to a magistrate, not a poll watcher, quicker 'n you can spit. Got it?"

Nods, some of them sullen, answered him, and he regarded them sternly for perhaps another ten seconds. Then he stepped back to his position on the sidewalk, watching the long line that stretched down the street and around the corner.

▼ ▼ ▼

"Langhorne!" Myltyn Fyshyr groaned, holding his right wrist as he flexed his ink-stained fingers.

He sat at a broad table, with a huge letter "B" on the wall behind him, and the line in front of him had halted for a few welcome moments while two of the registered poll watchers, each representing a different candidate, argued about whether or not the next man in line was entitled to vote in this precinct. He was grateful for the rest and the chance to work out some of the writer's cramp, but it was stupid of them to waste time on the argument. The voter in question still had to show his certificate to Fyshyr, and Fyshyr still had to check his roll to find both his name and the certificate number, before he'd be allowed to vote. And the poll watchers would have the opportunity to cross-check Fyshyr's records before his ballot was counted.

And there were going to be a lot of those ballots.

"How many of these people *are* there?" he demanded of no one in particular.

"More than there were last election day, less than there'll be *next* election day," Clareyk Zahmsyn said philosophically from the chair beside him. Fyshyr glared at him, and Zahmsyn shrugged. "You know it's true. Unless the economy goes to crap again, anyway."

Fyshyr's glare intensified for a moment, but then he shrugged and nodded with a grimace. Lord Protector Greyghor had insisted, after the Jihad, that the constitutionally mandated property standards both to hold office and to vote had to be reduced to reflect the changes sweeping the Republic. He'd recognized those sorts of changes couldn't happen overnight, however, so he and the Chamber of Delegates had provided a schedule for relaxing the standards gradually. That meant the pool of qualified voters would increase with each general election for four sequential election cycles. This was only the second since his death, and the campaign had been as ugly as any Fyshyr could remember.

Siddarmarkian political campaigns tended to be . . . obstreperous at the best of times. Vilification was the norm for broadsheets and newspapers everywhere and the otherwise strict libel laws of the Republic suddenly ceased to apply, especially right here in Siddar City. Political rallies were always well attended, and this year they'd been especially well attended by the city guard, which had spent quite a lot of time—and not a few bruised heads—keeping things from getting out of hand when rival rallies met.

They'd failed in that effort, a couple of times. And at one point, it had taken over two days to completely restore order.

The cleanup from that one had taken two *five*-days, and Fyshyr didn't like to think about how many thousands of marks worth of damage it had done.

Even now, he could hear the chants of the opposing candidates' supporters from out in the street. Siddarmarkian law prohibited anyone from blocking a polling place; no law said they couldn't stand to either side, behind the city guard's cordon, and call one another names, however.

They were doing a lot of that, he thought grumpily.

He finished flexing his fingers and looked up as the poll watchers stopped arguing and the voter who'd waited patiently stepped past them and extended his certificate.

"Your name?" Fyshyr asked pleasantly.

"Bahkmyn," the man said. "Allyn Bahkmyn."

The question had been a formality, since the certificate carried its bearer's name, but Fyshyr always asked anyway. Already today he'd tripped up three fraudulent voters who'd been too stupid to memorize the name on their forged or stolen certificates. There was always some of that, most often spontaneous, although there seemed to be more of it—and more of it that had been bought and paid for—this time around, and all three of them had been taken away by the guard to face a magistrate. They'd have the option of accepting the mandatory five months of jail time from magistrate's court, or they could request a full jury trial. Of course, if a *jury* found them guilty, they'd serve a full year, not just half.

It was one way of sorting out the sheep and the goats quickly, since the "regulars" knew to take their five months and get it over with. There'd always be another election, after all.

He flipped through the pages of his portion of the roll for this precinct, found "Bahkmyn, Allyn" listed at 306 Blacksmith Lane, and checked the listed name, address, and certificate number against the one in his hand. Everything matched, and he handed the certificate back to Bahkmyn. Then he took the next printed ballot from the stack beside him, recorded the number next to Bahkmyn's name on the roll, initialed the bottom of the card, tore it off at the perforated line and dropped it through the slot in the top of the locked box at his elbow, and handed the rest of the ballot to Bahkmyn.

"Through the arch," he said—unnecessarily, he was sure—and jerked a thumb over his shoulder.

"Thanks," Bahkmyn grunted and headed in the indicated direction, ballot in hand.

He would mark the ballot, then drop it into one of the locked ballot boxes under the gimlet eye of yet another poll watcher. No one at the polling place would be allowed to actually look at his ballot—the Constitution guaranteed that—and his name would appear nowhere on it. The number from the ballot would be recorded when it was counted, however, as would the candidate for whom it had been cast. If Master Bahkmyn's eligibility to vote was later questioned, or if it turned out that his certificate number had been used by more than one voter, the ballot could be identified by the number Fyshyr had recorded and subtracted from the total count. But those were the only circumstances under which the Republic was entitled to know how any individual voter had voted, and the process required the Keeper of the Seal to obtain a formal order from a senior judge.

Fyshyr looked at the seemingly endless line coming towards him and groaned mentally. He'd be here for at least another six or seven hours, he estimated, although he'd be getting another relief break in the next twenty minutes or so, and he'd need it.

But however much you might carp and complain, it was worth it. It was all worth it. He knew some of the other realms of Safehold found the Republic's voting procedures amusing. The sort of nonsense to be expected out of a bunch of people so ignorant they actually *voted* to determine who ruled them. But that was just fine with Myltyn Fyshyr. Nobody ever promised the Republic's voters would always elect the right man as lord protector. But at least they got to *think* about it every five years, by God!

▼ ▼ ▼

The thick-shouldered man with the Weaver's Guild badge came stomping out of the tavern and started down the sidewalk, shouldering his way through the crowd. His expression was as surly as it had been before he went in to vote, and the city guardsman who'd intervened in the earlier quarrel pursed his lips as the younger fellow with whom he'd been arguing came out the door behind him.

The younger man paused long enough to make eye contact with the guardsman and raised his eyebrows as he twitched his head after the departing guildsman. The guardsman looked back levelly for a second, then ostentatiously turned away and looked up at the bronze wyvern on the flagpole across the street from the tavern.

The younger man looked at his back for a moment, then grinned, spat into the palms of his hands, and started down the sidewalk in the guildsman's wake.

▼ ▼ ▼

"Well, he won," Cayleb Ahrmahk observed, leaning back in the rattan chaise lounge and watching as Empress Sharleyan, Crown Princess Alahnah, Princes Gwylym Haarahld and Bryahn Sailys, and Princess Nynian Zhorzhet—who would be six next month—engaged Hauwerd Mahrak Breygart, his sister Alysyn, Princess Irys Aplyn-Ahrmahk, and their cousins Prince Hektor Merlin, Princess Raichynda Sharleyan, and Princess Sailmah in what was theoretically a game of rugby. The teams were understrength, but that didn't really matter, since *both* of them were busy trying to score against Nimue Gahrvai, who was tending goal in the deep end of the swimming pool. In deference to her merely mortal opponents, she'd dialed down the speed of her reflexes just a bit, but she was still holding her own handily, he noticed.

"Yes, he did," Merlin acknowledged from the chaise lounge beside his.

Nynian and Stefyny were stretched out on blankets, just far enough from the pool to avoid the frequent fountains launched from its surface, soaking up sun with an abandon which would have horrified an Old Terran dermatologist who didn't know about Federation nanotech. Interesting-smelling smoke drifted from the other end of the courtyard around the imperial family's private swimming pool where the Duke of Darcos and Sir Koryn Gahrvai, assisted by Ensign Sebahstean Mahlard Athrawes, ICN, officiated over the enormous grill upon which meat patties and wyvern and chicken breasts currently sizzled.

The smoke, Merlin noticed, with the perversity of outdoor grills the universe over, followed the chefs no matter where they squirmed to avoid it. And unlike his eyes, theirs watered—a lot—when it caught up with them.

Moments like this were as precious as they were rare, he thought, smiling as he soaked up the comfort like a drowsy cat. Of all the outcomes Nimue Alban had imagined when she first awoke here on Safehold and realized the task she'd assumed, this—finding herself surrounded by the joyous shouts of *children,* all of them "hers" in one sense or another—had not among them.

"Yes, he won," Kynt Clareyk acknowledged over the com. "It was a squeaker, though."

"It was, but he's got five years to firm that up," Cayleb pointed out. "I could wish he'd had a bigger margin, and it looks like the Chamber's going to be even more . . . factionalized than it was, but five years is still five years, Kynt. Let's not borrow trouble."

"Granted. Granted!" the Duke of Serabor agreed, looking out his Maikelberg office window as the sentries outside the Imperial Charisian Army's headquarters building were changed. "And a lot can change in five years. For the better, I mean."

"No, you mean it can change—*either* way," Nahrmahn disagreed from Nimue's Cave. "And it can. To be honest, I don't like some of the trendlines we're seeing, but we knew that going into the election. This is absolutely the best outcome we could've hoped for, Kynt. Aside from that factionalism in the Chamber, at any rate, and let's face it, that couldn't make things much worse on the legislative front!"

"*Even* that couldn't make things much worse, you mean?" Merlin inquired a bit sourly.

"Well, yes," Nahrmahn acknowledged. "I'm trying really hard to find a bright side to this, you know, Merlin. You're not helping."

"Not my job," Merlin said, rising from the chaise lounge and heading for the edge of the pool. "My job is always to be the voice of stern duty, my '*seijin* blue eyes' fixed unwaveringly upon the steady horizon, my calm hand upon the tiller, my—"

"Your overinflated ego, so humbly displayed," his wife's "voice" put in over her implants.

"Your self-admiration, so unblushingly disclosed," Nimue Gahrvai observed as he neared the edge of the pool.

"And your pomposity its own penalty!" Stefyny Athrawes concluded, as she rose from her tanning blanket, took four running steps, and pounced. She landed on his back, wrapping her arms around his neck from behind with a shout of laughter, and he hit the water just a bit harder than he'd originally intended to ... and just in time for every contestant in the water polo game to descend upon him.

It was a very good thing, he concluded later, that PICAs didn't need to breathe.

. II .
Five Islands,
Maddox Province,
East Harchong,
Harchong Empire.

The islands in the middle of the Mynkhar River had proved their worth yet again, Vicar Zherohmy Awstyn thought, looking out the carriage's window as the automotive chuffed across the river. Without them, this bridge could never have been constructed.

The Mynkhar was over two thousand miles long, from its far distant source in the Langhorne Mountains to its mouth on Fairstock Bay. Even in late summer, it was three and a half miles wide here at the city of Five Islands, seven hundred winding miles above Fairstock, but the reason Five Islands had grown into a major city in the first place was because it was the point at which the high road out of the Temple Lands crossed the river.

And it crossed it on the enormous Archangel Sondheim Bridge, broad enough for four freight wagons abreast, whose mighty stone piers were founded on the five islands strewn across the river's course which had given the city its name. The rail bridge used the same islands, running parallel to the high road. Looking out the window, Awstyn watched the draft dragons harnessed to a pair of massive eight-wheeled freight wagons throw up their heads in alarm as the smoke-spouting monster clattered past them, but they fell behind quickly.

Awstyn might still cherish a few apprehensions about the furious pace of the change Charis had unleashed upon the world, but he had to admit that the sheer exhilaration of traveling at almost forty miles an hour—although they'd traveled even more rapidly than that over much of his enormous journey—still filled him with wonder and delight. The poor draft dragons obviously felt rather differently about it. He chuckled at the thought, then looked out the other window, across the broad expanse of the river.

Even at the automotive's furious pace, it took almost three minutes to cross the wide stretch of dark brown water, and he was uncomfortably aware that the bridge beneath him, supporting the massive weight of the automotive and its rails, was made of timber. Yet another bridge was currently taking form on the far side of the high road, and when completed it would cross the river in bounds of solid masonry and good, honest stone, but that project would take years yet to complete. The trestle bridge—built by enormous gangs of engineers who'd learned their trade in the Mighty Host of God and the Archangels—had gone up far more rapidly, and Mother Church's own engineers assured him it was more than adequate to its task. It was still made of *wood*, though, and Awstyn was cursed with an active imagination. There were moments when he could picture massive iron bolts vibrating their way out of the wood, waiting until exactly the right moment. Or a horde of beavers chewing its way through the timbers themselves, undoubtedly urged on by the spicy savor of their creosote!

Stop that, he chided himself, watching a barge emerge from under the enormous trestle. *You're a* vicar, *for goodness' sake! Surely someone in your position should have a little faith, Zherohmy!*

He snorted at the thought, but he also couldn't suppress an ignoble spurt of envy. According to Bryahn Ohcahnyr, the Charisians were producing sufficient iron and steel to build *their* river bridges out of steel "girders" instead of wood, whereas the Temple Lands' foundries could produce no more than eighty or eighty-five percent of the rails needed by its expanding rail network. They were forced to purchase the remainder from Charis, and they had no capacity at all to spare for bridge "girders." Without the enormous number of modern foundries built during the final years of the Jihad, they couldn't have managed even that . . . which only underscored the vast scale of Charis' internal "industrialization." Not only were Delthak Enterprises and its steadily growing field of internal competitors sufficient to meet their empire's internal needs, they remained very much iron master to the world, aggressively competing with one another to supply other realms' needs.

But that's changing, he reminded himself as the river fell behind and the automotive's headlong pace began to slow. Just building all these railroads—he'd traveled almost two thousand miles, in barely more than two days, from Zion to reach Five Islands—drove an ongoing, apparently never ending, frenetic expansion of the steel industry. And that had its own ripple effect throughout the entire economy.

And produces Shan-wei's own hell on earth, sometimes, he thought grimly.

Like so many things on Fallen Safehold, "industrialization's" advantages brought problems of their own. On balance, the advantages appeared to outweigh the problems, but that made the problems no less severe.

Mother Church had mandated that the Temple Lands' foundries, mines, and manufactories emulate the codes Charis had adopted for the safety of employees. She'd fully embraced the prohibitions on child labor, the apprentice training programs that were open to all, not just members of a closed guild, and the educational opportunities for their workers' children. And she'd *especially* taken to heart the advice of the Charisian experts Delthak had made available—with amazing generosity, considering the bitterness of the conflict—almost before the Jihad's smoke had faded. They'd been well-paid, those experts, but they'd been more than worth it, and not just because of the new techniques they could teach. One of the things they'd most strongly emphasized was the need to minimize as much as possible of the health impact of the new processes. Blast furnaces and coal mines both produced enormous quantities of slag, other manufactories produced their own contamination, and the volume of smoke from a steel manufactory had to be seen to be believed. There were steps that could minimize damage to the land and water around the manufactories, but nothing could completely alleviate it. And some workers were foolish enough—or stubborn enough—to resist wearing the safety gear Mother Church required, at least at first. Coal miners had used the face masks required by the *Book of Pasquale* as protection against the curse of black lung since the Creation, however, and experience soon brought the new manufactories' workers around.

Either that, or they found other employment, because Mother Church's inspectors gave them—or their employers—short shrift for repeated violations. Much though Awstyn continued to worry about the Church of Charis and its impact on the world, he was deeply grateful for the way in which the Charisians had clearly thought through the impact of their innovations.

It was a pity that people in places like Harchong and Desnair, or even some places in Siddarmark and the Border States, didn't seem to *care* about that impact.

His mouth twisted bitterly at that thought. His sense of compassion, his need to serve others' needs, was what had drawn him to Mother Church in the first place, and he hated the thought of what rulers like Emperor Zhyou-Zhwo and Emperor Mahrys were not simply permitting, but actively inflicting upon their subjects. Grand Vicar Tymythy Rhobair had followed in Grand Vicar Rhobair's footsteps in denouncing those abuses, and Mahrys, at least, had piously promised to do "all in my unfortunately limited power" to alleviate them. Zhyou-Zhwo hadn't even bothered to reply, and that ominous silence only underscored the totality of the break between the Church of Harchong and Mother Church, whatever Zhyou-Zhwo and Kangsya Byngzhi, his tame archbishop, might claim.

But, he reminded himself, that wasn't true everywhere in Harchong, and if God and Langhorne were good, perhaps it wouldn't be true forever in the rest of that bloodied and battered empire, either.

The buffers between the carriages banged as the automotive entered the outskirts of Five Islands proper and began to slow, and he sat a bit straighter in his seat, watching buildings begin to flow past his window.

▼ ▼ ▼

"I trust the men are prepared to behave themselves, Syizhyan," Medyng Hwojahn, Baron Wind Song, murmured as the automotive banged and clattered to a hissing halt in the Five Islands Station.

"My Lord, the men are *always* prepared to behave themselves," Lord of Foot Syizhyan Lung replied. He gave his superior a sidelong look and puffed his magnificent mustache. "When was the last time they embarrassed you in front of an important visitor?"

"There's always a first time for anything," Wind Song replied with a smile. But then his expression sobered a bit. "And I'm not happy about what we're hearing about the men's reaction toward Mother Church. Mind you, I can't blame them for it, but we can't have them painting with too broad a brush. Especially not where our genuine friends, like Vicar Zherohmy and the Grand Vicar, are concerned."

"I take your point, My Lord." Lung nodded. "And I've already had a word with the escort's officers. And, more to the point, with their noncoms!" He and the baron both smiled at that. "I don't think anyone's going to forget we wouldn't be here without Mother Church's support, but you're right. The mood is turning really ugly where the Church of *Harchong* is involved."

"I know," Wind Song said sadly, remembering the fervency with which the Mighty Host of God and the Archangels had set forth in Mother Church's defense those ten or twelve long years ago.

He'd been younger at the time, filled with much of the same fervor, yet he'd known even then that the Church in Harchong bore precious little resemblance to the one Langhorne and Bédard had decreed before the rise of the Fallen. Today, that difference was greater than ever, and the fact that Grand Vicar Rhobair and Grand Vicar Tymythy Rhobair had done so much to restore the vision of Langhorne and Bédard outside Harchong only made the rift even more obvious.

"So long as they remember that," he said more briskly. "Although," his eyes narrowed, "I don't want to hear any more 'rumors' about burned rectories or priests who 'disappear' when our men arrive in the parish, either."

"I take your point again," Lung replied. "Mind you, My Lord, I think a lot of those priests—the ones bright enough to see lightning and hear thunder—scampered for it the instant they heard we were coming. Doesn't mean a goodly lot of them didn't fall foul of our lads, though. I'll see to it the wick stays turned up for any of them who feel like taking personal revenge."

"Good. Good Syizhyan!" Wind Song patted the younger man on the shoulder as the train came fully to a halt and a captain in the orange colors of a vicar's armsman hopped down from the lead carriage. "Now, let's go make a good impression on our visitor!"

▼ ▼ ▼

Zherohmy Awstyn descended the carriage steps and the waiting trumpets blared the instant his foot touched the wooden platform. The entire station smelled of sawn wood, tar, creosote, and fresh paint, and he suspected the clatter of tools would resume the instant he got his own august presence decently out of the way.

The Rebellion had swept through Five Islands before Earl Rainbow Waters and his veterans were able to intervene. It had been less violent than other places, with a lower casualty total, but altogether too many people had died anyway. Worse, most of the city's storehouses and waterfront warehouse district had burned. That had been particularly pointless, with winter coming on, and it had contributed to far more deaths from starvation over the bitter months of ice and snow. But the conflagration had also cleared a broad swath along the riverbank, and Rainbow Waters' engineers had chosen the spot for the Five Islands Station with care. The broad streets which had served dragon-drawn freight wagons for centuries converged on what had been the warehouses, giving good access to the rest of the city; the station's planned switching and freight yards would mesh nicely with the river wharves; and new warehouses were going up on all sides. The freight hauled by the gleaming line of rails already challenged that delivered by canal and river barge, and that challenge was likely to grow in months to come.

At the moment, Five Islands was effectively the capital of East Harchong, although Rainbow Waters had been careful—so far—to avoid bidding formal defiance to Zhyou-Zhwo and the government in Yu-kwau. Everyone understood how unlikely it was that that could last, given the intransigence with which Zhyou-Zhwo had chosen to proclaim his own position vis-à-vis Rainbow Waters' "invasion" of his realm. Clearly, the emperor would prefer to see entire provinces burned to the ground rather than have his subjects rescued by someone as disloyal as Rainbow Waters!

You might *be doing the man a disservice, Zherohmy,* he reminded himself. If he was, however, it was a very *minor* disservice, as Vicar Haarahld's instructions had made abundantly clear before he set out.

But there'd be time enough for that, he thought, beaming with genuine pleasure as Baron Wind Song stepped up to him through the blare of trumpets. He extended his hand, and the baron bent, kissing his ring, then straightened.

"It's my pleasure—mine and my men's—to welcome you to Five Islands Station, Your Grace," he said and smiled, waving one hand at the escort standing at rigid attention. Their uniforms were immaculate, their perfectly maintained weapons gleamed in the bright afternoon sun, and every one of them had the solid look of the veterans they were. "The farthest west station on the Zion Line . . . for now." Wind Song's smile grew broader. "Lord of Horse Rungwyn is surveying the route to Chyzan even as we speak."

"Why am I not surprised?" Awstyn replied, shaking his head with admiration. "I'm impressed, My Lord. *Very* impressed."

"It wouldn't have been possible without Mother Church," Wind Song said much more somberly. "Believe me, every man in the Host understands how much we owe to the Grand Vicar and the Vicarate."

His last sentence said more than just the words it contained, and Awstyn nodded.

"I understand, My Lord."

"I'm glad." The baron inhaled, then straightened and gestured to the waiting horse-drawn carriages. "My uncle is eager to see you, Your Grace. I had to argue with him to convince him to wait for us at the palace."

"He's not well?" Awstyn's eyes darkened with concern.

"He's not ill, Your Grace," Wind Song said quickly. "But . . . he's not as young as he was, either. He turned seventy-one in April, and we worry about him—every man in the Host. He's that kind of man."

"I understand, My Lord," Awstyn repeated softly, in a very different tone. He signed Langhorne's scepter, then put his hand gently on Wind Song's shoulder. "In that case, let's not leave him wondering what's become of me!"

▼ ▼ ▼

Tyshu Daiyang had been only sixty years old when he assumed command of the Mighty Host of God and the Archangels. That was quite young for someone of his rank in the Imperial Harchongese Army, and he'd been a physically robust man—a handsome man, with sleek, thick hair, darker even than usual for a Harchongian, and the powerful hands and wrists of a swordsman. But now, twelve years later, his hair had gone completely silver and his once robust physique had grown increasingly frail.

It wasn't just the years, Awstyn thought as Mangzhee Zhang, Earl Rainbow Waters' majordomo, escorted him and Baron Wind Song into the earl's working office. The earl had spent his strength like fire looking out for "his" men when their emperor and their Church cuffed them aside.

It showed.

Zhang, on the other hand, radiated a certain indestructibility. Not so very many years ago, he'd been Regimental Sergeant Major Zhang, and most of Rainbow Waters' staff still referred to him as "the Sergeant Major." He looked like a sergeant major, too, although he'd been surprisingly literate for a peasant when he was swept up for the Mighty Host. His parish priest, who'd had pronounced Reformist tendencies for a Harchongese cleric, had given him extra tutoring, and he'd shown a strong aptitude for the mathematics made available by the new "arabic numerals."

He was also fiercely devoted to Rainbow Waters, and his attitude was obviously more protective than the last time Awstyn had visited the earl in the Temple Lands, before the Rebellion. That was an ominous sign, the vicar thought, as Rainbow Waters laid a hand on his desk and unobtrusively used his arm to lever himself to his feet.

"Your Grace," he said.

There was genuine welcome and warmth in his voice, and it, at least, was as strong as ever. Awstyn crossed quickly to the desk, trying to conceal his concern as he held out his hand. The tremor in the earl's fingers as

he took the hand before kissing the ring was almost—
almost—more imagined than real.

"My Lord," he said, clasping forearms briefly but
warmly after the ceremonial kiss. "It's good to see you."

"And to see you, Your Grace." Rainbow Waters inclined his head, then waved gracefully at the comfortable armchair at the corner of his desk. "Please, sit."

Awstyn sat rather more quickly than he might have
under other circumstances, because he knew Rainbow
Waters would remain standing until he did. He refused
to embarrass the earl by urging him to get off his feet,
but that didn't mean he couldn't speed the process.

"Thank you, My Lord."

He settled into the chair and Zhang offered whiskey
with as much quiet efficiency as if he'd spent his entire life in service to one of the great families of Harchong rather than working a rocky patch of farmland
in southern Thomas Province. Awstyn accepted a glass
gratefully. Rainbow Waters had always kept an excellent cellar, even in exile, and the blended whiskey went
down like thick, smooth, biting honey.

Rainbow Waters took a smaller sip from his own
glass, then tipped back in his chair and Awstyn considered their surroundings.

The earl had taken over the Archbishop of Maddox's
palace, across the city's central square from the cathedral. The prelate was currently ensconced in Yu-kwau
with Archbishop Kangsya, who'd become the primate
of a breakaway church, whatever he might say in his
official correspondence with the Temple. Since he no
longer needed a house in his archbishopric and the earl
did need an administrative center for the area under his
protection, Rainbow Waters had availed himself of the
archbishop's residence. It was big enough to house his
entire administration and its staff, and like more than
one archbishop's or bishop's palace in Harchong, it had
been built with an eye towards security and defense.

The earl had an official office one floor up from the
magnificent foyer, but that was mainly for show. He
preferred something smaller and more informal for his

working days, so he'd converted what had originally been a small side chapel off the archbishop's library. It retained most of its original sumptuous furnishings, which surprised Awstyn a little bit. He would have expected a vengeful peasantry to have looted it as an act of defiance to the Church which had sided with its oppressors for so long. Langhorne knew it had happened to enough other churches and monasteries and convents.

"How was your journey?" Rainbow Waters asked after a moment.

"Amazingly smooth and efficient," Awstyn said with genuine enthusiasm. "Not as smooth or as comfortable as a well-fitted barge, but *far* faster. And we made the entire trip without a single mechanical problem! I think that may have been even more impressive to me than the speed. And I noticed that the . . . the 'double track'—" he paused for a moment, making sure he had the right term, and the earl nodded "—has been completed for almost half the entire route."

"It's true the men have done amazingly well." Rainbow Waters smiled warmly, his lined face showing his genuine affection for and pride in his men. "We trained some excellent engineers during the Jihad, and I'm sure all of them find building railways and bridges far more satisfying than laying land bombs or building earthworks."

"I know they do," Awstyn said sincerely. "You—and they—have a great deal to be proud of, My Lord. Not only have you reestablished order and something like genuine public safety in so much of Langhorne, Maddox, and Stene, but with the railways and the other projects, you're giving these people something even more precious: *hope*."

"I like to think so." Rainbow Waters' voice was soft and he turned his chair sideways to look out the window at the brilliant blue sky, the peaceful pedestrians and traffic of the central square, the towering steeples of the cathedral facing the palace he'd appropriated. "I like to think at least something good could come out of this."

"My Lord, it's not given to mere mortals to accomplish tasks that would daunt even an Archangel by merely snapping our fingers. All we can do is the best we can do, and that's what you've always done. The Grand Vicar and Vicar Haarahld didn't send me all the way out here just to represent them officially on the first Zion-to-Five Islands automotive. That would probably have been enough for them to ship my deplorably youthful carcass off, you understand," he smiled broadly. "But they've also sent messages and reports, and there are several issues they wish you and me to consider jointly while I'm here. To be honest, the Grand Vicar and the Chancellor are increasingly of the opinion that it's nearing the time for you and your Host to officially proclaim your independence of the Emperor."

Rainbow Waters' face tightened. He stayed motionless, still gazing out the window, for several seconds while the steady ticking of the clock on the mantel sounded clearly in the quiet.

Awstyn leaned back, letting him digest that last sentence, and for once he was grateful the Vicarate had passed over him when it named Haarahld Zhessop to succeed Tymythy Symkyn as chancellor. As one of Symkyn's closest assistants, Awstyn might have aspired to the post himself, but he'd been only forty-one at the time. The vicars had wanted more age, more maturity—less impetuosity, though they'd been too tactful to say so—in the office of Mother Church's chancellor, and Zhessop had been an excellent choice. An experienced diplomat and a good man, he was also sixty-one when he was chosen and he'd made it quietly clear to Tymythy Rhobair that he intended to step down by the time he was seventy. By then, Awstyn would be fifty, more than old enough to assume the post. And in the meantime, he would function as Zhessop's senior deputy, accruing additional experience along the way.

But for now, he was still in the position of someone who got to advise rather than take responsibility, and there were times—like now—when he was guiltily aware that he was just as happy with that state of affairs. To be fair, he thought Zhessop and the Grand Vicar were right about the timing, but that wasn't going to make the decision any more palatable for Rainbow Waters.

"May I take it from the fact that you've brought this up that His Holiness and the Chancellor are . . . advising me to make that proclamation?" the earl asked finally.

"My Lord, you're the effective ruler of almost a quarter of North Harchong," Awstyn said. "All of us regret the circumstances which made it necessary for you to take the steps you've taken, but before God and the Archangels, you had no choice." The earl looked at him, and he met those dark eyes steadily. "God—and Mother Church—placed you in a horrendous position, My Lord, and despite that, you've always comported yourself as a man of honor and as a faithful son of Mother Church. Neither the Grand Vicar nor the Chancellor are suggesting you take this step to . . . enhance your own position or your own authority. Their belief, however, is that your name and reputation, more than anything else, are truly the glue that holds East Harchong together."

Rainbow Waters half raised one hand, as if in a gesture of protest, but Awstyn shook his head.

"No, My Lord—it's not your men. Or, rather, it *is* them, but only because you lead them and because so many of them would rather die than disappoint you. Do you think Mother Church's confessors don't know how they *talk* about you? 'The Earl,' they say, the same way they called Grand Vicar Rhobair 'the Good Shepherd.' I'm not saying they think of you the same way they thought of him. Don't think that for a moment! But they trust you, they honor you. In fact, most of them *love* you, because they know you've always taken their part, looked after them. Langhorne knows how many of the Mighty Host's officers abandoned them, took Emperor Waisu's offer of passage home to their families, their lands and estates . . . as long as they came home without their men. You didn't. Instead, you fought for them. They know that, and that's why it's your authority, more than anything else, which prevents many of your men from seeking vengeance just as mercilessly as any of the rebels who may have fled from their bayonets."

Rainbow Waters lowered his hand. He gazed at the vicar for a moment, then shrugged and sat back once more, placing his forearms neatly along the armrests.

"There may be . . . something to that," he said finally. "The Archangels know they needed someone to take their side after they fought their hearts out! It shames me to say that until the Jihad, I was as oblivious to the circumstances of their lives as most of my fellows. I'm not anymore." He smiled with brief, bitter whimsy. "I suppose *something* good can come even out of something like the Jihad."

"But I'm not a king, not an emperor, Your Grace."

"Uncle," Baron Wind Song said, speaking for the first time, "no one says you are. But I think I understand what the Grand Vicar and the Chancellor—and Vicar Zherohmy—are saying."

Rainbow Waters looked at him, one eyebrow raised, and Wind Song shrugged.

"Uncle, you—you and the Host—have accomplished so much. The population of the area under your protection is actually greater now than it was before the Rebellion, and you know the reason for that as well as I do. It's because anyone who could, nobles as well as peasants, have fled Central Harchong to join us here because they know you and the Host will *protect* them. And the Host looks to you, not to the Emperor. Not even to the Grand Vicar. *To you.* And what they hear coming out of Yu-kwau is the Emperor's declaration of war on you—and through you, on all of them—simply because they stopped the killing. That doesn't even count the railways, the canals our engineers have rebuilt, the housing we've thrown up, the draft animals and plows we've brought in. They *stopped the killing,* Uncle, and that gives them a sense of pride even their record in the Jihad couldn't. But they've seen too much, had too much taken away from them. They need the assurance that they won't be . . . sold out in the end this time the way they were *last* time. That their officers and the civil officials working with them aren't still proclaiming their loyalty to the Crown in hopes of finding pardon *from* the Crown . . . and leaving them twisting in the wind when Zhyou-Zhwo and that bastard Snow Peak finally get around to invading."

"I would never do that!" Rainbow Waters snapped.

"Of course you wouldn't, Uncle. Do you think I, of all people, don't know that? And the men in the ranks don't think you would, either. But, forgive me for saying this, you aren't getting any younger." Rainbow Waters' eyes darkened, not with anger but with some other emotion. "What I think the Grand Vicar and the Chancellor are seeking here is an open proclamation—one that will burn the bridges of the entire Host, whatever happens to *you*—to prevent whoever succeeds you from doing that to them."

Rainbow Waters gazed at his nephew for almost a full minute, then turned his eyes back to Awstyn.

"*Is* that His Holiness' thinking?"

"In large part, yes, My Lord." Awstyn raised his hand, waving it between them. "Oh, there are other aspects to it, as well. You and the Host are doing incredibly well here, but the truth is that all our reports are that the United Provinces are accomplishing even more, courtesy in no small part to the 'Ahrmahk Plan' and the investment it's made possible."

Awstyn kept his expression serene, his voice calm, despite his ongoing personal unhappiness over the souls he knew were inevitably straying to the Charisian side of the schism as a consequence of all the Empire and Church of Charis had done for them and their families.

"Many potential investors, in both the Temple Lands and the Border States who might otherwise see opportunities for investment here in East Harchong—the kind of investment you need if you hope to maintain the upward trajectory you've managed to create—hesitate to seize those opportunities because they fear that if they invest with you, and if the Emperor ultimately reasserts his authority in these provinces, all of their investments will be lost. By the same token, I doubt any of them genuinely believe Snow Peak and his army could retake East Harchong from you and your veterans, especially with Mother Church, Vicar Allayn, and the Army of God standing at your back. If you formally declare the independence of East Harchong, much of that investment will begin moving your direction. And on a legal front, Mother Church, the Temple Lands, and the Border States, could then open formal diplomatic relations with you, leading to all manner of other possibilities.

"No one who knows you believes for an instant that you've done all of this—" the youthful vicar waved his arm to indicate not just the office but the city and the province beyond it "—for personal power or even to punish Zhyou-Zhwo for the edict that exiled you and all your men. We aren't urging you to declare East Harchong's independence so you can set up as some sort of emperor in Zhyou-Zhwo's place. Our concern is that even now, years after the Rebellion's start, so much of North Harchong is in limbo. The United Provinces are beginning to restore order in the west and expanding slowly into the western reaches of Tiegelkamp, and all of our reports indicate they've already accepted that there can be no return to the Crown's authority. Now you're doing the same thing in the east, and however much you may recoil from the thought, it's time to make your break with Yu-kwau formal and official, as well."

"Uncle, he's right," Wind Song said quietly. "And you know as well as I do that no other outcome's ultimately possible. Langhorne knows we've discussed it often enough!"

"Perhaps."

Rainbow Waters raised one hand, pinched the bridge of his nose, massaged his eyebrows. Then he lowered it again and looked at Awstyn.

"You and Medyng may well be right, Your Grace. I don't know how much additional impact a formal declaration could have, but God knows none of the Host could ever return to the Crown's authority in safety. And, to be honest, the very thought of allowing the same people who created the conditions for the Rebellion in the first place to return to their places here sickens me. But I've been so clear, so forceful, on the point that I'm not seeking a crown of my own. What you're suggesting is, in many ways, a renunciation of that promise on my part."

"I rather thought you might feel that way, My Lord, and the fact that you do does you as much credit as any of your previous actions. May I suggest a possible avenue?"

"By all means, Your Grace!" Rainbow Waters tipped back in his chair once more, watching the vicar intently.

"My Lord, you can't avoid some of the appearance that concerns you. I'm sorry, but there simply isn't a way to do it. What I would suggest, however, is that you announce that the rupture with Yu-kwau is obviously irreparable because of what Zhyou-Zhwo is proclaiming. That he's made it abundantly clear a return to the authority of the House of Hantai on any peaceful terms is impossible. Because of that, you have no choice but to accept the situation *he's* created and proclaim the independence of East Harchong. However, at the same time you do that, you also proclaim the creation of a Harchongese parliament, similar to the one the Charisians have established. As the commander of the Host, you'll retain the . . . executive authority, I suppose you might call it, but your new parliament will contain a lower house, elected from and by your enlisted and noncommissioned personnel, and an upper house, elected from and by your officer corps. Exactly how the houses would be arranged, what their relative positions would be, would have to be worked out in advance, but its goal should be made very clear and very simple: to take a page from Siddarmark's experience and proceed, in consultation and coordination with you, to enact a written constitution for the provinces under your protection which lays out the relative powers of the executive and the two houses. And if that constitution grants the parliament what the Charisians call 'the power of the purse' and the authority to approve or reject treaties between

East Harchong and the rest of the world, I think the men and officers of the Host will heave a vast sigh of relief."

"And what about the civilians in the 'provinces under our protection'?" Rainbow Waters asked. "If they find themselves excluded from this new parliament, this new constitution, why shouldn't *they* conspire with Zhyou-Zhwo to restore his authority? They aren't the ones who invaded his territories, after all."

"No one says the houses of parliament established after the constitution is proclaimed have to be identical to the ones that *write* it, Uncle," Wind Song pointed out. "The Host, as the guarantor of peace and stability, can proclaim the constitution by right of possession, but they can also constitute the ultimate parliament any way they wish under that constitution."

"Yes!" Awstyn said enthusiastically, delighted by Wind Song's support.

Not only was the baron Rainbow Waters' most trusted advisor, he was also the earl's obvious heir apparent. Rainbow Waters' wife, Hyngpau, had defied all of her relatives to join him in his exile, but much as the two of them loved one another, they'd never had children. That made Wind Song, his only sister's eldest son, his heir under Harchongese law. More importantly, Wind Song's faithful service in the Jihad and since made him the earl's only possible successor in the eyes of the *Host*, as well. If he got behind the proposal and pushed, clearly accepting whatever limitations on his own future position the new constitution might impose, it had to weigh heavily with his uncle.

"My Lord," the vicar continued, "I could see a mix in which the lower house of any future, permanent parliament consisted of commoners who meet property qualifications, such as landownership or income, and also of all of the enlisted and noncommissioned personnel of the Host. In other words, all of your men and the nonnoble civilians who meet those qualifications would share the franchise and be eligible for seats in the lower house. By the same token, your officers could be granted noble status and assigned seats on that basis."

"Or *their* seats could be elective, too, Uncle. We could limit eligibility for them to those who hold patents of nobility or served as officers in the Host, past or future, but they could still be required to stand for election by all franchized voters, as well," Wind Song said, and Rainbow Waters arched an eyebrow at him.

"Should I assume you've been reading more of that Charisian drivel about the rights of man, Nephew?" he asked, but his tone was light, affectionately teasing, and Wind Song shrugged.

"Men do have rights, Uncle. You're one of the people who taught me that. I'm only saying that if a commission in the Host and a patent of nobility, however great or minor, qualifies a man for a seat in this 'upper house,' and if they, too, have to stand for election, then we give every man in East Harchong a potential place at the table. The chance to speak their minds in the halls of power."

The baron shook his head, his eyes somber.

"You've seen how our men reacted to the land Grand Vicar Rhobair gave them. The men in the Host right now left that land only because of their trust in you, and if they hadn't left it, they would have defended it to the death against anyone who tried to take it from them. Do you really think, after all that's happened since the Jihad, since the Rebellion and the anathemas Zhyou-Zhwo and Byngzhi have thundered from Yu-kwau, that if we gave the same incentive, the same hope, the same sense that they're men, not just 'serfs' and peasants—not just *property*—to every civilian who's turned to us for protection, *they* wouldn't fight to keep it, too?"

It was very quiet in the office, so quiet the traffic sounds came clearly through the window and the clock sounded like thunder.

FEBRUARY YEAR OF GOD 909

·✦·

. I .
Protector's Palace,
Siddar City,
Republic of Siddarmark.

"Place your left hand upon the *Writ*."

Archbishop Dahnyld Fardhym was almost seventy-two years old, but his voice carried clearly on the afternoon air. He stood on the balcony of Protector's Palace, looking out over the square where so many thousands had died in the Sword of Schueler's attack on the Republic's government. Today, that square was packed not with rioters, but spectators, with strategically located, specially trained priests prepared to relay whatever was said upon the balcony. They faced a rather more demanding task today, however, because many of that enormous crowd were . . . restive. Klymynt Myllyr had been reelected Lord Protector only by a narrow margin, and not everyone in that crowd had voted for him.

Myllyr looked out across the square, then placed his left hand upon the beautifully embossed copy of the *Writ* and raised his right. A wyvern drifted high overhead, riding the updrafts from the city's paved areas, and the faintest of breezes stirred Myllyr's hair.

"Do you, Klymynt Myllyr, solemnly swear before God and the Archangels to faithfully discharge the duties and responsibilities of the office to which you have been elected?" Fardhym asked.

Myllyr waited a moment, long enough for the relays in the crowd to repeat the words.

"I do."

"You will see that the Constitution is fully and fairly enforced?"

"I will."

"You will maintain the Army and preserve the safety of the Republic and its citizens against all enemies, domestic and foreign?"

"I will."

"You will account the Republic's state and condition—fully, freely, and accurately—to the Chamber of Delegates no less than once per year?"

"I will."

"And do you swear upon the *Writ* and your own soul that you will honor, keep, meet, and discharge all of the promises you have just made?"

"I do so swear," Myllyr said levelly, looking into the archbishop's eyes.

They stood for a moment, and then Fardhym stepped back a pace with the bound *Writ* and bowed.

A thunderous roar went up from the square, startling wyverns and birds roosting on rooftops and cathedral spires. It was the traditional acclaim of a new lord protector, but loud as it was, it was weaker than it ought to have been, and here and there in the crowd banners blossomed with slogans that were less than complimentary to the man being cheered.

▼ ▼ ▼

"Well, thank God that's over!" Lord Protector Klymynt said, an hour later, as he strode into the well-appointed guest chamber on the side of Protector's Palace that faced the square. He handed the Sword of State to an aide and grimaced as he shrugged out of the heavy, old-fashioned, thickly embroidered tunic he'd been forced to wear in the August heat.

"Oh, I don't know," Cayleb Ahrmahk replied, turning from the window with an off-center smile. "As coronation ceremonies go, it didn't seem all that arduous."

"Please, Cayleb!" Daryus Parkair said with a shudder which wasn't entirely feigned. "*Don't* call it a 'coronation'! That's the last thing we need to hand the opposition."

"Well, that's what it was." Cayleb's smile broadened. "For a purely limited reign, of course, what with all of those deplorably republican traditions you have." He shook his head. "Never do for an old-fashioned despot like myself!"

Myllyr snorted and crossed to the bar against the chamber's back wall. He opened the top of an insulated, wood-paneled chest and took out one of the bottles of beer which had stood on the block of ice from the Palace's icehouse, opened it, and crossed to stand beside Cayleb.

"I don't think that's how all those Harchongians think of you—any of 'em," he said. "The ones who like you seem to think you're even more republican than *we* are, and the ones who *don't* like you think you and Sharleyan are both scheming manipulators, playing the credulous fools who trust you like fiddles."

"We always were sadly transparent." Cayleb shook his head, and Myllyr snorted again. Then he took a long swallow of beer.

"Heard the catcalls out there, didn't you?" he asked more abruptly.

"A few," Cayleb conceded in a less mischievous tone.

"Trust me, there'd have been more if the Guilds could've gotten themselves properly organized." Myllyr shook his head, looking out the window as the square continued to empty. "I'll be honest—if I hadn't known Flahnairee would have killed the Bank in a minute if he'd won, I'd never have run again. I know I owe it to Greghor and Henrai—and the rest of the Republic, of course, whether it appreciates it or not—but it's going to be a bumpy ride, these next five years."

"I know." Cayleb sighed. "I hate it. And you know we'll do everything we can to help. But somehow, it seems that the more we try to help, the worse it gets."

"There are a lot of factors tied up in that, Cayleb," Samyl Gahdarhd said. He'd followed Myllyr into the guest chamber. He also continued in the office of Keeper of the Seal, although his hair was much more heavily streaked with white and his face was more lined than it had been. "Some of them may be things we can do something about. Others?" He shrugged. "All we can do is try to ride it out."

"Like those frigging idiots out West," Myllyr said, still looking out the window, and his own western origins only made him more bitter. The violence which had flared back up after Maidyn's assassination might have burned itself out again, more or less, in the western provinces, but the political corruption was only growing even more entrenched. "But at least it looks like we *may* be starting to turn the corner on the Bank."

He hadn't turned from the window as he spoke. Now Cayleb glanced at Gahdarhd, and his lips tightened at the keeper of the seal's very slight headshake.

"Are you at a point where we could make our version of the 'Ahrmahk Plan' work?" he asked after a moment.

"That's a better question for Bryntyn and Brygs." Myllyr rubbed his scarred left cheek through the concealing beard. "I just don't know if we've . . . stabilized things enough."

Cayleb nodded. Bryntyn Ashfyrd was Myllyr's replacement as Chancellor of the Exchequer. He was hardworking and bright, but he was more of what Merlin called a "policy wonk" than a politician. Zhasyn Brygs might actually have been a better choice for Chancellor, given his political acumen, but he couldn't be spared from his job as the Central Bank's governor. Although there had to be times when he wished he could have had some other—*any* other—job, whether he could be spared or not.

"The truth is that the Ahrmahk Plan is still a two-edged sword here in the Republic," Gahdarhd said, and shook his head again, harder. "I *wish* I understood how so many people could be so damned blind to how much we owe Charis!"

"Forgive me," Cayleb said gently, "but I think part of the problem is that they *aren't*." Gahdarhd raised an eyebrow at him, and he shrugged. "You know the saying, Samyl: gratitude is a garment that chafes. And rightly so, especially if people keep throwing it into your teeth."

"You and Empress Sharleyan've never done anything of the sort!" Myllyr said sharply, turning from the window at last.

"Haven't we?" Cayleb looked at him levelly. "We've certainly tried not to, but there are a lot of Siddarmarkians who think we're doing our damnedest to direct the Republic's policy. And they think we're trying to do it because we think the Republic *owes* us." His expression was completely serious now. "You only wound up in the Jihad because there *was* a Jihad, and that happened only because Clyntahn came after *us*, Klymynt. Maybe he would've attacked the Republic anyway. In fact, I'm pretty sure he would have. But when he did it—and the way he did it—evolved out of his war against Charis. And without you as an ally and as a means to take the war to the Church here on the Mainland, we couldn't have won. Not the way we did, anyway. So, yes, we shipped in food, we shipped in new industrial processes, we shipped in troops, but the price the Republic paid in blood outweighs *anything* we could've done. I think most of your citizens understand that, and if they do, and if they genuinely believe we're trying to direct your policies, then they have every right to resent the *hell* out of us."

Myllyr looked at him in silence for several seconds, and Cayleb knew he was remembering conversations with Mahlkym Preskyt. The Charisian ambassador might not be a member of the inner circle, but he was a very intelligent man. He'd made almost exactly the same points to Myllyr more than once, but this was the first time *Cayleb* had said them to the lord protector directly and personally.

"He's right, Klymynt," Gahdarhd said. Myllyr glanced at them, and the keeper of the seal shrugged. "I said I don't understand how they could be so blind, but that's because reason ought to triumph over what Cayleb's just said. Unfortunately, it doesn't. And the fact that we just seem to keep staggering along without ever getting our feet back under us isn't helping one bit. It's been going on for *years* now, and every time it looks like we're turning the corner, something else happens. No wonder people like Hygyns are making ground!"

Myllyr looked like he wanted to spit, and Caleb didn't blame him.

The lord protector had served in the quartermaster's corps during the Jihad after the serious wounds he'd suffered trying to stop the Army of God's advance down the Stylmyn Gap. Zhermo Hygyns, on the other hand, had served in combat commands throughout the Jihad, rising to the rank of brigadier general by the end of the war. He'd performed . . . competently, if not brilliantly, but there were those—quite a lot of those—who pointed to his combat experience and contrasted it with Myllyr's "rear echelon" experience . . . conveniently forgetting how he'd come to be wounded in the most desperate campaign of the entire Jihad.

Hygyns hadn't been shy about playing upon his combat record when he entered the rough-and-tumble of the Republic's political strife. The fact that he'd been one of the senior officers Daryus Parkair sent to Tarikah to deal with the unrest there was another factor in his favor. The violence had been in the process of dying down by the time he arrived, if only because the remaining Temple Loyalists had been driven out by the Siddar Loyalists, leaving them with no one to lynch, but he'd earned quite a lot of political support in the western provinces because of his "man on a white horse" status. The flare of violence which had followed Lord Protector Henrai's assassination had only enhanced that reputation as he took steps—firm ones, admittedly—against it. Since then, however, he'd resigned his active-duty commission to enter politics, and he was doing dismayingly well in his new career. He did have his critics, even in Tarikah, but there was no denying his popularity in the West, and his star was obviously rising on the national level, as well. He hadn't been a candidate against Myllyr in the election just past—that had been up to Rohskoh Flahnairee, who'd headed the Oil Merchants' Guild before challenging Myllyr—but it was obvious which job he had his sights set upon in the fullness of time.

"I know you don't like him, Klymynt," Gahdarhd went on as the lord protector grimaced. "I don't much like him myself. But he represents those people Cayleb's talking about, and he's getting more popular."

"That's how we read it from Tellesberg," Cayleb said. Myllyr and Gahdarhd both looked at him. "We do try to keep up with events here, you know," he told them dryly, and it was Gahdarhd's turn to snort, and not entirely with amusement.

"I promise we don't have hordes of *seijins* scattered through the Republic spying on you," Cayleb continued, truthfully, as far as it went. SNARCs weren't *seijins*, after all. "But from what we're seeing, he's got a damned good chance of being elected Governor of Tarikah next month."

"I wish you weren't right about that," Myllyr growled. "Draifys has been on thin ice ever since Henrai's assassination. Those bastards Ohlsyn and Zhoelsyn have been working to cut his throat from the beginning, and too many people who disagree with the two of them blame Draifys for 'letting' Henrai be killed, as if it was somehow his fault!"

"Exactly." Cayleb nodded. "And those same people credit Hygyns with stepping on the flames when they sprang back up. And we have reports he and the Syndicate crowd are very *comfortable* with each other."

"And if Samyl had proof of that, the bastard'd be in jail!" Myllyr sounded even more disgusted. "Unfortunately, he's too damned good at hiding the payoffs."

"I'm sure," Cayleb said.

In fact, however, the reason Hygyns was "too damned good" at hiding the payoffs was that there *weren't* any. Not financial ones, anyway. Zhermo Hygyns might be as ambitious and unscrupulous as they came, yet so far, at least, he'd steered clear of the sort of bribery and graft men like Mahthyw Ohlsyn and Maikel Zhoelsyn doled out. But that hadn't prevented him from using the troops under his control to break up more than a few demonstrations—and, to be fair, riots—aimed at Ohlsyn and Zhoelsyn's Western Syndicate paymasters.

The land speculators who'd succeeded in snapping up so much of the consecrated farmland of Westmarch and Tarikah had converted their holdings into massive commercial operations of the sort the Republic had never before experienced. Along the way, many once-independent farmers who'd been frozen out had been reduced to little more than sharecroppers, often on land which had been in their own families for generations. That generated resentment, and the "Western Syndicate," as the alliance of landlords had been dubbed, had turned to the Army when some of that resentment spilled over into active resistance.

To his credit, Hygyns hadn't set out to be the Syndicate's leg-breaker, but he'd made no distinction between irate farmers protesting their new status as slightly better off serfs and Siddar Loyalists burning out Temple Loyalists' farms and families. That had brought him glowing recommendations and support from the Syndicate's political allies. They'd been smart enough not to offer him money, but they'd offered him plenty of validation and ego-stroking. In the process, they'd captured his ongoing support for their positions without paying him a single copper mark.

"As Samyl said, we're just going to have to ride it out," the lord protector said after a long, fulminating moment.

"And I hope the fact that I came and Sharleyan didn't isn't going to make that harder," Cayleb sighed.

"What was that phrase Merlin came up with? A 'lose-lose situation,' wasn't it?" Gahdarhd said sourly, and Cayleb nodded.

He and Sharleyan had decided only one of them should attend Myllyr's inauguration. Indeed, they'd strongly considered both simply staying home. In the end, they'd decided Myllyr needed a public display of their support, now that he'd won reelection in his own right, as part of the groundwork for the eventual implementation of the Ahrmahk Plan's Siddarmarkian variant. At the same time, they'd wanted to avoid looming behind him and giving additional grist to the "Charisian puppet" caricature Flahnairee and his backers had used against him. That was also the reason Cayleb had left Merlin home with Sharleyan and the children. His reputation as a "puppetmaster" was even stronger (and far more sinister) among the anti-Charis crowd. Unfortunately, as Gahdarhd had just pointed out, there was a downside to that, too, with another element of the anti-Charis segment pointing out that both monarchs had so recently traveled to Dohlar for the funeral of a mere earl—and one who'd been a leading military commander on the other side of the Jihad, to boot! That showed Charisian priorities pretty damned clearly, didn't it?

"The best we can do is the best we can do," he said finally. "It probably won't hurt for me to get my posterior back to Tellesberg as soon as I can, but stay in touch. Ambassador Preskyt has our full confidence, and you know that anything we *can* do, we will. If anyone owes anybody anything because of the Jihad, Charis owes Siddarmark, not the other way around. There may be some people here in the Republic who're having trouble remembering that, but we aren't."

. II .
City of Tellesberg,
Kingdom of Old Charis,
Empire of Charis.

The enormous gray-colored airship drifted down the cobalt-blue sky, propellers spinning like silver discs in the brilliant sunlight. The *Duchairn*-class airship's gas-bag was two hundred and sixty feet long and fifty feet in diameter, and the hum of its propellers was clearly audible although its Praigyr engines were silent.

As it neared the ground, those waiting for it did hear a soft, sibilant roar, however. It was the sound of venting hydrogen as it decreased its lift. It drifted still lower, turning into the wind, propellers slowing as it came to a near halt, balanced between their remaining thrust and the breeze pressing against its streamlined but bulbous prow. Mooring ropes fell from its cabin and waiting ground handlers pounced. Four of them were made fast quickly to massive, vehicle-mounted winches, and vaporized kerosene burned with a seething roar of its own as the Praigyr-powered winches began to take in slack.

The airship—it was low enough now to read the name emblazoned across its cabin: *Zhasyn Cahnyr*—stopped venting hydrogen and its propellers slowed to a halt as it once again became captive to the earth.

▼ ▼ ▼

"Langhorne, that was *fantastic!*" the tall, brown-haired young man said enthusiastically as he bounded over to the waiting steam carriage. "Eight days! The entire trip took just *eight* days, *Seijin* Merlin! And that was with the . . . the 'layover' in Tarot!"

Merlin Athrawes nodded gravely. Lywys Whytmyn would be nineteen in two more months. That made him the Old Terran equivalent of seventeen. He might be very tall for a Safeholdian, barely four inches shorter than Merlin himself, but he was still only nineteen. And he'd just completed an eight-day trip—by *air*—from Gorath to Tellesberg. Small wonder that he was . . . excited.

Despite that, the youngster reminded Merlin in many ways of another nineteen-year-old he'd met here in Charis, almost twenty Safeholdian years ago. He and Cayleb were very much of a height—Cayleb was a little taller—and their coloring was similar. Young Whytmyn had his grandfather's chin, though, and something about his eyes reminded Merlin of Lywys Gardynyr, as well. Tall as he was, he had a lot to live up to before he could challenge his grandfather's moral stature, but he seemed a smart, focused fellow. The early signs were good, Merlin thought.

"I'm glad you enjoyed the flight," he said out loud. "What did you have to promise your mother to be allowed to make it?"

"Nothing!" Whytmyn said emphatically.

"Really?" Merlin arched an eyebrow at him. "No doubt that explains why your sister and your cousins are coming by sea?"

"Well, maybe she just thinks boys are more expendable," Whytmyn shot back, and Merlin chuckled. "Truthfully," the young man went on, "I didn't have to promise anything I wouldn't have had to promise her anyway."

"Such as?"

"No leaning out of windows over the ocean, for one thing!" Whytmyn laughed. "And she made me turn out my pockets to show there were no candles in them before she let me go on board."

"I see."

"Seriously, *Seijin*, she took it better than I expected." Whytmyn's expression sobered. "I don't think she's completely comfortable with all the changes in the world, but she knows you can't put a wyvern back into the egg. You're right, she wasn't ready to let the girls come the same way—and she told me to thank you, as well as Their Majesties, for sending *Seijin* Cleddyf to escort them." He smiled gratefully at Merlin. "All of us appreciated that, because we know they couldn't be safer with *anyone*. But she told me, before I left, that she knew she'd have to let me do 'crazy things' sooner or later, so she might as well start now. And she said she hoped I'll grow up understanding the changes better than she ever could."

"I see," Merlin repeated, his expression thoughtful.

The inner circle had pulled back on the use of the SNARCs since the Jihad. Some individuals and groups were too important, too potentially threatening, to be left unobserved. But they'd tried to strike a balance between intrusiveness that could and couldn't be avoided. Merlin had never been comfortable about spying on personal and intimate moments, and he and the inner circle—even Nahrmahn—had relegated more and more to Owl now that the AI had developed full sentience. They relied upon him to filter the content, and unlike his organic friends, he could genuinely erase or lock records—even in his own memory—that had no bearing on the inner circle and its mission.

Despite that, Merlin had watched Whytmyn growing up, and what the young man had just said only increased his respect for his mother, Hailyn.

"I think she understands it better than she thinks she does, Master Whytmyn," he said now. "She's a very smart lady, and her and your father's willingness to send you to the Royal College shows a pretty firm grasp of the shape of things to come, I think."

"Please, *Seijin* Merlin," Whytmyn said. "You've known me since I was *six*. Do I have to be 'Master' Whytmyn?"

He looked at Merlin, his eyes very steady, and Merlin smiled slowly.

"At the moment, I'm acting in my official capacity, collecting you for Sharleyan," he pointed out. "As such, it behooves me to abide by all those stuffy rules. But, if you insist, after we get you settled, if you want to be 'Lywys,' it's all right with me. As long as I'm 'Merlin' to you."

"Well, of course." Whytmyn's voice, which was quite deep for a youngster of his age, although nowhere nearly so deep as Merlin's, seemed to slide higher for a moment. Then he cleared his throat. "I'd be honored."

"As you say, I've known you and your family a long time," Merlin said more gently, resting a hand on his shoulder for a moment. "Your grandfather was one of the finest men I ever met. Grow up to be the man he was, and the honor will be *mine,* believe me."

▼ ▼ ▼

The Praigyr-powered steam carriage rolled quietly into the Tellesberg Palace courtyard, and a small phalanx of greeters gathered at the top of the broad, shallow steps.

Cayleb was en route home from Siddar City, but Empress Sharleyan stood flanked by Crown Princess Alah-nah and Stefyny Athrawes. Alahnah had nine-year-old Gwylym in hand, and Stefyny had corralled Bryahn, the more fractious of the twins. Six-year-old Nynian Zhorzhet held Sairaih Hahlmyn's hand, gazing gravely down the steps, and Prince Domynyk, who'd turn two in another five-day, paid absolutely no attention from Gladis Parkyr's arms.

Merlin got out of the front seat and opened the pas-senger side door. Young Whytmyn climbed out of it and tugged the hem of his tunic down. Then he nodded his thanks to Merlin and waved courteously for the *seijin* to proceed him. Merlin smiled, then led the way up the stairs, and Sharleyan extended her hand as Whytmyn approached.

"Master Whytmyn—Lywys," she said with a smile, and that smile turned impish as he bent over her hand and kissed it with a flourish the most polished courtier couldn't have bettered. He straightened and his cheeks turned ever so slightly pink as he saw the twinkle in her eyes, but she squeezed his fingers firmly before he released her hand.

"You are most welcome in our home," she told him. "It's good to see you again, and good to know you'll be spending some time with us. We've arranged quarters for you here in the Palace for now. When Lyzet, Zhosifyn, and Zhudyth get here—and Rahnyldah, of course!— we'll probably arrange for all of you to be quartered with Archbishop Maikel or Bishop Paityr. Wherever we end up parking you, we expect to see a lot of you here, however. I trust that's understood?"

She gave him a moderately stern look, and he nodded.

"Yes, Your Majesty," he said meekly. *Suspiciously* meekly, in Merlin's opinion. "Mother made me promise to give you her greetings, to thank you for 'putting up with me,' and to tell you that she trusts me entirely to your hands. And she also said something about behav-ing myself because if I don't, after you get done with me she'll make my life *truly* miserable."

"A wise woman!" Sharleyan chuckled. "I've *always*

liked her. And, trust me, I'll take her advice where you're concerned, young man!"

"I know you will, Your Majesty," he told her with a grin, and she smacked him lightly on the shoulder. Then she turned and waved at the rest of her family.

"So, with that out of the way, say hello to the rest of the menagerie and we'll get you settled and unpacked before dinner!"

JUNE YEAR OF GOD 909

·✦·

. I .
Iythria Automotive Works,
City of Iythria,
Duchy of Kholman,
Desnairian Empire.

"Impressive—most impressive, Sir Dunkyn!" Mahnan Zhyng said, as the smoking behemoth came crawling out of the enormous shed. More smoke streamed from the louvers in the shed's steeply pitched roof. The automotive's bell rang loudly, clearly, and Zhyng smiled. "His Majesty will be delighted!"

"It's certainly to be hoped he will, Master Zhyng," Sir Dunkyn Paitryk, the managing director of Iythria Automotive Works, said as he shaded his eyes against the bright afternoon sun. The automotive's polished brass work was almost blinding. "We're proud of it, anyway."

"And well you should be," the Harchongian said firmly, looking up at the substantially taller Desnairian. "I probably shouldn't admit this, but the automotives our manufactories are producing remain . . . less than satisfactory. Carriages and rails, yes; those we can manage. But the automotives themselves?" He shook his head, his expression much less cheerful than it had been.

"I'm sorry to hear that." Paitryk's own expression was admirably grave, although the news was scarcely unwelcome.

"Master Nengkwan is making progress, but the accursed Charisians left before our artisans were fully trained. The problems have been less severe in the foundries themselves, but our automotive works have issues with the . . . tolerances." Zhyng frowned. "I suspect that means more to you than it does to me?"

"I'm familiar with the problem, yes," Paitryk replied. In fact, he was much more familiar with it than he'd been four or five years earlier, before he became one of Symyn Gahrnet's senior deputies. They never had enough inspectors, and their calipers and measuring rules simply weren't as precise as the ones Charis produced, which only made the problem worse. But they were dealing with it, he reminded himself. One way or the other, they were dealing with it.

"And I can't say I'm surprised the Charisians left your workers less than fully trained," he went on.

Of course, he added silently, as Zhyng scowled in obvious agreement, *if your idiot emperor hadn't kicked them out of his empire, that might not have happened.*

He scolded himself for the thought, but that didn't make it untrue. And the fact that there'd never been any Charisians to throw out of Desnair only fueled his scorn for Zhyou-Zhwo's decision. If the idiot had only waited another few months, the equally idiotic Charisians would almost certainly have trained the Harchongese workmen up to Charisian standards. But had Zhyou-Zhwo thought about that? Of course not!

Just as well he didn't, though, really. If he had, he might not be such an eager customer for our automotives! And there is *the matter of my commission on every one they buy from us.*

Paitryk was related to half a dozen major aristocratic families by blood or marriage, but despite the "Sir" in front of his name, there were far too many heirs between him and any of those families' titles. It would have taken a plague of Grimaldian proportions to empty enough shoes to do *him* any good!

His service as a youthful colonel in the Jihad had been honorable—and avoided the Army of Justice's debacle—but no one had won many titles or honors from *that* war, which had foreclosed the most customary Desnairian path to noble position. Given his meager prospects, he'd decided early on that he couldn't afford the traditional disdain for wealth earned in "trade," yet he had sufficient good blood to be an acceptable interface between the grimy, oily world of "industrialization" and those relatives of his.

His current perspective gave him rather less patience with his relatives these days, however, and even less with Zhyou-Zhwo.

"It might be possible for some of our artisans to visit Harchong and help train yours," he said now. Zhyng brightened perceptively. "I'd have to discuss the idea with Baron Iythria, of course."

"Of course! In fact, I should admit that Master Nengkwan suggested in his latest semaphore messages that Earl Sunset Peak would appreciate any assistance in that regard that I might be able to entice you and the Baron into sharing with us."

"I understand," Paitryk said. "And I'm sure he'll provide any assistance he can. Of course, we *are* heavily taxed ourselves with our expansion efforts. We'll break ground on the third production line here at Iythria in August."

"No doubt," Zhyng agreed with a nod, and Paitryk nodded back as they both focused on the gleaming black-and-red automotive once more.

Symyn Gahrnet, who'd been rewarded with the vacant title of Baron of Iythria for his efforts, had accomplished more, and accomplished it more rapidly, than Paitryk had really believed they could when they first set out. On the other hand, Paitryk's original expectations hadn't allowed for the unanticipated assistance of Stywyrt Showail and Dymytree Shallys. The two renegade Charisians had proven worth every one of the exorbitant heap of marks Iythria and the Crown had showered upon them, although Paitryk didn't much care for them. No, that wasn't fair. He didn't care for *Showail* at all, but Shallys wasn't bad. Unfortunately, Shallys was a shipbuilder, not a foundry master or an automotive maker.

Showail was both those things, and that meant Paitryk

had to put up with him. Worse, he'd had to accept the man's condescending "expertise." It hadn't been the easiest thing he'd ever done, but he had to admit he'd learned Langhorne's own lot from the Charisian turncoat. And he'd also come to suspect that Showail himself had learned quite a lot about automotives as he went about building the first Desnairian automotive work. He'd seemed suspiciously short of hands-on experience, but he'd arrived with a trunk full of plans and sketches. He'd been creatively vague about how they'd come into his possession, but fortunately for him, Emperor Mahrys declined to recognize Charis' ridiculous "patent laws." And whether Showail had ever before built an actual automotive, he'd known exactly how to turn those plans into actual buildings and machinery. He might be a loathsome individual, but he was competent. Not too surprisingly, since he'd been a highly successful foundry master in Charis during the Jihad . . . until he'd fallen afoul of those pesky "patent laws" and the ridiculous Charisian rules against child labor. That was the reason he'd been driven out of business—and financially ruined—by no less than the great Duke of Delthak himself.

That would have been more than enough to recommend him to both Zhyou-Zhwo and Emperor Mahrys, all by itself.

But this automotive was the product of the second automotive works Showail had built here at Iythria, and there was another under construction outside Desnair the City. The decision to put the newest works there had met with an unusual degree of resistance to an imperial decree, but Paitryk suspected Mahrys had chosen Desnair the City as its site because of his preference for Geyra. He knew blast furnaces, steel manufactories, and automotive works were essential, but that didn't mean he wanted to look out the window and see them.

A gentleman—and an emperor—had to draw a line somewhere.

Paitryk was unhappily aware that Desnair's rate of industrialization lagged far behind that of Charis or neighboring Dohlar. For that matter, even Silkiah had pulled slowly but steadily ahead. It was harder to decide about Siddarmark. Desnair might be holding its own against the Republic, but that was hardly reassuring, given Siddarmark's recurrent economic woes. And it would be a long time before Desnairian engineers and artisans were ready to begin producing their own designs. This automotive, for example, was at least a generation behind the latest Delthak Automotives model. In fact, it was probably farther behind than that, given the breakneck rate at which Delthak kept insisting on *improving* things.

It was, however, far better than anything Harchong had yet managed to produce, and if Desnair's expansion was slower than that of Charis, it, too, was gathering speed. And, unlike Charis, managing to do it without upsetting the social order God and the Archangels had decreed. Artisans were artisans, not men of blood. They were clearly necessary, and they had to be paid accordingly, but they were equally clearly un-fitted to discharge the Crown's wishes and desires. Perhaps some of them would rise above their origins in the fullness of time—the ones with the most talent, the most value. Paitryk himself had been promised a barony, at the least, awaited him, assuming he continued to discharge his own duties as well as he had. With that in mind, he was prepared to grant even the most commonly born at least some recognition of their accomplishments.

"We'll spend the rest of today and tomorrow running it around the test track," he said now as he and Zhyng turned and began walking down the boardwalk towards the rails. "There's always a bit of 'wearing in' for an automotive fresh out of the shop, and this is the first one off of this line. Besides, we need to be especially confident this one's ready before we turn it loose."

Zhyng nodded vigorously. This was the twelfth automotive Harchong had purchased from Desnair, which had contributed significantly to Iythria Automotives' expansion. What made it special was that it was the first which wouldn't be delivered to its buyers in parts by sea and assembled by Desnarian artisans after arrival. (It would have been better to ship them assembled, had any Desnarian or Harchongese steamship been large enough.)

As of the first of the month, however, the rail line paralleling the Mahrosa and Sherach Canal ran all the way from Iythria to Symarkhan on the Hahskyn River. It was single-tracked with only occasional sidings the entire way, and there were more than a few trestles Paitryk wouldn't have cared to cross, but it existed—over three thousand miles of track, which equated to almost ten *million* rails. Desnair and, by default, the Harchong Empire had adopted lighter rails than Charis, but that still equated to close to 380,000 tons of hot-rolled steel rails, the vast majority of which had come out of Harchongese or Desnairian foundries. Even Desnair would have been hard put to come up with the labor gangs who'd built that line, but Zhyou-Zhwo had found them. And his supervisors and overseers had pushed the work at a furious pace, aided by the fact that the canal right of ways were more than wide enough to accommodate the tracks for almost all that length. If they'd had to dig and blast the roadbed, the task would have taken years longer to complete.

Nor could they have accomplished it without the Desnairian rails. Zhyou-Zhwo didn't need to know about the additional rails Baron Iythria had quietly purchased from Charis through Dohlaran and Silkiahan middlemen to fill the Harchongians' voracious orders, and Paitryk devoutly hoped Zhyou-Zhwo would continue to believe all of them had come out of domestic Desnairian production. Actually, he calculated that there was a pretty fair chance of that. He was positive Mahnan Zhyng, for one, had absolutely no intention of informing his emperor that the hated Charisians had actually manufactured about ten percent of his "Desnairian" rails.

"We'll turn it over to your drivers once we're confident we've found and corrected any potential faults, and our people will make sure they're fully familiar with the

controls before we do," he said as the automotive came
to a halt in a drifting reek of coal smoke.

It stood, panting, oozing tendrils of steam. The sight
and the sounds filled Paitryk with a sense of pride and
accomplishment he once would have denied he might
feel over mere machinery, and his nostrils flared appreciatively as he inhaled the scents of creosote, tar, coal,
and hot iron. Half his relatives undoubtedly looked
down upon him scornfully, assuming they ever thought
about him at all, but that was all right. Whether they
liked it or not, *this* was the future, and he meant to be
far more than a mere baron before he was done.

"The test runs will make sure we don't have any mechanical problems," he continued, "but, to be on the
safe side, Baron Iythria has instructed me to send one of
our own automotives and a repair carriage along on the
run to Symarkhan."

"Thank you!" Zhyng beamed. "That's very generous
of you. And unexpected, too! I'm sure Earl Sunset Peak
will be most grateful."

"I'm glad to hear that, but please tell the Earl he's
entirely welcome. I know you've brought your own artisans to take delivery, and I'm sure they won't encounter
any problems they can't deal with." One had to be polite, especially to Harchongians, even if it did require a
blatant disregard for truth. "But we pride ourselves on
both our workmanship and on giving good value for
Emperor Zhyou-Zhwo's marks. It's possible a more serious fault may get by our inspections. If it does, our
people will be on the spot to make it right for His Majesty."

Zhyng smiled even more broadly, and Paitryk gestured to the steep iron steps up into the automotive's
cab.

"And now, Master Zhyng, would you join me aboard
the Emperor's newest automotive for its first run around
the track?"

FEBRUARY YEAR OF GOD 910

✦

"Well, we don't look *too* bad for a pair of old farts," Domynyk Staynair, the Duke of Rock Point, observed as he leaned on his cane, looking out the window of the new eight-story headquarters of Delthak Shipbuilding.

"'Old farts'?" Sir Dustyn Olyvyr, Chief Constructor of the Imperial Charisian Navy, repeated. "Who are you calling old?!"

"You, actually, you decrepit old wreck," Rock Point replied with a chuckle, looking over his shoulder. "My God, man! You're almost *five months* older than I am!"

Olyvyr made a rude noise and stepped up to the window beside him. They looked down from it at the always-bustling vista of Delthak Shipbuilding's Larek Yard.

It was impossible to recognize the once-modest town which had given its name to the sprawling—and still growing—city at the mouth of the Delthak River, where it flowed into Howell Bay. The wooden wharves where fishermen had once landed their catch had disappeared into massive stone quays, hulking warehouses, gaunt gantries, and vast workshops, and drydocks, construction slips, fitting-out docks, and the rail lines that served them stretched for over five miles.

The river estuary was really too shallow for ships the size of the ones Delthak was building now, but Duke

Delthak's ever-inventive artisans had an answer for that, too. As Rock Point and Olyvyr looked southeast from their vantage point, they saw the enormous barge of a continuous-chain, steam-powered dredge. The bottom was sand, mud, and shells, and a steady cascade of liquid-streaming mud avalanched from the dredge's bucket shovels onto the second barge, moving in tandem with it. A third barge, loaded to the gunnels with shell-laden sand and mud, moved ponderously towards the cement works on Fish Island under the urging of a bluff-bowed steam tug. Yet another barge had just come over the horizon from the west, returning from Fish to await its turn at the dredge.

There were limits to what could be accomplished, however, and it wouldn't be so very much longer before some of those limits might become a problem. The *Thunderbolt*-class drew twenty-five feet of water at its designed draft, and Howell Bay's deep channel depth at low water was only about thirty-two feet. Here, close to the mouth of the Delthak, it was a good eight or nine feet shallower even than that, so launches at low water could be problematical. There was a reason Delthak was expanding its Eraystor Yard, because although Eraystor Bay was much smaller than Howell Bay, it was also deeper.

For now, however, the Larek Yard was sufficient for even the Navy's biggest ships, and even if it eventually became impossible to build the largest capital ships here, there'd always be a need for the cruisers Larek *could* build. And Larek was far more convenient than Eraystor to the sprawling Delthak Works, which remained the heart and soul of Delthak Enterprises.

"Could you have imagined this that first day when Merlin sat down with you at King's Harbor?" Rock Point asked now, and Olyvyr barked a laugh.

"If I'd even *tried* to imagine this then, I'd have run the other way babbling hysterically! And if I'd told Ahnyet where this was truly going to lead, she'd have called the Bédardists and had me committed!"

"It does rather boggle the mind, doesn't it?" Rock Point's tone was almost whimsical, his eyes steady as he watched the dredge buckets ripping away at the bottom of the bay. "Galleys. We were still building *galleys,* Dustyn." He shook his head. "I remember when a twenty-four-gun galleon seemed like the terror of the seas!"

"Because it was," Olyvyr said.

He moved a little closer to the window, looking down at the nearest building slip, the one named for Commander Urvyn Mahndrayn. There were other slips, named for other people they'd lost to the Jihad, but few of them had hurt as much as Mahndrayn, and the fact that he'd been murdered by his own cousin only made it seem perversely worse, somehow.

Olyvyr's mouth tightened at that familiar memory, but then he shook his head with a smile, instead. The Urvyn Mahndrayn Slip had produced more than one new ship, including HMS *King Haarahld VII.* She'd been the very first armored cruiser ever laid down on Safehold, although the disastrous fire at the Delthak Works and an unusual case of faulty machinery meant her sister ship, HMS *Gwylym Manthyr,* had been completed before her. And yet another innovative vessel was building in that slip as he watched.

At the moment, she was only an ungainly heap of girders and ribs, streaked with rust. She lay there with all the elegance of a foundry scrapyard, and the piles of building materials heaped about in what looked like utter disorder only strengthened that impression. But Olyvyr's eyes saw the organization underlying the chaos, the polished efficiency of the most skilled shipbuilding work force in the world, and he felt a familiar sense of awe as he absorbed it all again. The clatter of pneumatic-powered rivet guns must be deafening down in the slip, although it was lost in the general background by the time it reached the office window. On the other hand, the contacts Owl had provided to allow him to view imagery over the SNARC network had also corrected his nearsightedness. More than that, the current version provided the equivalent of a good pair of Old Terra binoculars. Now he zoomed in on the construction workers, watching their skilled rhythm. And some of them were using the newly developed acetylene welding equipment, although that process was still novel enough that not even Sir Dustyn Olyvyr was going to trust it for critical structural components.

As he watched, dockside cranes lowered a fresh load of hull plates into the slip, and he saw one of the foremen on the scaffolding, arm-waving directions to the crane operator. It was hard to believe, even for him, that those unprepossessing beginnings would eventually become a brand-new *Falcon*-class scout cruiser. Albeit one with a difference.

"Doesn't look like much, does she?" he said out loud.

"Not yet," Rock Point agreed. "Of course, even when she's finished, the really impressive bits won't be out where people can see them."

"I would've liked to put the geared turbines into her, too," Olyvyr said wistfully.

"There are times you remind me of Ahlfryd," Rock Point said with a bittersweet smile. "Always want to play with latest toys."

"Well, as one old fart to another, I'm not getting any younger. I don't want to miss it!"

"*Younger*—pshaw!" Rock Point scowled magnificently. "You've got decades left yet!"

Olyvyr glanced at the duke, but he had to acknowledge Rock Point's point. They'd both received Owl's nanotech, and despite their advanced ages—although, to be fair, they were barely in their early seventies in the standard years of dead Terra—they were in excellent health. In fact, they were in sufficiently excellent health that they had to remind themselves to complain about the aches and pains they ought to have had. Not too often, of course. They were, after all, noble and stoic individuals.

He chuffed a laugh at that thought. Rock Point arched an eyebrow, but he shook his head without explaining.

"Sooner or later, you and Cayleb—and Merlin—are going to have to let me build one with turbines," he said instead.

"Trust me, it's going to be later." Rock Point shook his head. "Do you think I wouldn't love to be out there charging across the ocean at thirty-five or thirty-six knots? Of course I would! But we're not going to introduce that kind of speed until someone else does or we have to. Keeping advantages tucked up our sleeves was what kept us alive during the Jihad, and I'm not real interested in changing course on that anytime soon."

"Granted," Olyvyr sighed. "*Granted!* Although," his gaze sharpened, "firing her boilers with oil's a pretty damned significant change in its own right."

"It may take the other navies a while to realize that, though," Rick Point pointed out. "They haven't had the chance to play around with it a lot."

"Um." Olyvyr pursed his lips, then shrugged. "You're probably right," he conceded. "All they'll see—at first, at least—is that oil's one hell of a lot cleaner."

He shuddered, recalling the clouds of coal dust that coated every surface with filth whenever a ship refilled her bunkers. Charisian naval bases had developed steam-powered machinery to make it both easier and much faster, but nothing could magically erase all that dust. Oil produced no dust, and refueling would be as simple—and fast—as attaching the fuel hoses and then standing back while the oil gushed into the tanks.

That much would be pretty evident to most people. What they might be slower to realize was how much cleaner oil *burned.* Just avoiding the thick, choking, vision-blocking clouds of coal smoke would be a huge boon to signaling and maneuvering safety at sea, but just as importantly, the stokers aboard an oil-fired ship wouldn't have to draw and rake their grates at regular intervals to clear them of clinker the way a coal-fired vessel's stokers did, either. They could maintain maximum steam pressure for as long as their feedwater and fuel lasted, rather than periodically reducing speed while their fireboxes were cleared. Well, they'd still have to clean the boilers themselves of scale from time to time, but that was part of any ship's regular maintenance schedule, not something that needed to be done every few hours. And converting to oil would reduce the complement of a *Falcon* by over twenty percent just by eliminating all the stokers who sweated and strained heaving coal into the ships' roaring furnaces. *That* wouldn't hurt a thing, either.

And what would be even less obvious to those other navies was the fact that oil contained far more caloric energy than coal on a pound-for-pound basis. Ten tons of oil provided the same potential energy as fifteen tons of coal, but the efficiency differential in a steam plant was actually about 1.7-to-1 in oil's favor, once the handling advantages of oil were factored into the equation, so a ship with a cruising radius of five thousand miles using coal would increase its radius by thirty-five hundred miles, assuming equal weights of fuel. And on top of all that, oil "packed tighter" than coal. Given that the volume of 1.7 tons of anthracite was a bit over forty-nine cubic feet and the volume of a ton of oil was only about thirty-eight cubic feet, and allowing for the efficiency differential, an oil-fired ship could pack the same "energy bank" into less than half the volume. The saving in weight would be even more significant, as would the fact that oil could be carried in tanks located low in the ship, which would have huge advantages for stability. And the design of any warship was always a study in tradeoffs. Anything that cost less weight *and* less volume was worth its weight in gold to someone like him.

Indeed, about the only downside was that current designs used coal bunkers as additional side armor against enemy shell fire. Olyvyr would miss that, but he could more than live with it in light of all the advantages oil conferred.

"Merlin and I have seriously discussed finding a handy spy somewhere and spoon-feeding him *all* the reasons we're thinking about going to oil," Rock Point said. Olyvyr raised an eyebrow at him, and he chuckled.

"Of course we have! Hell, Dustyn! If anyone out there wants to emulate us, I'll stand on the spire of Tellesberg Cathedral and cheer about it!" The duke smiled sardonically. "Thanks to Zhansyn Wyllys and SD&R, we've got the beginnings of a genuine petroleum industry . . . and they don't. That probably means most of the potential

competitors out there will stick with coal even if they figure out the advantages, because they know they have an
assured supply of it, which isn't the case with this newfangled 'oil-fired' machinery. But some of them may not
stick it out if we feed them the word on all the wonderful
advantages it'll give *us*. In which case—" his smile turned
wicked "—they'll have to build their own oil industry, and
think how *that* will contribute to the Nahrmahn Plan."

"It couldn't hurt any, that's for sure," Olyvyr said.

"And that's the name of the game," Rock Point said,
his smile fading, and Olyvyr nodded.

Neither of them did anything dramatic, like looking
at the calendar on the office wall, but they didn't have
to. If their most pessimistic timing for the "archangels'"
return proved accurate, they had little more than five
years in hand.

. II .

City of Zhynkau,
Boisseau Province,
United Provinces.

"I do trust we've done enough to avoid panic," Runzheng Zhou said, raising the custom-made double-glass,
a gift from Duke Delthak that was small and light
enough for a man with one hand, and sweeping the
southern horizon again.

"I believe that's the fourth—no, forgive me, the
fifth—time you've said that this afternoon, My Lord,"
a dry voice observed, and Baron Star Rising lowered
the double-glass and looked at the man behind him. "I
understand your concern, My Lord," Bishop Yaupang
continued more gently, "but after this long with one 'infernal' Charisian innovation after another, I really doubt
anyone's going to run about screaming and flapping his
arms like a headless wyvern. And I promise you, every

one of my parish priests has spent the last two five-days preparing our flock for the visitation."

The two of them stood on the patio outside Star Rising's office. The day was warm and sunny, with a moderate breeze out of the northwest. There might be a hint of rain in the clouds just visible on the western horizon, but probably not. And even if there were, it would be hours before the weather got here. Of course, given what they were waiting for, any "weather" might be a less than desirable thing to have.

"I know you've been . . . priming the pump," the baron said after a moment. "And I'm probably fretting because of my own nerves. Actually, what I'm most afraid of is that this is going to end in a spectacular crash." He grimaced. "The Delthak representatives were clear enough about the consequences of sparks in unfortunate places when they built the gasworks!"

"There do seem to be some significant . . . downsides to some of our Charisian friends' new toys," Yaupang Lyauyan acknowledged. "On balance, however, I think those are far outweighed by the advantages. And let's be honest, My Lord, there've always been uncountable ways for men to kill themselves using totally mundane tools no one would ever suggest could conceivably challenge the Proscriptions! In fact, the amazing thing is how many more people all these Charisian innovations let us feed and clothe and house in something approaching decency." There was no twinkle in the bishop's eye now. "The people of the United Provinces have never been so healthy or so well-off in their entire lives, My Lord."

Star Rising nodded soberly, because it was nothing but simple truth. Oh, the United Provinces were experiencing their share of painful adjustment, especially as the guilds' trained craftsmen found themselves increasingly challenged by Charisian-style manufactories. They were handling the dislocation well, though, all things considered. Only a minority of guildsmen had decided to actively oppose the changes, and no one paid them much heed. The overwhelming majority of the United Provinces' citizens had embraced those changes enthusiastically, and along the way, they seemed to be importing a remarkably Charisian attitude, as well. It would be decades, at least, before Harchongese peasants and ex-serfs fully assimilated the sturdy, *confident* independence of their Charisian mentors, but that very lack of confidence—of that assurance that no one could take *their* independence away—only made their attachment to it even stronger. They knew exactly what they could lose, and Langhorne help anyone who ever tried to cram them back into their pre-Rebellion servility!

And the militia's turning into a pretty damned good army, *come to that,* he reminded himself. *So anyone who tries that cramming would have to comb a lot of bullets out of his beard first!*

"You know," he said, raising the double-glass again, "I never really considered how good it would feel to totally overturn the entire basis of Harchongese society." He smiled whimsically, eyes sweeping the heavens while the breeze flowed over them. "I'm sure most of my ancestors are lining up in Heaven to kick my arse as soon as I arrive!"

His back was to Lyauyan once more as he spoke, so he didn't see the bishop's smile or note its warmth.

"Oh, I don't think they'll be quite that irate with you, My Lord," Lyauyan reassured him. "Only a *little* irate. No more than a severe scolding."

"I can tell you never met my grandfather," Star Rising said dryly. "He wasn't like those pigs in Tiegelkamp, but he had a pretty firm notion of what was due him from his serfs and the peasants renting land from him. Had a pretty firm notion of what was due him from disrespectful *grandsons,* too, now that I think about it." The baron chuckled. "I remember one time—"

He broke off and stiffened, peering even more intently through the double-glass, then lowered it and looked at Lyauyan again.

"Our visitors are arriving, My Lord Bishop. I think we should head down to greet them."

▼ ▼ ▼

"By God, Master Ahzbyrn, could that be—? Is it possible—?"

Lieutenant Ahlyxzandyr Krugair, Imperial Charisian Air Force and commanding officer of His Majesty's Airship *Synklair Pytmyn*, grabbed his executive officer's sleeve with his left hand and pointed out the curved expanse of the glass windscreen at the river mouth town. It was toy-like with distance, its roofs bright patches of color against the green, brown, and tan of the earth. The dark blue waters of the Yalu Inlet, turning lighter blue and green as they shoaled, stretched away on *Synklair Pytmyn*'s starboard side as she made her way directly into the northwesterly breeze.

"Can't be, Sir." Lieutenant Ahlbyrt Ahzbyrn shook his head emphatically. "Why, if that were Zhynkau, it would mean Ensign Braiahnt actually knew his arse from his elbow! And since we all know *that* isn't true, that must be . . . Tellesberg. That's it! It's *Tellesberg*."

"With all due respect, Sir," despite his choice of words, a disinterested observer might have noted that Ensign Mahrtyn Braiahnt, *Synklair Pytmyn*'s youthful navigator, didn't actually sound all that respectful, "I'm not the one who steered a reciprocal of the compass heading his hard-working, always accurate navigator gave him for five and a half hours before he noticed his error."

Ahzbyrn looked at him, and Braiahnt raised both hands.

"I'm not naming any names, Sir," he pointed out. "On the other hand, you might want to reconsider your identification of our landmark."

"Well, I suppose it *could* be Zhynkau," Ahzbyrn said after a moment, his expression severe. "After all, I've never visited the place before, so I might have been guilty of some small . . . misidentification of our landfall."

"That's very big of you, Ahlbyrt," Lieutenant Krugair said with a chuckle, then nodded to Braiahnt. "Well done, Mahrtyn. *Very* well done!" he said warmly, and the ensign, who'd just turned nineteen four months earlier, beamed.

In fact, he'd done extraordinarily well, although he'd

been helped by the inlet itself. It was the sort of land-mark that was hard to miss, and all he'd really had to do was follow it once he found it. On the other hand, he'd found it unerringly in the first place, and he'd spent quite a few hours along the way making detailed sketches of topographical features. There weren't many of those on over-water flights, but islands and coastal features could be extremely useful to navigators.

Shooting his noon position was always an exciting proposition for any airship navigator, requiring him to climb the ladder through the airship's gasbag to the glass dome at its apex, and it had a certain special edge for young Braiahnt. The good news was that he had absolutely perfect visibility from his dome—he could even open it and take his sights in the open air if he wanted to. The bad news was that *Synklair Pytmyn* rou-tinely operated at up to 11,000 feet, much higher than the original *Duchess of Delthak*. At that altitude, aver-age air temperature was only about twenty degrees . . . which could feel *much* colder with a sixty-mile-per-hour headwind. Beyond the airship's cabin, which was heated with the exhaust from its twin Praigyrs, it was colder than Shan-wei's smile . . . and Braiahnt was an Old Charisian who'd never even seen snow before he joined the Air Force. He tended to dress up like a Raven's Land reindeer herder before he started up the ladder.

His noon positions were always spot-on for accuracy, but no navigator wanted to rely solely on a once-a-day position fix, and that was especially true for an airship. *Synklair Pytmyn* moved far greater distances in a day than any galleon or steamer, and she was even more sus-ceptible to headwinds—or tailwinds—which meant even a small error in heading or speed estimate could lead to major discrepancies in position. So any airship navigator wanted all of the landmarks he could find along the way for position checking as a corrective for drift, as well.

There *weren't* very many landmarks in long over-water flights, which was what made them so challeng-ing, but from *Synklair Pytmyn*'s altitude, the crew could theoretically see for well over a hundred miles. Making out details at that sort of range was impossible, even with the best double-glass, but islands could at least be sighted and steered for, and one of the required qualifications for any airship navigator was the ability to make accurate sketches. Braiahnt had filled his logbook industriously with one sketch after another on the long flight up the Gulf of Dohlar from the airship terminus at the naval base at St. Haarahld's Harbor.

Krugair was sure at least a score of merchant skippers must have pissed themselves when they looked up and saw the airship driving steadily westward above them. In fact, if anyone had asked, he would have been forced to admit he'd actually altered course slightly, from time to time, to be sure they passed overhead. After all, he'd told himself virtuously, one of the Air Force's primary tasks in wartime would be scouting for enemy shipping. It only made sense to practice that now, didn't it?

They'd passed over Talisman Island without slowing, although they'd been authorized to stop there if necessary. *Synklair Pytmyn*'s fuel state had been fine, though, and they'd had plenty of lift in reserve. Besides, Talisman wasn't all that large, wind conditions could be tricky, and avoiding avoidable risks was high on Ahlyxzandyr Krugair's to-do list.

Krugair had enormous faith in his ship and in his ship's company, but there was no denying that airships were fragile and . . . chancy. He remembered his father's favorite saying: "There are old seamen, and there are bold seamen, but there are no old, bold seamen." If that was true of those who sailed the world's seas, it was even more true of those who sailed Safehold's skies, and Krugair had every intention of getting much, much older.

"I suppose we should wake up Lieutenant Pahlmair," he observed now, and uncapped one of the voice pipes. He blew down it to sound the whistle at the far end, then waited.

"Pahlmair," a growly voice floated back up with the hollow-edge voice pipes always imparted.

"Zhynkau's in sight, Kynyth," Krugair replied. "Looks like we'd have sighted it sooner if there wasn't a bit of ground haze. I'd estimate about seventy miles, so we should be overhead in about two, two and a half hours, given the current headwind."

"We actually found it?" Lieutenant Pahlmair, *Synklair Pytmyn*'s engineering officer said, and Krugair looked over his shoulder to grin at Braiahnt.

"I'll have you know Mahrtyn is on the bridge and he heard that," he said severely down the voice pipe.

"Oops," Pahlmair said with remarkable tranquility. "I'll pass the word to the Bo'sun," he went on in a crisper tone. "I just hope the ground crew's ready for us. I'd hate to come all this way and then blow up on our final approach."

"Oh, *thank* you for that ray of sunlight!"

"What I'm here for, Skipper."

▼ ▼ ▼

Star Rising and Lyauyan reached the landing ground outside Zhynkau with time to spare. They joined the other spectators, who moved aside respectfully to give them room, craning their necks to gaze up at the floating marvel drifting steadily towards them across the heavens. Star Rising listened carefully, but the murmurs he heard were filled with awe and admiration, not alarm, and the bishop gave him a mildly triumphant look.

"Well, they wouldn't have believed *me* if I'd told them it was non-demonic," he said quietly. "After all, I'm just a layman."

"But a very well-thought-of layman, my son," Lyauyan told him soothingly.

"I appreciate the reassurance, My Lord," Star Rising told the younger man dryly.

"You're most welcome, My Lord," Lyauyan replied with a twinkle.

The two of them fell silent as the airship neared the ground. It pitched ever so slightly as it pushed its bluntly rounded nose into the wind, and Star Rising saw the . . . "control surfaces" on the cruciform tail working like a ship's rudder but in multiple dimensions. It was fascinating to watch, and then it was coming slowly overhead, casting an enormous shadow over the landing ground and the raptly watching audience, and the mooring lines plummeted from the cabin slung under the "haze gray" gasbag.

The waiting uniformed Charisians—the Air Force's uniforms were the same color as the Imperial Charisian Navy uniform but cut like those of the Imperial Charisian Army—pounced on the lines as they thudded to the ground. The Harchongians they'd trained to assist raced to join them, and the free ends of half a dozen lines were passed through the mooring bollards which had been driven deep into the earth.

The airship's lift and the pressure of the wind pulled against the bollards, but they held firm, tethering it, while the remaining lines from nose section and tail were passed to the steam-powered, wagon-mounted winches which had been shipped in by sea. One of the ground crew, standing well in front of the airship where the crew could look down and see him through the curved windscreen, waggled semaphore flags, and the airship's propellers went still. Then they heard the rushing sound of venting hydrogen as the airship slowly reduced its buoyancy while the winches gathered in the slack.

"That's incredible," Star Rising said quietly, and the bishop nodded. For once, even he seemed abashed.

"It truly is," he said. "And I'm sure those people in the South will insist we're cavorting with demons. But, do you know, My Lord, I really don't *care* what they say. What this—" he jutted his chin at the airship settling steadily towards the ground "—proves to me is that those people don't have a clue what they're talking about. I wish with all my heart the Rebellion had never happened and all those people had never died, but what's coming out of it, at least here in the United Provinces, couldn't have been born any other way. It just . . . couldn't."

"Not given the way men's hearts work," Star Rising said sadly. "But, you know, my wife had hard pregnancies, all three of them. I would've done anything to make that easier for her. But neither she nor I would give up those children for anything. And we're not going to give up this child—" the sweep of his good arm took in not just the excited crowd around them but all of the United Provinces "—either." He looked back at the bishop, his eyes dark and determined. "Not for *anything*. And not to any*one*."

.III.
Saint Sanzhung's Church,
City of Zhutiyan,
Chynduk Valley,
Tiegelkamp Province,
North Harchong.

Tangwyn Syngpu swallowed hard, trying to remember if he'd ever been this scared.

Surely he must have been, hadn't he? There'd been that time in Tarikah, for instance, when the Charisian shell had exploded so close his head had rung for a full five-day. Or the first time he'd gone into combat, heard the hissing sound of rifle bullets crackling past, the sodden thud when they found a target—then the screams, the blood, the writhing anguish of men he'd known and trained with for endless months. That had been bad.

But those fears had become old friends. They didn't go away, just because a man had survived. In fact, in some ways they got worse. But they were . . . known quantities. They didn't creep up behind a man, take him by surprise when he wasn't looking. Not anymore. But *this*—!

He looked around the packed church. It was no cathedral, but it was bigger than any church he'd ever attended back in Thomas, before the Jihad. Its stained-glass windows were far finer and grander than the muddy-hued ones he'd grown up with, and so were the mosaics of Langhorne and Bédard. Back home, the best the local artist had managed had been almost cartoonish compared to these. Now he truly had the sense that the archangels looked down on him, yet they seemed less judgmental and more welcoming than they'd ever seemed in the mountains of his homeland. Maybe that was because he knew the priest whose church this was wasn't going to side with the local baron when he decided to drag some peasant maid off for his pleasure.

His eyes shifted to the young man standing at his left as that thought went through his mind. Tangwyn Syngpu would never forgive what men had done to his daughter, but God had given her a husband who didn't care that she'd been passed from man to man to be used and abused for their pleasure. Who loved her bastard daughter just as much as he loved the son she'd borne to him. So maybe Father Yngshwan and Yanshwyn were right. Maybe what God had in mind mattered more than what Mother Church allowed to happen.

He looked to his right.

Zhouhan Husan looked just as nervous—and just as out of place in his tailored tunic—as Syngpu felt. At least Yanshwyn had supported him when he put his foot down and insisted that he'd been born a peasant and he'd dress like a peasant. A well-off, prosperous peasant, perhaps, but still a peasant, without the elaborately cut tunic or the fancy hat of a noble or even a squire like Miyang Gyngdau. Not that he'd managed to make that stand up completely. His "peasant" tunic was made of finer cloth than he'd ever owned before, and the embroidery on it was incredible. He'd never imagined anything like it! It was far too splendid for the likes of him, and creating it had made hours of work for Yanshwyn, Madame Gyngdau, and at least half a dozen other women of Zhutiyan.

He'd argued about it, of course. They'd had far better things to waste their time on than trying to pretty up a battered old peasant like him, and he'd told them exactly that. But he'd also retreated in ignominious defeat at the outcry he'd provoked. They'd insisted, and they'd made it clear they weren't brooking any defiance on his part, either. And when he'd commented on it to Yanshwyn, shaking his head in bafflement, she'd only shaken her own head and smiled at him through a glitter of unshed tears.

"No," she'd said. "I don't suppose you do understand why it's so important to them, do you?" She'd risen on her toes to kiss his weathered cheek, then leaned her own cheek against his chest. "I love you very much, you know," she'd said, and after that, all the embroidery and all the fuss hadn't bothered him at all.

But now—!

"Stop fidgeting, Tangwyn!" Husan hissed in his ear. "You look like you've got ants in your breeches!"

"I'm not fidgeting!" he hissed back.

"Are, too!"

"Am not!"

"Are!"

"Am—!"

"Both of you shut up," Father Yngshwan said severely. They looked at him quickly, like guilty little boys, and he shook his head. "There are times I'd rather herd cat-lizards than you two," he continued in a quiet voice no one could hear through the background murmur of conversation that filled Saint Sanzhung's. "If I didn't know how it would piss off Yanshwyn, I'd kick both of you out of my church and you wouldn't get back into it without at least a five-day of penance!"

"He started it," Syngpu muttered.

"Not . . . one . . . more . . . word," Father Yngshwan growled, but his lips quivered on the edge of a smile.

Syngpu nodded and started fiddling with the cuffs of his tunic, instead. He didn't know what was taking so long, but it always seemed to work this way. When he'd married Shuchyng all those years ago—God, had they both really been only sixteen?—she'd been late then, too. Was it some sort of conspiracy? A tradition nobody let the men in on? The tiny, tiny chapel in which he and Shuchyng had exchanged their vows without benefit of clergy had been cold and windy that day. He remembered the way her cold cheeks had flushed, how she'd been bundled up against the cold, how she'd smiled as the two of them promised the Archangel Bédard they would love and cherish one another.

And they had, until the Mighty Host took him away from her. Until she died, while he was half a continent away. The remembered grief, the anger, the self-hatred rose up in his throat again for a moment, but then he heard another voice.

"*Let it go, Tangwyn,*" Yanshwyn said gently in the back of his mind, and now there was another voice. Shuchyng's, he realized, whispering his name. It was the first time he'd heard her voice in over five years. He'd heard it often—in his mind, in his heart—after the Mighty Host claimed him. But not since he'd learned of her death. Not since he hadn't been there when she'd needed him most. She'd left him, then, and his eyes burned as he heard her now. Heard her telling him exactly what Yanshwyn had . . . and heard the love in her voice, too.

I'm sorry I wasn't there, he told her. *I would have been, if I could have. Truly I would!*

I know that, that loving ghost told him. *I knew that then. How could I not have? And you came for Pauyin. You* came *for her, Tangwyn.*

But it wasn't enough.

Yes, it was. And now it's time for you to let me go.

No, never!

Not that *way,* the voice was almost laughing this time. *I* didn't say *forget* me, *Tangwyn. But let me go so that you can go on. Don't you know that's what I've always wanted for you?*

He blinked against the sudden blur of tears, and she was gone. Had she ever really been there? Or had it all been his imagination? Just a way for him to lie to himself, let himself off the hook?

No. Perhaps she hadn't really come to him once more, but what he'd heard was what she would have said if she had. He knew that now. He knew that this was what she would have wanted for him, just as she would have wanted Baisung for her daughter.

The faintest echo of a loving laugh ghosted through his mind, and he smiled despite the tears.

And then the organ soared into life, the choir's voice rose, and he turned towards the back of the church as the doors opened and Yanshwyn Gyngdau came through them on her brother-in-law's arm. She was past the bloom of her youth, just as he was. Life had left its marks upon her, the first streaks of white had touched her hair, and her face would never have spurred a poet's pen, even when she'd been a young woman. But she moved with regal grace, her small head carried high and proud. The faint lines around her eyes spoke of character and wisdom, laughter and tears, and those eyes—those beautiful eyes—were only for him as she glided towards him down the central nave. There were flowers in her hair, a bouquet in her arms, her gown the white of mountain spike-thorn, even more magnificently embroidered with highland lilies than his own tunic, and she was the most exquisite thing he'd ever seen.

His heart went into his throat, and he knew she couldn't be for him. Surely she couldn't! He was a peasant, a shepherd, rough and unfinished. And she . . . she—

The bridal party reached him, and Miyang took her hand from his forearm and placed it on Syngpu's.

"Take care of her," he said softly, under the music and the voices. "My brother was a fine man. I never thought I'd see her find another just as fine, Tangwyn."

He touched Syngpu's upper arm lightly, then stepped back beside his wife. Rouchun was already dabbing at happy tears, and she smiled at Syngpu as she nodded agreement with her husband.

Then Yanshwyn was beside him, and the two of them turned, standing side by side, to face Father Yngshwan. She was so tiny, half Shuchyng's size, if that, and a part of him wanted to enfold her in his arms and wrap himself around her like a fortress. But another part of him felt the strength of her, the strength which had reached out to him and told him there was love enough in the world for them, too. That they neither needed to forget they'd both loved others before they met nor doubt their love for one another now.

The choir reached the end of its anthem. The organ fell silent, and Saint Sanzhung's Church was suddenly still and very, very quiet.

"My children," Father Yngshwan said into that stillness, "Tangwyn and Yanshwyn have come before you to pledge their lives to one another. We live in perilous and frightening times, and all of us know how much of our safety we in the Valley owe to Commander Syngpu. Just as we know how tirelessly Yanshwyn has labored as both scholar and healer, the endless miles she's traveled to distribute food and medicines wherever they were most needed. And so the joy they've found in one another is our joy, as well. Yanshwyn was born here in the Valley; Tangwyn came to us from far away, in the hour of our greatest need. Now both of them are ours, so let us join them and rejoice as they make one another their own."

He raised his hand in benediction, signing the Scepter of Langhorne. And then he began from memory, without so much as glancing at the prayer book the acolyte held beside him.

"And now, dearly beloved," he told Saint Sanzhung's hushed church, "we have gathered together here in the sight of God and the Archangels, and in the face of this company, to join together this man and this woman in holy matrimony; which is an honorable estate, instituted of God and the Archangels, signifying unto us the mystical union that is between God and His Church; which is a holy estate which the Archangel Langhorne adorned and beautified with his presence in his time here upon Safehold, and is commended of the Archangel Bédard to be honorable among all men: and therefore is not by any to be entered into unadvisedly or lightly; but reverently, discreetly, advisedly, soberly, and in the fear of God. Into this holy estate these two persons present come now to be joined. If any man can show just cause why they may not lawfully be joined together, let him now speak, or else hereafter forever hold his peace."

AUGUST YEAR OF GOD 910

·✦·

. I .
Siddar City,
Republic of Siddarmark,
and
Tellesberg Palace,
City of Tellesberg,
Kingdom of Old Charis,
Empire of Charis.

Rain drummed on roofs, gurgled along gutters and splashed down downspouts, and battered pedestrians and freight wagons. Umbrellas moved along the sidewalks, many of them bright splashes of color against the rain-washed gray and brown of stonework or the dark umber brick of Siddar City. Ever-increasing numbers of "bicycles" had made their way to the Mainland, and their riders swerved in and out of more traditional traffic, bumping up onto and off the sidewalks, as often as not, with their customary lack of concern for others. The rain was heavy enough to reduce visibility significantly, which made their normal antics even more disruptive, and Dustyn Nezbyt grimaced out the boardroom window at them.

"This weather sucks," he growled to the man standing next to him.

"I'm not too partial to it myself," Zhak Hahraimahn acknowledged, "but is there a particular reason it bothers you today?"

"Well, mostly because Mahtylda and Aileen and I are

supposed to take *Triumph* out on the Bay tomorrow."
Nezbyt looked at the taller Hahraimahn and twitched
his head out the window. "You really think Mathylda's going to enjoy herself sailing around out there in
weather like this?"

"No, not really." Hahraimahn's lips twitched, although his voice remained admirably grave.

Mahtylda Nezbyt was an attractive woman, but she
did have a temper and she regarded Nezbyt's 150-foot
sloop with mixed feelings at the best of times. The fact
that she suffered from seasickness was a factor in that,
of course. On the other hand, she obviously saw the
yacht as a symbol of her husband's success, and she was
well known in their marina for the parties she threw . . .
as long as she didn't have to actually take *Triumph* out
to sea. Her daughter, Aileen, on the other hand, was an
enthusiastic sailor.

"It may clear," he said helpfully. Nezbyt rolled his
eyes, and Hahraimahn chuckled. "I didn't say it *would*
clear; I said it *might*."

"I believe the proper response is 'Not a chance in
hell,'" the other man said glumly, turning back to the
window. "About the only way it could get worse would
be to have one of those damned bicycles of yours run
me down on the way home to face her. Although, come
to think of it, that might be the better alternative!"

"Don't get me started on those things!" Hahraimahn
snorted. "They're making me buckets of marks, and the
Pasqualates love them. Apparently, riding the damned
things is really, really good for your heart. But they have
got to be the worst 'improvement' Charis ever inflicted
on us!"

"Might be putting it a *little* strongly," Nezbyt disagreed, but it was also his turn to chuckle, and Hahraimahn gave him a moderate glare as he realized he'd
risen to his friend's bait. But, damn it, it was true.

And the fact that quite a few of those bicycles did
come from his own manufactory didn't make him any
happier about their irritation quotient. The damned
things were a menace, and draft dragons hated their

jingle-jangling bells. For that matter, *he* didn't much care for the racket, either! Besides, even with the "home-field advantage"—and the eight percent import duty the Chamber of Delegates had slapped on imported goods—Charisian-made bicycles were very competitively priced, even here in Siddar City.

And everybody knows Charisian products are better than anyone else's, he thought grumpily. *Idiots will pay a premium for the Charisian name, and especially the Delthak label! And their local dealers aren't shy about playing that up, either.*

The truth, he knew, was that most often Charisian products, and especially those bearing the Delthak label, *were* better than anyone else's. Even worse, from the perspective of Delthak's competitors, the Charisian duke required any of his Siddarmarkian representatives to have what he called "service departments" in-house. If one of their products broke or needed routine repair, they were expected to handle it, and their fees were lower than most Siddarmarkian artisans would have charged. Not only that, many of their products were guaranteed for up to a full year from date of purchase. Indeed, some were guaranteed for as much as *five* years! If they broke during that period, Delthak would repair or replace free of charge, unless it was obvious the product had been grossly abused by the buyer.

How was anyone supposed to compete with *that*?

Sneaky bastards, he thought, with a smile that was only half humorous. *Probably couldn't get away with it without the head start they got during the Jihad.*

Hahraimahn's father had been Greyghor Stohnar's senior representative on the Council of Manufactories he'd established to fight the Jihad. That was where Hahraimahn and Nezbyt had met, actually. Nezbyt had been an up-and-coming young manager with the Exchequer and he'd worked with both Zhak Hahraimahn, senior, and an army officer named Klymynt Myllyr while Zhak Hahraimahn, junior, had been his father's chief assistant.

The elder Hahraimahn had also worked closely with Ehdwyrd Howsmyn before Howsmyn became the Duke of Delthak, and he'd always spoken warmly and admiringly of the man. Well, Zhak, junior, respected and admired Delthak, too, but he'd always been a bit less comfortable than his younger brother, Ghordyn, with the headlong pace of innovation. Obviously, they had to adapt themselves, but the sheer rate of change was enough to make anyone nervous, and Hahraimahn more than suspected that it had contributed a great deal to Siddarmark's . . . erratic performance over the last ten or twelve years. You simply couldn't overheat a realm's entire banking and investment structure, not to mention its manufactories, by cramming such fundamental *change* at it that way without consequences.

Ghordyn, predictably, pointed out that Charis had managed that quite nicely. Of course, Charis also had the Mohryah Lode, didn't it? And Charis was the one driving the entire rush forward as if there were some sort of time limit on it. If they'd only *slow down,* even briefly, the rest of the world—and the Republic of Siddarmark, in particular—might get a chance to draw a deep breath and settle down.

Ghordyn preferred to shoot the rapids right along with the Charisians, so he and his older brother had divided their father's holdings between them. So far, it seemed to be working out for Ghordyn. He'd certainly been more fortunate than many another investor, at any rate. The older Hahraimahn brother, on the other hand, had opted for slow and steady. He'd expanded his manufactory base, but at a considerably slower pace than he might have, with the result that he hadn't been badly hurt by any of the seemingly inevitable swings between boom and bust.

And that's why Myllyr had picked him for this, he thought sourly. He wished he could have figured out a way to decline the "honor," but that had never been going to happen. And Hahraimahn couldn't really blame him. The lord protector wanted people he knew weren't going to go dragon wild, which was why he'd tapped Nezbyt as chairman and Hahraimahn as vice-chairman.

Thunder rumbled overhead, and he looked away from

the window. The chairs around the long, polished table behind them had filled steadily while they stood gazing out into the rain, and he nudged Nezbyt's shoulder. The shorter, auburn-haired man looked over his shoulder, inhaled, then gave Hahraimahn a resigned look.

"Time to get this dog-and-dragon show on the road," he muttered, then squared his shoulders and walked to his place at the table's head.

"Gentlemen," Nezbyt said as Hahraimahn settled into his own chair at the other end of the table, and a chorus of murmured responses came back to him. He smiled with more cheer than he actually felt, picked up the gavel, and rapped it once, lightly, on the table.

"As they say in the Chamber," he said, "this first meeting of the General Board of the Trans-Siddarmark Railroad will come to order." He glanced at Zhasyn Brygs, the board's secretary. "I know we don't have any minutes to read, Zhasyn, but I don't think it would hurt a thing for us to go over the Lord Protector's instructions before we start making any actual plans."

▼ ▼ ▼

"I could wish Myllyr had picked someone else to chair this thing," Merlin Athrawes said.

It happened to be raining in Tellesberg, as well, although it was a far gentler rain than Siddar City's drenching downpour, and the windows were open to admit the damp, cooling breeze. He sat tipped back in his armchair with a foaming beer stein in his right hand and a bowl of his favored fried potato slices at his left elbow, and wiggled the toes of his sock feet at his wife.

"Really?" she said as the toes waved at her. "This is what the mighty *Seijin* Merlin does when there's no one around to be impressed? Sits around drinking beer and waving his feet in the air?"

"I am not 'waving them in the air,'" he said with meticulous accuracy. "They are, in fact, propped on an ottoman. And I trust you will note that there aren't even any holes in my socks." He sniffed. "It doesn't get much more genteel than that, Madam!"

"Not in your case, anyway," she agreed with a smile, and someone chuckled over the com link. It sounded like Ehdwyrd Howsmyn.

"I find myself more in agreement with Merlin than with you on this one, Nynian," Cayleb Ahrmahk said. "Sorry. And I'm sure Sharleyan will take your side when she gets here. For now, though," his tone turned more serious, "I think I agree with him about Nezbyt and Hahraimahn, too."

"I'm not sure I do, really," Duke Delthak said, and one of Merlin's eyebrows rose.

"Nezbyt doesn't have a lot of hands-on experience in the boardroom, Ehdwyrd," he pointed out. "He's a bureaucrat. A pretty good one, based on his record during the Jihad, but basically an Exchequer weenie. I don't know how good a job he's going to do riding herd on something like this."

"At least he's a reasonably honest bureaucrat," Nahrmahn observed. "He could've made a ton of money managing that contract portfolio for Stohnar and Maidyn during the war. God knows enough other government officials did!"

"I didn't say he wasn't honest, Nahrmahn," Merlin replied. "Although he did scarf off a few feathers for his nest, you know. It was all small change, but he managed to rake off a little."

"But Nahrmahn has a point," Nynian countered. "Since the Jihad, all of his accounts have balanced almost perfectly. He's still a little too friendly with some of the manufactory owners and bankers he worked with during the war—Hahraimahn's a case in point, as a matter of fact—but I think he'd feel genuinely insulted if anyone offered him any kind of overt payoff. And the main point in his favor is that Myllyr knows and trusts him."

"And the same thing is true about Hahraimahn," Delthak added. "That Myllyr knows and trusts him, I mean. And to be fair, Myllyr's obviously aware Nezbyt's a bean counter and not a fearless captain of industry. That's why he paired him and Hahraimahn in the

Board's two top slots. Nezbyt's the guy who's going to represent the government's—that is to say, Myllyr's—position and Hahraimahn's as much his technical advisor as his second in command."

"Maybe, but Hahraimahn's not exactly a hotbed of innovation, either, Ehdwyrd," Merlin noted.

"No, he's not, but maybe that's not what we need right now. I wish Myllyr hadn't held out for this approach in the first place, but if we're going this route, it may not hurt to have someone who's more 'slow and steady' at the helm."

"Ehdwyrd may have a point," Nahrmahn put in from his computer. "Two of them, actually. We could've had a much bigger footprint out of this if we'd gone with the same sort of 'Ahrmahk Plan' we used in the United Provinces. But if we're not going that route, somebody like Nezbyt and Hahraimahn are more likely to instill confidence in the more . . . skittish members of the Siddarmarkian business community."

Merlin pursed his lips and looked at Nynian. She was curled on the couch, a glass of wine on the end table at her elbow, her legs folded under her, and the book she'd been reading while they waited for the rest of the conference to assemble facedown in her lap. Now she looked down at it, tracing the cover's embossed title with an index finger, and her expression was thoughtful. After a moment she looked up and nodded slowly to him.

<Well, sweetheart, if you and Nahrmahn both agree with Ehdwyrd, there must be something to it,> he murmured over their private channel.

<For a beer-swilling lout, you do have your perceptive moments, don't you?> she replied with a smile, and it was his turn to chuckle.

"The thing that bothers me the most in the first place," he said to the other members of the conference, "is that Myllyr *is* going to go 'slow and steady.' The clock's ticking."

"And if we blow up the Siddarmarkian economy all over again, the clock will stop where the Republic's concerned," Delthak pointed out. "I don't like this approach either, and like Nahrmahn says, I'd like to have a bigger footprint, with something more like the United Provinces, but it's remotely possible he knows his business better than we do."

"It's possible he doesn't, too," Cayleb said a bit acidly, then inhaled deeply. "But, either way, it was his decision and none of us could find a way to change his mind."

Merlin smiled in sour agreement, then treated himself to another swallow of the beer a PICA didn't really need.

Henrai Maidyn's Central Bank was working . . . after a fashion at least. Not without a lot of pain and resentment, but working.

The act which had established the Bank had also created the Asset Guarantee Trust, a special account within the Exchequer, funded jointly by the Central Bank and the trust's member banks, and authorized the Bank to guarantee the deposits of any member bank. In return, any bank which associated itself with the trust and accepted the guarantee had to meet certain criteria. They had to maintain a mandated ratio between debt and actual deposits and they also had to open their books to the Exchequer and the Central Bank's auditors.

The AGT didn't have to accept a bank, and if a member bank's debt-asset ratio looked too bad, the Central Bank could liquidate it entirely, but there'd been several carveouts within the legislation which created the new institution. If the Central Bank ordered a bank liquidated, the Exchequer had to absorb the difference between its assets and what it owed *all* of its creditors, not just its deposit holders. If a member bank of the AGT actually failed, the Exchequer actually made out better; it had to pay depositors, if any, but other creditors were reimbursed only out of the bank's assets—and only after all depositors had been paid—under the terms of a new, more draconian bankruptcy law. That created a disincentive on the part of the Central Bank to order the liquidation of shaky banks as a first option, which had been exactly what some of the legislation's sponsors had wanted, and meant the preferred solution was to manage mergers between weaker banks and stronger ones.

The same legislation gave the Central Bank pretty draconian authority over banking and loan activities in general. Even banks which opted not to join the AGT—and they had the right not to; that was another carveout provision of the Act—were still required to abide by the new banking regulation. That was vastly irritating to some of the wheelers and dealers—not to mention the fly-by-night speculators—who had dominated far too much of the Siddarmarkian stock market after the Jihad and the collapse of the House of Qwentyn. They weren't required to maintain the same ratio between debt and assets as the members of the AGT, but the revamped bankruptcy laws and the efforts to rein in the more extravagant practices were having an effect even there. And, unpopular as the Central Bank remained with large segments of the Siddarmarkian business community, depositors loved the AGT. Banks which opted out of the Guarantee Trust had seen a steep decline in deposits, which exerted a steady pressure on more and more of them to bite the bullet and sign on.

With that process underway, and after a year in office in his own right, Myllyr had decided the Republic was finally turning the corner. At least some of the groundswell of anti-Charisian sentiment had faded as the Siddarmarkian economy seemed to be stabilizing, and the lord protector had been far more amenable to Cayleb and Sharleyan's offer of a Siddarmarkian Ahrmahk Plan. But he'd remained leery of the sort of individual loans the House of Ahrmahk had made in the United Provinces. He'd been afraid a sudden influx of Charisian money might undo some of the stability the banks had achieved, especially since it would have been seen as direct competition to those banks at a time when the Central Bank was already restricting their activities. Indeed, some would see—or *claim* to see—the new regulations as having been *designed* to create a fresh opportunity for those nefarious Ahrmahks. As he'd pointed out, that might well kick up the embers of that anti-Charisian resentment, not to mention the potential negative consequences for the economy in general.

And so the Trans-Siddarmarkian Railroad had been born as a joint private-government enterprise. Its ambitious charter was to build a rail net which would connect every major Siddarmarkian city and stretch from Siddar City itself through Tarikah and the Border States all the way to Zion. That was a gargantuan task. "Just" the line from the capital to Lake City in Tarikah would require over two thousand miles of track, several hundred miles longer than the original "Transcontinental Railroad" of Old Terra between Nebraska and California. The rest of the proposed network would require many times that trackage, which would take years and cost millions upon millions of marks to lay, and both of those were good things from Klymynt Myllyr's perspective. It would funnel all those marks into employment and the expansion of the Republic's domestic steel industry, and it would provide that economic engine for a long time.

It was a bit too much like Emperor Mahrys and Zhyou-Zhwo's "five-year plans" for Merlin's tastes, though. And it was focused on only one aspect of the overall Siddarmarkian economy, unlike the situation in the United Provinces where the Ahrmahk Plan had made loans available to entrepreneurs pursuing a broad spectrum of opportunities. Myllyr's proposal lacked much of the synergistic effect which both the United Provinces and Dohlar were exploiting to such good effect.

He'd been quietly, stubbornly adamant, however, and so the TSRR had come into existence. Behind the scenes, Cayleb and Sharleyan—operating through Delthak Enterprises—had provided over seventy percent of the corporation's initial capitalization. Keeping that "behind the scenes" had been another of Myllyr's suggestions, since it kept Cayleb and Sharleyan officially out of the public eye and helped play down the inevitable "puppet master" allegations, but the Mohryah Lode had underwritten much of Delthak Enterprises' investment.

The rest of the capitalization had been raised from Siddarmarkian investors and government bond issues, and the General Board's membership was heavily skewed in the Republic's favor. Despite the amount of Charisian money involved, Charis held only two of the seven voting seats on the board. Myllyr appointed the chairman and the vice-chairman, as well as the non-voting secretary-treasurer. He'd selected Zhasyn Brygs for the latter position, in addition to his duties as the Governor of the Central Bank, which struck Merlin as a bit cumbersome. Myllyr's theory was that it would ensure both that the Bank's view was represented and that it knew precisely what was happening at all times but without exerting overt control. Merlin's theory was that Brygs was likely to be badly overworked . . . at best.

Time would tell about that, however, and the other three voting members were elected by the Siddarmarkian investors. In theory, that gave the united front of the Charisian members and Myllyr appointees a four-to-three advantage, but if the time came when Myllyr (or his successor) differed with the Charisian perspective, things could get . . . messy, Merlin thought.

"You're right about whose decision it had to be in the end, Cayleb," he said. "And you have a point, too, Ehdwyrd. We've been looking in from the outside, and the SNARCs give us more reach than Myllyr's got, but he's a Siddarmarkian, and we aren't. So maybe he does know best. And either way, we're going to be laying a lot of track. Not as much as we might otherwise, and I do wish the Republic was going to be looking at other opportunities—they've got all those potential oil fields in Westmarch and Thesmar, for example. But at least it looks like their economy's going to be growing again. That has to be a good thing."

"It's a lot better than what we had before, at any rate," Nahrmahn agreed. "And this is going to bolster the industries we'll need most when the time comes to actually start building the canal in Silkiah."

"Which is the name of the game, really," Cayleb pointed out. "And, since it is, and since there isn't a lot more we can do about Siddarmark at the moment, I'd like to take a look at what's going on in Desnair and South Harchong. Have you had an opportunity to review Owl and Nahrmahn's latest projections, Merlin?"

"I'm afraid not," Merlin admitted. "I've been focused on the Republic and North Harchong, I'm afraid."

"I figured." Cayleb's com image shrugged. "We can cover a lot more ground now that we have so many people to delegate stuff to, but it does mean none of us can stay as on top of everything as we used to."

"Forgive me, Your Majesty," Owl said, "but I'm very much afraid that you couldn't 'stay on top of everything' the way you once did under any circumstances. In many ways, the Nahrmahn Plan is much more complex than managing the Jihad was."

"And our poor protoplasmic brains have neither the computing power nor the memory storage you and Nahrmahn do," Cayleb agreed. "Although I noticed you're too tactful to point that out."

"Actually, Your Majesty," the AI replied, "I believe I did point it out. Tactfully and only inferentially, of course."

Cayleb chuckled and shook his head.

"Point taken," he said, then turned back to Merlin. "What I wanted to discuss with you is the way the two of them, and especially Zhyou-Zhwo and Snow Peak, are starting to get that army of theirs armed with modern weapons. They're still awfully light in artillery, but small arms production is climbing, and—"

MAY YEAR OF GOD 911

·✦·

. I .
Ironhill Mountains,
Barony of Deep Valley,
Kingdom of Old Charis,
Empire of Charis.

"This is nice, Braiys," Cayleb Ahrmahk said.

He looked up at the patches of cloudless blue sky visible through the occasional hole in the canopy of nearoaks as the winding trail snaked its twisty-turny way through the thick woodland of Deep Valley. They were five hours from Tellesberg by train; the air was cool and refreshing for Old Charis, this high in the Ironhill Mountains' foothills, especially in the dense shade, and he inhaled deeply, swelling his lungs.

"I don't get out enough," he added a bit wistfully.

"I believe that comes with the Crown, Your Majesty."

Sir Braiys Sohmyrsyt, Baron Deep Valley, was a small, wiry man, ten years older than Cayleb, with an infectious smile. He was also one of Cayleb and Sharleyan's staunchest supporters, although he'd never heard of anyone named Nimue Alban or something called the Terran Federation. He did know a thing or two about his emperor, however, and when word of the slash lizard stalking his barony's flocks of sheep reached him, he'd known exactly what to arrange as a belated birthday gift to his crown princess.

"If I'd known I'd be spending so much time in offices and council chambers, I wouldn't've taken the job," Cayleb replied now. He lifted the canteen from his saddle bow and swallowed appreciatively, then recapped it and looked at Deep Valley. "There was a time, you know, when I spent every minute I could steal hunting."

"I think someone mentioned that to me, once," Deep Valley said dryly. Saying Crown Prince Cayleb had been an avid hunter was like saying Howell Bay was a bit damp. "Maybe even twice, now that I think about it. And I wouldn't want to say anything unbecoming or undutiful about daughters and chips off the old block."

"But at least Alahnah has a *modicum* of good sense," Major Athrawes put in from the other side of Cayleb's horse.

"You only say that because she's prettier than I am," Cayleb said with a grin, and Merlin shook his head.

"I only say that because she's *smarter* than you are," Merlin shot back. "The day I met you, you'd just finished killing another slash lizard—with a spear, if I recall correctly." Merlin gestured at the massive double-barreled, over-and-under rifle in Cayleb's saddle scabbard. Handbuilt by Taigys Mahldyn, it fired a massive .625 caliber round at a velocity of almost two thousand feet per second. "That's a *far* better choice, believe me!"

"But much less satisfying," Cayleb said with a devilish glint. "I'm a traditionalist at heart, you know!"

"That's not how people like Zhyou-Zhwo put it, Your Majesty," Deep Valley said.

"Well, in *some* ways," Cayleb amended. "In other ways, change is good."

"And Sharleyan's comment about 'little boys with toys' didn't have anything to do with this sudden onset of sanity?" Merlin inquired, pointing at the rifle again.

"She may have said a little something on the subject," Cayleb conceded. "And something else about daughters and setting *good* examples, now that I think about it. Or I think she did, anyway. I wasn't really paying attention at the time, you know."

"It's fortunate no one present for this conversation would dream of recounting it to Her Majesty," Earl Pine Hollow said, rubbing his chin thoughtfully. "It would make interesting blackmail material the next time the debate on the Council gets a bit heated, though, wouldn't it?"

"Trahvys, it would pain me deeply to imprison you in a lonely tower somewhere for the rest of your days, but if push came to shove, I *would* do it."

All four men laughed, and Merlin shook his head. It truly was rare these days for Cayleb—or Sharleyan—to get away from the daily grind of their imperial duties. But while Sharleyan was just as avid a shooter as he was, she preferred target ranges to hunting. She never had understood the appeal of waiting all day in a rain-drenched shooting blind for a prong buck or a jungle lizard that might never happen by anyway. She did enjoy horses, though, and she would have come along today, if only for the ride, if Prince Domynyk Maikel hadn't decided to catch the flu. At three and a half—in Safeholdian years; he was barely thirty-eight Standard Months old—he remained six or seven Safeholdian months too young for the nanotech which protected the older members of his family. The rest of the Federation's pharmacopeia could be deployed in his defense, of course, but it worked considerably more slowly, and at the moment he was a very unhappy toddler. Cayleb had almost stayed home with her, but she'd shooed him out the door. Officially that was because today had been organized for Alahnah, not him, and she'd announced she was staying home if her father was. Actually, it was a joint wife-and-daughter conspiracy to get him out into the open air.

And he deserved it. There were still traces of the impetuous teenager Merlin Athrawes had met twenty-one years ago, in woods very like the ones around them today, but he reminded Merlin more every day of his father. Haarahld Ahrmahk had taken his responsibilities seriously—more seriously than even Merlin had realized, until after King Haarahld's death—and he'd taught his son to do the same. Emperor Cayleb would never have considered Crown Prince Cayleb's tendency to play truant. Although, to be fair, Cayleb *had* been discharging his responsibilities the day he and Merlin met. The fact that he'd chosen to discharge them with a lizard-hunting spear—on foot—might have been just a tad *irresponsible*, but he had been acting to protect his future subjects.

Which, of course, had been the only reason—the self-less and *noble* reason—for his expedition.

Merlin chuckled as he recalled Lieutenant Ahrnahld Falkhan's rather pithy comments when he'd discovered what they were actually hunting. The hard-pressed Marine lieutenant who'd commanded Prince Cayleb's security detail had put up with a lot from his fractious charge, and Merlin had listened through the SNARC remotes as the two of them "discussed" Cayleb's agenda that day. The prince had been less than fully forthcoming about his plans before they left Tellesberg, and Lieutenant Fhalkhan had come within a whisker of turning them around when he found out what sort of "game" Cayleb proposed to hunt. But Cayleb Ahrmahk had been a force to be reckoned with, even at nineteen. Of course, if Falkhan had known about the assassins who'd arranged for Cayleb to hear about the man-eating slash lizard in order to draw him out, not even Cayleb's stubbornness could have prevailed over his sense of duty.

Nor had time changed that sense of duty, which was one reason Brigadier *Sir* Ahrnahld Falkhan was now the commanding officer of the Charisian Imperial Guard. He walked with a limp to this day because of the thigh wound he'd suffered in the assassination attempt, and he retained his rank in the Imperial Charisian Marines, but he'd been the obvious choice to head the Imperial Guard when Ahdam Ropewalk finally surrendered that post.

He'd also personally handpicked the Marine bodyguards assigned to Crown Princess Alahnah. The heir to the Crown was protected by the Marines, not by the Imperial Guard; that part of the pre-imperial Charisian tradition continued to hold, although Lieutenant Ahlbyrt Bynyt, the commander of Alahnah's detachment, was a Chisholmian, not an Old Charisian. Aside from that minor technicality, he reminded Merlin a great deal of a younger Ahrnahld Falkhan.

Which was a source of great comfort to him, since even a PICA could be in only one place at one time. At the moment, Alahnah and a handful of friends closer to her own age than a stodgy old father like Cayleb, had ridden ahead under Bynyt's watchful eye, eager to reach the lodge where Ahlys Sohmyrsyt, Deep Valley's daughter, waited to greet them.

Personally, Merlin thought that eagerness had more than a little to do with Alahnah's special guest. She'd arranged for Stefyny to invite him in the fond belief it was possible her parents might not detect her own hand in the invitation. He wondered how she was going to react the day she discovered the truth about the archangels and the inner circle and realized her parents had had access to Owl's SNARCs from the day she was born.

Actually, remembering Nimue Alban's long-ago girlhood, he had a pretty fair notion how she was going to respond to learning about that particular unfair advantage on their part.

"How much farther to the lodge, Braiys?" Pine Hollow asked, although, like Merlin and Cayleb, he knew the actual distance to the foot, courtesy of the SNARCs and their com implants.

"Maybe another forty-five minutes or an hour," Deep Valley said, after glancing around to check his landmarks.

"Good!" Cayleb said. Deep Valley raised an eyebrow at him, and Cayleb smiled wickedly at Merlin, then waved at the half-dozen Imperial Guardsmen flanking them as they made their way along the trail. "I'm looking forward to seeing Ahlys again, of course, but honesty compels me to admit that that's not the only reason I'll be glad to get there. As I believe I asked a certain Marine once upon a time, many years ago, how are we going to hunt anything if we take a great thundering herd of bodyguards along?"

He chuckled at Merlin's expression, then sobered—a bit—and shrugged.

"I know we can't really ditch them completely, but once we get to the lodge, I'm definitely stripping down a bit. I think we could probably trust Merlin to keep me intact, and he's at least a little quieter in the woods than those fellows." He twitched his head at the Guardsmen. "I think we'll just leave most of them at the lodge."

"We will, will we?" Merlin asked.

"Oh, trust me, we *will*," Caleb told him firmly.

▼ ▼ ▼

"So, what do you think of the Ironhills?" Alahnah Ahrmahk asked the tall, brown-haired young man riding beside her.

"Impressive, Your Highness," Lywys Whytmyn replied. "We don't have as many mountains in Gorath as you do here in Charis. And Thirsk's actually pretty flat. I mean, I love it—don't get me wrong! But I have to admit I like this." He waved one hand to indicate the trees and slopes around them. "Back home, mountains like this would be covered with snow by midwinter, though. I'm guessing not so much here?"

"Not so much, no," Alahnah acknowledged. "Technically, this is still summer—we won't officially start into fall for another couple of five-days—but we don't get much snow even in August, despite how far south we are. Not on this side of the Iron Hills, at least. If you want to see *snow,* you should come visit us in Chisholm!" She shivered theatrically. "Gwylym and Braiahn love snow, but not me. I'm my father's girl where cold weather's concerned, and so is Mom, really." She grinned. "She's not going to admit it where any of her Chisholmians can hear her, but she's the one who insisted that the half-year we spend in Tellesberg just happens to be the middle of winter in Cherayth! We'll be leaving for Chisholm the middle of next month."

"I can't fault her timing." Whytmyn chuckled. "It must be odd, though, moving everything back and forth twice a year."

"Well, we don't actually move *everything,*" Alahnah pointed out. "That's sort of the point, really. We leave Earl Pine Hollow home here in Tellesberg while we're in Cherayth, and we leave Earl White Crag in charge in Cherayth when we're in Tellesberg. And that way neither kingdom feels like it's being frozen out in terms of political influence." She shrugged. "It's awkward, although Mom and Dad both say it was a lot worse before we had steamships that can get dispatches from Chisholm to Old Charis in just nine or ten days. Or if it's something that can be trusted to the semaphore, it can get here in as little as two days, if everything works right."

His eyes widened. The Charisian Empire was wrapped around half the planet; it was literally true that the sun never set on the Charisian flag. He'd always assumed that had to have major implications for its internal communications, and it was clear from what Alanah had just said that it did. But that was a far shorter message turnaround time than he would have believed was possible. His surprise showed, and she shrugged.

"We've got semaphore chains clear across Zebediah now, so the dispatch boats only have to cross the water gaps between Chisholm and Zebediah and then between Zebediah and Silverlode. Same thing's true for Corisande and Zebediah, really, and for Tarot, the water gap's barely three hundred miles across the Tranjyr Passage. On a good day, Dad and Mom can get a message to King Gorjah in Tranjyr in less than *one* day! In fact, the record from Tellesberg to Tranjyr is just under fifteen *hours*. A lot depends on timing and weather, of course. Semaphores don't work very well in the dark or if there's any fog around, so the actual transmission time between Cherayth and Tellesberg is usually at least three days, even at the best of times. But it works, and the promise to move the capital back and forth was a pretty important part of Dad's marriage proposal, really. Thinking ahead that way's one of his strengths. Mom's, too, of course, but Dad's the most . . . foresighted person I know. I keep watching him, trying to figure out how it works since it's going to be my job someday, but I haven't nailed it down yet. I will, though!"

Whytmyn nodded. His expression was merely thoughtful, but his eyes had sharpened as she spoke. He was three years older than she was—she'd turned seventeen last month and he'd celebrate his twentieth birthday next five-day—but she didn't seem that much younger. That was probably to be expected, given her parents and the job she knew would one day be hers, but that made it no less impressive when he listened to her.

Part of it might simply be that she was *Charisian*, though, he thought. She was arguably the most nobly born young woman in the entire world, but she seemed unaware of it. Or, no, that wasn't quite right. She was *aware* of it, and she conducted herself in the public eye with an easy grace and a calm assurance that commanded deference without ever having to demand it. He suspected she'd learned that more from her mother than father, since Cayleb's style was rather more . . . free-form than the majority of Safeholdian monarchs. But there wasn't an arrogant bone in her body. He was sure of that, and he wondered if she had any idea how remarkable that was.

It was genuinely possible she didn't. Charisians in general—and Old Charisians, in particular—were unlike anyone he'd ever known growing up. Dohlar was nothing like Desnair or—thank God!—Harchong, but Dohlaran grandees knew *exactly* who they were and made damned sure everyone else was equally aware. Thankfully, he'd grown up as his grandfather's grandson, and Earl Thirsk had possessed very little patience with that sort of attitude. Probably because he'd had to deal with so much of it during the Jihad. Whytmyn's cousin Ahlyxzandyr had inherited the Thirsk title, and, despite his youth—he was only seven years older than Whytmyn—he was clearly following in their grandfather's footsteps, much to the chagrin of certain of those other grandees. The fact that Thirsk—a mere earldom—had more influence these days than any of the kingdom's duchies only made that worse, in their eyes. And the "Thirsk contamination," as King Rahnyld liked to call it, was spreading to other noble families as well. Everyone told Whytmyn that—more often than not in terms of profound disapproval—so he had to believe it. It seemed to be spreading just a bit slower than a Mountains of Light glacier, however.

But Old Charis wasn't like that. Oh, no Old Charisian was going to just walk up to Crown Princess Alahnah! He knew that, too. Yet virtually everyone, from the most commonly born longshoremen on the Tellesberg waterfront to the most nobly born duke in the entire kingdom, regarded her as their favorite younger sister. They respected her, and they admired her, and they loved her, but they weren't in *awe* of her . . . and she saw absolutely no reason why they should be.

He thought about that now, glancing away from her while she turned to say something to the tiny fair-haired girl riding to her right.

Gladys Frymyn was five months younger than Alahnah, and much shyer. Not that there was anything wrong with her brain! Her mother had invented the double-glass, the angle glass, and the Imperial Navy's "rangefinder." She continued to forge ahead in optics of every sort, and Gladys was just as smart as Doctor *Zhain* Frymyn. Her interests lay elsewhere, however, and she'd become one of Dahnel Vyrnyr's star students and research assistants. Outside the Royal College, though, she was much less self-assured, and the fact that she was as petite as her mother, which made her look even younger than her age, didn't help. It was like Alahnah to make sure she was included in the conversation rather than let her withdraw into what she herself called her "nerd corner."

Whytmyn had no idea who'd invented that word— "nerd." He suspected it had been *Seijin* Merlin, although Cayleb tended to leave new words and mangled language in his wake, as well. Whoever had invented it, though, it was the perfect way to describe Gladys, and he was glad Alahnah was unwilling to let her withdraw.

"She does that well, doesn't she?" a voice asked.

"I didn't realize you'd noticed me noticing," he replied, smiling at the young woman riding on his other side.

Her hair was far darker than Gladys', her eyes were gray, not blue, and she was seven years older and five inches taller.

"I'm *Seijin* Merlin's daughter," Stefyny Athrawes replied with a rather broader smile, "and she's my crown princess, not just my friend. It's my job to notice things where she's concerned."

Her smile faded and she looked at Alahnah's back as the princess laughed at something Gladys had said.

Whytmyn wondered if she realized how much her own expression revealed in that moment. How much true and deep affection . . . and how much protectiveness. He'd heard the stories about her, had some idea—intellectually, at least; he knew damned well that no one who hadn't been there could truly understand—of what she'd endured in the Inquisition's concentration camp. And he knew how, after surviving all that, she'd still lost the birth-father she'd challenged the Punishment itself to save.

Yet all of it had left her unbroken. Not un*scarred,* he knew that had to be true, but unbroken. And perhaps it was what she'd experienced, what she'd lost, as much as the example of the adoptive father she clearly loved just as deeply, that made her so fiercely protective herself.

"You love her a lot, don't you?" he heard himself saying, and her eyes flipped back to him.

"She's my friend," she repeated after a moment. "And I guess you might say looking after the Ahrmahks is the family business."

"And the world's a lot better off because you're so good at it," he said quietly. She arched an eyebrow at him, and he shrugged. "They're the reason Zhaspahr Clyntahn's Inquisition didn't win," he said, "and Merlin is the reason they lived to stop him." His own expression was somber. "I never experienced anything like you and your brother went through, Lady Stefyny, but without *Seijin* Gwyliwr and *Seijin* Cleddyf, my entire family would probably be dead. You might say—" he grinned suddenly "—that the Whytmyns and Mahkswails are big *seijin* supporters!"

"Really?" She shook her head and smiled back at him. "Imagine that! It seems you and I have something in common. Besides—" her smile turned a bit impish "—liking Alahnah, I mean."

▾ ▾ ▾

"Princess looks like she's having a good time," Corporal Strathmohr commented. He and Sergeant Adkok had the rear of the small party, riding along behind the crown princess and her guests. Lieutenant Bynyt and Corporal Wynstyn Draifys rode at the head of the party with one of the guides Baron Deep Valley had provided, and Corporal Ohtuhl took point, a hundred yards ahead of them and well out of sight on the winding trail, with the second Deep Valley guide.

"Does appear that way," Sergeant Adkok agreed. Like Strathmohr's, the sergeant's eyes never stopped their regular sweep of the woodland to either side of the trail. At forty, Jyrohm Adkok was the oldest member of Crown Princess Alahnah's personal detail, and he'd known her literally since babyhood.

"Have to wonder if she thinks she fooled anyone, though," Strathmohr said.

"You mean having Lady Stefyny invite him along?" Adkok said dryly. "Might be one or two reindeer herders up in the Snow Crests she fooled. Somehow I don't think she put anything over on Their Majesties. And I *know* she didn't fool the *Seijin*!"

"Well, of course not!" Strathmohr's lips twitched as he looked off into the woods. "*Nobody* fools the *Seijin*, Sarge!"

"Guess not," Adkok agreed. "Probably just as well, don't you think?"

"Do I *look* stupid?"

"Maybe not *that* stupid," the sergeant said in a thoughtful tone, and Adkok chuckled. But then his expression sobered a bit.

"I don't like these woods, Sarge," he said.

"Me neither," Adkok acknowledged. "Visibility's a lot lower than the Lieutenant and I thought it'd be from the descriptions." He frowned, then shrugged. "I guess the good news is it's not real likely anyone'd be stupid enough to try anything with the *Seijin* riding herd on us." He snorted. "Didn't work out real well, the last couple of times somebody did."

▼ ▼ ▼

"Damn it," Cayleb said mildly, releasing his horse's cannon. The big gray lowered its forehoof, but it didn't put it back down on the trail. Instead it kept its lower leg cocked, the hoof just off the ground, and turned its head to snuffle his hair affectionately as he sheathed the knife he'd used to pry the small stone from its hoof. The emperor shook his head and patted the gelding's neck, then looked up at Baron Deep Valley.

"The damned rock was caught in the collateral groove and the frog's bruised pretty badly," he said, tossing the baron the stone. "If Gray Wind weren't so stubborn, he'd have pulled up lame at least fifteen minutes ago."

"Would've been nice if he'd let us know when he picked it up," Merlin agreed. The *seijin* stood on the trail beside Cayleb and shook his head. "And speaking of stubborn, I wouldn't want to say anything about horses taking after their riders or anything."

"Really?" Cayleb looked at him. "That would be a first." He patted the gelding's shoulder and frowned. "I don't like how much he's favoring it. I think the bruise's even worse than I thought it was at first."

"Hairahm!" Baron Deep Valley called, and a grizzled-looking man in hunting leathers touched a heel to his horse to trot up beside him.

"Yes, My Lord?"

"His Majesty's not going to be riding that horse anymore this afternoon."

"No, My Lord," Hairahm Fyrnahndyz, Deep Valley's senior huntsman agreed, and swung down from the saddle. "Take mine, Your Majesty," he said.

"Oh, don't be ridiculous!" Cayleb replied. "This is why Nanny Merlin insisted on bringing along remounts even for a jaunt this short. I, in my infallible wisdom, knew we wouldn't need them. You may have noticed, however, that Merlin's just a bit smarter than me sometimes?"

Fyrnahndyz darted a quick look at Merlin, who only shook his head, his expression resigned.

"Don't answer that," Cayleb said with a grin. "Her Majesty keeps telling me I shouldn't put people in positions where they have to choose between diplomacy and honesty. At the moment, however, what matters is that because of the *Seijin*'s foresight, we brought along extra horses, so there's no need for me to take yours."

"But—" Deep Valley began, then stopped as Cayleb shook his head.

"As I believe we were saying earlier, I can't get away with traveling as lightly as I did back when I was a mere heir to the throne. That whole thundering herd can't be more than fifteen, twenty minutes behind us. It won't hurt me to cool my heels until they catch up. For that matter," he patted Gray Wind's shoulder again, "the wait might help me remember to be a little more attentive next time around. I should've realized he was pulling up lame before it ever got to this point."

"As you say, Your Majesty," Deep Valley said after a moment and climbed down from his own saddle.

Merlin nodded unobtrusively to Corporal Boyke Cohlmyn, the senior of the Guardsmen currently attached to Cayleb, and Cohlmyn nodded in response, then turned his horse and trotted back the way they'd come to fetch the support party following along behind. They could have been closer, but Cayleb had deliberately ridden on ahead, putting a little space between him and the healer, the secretaries, the additional Guardsmen, the extra horses, and all the other impedimenta which accompanied him wherever he went. The entire collection—except, possibly, for the secretaries—was a colossal waste of time, in his opinion. By now, all the world knew that someone under Merlin Athrawes' protection didn't need anyone else's. He'd said as much,

on more than one occasion and more than a little petu-
lantly, but Sharleyan only looked at him *that* way whenever he did.

"It makes them feel better," she'd say . . . and that
would be that.

"And while we're waiting," he said now, "did anyone
brin—"

It was fortunate, he thought later, that no one realized he'd broken off in mid-word a fraction of a second
before Merlin whirled, dropped his horse's reins, and
hurled himself up the trail.

▼ ▼ ▼

It wasn't Lieutenant Bynyt's fault.

He and his detachment had done everything right,
and the entire excursion had been blessedly uneventful.
Until he heard the hideous scream, at any rate.

He knew what it was the instant he heard it. He was
a lieutenant, but like many Marine officers, he'd started
as a noncom, and a very youthful Corporal Bynyt had
served under an equally youthful emperor in Cayleb's
Corisande campaign.

He'd heard the shriek of dying horses before.

His head came up as the same sound ripped around
the bend in the trail towards him again. He couldn't be
certain, but it sounded like a second horse this time, and
his hand dropped automatically to the revolver at his
side.

"What the—?" the guide riding just ahead of him began.

"*Adkok!*" Bynyt bellowed over the other man, boot-
ing his own suddenly panicky horse as he forced it back
under control and turned it broadside across the trail.
"*Get her out of here* now!"

▼ ▼ ▼

Alahnah Ahrmahk's head snapped up as the unearthly
sound interrupted her conversation with Gladys Frymyn. She'd just started turning towards it when Bynyt
shouted, and Jyrohm Adkok responded instantly.

"*Go,* Your Highness!" the sergeant snapped. "Back to your Father—*now*!"

His horse crowded suddenly up beside hers even as he spoke. No, not beside hers, she realized; *between* hers and whatever had made that dreadful sound. And his revolver was in his hand.

"What—?" she began, then closed her mouth with a snap. She was her parents' daughter and she'd been ruthlessly drilled in what to do when bodyguards started snapping orders. So instead of arguing, she nodded once, reined her horse around, and drove in her heels.

The mare tossed her head in surprise, then gathered herself and launched back down the trail.

Frahnk Strathmohr's gelding was half a length ahead of the mare as the corporal responded automatically to his training and his standing orders. He was Alahnah's close cover, the bodyguard assigned to stick to her whatever happened . . . and to always be *between* her and the threat. He had no idea what was coming down the trail towards them, except that it was a threat. It might be assassins, it might be kidnappers, it might be *anything*. He didn't know, but the drill for this situation was clear. Whatever was behind them, it was behind them, and that made it the rest of the detachment's responsibility. His job was to clear the trail before her, and anything waiting ahead of them would have to go through him to reach her.

Lywys Whytmyn was a heartbeat behind the Marines in recognizing the threat—or that there *was* a threat, at any rate—because he lacked their trained and honed hyper-awareness. When he did, he wheeled his own horse around, but he held the gelding back long enough for Gladys and Stefyny to follow on Corporal Strathmohr's heels. He waited to be sure they'd turned back, then darted a look over his shoulder at Adkok.

"Go, My Lord!" the sergeant snapped, not even looking in his direction. He'd holstered his revolver . . . but he'd also dismounted, and now he pulled the M987 rifle from his saddle scabbard.

"But—"

"Get the *fuck* out of here!" Adkok snarled. "This is *my* job—you get your ass down that trail and help watch her back!"

Whytmyn stared at him for one more second, then swore vilely, clapped in his heels, and went thundering after Strathmohr and the women.

▼ ▼ ▼

"Oh, *shit*!" the guide gasped as the equine scream ended abruptly and they heard another sound: a deep, whistling bellow that ripped through the woodland like an avalanche.

"*Dragon*!" the man shouted, turning his horse to flee. "It's not a slash lizard! It's a Shan-wei–damned *drag*—!"

He never finished the sentence.

Corporal Draifys was closest to the bend in the trail. He was still drawing his revolver when twenty feet of gray-green, scaly hide exploded around it behind a gaping maw of foot-long bloody fangs. A taloned paw, bigger than a grown man's chest, slashed out, and it flung the Marine from the saddle like a broken, bloodied puppet.

The guide was closer than Bynyt, and the hideous jaws closed on him with a wet, dreadful crunch even before Draifys hit the ground. His scream of fear died stillborn as the great dragon reared up, tossed its head and hurled his mutilated body aside, and the same foot that had killed Draifys slashed out at the man's rearing, panicked horse.

The talons raked once, ripping the horse's belly open, and it shrieked as it was disemboweled. It went to its knees, then collapsed completely, and the great dragon whirled towards Bynyt.

The Marine had thrown himself from the saddle of his rearing horse, his revolver was up in a two-handed shooting stance, and thunder rolled as the dragon turned.

The first bullet smashed into the dreadful predator's shoulder while it was still turning. The second took it in the chest. The third hit the base of its neck, the fourth hit it just above its right eye and bounced off the inches-thick bone of its skull.

There was no fifth shot.

A fully mature great dragon was two and a half tons of ravening fury. Lieutenant Ahlbyrt Bynyt knew he couldn't stop it with a revolver, but he was a Marine, and his crown princess—and his emperor—were some-where down that trail behind him. His revolver was still up, his finger squeezing the trigger, when the dreadful jaws closed yet again.

▼ ▼ ▼

Sir Braiys Sohmyrsyt was still staring at the spot where Merlin Athrawes had vanished when he heard the first shot, faint with distance.

"*Alahnah!*" Cayleb shouted, then whirled back to Hairahm Fyrnahndyz as three more rapid shots rolled toward them. "Horse—*now*!" he barked.

The huntsman stared at him for one stunned instant, then threw him the reins and held the stirrup for his emperor.

"No, Your Majesty!" Deep Valley shouted, crowd-ing his horse up beside Fyrnahndyz' mount as Cayleb vaulted into the saddle. "We can't *risk* you! Not when we don't even know—!"

Cayleb only reached past him, yanked the heavy rifle from Gray Wind's saddle, and drove in his heels. The baron looked after him for a moment, then swore and went thundering after him with every Imperial Guards-man at his heels.

▼ ▼ ▼

Great dragons were the apex hunters of Safehold. De-spite their name, they were carnivores, more closely related to the slash lizard Cayleb and his party had ex-pected to be hunting than to the herbivore hill or jungle dragons. In fact, they looked very much like overgrown slash lizards, although they were very nearly twice as large and covered in thick, well-insulated hide rather than fur. They were little more than a third the size of a jungle dragon . . . but jungle dragons could reach fifteen or sixteen tons. Great dragons were the most dreadful and feared predators in the entire world, better than twice the size of the largest Old Earth polar bear ever measured. Their mere presence was enough to drive any other predator from any range they claimed—not even a slash lizard would challenge them—and not just because of their size or their ferocity. Huge as they were, they were also blindingly fast, agile, savagely territorial, and smart.

And mated pairs hunted as a team.

▼ ▼ ▼

Alahnah Ahrmahk heard the great dragon's bellow, and then the sound of shots, behind her. She'd never heard a hunting great dragon before, never heard its challenge scream when its territory was invaded. She didn't know what she'd heard even now, what her bodyguards were firing at, but her heart froze as she realized only one of them was shooting at all.

Her eyes stung and she blinked furiously, trying to clear them of tears. Her Marines had protected her since she could walk. They were family, uncles she'd always known were there to keep her safe from any harm. Now she was running away, fleeing without even knowing what she fled from, and they were *dying* behind her. She knew those men—she knew they would stand together in the face of Hell itself, so if only one of them was shooting, it was because only one of them was still alive.

And she was running away. Abandoning them. She knew the story of how her mother's Guardsmen had died almost to the man, saving her from assassination at the Convent of Saint Agtha. She'd always known it could happen to her Marines. But her mother had stood and fought beside her protectors, and she . . . *she* was running *away*.

Not even knowing that was her duty, her overriding responsibility, could make it hurt a single bit less.

Her mare shied suddenly. Its head came up, it stumbled, and Alahnah Ahrmahk's eyes widened in horror as the great dragon's mate exploded into the trail ahead of her.

Something a great dragon's size didn't have to be an ambush hunter, but that didn't mean it couldn't be one, and Frahnk Strathmohr never saw it coming. It erupted from his left, out of that restricted visibility he hadn't liked, and it was five times the size of the horse under him. It bowled the gelding over effortlessly, Strathmohr flew from the saddle and smashed headlong into a tree. His neck snapped, his body bounced back, thudded limply to the trail, and the great dragon hissed like a steam automotive as it twisted around toward Alahnah.

Old Charisians were seamen, not horsemen, but *Chisholmians* were another matter, and Alahnah Ahrmahk had been thrown up onto her first pony almost before she could walk. Once she was in the saddle, she was a centaur, yet not even she could hold the mare when they found themselves face-to-face with a six-limbed horror from Hell. The horse screamed in panic, twisted impossibly around on its haunches.

It bolted back the way it had come, and Alahnah cried out as her head struck a low-hanging branch. It was only a glancing blow, but it was more than enough to stun her, and she lost the reins as she reeled in the saddle.

It was all she could do to stay with the mare; she didn't have a prayer of controlling it.

▼ ▼ ▼

Fresh thunder rolled behind him, and Lywys Whytmyn twisted his head around, daring to look back, away from the trail ahead of him.

Jyrohm Adkok's job was to cover his crown princess' escape, and he'd dropped behind a downed tree to one side of the trail, rifle ready, to do just that. The Mahndrayn-97 was a powerful weapon, firing a 350-grain bullet at over twenty-four hundred feet per second. It was a superb mankiller, famous for its lethality and accuracy, and Adkok was an expert shot.

But for all its virtues, the M897 had never been intended to take down a two-and-a-half-ton monster.

Sergeant Adkok knew how little hope of stopping a great dragon with it he had. He recognized that in the instant he saw the nightmare flowing down the trail towards him like a tsunami.

He was off the trail, out of the great dragon's immediate path, and its attention was obviously on the horses fleeing before it. It probably didn't even realize he was there . . . and if it did, it clearly didn't care. All it wanted was to storm past him, destroy the impudent pygmies who'd invaded its newly claimed range.

He knew that, too, but his princess was ahead of the monster, not safely to one side, and a tiny corner of his mind noted the blood welling from the wounds Bynyt's revolver had left, knew his lieutenant had at least marked his killer.

Now it was his turn.

The enormous predator drew level with him at less than fifty yards' range, and he squeezed the trigger.

The great dragon's head twitched sideways under the impact of the next best thing to five thousand foot/pounds of energy. The spitzer-pointed bullet smashed home less than an inch from the base of its triangular left ear, where the bone was thinner. But it was swinging its head as he fired, changing the angle, and not even that mighty round could penetrate its skull, despite the skill with which it had been placed. It could only *hurt* the monster, not kill it, and it shook itself and slid sideways, squalling in pain and fury, as it braked and pivoted towards whatever had attacked it.

Adkok worked the bolt.

The Imperial Charisian Army—and the Imperial Charisian Marines—routinely practiced the "mad minute drill," an exercise which required marksmen to fire as many aimed shots as possible in one minute. The ICA record was thirty-five aimed shots and thirty-five hits. Adkok's best personal record was thirty-two, just over one round every two seconds.

Today, his second shot was barely a second behind the first.

The great dragon was still turning when the second bullet hammered its forehead, the only part of its head presented to the sergeant as it turned. It was a direct, no-deflection hit, but the forehead was also the thickest part of the creature's skull. Bone broke as the bullet blasted a divot out of it, but it didn't penetrate, and then the dragon had turned, faced Adkok fully.

It launched itself straight at him.

Sergeant Jyrohm Adkok, Imperial Charisian Marines, fired his last round with the muzzle of his rifle twenty-three inches from the great dragon's gaping jaws. The bullet ripped into the creature's mouth, penetrated its palate, slammed up into its skull . . . but it missed the brain.

The dragon shrieked as its left eye socket exploded in blood, instead. It twisted with the sudden agony, but it hit Adkok's fallen tree like a two-and-a-half-ton battering ram. The log flew aside and the hideous jaws yawned wide, but the impact had already crushed the sergeant's ribs, shattered his spine.

He was dead before they closed upon him.

▼ ▼ ▼

This part of the trail was straighter than the rest of it, and Lywys Whytmyn's gorge rose as he looked back. He would never forget the glimpse he had of the great dragon mauling Jyrohm Adkok's body, but the sergeant had hurt it, hurt it badly enough to divert it at least momentarily from its other prey. Its rage was obvious as it rent and tore its tormentor, and the young Dohlaran felt the hot burn of shame as he galloped down the trail, abandoning the Guardsman. But he also remembered the last thing Adkok had said to him. He wasn't going to waste the respite, however fleeting, the sergeant had purchased with his life, and he urged his horse to even greater speed as he galloped after Alahnah and the other women.

He thundered around a bend in the trail, and his head came up as someone screamed. He caught a glimpse of a horse stumbling, going down. A small, long-haired body flew through the air as Gladys Frymyn was thrown from its saddle. She hurtled headfirst into the trees beside the trail and cried out again as her shoulder slammed into the bole of a massive nearoak and shattered. She bounced back only to hit a heaved-up slab of rock, then slithered limply to the ground, and terror filled Lywys Whytmyn.

He'd never imagined feeling so frightened in his entire life. All he wanted to do was to run, to go *on* running, just as hard and as fast as he could. But instead he started to rein in, already preparing to dismount.

And that was when Alahnah's mare came bolting back up the trail.

The princess reeled in the saddle, blood streaming from a gash on her forehead, and Whytmyn's heart froze as he realized she was barely able to cling her mount . . . and that it was galloping straight back towards the great dragon which had killed Adkok.

"*Go!*" someone screamed.

His eyes darted towards the voice, and he saw Stefyny Athrawes standing in the trail. He hadn't even seen her dismount, but she'd sprinted to Gladys' side, and somehow she'd snatched the rifle from her own saddle scabbard. It was identical to the one Taigys Mahldyn had built for Cayleb Ahrmahk.

"*Go!*" she screamed again, pointing after Alahnah with her free hand, then went down on one knee beside the unconscious girl. Whytmyn had one more glimpse of her, calmly breaking the rifle open, checking the loads, and then he'd whirled his own mount around and gone galloping after Alahnah.

▼ ▼ ▼

Alahnah's mare rounded the bend.

The princess was barely conscious, staying in the saddle more by instinct than by intent. But good as those instincts and her training were, she almost lost her seat as the mare came face-to-face with the wounded great dragon.

Alahnah never realized, then or later, how merciful her semi-consciousness actually was. It kept her from seeing the tattered, brutally mauled, half-eaten remnant of Jyrohm Adkok's body. But it also precluded her exerting any sort of control over the mare as the terrified horse swerved yet again and went galloping headlong into the woods beside the trail.

She was aware enough to lean forward, lying flat, wrapping her arms as far around the horse's neck as she could. Branches whipped over her, slammed her from either side, battered her black and blue, but they couldn't sweep her from the saddle. She managed to stay with the horse, yet a corner of her wavering, half-stunned brain realized it was only a matter of time before the mare went down over a fallen trunk or smashed headfirst into one of the towering nearoaks. And when that happened—

She managed to turn her head partway, and her heart rose in her throat as she saw the great dragon charging after her.

It was far, far larger than the mare. It couldn't fit through the eye-of-the-needle spaces the horse could thread, but it didn't have to, either. It tore through the dense, low-growing tangles of the needle trees which looped through the nearoaks like one of Duke Delthak's steam-powered bulldozers, splintering the undergrowth aside. The obstacles slowed it, but they couldn't stop it, and even hindered as it was, it was gaining.

▼ ▼ ▼

Stefyny Athrawes watched through the SNARC's remotes as the smaller of the great dragons, the one which had killed Corporal Strathmohr, rampaged up the trail in the wake of Alahnah's mare. It had lingered to finish killing Strathmohr's horse, which was the only reason Alahnah had escaped it, and Stefyny knew she and Gladys wouldn't. Just as she knew what had happened to Sergeant Adkok.

But unlike Adkok, she also knew exactly what—and where—the great dragon was ... and *her* rifle was no M897.

She settled into a kneeling position behind the upthrust of rock Gladys had hit and leveled the heavy double rifle across the stone. That rifle weighed over fifteen pounds—it had a *lot* of recoil to absorb—and she wanted all the support for it she could get. She normally preferred the prone position for precision shooting, but the recoil of the massive .625 round would almost certainly have broken her collarbone, despite the rifle's weight. Besides, she couldn't be positive the predator would come straight in. If it swerved at the last moment, came around her flank, she needed to be able to adjust quickly and—

The great dragon charged around the bend. Fast as it came, it wasn't at full speed. Its head was up, tracking from side to side, and great dragons hunted as much by sight as by smell. Stefyny's horse had fled into the woods, but Gladys' struggled to get up, squealing with the agony of a badly broken leg. Its struggles attracted the great dragon's attention, and it slowed, then flowed through dappled shadow and shade towards the crippled horse like a huge, dark shadow of death.

The gelding saw it coming. It lunged one last time, fighting to rise and run, then screamed in terror just before the dragon hit it, and Stefyny felt her mind try to crawl into a hole and hide as the monster ripped into the hapless mount. At least the screaming stopped quickly, but the ghastly, wet, rending sounds seemed to go on much longer. A part of her hoped they'd go on still longer, keep the great dragon distracted. But then its gore-dripping muzzle came up. Its head swiveled in Stefyny's direction, she heard the boiler-steam hiss of its territorial fury, and it launched itself straight at her and the unconscious Gladys.

She drew a deep breath, exhaled half of it, and wrapped the hours she'd spent on rifle and pistol ranges with her mother and father around her like a cloak. Her entire world focused down to the sight picture, and the sudden thunderbolt bellow as the trigger broke, and the brutal recoil that hammered her shoulder, surprised her, exactly the way they were supposed to.

The great dragon's enormous head flew up as the thousand-grain bullet smashed into its forehead. It struck almost exactly where Adkok's bullet had hit its mate, but Adkok's bullet had carried 4,665 foot/pounds of energy; Stefyny's carried 9,800, more than twice as much.

It slammed through the massive bone like an awl, and the great dragon's whistling shriek died in mid-breath. It stumbled, feet going out from under it, and drove forward like an out-of-control cruiser. Its snout plowed a furrow through the leaf mold, careering toward Stefyny as if determined to complete its charge even in death.

It slithered to a halt, ten feet from her, and quivered, legs still thrashing. She watched it for a moment, then stood, astounded to discover that her own knees didn't even tremble. She stepped a few feet closer to the enormous carcass, then put the muzzle of the rifle two feet from its skull, an inch in front of its right ear, and squeezed the trigger again.

▼ ▼ ▼

Lywys Whytmyn bent as low in the saddle as he could, whipping the gelding's flank with the ends of his reins to urge it to even greater speed.

The horse was willing enough, he reflected in the jagged bursts of thought burning through his desperation. Or perhaps it just hadn't realized what they were pursuing as they charged along the path the great dragon had ripped through the forest. The footing was treacherous even there, and the chance of the horse going down was terrifyingly high at his furious pace, but it was the only way he could possibly catch up. He didn't know what he was going to do if he did catch up. He'd never hunted slash lizards before, and Emperor Cayleb and his friends had been exquisitely tactful about his choice of weapons. The custom-made rifle—it had been his grandfather's, made to his exact measure by the great

Delthak gunmaker Mahldyn, and it was one of Lywys Whytmyn's most prized possessions—was superbly accurate and more than capable of dropping any prong buck ever born. But it would have been out of its class even against the slash lizard they'd thought they were going to hunt, far less the great dragons which had decided to hunt *them*.

It was all he had, though, and he could never go home, face his family, without at least trying. Worse, he could never have faced his grandfather's ghost . . . or himself.

On the flat, the great dragon would have been faster, at least in a sprint, than his horse. Thanks to its need to batter its way through the needle trees, he was able to gain on it, but he knew it was gaining on Alahnah even more quickly. He could catch only glimpses of the fleeing mare between the tree trunks, but despite its terror, its strength was clearly beginning to fail. He had no idea how Alahnah had stayed with it this far. He'd ridden all his life, and he knew he couldn't have done it. But how much longer could—

The mare gathered itself to leap across a fallen tree.

It didn't make it.

Its knees hit an upthrust limb, it somersaulted in midair, and Alahnah flew out of the saddle, curling instinctively into a ball as she arced upward. The tree had torn a hole in the canopy when it went down, and scrub trees and underbrush had taken advantage of the sunlight, growing thick and luxuriant in the clearing it had made, denser and taller than the needle trees. She smashed into a young nearoak sapling, crying out as ribs broke, then thudded to the ground.

The great dragon paused to finish off her thrashing, crying horse.

She pushed herself to her knees in the underbrush, breathing around the knife-blade pain in her chest, and the great dragon's head rose, blood dripping from its jaws. It turned, craning its neck, looking for her with its single functional eye.

It found her, and she watched it settle, crouch on all

six limbs, prepare to pounce, and knew she was about to die.

CRAAACK!

Her head snapped around as she heard the rifle shot, and her eyes widened as she saw Lywys Whytmyn, standing on the ground, his prong buck rifle at his shoulder.

"*Run, Alahnah!*" he shouted, and squeezed the trigger again.

CRAAACK!

The bullet smashed into the side of the dragon's already wounded head. It was too light to inflict significant damage, but it was heavy enough to hurt, and the predator screamed in fresh, goaded rage. It turned towards him, and Alahnah realized what he was doing.

He couldn't kill it. He *knew* he couldn't. All he was trying to do was distract it, draw its attention. To goad it into chasing and killing *him* to give her a few more minutes to run.

"*Run,* Goddamn it! *Run!*"

CRAAACK!

Somehow, she clawed to her feet, unable to see through her tears, knowing what had to happen. Knowing she wouldn't escape in the end, anyway. It would kill him, and then it would kill her, and he would have died for *nothing*. But if he was going to try, then she had to try, too.

CRAAACK!

The great dragon shrieked, and then it was hurtling through the trees straight at Lywys Whytmyn. He stood his ground, watching it come, and squeezed the trigger yet again.

CRAAACK!

It was close enough he saw the bullet hit, saw the hide ripple and the blood splash away from the impact, and it didn't even slow. It only kept coming, and he drew what he knew would be his final breath and—

"*Down, Lywys!*"

The deep, resonant bass shout came from behind him.

He had one fleeting instant to begin to recognize it, and then Merlin Athrawes flew over his head in a running broad jumper's leap which had to be impossible even for a *seijin*. He traveled over forty-five feet through the air, hurtling through the leaves and scrub branches in his path like a boulder.

Whytmyn staggered back a stride as Merlin hit the ground perfectly, impossibly balanced, directly between him and the charging great dragon, and the *seijin*'s curved blade was suddenly in his hands.

The predator's head came up, its forefeet digging into the soft earth and leaves. Not in panic, but in surprise as the insignificant, puny mite appeared so abruptly in front of it.

And then it got another surprise as the battle-steel katana came down in a two-handed overhand stroke and the enormous skull which had laughed at Jyrohm Adkok's and Lywys Whytmyn's rifle bullets split in a steaming explosion of gray and red.

▼ ▼ ▼

"Merlin! Oh, *Merlin*!"

Alahnah stumbled out of the undergrowth, hobbling, arched forward around the stabbing hurt of broken ribs but holding out her arms. And then Merlin was there, his arms around her, one hand gentle on the back of her head as she pressed her cheek against his breastplate and sobbed. In that instant, she was six years old again, safe in the arms of her godfather, who would never— *ever*—let anything hurt her.

But she wasn't six anymore, and she knew what had happened to her Marines, and nothing would ever be the same again.

"I'm here, Bug," his deep voice rumbled in her ear, using the childhood nickname only he had ever bestowed upon her. "I'm here."

She wept even harder, but then, suddenly, she stiffened.

"*Stefyny!*" she gasped. "Gladys!"

"Stefyny is fine," he told her. "Gladys is hurt, banged

up quite a bit worse than you are, but I think she's going to be fine, eventually, too."

Alahnah sagged in relief, but then she pulled back, raising her head to stare up at him through the hazy veil of her tears. He'd never lied to her, but how could he—?

"How do you *know* that?" she asked, desperate to believe he wasn't just saying it to soothe her incipient hysteria.

"I'm a *seijin*," he told her with a crooked smile. This was *not* the time to be telling her about com links and wetware. "We *seijins* know these things."

"I'm sure you do," another voice said from behind him, and he and Alahnah turned. Lywys Whytmyn stood beside the downed great dragon, looking down at a split skull almost as long as Alahnah was tall.

"I'm sure you do," he repeated, looking up at Merlin. "But how did you get here so quickly? And how—?"

He gestured at that riven skull, and his eyes were dark.

"I know *seijins* can do wondrous things, Merlin, but there are limits in everything. *How* do you know Stefyny and Gladys are safe? And how did you get here in time to save our lives?"

Merlin considered the young man whose unwavering eyes looked more like Lywys Gardynyr's than ever. He'd always suspected there was a lot of his grandfather in young Lywys; now he knew.

Merlin Athrawes would be a long time forgiving himself for letting any of this happen. Intellectually, he knew his bitter self-condemnation was unreasonable. For that matter, he was no longer the only one with SNARC access and he wasn't the only one who'd been blindsided, but that didn't help his heart and emotions one bit. The SNARCs had swept the foothills for possible *human* threats, but it had never occurred to him to check for *non*human dangers. He'd fully intended to keep a remote hovering overhead when they eventually set out after the slash lizard Baron Deep Valley had invited them to hunt. Not even slash lizards would attack a party the size of the hunting expedition without severe provocation, however, so he'd seen no rush to start looking for them yet.

But great dragons weren't slash lizards, and they *would* attack anything that even looked like infringing upon their range.

This pair must have moved in only in the last five-day or so, or Deep Valley's huntsmen and foresters would have known about them. Great dragons were seldom shy about keeping their presence a secret. He didn't know—they'd probably never know—what had attracted these two to this stretch of foothills. The hunting was more than adequate for a slash lizard or two, but feeding a pair of great dragons would have stripped it of prey fairly quickly, although they might well have expected the nearby flocks of sheep to help keep them fed. He wondered if they'd located a likely spot for a lair. It was early in the year for them to be thinking about breeding, but not *too* early, and breeding great dragons split the child-rearing duties. The dam stayed home, nursing their young, guarding the den, while the sire ranged broadly, finding prey, killing it, and dragging it home. In fact, they usually limited their hunting in proximity to the den, because they needed to leave prey for their young to practice hunting as they became more venturesome. And if that was what had drawn them here, that might explain why they'd been hyper-territorial even for great dragons.

But whatever their reasons, he was the one who hadn't spotted them. Who'd let them get close enough to kill Bynyt and all of his Marines . . . and come within an eyelash of killing Whytmyn and Alahnah.

And they *would* have killed Alahnah, before even Merlin could have reached them, if Lywys Whytmyn hadn't deliberately drawn the attack down upon himself, knowing it would kill him.

Yet he couldn't dwell on that now, because Whytmyn's questions demanded answers, and there were likely to be other questions, as well. Like how he'd known what was happening and exactly where to go. How he'd gotten here so quickly on two feet, when the mounted rescue party was still ten minutes away. How he'd downed a great dragon with only a sword.

It's the krakens all over again, he thought, remembering a hot, sunny afternoon on Helen Island. *And Cayleb and the damned slash lizard, too, for that matter! But with a lot more witnesses this time. Thank God none of the others saw me moving after I killed the governors, but Lywys and Alahnah sure as hell did!*

"Those are very good questions, Lywys," he said after a moment. "I could say this is all *seijin*'s business, but I owe you more than that. We all do. Without you, none of this would matter because not even I could've gotten here in time to save Alahnah. And I know exactly what you did . . . and why. Trust me, this afternoon, you've repaid any debt you or your family may ever have thought they owed Cleddyf or Gwyliwr. Or me."

"I—"

The young man broke off, looking at the rifle still in his hands, then raised his head again.

"I tried," he said. "But without you. . . ."

"A team effort, then."

Merlin unwrapped his right arm from Alahnah and extended his hand. Whytmyn glanced at it for a moment, then clasped forearms with him, still looking steadily into his eyes.

"And because it was a team effort," Merlin continued, "you—both of you—are going to have to learn a secret. A secret men and women have died to keep. The most important secret in the entire world." He gripped Whytmyn's arm firmly, holding those steady eyes with his own. "You've earned the truth, and I promise that's what you'll be told, but I can't tell you right now. Cayleb will be here in just a few more minutes, and Baron Deep Valley and everyone else with him. This is something that needs to be discussed in privacy, and I badly want Archbishop Maikel and Bishop Paityr to be part of that discussion."

Something like relief flickered in the backs of Whytmyn's eyes as he heard those two names, and he nodded.

"And in the meantime," Merlin said in a much more resigned tone, looking down at the mountain of dead great dragon, "I see the legend of *Seijin* Merlin is about to get a fresh infusion." He shook his head and looked back up, smiling wryly at both of them. "I suppose it was inevitable. I haven't done anything this . . . splashy in years now."

"'Splashy,'" Whytmyn repeated, and startled himself with a laugh. "I guess that's *one* way to describe it."

"Just do me one favor, both of you," Merlin continued as they heard the sounds of horses forcing their way through the woods towards them.

"What?" Alahnah asked, looking up at him.

"*Please* don't get carried away oohing and ahing about this." He shook his head. "In fact, if both of you could just tell everyone you're in such a state of shock you don't remember exactly what happened, that would be wonderful."

They stared at him, and he shook his head again.

"I've spent the last dozen years living down the 'sinister, supernatural, demonic *Seijin* Merlin' narrative. I really, *really* don't want to start that whole thing up again!"

. II .

Archbishop's Palace,
City of Tellesberg,
Kingdom of Old Charis,
Empire of Charis.

Sharleyan Ahrmahk stood as Lywys Whytmyn followed Alys Vraidahn into Maikel Staynair's study. Mistress Vraidahn, who'd been Staynair's housekeeper for almost thirty years and had become an official house mother for all of the Dohlaran nobles attending the Royal College, had greeted him with a huge embrace, kissed his cheek, and then insisted on personally escorting him, rather than letting him find his own way to the study he'd visited so many times.

He stepped through the door, past Major Athrawes,

then paused as Sharleyan walked straight to him and wrapped her arms around him. He stood for a moment, frozen, as she laid her head on his shoulder. Then his own arms went around her.

"Thank you," she said softly. "*Thank* you for my daughter's life."

"Your Majesty, I—" Whytmyn broke off, looking over her head with a helpless expression as Cayleb and Alahnah rose from their own chairs. Then he drew a deep breath. "Your Majesty, it was Merlin who saved *both* of us. I only sort of . . . got in its way."

"And don't think I haven't already thanked *him*, too," Sharleyan replied, never taking her head from his shoulder. "My family's had a lot of practice thanking him. But you're the only reason he had time to get there. And I know exactly what you did, Lywys. It was a lot more than 'just getting in the way.'"

There was an odd note of assurance in her voice, he thought. As if she spoke from *personal* knowledge.

"It was, indeed, my son," Archbishop Maikel said, entering the study from a side door with Bishop Paityr Wylsynn.

Sharleyan released Whytmyn with a last squeeze and stepped back as the Dohlaran turned to face the prelates. Staynair extended his hand, and Whytmyn bent to kiss his ring, then straightened.

"I understand you're here for an explanation," Bishop Paityr said as the younger man turned towards him. He didn't offer his own ring, only waving his hand for Whytmyn to stay where he was, but he did smile in welcome. In fact, it looked almost more like a *grin* than a smile, Whytmyn thought.

"The *seijin* is very good at making explanations," Wylsynn continued with that almost impish expression. "He's had a lot of practice. In fact, he made exactly the same explanation to me in this very study."

"He did?" Surprise startled the question out of Whytmyn, and the bishop chuckled.

"Oh, yes! Not that he didn't get a few surprises of his own out of the conversation."

"Don't tease the boy, Paityr!" Staynair's admonition sounded stern, but it was accompanied by an undeniable twinkle. "Curiosity's eating him alive, and no wonder! His introduction to the secret was just a bit more traumatic than yours, if I'm remembering correctly."

"That's certainly fair," Wylsynn agreed more soberly.

"Then why don't all of us find chairs and let Merlin get started doing that explaining.

▼ ▼ ▼

"This is going to take some getting used to," Lywys Whytmyn said, the better part of three hours later, looking back and forth between Merlin, the archbishop, and the emperor and empress.

"Is that what they call 'Dohlaran understatement'?" Alahnah Ahrmahk asked from the chair beside his.

Her expression was even more thunderstruck than his, but then again, he hadn't just discovered he'd lived his entire life in the very midst of what was probably the greatest secret in human history without ever even suspecting the truth.

"Merlin," the princess continued, turning with the caution of three broken, tightly strapped ribs, to the tall, broad-shouldered *seijin* she'd just discovered had once been a woman named Nimue Alban—the woman her own middle name memorialized. "I've always known you and Nimue are more than human. I just . . . just never suspected how *much* more!"

"We are what we are, Bug," he told her, touching her cheek with the hand which had tied one of the pokers from the archbishop's fireplace tools into a knot in a casual demonstration of his genuinely superhuman strength.

"More importantly, Alahnah," Staynair said gently, "they are *who* they are. Yes, their bodies—their PICAs—let them accomplish 'impossible' feats, but it's the minds, the *souls*, inside those bodies that make them the remarkable people they are."

"Spare our blushes, Maikel," another voice said dryly from the "com" lying on one corner of Staynair's desk.

"Poor old Merlin's stuck in the same room with you, but *I* can always just turn off the com if you get too mushy."

Alahnah surprised herself with a giggle, and Bishop Paityr smiled encouragingly.

"I admit it's difficult not to venerate the pair of them, Your Highness," he told her. "Fortunately, as you just heard, they don't approve of that attitude. And given that you've been exposed to Merlin's so-called sense of humor for your entire life, I'm sure you can understand how we get past our initial awestruck response to the truth."

"I don't have that advantage, My Lord." Whytmyn shook his head. "I think it's going to be harder for me. And it's going to be even harder to wrap my mind around the truth about Langhorne and the Church!"

"It always is, my son." Staynair's tone was compassionate. "And that's the true reason we try to be so insanely cautious about revealing that truth to just anyone. Not everyone takes it as well as the two of you have."

"I can believe that, Your Eminence," Whytmyn said slowly, his eyes suddenly intent as he looked at the archbishop, and then at Cayleb and Merlin. "And I have to wonder what would have happened if we hadn't taken it so well?"

"It would've been ... messy, Lywys," Merlin said, looking at him levelly. "There was a time when our only real option would have been the one I'm sure just occurred to you."

"You mean you would've had to kill us." Alahnah's voice was soft and her eyes were huge and dark as she looked at her mother and father, but those eyes were also unflinching, and Merlin felt a fresh swell of pride as she proved once again that she was her parents' daughter.

"Once, yes," he acknowledged, equally unflinching, before either of them could speak. "We have other options now, though."

"What sort of 'options'?"

"We try *so* hard not to tell anyone we aren't certain

can handle the truth," Sharleyan said, taking her daughter's hand in hers. "Sometimes, though, despite everything, we're wrong about that." She shook her head, her eyes suddenly soft with tears. "One of them was Ruhsyl."

"Ruhsyl?" Whytmyn repeated, his tone suddenly sharper. "Excuse me, Your Majesty, but do you mean Ruhsyl *Thairis*? Duke Eastshare?"

"Yes," she said sadly. "He didn't—he *couldn't*—accept the truth about the Church. He tried. I think he really and truly *tried,* as hard as he could, because he loved me so much. But he couldn't."

"Mama, Uncle Ruhsyl *died,*" Alahnah said, her eyes wide with horror. "Did you—you and Daddy and Merlin—?"

"No, Alahnah. Ruhsyl didn't die," Merlin said, his own expression as sad as Sharleyan's. "I'm not sure what actually happened isn't almost as bad, in a way, but we didn't have to kill him. His 'heart attack' was nothing of the sort, although it's not the healers' fault they couldn't find a pulse when they examined him, and he's in Nimue's Cave right this moment, in the same sort of cryo sleep as the colonists who came to Safehold before the 'Creation.' He'll be just fine—physically—the day we can wake him up again. But we don't know how long that will be, and it's entirely possible everyone he ever knew will be gone by then."

Whytmyn swallowed hard, trying to imagine what that would be like. To awaken fifty years, or a hundred—or, like Nimue Alban herself, a *thousand*—years into an unknown future. Merlin was right, he realized. It might almost be better to have died.

"That's the true quandary, Lywys," Cayleb said, and Whytmyn looked at him. "We can't tell anyone we don't already totally trust—only the people who are closest to us or to other members of the 'inner circle.' Yet we always know that the instant we tell them—tell our friends, people we *love*—we may sentence them to something like what happened to Ruhsyl." He shook his head, his own eyes sad, haunted. "Ruhsyl would have *died* for

Sharleyan, for any of us, and we would have died for him. But in the end, we pushed him that one step too far, and I will always regret the fact that I was the one who cast the deciding vote."

"You couldn't have known," Sharleyan said softly.

"No," Cayleb replied bleakly. "But you were against it. I should have listened."

"And if I'd been positive, I wouldn't have agreed with you in the end," she said unflinchingly. "We're not arch-angels, love. All we can do is the best we can do, and that's what you've always done."

"Are . . . are there very many others who reacted that way?" Whytmyn asked.

"No." Merlin shook his head. "No, there are actually only a very few—fewer than I would've expected, really—and we've been expanding the 'circle' for years now. Of course, we haven't expanded it very quickly, and the Brothers of Saint Zherneau still vet our candidates for us. They're very good at it—they've been doing it for a long time—and we normally think long and hard before we tell anyone. For that matter, we practically never deviate from the Brethren's original policy of never telling anyone before their thirtieth birthday. Usually, at least. Sometimes, though, events . . . force our hand."

"That's one way to put it," Cayleb said dryly. Whytmyn glanced at him, and the emperor chuckled. "They didn't tell *me* the truth—not the complete truth—until I'd been king for almost four months! I'd been cleared for Merlin's original 'the *seijin* sees visions' story, and that's still incredibly useful to us, but the Brethren didn't really want to tell even me the full truth. They just didn't have much choice."

"Fair's fair," Merlin said mildly. "Maikel hadn't told *me* about 'Saint Zherneau' until the day we both told you!" He looked at Whytmyn. "Trust me, there are plenty of layers to this onion, Lywys."

"And Cayleb didn't tell *me* the truth—the full truth— until after Saint Agtha's," Sharleyan added. "The problem is that it's not something you can *un*-tell someone, which is why we have to think so very carefully before we tell anyone."

"And if one of us, even both of us, hadn't been willing or able to accept it, we would've had 'heart attacks,'" Whytmyn said.

"Not necessarily." Merlin shook his head. "Or, not in the way you may be thinking, at any rate. Yes, you would've had to 'die' as far as the rest of Safehold knew. That's what I meant when I said it would have gotten messy, especially if both of you suddenly dropped dead at the same time so soon after the great dragons. But it was Ruhsyl's choice to go into suspended animation. We would have been perfectly willing to keep him under what I suppose you'd call 'house arrest' in Nimue's Cave, where he would have had access to all of our books and records, and even to the SNARCs. We've done *that* in a few cases, as well. When we could cover for the person involved's extended absence, we've even brought some of them home again after they'd had a chance to fully examine the evidence. We couldn't explain away that long an absence in his case, though. And, even if we could have, I think it hurt him too much to know the truth when he couldn't *accept* the truth."

"Ruhsyl never gave less than his complete heart to anything he believed in," Sharleyan said sadly.

"That's true," Bishop Paityr said, but his tone was brisker, more bracing than hers had been. She looked at him, and he shook his head with a sympathetic smile. "It *is* true, Sharley, but as I believe you just said to Cayleb, all we can do is the best we can do, and that's exactly what you've always done, too. So instead of dwelling on the occasional inevitable moments when we come up short of divine perfection, let's focus on what happens when things go right. Like tonight." He smiled warmly at Whytmyn and Alahnah. "It seems to me it's pretty clear neither Lywys nor Alahnah is going to opt for state confinement in the Cave!"

"I believe you can safely assume that, My Lord," Whytmyn said dryly. "Of course, if you hadn't pulled out that 'Stone of Schueler' you'd only have my unsupported word for it."

"Handy things to have around, those 'holy artifacts,'" Wylsynn agreed. "Especially since most of the 'genuine' artifacts really do work. Of course, there's a downside to it, as well. That sort of evidence of divine intervention does give the stamp of approval to Mother Church, doesn't it?"

"Yes, it does. But it sounds to me like it can also turn around and bite the 'archangels'' original plan," Whytmyn observed. "Like now, and the Stone."

"It's still going to take getting used to," Alahnah observed.

"Oh, trust me, that's something all of us understand!" Her mother gave her a quick hug. "All of us except Merlin and Nimue, at any rate."

"I believe you can safely assume the Commodore's explanation to me—or mine to Nimue, now that I think about it—carried its own *'what* did you say?' quotient," Merlin assured her. "And I believe I just mentioned Maikel's little surprise, for that matter." He smiled at Alahnah. "Fortunately, you've got a pretty good support team to help you cope with it."

"To help *both* of you cope with it," Cayleb said. "I think it would be a very good idea for all of us to take a family vacation in the wake of what just happened in Deep Valley. It'll let us get away from the Palace for a bit and give us the opportunity to answer some of the dozens of other questions I know from personal experience are going to occur to you, Alahnah. I'm thinking that we might take the *Ahlfryd* out for a five-day cruise or so."

His daughter nodded, slowly at first, and then harder.

"I think that would be a really good idea, Dad. Because right this minute, I'm still pretty dazed. I'm sure a lot of those questions are going to come along the instant I get over the stunned part of all this."

"Of course they will. They always do, trust me!" her father assured her. "And because that's true," he added with a wicked smile, "I suppose we'd better invite Lywys along so we can deal with *his* questions, too. Does that sound like a good idea to you?"

"Yes," Crown Princess Alahnah Ahrmahk said with commendable steadiness despite her slight but unmistakable blush. "Yes, Dad. I think it sounds like a *very* good idea."

AUGUST YEAR OF GOD 911

·◆·

.I.
Five Islands,
Maddox Province,
East Harchong,
Harchong Empire;
and
Nimue's Cave,
Mountains of Light,
Episcopate of St. Ehrnesteen,
The Temple Lands.

"Sergeant Major?"

Mangzhee Zhang looked up from the ledger with a frown as Tyngchen Zhu opened his office door and scurried through it. Zhu was in her late thirties, the widow of one of Earl Rainbow Waters' veterans, and the quality he most strongly associated with her was calm. Or serenity, perhaps. She'd seen—and survived—enough that nothing seemed to faze her, and while her official title was simply "chambermaid," she functioned as the assistant housekeeper and when old Madam Chyrzhi finally retired, she would undoubtedly move into that spot on a formal basis.

But that serenity seemed in short supply this morning.

"What is it, Tyngchen?" he asked.

"Zungnan needs you," She was actually wringing her hands, and Zhang realized she hovered on the edge of tears. No, that there *were* tears in her eyes. "He needs you now in . . . in the Earl's bedchamber."

The majordomo stiffened.

Countess Rainbow Waters was due back from the Temple Lands on the afternoon steam automotive, and the earl had announced that he intended to meet her at the station. He'd been more tired than usual for the last two or three five-days, and Zhang and Zungnan Tyan, his valet, had joined forces, presenting a joint front and insisting that in that case, he needed to catch a quick nap first. But from Tyngchen's expression—

Mangzhee Zhang shoved to his feet so violently his chair crashed over onto its back and headed out of his office at a run.

▼ ▼ ▼

"I'm so sorry, Aunt Hyngpau," Medyng Hwojahn said, wrapping his arms around her. "Sahmantha and I got there as quickly as we could, but he was already gone. In fact, he was gone when Zungnan went to get him up."

Hyngpau Daiyang nodded, pressing her face into his shoulder. There were no tears—not yet. She would save those until she had seen her husband. But that didn't mean there were none in her heart.

"I was at the Palace when they found him, Hyngpau," Sahmantha Hwojahn said.

Anything less like a typical Harchongese woman than Baroness Wind Song would have been hard to imagine. She was three inches taller than the countess, with dark blond hair, brown eyes, and a pronounced Temple Lands accent, but she'd adopted traditional Harchong fashion enthusiastically after her marriage. Indeed, Countess Rainbow Waters' elegant, Zion-made gown was far more "eastern" than anything the baroness was likely to wear these days.

And she'd known Earl Rainbow Waters since she was twenty-two years old . . . and come to love him just as much as her husband did.

"I got there even before Medyng," she continued. "I

know it's probably not a lot right now, but I think he went very peacefully." Her voice trembled, and Countess Rainbow Waters reached out a quick hand to her without ever withdrawing from her nephew's embrace. "He just . . . went to sleep," Sahmantha said, blinking on tears of her own. "And he woke up with God, not us."

"You're wrong, my dear," the countess told her, squeezing her hand. "It means a great deal, knowing he had such an easy end." She inhaled deeply. "After what those . . . those *bastards* did to him and the entire Host, he deserved to go easily. And you're right about where he is right now, but, oh, I already *miss* him so!"

"We all do," Wind Song said. "I think it'll be a long time before we realize everything we've lost with him, but we already know that much."

"We should've had at least ten more years," the countess said, still holding Sahmantha's hand and closing her eyes. "At least ten. Clyntahn and that pig Zhyou-Zhwo took those from us, too. Along with *so* much else."

"Yes, they did," Wind Song agreed. "But in the end, it cost Clyntahn his life—not to mention his immortal soul! I'm fairly sure Langhorne's not going to be all that eager to welcome Zhyou-Zhwo, either. And whatever the Archangels have in store for him in the *next* world," the baron's voice held nothing but grim satisfaction, "Uncle Taychau made damned sure he wasn't going to enjoy his life in this one! How many men can lose half a continent out of sheer stupidity?"

"That's Taychau talking," the countess said with a watery chuckle, hugging the nephew who'd long since become the son she'd never had.

"No, Aunt Hyngpau," he told her. "That's *history* talking."

▼ ▼ ▼

"He's right about that," Nahrmahn Baytz said somberly, and Merlin nodded.

He'd made the flight to Nimue's Cave from Chisholm, where Cayleb, Sharleyan, and their children were currently ensconced, to collect a rather special birthday present for Domynyk Maikel. The boy was only four years old, which was still on the young side for the complete, upgraded Federation nanotech he'd designed for the rest of the inner circle. The mil spec self-repair nanites could be more than a little too aggressive, especially the way he'd tweaked them, for a child. But Owl had long since whipped up a version that upgraded the standard childhood package only slightly. It would make him equally disease-resistant and provide a somewhat gentler regeneration capability, and he was finally old enough to receive it. There'd been no need for Merlin to come collect Domynyk Maikel's injection in person; Owl was more than capable of delivering it so stealthily no one would ever notice. But he liked to touch base with the cave physically every few months.

Maybe even more important than that, though, was how much he enjoyed excuses to strap himself into the recon skimmer. There were a lot fewer of those than there'd been during the Jihad.

"I do wish he and his wife had had those extra years, though," he continued now, sitting back in one of the chairs at the circular table. "Not just because they deserved them, either. We needed him, Nahrmahn."

"No, we'll *miss* him," Nahrmahn corrected gently. "Wind Song's ready, Merlin. He's been ready for years now. I know he hates the very thought of stepping into the Earl's shoes, but that's only because they were his uncle's shoes and he wishes Rainbow Waters was still here to fill them. Do you really think any of East Harchong's policies are going to change?"

"No," Merlin said after a moment, and Nahrmahn nodded.

"Of course they aren't! Why should they? That parliament notion Tymythy Rhobair and Vicar Zherohmy sold to Rainbow Waters was brilliant, and we didn't even have to suggest it to them!" The avatar's lips twitched, despite his somber mood. "And Wind Song's contribution to the new franchise qualifications was inspired."

"I suspect the constitution they voted out gave the

executive a little more power than he or his uncle expected," Merlin observed.

"Actually, I suspect it may be a little more power than he or his uncle *wanted*," Nahrmahn replied.

"Probably." Merlin nodded. "Mind you, I think he'll find out he needs it, whatever he may've thought he wanted. But you're right about how smart the lot of them were. The people of East Harchong *are* invested in their own rule now, and they *will* fight to the death to keep it, and they couldn't have a better head of state for that than Wind Song. Only I guess we should really start thinking about him as Rainbow Waters. After all, he's the earl now, isn't he?"

"Legally, under the terms of his uncle's will." Nahrmahn shrugged. "Personally, I make the odds sixty-forty he lets the title lapse. It's not like he or any of his descendants will ever regain the earldom, anyway. And I think . . . I think he doesn't want there to be any confusion about which 'Rainbow Waters' they're talking about when they start writing the history of everything the Earl managed to accomplish."

"You don't think that will disappoint his aunt?"

"I think his aunt thinks he's his uncle's true memorial," Nahrmahn said. "And if he wants to let the title go, let it 'stay with' the Earl, I think she'll understand."

"Won't hurt anything for him to stand in his own right, either, I suppose." Nahrmahn arched an eyebrow, and Merlin shrugged and then smiled. "In the history books, I mean. God knows he already stands on his own where the Host—and now their Parliament—is concerned!"

"That's true." Nahrmahn nodded. "Like I say, we'll miss the Earl, but overall, I think East Harchong's in excellent hands, Merlin. Sure as hell better hands than *South* Harchong, anyway!"

NOVEMBER YEAR OF GOD 911

·◆·

.I.
Room 307,
King Haarahld VII Hall,
Royal College Campus,
and
Archbishop Maikel's private chapel,
Archbishop's Palace,
City of Tellesberg,
Kingdom of Old Charis,
Charisian Empire.

"Oh, *thank* you both for coming!" Princess Rahnyldah said, looking up from the opened books and drifts of notepaper which festooned the library-style tables. "If I don't get this equation nailed down for Doctor Mahklyn, he is *so* going to pin my ears back in class tomorrow!"

"Oh, don't be silly!" Crown Princess Alahnah replied with a laugh. "First, I'm sure we can turn up whatever you're looking for. Second, he likes you too much to do any ear-pinning even if we don't."

"Easy for you to say," Rahnyldah retorted, looking up at her far taller friend. Alahnah, at seventeen, was clearly still growing. She was also already four inches taller than Rahnyldah, who'd decided to stop at five-two. "He's known you since you were a baby. Besides, you're a *crown* princess, with all sorts of executioners and stuff. I'm only the spare heir. Nobody's afraid of *me*!"

"Only the people who know you and realize what a terrible temper you have," Lywys Whytmyn said from behind Alahnah as he followed her into the otherwise unoccupied classroom. He smiled as Rahnyldah made a rude gesture in his direction. While he never forgot she was currently second in the line of succession for the Dohlaran throne, they'd grown up together and she was very much his "kid sister."

"I do *not* have a terrible temper!" she told him now. "I haven't asked Rahnyld to lock anyone in the tower in, oh, two or three years now."

"Oh, very reformed, Rahnee!" Lywys chuckled as Lieutenant Makahfee, the new commander of Alahnah's protective detail, stepped through the door on his heels. The Marine's eyes swept the room quickly but thoroughly, and he crossed to open the door in the west wall and poke his head through. He gave the small cluster of study cubicles a searching glance, then closed the door, drew himself to semi-attention, bowed respectfully in Alahnah's direction, and withdrew, shutting the hall door behind him.

She watched the door close, and her eyes were sad for a moment. She liked Dahnyld Makahfee. She liked him a lot. But there were times when she missed Lieutenant Bynyt and especially Sergeant Adkok so much it hurt. She'd had almost six months to become accustomed to her new Marines, yet that memory could still ambush her unawares.

Rahnyldah watched the door close, as well, then giggled. Lywys looked at her, head tilted and eyebrows arched in surprise, and she shook her head.

"You really thought I wanted *you* to help me with a *math* problem, Lywys?" Her expression was pitying and she rolled her eyes. "*Please!*"

His own eyes narrowed, then flipped sideways to Alahnah. The imperial family had returned to Tellesberg from Cherayth only two days ago, and this was Alahnah's first day back at the College. To be honest, he'd wondered why Rahnyldah had sent him such an urgent plea for assistance, especially since he'd seen her at supper in the Archbishop's Palace just last night and she hadn't said a word about it then. Now. . . .

"The light dawns!" Rahnyldah laughed.

"I have it on the best of authority that *all* men are a little slow," Alahnah said dryly, giving Rahnyldah a quick hug.

"The empirical evidence would seem to support that hypotheses," Rahnyldah intoned in a rather good impersonation of Doctor Hahlcahm.

"Yes, it does, and I owe you for this one, Rahnee."

"Yes, you do, Lahna," Rahnyldah agreed, squeezing her back. "Don't worry, I won't ask for anything big. Maybe . . . oh, a mutual defense treaty or something else small."

"Sounds about right," Alahnah agreed with a chuckle. "Now *scoot* . . . please."

Rahnyldah snorted, but she also waved and disappeared through the door to the study cubicles. There was no other entry or exit to or from the cubicles, which was one reason she'd chosen Room 307. She and Alahnah had known the Marines would settle for guarding its external access points.

The door closed behind her, and Lywys turned his somewhat wary attention to Alahnah.

"And just what, if I can ask, was that all about?"

"Lord help me, you *are* slow, aren't you?" Alahnah said, and opened her arms to him.

He hesitated just a moment, but then his own arms went around her and he held her tight, bending to press his cheek against her sweet-smelling hair.

"It's been a long four months," he said a bit huskily, feeling that lithe, slender body pressed against his own.

"You mean it's been a long *five* months . . . and one five-day, including travel time," she said against his chest. "But who's counting?"

He chuckled, the sound rumbling through his chest against her ear, and she smiled.

"I've wanted to do this for the *longest* time," she continued. "I mean, thank *God* for our coms, but they're no substitute for *this*."

"No, they aren't," he agreed. "But it's been kind of eye-opening in a lot of ways, you know. Grandfather always did wonder how your mom and dad seemed able to read each other's minds even when they were half a world apart! Little did he know."

Alahnah snorted, remembering the endless hours she and Lywys had spent on the com during her four-and-a-half-month sojourn in Cherayth. They'd had fewer—and much briefer—opportunities on the *Ahlfryd Hyndryk* in transit to and from Chisholm. She'd wondered, too, about her parents. Not how they'd read each other's minds but how two people who obviously loved one another so dearly could have stood to be apart so long during the Jihad. Now she knew. It must still have hurt, but at least they'd been able to see one another, *talk* to one another.

And so had she and Lywys.

Now she gave him one last squeeze, then stood back so that she could look up into his face. She was going to be taller than her mother—she got that from her father—but Lywys was actually an inch taller than Cayleb. That was nice, she thought.

Now she gazed up into his eyes, and thought about all those conversations. Thought about how he'd been there for her, despite the different time zones, whenever she woke in the night, weeping brokenheartedly for her dead Marine protectors. How they'd laughed at each other's jokes. How they'd marveled with one another over the incredible vista of human history which had been opened to them. The way they'd seen all of her parents' actions slotting into the strategy which must someday bring down the Church of God Awaiting and the *Holy Writ* in which an entire world believed.

She'd talked to him about things she'd never dreamed of discussing with another. Things she hadn't been able to talk even to her parents about as she realized how horribly it hurt to discover that the Church in which she'd believed her entire life was founded upon a lie. That all of the millions of innocent people who had died in the Jihad had been slaughtered in the service of that lie.

And that it was very possible the world—or *their* world, at least—was going to end barely four years from this very day.

As she looked into his eyes, she saw the memory of those conversations, and of the other conversations, they'd had as well. The ones about dreams and hopes. The ones about friendship and how friendship could change, deepen.

"It's so good to see you," she said now. "I mean to really *see* you, with my own eyes. Know you're really here."

"Likewise," he said softly, raising a hand to the side of her face. Then he smiled. "We were already going to see each other at dinner tonight, though, you know."

"You're an idiot," she told him, putting her hand over his to press her cheek more firmly into his palm.

"I'm male." He shrugged. "I'm doing the best I can."

"God, that's scary!" She shook her head.

"I understand it gets worse as we get older and our brains ossify," he told her very seriously.

"Wonderful."

"I know. At the same time, in my slow male way, I'm still wondering exactly why we had to get Rahnee involved in all this. I mean, I thought we'd agreed to be 'discreet.'"

"If you think Rahnyldah hasn't already figured out how we feel about each other, you're not just slow, doof!" Alahnah shook her head. "She'd figured it out before we ever left for Cherayth."

"Well, okay. I can see that." He nodded. "But why the charade?"

"I could say it's because we had practically zero opportunity to cuddle before I got whisked off to Cherayth, and that would be true. But the real reason is because I wanted to be standing this close to you—alone—when I asked you a question," Alahnah said, and the humor had fled from her expression and her voice was soft.

"You could've done that at the Palace tonight," he pointed out. "Your mom and dad have to know how many hours we've spent 'alone together' on the com. I don't think they'd have begrudged us a minute or two of physical privacy. Or maybe they *would* have," he added with a crooked grin, "if they'd figured out how much lost 'cuddling' I'd like to make up for!"

"Of course they wouldn't have, but I don't want them to know about this conversation until after we've had it."

"Alahnah, Merlin has a SNARC remote parked on top of you twenty-six hours a day! They're not going to know we talked?"

"No, they aren't. Or not what we talked *about*, anyway. Mom and Dad don't spy on the people they love any more than they have to, so they've put Merlin and Owl in charge of my security and Merlin has Owl privacy-filtering my conversations. Oh, if they ask, Owl will tell them you and I spoke to each other, but not what about. If they really want to know that, they'll ask *me*."

Lywys nodded slowly, but his eyes were intent as he absorbed her own focused intensity.

"Okay, I can see that," he said. "But why don't you want them to know we've talked?"

"It's not that we've talked, it's what we've talked *about*," she replied, and his eyes narrowed as she looked down again, fingers playing with the pleats of her gown. That sudden break of eye contact was very unlike the Alahnah he knew.

"Which is?" he asked gently.

"Which is—" she looked back up "—what we want to do about the way we feel about each other."

His nostrils flared, although he couldn't pretend even to himself that he was really surprised. It was just something he'd very carefully kept himself from thinking through.

"Lahna, I know what I *want* to do." He caught both her hands in his and squeezed. "I think it's what I wanted to do even before the hunting trip. But you're a crown princess. And not just *a* crown princess; you're *the* crown princess. Your parents are the most powerful monarchs in the history of Safehold, and I'm the grandson of an earl without any titles—or any prospect of any titles—of my own. And twelve years ago, our families were shooting at each other! There's no way your parents could agree to let you marry someone like me."

"My God, you *are* an idiot," she said softly, an edge of loving tears in her voice. "You think my parents wouldn't *let* me marry you?! Lywys, they love each other to pieces. You think they wouldn't want that for me, too?"

"I'm sure they would, but they're rulers, Lahna. Sometimes they have to make decisions they don't want to make. Like what happened to Duke Eastshare, for God's sake! I admire them and I respect them more than I could possibly say exactly, because they've never flinched from making those decisions. But there's no way they could waste your hand on a Dohlaran nobody, no matter who his grandfather was."

"First of all, you're not a nobody and never have been!" she said just a bit sharply. "Second, who are they going to marry me off to as a diplomatic masterstroke? Emperor Mahrys' son? *Zhyou-Zhwo's* son? Please! *Not* going to happen, and even if it did, I'd slit my wrists on the way to the cathedral! And there's not anybody else they want or could conceivably need a dynastic alliance with. I mean, the Republic doesn't have a royal family, so that rules Siddarmark out. And Silkiah's a nice place, but it's going to be pretty firmly in the Charisian orbit no matter what. So the only 'diplomatic' consideration would be Prince Rohlynd—who, I'll grant you, is about the right age—to solidify Tarot's loyalty to the Empire. But that doesn't seem like a pressing concern at the moment, even if he didn't already seem very attracted to Fhrancys Breygart, and aside from Rohlynd, there's *nobody* else on the horizon. In fact, if we're waiting for the right dynastic partner to come along, I'll die an old maid, and I wouldn't like that."

"No, I can see that." His voice was a trifle unsteady and his lips twitched.

"Well maybe you're not a *complete* idiot then." She shook her head, but she also squeezed his hands more tightly.

"If you want to marry me," she told him quietly, "Mom and Dad will say yes in a heartbeat. I'm not worried about that. I'm worried about some . . . other things."

"I'm not sure marrying me would be a wonderful idea—politically, I mean," he argued with stubborn integrity. "You may be right about dynastic marriages, but I can see all kinds of downsides to a marriage between the Charisian crown and Dohlar."

She nodded, and the eyes she'd inherited from her father softened. It was like him to worry about the consequences of something they'd both discovered over the months just past that they both wanted so badly. And although he'd never admit it, possibly even to himself, there was another factor. He genuinely was a "nobody" in the eyes of altogether too much of the world, and the people behind those eyes would undoubtedly think of him as a fortune hunter. Or of her as a flutter-headed little girl who thought with her hormones.

He obviously wasn't prepared to see that happen.

"Lywys, aside from a few illiterate shepherds up in the Iron Spines back home in Chisholm, there aren't two people in the entire Empire who don't know you saved my life. You think that's not going to cut any ice with my future subjects? Because I damned well promise you it does with me and my parents!"

"It wasn't me, it was Merlin!" Lywys protested.

"Who wouldn't have gotten there in time without you," she said relentlessly. "And the reason you were there was because you chased that monster through the woods *knowing* you couldn't kill it, *knowing* no magic *seijin* was going to arrive in the nick of time, and then you *stood* there on the ground shooting at it to give me time to run when you knew it was going to kill you where you stood."

Her eyes glistened with tears and her voice quivered.

"My mother and father told me years ago that the true test of love is knowing the other person will always be there for you, no matter what. Well guess what? I'm luckier than a lot of people, because I *know* the man I love *will* be there. That he'll stand beside me just like my father stands beside my mother, even in the face of Hell itself, *because he's already done it*. So don't you tell me marrying you is a bad idea, Lywys Whytmyn! Only tell me that if you don't *want* to marry me."

"Of *course* I want to marry you!" he said, sweeping her into his arms once more. "I want that more than anything else in the world, because whatever you may think, I'm not really an idiot, and I know nobody could *deserve* to marry you. I just . . . I just can't help looking at the obstacles."

"There are obstacles, and then there are obstacles." Her voice was a little muffled in his crushing embrace, and he eased up enough for her to step back and look up at him again, still from the circle of his arms.

"You're absolutely right about how a lot of the rest of the world will look at this," she said then, and despite her youth, he heard her parents' pragmatism in her voice. Then again, he reminded himself, she was barely a year younger than her father had been the day he met Merlin Athrawes in the woods.

"I don't care about most of those 'obstacles' of yours, and I don't think Mom and Dad will care about them either," she continued. "That doesn't mean they aren't real, though, and the biggest one is the problem that you're Dohlaran. I don't think that's going to matter to most Charisians, although you and I both know there are some Charisians who're never going to forgive Dohlar for being 'Clyntahn's cat's-paw.'" She shrugged. "Stupid of them, but hate and grief make people do and feel stupid things.

"That's not the real problem, though, because those Charisians are a minority, and by the time I'm inheriting any thrones, most of the people who think that way will be safely dead. And I don't really think Rahnyld or Duke Fern will have any serious problems with the notion of a dynastic alliance between the House of Thirsk and the House of Ahrmahk. Neither of them is that stupid. Oh, Fern might wish I'd decided to marry Rahnyld, instead, but he's a realist. Besides, Rahnyld wasn't involved with any great dragons and me, and the truth is that whether he wants to admit it or not, Fern is a romantic at heart."

"Really?" Lywys asked dryly. "Odd. I'd never noticed that melting, gooey part of him before."

"Not my fault if you haven't been paying attention," she replied with a grin, but the grin faded quickly.

"No, the problem will be Siddarmark, because a lot more Siddarmarkians hate Dohlar. And for a lot better reasons, when you come down to it. I know it wasn't your grandfather's idea—and it sure wasn't yours. For that matter, *Rahnyld* was a schoolboy when it happened, so it wasn't his, either. But they haven't forgiven or forgotten, and the way Dohlar's taken off industrially—and how close Dohlar and the Empire've gotten since the Jihad—really grates with those people. If I marry you—if we even make any formal announcement that I'm *going* to marry you—the people who already hate Dohlar—and a lot of the same people already resent 'Charisian interference' in the Republic, for that matter—will have what Aunt Mairah calls a 'hissy fit.' I wouldn't mind about that, if the Trans-Siddarmark Railroad wasn't still in its formative stages. Or if the Silkiah Canal wasn't hanging fire. Grand Duke Kahnrad's not the only person who's figured out Dohlar's the other logical partner for the canal. If we get married, or even betrothed, before *Siddarmark* and Charis break ground on the canal, the consequences could be . . . unfortunate."

Lywys nodded gravely, any temptation to smile at her characterization of Duke Fern less than a memory as she laid out her reasoning. Obviously, she'd given this a lot of thought, but she wouldn't be eighteen for another four months. That was barely sixteen in the years of murdered Terra. He was astounded by her ability to stand back and analyze the complicated and volatile world of diplomacy so clearly and to summarize it so concisely.

Which I shouldn't be, given her parents, he thought with a deep sense of pride in her and of the even deeper respect *for* her. *Now that I know about DNA, I have to wonder if there's a gene for this. If so, she obviously got it from* both *sides!*

"It sounds to me like you just explained exactly why we *can't* get married," he said, after a moment. "On the other hand, knowing you as well as I do, I'm sure you have a plan to deal with it, even if I can't imagine what it might be."

"That's because I don't have one. Not for marrying you in Tellesberg Cathedral anytime soon," she admitted, meeting his gaze without flinching. "I *want* to—oh, how I want to! I want to walk down that aisle in front of all those hundreds of people and stand in front of that altar beside you and tell God—not the frigging 'Archangels,' but *God*—that I am and will always be your wife, forever! But it's not going to happen until we break ground on the damned canal. Less because we need the canal than because we need to patch up the relationship with Siddarmark the canal will represent."

"Then why—?" he asked slowly, looking down at her.

"Because we may be running out of time," she said very, very softly. "If the 'Archangels' *are* coming back a thousand years after the Creation, and if they don't react the way we all hope and pray they will, I'll never see my twenty-second birthday." His arms tightened around her again, but her eyes never flinched. "If there's one family on the face of Safehold which will *have* to be destroyed if they try to reestablish the Proscriptions, shut down industrialization, it's mine. They can't leave us alive, if that's the way they react. I realized that the minute Mom and Dad and Merlin explained it to us. In that respect, I'm Nimue Alban and they're the Gbaba all over again, Lywys.

"But you don't have to be. Some of the new '*Rakurai*' are bound to splash onto Dohlar, given how enthusiastically the Kingdom's been industrializing. But if you go home, if we arrange to grow 'estranged' from your family—and I'm sure Mom and Dad would do that for your parents, your aunts and uncles, even if we could never explain to them *why* they're doing it—then you and the other people you love may not have to be on the 'Archangels' list.

"So you can go home," tears glittered on her lashes, "and a part of me wants you to do that, *so* badly. Wants you to get as far away from me, from my family, as you can. But the selfish part of me wants you to stay, and if we have only four years, then . . . I . . . *want* . . . those . . . years, Lywys." She looked up at him. "I can't announce our betrothal, not marry you the way I want. Not right now, and I may never have time to do that, to give us and your family that, but I want that time with you. I want to share it with you, to know you and I *are* husband and wife, whatever the rest of the world knows or doesn't know. And the question I needed to ask you standing here, with you, is whether or not that's what you want."

▼ ▼ ▼

The moon rode high and silver in a heaven of cobalt blue velvet, and the stars of Safehold were a magnificent diadem, draped across the night. It was cool, for Charis in November, and the private chapel's open windows admitted the gentle night breeze that fluttered the candle flames.

It wasn't an enormous chamber, although archbishops, as a rule, had larger chapels than mere bishops, and at the moment it was crowded. Indeed, it was far more crowded than the casual beholder might have guessed.

Maikel Staynair stood there, smiling as the young man standing at the sanctuary rail turned to watch an even younger woman enter the chapel. She wasn't on her father's arm, because her father already stood at the groom's elbow as his best man. She was on the arm of a very tall man whose sapphire eyes glittered in the candlelight. That had been her parents' choice, not her escort's, although Alahnah had agreed with tears in her eyes that if any living being deserved to stand sponsor to this marriage, it was Merlin Athrawes.

Nynian and Stefyny Athrawes, the Duke of Delthak and his wife, Earl Pine Hollow, Duke Rock Point, Rahzhyr Mahklyn, and a dozen other members of the inner circle filled the chapel to capacity. They'd arrived in ones and twos, using the hidden tunnels between Archbishop's Palace and Tellesberg Cathedral and Tellesberg Palace. And all across Safehold, other men and women who'd joined the inner circle's battle attended over their coms, filling the chapel with their presence.

The archbishop reached out to take the hands of the young man and the young woman before him.

"Lywys and Alahnah," he said quietly, "you've come here to become man and wife, whether or not the rest of the world ever learns of that decision on your part. I honor you for it, and I'm honored that you've asked me to marry you. And that despite having learned the truth about the Church of God Awaiting your faith in God Himself has never wavered. I believe in the validity of the sacraments of the Church of Charis, because those sacraments represent the beliefs and the deep and abiding faith of uncountable men and women and children who have been able to know God only through the distorting prism of the Church of God Awaiting. That makes Him no less God and them no less His children, but you know the truth of the Church. And so, at your request, we will use an older liturgy, one that speaks of the God Nimue Alban and Jeremiah Knowles brought to Safehold with them. The liturgy Merlin and Nynian chose when *they* wed. Are you prepared for us to begin?"

They looked at one another, then back at him and, as one, they nodded.

"Very well, my children."

He squeezed their hands and drew a deep breath.

"Dearly beloved, we are gathered together in the sight of God and in the face of this company to join together our son Lywys and our daughter Alahnah in holy matrimony; which is an honorable estate, instituted of God, signifying unto us the mystical union that is betwixt Christ and his church; which holy estate Christ adorned and beautified with his presence and first miracle that he wrought in Cana of Galilee, and is commended of Saint Paul to be honorable among all men: and therefore is not by any to be entered into unadvisedly or lightly; but reverently, discreetly, advisedly, soberly, and in the fear of God. Into this holy estate Lywys and Alahnah come now to be joined. If any man can show just cause, why they may not lawfully be joined together, let him now speak, or else here after forever hold his peace."

The ancient words, the words Eric Langhorne, Adorée Bédard, and Maruyama Chihiro had stolen and twisted so many centuries before, rolled through the private chapel on the deep, velvety music of his superbly trained voice, and Alahnah Ahrmahk and Lywys Whytmyn held their heads high as they stood side-by-side before him . . . and the future.

MARCH YEAR OF GOD 912

◆

. I .
Ananasberg,
The Stylmyn Gap,
Moon Thorn Mountains,
Mountaincross Province,
Republic of Siddarmark.

"I'm telling you, Kynyth, this crap is going to get somebody *killed*!"

Aivahn Ohgylsbee's Zebediahan accent was more pronounced than usual as he glared at the length of rail. It had just been unloaded from a flat car piled high with identical rails, and his eyes were unhappy as yet another charge of Lywysite roared from the excavation for the Trans-Siddarmark Railroad's roadbed between the capital and the rebuilt city of Guarnak.

"It's not quite that bad," Kynyth Sahnchyz objected. Ohgylsbee shifted his glare from the rail to his putative superior, and the Siddarmarkian raised one hand in a placating gesture. "It's not going to get anyone killed . . . as long as our on-site inspectors catch it before the track gets laid," he amended his earlier statement. "If this'd gone into one of the sections without being spotted, then, yeah, it could've—*would*'ve—been bad."

Ohgylsbee glared at him for another long moment, then drew a deep breath, nodded, and kicked the offending rail. He was careful to use the heel of his boot, because he liked his toes unbroken, but his lip curled with contempt as Sahnchyz joined him in glowering down at it.

"For Hasting's sake, this thing doesn't even match the

profile," Ohgylsbee said, "and the son-of-a-bitch is *cast iron,* not steel! How the hell did they get this past the inspectors farther up the line?"

Sahnchyz glanced up at him, then sighed. Ohgylsbee was one of the best engineers he'd ever known—he was certainly better than Kynyth Sahnchyz, at any rate!—which was the main reason he was one of Duke Delthak's personal representatives to the TSRR. But in some ways, he was a child.

No, that's not really fair, the Siddarmarkian reminded himself. *What he is, is an honest man who's used to dealing with honest suppliers.*

"Are you asking that as a serious question, or a rhetorical one?" he asked. Ohgylsbee looked up from the rail. "I mean, both of us know who sent it to us."

"I don't really expect better than this out of Hymphyl," Ohgylsbee growled. "I mean, it's a little bareknuckle even for him, but we're talking about *Hymphyl,* for God's sake. I just don't understand how the inspectors didn't catch it."

"They didn't catch it because someone told them *not* to catch it." Sahnchyz's own anger made his voice come out harsh, choppy. "And they probably got paid pretty well to look the other way, too."

"You think it's gone that far?" Ohgylsbee asked with a frown.

"Look, I know you probably don't have a lot of experience with this kind of stuff back home in Charis," Sahnchyz began, "but—"

"Kynyth, my family's from Zebediah," Ohgylsbee interrupted, "and before Emperor Cayleb kicked his arse out, Tohmys Symmyns was about as sorry—and corrupt—an excuse for a grand duke as ever existed. My family were serfs under the old League of Corisande, and we saw the shit-end of every stick there was. Bit different since Their Majesties put in Grand Duke Hauwyl, but, trust me, I know about corruption and I know about corner-cutting. Hell, I even know about bribery and kickbacks! What I *don't* know is why anyone's letting them get away with it on something this important to the entire damned Republic. And what I'm *afraid* of is that it's only going to get worse. Right now, it's more of an irritation than anything else, but if other subcontractors start pulling this kind of crap, it's going to be a *significant* problem down the road."

Kynyth Sahnchyz revised his opinion of Charisian naivety as he saw the bitterness in Ohgylsbee's eyes.

"I don't know how bad it's going to get," he admitted unhappily. "Trust me, I'll be sending a report up the line, but I don't know how much good it'll do. Our good friend Hymphyl has what they call 'friends in high places,' and I suspect at least some of them work for—or with, at least—the General Board."

"Any of those friends have a name?" Ohgylsbee asked, his eyes narrow.

"Maybe," Sahnchyz said. "I'm not throwing around any names above Hymphyl without something a lot more like proof to go on, but somebody's steering contracts. That's the only explanation for this. And it's the reason sending my report's not likely to do a whole frigging lot of good."

It was his turn to kick the rail, and Ohgylsbee frowned.

"You really think no one'll pin his ears back if you report it? Believe me, I'll be delighted to sign off on your report if you think it'll do any good!"

"I'll take you up on that, and I'm sure he'll get his knuckles smacked, but I don't expect anything more than that."

"Kynyth, this thing is *cast iron*. No way it meets spec!"

"Not for Trans-Siddarmark, no," Sahnchyz agreed. "But I'll guarantee you I know what'll happen if anyone really does come back on him about it. It'll turn out it was a 'clerical error' and we got sent the wrong shipment."

"Wrong shipment?"

"Sure. It'll turn out this piece of crap was supposed to go to one of the trolley lines, or some of the light rail going in at some manufactory." Sahnchyz kicked the rail again. "The General Board may've specified first-quality steel, thirty-five pounds to the foot, but we don't have the kind of universal code enforcement you have in Charis. For that matter, we're still producing a lot more iron and a lot less steel than you are, and a lot of the lighter traffic's running on iron for right now. The rails won't last as long, and I sure as hell wouldn't try to run any heavy freight over them or put any fast automotives on them, but they can be turned out domestically and a lot of palms are being greased to use them wherever we can. So, if Hymphyl gets hammered over this, he'll just say his warehousers loaded the wrong shipment on the wrong flatcar. He'll fall all over himself apologizing for it, replace it with the *right* rails, and probably offer some kind of half-arsed discount on the next shipment as a 'voluntary refund for the inconvenience.' And that'll be that. No harm done, everything's been made good, and everybody's happy. Except maybe you and me."

"Shan-wei." Ohgylsbee shook his head. "If anybody tried that back home, they'd better have *tons* of paperwork to back it up. And odds are, somebody'd still see the inside of a cell before it was all over!"

"I wish it worked that way here, too, but it doesn't. Not yet, anyway." Sahnchyz shrugged. "And the good news is that, so far, anything that gets by the initial inspection's being caught by our inspectors here on-site. If it doesn't get any worse, we can cope with it."

Ohgylsbee nodded slowly, without saying another word, but his expression spoke volumes, and Sahnchyz found himself trapped between resentment and agreement. Kickbacks, graft, even outright bribes had become part of the Siddarmarkian business world in the superheated, credit-fueled bubble that had followed the Jihad. He didn't like it, and he liked it even less when an outsider like Ohgylsbee saw all the dirty linen. But that didn't mean he appreciated the way he was sure most of Charisians thought about the Republic these days.

And you appreciate it least because you suspect they're right *to think that way,* he told himself. *Too damned bad you can't do a frigging thing about it besides write reports that arsehole Kartyr will sit on.*

"So, what do you make of Sahnchyz' analysis, Ehd-wyrd?" Cayleb Ahrmahk asked.

He was tipped back in his rattan chair with a straw hat pulled low to shade his eyes. He was also simply dressed, in clothing that was well-worn—indeed, Shar-leyan was fond of calling it "ratty"—and comfortable. In fact, he looked like any commonly born angler as he talked quietly to the empty space about him.

There was quite a bit of that empty space at the moment as he sat on the private dock, shaded from the wester-ing sun by a gently flapping canopy while the striped float of his fishing line bobbed on the gentle swell. *Seijin* Merlin was "temporarily away," but the other members of his personal detail had closed off the end of the dock from the landward side, leaving him its entire length as a welcome bubble of privacy. With his eyes closed, the contacts he still hadn't had the time and opportunity to exchange for implants relayed the SNARC remotes' view of the riflemen perched up on the nearest rooftops with rifles and telescopic sights.

All right, maybe not "any commonly born angler," he thought wryly. *But I can at least* pretend.

"I think he knows what he's talking about," the Duke of Delthak said grimly over Cayleb's com earplugs. "And I think it's going to get worse."

"Really?" Cayleb looked at his float, then twitched his rod a little. Not that he really anticipated attracting any of the harbor's fishy denizens. Any true angler knew that wasn't the real object of the exercise, anyway.

"Really." Delthak didn't sound any more cheerful. "In

fact, I could lay pretty good odds I know who he was talking about."

"Ah?"

"It's not that hard, Cayleb. Wouldn't be even without the SNARCs! He's absolutely right about Inosyncio Hymphyl. That man's a corner-cutter to the core, and he never found an opportunity for graft or bribery that he didn't take. But he couldn't be getting away with this where Trans-Siddarmark is concerned without what Nahrmahn and Owl call an 'enabler.' And that's got to be Kartyr Sulyvyn."

Sulyvyn's name came out in exactly the same tone Delthak used whenever Stywyrt Showail's name entered a conversation, Cayleb noted.

"The name's familiar, but I can't quite place it," he said. "From the direction of this conversation, should I assume he's associated with the Trans-Siddarmark Railroad one way or another?"

"Oh, yes. You certainly should." Delthak swiveled his chair, looking out his office window across the vista of blast furnaces, cranes, tram lines, canal wharves, and an ever-growing number of steam dragons—what someone from Old Terra might've called a steam-powered truck or lorry.

"I know you haven't spent as much time looking at the nuts and bolts in Siddarmark as Nahrmahn and Nynian and I have," the duke went on, "but you've at least got the general picture."

"I believe you may safely assume that," Cayleb said dryly.

"Well, I was struck by a couple of terms Merlin and Nimue have taken to using in their discussions with Nynian and Nahrmahn, so I went and did a little research. And, as usual, our *seijin* friends have come up with useful labels."

"Which would be?"

"'The Wild West' and 'robber baron,'" Delthak replied.

"I think I can guess what 'robber baron' means. 'Wild West,' though?"

"It's a reference to a wide-open frontier that existed once back on Old Earth," Delthak said. "One where 'law and order' hadn't caught up with the people expanding it and the only real limit was what you figured you could get away with until someone shot your sorry arse, and I'm afraid that describes the Republic pretty damned well, in a lot of ways.

"When the House of Qwentyn went down, it did even more damage than we thought at the time. Not immediately, and not in and of itself. It was more like . . . opening a door, and all of the social unrest from the Jihad's displaced refugees, coupled with the possibilities—and challenges—of the new technology, crashed right through it. It was every man for himself and there really wasn't any governing law about patents or usury or commercial law in general. The legal aspects had always been provided by the Church's law masters, and the law masters didn't have a clue how to deal with all the new concepts we'd introduced here in Charis. Not just the ones since Merlin, but for the last forty or fifty years. I don't think any of us, including Merlin, realized just how significantly our law codes and commercial practices differed from those of the Mainland even before he and Paityr got hold of them.

"After the Jihad, the Church found itself displaced from its traditional role of lawgiver and the Qwentyns had effectively disappeared as the governor that moderated the . . . ferocity of the Siddarmarkian financial sector. I'll be honest, some of the practices that got by were enough to curl my hair, and there are actually more than a few subterranean faults in the Republic's economy even Henrai Maidyn hadn't identified.

"One fault Maidyn *did* identify are the 'robber barons' who took advantage of that 'Wild West' window to build their own empires. Some of those empires are built on foundations of sand, and someday soon, a lot of them are likely to come crashing down. The Republic's going to get hurt when that happens, although I do think the Bank and the Asset Guarantee Trust are huge steps in the right direction. I can't tell you how much

I wish Henrai hadn't gotten himself killed before he'd had time to put through the stock trading regulations he'd wanted, as well, and the fact that he didn't could be a very bad thing in the end. But overall, Siddarmark's economy's in a lot stronger situation than it was two or three years ago.

"Unfortunately, a lot of those fly-by-night operators are still out there, and Kartyr Sulyvyn's one of them—one of Merlin and Nimue's 'robber barons,' which doesn't have a damned thing to do with titles of nobility. Sulyvyn owns bits and pieces of dozens of manufactories or other businesses—including Hymphyl Ironworks—but what he really does is . . . facilitate transactions. He specializes in putting together deals, acting as other people's agent to organize complex, large-scale operations. Which is how he became one of the General Board's senior purchasing agents."

"I thought I knew that name," Cayleb said.

"In some ways, it's hard to blame Nezbyt and Hahraimahn for giving him the slot." Delthak, Cayleb noted, sounded like he didn't find it difficult at all but was doing his damnedest to be fair. "Nezbyt's basically a bureaucrat, without a lot of marketplace experience of his own. And Hahraimahn's always been a manufacturer. He sells stuff to other people. Aside from raw materials, he certainly doesn't *buy* stuff—finished product, stuff I mean—in enormous quantities. Or such diverse *kinds* of stuff. Worse, before he ended up on the General Board, he'd never dealt with anything remotely as big as Trans-Siddarmark. I mean, we're talking about *millions* of marks here, Cayleb. That's serious money, and nobody in the Republic was ever involved with anything this big before, even during the Jihad. The Council of Manufactories coordinated scores of smaller suppliers for the Army, but no one ever imagined a single entity *this* size.

"So it's not unreasonable for Nezbyt or Hahraimahn to look for someone who's spent years 'facilitating' large-scale purchasing and supply agreements. The fact that Sulyvyn and Nezbyt worked together during the Jihad and Sulyvyn figured out how to stroke Nezbyt's ego only made that an even more comfortable fit. But what neither Nezbyt nor Hahraimahn have realized, I think, is that eighty or ninety percent of the time when Sulyvyn 'facilitates' a deal, he does it by buying from one of the enterprises he owns a piece of, *through* another one of the enterprises he owns a piece of, for delivery *to* a third enterprise he owns a piece of. And at every stage in the process, he rakes a little 'finder's fee' off the top. You don't need to take a really big percentage of a couple of hundred million marks to start racking up some big totals, Cayleb. And the son-of-a-bitch isn't shy about spreading some of those totals around to protect his cash cow."

"We have proof of this?"

"Yes, and no," Delthak said unhappily. "Yes, Nahrmahn and Owl and I have proof. And, no, I can't present it in court. It's that sort of evidence. You know—the sort that comes from our mysterious *seijin* friends."

"And we really don't want Myllyr to think we have our *seijins* spying on him," Cayleb observed glumly.

"That's one way to put it. Daryus and Samyl Gohdard would probably take our word for it, at least enough to open an independent investigation of their own. Myllyr won't, not without Nezbyt's signing off on it. Because Myllyr trusts Nezbyt, and *Nezbyt* trusts his cronies."

"Is that because Sulyvyn's paying Nezbyt off?" Cayleb's tone was considerably grimmer, but Delthak shook his head.

"As far as we can tell, no. Not directly," the duke said. "During the Jihad, yes, Nezbyt did skim a little. It wasn't a huge amount, and overall he did a damned good job, so Nynian and Nahrmahn didn't worry about it at the time. They had a lot bigger and more dangerous krakens to deal with. *Since* the Jihad, it doesn't look to us like he's still on the take. But what he did do was establish wartime relationships with a lot of people, including Sulyvyn and a couple of others who are at least as shady as he is. They worked with him, he came to know them, and he's . . . comfortable around them. And they, by and large, are smart enough not to offer him explicit payoffs, because that would probably set off his own internal alarms. So instead, they give him 'gifts.' One of Sulyvyn's manufactories re-coppered his yacht for just the cost of the copper . . . and discounted that pretty steeply. Another one introduced his wife to one of the most exclusive milliners in Siddar City . . . and quietly arranged to pay a third of her expenses without ever mentioning it to her. *She* thinks she's just a really good shopper who finds better deals than any of the other women she knows and prides herself on it."

"That sounds like 'explicit payoffs' to *me*," Cayleb growled.

"Nezbyt doesn't actually know about some of them—like the one with his wife's milliner," Delthak pointed out. "What he knows there, is that one of his 'friends' guided his wife into the store where she finds exactly what she wants at the price she wants, but then she *pays* for it . . . so far as Nezbyt knows. So what these guys are doing is they're building this relationship of friendship and trust with him, which leaves him disinclined to go looking for anyone else, and the fact that the Trans-Siddarmark's charter doesn't require a bidding process for most of its transactions keeps anyone else from crowding their way in into that relationship."

"What about Zhasyn Brygs?" Cayleb asked.

"Brygs is too busy," Delthak said flatly. "Just being Governor of the Central Bank and director of the Asset Guarantee Trust would be more than enough to keep anyone running twenty-six hours a day. With the role of secretary-treasurer for Trans-Siddarmark thrown onto the stack, he can't possibly look at everything he ought to be looking at, and guess which one of his hats gets the shortest shrift? You may recall that we both suggested to Myllyr as firmly as we could that this might pose some small problems farther along the line? Well it turns out we're very smart people, because that's exactly what it's doing. He doesn't have the time to peruse every contract and every major deal, so some of them don't get reviewed at all and others get reviewed by his or Nezbyt's clerks, not all of whom are as honest and upright as Brygs."

"Crap."

"One way to put it," Delthak acknowledged.

"How bad is it, really?"

"Not good, but I have to admit it's not cata-strophic . . . yet. The rats in the woodwork are probably increasing Trans-Siddarmark's costs by around fifteen percent, maybe a little more, but that's not a lot, by Mainlander standards. Like I say, with this many mil-lions of marks floating around, even relatively low levels of graft and kickbacks rake in *buckets* of money. By and large, though, the service aspects of their contracts get discharged effectively and on time—it's kind of like it was in Harchong before the Jihad. Once the right palms get greased, things can be accomplished with amazing efficiency. It just doesn't come *cheaply*.

"So I'm not really concerned about whether or not Trans-Siddarmark can get the job done. Our inspectors have to downgrade and reject more and more substan-dard supplies, but so far, I think they're staying on top of that. Mind you, if it continues to get worse, that may not be the case forever.

"What I'm really worried about?" The duke puffed his lips and shook his head, and his eyes were dark as he looked out over the bustling industry around his of-fice. "What I'm really worried about is the knock-on ef-fect if—*when*—the Republic hits another recession. The amount of corruption inside Trans-Siddarmark's grow-ing steadily, and it's a private-*public* corporation, Cay-leb. If the shit hits the fan, as Merlin is fond of saying, where the Republic's economy is concerned and people in the business community find out the level of corrup-tion their own government's apparently winked at, pub-lic trust in all of Henrai's reforms will take a serious hit. And the one thing all of my research's convinced me of is that economies depend a lot more on perceptions than realities. Consumers make purchases based on their perception of their need and opportunity, but also on the basis of their optimism about the future. Manufactory owners do the same thing. When that optimism evapo-rates, drops to the kind of level we're still seeing to some extent in the western provinces, the entire economy tanks. And if that happens, and evidence of widespread corruption—and God knows, there's plenty of it *outside* Trans-Siddarmark!—hits the newspapers and broadsheets, the consequences could be . . . dire."

"In that case, we need to tell Myllyr about it now," Cayleb said. "I mean, I know the circle's delegated this to you, Nahrmahn, and Nynian, but it sounds to me like we don't have much of a choice!"

"I'm already making my concerns known, Cayleb. I've sent Myllyr and Chancellor Ashfyrd several memos detailing concerns of my own inspectors and supervisors, like Ohgylsbee. And I've shared as much evidence of what's going on with people like Sulyvyn as I can without getting into any of those sticky questions about just how I acquired it. And it's not doing much good."

"Why not?" Cayleb demanded.

"Because Nezbyt trusts Sulyvyn—and all the other Sulyvyns he's doing business with—and Myllyr and Ashfyrd both trust *Nezbyt*. And the hell of it is that in terms of anything overtly illegal, or even significantly and knowingly corrupt, Nezbyt really is an honest man, so it's hard to fault Myllyr and Ashfyrd for trusting him. The problem is that they're also trusting Nezbyt's *judgment,* and I don't think they can separate personal honesty from judgment and realize Nezbyt can possess one without necessarily having the other.

"In Ashfyrd's case, that's because he was never really a politician until Myllyr tapped him to head the Exchequer. He's always been a nuts-and-bolts fellow, a lot more comfortable dealing with numbers than people, mostly because he *understands* numbers . . . and he's not so sure he understands people. I guess I'm saying he's got really good bureaucratic skills but not very well honed political instincts, which makes him a bit like Nezbyt, in a way. He *trusts* people, Cayleb, at least until they damned well prove he can't, and that can be a good thing. Or not.

"And Mylyyr's like Ashfyrd, in a lot of ways. He never really wanted to be a politician, either, and he only ran for Lord Protector in his own right because he thought he owed it to Henrai and the Republic. He'd a lot rather be back at the Exchequer himself . . . or at home, raising petunias or something. But that means that despite his office, *he's* not a skilled political operator, either. He's got some good advisors, and he listens to them, but he not a political animal at heart. Worse, in this case, he's known Nezbyt a long time. He considers the man a personal friend and a colleague from his own Exchequer days, and the truth is they always worked well together there, so he doesn't see any reason they shouldn't now."

The duke paused, glowering out his office window. The vista didn't have its usual encouraging effect today.

"At any rate, Myllyr's not prepared to question Nezbyt's honesty—or judgment—without more evidence than we can plausibly give him. And, to be fair, so far despite the graft and all the . . . irregularities, Trans-Siddarmark's growing like a house on fire. It's far and away the most successful project in Siddarmark and there are a lot of other infrastructure projects and manufactories riding its coattails. Nobody in Siddar City—or Protector's Palace!—wants to do anything to kill the golden wyvern."

"Crap," Cayleb repeated, and Delthak chuckled harshly.

"Look at the bright side," he suggested.

"*What* bright side?" Cayleb growled.

"So far, Trans-Siddarmark *is* being successful. Not as successful as a fullbore Ahrmahk Plan might have been, but still pretty damned successful. So, despite any apprehensions I may nurse, it looks like we're getting the job done." Almost despite himself, Cayleb began to nod as the duke continued. "And if the wheels ultimately do come off, there's no Zhaspahr Clyntahn waiting to send in the Sword of Schueler to finish off the Republic. So nothing we're talking about here represents an immediate and significant threat to Siddarmark."

Cayleb nodded more emphatically than before, and Delthak smiled thinly.

"Yet, at least," he added, and the emperor stopped nodding with a glare.

AUGUST YEAR OF GOD 912

·✦·

. I .
HMS *Crag Reach* and HMAS *Bryntyn Hahlys,* Charis Sea.

"There she comes, Sir," Captain Brahdryk said quietly. Admiral Sir Bruhstair Ahbaht looked up, and the much taller captain raised a hand and pointed. "There, Sir. About thirty degrees off the larboard bow. And only an hour or so behind schedule. Not bad given the weather."

Ahbaht followed the pointing finger, then nodded.

"Got it, Captain," he said, then shook his head. "My eyes aren't as young as they used to be. Then again, neither is any of the rest of me."

"You seem to be doing just fine to me, Sir," Brahdryk said dryly. "Especially judging by the spades tournament."

"So I count trump. When you get to be my age you have to, because you sure aren't going to just *remember* what's been played!"

Ahbaht grinned, and it was Brahdryk's turn to shake his head.

Sir Bruhstair commanded the Imperial Charisian Navy's Fifth Fleet, homeported on Eraystor Bay and often referred to as "Home Fleet." Duke Rock Point hadn't exactly picked his fleet commanders—and especially Home Fleet's commander—by plucking names randomly from a hat, and despite Bruhstair's easy-going sense of humor, he was a very, very smart fellow. He'd also built a remarkable record during the Jihad, and the Navy's grapevine assigned him quite a few psychic talents. According to those who had served with him, those talents included the ability to read cards' faces from their backs. Sir Bruhstair had been aboard *Crag Reach* for less than a five-day in preparation for today's exercise, but nothing Brahdryk had seen from his own spades games with the admiral challenged that particular rumor.

"I'll try to remember how aged and infirm you're getting the next time you trounce me, Sir."

"It's a senior officer's duty to teach his juniors to cope with adversity, Captain." Bruhstair patted his forearm with a fatherly air.

"And some of them do it better than others, Sir," Brahdryk replied.

Bruhstair chuckled, but neither of them had looked away from the gray shape blending out of the overcast while they spoke. Frankly, the admiral—like Brahdryk, judging from what the captain had said—had had his doubts about whether or not the airship would even be able to find them, given the weather.

Crag Reach was four hundred miles north of Rock Shoal Bay, almost equidistant between Sea Dragon Point and Tairayl Island. That put the armored cruiser pretty close to the center of the Charis Sea, but the Charis Sea wasn't all that huge. She was only about a hundred and sixty miles from the closest land, which was far enough to keep her out of the normal shipping lanes for the duration of the exercise, but that shouldn't normally have made her a challenge for an airship to locate. Visibility wasn't good, however. It had been coming and going all day, and Lieutenant Commander Klymynt, *Crag Reach*'s navigator, estimated the cloud base had dropped to no more than twenty-five hundred feet. That limited the airship's ceiling and thus its visual range, and the occasional bouts of mist rolling across the sea's surface didn't make things any better.

But finding ships at sea is one of the things they're trained to do, he reminded himself, raising his double-glass and turning the focusing wheel to sharpen the image. *And they're getting damned good at it.*

There were times when Bruhstair Ahbaht wondered where—or if—the headlong changes were finally going to slow.

Or at least stop accelerating.

"They're signaling, Sir," another voice said, and Ahbaht lowered the double-glass to glance over his shoulder at Lieutenant Ohtys Chandlyr, *Crag Reach*'s signals officer. As the youthful lieutenant spoke, he was peering through a much more powerful double-glass swivel-mounted on the bridge wing railing, at the tiny, bright point of light blinking from the approaching airship, and Ahbaht wondered if the airship's crew felt as nervous about that as he would have.

Crag Reach was equipped with the latest and most powerful version of the Imperial Charisian Navy's new calcium "searchlights," and the torrent of brilliance they poured out was almost incredible. They did it, however, by directing a gas jet of combined hydrogen and oxygen onto a calcium "candle" to heat it to an enormously high temperature at which it radiated a blindingly white light. The candle was backed by a brilliantly polished mirror and had a focusing lens, both designed by Doctor Frymyn at the Royal College, that projected an almost solid-looking beam of light. The big fifty-inch lights could pick a small boat out of the darkest night—assuming otherwise clear visibility—at ranges of up to two miles, but first the searchlight crew had to know it was there. As a means of *finding* things in the dark, the searchlight still came in a distant second behind illuminating rockets or the recently developed "star shell" which could be fired from a ship's artillery.

The much smaller twenty-five-inch lights, however, had proved incredibly useful as a means of communication. Unlike signal flags, which could be used only in daylight, the signal lamps could be seen even in darkness. They also burned through mist—to some extent, at any rate—and were much more reliable and brighter than the heliographs previously in use. That didn't mean the heliograph had suddenly become obsolete, but one simply couldn't count on having the sun available—or in the right spot—when one needed it. Hence the "calcium lights."

But the new lights produced an enormous amount of heat, and an airship was one vast bag of highly flammable hydrogen. The prospect of blinking away with a calcium light in such close proximity to that potential explosion was enough to make anyone think twice. Although, he supposed, at least an airship had an effectively unlimited supply of hydrogen.

The important thing from his perspective, however, was that the new signal lamps meant an airship could communicate with another airship, the ground, or a warship like *Crag Reach* from much greater distances. The light could be seen—and read—from as much as twenty or thirty miles, even in daylight, although that was under ideal conditions. If the airship was between its intended recipient and the sun, the greater brightness of the sun tended to "white out" everything else, and haze, rain, or cloud knocked back visual range severely. But it was still better than anything anyone had ever had before, and vastly superior to the message capsules that went up and down the tethers of a warship's kite balloon.

And that promised a revolution in naval operations.

At their normal altitude of eighteen hundred feet, kite balloons already extended a ship's visual horizon from barely ten miles to almost sixty. For an airship at nine thousand feet, the visual horizon was over a hundred and sixteen miles, which gave it a scouting "bubble" almost two hundred and fifty miles across. That was in perfect weather, which was seldom obtained, but the boost in sighting distances was huge under *any* circumstances.

Previous trials had clearly demonstrated the scouting potential of an airship. With the latest version of the Delthak Works' Praigyrs, an airship could attain a maximum speed of almost seventy miles per hour in still air. That was three times the best speed the fastest steamer could maintain which meant it could search well ahead of any fleet or squadron and cover the distance back to it far more rapidly than any surface vessel possibly could. For that matter, squadrons of them operating together to form signal chains, as light scouting vessels had done for decades, could relay messages over enormous distances at incredible speeds. And that meant any fleet commander who could deploy a screen—a scouting line—of airships was far less likely to find himself suddenly surprised by an enemy's appearance.

The way one Sir Bruhstair Ahbaht had found himself surprised in Hahskyn Bay.

His jaw tightened with the remembered pain of what had happened to his squadron there, but it was an old and familiar anguish. His double-glass never wavered as he watched the blinking light, easy to pick out against the gray envelope of the airship's gasbag.

"*Bryntyn Hahlys* reports ready to proceed with the exercise, Admiral," Chandlyr said.

"Then I suppose we should be about it," Ahbaht said. "Please signal Lieutenant Zhasyn to commence at his discretion, Lieutenant."

"Aye, aye, Sir," Chandlyr replied, and Ahbaht heard the signal lamp's shutters clatter with the rapid, staccato, syncopated rhythm of the lieutenant's skilled hand.

He thought about the airship's name as he listened. *Bryntyn Hahlys,* one of the Imperial Navy's first aeronauts, had performed brilliantly at the Battle of Gorath. Although he'd been only a petty officer at the time, he'd clearly had an illustrious career in front of him. But that promise had never been fulfilled, courtesy of a climbing accident in Chisholm's Iron Spine Mountains which, unfortunately, had provided the Imperial Charisian Air Force with yet another name for one of its airships. And the irony of that name was particularly bitter, considering who'd been named to head the Admiralty's Office of Aeronautics.

Now Hahlys' namesake altered course, sweeping majestically around to approach *Crag Reach* from astern, and Ahbaht moved farther out on the bridge wing to keep the airship in sight. Fortunately, the wind pushed *Crag Reach*'s funnel smoke to starboard, clearing the range as the airship moved closer.

The admiral lowered the double-glass for a moment, looking aft at the large, flat raft, following in the armored cruiser's wake at the far end of the towing hawser. He could have wished that hawser was a little longer, but at least there were no actual explosives involved in today's experiment. And the exercise parameters called for the airship to make its final approach at an angle, cutting across well astern of *Crag Reach*.

And it's worked just fine in all the tests ashore, he reminded himself. *No point borrowing trouble by assuming the worst before it actually happens, Bruhstair!*

▼ ▼ ▼

Lieutenant Markys Zhasyn stood with his hands clasped behind him, looking down through the windscreen at the toy boat below, and tried not to worry. It wasn't the easiest thing he'd ever done because, technically, the Imperial Charisian Air Force "belonged" to the Navy. That was something of a sore point for some Air Force officers, although Zhasyn wasn't one of them.

Mostly.

He understood why the Navy—for painfully obvious reasons—was, and always would be, the senior service for the Charisian Empire, and much as he loved *Hahlys*, and however "airship crazy" he might be, the Air Force wasn't, and never would be. Airship design had advanced incredibly in just the last few years, but nothing could change the fact that they were fragile and weather-limited in ways surface vessels weren't. Yet despite that, their operational "model" was clearly far closer to the Navy's than it was to any army, so it was inevitable that the Admiralty had staked its claim early. And at least they'd created the Office of Aeronautics, headed by the Seventh Sea Lord. It might seem a little odd for airmen to answer to a *sea* lord, but it meant they were represented at the apex of the Navy's command structure. And while the officer who currently held that position was a mere commodore—and the youngest of the sea lords, to boot—he was also the most highly decorated aeronaut in Charisian service. Commodore Makadoo had piloted HMS *Gwylym Manthyr*'s kite balloon during the Battle of Gorath Bay and he'd spent the next four years working directly with Delthak Enterprises in the design process which had led directly to the *Duchess of Delthak*. Indeed, he'd left the Delthak engineering team only to assume command of the *Duchess* as Charis' first airship commander, and he was the one who'd written the training syllabus for all the other airship COs . . . including Markys Zhasyn. He'd clearly "paid his dues" on the technical side, as well as in combat, and he was also one of the officers who'd advocated most strongly for the creation of the Air Force.

That had been a tough fight, but they'd won it in the end—mostly. Air Force officers were still naval officers, but the Admiralty had ruled that the Air Force itself had to be commanded by someone who wore an aeronaut's wyvern wings on his chest. Someone who understood the operational realities and limitations of airships. Rear Admiral Aizak Cupyr had been a later convert than Makadoo, but he was as fiercely dedicated to the air as anyone in Charisian uniform, and under his command, the Air Force had been granted the same status as the Navy's six numbered fleets.

Yet there were plenty of Navy officers who didn't think the aeronauts deserved their special status, and that was what had Zhasyn worried as his command bored steadily through the air towards *Crag Reach*.

From everything Zhasyn had heard, Sir Bruhstair Ahbaht wasn't one of the people who wanted to strangle the Air Force in its crib. Not only that, Admiral Cupyr had served under him as a junior ship commander at Hahskyn Bay and again at Shipworm Island, which would probably incline him to actively support the Air Force. But if *Bryntyn Hahlys* managed to screw up today those *other* officers would shake their heads sadly while pointing out that they'd always known those newfangled airships were bound to come to a bad end. And, alas, Lieutenant Zhasyn's sad failure demonstrated precisely why it was a *terrible* idea to give the airmen so much independence.

Just getting here had been an adventure, given visibility conditions. And the rain. Fortunately, it wasn't raining here, and they'd encountered none of the violent thunderstorms that could swat an airship like a bug, only easier. They *had* run into quite a bit of rain, however, and he'd had to drop a lot of ballast to compensate for the weight of the rain which had coated the gas bag. Now that the active rain had ceased and the bag was drying, he'd been forced to vent more hydrogen than he really liked to keep from going too high and losing sight of the sea in the clouds. Of course, that particular problem was going to pretty much fix itself shortly, and—

"Fifteen minutes, Skipper," Lieutenant Mytchail, *Hahlys'* executive officer, said quietly from beside him.

"I know." Zhasyn nodded, then glanced at Mytchail. "*Please* don't embarrass us in front of the Admiral, Lohgyn!"

"Um, excuse me, Skipper, but isn't that pretty much up to Inzioh?"

Lieutenant Inzioh Bryttyn was *Bryntyn Hahlys'* navigator, which—through a process of logic Zhasyn didn't fully understand—had put him in charge of the critical aspect of today's exercise.

"And I've already discussed this with Inzioh," Zhasyn said, nodding again. "Now I'm discussing it with *you,* in the hallowed naval tradition of pointing out that the executive officer is responsible for everything that happens aboard his ship. And that shit flows downhill."

"Oh! I see." Mytchail's lips twitched and he looked away. "I'll just go keep an eye on him and encourage him, why don't I?"

"I think that would be a wonderful idea," Zhasyn agreed, and watched Mytchail head aft. Then he looked at the altitude coxswain at the elevator controls.

"Something amuses you?" he asked mildly.

"Oh, no, Sir!" the petty officer replied quickly, banishing what had certainly looked like a grin.

"Good," Zhasyn said, and turned his attention back to the steadily growing toy below.

▼ ▼ ▼

"Do you really think this is going to work, Sir?" Brahdryk asked in a thoughtful tone as he and Ahbaht watched the airship turn from a tiny model, no bigger than a man's hand, into an enormous behemoth, fully as large as—if far, far lighter than—*Crag Reach,* herself.

Ahbaht looked at him, and the captain shrugged.

"I mean, even if the trial works perfectly, do you really think it'll be practical under operational circumstances?"

"That's an excellent question," Ahbaht acknowledged after a moment. "And the answer is that no one knows. I don't think there's any question about airships' reconnaissance value, but this is a bit different. I'm pretty sure it *should* work—assuming it's practical at all—the first time or two. After that?" He shrugged. "A lot will depend on how low they have to come in, and a lot more will depend on what sort of weapons someone else comes up with to shoot them down." His eyes darkened. "We saw plenty of inventiveness like that out of the other side during the Jihad."

"That's what I was thinking, really," Brahdryk said. "I think some people tend to get all caught up with how inventive Duke Delthak's and Baron Seamount's people were and forget how . . . ingenious people like Thirsk and Lynkyn were. And let's not even get started on *Zhwaigair*!"

"Well, at least we'll know shortly whether or not it's practical under ideal conditions," Ahbaht said philosophically.

▼ ▼ ▼

"Steady!" Inzioh Bryttyn said loudly into the voice pipe. "That's perfect!"

"Aye, aye, Sir," the petty officer on the rudder wheel replied, and Bryttyn turned back to the eyepiece.

The sight was a simple device, provided by the Royal College and the Office of Aeronautics' own engineers. Unfortunately, it had to be mounted in the airship's very nose, well away from her bridge, and its accuracy depended on its ability to correctly estimate both *Bryntyn Hahlys'* altitude and her speed over the sea beneath her and set those values on the sight's adjusting knobs. Crosswind would be a factor, as well, although not a very great one, given the relatively modest altitude at which the weather had forced them to approach. And at least the wave pattern, combined with *Crag Reach*'s flag and her funnel smoke, gave him a crude yardstick of wind conditions at sea level.

The airship was equipped with an "altimeter," a closed, mercury-filled tube—rather like a barometer, in many ways—which calculated height by measuring air pressure. It wasn't perfectly accurate, but it was generally adequate when it came to determining altitude. Speed was trickier. *Bryntyn Hahlys* was provided with what Doctor Vyrnyr from the Royal College had dubbed a "pitot tube," similar to the one which had been developed for the earlier steamships, but more accurate, which allowed Bryttyn to be confident of the airship's speed through the air about it. Speed *over the ground* was trickier, given the chance of headwinds, tailwinds, or crosswinds . . . or all three in combination! That was why *Bryntyn Hahlys* had also been given a rangefinder which—in theory, at least—should have let him take timed ranges on *Crag Reach* as they approached. The rate at which the range decreased would have allowed him to judge their speed with acceptable accuracy. Unfortunately, visibility had been too poor for that until after they'd turned onto their final approach. That left him too little time for the *series* of ranges he would have required, so he'd just have to hope he'd estimated it correctly.

And if I didn't, the Skipper is so *going to rip me a new one,* he thought as he watched the raft edging towards the crosshair. *I really don't want—*

The raft reached the crosshair, he yanked the big handle, and HMAS *Bryntyn Hahlys* leapt upward.

▼ ▼ ▼

"*Yes!*" Sir Bruhstair Ahbaht said as the airship surged suddenly higher as its weight was abruptly reduced by a ton and a half.

Its altitude was down to three thousand feet when it dropped. From that height, it took the six plunging objects fourteen seconds to complete their fall. They were painted white, which made them easy to see against the dark gray sky, and they'd dropped nose-first from the individual cells in which they'd been stored. Each of them weighed five hundred pounds, about the same as one of *Crag Reach*'s ten-inch shells, but they were both longer and thinner, and they'd been fitted with stabilizing vanes, like the fletching of some squat, bullet-shaped arrow.

He hadn't been prepared for the whistling sound they made, although he should have been. He'd heard more than enough shells rumble overhead as they reached the end of their journey, after all. But somehow—

His thought broke off as the projectiles—the Office of Aeronautics had christened them "aerobombs," although he was confident that would be shortened simply to "bomb" with indecent haste—struck. They came down in a line that crossed the target raft at an angle, following the base course of the airship. The first two landed short and the last one landed long, but the other three "aerobombs" smashed directly into the raft. He heard the crashing thuds even over the sounds of a ship underway, and his eyebrows rose. That was a higher percentage of hits than he would have been willing to predict. On the other hand, the airship had been supposed to drop from *six* thousand feet, not three.

Yes, she was. On the other hand, she only dropped six of the damned things. Full load, even with maximum fuel on board, and she could carry four times that many. And—

"That's a lot better than I expected, Sir Bruhstair," Captain Brahdryk said.

"Better than I expected, too," Ahbaht acknowledged. "On the other hand, they dropped lower than planned and we weren't doing a thing to make their job any harder." He shrugged. "Steaming at fifteen knots in a straight line without even trying to dodge isn't the sort of thing someone who knew what was coming would be likely to do."

"No," Brahdryk acknowledged. "On the other hand, they only had six aerobombs on board. On actual operations, they'd have a lot more," he continued, speaking Ahbaht's own thoughts out loud. "And they'd hit the *deck*, not the belt."

"Yes, they would." Ahbaht nodded, because that was a very good point.

Even at extreme range, shells fired at a ship came in on low trajectories, because there was a practical limit to the range at which one ship could hit another. In theory, *Crag Reach*'s guns could have reached a target at fourteen thousand yards, but no gunnery officer could actually *hit* another ship at an eight-mile range. Her best realistic range couldn't exceed much over five or six thousand yards, and that meant virtually all hits would be on the sides of their targets, and that any shell which did hit a ship's decks would strike at a shallow angle and tend to skip like a stone thrown across a pond.

Obviously, therefore, a ship's side had to be heavily armored, and her decks . . . didn't. Which was good, since a ship had so much more deck area than side area. *Crag Reach* was almost five hundred feet long, with a beam of eighty feet. Her citadel—the portion of her hull protected by armor—was just over three hundred feet long and her armored belt was approximately fifteen feet deep. That meant both belts *combined* contained 9,000 square feet of armor. Her armored deck was just over seventy-six feet wide, however, which gave *it* an area of 23,100 square feet. That meant each inch of deck armor cost well over two and half times as much tonnage as an inch of side armor, so no designer wanted to add any more of it than he had to. Cutting half an inch off the deck armor let him increase the side armor—the armor that would actually be *threatened*—by almost an inch and half.

But an "aerobomb" would arrive on a very steep—indeed, on a *vertical*—trajectory. It would strike at a direct right angle and deliver all of its force to the deck, not skip across it.

"How does the drop speed compare to our guns' muzzle velocity, Sir?" Brahdryk asked.

"From the height they actually dropped at, I don't know," Bruhstair confessed with a shrug. "According to what I was told when I discussed the exercise with Admiral Cupyr and Commodore Makadoo, if they'd dropped from their intended altitude, the 'aerobombs' would've been traveling at between a fifth and a quarter of a ten-inch's muzzle velocity."

"Ouch."

"I agree, given that we've only got about two inches of deck armor."

Brahdryk nodded. *Crag Reach*'s main belt was better than three times that thick.

"And there's not any reason they couldn't make the damned things bigger," Bruhstair continued. "Commodore Makadoo was kind enough to share the numbers with me. A five-hundred-pound aerobomb falling from five thousand feet would have about the same impact energy as a shell from one of our eight-inch guns. Of course, the eight-inchers don't hold a candle to what the ten-inch can hand out, but that's still impressive. And if they dropped a *thousand*-pound aerobomb, it would have twice the impact energy. For that matter, they're playing around with a *two*-thousand-pound monster." Brahdryk's eyes widened, and Bruhstair didn't blame him. "If they dropped one of those things from five thousand feet, it would hit with about five times the eight-inch shell's force. And it would be delivered directly to the deck."

"Shan-wei," Brahdryk murmured, and Bruhstair shrugged.

"Frankly, I don't expect the chance of scoring a hit

from that high to be very good under actual combat conditions, but any hits that do land—especially if they weigh a *ton* apiece and they're filled with Composition D—are likely to be . . . I suppose 'devastating' would be a pretty good choice of words. And, theoretically, I don't see any reason they couldn't build one of the things to weigh as much as two or even *three* tons. The *Duchairns* can carry almost seven tons at maximum range. If they cut back on the range, they can increase that a bit, but at full load, her fuel only weighs about seven thousand pounds, so there's the trade-off. But they're already projecting that the next class of airship will be even bigger with an even bigger capacity. So say they get it up to ten tons and load one of them up with five two-ton aerobombs?" He shook his head. "Even a five-hundred-pounder would punch through our deck armor. A two-*ton* aerobomb would punch through the deck like an awl and keep going straight out the keel!"

Brahdryk shook his head, his expression almost numb, and Bruhstair smiled with very little humor.

"So I suppose you can see why Duke Rock Point and Their Majesties think it would be a really good idea to not let anyone else figure out what we're up to . . . or how to do it to *us*."

MARCH YEAR OF GOD 913

◆

. I .
HMS *Seeker*,
Hannah Bay,
and
Ducal Palace,
City of Carmyn,
Grand Duchy of Zebediah,
Empire of Charis.

"Permission to come on the bridge, Captain?" the wiry young man asked.

Commander Edwyrd Chermyn looked over his shoulder as HMS *Seeker*, a *Falcon*-class cruiser of the Imperial Charisian Navy, steamed steadily down the center of the passage between Grass Island and Dolphin Island. The sun was high overhead, heating the decks like an oven, and the banner of *Seeker*'s funnel smoke hung heavy in the air. Even the seabirds and wyverns, wheeling around the cruiser in winged kind's perpetual optimism that something tasty would turn up in her wake, seemed heavy and sodden with the heat.

Hannah Bay without a wind was the closest approximation to hell Commander Chermyn ever hoped to experience, even for a boy from Old Charis.

It was also the approach to the place he called home.

"Permission granted, Your Highness," he said now, and Daivyn Daikyn stepped out onto the bridge wing beside him.

"How much longer, Edwyrd?" Daivyn asked, taking

off his broad-brimmed hat long enough to fan himself and then hurriedly putting it back on as the sun beat down on the crown of his unprotected head.

"We're making a good fifteen knots, so call it just under eight hours," Chermyn said, and smiled quizzically. "About the same length of time it takes every time you ask me that."

"I've only made this trip with you three times before," Daivyn shot back with a grin, "and this is the first time I've made it on a ship you commanded. I figured you might be less . . . stodgy than some of your earlier captains and open the taps a bit."

"'Open the taps' is an unbecoming piece of engine room slang which a properly reared ruling prince shouldn't know," Chermyn said severely.

"Maybe not a 'properly reared' ruling prince, but what, precisely, does that have to do with *me*?" Daivyn inquired.

"I know Irys and Hektor did their very best with you." Chermyn shook his head. "All that effort for nothing!"

"Absolutely!" Daivyn agreed enthusiastically. "Don't forget, I had Cayleb's example, too."

"True," Chermyn conceded.

"Well, there you are." Daivyn shrugged. "And, having established that I'm a less-than-proper prince, I can use whatever unbecoming slang I want."

"Until Irys hears you doing it, you mean?"

"Of course I do. You think I'm dumb enough to use it when she's around?"

Daivyn grinned infectiously, and Chermyn shook his head. That smile could charm anyone—probably even a Zebediahan, assuming the Zebediahan in question didn't shoot before he saw it—and Chermyn was still astonished at times to realize it was totally sincere. The prince would be twenty-eight years old in four months, but he'd never lost that bubbling zest for life, which was really remarkable when one considered that he'd been orphaned when he was only eight and spent the next two years knowing his own life hung from a thread. He'd been too young to fully understand the reasons for that, but he'd always been an intelligent, observant child. He might not have understood why Zhaspahr Clyntahn considered his assassination at "Charisian" hands a useful tool, but he'd been far from blind to the peril in which he stood. Surely that had to have left a mark, left the bitterness of that fear in its wake.

Yet it hadn't. Somehow, it hadn't. There were dark spots in there, Chermyn knew, but they were very tiny.

"Speaking of 'dumb,'" the commander said now, "might I ask where Tobys is? Since, after all, we are going to be arriving in Carmyn this afternoon and I'm sure Father would like to keep you alive."

"Don't be such a pessimist!" Daivyn scolded. "Nobody's even shot at me *once* in Carmyn on the last three visits."

"Always a first time," Chermyn replied, "and this is the first time Frahncheska's been home in almost five years. I've seen her once—no, twice—in all that time, and I'd really hate for her homecoming to be spoiled by a state funeral."

He smiled, but there was more than a trace of seriousness in his voice. The House of Daikyn was not universally beloved in Zebediah, and for very good cause. Those causes had nothing at all to do with Daivyn, but embittered people seldom relied upon anything so pallid as logic or reason.

"I understand what you're saying," Daivyn acknowledged, but he also shook his head. "And I can't blame some of them for wanting my head, Edwyrd, but I honestly don't think anyone's likely to try taking it. Still, I promise—Tobys has given me the lecture, I've listened, and I won't be going anywhere without your father's permission and half a battalion or so of bodyguards." He grimaced. "Makes it a little hard to roam the markets incognito."

"That's sort of the point," Chermyn replied. "And while I wouldn't want you to get a swelled head or anything, I'm fond of you myself. Not to mention the fact that if I let anything happen to you, Irys and Hektor will have *my* head."

"Nonsense. They'd blame me for it. Besides, Tobys will flatten me and drag me home over his shoulder if he thinks I'm doing anything I shouldn't. No respect for authority at all, that man!"

Chermyn snorted. Lieutenant Tobys Raimair had headed Prince Daivyn's personal guard for the last seventeen years, and he probably would "flatten" his prince in an instant if he thought Daivyn was in danger. In fact, according to reports, he'd done something very like that during Daivyn's and Irys' escape from Delferahk.

"I don't think it's 'authority' he has any trouble respecting," the commander said.

"I think that was probably an insult," Daivyn said suspiciously.

"Nonsense! I have plenty of respect for authority, too."

▼ ▼ ▼

Frahncheska Chermyn watched the sleek cruiser slide smoothly alongside the stone quay without benefit of tugs. Mooring lines went ashore, dropped over bollards, and windlasses took up tension, nuzzling *Seeker* more firmly against the fender-protected pilings. The smells of the harbor were stronger than usual in the hot, windless late afternoon, and her nostrils flared. Not all of those smells were pleasant, but they were familiar and comforting.

"He did that well," her Aunt Mathylda—known on formal occasions as Her Grace, Mathylda, Grand Duchess of Zebediah—observed with maternal pride. She was a slender, silver-haired woman with wise brown eyes that laughed a lot. She was also the only mother Frahncheska had ever truly known.

"Of course he did it well!" she replied. "He wouldn't dare *not* do it well knowing you were standing here watching."

"I am fierce, aren't I?" Mathylda said reflectively.

"Oh, horribly so," Frahncheska reassured her.

"You're always such a comfort to me, dear. None of the boys ever understood me half as well as you did!"

Mathylda gave her a quick hug. "That's why I missed you so much."

"Well, I'm home now." Frahncheska hugged her back. "I loved Tellesberg, and I'm going to miss the College, but the truth is, I'm happier here, heat and all."

"Only because you were so young when we were first stationed here. You never had a chance to learn what a reasonable climate was like, poor baby," Mathylda said, and Frahncheska shook her head.

Mathylda Chermyn had been born about as commonly as anyone could, and no one had warned her she might one day become a grand duchess with almost eight million subjects. To this day, even after eighteen years in the Ducal Palace, she still thought of herself as the wife of a Marine first and a ruler's consort second. Or third. That had never kept her from doing her job, though, and Frahncheska was pretty sure she clung to the memory of that Marine's wife to help herself remember her humble origins when she dealt with all those other common-born subjects for whom she'd become responsible.

And that was one reason, among many, that the people of Zebediah loved her. Of course, if anyone ever mentioned that to Aunt Mathylda, she simply pointed out—rather tartly—that Zebedia would have been prepared to love *anyone* who replaced Tohmys Symmyns. Which, as far as Frahncheska could determine, was also true.

She shook her head at the thought as the brow ran out from the wharf to *Seeker*'s side. The cruiser towered over the three naval schooners anchored farther out into the harbor. There were fewer sailing vessels left in commission every year, and Frahncheska knew her cousin Edwyrd felt a certain nostalgic regret for that. She supposed she should have, too—schooners were certainly *prettier* than steamships—but four years at the Royal College had thoroughly infected her with the Charisian drive for innovation and ever-increasing efficiency. More than that, she'd studied with Doctor Wyllys. She understood what the Imperial Charisian Navy's new oil-fired boilers meant for cruising ranges, and so she knew the endurance which had given those schooners their additional lease on life in naval service was about to become far less relevant.

She truly was glad to be back, though. Carmyn was little more than a large town compared to Tellesberg, and it was undeniably provincial, but it was also the place she would always think of as home.

"Looks like Daivyn's about to disembark," Mathylda observed, watching the uniformed guardsmen coming to attention at the landward end of the brow.

"Yes," Frahncheska half sighed, shaking her head. Mathylda looked at her, and she grimaced. "I just hate it that we have to worry so much about someone wanting to hurt him, Aunt Mathylda. It's just so . . . so *stupid*."

"Frahncheska, not even your uncle runs around Carmyn without bodyguards. He won't let you or me do it, either. Do you really expect him to let anything happen to *Daivyn* on our watch?"

"It's not quite the same, Aunt Mathylda," Frahncheska pointed out, looking at the pair of guardsmen who'd accompanied them down to dockside. "We have two bodyguards; by my count, Daivyn has *eleven*, even before you add Tobys and Sergeant Wahltahrs to the mix. That's an awful lot of guards to drag around everywhere he goes."

"Better to inconvenience him than let him go home dead," Mathylda said a bit acerbically, but then she smiled. "I'm sure he'll be happy to know such a lovely young lady sympathizes with his plight, though."

"Oh, I'm sure!" Frahncheska bubbled a laugh. "We've known each other since he was eleven and I was *almost* nine. I don't really recall which of us kicked the other in the shins that first day, but it was probably me. Not that he didn't make up for it later! And the *last* time we visited Manchyr, I had that hideous acne. My entire face was one huge blotch, and all I wanted to do was hide under a barrel somewhere! Somehow I don't think he'd be all that impressed if I started batting my eyes and languishing in his direction after all these years."

"But that was before you went off to school." The teasing gleam in Mathylda's eyes was stronger than it had been. "He hasn't seen you in almost five years, dear, and you've done some growing up since. Some filling out, too, now that I think about it, and—" she cocked her head, studying her niece's countenance closely "—that acne of yours has cleared up without a trace. More to the point, he's visted here twice since you left and he's asked about you each time, you know."

"Oh my God! Not *twice* in five years, Aunt Mathylda?!" Frahncheska widened her eyes. "Why, after paying someone *that* kind of attention, he'll have to marry the girl!"

"I don't think the situation's quite that dire," Mathylda replied dryly. "But he *is* going to be glad to see you, I think. He's missed you, just like the rest of us."

"Well, I'm home now, and I'm not going anywhere else," Frahncheska said firmly. "Except maybe back to Tellesberg for a semester or two in a couple of years. Doctor Wyllys is talking about opening a subsidiary of Southland Drilling here in Corisande. Father Ahmbrohs says there should be a good-sized oilfield between Dragon Bay and the Wyvern Ridges."

"You're planning on going into business?"

"Well, a girl can't live off her family's generosity forever, Aunt Mathylda! Besides, you know I can't resist a challenge. And that's your and Uncle Hauwyl's fault."

"Guilty, I suppose." Mathylda shook her head. Then she nodded towards the moored ship. "I know Edwyrd's not coming ashore until he's finished arranging for fuel and water, so you and I should go collect Daivyn, tell him hello, and get him safely to the Palace."

▼ ▼ ▼

"See, Tobys? All the way to the Palace, and not a shot fired."

"This time," Tobys Raimair replied deflatingly, and Prince Daivyn shook his head.

"You're only this way because you're not going to admit not everyone in Zebediah wants to kill me. Well, and because you have absolutely no sense of humor, too, I suppose."

"First, I'm thinking as at least, oh, half a dozen Zebediahans—maybe even a whole dozen—probably don't want to kill you. Second, didn't think a sense of humor was required for the job, Your Highness."

"It's not required for a *bodyguard,* Tobys," Daivyn told him with a smile. "It *is* sort of required for a curmudgeonly old nanny . . . who's spent too many years keeping me alive."

"Imagine I can go on doing that a while longer, assuming you don't do anything stupid. Your Highness."

Daivyn laughed, then stepped out onto the long, covered balcony that ran the entire length of the Ducal Palace's southern façade. It was positioned to provide as many hours of shade as was physically possible this close to the equator, and a breeze had sprung up, offering a certain blessed relief to the day's fierce heat.

"I wish we could've come by airship," he said over his shoulder. "I really like Edwyrd, and *Seeker*'s a beautiful ship, but an airship would've been a lot faster."

"At least until it fell out of the sky or blew up," Raimair agreed. "That'd be exciting, I guess."

"I am a reigning prince, you know," Daivyn told him. "Sometimes I think you and Phylyp have a little trouble remembering that."

"Oh? Was it the Earl who put his foot down about that? Here I was thinking it was Princess Irys."

"I'm sure I have no idea at all what you're talking about."

"Princess Irys," Raimair said helpfully. "You remember her, don't you? Tallish? Chestnut hair? And the fact that, like any sane man, you know better than to cross her? I mean, *I'm* not going to argue with her, and I don't rightly remember the last time *you* did, now that I think about it.

"I keep forgetting how hot it gets here," Daivyn said, pointedly changing the subject as Raimair joined him on the balcony. "I think of *Manchyr* as 'hot.' This is something else again!"

"Something else like, oh, the hinges of hell?" Raimair offered.

"Actually, yes." Daivyn smiled at him. "I'm glad it's cooler now, though. Especially if the Grand Duke's serious about eating on the terrace."

"I misremember the last time His Grace *wasn't* serious when it came to eating, Your Highness." It was Raimair's turn to smile. "That man was a Marine for too many years to take mealtimes for granted."

"Then I guess I'd better change and get my royal posterior down there."

▾ ▾ ▾

"Whoa!"

Daivyn Daikyn braked hard, but not quickly enough to avoid the collision. The unfortunate victim of his impetuosity bounced with an "Oof!", stumbling backwards down the steep stone steps, arms windmilling, and his hand shot out to catch her before she could fall.

"Sorry!" he said. "I was in too big a hurry! Are you all right, Frahncheska?"

"Unbroken, I think," she replied a bit breathlessly, checking carefully to be sure that was true. The impact had caught her by surprise, and he was a surprisingly solid weight for someone so wiry. On the other hand, she'd just discovered there was quite a lot of muscle packed onto that slim frame. He was a small man, barely two inches taller than she, but his grip on her forearm had caught her effortlessly before she could fall.

"I really am sorry," he said contritely.

He released her arm cautiously as she came back on balance. He really had hit her hard, though, and he watched her carefully as she got herself back together, because it was obvious the impact had shaken her more than she cared to admit.

She was taller than he remembered, he thought. Then again, she was more than three years younger than he was. She'd been only eighteen—barely sixteen in the years of a planet called Old Terra, of which neither of them had ever heard—when she went off to the College, and he hadn't seen her in almost five years. As he looked at her, trying to find the little girl who'd played screaming games of tag with him—not to mention a tough short-stop's position—on visits to Manchyr with her aunt and uncle, he realized she'd changed in those five years.

In fact, she'd changed a *lot*.

"I never did learn to slow down," he continued. "Except on formal occasions, of course." He grimaced. "I usually do a better job of not running over people, though."

"I know." She nodded. "On the subject of not running over people, however, where's the shadow that follows you everywhere and makes sure nobody runs over *you*?"

"Tobys?" Daivyn chuckled. "Even Tobys is willing to let me out of his sight here in the Palace. He says the Ducal Guard would never dare face your uncle again after something happened to me on their watch."

"Does he?" Frahncheska smiled. "That's pretty much what Aunt Mathylda says, too. And not just because it would be a major diplomatic faux pas. They actually like you quite a lot, you know."

"Well, of course they do." He released her forearm and offered her his elbow, escorting her the rest of the way down the winding flight of steps to the shaded terrace. Her head topped his shoulder by a comfortable margin, but she did it without towering over him, he noticed, which felt nice for some reason. "I'm a very likable fellow. Except for those unreconstructed Zebediah-ans who continue to hold my father against me."

He said it lightly, but she cocked her head at him. The edge of regret in that last sentence was more poorly hidden than he'd thought.

"It's not really so hard to understand, is it?" she asked. "I'm not saying it's reasonable or that you deserve it, because it isn't and you don't. But it's very human of them."

"Oh, I know. And I don't really blame them for it. I don't lie awake at home in Manchyr fretting about it, either. It's only when I'm actually here in Carmyn that I realize how . . . depressing it is to know so many people

I never even met hate me just because of who I chose as a father."

"Is it that?" Frahncheska paused, drawing him to a stop at the foot of the stairs in the shade of a massive tree. A much more youthful prince's initials were carved into its bark somewhere, he recalled, as he looked up into its branches.

"Excuse me?" He raised an eyebrow, looking down into her gray-green eyes. They were large and dark, and he realized that this truly wasn't the schoolgirl he'd teased and played tag with in Manchyr or on his much rarer visits to Carmyn.

"Is it really depressing because they hate *you*? Or is it because you know they still hate your *father*?"

He started to reply quickly, dismissively. But then he stopped and looked at her more intently, and his own eyes narrowed as he considered what she'd just said and realized no one else had ever asked him that question. Not even himself.

"I . . . don't know," he said after a moment, his tone serious. "I never really thought about that."

"Not consciously," she told him, squeezing his forearm gently. "But I remember you and Irys talking about him when we were all younger. I remember how much you loved him."

"I don't really remember him very clearly anymore," Daivyn said softly, looking away from her. "I think I remembered him a lot better then, but now he's just . . . slipping away. That bothers me, sometimes."

"Daivyn, you were only seven when he died. Of course you don't remember him as clearly as you'd like to! I never even *met* my father, though. I don't have any memories of him at all. Or of my mother, really." He looked at her quickly, and she shook her head. "I regret that, but it's not like I didn't have Uncle Hauwyl and Aunt Mathylda! I may technically be an orphan, but trust me, I *have* parents. Still, maybe that does give me a little more insight. I remember thinking how much I envied you and Irys that you'd at least *known* your father, and I know her memories of him have to be stronger than yours. But one thing you obviously did remember was that he loved you and you loved him. Maybe to other people he was a prince, and maybe to other people he was a bloodthirsty tyrant, but to you, he was your father. And you never got the chance to grow up with him, or to learn to know him. For that matter, you never had the chance to know whether or not what everyone else says about him was the only truth in his life. Or to defend him, if it wasn't."

His gaze locked with hers, and she shook her head again, more gently.

"Daivyn, how could it not feel like they're attacking him when he's not even here to defend himself? And how could you not feel like that's an attack on the loving father you knew and not the conquering prince *they* knew?"

"You may be right about that," he said slowly. "There's certainly some truth to it, at any rate." He gazed at her for another moment, then shook himself and smiled suddenly. "Is that one of the things they taught you at the College?"

"I will have you know, Your Highness," she told him, elevating her nose, "that I studied geology and chemistry at the College. My deep and profound understanding of human nature results solely from the keenness of my powers of observation and the power of my own intellect."

"My God, you got that all out without cracking a single smile! I am awed."

"And well you should be," she told him with a laugh.

He laughed with her, but there was an odd edge to his gaze, as if he'd never truly seen her before. An edge which, for all of the keenness of her powers of observation, went by her unnoticed.

"I'm pretty sure they'll be setting up for supper by now," she went on, still holding his forearm and towing him back into motion towards the stone tables at the center of the terrace. "Come on! I'm starving—let's go steal some 'samples' of the roast lizard!"

JUNE YEAR OF GOD 913

·◆·

. I .
Zhutiyan,
Chynduk Valley,
Tiegelkamp Province,
Central Harchong.

"Tangwyn, you have to *rest*."

Yanshwyn Syngpu's voice was soft enough no one else could have heard it through the background of moans, but her eyes were dark in a deeply worried face as she gazed up at her husband.

"I can't. Not yet," he said.

"You have to!" she said more fiercely. "How much good will you do any of us if you *collapse*?!"

"Not going to collapse." He produced a smile. "I was lots tireder than this during the Jihad."

"I doubt that," she said flatly. "And when you were more tired than this before, had you also been *wounded*?" Her tone was even flatter. "And were you the commander in chief?"

He started to reply quickly, then made himself stop as her eyes dared him to lie about it.

"No," he admitted finally. "But that only makes it more important for me to be here. These are *my* boys, Yanshwyn! I'm the one who got them *hurt*!"

"For a smart man, you can be really stupid—did you know that?!" she snapped. "*You* didn't get anyone hurt, and a lot more of them would've been *killed* without you! Now I'm done arguing." She looked at him very,

very levelly. "You *are* going to rest, and Miyang and Father Yngshwan both agree with me on this. The last thing any of us need is you collapsing, and *don't* tell me how tired you were during the Jihad!"

He looked at her, then turned away, looking at the enormous barn where they'd danced that first dance together. The hay bales were gone, and the plank floor had been turned into a hospital. There were over four hundred men on that floor, every one of them wounded, and every one of them wounded under his command.

And another three or four hundred of their companions had been left behind, dead. Dead or captured, and captured was probably worse, given the "examples" Grand Duke Spring Flower and Baron Qwaidu would make of them. The anguish of that loss ripped through him again, but then he made himself look back down into the exhausted, frightened, loving, furious eyes of his wife.

"All right," he conceded finally. "A few hours."

"At least eight." Her voice was a bit less flexible than steel. "And that's not just from me, you stubborn, stiff-necked, falling-down idiot! It's from the healers, too. So we're not going to discuss it . . . *are* we?"

He hovered on the brink of arguing, but he knew she was right. He didn't *want* her to be, but wanting never changed anything, now did it?

"All right," he said. "Let me just tell Zhou—"

He broke off, his jaw clenching, and felt himself sway drunkenly, ever so slightly. No one else would've noticed, but Yanshwyn did. Her arm went around his waist instantly, and he was astonished yet again by the strength of that delicate-boned body as she steadied him. He closed his eyes and let her hug him for a moment, then shook his head.

"Let me just tell *Baisung* I'm going," he said, and his voice was almost normal. It didn't fool her. He would never be telling Zhouhan Husan anything ever again. Not after today.

"I already told him you would be," she said softly, her own eyes gleaming with tears and her arm squeezing again. "Now come on, Tangwyn. You really do need to rest, and you know it."

He nodded wearily, admitting defeat—*another* defeat—and let her lead him from the barn.

▼ ▼ ▼

The moonless night outside the town hall was dark and still, pressing down on Zhutiyan like a hand. The window was open. They could hear the sounds of insects, of night wyverns, of the wind. It was all so . . . peaceful. Normal. But the reality was something else entirely.

"So how bad is it, really?" Mayor Ou-zhang said, looking around his study.

No one answered the mayor for a second or two, but then Syngpu inhaled deeply. Yanshwyn had been serious; she'd put him to bed and she'd left him there. Not for eight hours, but for almost ten, and the fact that he'd slept that long proved how badly he'd needed to. Despite that, he felt almost worse than when he'd gone down, at least physically. The shoulder wound was worse than he'd been willing to admit to himself. He was fortunate there'd been no bone damage and there were no early signs of infection, either, but the healers had given him Pasquale's holy hell for how hard he'd pushed it. They'd also loaded him up with pain root—which might have had a little to do with how long he'd slept—and made him swear he'd use the sling. Worse, they'd made him promise *Yanshwyn* he would.

Beside that, the hip was only a bruise. Enough to make walking painful and slow, but no worse than that.

Which meant that now, as he looked out into the night from the same study window he'd looked out that first day, the mayor's question rolling through his brain, he was rested and fresh enough to feel the other, greater pain of so many dead and wounded. That was a pain no medicine could quell. But Yanshwyn had been right about the other reasons he'd needed to rest, and he drew the strength of his wife around him as his eyes came back from the window to the people sitting in that study with him.

"It's not good, and that's a fact," he said grimly. "It's not so terrible just now, aside from all the lads we've lost, but looking forward, it's not good, Zaipau. Not good."

The weary, strained faces around him tightened, but he owed them the truth.

"I sat down with Baisung, after Yanshwyn finally let me out of bed." His wife looked up, her pen pausing for just a moment, and he smiled at her. "He was almost as tired as I was when the lot of you made me turn in," he continued, then, "but we're pretty much in agreement about what happened.

"The nub is that Spring Flower and Qwaidu must've gotten a shipment of new-model rifles from Yu-kwau after all. We captured some of 'em. Most of them're knock-offs of the St. Kylmahn, just like ours. But a couple of them're like the ones the Charisians were using at the end of the Jihad, with magazines that hold six rounds." He shook his head, his eyes bleak. "Don't know how many of those they've got, but *any* are too many.

"The ground's still on our side. Losing Zhyndow exposes us a *little* more than we were, but we can handle that. What we can't handle are the numbers, especially if he's getting more of these new rifles. It's not just the magazines, either."

Heads nodded. The men—and woman—in this room understood exactly what he meant.

Baisung Tsungshai had, indeed, gotten the rifle manufactory back up and running, although the lack of iron and the fact that he had only charcoal, not coke, made it impossible to produce steel—even if any of them had known how to do that in the first place—and the absence of steel prevented any sort of large-scale weapons *production*. What he had been able to accomplish was to produce the spare parts to keep all of the rifles they did have in good repair. He'd been able to set up his powder mill, as well, and that was one of the bright spots, because its output met their needs comfortably and had allowed them to build up a substantial reserve. And if the Valley was practically devoid of iron ore, there were significant deposits of lead in the mountains above Haudyn, and they had plenty of bullet molds.

No, spare parts, gunpowder, and bullets weren't a problem. Percussion caps, unfortunately, were.

No one in the Chynduk Valley knew how to make them, and so, Tsungshai and the artisans he'd trained had been forced to convert the caplock St. Kylmahns into flintlocks. There were plentiful supplies of flint in the Valley, and flintlocks at least had the virtue of being simple to build and maintain.

They also had at least twice as many misfires as a regular St. Kylmahn, and they were virtually useless in the rain.

That hadn't mattered while Grand Duke Spring Flower was similarly cut off from new-model weapons. But that clearly wasn't the case any longer.

"I'd like to tell you it was only the new weapons we didn't know they had, but the truth is, they surprised us, too," Syngpu continued, his voice heavy but unflinching. "We never—*I* never—expected Qwaidu to throw that big a column straight up the Valley. It cost him. Well, it cost his *men,* anyway, because Zhouhan and our boys *hammered* 'em before they broke through. The new rifles *were* a part of it, because I know Zhouhan didn't expect them any more than I would've. But it was the sheer numbers that did it. We're just lucky we managed to stop them at the Kwyfan Farm."

They nodded in agreement yet again, but Miyang Gyngdau seemed to hover on the brink of saying something in reply. He didn't, and Syngpu breathed a silent sigh of gratitude. He suspected what the squire had wanted to say, but Tangwyn Syngpu wasn't the reason the invaders had been stopped at the crossroads twenty-odd miles northwest of Zhyndow. Oh, he'd gotten there in time to take command—and to get his idiot self shot—but it was the lads. It was the men he'd trained, the ones who'd come to the Valley with him and the Valleyers who'd been prepared to die where they stood. The man who'd stood at his back like a stone wall. A stone wall that screamed and bled and died but would *not* retreat. *They* were what had stopped the bastards.

"We're not getting Zhyndow back, though," he continued grimly, hoping he didn't show how grateful he was for Gyngdau's silence. "I'd like to, but we're not. And truth is the Valley's narrower at Kwyfan's. We can put a better cork into it there. And even if we wanted Zhyndow back, Qwaidu at least is smart enough to not let us have it. It's too good a staging point, and it cuts us off from the mountain lizard paths going east. With him holding Zhyndow and Syang—I guess he's officially 'Baron Cliffwall' these days—blocking the northern end at Ky-su, we're screwed."

He looked around the study again, saw the tightness of the expressions, the shadows in the eyes, and shook his head slowly.

"Wish I didn't have to say that. Wish it wasn't true. But the one thing I've always promised you was to be honest. They aren't coming through next five-day, or the one after that. They got hurt too bad themselves to try again for at least a month or so. But they'll be back. When they do decide to come through, we'll hurt them even worse'n we did this time. But they've got a lot more men than we do, and now it looks like they've got the new-model weapons to give 'em, we can't stop them forever. We can bleed 'em, and we could probably hold out—some of us—for months, even longer, up in the high coves. But that might be the worst thing we could do."

"Why?" Father Yngshwan asked quietly.

"Because the only bargaining point we have is to turn me and my boys over to Qwaidu and Spring Flower," Syngpu said bluntly. "We do that, he might be willing to settle for making the examples out of *us*. But if we try to hold out, fight some kind of guerrilla war, he'll burn this Valley from one end to the other, if that's what it takes. We've pissed him off too much, and we've been too much of an example—too much proof he's not some Archangel who can do whatever he wants with the wave of a hand. Bastard can't have that."

"We're not handing you—!" Yanshwyn began hotly, but Gyngdau stopped her with a raised hand.

"We're not handing *anyone* over *to* anyone anytime soon, Yanshwyn," he told her quietly, firmly. "And, if it comes to handing people over, Tangwyn, I don't think you're in any position to claim all the honors." He smiled thinly. "I'm pretty sure Spring Flower has a thought or two in mind for me, too. And Zaipu and Yngshwan, come to that. That doesn't mean you're wrong to be thinking about that possibility. But not yet. Not yet."

"I'm not educated," Syngpu said, reaching out to take Yanshwyn's hand. "Yanshwyn—she's been working on that, but seems to me she's still got a ways to go. But I can hear thunder and see lightning. My boys and I, we're ready to fight if there was even a *chance* we could hold in the end. Problem is, I don't think there is."

"Perhaps we could send for help?" Father Yngshwan said.

The others looked at him, and he raised both hands almost as if in a gesture of blessing. His eyes were much calmer than anyone else's, too. It would have been too much to call them serene, but there was . . . an acceptance in them Syngpu knew he couldn't have matched.

"Send where?" Gyngdau asked almost gently. "To whom? And how?"

"If what we'd heard about the 'United Provinces' before Cliffwall closed the passes is accurate, they have to be expanding our way," the priest said in a reasonable tone. "It would make a lot of sense for them to secure enough of Tiegelkamp to control everything west of the Chiang-wus, and controlling Cliffwall Pass and the Valley would be a very good way for them to do that."

"Even if they're expanding our way, they aren't here yet, Yngshwan," Ou-zhang pointed out. "I'm sure they have their own priorities closer to home, too. And even if they didn't, how are we supposed to invite them to come rescue us?"

"There are those lizard paths Tangwyn mentioned," Father Yngshwan pointed out. "They lead west, as well as east. And it's still only June."

"You're serious," Gyngdau said.

"Of course I am," the priest said calmly, and smiled.

"First, because I'm a priest! I'm the sort of fellow who *looks* for miracles. Second, because the people of this Valley are too good and care about each other too much for me to believe God and the Archangels aren't going to remember that bit about helping those who help themselves. And, third, because I will be *damned* if I sit here and listen to people I love talk about handing themselves over to that butcher Spring Flower just to buy a little more time, a little mitigation, for the rest of us." He shook his head. "Believe me, if you don't want to hear anathemas thundered from my church, you're not going to even *think* about that possibility until we've tried everything else."

He looked around the faces, and his eyes were as hard and as stubborn as anyone else in that study had ever seen as he let the silence linger for a good ten seconds.

"I trust all of that was clearly understood. Or do I need to go back and explain the hard words?"

"Yngshwan, it's not that we *want*—" Gyngdau began, then broke off as someone rapped lightly on the study door.

He and the others looked at each other. It was very late, only a few hours until dawn, and everyone knew how little they needed any interruptions while they coped with the oncoming tide of disaster.

Whoever it was rapped again, and the squire sat back, shook his head, and waved at the mayor.

"What?" Ou-zhang called, raising his voice.

Then the door opened, and every person in that study froze as a man stepped through it. They'd never seen him in their lives, yet they recognized him instantly. It wasn't very difficult, because he was very tall, with black hair lightly dusted with silver, and his eyes were impossibly dark in the lamplight. He wore a blackened breastplate badged with the black, gold, blue, and white of the House of Ahrmahk, and he swept a graceful bow into the stunned, motionless silence. Then he straightened, stroking one of his fiercely waxed mustachios.

"I apologize for interrupting without any warning, but I believe we may need to talk," Merlin Athrawes said.

"You think Star Rising and the others are really ready to move that much farther east?" Cayleb Ahrmahk asked over the com as Merlin leaned back in his flight couch. The imperial family was back in Chisholm, accompanied by Lywys Whytmyn, and Merlin shrugged as the recon skimmer sped west to rejoin them.

"I think they'll be more than a little surprised by the timing, but it's not like this isn't something they've been talking about—with us, as much as with each other—for a while. *We've* been talking about it amongst ourselves even longer than they have, if you'll recall, but their parliament's been putting the pieces together for almost three years now!"

"Yes, but while they were talking about it and putting pieces together, Spring Flower wasn't handing out modern weapons to his thugs, either," Cayleb pointed out. "And they just got finished 'digesting' Shang-mi and the Show-wan Hills. That gives them rail communications that far east, which is nothing to sneer at. But it also means they're still a good three hundred miles west of Jai-hu at the other end of a high road that hasn't been properly maintained in almost fifteen years, Merlin. And that's at the western end of the Cliffwall Pass. Which is still a good four hundred twenty miles—*air*-miles—from Ky-su. That's close to a thousand miles beyond Jai-hu, given the way the road twists and turns, and it's going to be a long time—probably years—before they could get a rail line that far forward! Will they really want to go that far east to get involved in somebody else's fight now that it's not just an academic proposition? Especially when the somebody else in question's opponents have *modern* rifles now?"

"Only for some values of 'modern,' Cayleb," Nahrmahn pointed out. Cayleb snorted and glanced across the bed chamber to where Sharleyan sat slowly, steadily, brushing her dark black hair. She saw him in the mirror and shook her head with a reflected smile.

"They're a hell of a lot more 'modern' than anything the folks in the Chynduk Valley have at the moment," he told Nahrmahn.

"And they're either locally produced versions of the St. Kylmahn from South Harchong or that half-arsed Desnarian version of the Mahndrayn Showail ripped off for Mahrys," Sir Koryn Gahrvai put in.

He and Nimue had just finished tucking the five-year-old twins into bed and young Alyk Gahrvai, who would be two years old next month, sat in his mother's lap as Nimue leaned back in the enormous recliner Delthak Enterprises had designed and built to her specifications. Gahrvai stood looking out the window at the gaslit palace grounds, and his eyes were sober.

"And your point is?" Cayleb asked slowly.

"I have several of them really," Gahrvai said. "First, the reason we sent Merlin to talk to them in the first place was that Syngpu's right. If we don't intervene—if the United Provinces don't intervene—the Valley's going down. We're in agreement that that would be a Bad Thing, yes?"

He looked around at the circle of faces projected into his vision, eyebrows arched.

"Of course it would," Maikel Staynair said from Tellesberg, where it was bright daylight. "We've been watching that island of stability for years now. Just look at all the good they've done. We can't let that be torn down and thrown away, even irrespective of the human cost!"

Several other people nodded, and Gahrvai snorted.

"All right, that brings me to my second point. If *we're* going to get involved, then it only makes sense to get the United Provinces involved for a lot of reasons, but two of them seem especially important to me. First, Merlin's plan to keep the Valley alive will work even better than I expected it to, but we simply can't give them enough help that way to prop them up forever. So we need the

UP to be the foundation for the sustainability of whatever we do. And my second reason's just as sound, I think. We've been working with Star Rising and the others for years now, and one of the reasons we have is that we want the United Provinces as big as we can get them, whether they know it or not."

More nods, and Merlin smiled up at the stars through his skimmer's canopy. He was pretty sure Star Rising, at least—and almost certainly Bishop Yaupang, as well—recognized precisely what their Charisian friends wanted to happen to their borders. They might not realize just how far Charis wanted them extended, and the thought of reaching all the way across Central Harchong to make contact with Baron Wind Song's East Harchong probably would have frightened them to death. But Tangwyn Syngpu wasn't the only person who recognized the defensive bulwark the Chiang-wu Mountains would provide to the United Provinces.

"Third point," Gahrvai continued, almost as if he'd been reading Merlin's mind, "this is the smartest thing the United Provinces could possibly do for their own security, especially now that Zhyou-Zhwo's finally getting better weapons into Central Harchong. He's out of his mind if he thinks that this will magically give him back control of Harchong—or even just *Central* Harchong— but that won't keep people like Spring Flower from being a hell of a lot more dangerous after he gets done 'enabling' the bastards. Keeping them on the far side of the Chiang-wus was already high on the United Provinces' to-do list, and it's damned well just gotten higher. Or will as soon as our *siejin* spies tell them about it, anyway!"

Merlin stopped smiling and nodded. Zhyou-Zhwo had finally established a conduit to Spring Flower and a dozen other "great nobles"—most newly created— fighting to "restore the imperial authority" in North Harchong. In fact, the *last* thing they wanted was the imperial authority restored, especially after so long. None of them had any desire to find his own ambitious growth constrained until he'd gobbled up as many of his competitors as he could and established the broadest possible borders for the new, independent kingdoms they fully intended to declare as soon as the pretence of loyalty to the crown was no longer useful to them.

Zhyou-Zhwo appeared blissfully unaware of that, however. Merlin doubted he actually was, although he might be wrong about that. Earl Snow Peak certainly understood it, but he much preferred to allow the endless dogfight and bloodletting to continue as long as possible before getting involved in it—assuming he got involved at all—with the new-model imperial army he was still building.

"Fourth point, this is our fault," Gahrvai's eyes had hardened. "We're the ones who let that bastard Fangzhin take over at Laichyng, and that means we're the ones who opened the door for Zhyou-Zhwo."

Merlin's non-smile went even flatter, because that was an excellent point. Yinzhung Fangzhin was another of the seemingly unending supply of warlords and brigands out to seize any territory he could get. He'd been more successful than most, however, although not yet on the scale of someone like Spring Flower. Partly that was timing, partly that was cunning, and partly that was luck. He'd been on the eastern fringe of the warlords fighting over the territory south of Spring Flower at the time of the ill-advised attack on the Zhyahngdu relief area. He'd seized the opportunity when his three unfortunate neighbors paid the price for challenging the Army of God and the Imperial Charisian Navy on the same afternoon and consolidated his own territory around the relatively small seaport of Laichyng, which lay just under three hundred miles from Saram Bay. It wasn't much of a seaport, although it was respectable in size, but he'd added the large farming town of Mangchu and reached an "understanding" with the smaller port of Dauku on the western flank of Cape Samuel.

Laichyng's total territory stretched three hundred and eighty miles, east to west, and about a hundred and seventy-five miles north to south, at its deepest. Despite its impressive dimensions, its population wasn't enormous, but it gave Zhyou-Zhwo and Yu-kwau an actual foothold in North Harchong, and both Cayleb and Sharleyan and Tymythy Rhobair had hesitated to crush Laichyng before he'd firmly established himself. It wouldn't have been much of a challenge to either the Army of God or the Empire of Charis, but they'd chosen to avoid providing Zhyou-Zhwo with a clear and unambiguous reason for war, and Baron Wind Song had been too busy expanding to the northeast and east to take his own forces that far south. For that matter, *he* didn't want to goad Zhyu-Zhwo into finally launching the invasion he'd promised for the last fifteen years, either. He was no more afraid of Snow Peak's army than the inner circle or Tymythy Rhobair, but, like them, he hesitated to inflict still more bloodshed, if it was avoidable.

Unfortunately, their restraint had allowed Laichyng to secure his control, and Grand Duke North Wind Blowing, Earl Snow Peak, and Zhwyfeng Nengkwan had found a way to get some of their more modern weapons into the hands of "their" nobles at last. Those newer weapons were finally beginning to accumulate in useful numbers and the rate of increase continued to grow. They—and Desnair—remained woefully short of Charis' production rates, but in certain areas—like rifles and ammunition—they'd almost equaled Delthak's wartime production rate from the Jihad. And since they were acquiring the weapons, they'd decided to charter third-party merchant ships, usually flagged in one of the Border States, to transport some of them to Laichyng. The newly fledged grand duke must've been sorely tempted to keep all of them for himself, but unlike many of the other "nobles" professing their loyalty to Yu-kwau and their distant emperor, he actually meant it. Not because he loved Zhyou-Zhwo, but because his coastal position meant the emperor was far better placed to give him genuine assistance . . . or cause him genuine grief if he got out of line. And so he'd kept enough of them to arm all of his own troops, with a ten percent reserve or so, and then begun shipping the rest overland to people like Spring Flower.

And as Gahrvai had just pointed out, that was because *they* hadn't acted before Fangzhin was firmly enough ensconced to play middleman for Zhyou-Zhwo.

"Since we let Zhyou-Zhwo back in, we have a responsibility to do something about it," the general pointed out.

"Blockading his weapon shipments would be one way to do that," Duke Rock Point growled. He'd made the same argument before.

Repeatedly.

"Yes, we could," Cayleb agreed now, with more patience than he actually felt. "*If* we want to piss off the Border States. *And* maybe the Republic. You did notice that Snow Peak was clever enough to go through Siddarmarkian shipping agents and drayage firms to move his guns, didn't you?" Rock Point made an exasperated sound over the com, and Cayleb's lips twitched. "I think we can be pretty sure how the Border States would feel about our seizing their ships as contraband during peacetime. But how do you think the anti-Charis part of the Republic would react if we started seizing or destroying those ships' *cargos*—the ones *they're* responsible for—the same way."

"Damn, I *hate* diplomacy," Rock Point growled.

"Granted. And I'm not saying I wouldn't prefer a nice, simple blockade myself," Cayleb acknowledged a bit sourly. "That's not on the table, though, and the whole purpose of Merlin's little trip is to do what we *can* do to help the Valley. What we're talking about now is getting the United Provinces involved, and that brings us back to the fact that if it comes to direct combat between the United Provinces and Spring Flower, we're looking at two wildcards. First, we have no idea how that will play out politically, given that Star Rising and the others could no longer claim they're simply acting in self-defense. Oh, they would be, in a lot of ways, but this time around they'd be engaging in combat with an intact grand duchy and a grand duke sworn to the Crown and fully supported by the emperor. That's a can of worms we haven't opened yet.

"And the second wildcard is that we don't know how the *UP* would make out against Spring Flower's and Qwaidu's new army. It could get really ugly, especially if they wound up having to fight their way through Cliffwall in the face of dug-in opposition."

"Can't answer the first one," Gahrvai said with a shrug. "I know what would happen with the second one, though."

"What, Koryn?" Sharleyan asked, brush paused in mid-stroke as her mirrored eyes met Gahrvai's across the com interface.

"Spring Flower and Qwaidu would get their arses kicked," Gahrvai said flatly. "And that would be even without us providing artillery support. *With* our artillery, it'd be a massacre."

"Really?" Sharleyan laid down the brush, and Gahrvai chuckled.

"Kynt? Care to weigh in on this one?" he asked.

"You seem to be doing adequately without my input," Duke Serabor said dryly. "I think you may be grossly pessimistic about how well the United Provinces would make out, though."

Several people chuckled, including Serabor, but then he sobered.

"The truth is, the UP could probably take anybody out there short of Wind Song's troops or the better Army of God divisions. Personally, I think they'd have a pretty good chance against Wind Song, and I know they'd go through Spring Flower and Qwaidu like shit through a wyvern. Might be a little ugly in the mountains, initially at least, but once they were through to the other side of Cliffwall?" He shook his head. "If they wanted to keep going west, they'd have Fangkau and Maichi within a five-day."

"Which really would send Zhyou-Zhwo ballistic," Nimue Gahrvai put in, hugging her daughter. "Mind you, I'm not convinced that would be a bad thing. I'm just saying he'd reach orbit without benefit of a recon skimmer."

"Damn, I'd pay good money to see *that*!" Hektor Aplyn-Ahrmahk observed.

"Shut up and stop encouraging them," his wife advised sweetly. He looked at her, and Irys shrugged. "They don't *need* your encouragement, and while I'm sure they're both right about the military aspects, Cayleb's right about the potential political downsides. And they may not see things quite as clearly as we do."

"Well, there's only one way to find out," Merlin observed. "And whatever Star Rising and his friends decide," the *seijin*'s expression hardened, "I think our friends in the Chynduk Valley deserve a little help. Besides," his tight facial muscles relaxed and he smiled again, "it'll be wonderful experience for *us* down the road, too.

"Assuming, of course, that it works."

AUGUST YEAR OF GOD 913

. I .
Chynduk Valley,
Tiegelkamp Province,
Central Harchong.

"Might want to get those signal fires lit, Commander Syngpu," Merch O Obaith observed.

Tangwyn Syngpu cocked his head, glancing at the dark-haired, blue-eyed young woman. In sunlight, that hair had auburn highlights, and he'd never imagined eyes as darkly blue as *Seijin* Merlin's had been that first night.

This was Merch O Obaith's third visit to the Valley, however, and she had eyes of exactly the same shade. He couldn't have seen them in the darkness, even if she hadn't been peering upward, but he knew that. And although she was also a good foot shorter than *Seijin* Merlin, there was no doubt in Syngpu's mind that she was just as deadly. And she was just as good at mysteriously appearing places. Syngpu *still* didn't know how Merlin—or *Seijin* Merch—came and went with such blithe ease and without a single one of his highly experienced and motivated sentries ever seeing a single thing.

Yanshwyn's right about that, he told himself. *Stop worrying about it and just be glad they've decided they're on* our *side.*

Although he *would* like to know how the *seijin* knew it was time to light the fires. The night sky was crystal clear and calm, with a torrent of stars blazing gloriously overhead through the thin mountain air, but it was also moonless and the only sounds *he* could hear were insects, birds and wyverns, and the gentle stir of the breeze.

He thought about asking her if she was sure about that. Then he shook his head mentally. Probably not a good idea. Instead, he looked over his shoulder at the grizzled old sergeant waiting patiently.

"Heard the *Seijin*," he said with a shrug. "Best be lighting them up."

▼ ▼ ▼

"I would love to know whose brilliant idea this was," Lieutenant Krugair growled as HMAS *Aivahn Hahgyz* bored through the night sky. He sounded a little strange, thanks to the bulky apparatus strapped to his face. "If I did, I could go break his kneecaps."

"It is sort of exciting. In a boring, frozen to death, can't-see-crap sort of a way," Lieutenant Ahzbyrn pointed out in an equally muffled voice, and Krugair glared at him.

The good news was that *Aivahn Hahgyz* was brand-new; the bad news was that they'd taken *Synklair Pytmyn* away from him—away from his entire crew, really—when they were assigned to the new ship. She was the first of the new *Moonraker* class: much longer but proportionately a bit slimmer than *Synklair Pytmyn*, with an aerodynamic fabric cover stretched over braided wire stringers around the cells of her gas envelope. With her newly up-rated Praigyrs (*every* Praigyr was up-rated from the one before it . . . and obsolete the moment it was installed), more efficient shape, and larger size, she was both faster than *Synklair Pytmyn* had been and structurally tougher. Her gas volume was over three times that of Krugair's earlier ship, and even though the stiffening inside her envelope and an extra pair of engines consumed precious weight, she could lift up to fifty passengers and almost thirty-five tons of cargo at her designed fuel weight. If she loaded her maximum fuel allowance, that fell to only twenty-seven tons.

She and her two sisters were also the first airships to be fitted with oxygen for high altitude operation, which imposed its own weight penalties, and Krugair had been very much in two minds when he heard about that! Instead of the nine to eleven thousand feet at which *Synklair Pytmyn* had operated, *Aivahn Hahgyz* could carry her crew to as much as twenty-two thousand. And Delthak was experimenting with something called a "pressurization system" which would draw power from her Praigyrs and—in theory, at least—mean the crew of *Aivahn Hahgyz*' follow-on classes might be able to operate that high without oxygen masks.

Frankly, Krugair would believe *that* one when he saw it. Although, he admitted, it *would* be nice.

At four miles, the air might reasonably be described as "thin," he thought now, rubbing irritably at the rubber mask. He hated the damned thing, although he had no intention of taking it off at the moment. Although, to be fair, they were nowhere near *Aivahn Hahgyz*' maximum ceiling, because rugged as the Chiang-wu mountains were, they averaged considerably lower than, say, the Mountains of Light. Mount Olympus, for example, was almost 38,000 feet high, whereas the tallest peak in the Chiangwus was barely 19,000. The average peaks were substantially lower than that—enough so that a mere 17,000 feet of altitude sufficed quite nicely . . . as long as Lieutenant Braiahnt didn't run them into any of the handful of mountaintops at or above their current height. There were only three of them within forty miles of their planned course, but with no moon, visibility was limited, which imposed a lower-than-usual speed. And the lack of moonlight made navigation interesting, too. Star shots were easy enough this high, as long as Braiahnt didn't freeze to death taking them—which was a genuine risk, since the air temperature at their current altitude was about one below zero—but picking out landmarks was not.

To say the least.

Oh, quit bitching! he told himself. *This is the most advanced airship in the world, and all you can do is complain because you've been assigned a* mission?!

He shook his head, although the possibility of encountering a mountain top wasn't the only reason he was less than delirious with joy. Even with the arctic clothing borrowed from the Army and the exhaust-based heating system built into the airship's cabin, he was colder than Shan-wei's heart. But at least they must be almost to their destination.

Of course he'd been telling himself that for the last forty-odd minutes. But if he kept *on* telling himself, then sooner or later he'd be right and—

"There, Skipper!" Ahzbyrn thumped him on the shoulder and pointed, and Krugair held up a heavily gloved hand with the upraised thumb the Empire's aeronauts had borrowed from *Seijin* Merlin as he saw the brilliant glow of the bonfires spreading across the valley floor below them.

"Good!" he said. "Start the spiral and let's start venting some gas."

▼ ▼ ▼

"You were right, *Seijin*," Syngpu acknowledged as an eye-tearingly brilliant pinprick of light flashed against the stars.

After the signal lamp attracted his attention, he could actually make out the faint loom of the enormous airship as it obstructed the stars above it. During the intervals *between* signals, that was. He couldn't see anything but the damned lamp whenever it was flashing.

He waited out the current round of blinking, then looked expectantly down at the *seijin*. He had enough trouble reading printed words.

"They'll start the drop in fifteen or twenty minutes," she told him with a grin. "They need to get a little lower first, since we'd rather not break anything we don't have to. They'll pop a green flare when they start the drop and a red one when they stop."

"Good of them," Syngpu grunted.

He'd come to the conclusion that *Seijin* Merch was considerably younger than *Seijin* Merlin. She certainly possessed a more . . . impish sense of humor.

On the other hand, it was best if they took the warning to heart, and he pulled out his whistle and blew a deafening blast.

None of his ground crew lingered when they heard the whistle. The Charisians' ingenious new "parachutes" sometimes failed. Even when they didn't, they came down fast and hard with their loads, and the cargo pallets were heavy. Since it would be difficult to dodge parachutes they couldn't see coming in the dark, as soon as they heard his whistle all of the groundmen darted under the heavily braced overhead cover of the shelters *Seijin* Merlin had suggested they build.

Syngpu himself waited, watching the huge airship's blot against the stars circle as it dropped steadily lower. It was a fascinating sight—one he knew he would never tire of—although it was far more spectacular when there was a moon. He was always a little nervous while they circled, too, he admitted to himself. True, the valley floor was over twenty-five miles wide at this point, and the walls were nowhere near as sheer as they were at other spots. The Charisians probably had more like thirty-five miles to play with at the altitude from which they made their drops. But if the wind took them or they drifted into the mountainside. . . .

They dropped lower and lower, spiraling downward. Then the spiral stopped and they headed straight down the long-axis of the valley, directly along the line of bonefires. Those fires had largely burned down by now, but they must still be plenty bright enough from that high up, and—

A green flare arced away from the airship and blazed against the night.

"After you, *Seijin*," Syngpu invited rather pointedly, indicating the shelter behind the two of them, and Obaith chuckled. Then she gave him a pantomimed curtsy and scampered—undeniably, she *scampered*—under cover.

He'd started down the steps behind her, shaking his head.

▼ ▼ ▼

"Airspeed twelve miles per hour, Skipper," Lieutenant Ahzbyrn said, and Lieutenant Krugair nodded in satisfaction. He didn't want to drop any more speed, because that could cause handling issues, especially during abrupt weight changes. But he didn't want to be moving too quickly when they dropped, either, because that would scatter their load all over Shan-wei's half-acre. Besides, there was a *river* down there.

"Commencing drop in one minute, Sir!" Chief Petty Officer Tymyns announced, straightening from the voice pipe that connected him to Lieutenant Braiahnt's position, which was rather farther from the bridge than it had been aboard *Synklair Pytmyn*.

Lieutenant Krugair nodded again, then checked his harness to be sure it was clipped to the safety ring. *Aivahn Hahgyz* was about to get a lot lighter. He'd lost twelve thousand feet of altitude during his circling approach, which had brought his command down to no more than three thousand feet above the Valley floor before he'd ordered the vents closed again. Not that they were going to stay closed. He'd hated giving up the hydrogen, but that was only reflex. He'd really like to be a little higher than five thousand feet, too, given the height to which the Valley's *walls* rose, but the maximum altitude for the ICAF's parachutes was only twelve hundred feet and he needed a little margin to work with, given what was about to happen to his ship's buoyancy. Even with two parachutes, the pallets would hit hard from this altitude. As for the hydrogen they'd dumped, it wasn't like they were going to need it for the trip home! In fact—

"Stand by to vent!" he ordered.

"Aye, aye, Sir. Standing by to vent."

"Very good."

Krugair's hand tightened on the bulkhead handrail, and then—

Despite the altitude, the flight from the United Provinces had been absurdly short by *Aivahn Hahgyz*' standards, and she'd loaded less than a quarter of her designed fuel load. The weight savings had been used for extra cargo, and now the first pallet dropped cleanly from her keel. The trio of parachutes opened quickly, and the heavily strapped pallet went floating downward.

"Commence venting!" Krugair commanded as the enormous airship *bounced* upward and the sudden added buoyancy slammed against the soles of his boots. His knees flexed, hydrogen roared as the vents opened wide, and he felt the shock as the next pallet dropped. And the next.

Theoretically, they could have dropped up to six tons on a single chute. That was what they'd trained do to back in Old Charis, but those drops had been at or near sea level. At five thousand feet the air density was little more than half what it was at sea level, and they were taking no avoidable chances with this load. Each of those pallets weighed approximately five tons, and *Aivahn Hahgyz* dropped four of them at one-minute intervals. During those three minutes, she traveled just over a half mile along the line defined by the signal fires.

Krugair ordered the vents closed again as the third pallet dropped, but *Aivahn Hahgyz* kept shooting upward. She simply couldn't vent gas rapidly enough to compensate for such a sudden, massive loss of weight *without* climbing, and she swept steeply higher, surging back to an altitude of sixteen thousand feet in a matter of minutes while her structure creaked and groaned about them. It probably would have been alarming as hell to a groundsman, but Krugair was delighted with the entire process. This was a stress his ship was specifically designed to withstand, and he'd experienced conditions just like it on the practice drops. And, for that matter, on the two he'd already made here! Besides, any aeronaut knew there was no such thing as too much reserve lift. He'd much rather have extra lift in hand and have to vent more gas than be forced to dump ballast to maintain altitude as they crossed the Chang-wus back into Boisseau.

And it was so damned much *fun*, to boot!

"All pallets away," PO Tymyns announced from the voice pipes as the airship began stabilizing at her new altitude. "Secured from cargo-dropping stations, Sir!"

"Very good," Krugair replied, unclipping his safety line and moving to a point from which he could see the illuminated faces of the altimeter and compass. "Come to a heading of south-southwest and increase speed to forty knots."

"Aye, aye, Sir. Coming to south-southwest and increasing speed to forty knots."

The engine room telegraphs clanged, the rpm of the four propellers—each with three blades, rather than the two of earlier airships—accelerated as the steam throttles were opened wider, and HMAS *Aivahn Hahgyz* sailed majestically across the stars as she circled back the way she'd come.

. II .

Town of Taizhow,
and
The Kwyfan Crossroads,
Zhyndow-Zhutiyan Road,
Chynduk Valley,
Tiegelkamp Province,
Central Harchong.

"Those bastards aren't going to enjoy this at all," Grand Duke Spring Flower growled with undisguised satisfaction as he glowered down at the map. "And I don't want any more reports about that son-of-a-bitch Syngpu being 'wounded,' is that understood?"

He raised his smoldering eyes to Zhailau Laurahn, and the man who no longer found it strange to think of himself as the Baron of Qwaidu nodded. He had more than enough bones of his own to pick with Tangwyn Syngpu.

"Dead on the ground or back here where he can be made a proper example of—one or the other!" Spring

Flower went on. "I'll settle for dead if I have to, but he's done us enough damage I want him here, where we can show everyone else what happens to people who screw around with us. So you tell the men he's worth five thousand marks to me alive but I'll cough up only *one* thousand for just his head!"

Qwaidu nodded again. If the notoriously parsimonious Spring Flower was prepared to come up with that kind of money, he was obviously serious. And he'd learned from others' example that rulers who promised rewards and then didn't deliver came to bad ends, so he wasn't just venting this time.

"I really want *all* their precious 'Valley Council' back here where they can be dealt with properly, if we can get them," the grand duke continued, "but I'll settle for dead for them, too, if I have to. The important thing is, we *end* this crap!"

Qwaidu nodded a third time. In his fairer moments, of which he had as few as possible where Tangwyn Syngpu, Miyang Gyngdau, Zaipu Ou-zhang, and Yngshwan Tsungzhi were concerned, the baron had to concede that the Valleyers didn't actually go out of their way to cause trouble outside the confines of their own Valley. The problem wasn't what they did; the problem was what they *were*: a prosperous, thriving community which refused to bend the knee or the neck to its betters. Specifically, they refused to bow before the Grand Duke of Spring Flower.

And, by extension, to His Majesty, Zhailau. Don't forget that! the baron reminded himself.

The *emperor* certainly wasn't going to forget. He'd made that clear enough. In fact, Qwaidu rather suspected the emperor and the rest of the imperial court in Yu-kwau saw the Valleyers as stand-ins for the United Provinces. Zhyou-Zhwo couldn't get at Boisseau or the other coastal provinces whose rail lines and manufactories were growing so robustly, so Chynduk would have to take the blows in their place.

That was fine with Qwaidu. He didn't care why Yu-kwau supported them against Syngpu, Gyngdau, and the others. All he cared about was that it did.

Of course, it was entirely possible his troops would catch neither Syngpu nor the other Valley leaders, but that was acceptable, too. Whether or not he managed to drag them out of their hidey holes, starvation and cold would finish off their resistance after he burned their barns and killed or ran off their livestock. He was under no illusion that he could get all of their barns or all of their animals, but with the new weapons from Yukwau, he could go wherever he wanted, and that meant he could damned well get enough of both to starve the bastards out.

"The only thing I'm still a little worried by are those reports of the damned 'airships,'" he said now, looking down and running his finger across the same map. "I know they're all half-arsed rumors of rumors, not anything solid. But the frigging Charisians *are* flying the damned things all over the damned world. There's plenty of confirmation of that! And there are enough rumors of people seeing them over Boisseau and the Chiang-wus to make me think there has to be something to them, Your Grace, and the terrain's going to give them enough opportunities to surprise our scouts and columns without someone sitting in a damned balloon and looking down on every move we make." He grimaced. "I'm not saying they could stop us, Your Grace. I'm just saying that if they really have one of the things, we're likely to get hurt a lot worse than we would otherwise."

"By a *balloon*?!" Spring Flower shook his head and made a sound of disgust. "Don't worry about any damned *balloons*. Earl Snow Peak assures me that all they can do is spy on us. And that assumes half the lies the Shan-wei–damned Charisians and their arse-kissing friends tell are true! How likely do you think that is?"

Actually, Qwaidu was prepared to think *most* of what the Charisians said was reasonably accurate. And the possibility that "all they can do is spy on us" was precisely what he was worried about. "Commander" Syngpu and his ragged-arsed peasants and serfs were masters of concealment and perfectly comfortable operating dispersed, shooting at him from behind stone walls and wood piles and then filtering away before he could put in a charge to overwhelm them. They were Shan-wei's own challenge to dig out of the woodwork at the best of times. If they had someone standing on the equivalent of the tallest mountain in the vicinity and shouting reports on Qwaidu's movements, they'd be even harder to spot before they opened fire . . . and a hell of a lot harder to catch once they did.

There were many things about Earl Snow Peak which inspired less than total confidence in the baron, including his estimates of the 'airships'' potential threat. It seemed reasonable to Qwaidu that anything which could carry people could carry people with rifles, which suggested they could at least harass the hell out of ground troops! But if they came close enough to shoot at his men, then his men could shoot back at them, and they finally had modern weapons to do it with. Weapons which still relied on black powder, rather than the 'smokeless powder' Charis was willing to provide to its friends, perhaps, but the new Desnairian rifle—christened the Harless, although Qwaidu would have preferred a different name, given what had happened to the Duke of Harless in the Shiloh Campaign—still gave a rifleman six shots as quickly as he could work the bolt. Seven shots if he started with one in the chamber. A few hundred of *those* firing upward should discourage any "airship"!

"Well, Your Grace," he said finally, straightening and standing back from the map table. "Time I was going. I'm hoping you'll be five thousand marks the poorer in a very few days now."

"So do I, My Lord." Spring Flower smiled thinly. "So do I."

▼ ▼ ▼

"Sir, we're starting to take some fire from the right flank."

Captain of Foot Rung looked up from his conversation with Sergeant Major Chaiyang. He'd been listening to the sergeant major very carefully, because while Hanbai Chaiyang might still be "only" a noncom, he was *the* noncom, as far as Baron Qwaidu was concerned. He was seldom far from the baron's side, especially these days, and when he was, it was because the baron had sent him to make sure there were absolutely no misunderstandings.

And after certain misadventures Zhungdau Rung's cavalry company had experienced at places with names like "the Yang-zhi Farm," misunderstandings with the baron were very high on the captain of foot's list of things to avoid.

"What sort of fire?" he asked the messenger now, acutely aware of Chaiyang's silent, listening presence.

"Captain of Bows Pyng said to tell you it's mostly long-range, harassing fire, coming from that belt of trees north of the farm, Sir. He estimates there could be as many as a hundred men in there. Maybe two hundred, judging from the powder smoke. He says he's pretty sure they're firing from prepared positions."

Rung pursed his lips and nodded slowly. He wasn't surprised, although that made the news no more pleasant.

In the wake of the Grand Duke's troops' last incursion into the Valley, they'd been forced to pull back to the ruins of Zhyndow to escape the galling sniper fire and hit-and-run raids the Valleyers had brought to bear. They could have stayed farther forward, but only at the cost of a constant, niggling stream of casualties, and that was bad for morale.

The downside of pulling back, however, was that the Valleyers had been given plenty of time to go over the ground and make their best deployments. Rung strongly suspected that having given them that time was going to prove expensive. But at least it was only his people's job to *find* the bastards. It was someone else's job to go in and dig them out.

He considered Pyng's message. He couldn't really call it a report, but the captain of bows had covered the essentials. And if he said there were over a hundred of the rebels in that patch of woods, there probably were. Kaujyng Pyng was the third officer to command

2nd Squadron's 3rd Platoon since Maizhai Rwan-tai got himself ambushed and killed. Neither of the other two had worked out. Well, in fairness, the second of them had gotten himself killed trying to break up a brawl over a woman before he'd had time to work out. And the court-martial had cost Rung three more troopers, as well. Couldn't have an officer getting himself killed by doing something stupid and then let the other half of the stupid walk away, could he? But Pyng was reliable. Solid.

Good. I won't have to waste more men sending them up that damned slope to confirm it!

It was time to turn the advance over to that "someone else," at least until the flank of the main road had been cleared for his cavalry.

"Message to Captain of Horse Lwanzhi," he said crisply, still aware of the silently listening sergeant major. "Inform him that my scouts have confirmed rebel riflemen in strength in the woods above the high road at the Kwyfan crossroads. My troopers will hold in place until his infantry can clear the trees."

▼ ▼ ▼

Captain of Horse Zhaigung Lwanzhi, the commanding officer of the Sochal Infantry Regiment, muttered balefully as he finished reading the brief note. He and Captain of Foot Rung were technically the same rank, and Lwanzhi's infantry regiment was twice the size of Rung's cavalry company. But Rung had been with Baron Qwaidu almost two years longer. That made him senior, and that was that.

On the other hand, Lwanzhi conceded, for a stupid fucking cavalryman, Rung wasn't that bad. He had at least part of a brain, anyway. And he was right. Screwing around in the woods wasn't what cavalry did best. It was what *infantry* did . . . damn it.

But at least all the men have Harlesses and not those crappy single-shot St. Kylmahns!

He scowled down at his map. It wasn't anything like as detailed as he would have preferred, but it showed the woods clearly enough. They were actually a chain of consecrated, interconnected second-growth woodlots that stretched for over twenty miles in a gentle arc along the contour lines above the Kwyfan Farm. If he'd been going to set up a delaying post, that's where *he* would have put it, too. And digging them out was going to be a genuine pain in the arse.

Best begin the way we mean to go on, he thought. *These bastards've already shown us it's going to cost to dig them out of anywhere, and Rung may be wrong about how many men they've got bellied down in there. Man could hide a couple of regiments in that much wood, if he really wanted to. So—*

"Tell Captain of Foot Raulai and Captain of Foot Zhweiau I need them," he growled at an orderly. "Now! We're burning sunlight here!"

▼ ▼ ▼

"Any idea what we did to draw the short straw, Sir?" Platoon Sergeant Mahnpyng Nyng-gi asked sourly as 1st Company started up the steep slope through the discouraging whistle of bullets with 3rd Platoon leading the way. Clouds of white powder smoke rolled through the trees atop the slope like an orphaned fog bank as the Valleyers bellied down up there sent those bullets down to greet them.

"No idea at all," Captain of Bows Kengbwo Gyng replied in an equally sour tone. He was about two-thirds Nyng-gi's age, but the two of them had been together for almost two years now, and Gyng had commanded 1st Company's 3rd Platoon for the last year and a half. "Most likely, we just did our job too damned well last time."

"Might be a good idea not to do it quite as well this time, Sir. Within reason, I mean." Nyng-gi's eyes were bleak as another of their privates went down. At least this one wasn't dead, although from his screams that might not be true much longer.

"I'll bear that in mind."

Gyng ducked as a bullet "wheeted" overhead. It probably hadn't been as close as it seemed to him, and he remembered the old adage. Any bullet you heard wasn't a problem.

He looked back over his shoulder and grunted in something as close to satisfaction as he could manage at the moment. The crossroads and Kwyfan Farm's buildings were close to four miles from the belt of woodland, but the main road ran along the northern edge of old Kyngswun Kwyfan's cultivated area. That put it within long rifle shot of the woods. Even if it hadn't, they couldn't afford to leave that many men up on their flank, ready to pounce on supply trains or reinforcing columns. Or, for that matter, to close in behind them if they ran into something as nasty as they'd hit last time and had to retreat.

Had he been given the option, he would have declined the honor of leading the way up that slope. He hadn't been, but at least Captain of Horse Lwanzhi believed in using however big a hammer it took. His entire 1st and 2nd Companies, each nominally three hundred men strong, were deployed, advancing behind a skirmish line as they swept up the slope. The regiment's remaining three companies waited in column on the southern edge of the road, far enough out to be safe even from Valleyer marksmen but close enough to support his leading companies if they needed help.

Hopefully, the stupid peasants could do the math. There might be the two hundred of them Captain of Horse Rung's troopers had estimated, but with *six* hundred infantry—all armed with the new magazine rifles—coming at them, it was time for them to be elsewhere.

Although, he thought grimly as another member of his platoon went down, they obviously weren't leaving until they were good and ready.

Just you stay where you are, then, if you want to be all bloody-minded about it, he thought venomously. *Let us get to* hand-bomb *range. Better yet, hang around until we can dangle you upside down over a slow fire!*

▼ ▼ ▼

"Bastards're hanging in there better than I expected," Captain of Horse Lwanzhi growled, watching through his spyglass—and wishing he had one of the double-glasses Baron Qwaidu and Captain of Horse Rung had managed to obtain.

"Maybe," Captain of Foot Renshwei said. "Might not be s' bad if they do, though. Probably nail more of 'em here, if they decide to make a real fight of it."

Lwanzhi grunted, because his second in command was right. And by their worst-case estimates, they had at least four times the manpower the Valley could afford to put permanently under arms. So they could afford to lose men. It wasn't written anywhere in the *Holy Writ* that they had to be *his* men, though.

"Looks like the skirmishers're just about up to the fence line," Renshwei observed, and Lwanzhi grunted again. The "fence" along the edge of the woodland scarcely deserved the name. It was intended to keep the Valleyers' sheep and cows from wandering into the woods, and there wasn't that much to attract them on the other side of it anyway. It was more of a reminder than an actual barrier, and it wasn't going to hinder his skirmishers much at all. Especially not with the formed lines behind them ready to lay down covering fire. In fact, in about another five or six min—

▼ ▼ ▼

"And . . . *now!*" Platoon Sergeant Taiyang snapped, and Corporal Tungkau yanked on the line.

Baron Qwaidu was quite correct that an airship couldn't shoot at people on the ground without having the people on the ground shoot back. Unfortunately for him, that wasn't the only way they could hurt him, because a five-ton, air-dropped pallet could carry an interesting assortment of things. For example, a Mark IV Mahndrayn rifle weighed just under nine pounds. Allowing for shipping materials and the weight of the pallet itself, a single pallet could deliver almost nine hundred of them. And each round of ammunition weighed about

1.6 ounces, so the pallet next to it could deliver ninety-six thousand rounds to keep those rifles fed in action.

At the moment, there were three hundred Valleyer infantry in those woods, all of them armed with Mark IVs and half of them armed with flintlock St. Kylmahn conversions, as well. They were the ones who'd been shooting at Captain of Horse Lwanzhi's infantry and producing all those clouds of powder smoke. Now they laid aside the flintlocks.

Nor had rifles been all Lieutenant Krugair and his airship had delivered, as Captain of Bows Gyng discovered—briefly—when Tungkau pulled the cord and the forty Shan-wei's sweepers spotted along the line of the fence detonated in a stupendous, rolling blast. Each of the directional mines hurled almost six hundred half-inch shrapnel balls into the faces of Lwanzhi's astounded infantry.

And then all three hundred Mark IVs went to deadly, aimed rapid fire, and unlike the black powder, six-shot Harless supplied by the Desnairian manufactories, the Mark IV Mahndrayn boasted a ten-round magazine and a much higher velocity—and flatter-shooting—cartridge. One that didn't emit billowing clouds of smoke to mark the shooter's position . . . or obscure his view of the target.

▼ ▼ ▼

"Shan-wei!" Zhaigung Lwanzhi swore as the entire line of the fence disappeared behind a rolling wash of explosions. He'd never faced the directional land-bombs the Charisians and their allies had used against the Mighty Host during the Jihad, but he realized what he had to be seeing as his entire skirmish line—and most of the rifle line behind it—went down like grass before a Charisian reaper.

Than the rifle fire started, right on its heels. The sheer volume, the crackling thunder of so many rifles firing independently as the men behind them picked their targets, was terrible enough. But there was worse. A heartbeat later, he realized there were no clouds of smoke. Which meant—

"Shan-wei take them to *hell*!" Lwanzhi snarled. Renshwei looked at him, eyes huge, obviously lagging behind Lwanzhi's thought processes, and the captain of horse managed—somehow—not to punch the man. It would have accomplished nothing, anyway . . . except to vent a little of his fury.

"Those are fucking new-model Charisian rifles up there!" he snapped instead.

"*Charisian?!*" Renshwei's eyes went even larger, and this time Lwanzhi did grab him by the tunic and shake him with one hand.

"Of course, Charisian, you idiot! Who *else* has 'smokeless powder'?!"

"B-B-But how?" Renshwei shook his head. "There's no way into the Valley!"

"No," Lwanzhi grated in agreement. "No, there's not, but—"

He broke off, his jaw clenching, then released Renshwei's tunic.

"There's no fucking way in on the *ground*," he said.

The captain of foot looked at him for a moment longer, then shook himself as understanding finally caught up.

"Those Shan-wei–damned airships!"

"Exactly."

Lwanzhi looked up the slope where the survivors of his leading companies had shown the good sense to fall back. In fact, at least half the survivors were running flat out, and he couldn't blame them. Of course, stopping and rallying them at the foot of the slope was likely to be a nontrivial challenge. On the other hand, screaming at them would at least give him something to do, because the one thing he damned well *wasn't* doing was to move a single yard farther along this road. If Baron Qwaidu wanted to send an advance up a single roadbed into the teeth of modern Charisian rifles and Langhorne-only-knew how many of those fucking land-bombs, then *he* could lead it, and this time around, Zhaigung Lwanzhi would tell him so in so many words. It wasn't as if—

▼ ▼ ▼

As it happened, Captain of Horse Lwanzhi was wrong about what he'd be discussing with Baron Qwaidu, because rifles and landmines weren't the only things which had been delivered to the Valley, nor had *Aivahn Hahgyz* traveled only by night. Lieutenant Krugair had never—quite—actually landed in the Valley. Without a proper ground crew, it would have been insanely risky to land a hydrogen-filled airship. It was, however, slightly less risky to come in close enough to the ground in daylight, with good visibility, for trained and athletic passengers—like members of the Imperial Charisian Army—to slide down ropes.

Most of those passengers had been experienced noncom instructors, including the training cadre from the Ruhsyl Thairis Center for Artillery at Maikelberg in Chisholm which had been sent in to teach Tangwyn Syngpu's militia the finer points of the ICA's M95 three-inch mortar.

Unfortunately for Captain of Horse Lwanzhi, they'd been very apt students.

OCTOBER YEAR OF GOD 913

·◆·

. I .
City of Yu-Kwau,
Kyznetzou Province,
South Harchong.

"I take it His Majesty was . . . unhappy, Your Grace?" Khaizhang Taiyang murmured as he poured tea into Grand Duke North Wind Blowing's cup.

The first councilor looked up at him with the eyes of a cat passing fish bones.

"I believe you might safely say that," he replied.

Taiyang dipped his head in acknowledgment and stepped back with the teapot while North Wind Blowing lifted the cup in both hands, inhaling the fragrance of the blend. At least losing the North hadn't interfered with his few creature comforts, he thought moodily. All the best tea blends had come from the South, anyway. In fact, the more he'd thought about it, the more he'd realized he was perfectly willing to leave the North to the maniacs slaughtering each other there. Everyone who'd ever mattered to him was either already safely in the South or dead, and he knew in his bones that Zhyou-Zhwo was never going to reassert the imperial authority north of the Gulf of Dohlar.

That had been evident even before the latest debacle.

Unfortunately, "His Supreme and Most Puissant Majesty" refused to accept that. After all, he could scarcely be "puissant," far less "supreme," with people who ought to be his subjects defying him.

There were times when Ahnhwang Hwei was sorely tempted to lay down the burden of his office. He would turn eighty-six in two months' time, and that was well past the age at which he should have retired to his estates to enjoy his golden years and his grandchildren. But those estates had been burned to the ground. All he had was what he'd been able to rebuild in the last nine years, and that wasn't nearly enough to leave to his family. Besides, he had at least some duty to the Empire, which included trying to keep some sort of a bridle on Zhyou-Zhwo's increasingly autocratic rule.

"I suppose you'd best summon the Earl, Khaizhang," North Wind Blowing sighed finally. "And remind him we're currently on the outs again."

"Of course, Your Grace," Taiyang bowed a bit more deeply, and his lips twitched ever so slightly. North Wind Blowing saw it, and despite his mood, he smiled back.

Briefly.

"Go—go!"

He took one hand from his teacup, waving it in a shooing motion, and Taiyang bobbed one more bow and vanished. The door closed behind him, and North Wind Blowing climbed out of his chair—cautiously; neither his bones nor his joints were what they had been—and crossed to the window with his tea. He stood sipping it, looking out over the sundrenched roofs of Yu-kwau, thinking about the future.

His own would be brief. Five more years, perhaps. Ten at the outside. That came to all men, in the fullness of time, although he was a bit more concerned than he'd once been about how the Archangels were likely to greet him on the other side. Not that there was much he could do about that at this point.

He grunted at that familiar thought and watched white sails and occasional columns of coal smoke drifting across the Bay of Alexov. Back home, in the North, the snow was probably already a couple of feet deep, he thought, looking at the white beaches, feeling the warmth. Why in God's name had Langhorne and the other Archangels settled his ancestors in such an . . . inhospitable place in the first place? There had to have been a reason. When he compared North Harchong's wheat fields, beet fields, and hog farms to the vista beyond his window, he could only conclude that his ancestors must have truly pissed off the Archangels somehow!

He snorted at the mild sacrilege, but it was true that the South was a much better place to live. And despite the fact that the southern lobe of the Empire contained barely a quarter of its total territory, it had boasted almost half the Empire's population even before the Rebellion. Given how many had died in the North, and how many had refugeed out to the South, the imbalance in population had to be even smaller than it had been. Indeed, he suspected the South's total population actually outnumbered the North's at last.

Of all the mainland realms, only Siddarmark and Desnair had more population than South Harchong, alone, and Desnair's edge was less than ten million, barely eleven percent of South Harchong's total.

He needs to be content with what he's got, he thought now, sipping tea. *We're never going to convince him of that, though.*

No, they weren't, and perhaps Zhyou-Zhwo was right, in some greater sense. Perhaps they did owe it to God to reclaim the ancestral lands of the Harchongese people and restore them to the relationship they were supposed to have with Him and His Archangels. But if that was what God wanted, then He'd best give the Emperor better tools—and better advisors—than he had now.

North Wind Blowing wouldn't be around to do that advising very much longer, which was why he'd been grooming his distant kinsman Hangwau Ge-yang, Earl of Cinnabar Hill, for the thankless task of replacing him. No doubt Cinnabar Hill would contrive to improve the family fortunes along the way—that was what one did with high office, after all—but he had more than mercenary motives for assuming North Wind Blowing's mantle.

Cinnabar Hill was a mere earldom, and in Queiroz, to boot, which had excluded its earls from any hope of wielding serious power in Shang-mi. Times had changed, however, and North Wind Blowing had changed with them, although he'd concealed that as much as possible. The grand duke had contrived to have Zhyou-Zhwo choose Cinnabar Hill as one of his trusted confidants and assign him as his first councilor's senior deputy despite—or, rather, *because of*—the "bad blood" between them. No one knew precisely what that "bad blood" stemmed from, but there were enough intrafamily feuds in Harchong to keep a thousand genealogists busy counting the bodies.

In this case, the bad blood was North Wind Blowing's invention, however. It was obvious Zhyou-Zhwo had retained the grand duke as first councilor mainly because he saw North Wind Blowing as an old, tired man, incapable of seriously restricting the imperial prerogative. Which was true, in many ways. Of course, there were more subtle ways of shaping policy than openly opposing a headstrong and arrogant emperor. And so Cinnabar Hill had been careful to disagree with North Wind Blowing upon occasion, both in public and in private conversation with the emperor, establishing that he was his own man. Or, rather, that he was independent of North Wind Blowing . . . and *Zhyou-Zhwo's* man.

Not even Cinnabar Hill's wife knew his true relationship with the grand duke, or how closely he and North Wind Blowing coordinated their policies. The only person who did know was Khaizhang Taiyang, who had "secretly" transferred his allegiance to Cinnabar Hill now that North Wind Blowing's penurious state suggested that Taiyang's own retirement might be a bit threadbare.

Everyone in Yu-kwau seemed aware of that treason on his part. Except North Wind Blowing, that was. Clearly additional evidence of how the old man's grip was slipping.

It's the best I can do, the grand duke thought now, watching those sails, wishing he was sitting on that beach, soaking up that sun. *I don't know if even Hangwau's going to be able to . . . restrain Zhyou-Zhwo, but he's my last gift to the Empire. And to the House of Hantai, come to that. If someone doesn't keep him from—*

The door opened and a tallish, dark-haired man stepped through it. Hangwau Ge-yang was always immaculately groomed, although he eschewed the aristocratic styles of the North in favor of the more comfortable and flowing Southern style. He was almost thirty years younger than the grand duke and he favored his mother's side of the family; that was where his height came from. He was also a partner in at least half a dozen manufactories, and North Wind Blowing knew he represented the future of the family in more than one way.

"You sent for me?"

"I did."

North Wind Blowing pointed at a chair, and Cinnabar Hill settled into it while the grand duke turned, still standing by the window, to face him.

"We have fresh messages from Spring Flower," North Wind Blowing told him with a grimace. "They say much the same thing as the earlier ones, only louder and more emphatically."

"Wonderful," Cinnabar Hill sighed.

"In fairness, it seems obvious Cayleb and Sharleyan did provide modern weapons to the rebels." The first councilor shrugged. "They can't have come from anywhere else, assuming they truly did use the 'smokeless powder' Qwaidu reports. And given his casualties, I'm inclined to think his reports are basically accurate."

"That would imply these 'airships' of the Charisians are less of a novelty and more of a useful instrument than we'd assumed," Cinnabar Hill observed.

"Among other things, yes." North Wind Blowing shrugged again. "All of our spies' reports indicate that even the largest of them can carry no more than fifteen or twenty tons, thirty at most—less than a single dragon can pull along the high road. And they're obviously hideously expensive—so expensive only a Charisian could afford them!—and fragile. So far, at least two of them have burned on the ground, although they haven't yet lost any in the air and so far as we know no one was killed in either of the fires. So I still don't see them having a fundamental impact on the movement of vast quantities of cargo. But sometimes even the largest avalanche can be set in motion by a single stone, and that would appear to be what happened here."

"I think you're right." Cinnabar Hill nodded. "And that leads me to wonder how far behind the airships the United Provinces' columns are following."

"Again, our spies indicate Star Rising and the others have no desire to find themselves caught at the end of an extended supply line in the Chiang-wus in the winter, so I think it's . . . unlikely we'll see any United Provinces troops in the Valley until late spring or early summer. But you're right, it *is* coming, and His Majesty will be . . . mildly incensed when it happens."

"*Mildly!*"

"Well, compared to how he's responded to a half-dozen other incidents I could mention." North Wind Blowing smiled briefly. "But he is decidedly unhappy at the moment. As far as he's concerned, Charis has just openly declared war upon the Empire."

"I don't think he's wrong," Cinnabar Hill said.

"Neither do I, but there are wars, and then there are wars, and it would serve the Empire far better to keep this one a war of manufactories and railroads. We're unlikely, to say the least, to best Charis in a war like that, but given what just happened to Spring Flower, the other sort of war—you know, the sort in which people actually shoot at one another?—would work out rather worse. And probably a hell of a lot more quickly."

"Uncle," Cinnabar Hill said, giving him the familial title of respect despite the distance of their relationship, "there's no way the Emperor will settle for status as the ruler of a secondary power. This is the *Harchong Empire,* the oldest, most powerful, most advanced, and most artistically talented realm on the face of Safehold!" The earl rolled his eyes. "He can never resign that position in favor of an empire of shopkeepers!"

"And, to be honest, I wish he didn't have to," North

Wind Blowing said flatly, looking back out the window. "This new world, the one coming to you and my children and my grandchildren—it's not one I like. But I can't stop it from coming, either, so perhaps it's best you're at least . . . in alliance with some of those shopkeepers, right here in Queiroz. But someone still has to steer, unless you really like ramming the ship of state into the rocks, so try to at least moderate your view of our glorious historical and artistic legacy where anyone else might hear you."

"Understood." Cinnabar Hill bowed without rising.

"All right." The grand duke crossed back to his desk, set his teacup on the saucer, and seated himself. "As you can imagine, Spring Flower's messages left him absolutely livid. It only proves once again, even more emphatically, that Charis is the root of all evil in the world. Not just the reason the order God and the Archangels intended was overturned in the first place, but the malign influence determined to stamp out any chance of *restoring* the rightful order. And, as I say, in his view we're now actively at war with Charis. Indeed, he'd prefer to commence active operations immediately."

"Please tell me you're jesting."

"No." North Wind Blowing shook his head and leaned back in his chair. "Fortunately, for once, Snow Peak and I are on the same page. For that matter, Earl Sunset Peak's at least as aghast at the notion as you and I. In fact," the first councilor allowed himself a small smile, "I believe the good Earl did himself a certain amount of damage this morning."

"Oh?" Cinnabar Hill perked up.

"Oh, yes. I fear he allowed his dismay at the thought of open hostilities with Charis to . . . color his attitude."

"Well, that was certainly stupid of him."

"Now, now!" North Wind Blowing shook an admonishing finger. "The news came at him as a surprise." He smiled again, more broadly. "I fear the memo I sent him before the Privy Council meeting went astray somehow." He shrugged. "These minor clerical errors do happen."

"I'm taking notes, Uncle."

"Good." North Wind Blowing smiled again, but then his expression sobered. "Fortunately, Snow Peak and I were a bit more adroit. We pointed out to His Majesty the way in which the existence of the Imperial Charisian Navy constrains our ability to take any war to them. He argued in return that Emperor Mahrys would undoubtedly stand with us against the Charisian contagion, but we pointed out that Emperor Mahrys' navy is almost as nonexistent as our own."

"And—?" Cinnabar Hill asked as the grand duke paused.

"And so, we decided to divert him into another direction. Mind you, I'm not certain we've succeeded in the long-term, but for now it looks promising. You see—"

. II .
City of Tellesberg,
Kingdom of Old Charis,
Empire of Charis.

"So, what do you think of North Wind Blowing's brainstorm, Dunkyn?" Duke Rock Point asked as he settled back into his comfortable wingback chair with his whiskey glass.

"I think he's cleverer than I thought he was," the Earl of Sarmouth said, dropping into the facing chair across the crackling fire's hearth with a matching glass. "Whether or not the strategy will work's another matter. I don't really have an opinion about that, but he has to've been thinking about this one for a while, and as political legerdemain goes, it's pretty impressive."

"That's one way to put it," Rock Point said dryly. "Although, I'll grant you that if they can keep Zhyou-Zhwo tied up in it, it will at least keep him from doing anything stupid. Anything else stupid, I mean. I just doubt they'll be able to do it."

"I don't know about that," Sarmouth said thoughtfully. "There *is* a certain underlying logic to it."

"Oh?" Rock Point raised one white eyebrow. "And how well did that work out for Alfred von Tirpitz and Wilhelm II?"

"I didn't say it would 'work out' for Zhyou-Zhwo." Sarmouth smiled slightly. "What I said is that there's a logical model for it, and that's true. Of course, as Cayleb's become fond of saying 'logic is an organized way of going wrong with confidence.'"

"Thank you, Doctor Kettering," Rock Point growled, and Sarmouth raised his glass in salute.

"The point here, though," he said, "is that North Wind Blowing and Snow Peak could care less if it works. They just want Zhyou-Zhwo to go off in a corner and play with it as a way to keep him from doing something a lot worse."

"Um." Rock Point sipped his own whiskey appreciatively while he thought about it.

When Alfred von Tirpitz and Kaiser Wilhelm came up with the notion, they'd called it the "*risikoflotte*"—the "risk fleet." Like most of the rest of nineteenth-century Old Terra, Wilhelm had believed it was the British Navy which had allowed Great Britain to build the greatest empire in human history. And, on the face of things, it was hard to fault the world's reasoning. The corollary, that only offsetting that maritime power could give anyone else a fair shot at empire, might have been more suspect, but it, too, had seemed reasonable at the time. Yet Imperial Germany would never be able to outbuild the Royal British Navy; that was a given. So, how did an ambitious imperialist neutralize the unfair advantage all those ships had bestowed upon his imperial cousins?

Von Tirpitz, who'd had a love-hate relationship with all things British, had provided his emperor with an answer. Germany couldn't build a navy big enough to fight the Royal Navy and win, no. But it could build a navy big enough to give Great Britain one hell of a fight. A big enough fight, perhaps, to erode the Royal Navy's supremacy and allow the British Empire's *other* competitors to snatch away Britannia's crown. And if Germany built a navy that size, Britain would be loathe to risk the consequences of an actual war with Germany. Hopefully, the *risikoflotte* would force Great Britain to support Germany diplomatically—or, at least, to not actively oppose German diplomacy—without ever firing a shot.

It hadn't quite worked out that way.

"Do you think they can actually convince Zhyou-Zhwo he could build a navy big enough to make us break a sweat?" the duke asked finally.

"I think they can convince Zhyou-Zhwo—temporarily, at least—of anything that suits his prejudices," Sarmouth said seriously. "And at the moment, this suits his prejudices."

"To be fair, we're in a bit of a different position from Great Britain," Rock Point said slowly. "We don't really have a single strategic center. Or peripheral areas we can risk, for that matter. Chisholm and Corisande aren't India or the China Station, and we don't have Japan to watch our back in the Pacific, either. We'd have to maintain sufficient forces on distant stations to protect our core citizens."

"Like I say, a logical model." Sarmouth shrugged. "Personally, I don't think they have a chance in hell of pulling it off, but look at it this way—it plays perfectly into the Nahrmahn Plan. Just think of how the shipbuilding programs in Germany 'grew' Krupp! Of course, old Alfred couldn't hold a candle to our Ehdwyrd, but that wasn't his fault."

"No, it wasn't," Rock Point acknowledged.

"And so far, the Nahrmahn Plan does seem to be working," Sarmouth pointed out rather more somberly. "Not as well as any of us would like, especially given the way Siddarmark seems to keep stuttering along. But any Archangel that comes back now's going to find the cat well and truly out of the bag. Maybe not in terms of technology, but at least as far as industrialization is concerned."

"The problem, of course, is that the aforesaid Archangel may not *care*," Rock Point pointed out grimly, and Sarmouth nodded.

The clock continued to tick, and the earl knew Rock Point felt the coiling tension just as much as he did. In a little over one month, it would be Year of God 914. If the "Archangels" truly meant to return *exactly* a thousand years after the Day of Creation, they would arrive on God's Day—which was the traditional anniversary of the Day of Creation and always fell on the thirteenth day, the third Wednesday of the month, in 915. Even allowing five months' leeway either side, that meant they *could* turn up as early as February 915 or, at the latest, by February 916.

That wasn't a lot of time.

Silence hovered for several seconds, and then Rock Point chuckled suddenly. The sound was harsh, and Sarmouth cocked his head.

"What?" he asked.

"You're right about the Nahrmahn Plan," Rock Point told him. "About the way a Harchongese 'risk fleet' would help push it along, I mean. And, for that matter, about the way it's working in places like Dohlar, Silkiah—even Desnair—not just here in Charis. But a thought just occurred to me. What we've been doing—?"

He paused, eyebrows arched, until Sarmouth nodded for him to continue.

"The Nahrmahn Plan's our own *risikoflotte*, Dunkyn," the duke said very, very seriously. "I'm not saying we have a better strategy. I'm just saying that that's what it is. Oh, not because we could fight the bastards and hope to do much more than scuff their paint—we'd be in a lot worse mess than Scheer at Jutland if we tried that!—but because what we're betting on is that they'd have to do so much damage to Safehold to eradicate what we've done that they'll decide to throw in the towel. If I'd thought I could suggest a better approach, I damned well would have—don't think I'm not saying this isn't the best one we've got. I'm just saying, well—"

He shrugged.

"That when our illustrious German ancestors tried their variant on the plan it didn't work out very well, you mean?" Sarmouth asked dryly.

"More or less." Rock Point nodded.

"I can never thank you sufficiently for sharing that thought with me," Sarmouth said. "And here I thought I was going to sleep tonight!"

"Always here for you, Dunkyn," Rock Point said with another, much lighter chuckle. "Besides, I don't like to complain, but too much sleep always leaves you loggy and so cranky in the morning."

MARCH YEAR OF GOD 914

✦

. I .
Boardroom,
Trans-Siddarmark Railroad,
Siddar City,
Republic of Siddarmark,
and
Royal Palace,
City of Cherayth,
Kingdom of Chisholm
Empire of Charis.

"Good morning, Zhak!" Dustyn Nezbyt said, smiling and crossing the boardroom with a hot cup of tea in his left hand while he extended his right to Zhak Hahraimahn. "Talk about your miserable weather—!"

"It is pretty bad," Hahraimahn agreed with a certain fervency, clasping forearms with him.

March was still winter, and Siddar City was still Siddar City. The city's workers' endless battle against snow clearance was clearly in a losing phase, at the moment, and Hahraimahn crossed to the Charisian-style iron stove built into the conference room's old-fashioned hearth. He held out his hands, warming them above the heat rising from the coal-fired stove while he listened to the wind blustering about the eaves.

"The streetcars are still running . . . for now," he said

over his shoulder. "It's looking pretty bad, though. I'm not sure we'll have a quorum today, after all."

"Can't say I'm really surprised. Tea?"

"Please!" Hahraimahn rubbed his hands together harder, and Nezbyt chuckled as he crossed to the side table where carafes of tea steamed gently over the spirit burners.

"Real tea? Or cherrybean?" he asked.

"Do I look as effete as you? There is no 'tea or real tea.' There is only cherrybean and pale, muddy water, especially in weather like this! And don't dilute it with any of that cream or sugar."

Nezbyt chuckled again, poured, and carried the second cup across to the shorter, stockier Hahraimahn. Hahraimahn took it gratefully and sipped. Then he turned his back to the stove, looking across the boardroom at its handsome furnishings. An enormous painting of one of the TSRR's steam automotives thundering across a mountain trestle bridge dominated the decor. Mahtylda Nezbyt had suggested the artist, and while Hahraimahn wasn't prepared to back her judgment in all things, this time she'd been right. The painting caught the majesty and energy of the Republic's rapidly expanding rail net almost perfectly.

It would have been nice if everything else about the TSRR's operations had gone as smoothly as picking an artist. Of course, no one could put something this size together without making a few mistakes, hitting a few rough spots.

"The weather may not be an altogether bad thing," he said now, still looking at the painting. "Mind you, I'll be really pissed if I came seven blocks in the middle of a blizzard and we don't have a quorum, anyway! But there's something I wanted to mention to you before the meeting."

"Oh?" Nezbyt sipped more tea, looking at him across the rim of the cup.

"Zhaikahbsyn buttonholed me at the club Thursday. He's not happy about some of the contracts."

"Really?" Nezbyt rolled his eyes ever so slightly, and Hahraimahn grimaced.

"I know he's been complaining about quite a few things, but I think he's genuinely beginning to be a little alarmed."

"Zhak, Zhaikahbsyn's always going to be 'a little alarmed' over something! And he's not exactly at the heart of the stock market or any of the banking cartels."

Hahraimahn nodded at Nezbyt's point. Points, really.

Lainyl Zhaikahbsyn was the second-youngest member of the General Board. Only Lawrync Ashtyn, one of the two Charisian members, was younger, and like Ashtyn, Zhaikahbsyn was more of an engineer than a banker. A self-made iron master, he'd enthusiastically adopted the Charisian technologies during the Jihad, and he was smart. Shan-wei, but he was smart! Yet a man couldn't be smart about *everything,* and Zhaikahbsyn had been wringing his hands over the Republic's economy for years now. His concerns hadn't all been simple alarmism, of course. Langhorne knew there'd been more than enough bumps and potholes along the road! But there'd been a lot of Wyvern Little's falling sky in many of Zhaikahbsyn's complaints, too.

"I know he's always looking out for the next downturn," Hahraimahn conceded. "But I'm hearing some rumbles from other sources, as well. I think this may be something we need to look into, Dustyn. If only so we can tell people like Lainyl we have!"

Nezbyt's lips had thinned as he listened, but he relaxed—a bit—at Hahraimahn's last sentence.

"Zhak, TSRR's the biggest single commercial enterprise in the history of the Republic. I mean, we have thousands—*scores* of thousands—of shareholders, and we're operating on a scale no one except Mother Church *ever* operated on before. I'll be honest with you, I don't have a clue—I doubt anyone does—just how many people we actually have working for us at this moment, and the pace and the scale are both still growing. I know things were more . . . intense during the Jihad, and God knows we were expanding manufactories even faster than we are now. Having a Shan-wei–damned army invading your territory has that effect."

He smiled sourly, and Hahraimahn snorted in agreement.

"But even then, if you look at the absolute numbers, nobody in the Republic—no single manufactory, not even any single *consortium* of manufactories—has ever operated on the scale we're operating on. We've got more workers, we've got a much bigger cash flow, and we're snapping up every steel rail we can buy, beg, borrow, or steal. I've got to tell you, there's *going* to be some skimming and there's going to be some nest-feathering out there. There has to be, given human nature and the scale of this project. The only things in history that could even compare to what we're doing are building the high roads and the canals, and both Mother Church and the Republic had the *Holy Writ*'s instructions where those were concerned. Not only that, the Church had the tithes to pay for them, and everybody involved had centuries to build them. We're doing this 'without benefit of clergy' and our completion date's only *twenty years*. We're going off in way too many directions at once for anyone to stay on top of everything, and that's likely to get worse once the Silkiah Canal project starts competing with us for management talent—and investors, for that matter! When the bond issue for that hits the markets in September, things will get *really* crazy."

"I understand all of that," Hahraimahn said. "You're preaching to the choir about the size and the speed of this whole thing. And I agree with you about human nature, too. For that matter, I think Zhaikahbsyn does. But he does have a point when he says the fact that we can't *stop* it doesn't mean we don't have a responsibility to at least hold it to manageable levels!"

"Which is what we're doing." Nezbyt shrugged. "Orlynoh's helping me keep an eye on things, and I'll have him sit down and discuss Zhaikahbsyn's concerns with him."

Hahraimahn nodded again, in approval. Orlynoh Archbahld was Nezbyt's executive assistant, another veteran of the Exchequer. He knew his way around facts and figures, and he wasn't just smart and efficient. He also had the political bureaucrat's skill set needed to stroke ruffled feathers.

"I'm inclined to wonder, frankly, though," Nezbyt continued, "how much of Zhaikahbsyn's concerns have to do with contracts *he* is or isn't getting." Hahraimahn arched an eyebrow, and the chairman waved one hand quickly. "I'm not saying he's running crying to the General Board to try and make us throw business his way! I don't think he'd object if we did that, but he knows the Lord Protector and Chamber cut the General Board out of the actual contract-awarding process specifically to prevent any of us from favoring ourselves or our friends, and I think he's in favor of that. But he'd be more than human if he didn't feel aggrieved if he genuinely thinks there's favoritism involved in the contracts that are being awarded . . . but not to him."

"That . . . could be a factor," Hahraimahn conceded slowly. "I don't think it is. Or, at least, I don't think *he* thinks it is, if you take my meaning. But it could be. As far as I know, all of his manufactories are working at pretty near full capacity right now, but it's true he's not expanding as quickly as some of the others. So he may be feeling a little pinched. A little . . . squeezed out."

"I'll have a talk of my own with Orlynoh before he calls on Zhaikahbsyn," Nezbyt promised.

▼ ▼ ▼

"He damned well *should* have a talk of his own with Archbahld," Ehdwyrd Howsmyn growled over the com. "Just not the talk he's *going* to have!"

"I agree, but Archbahld's more a symptom of the problem than the problem itself," Nahrmahn Baytz put in from Nimue's Cave. "If he was all we had to worry about, I *wouldn't* worry about it."

"It's not an ideal situation," Cayleb said, looking out his and Sharleyan's chamber's window at snow that was even heavier than that falling on Siddar City . . . although, thankfully, without the powerful winds. "In fact, I'll go farther than that and say I don't *like* the situation. But let's be fair here. We've never liked the way Myllyr set up the Trans-Siddarmark Board. And Nezbyt's got a point. They're laying a *ton* of track, Ehdwyrd. Anything going that fast on that scale is going to be messy. We saw enough of that right here at home during the Jihad, even with honest supervisors—and *SNARCs*—keeping an eye on things!"

"I know—I know!" Duke Delthak waved both hands. "But this is . . . this is *systemic,* Cayleb."

"It's always systemic, or else it doesn't happen," Sharleyan pointed out. "I'm not trying to downplay anything you're saying, Ehdwyrd, because the truth is I agree with you. But I think what Cayleb's saying is that from *Nezbyt's* perspective, if it isn't broken he shouldn't be trying to fix it. And he doesn't think it's broken."

"I know. And, overall, he may have a point," Delthak conceded. "After all, the Republic's entire economy's in a lot better shape, and Ashfyrd's announcement that the Exchequer's finally launching the Canal Consortium bond issue's bound to help that along. So I have to agree everything seems to be trending upward. It's just that there are still . . . management issues, especially on the political side, that worry me. The Central Bank's getting steadily better, but it's still making things up as it goes along. Its Board of Governors has made its share of missteps, and its enforcement of the new credit regulations is . . . erratic. Brygs is doing his best—and, by the way, the sheer demands the Bank puts on his time are why he's relying so much on Paidrho Ohkailee to oversee people like Sulyvyn—and Ashfyrd's backing him to the hilt. But they're still training regulators and inspectors. They don't have nearly enough of them yet, and too many of the ones they do have don't see any reason they shouldn't make a little on the side for their efforts. That means there's still a lot of playing fast and loose at the margins, and it's going to be a while before they get a handle on that.

"That worries me, but, frankly, completely irrespective of enforcement . . . foibles, the Bank's basic policies are too restrictive in some areas. Their demand for collateral and the limits they've imposed on debt-asset levels for creditors mean smaller investors are finding it harder to qualify for loans. That's starving entrepreneurship and the development of the small business sector. But, at the same time, Ashfyrd—and Myllyr, I think—are subscribing to the 'too big to fail' mindset where other loan and credit decisions are concerned, and Brygs is working inside their policy directives . . . even when that can mean looking the other way. The Bank's granting extensions and exemptions for the consortiums and corporations they 'can't afford to lose.' And if that's true where something like the Hahraimahn association or Hymphyl Ironworks is concerned, it's even truer about something like the TSRR.

"I'm concerned about that, for a lot of reasons. For one thing, I think we're actually seeing an . . . erosion of the marketplace's faith in the rule of law, despite the increase in regulations. Siddarmark's never made a Dohlaran level of commitment to a thorough overhaul of its commercial law codes and patent law. That was one of the things Henrai Maidyn was still fighting for when that idiot killed him. I'll admit Myllyr and Ashfyrd've continued the fight, but not everybody's onboard with that. What Nahrmahn and I are seeing is a growing willingness to 'game the system' as the regulations get more restrictive, coupled with that 'too big to fail' attitude which keeps major financial stakeholders from getting hammered the way the little guy does when they get *caught* gaming it. That means the little guy's likely to lose faith in the impartiality of the system, which could have . . . negative implications down the road. For example, Zhermo Hygyns. Now that he's decided to throw his hat into the ring and challenge Myllyr for the protectorship, this is exactly the sort of issue he'll fasten on. And he won't feel particularly constrained by the truth or any kind of faceted analysis when he does!"

"The best we can do is the best we can do," Cayleb said philosophically. "Unless we want to start using *seijin*-style techniques to drop something like Kartyr

Sulyvyn's second set of books on Brygs' desk in the middle of the night, we can't do a lot more than we already have. And to tell the truth, Ehdwyrd, Archbahld and Sulyvyn aren't remotely number one on my list of concerns. I mean, all of that's important, and so is encouraging the rule of law any way we can, but at the moment Trans-Siddarmark's pushing the Nahrmahn Plan harder than any other single non-Charisian entity on the entire planet. Could I could wish the rest of the Republic's economy was taking off the same way? Of course I could! But let's be grateful for what we've *got,* because it's one hell of a lot better than what we had a couple of years ago. And while I could wish we were already digging canal bed in Silkiah, at least we'll be starting on it by the beginning of next year. But let's be honest here. I think all of us are finding things to worry about—maybe even *obsessing* about things to worry about—where things like the Canal are concerned to help us avoid another time limit we don't much like to think about."

Silence fell on the com net, and Sharleyan reached across to squeeze her husband's forearm. He put his free hand over hers and smiled crookedly at her while they listened to that silence.

"You're right," Delthak acknowledged finally. "That doesn't mean what we're worrying about isn't valid, but it does kind of put things into perspective, doesn't it?"

"Maybe. And maybe I'm just feeling a bit . . . frazzled at the moment. But the truth is, we're headed into the final stage of the first phase of the Nahrmahn Plan, one way or the other. And I think we'll just have to let the Republic take care of itself. It only has to hold together for another two years and then we're either golden or it doesn't matter for at least another seventy years."

MAY YEAR OF GOD 914

·✦·

Zhutiyan,
Chynduk Valley,
Tiegelkamp Province,
North Harchong.

"—so I don't think Qwaidu and Spring Flower're going poke their greasy fingers at the Valley again this year after all," Major Fraidareck Bulyrd said with a broad grin, leaning back on the other side of the trestle table with his mug of beer. "By now, they have to know the United Provinces're on their way. If Qwaidu was coming, he'd've been here already, trying to beat them, but the truth is he's already missed the turnip wagon."

Tangwyn Syngpu sat on the other side of the table. It stood on the veranda of the sturdy cabin which had been run up to give him a proper headquarters building, and he waved his own mug of beer in agreement. Of course, the Charisian sitting across from him was one of the main reasons that was true. Bulyrd had been a guest here in the Chynduk Valley for over seven months, ever since he'd shinnied down a rope from the enormous airship floating overhead. He'd overwintered in the Valley—which, he'd explained, hadn't been as severe hardship for him as for some of his fellows, since he'd actually been born in northern Chisholm—and Syngpu was the first to admit how much he and his militia had learned from their Charisian advisors.

And Bulyrd and Sergeant Major Rahdryk Hamptyn had managed to do it all without ever "talking down" to the ex-serfs and ex-peasants they were teaching about modern weapons and tactics.

Bulyrd had spent even more time with Syngpu, in deep, private conversations which had taught the ex-sergeant of the Mighty Host just how big a difference there was between the knowledge of an experienced field grade officer and a sergeant. Looking back from what he knew now, some of his own earlier decisions appalled him, but Bulyrd had waved away his self-criticism.

"Something Duke Serabor's always emphasized, Tangwyn," the Charisian had said. "If it's stupid and it works, then it wasn't stupid in the first place. What we're talking about now—the stuff you and I are discussing—that's the icing on the cake. That's what helps you do in the other guy quicker, with fewer of your guys getting hurt in the process. And it does help with the logistics and the planning and all that crap. But what you've demonstrated you had from the beginning was the instinct and the common sense. Give me a good, solid sergeant who knows his troops, knows his weapons, knows his ground, and is bloody-minded enough to break the neck of anyone who comes at him over an 'educated' officer who runs from the smell of gunsmoke any day. Langhorne's honest truth, I'd be totally satisfied serving under your command, and I'm not just blowing smoke up your arse when I say that."

Over the months, Syngpu had been forced to accept that Bulyrd actually meant that, but that didn't change his own profound gratitude for everything the major and his cadre of experienced noncoms had taught them.

And, of course, for the weapons the Charisians had provided without even discussing a price tag.

"I'll agree the two of them have missed the wagon," Syngpu said now, "but I'm less convinced they'll realize that. We know they've been recruiting, and the Emperor's been shipping in every gun he could lay hands on. Don't they almost *have* to make another try to keep him happy?"

"No," the woman at the end of the table said. He looked at her, and she shook her head. "What they're going to do is to *not* try again . . . and tell Zhyou-Zhwo they did. Oh, they'll probably march up and down and make a lot of smoke firing off a couple of tons of ammunition at nothing in particular so it'll look good, but they aren't going to screw around with your boys again."

"If you say so, *Seijin* Merch." Despite himself, Syngpu couldn't quite keep all of his doubt out of his voice, and she rounded her eyes at him and stuck out her lower lip. She even got it to quiver.

"Don't you love me anymore, Tangwyn?" she asked sadly.

Major Bulyrd hid his face behind his beer stein with commendable speed, although his shoulders did quiver just a bit.

"Were you my daughter," Syngpu told her, "the seat of your breeches and a birch wand would be old, *old* friends by now."

"*Bully!*" she said, and grinned impishly at him. "Bet you *were* a strict father, though. You know I've been talking to Pauyin, too, don't you?"

"Near as I can tell, you talk to *everyone*," he said philosophically. "How you find time to get any *seijin*-ing done is more'n I can say."

"There's something they teach us *seijins* to do. It's called 'multitasking.' And one reason I talk to so many people is because that's one way you learn things. Frankly, I enjoy it a lot more than I do creeping around in the shrubbery and spying on people. Not that I don't like to keep my hand in on the creeping around in the shrubbery bit."

"That much I believe," he said with feeling.

To this day, no one had *ever* seen Merch O Obaith arrive in the Chynduk Valley, and she'd become a fairly regular visitor. Including during the very heart of winter, when Cliffwall Pass was head-high on a dragon with snow. Clearly, she was no respecter of weather. The fact that she obviously found it child's play to evade his sentries didn't bother him. Or, rather, it didn't bother him as much as it once had. Figuring out how she danced through the blizzards without ever even catching a *cold* was something else.

"But getting back to unimportant things, like, oh, Baron Qwaidu's army," the major said, lowering his beer mug once he was certain it was safe. "I'd be inclined to think the same thing, Tangwyn, even without the reports from the *seijin's* spies. And one thing I can tell you for certain is that we never got bad information from a *seijin* during the Jihad. Nobody's spies get *everything* right, but if a *seijin*—even *Seijin* Merch—tells you he or she knows something, you can put it in your lockbox under your bed."

"My head knows that," Syngpu said. "It's the rest of me's having a little trouble with it. Sort of got into the habit of expecting the worst. Comes natural to a peasant, I guess you'd say, but it also meant I was never surprised when it happened anyway."

"Not a bad attitude, as long as you don't let it paralyze you," Bulyrd said, and *Seijin* Merch nodded in agreement.

"No it isn't," she said, "and as far as I can tell, you never did, Tangwyn. But the main point right now is that between your boys and what the Major and his boys could teach them, I'm pretty sure you've convinced Qwaidu, at least, that he *never* wants to come back to the Chynduk Valley. And if he did," her kraken-like smile was not in the least impish now, "he'd probably get to stay this time. At the bottom of a nice, deep hole. If we're feeling generous, we might even put a marker on it. Probably not, though."

There was no mistaking the satisfaction in her voice, and Syngpu smiled at her across the table while the breeze played with loose strands of auburn hair which had escaped her braid.

And she was right about what would happen if Qwaidu was stupid enough to try again, he thought.

He'd come to the Valley with just over four thousand men, and over six hundred of them had died defending it. Despite that, his present roster strength when the militia was fully mobilized was up to almost *nine* thousand. Of course, he couldn't keep all of the men under arms, because most of them were also the farmers who kept the Valleyers fed, but they worked their farms cooperatively so that he could keep a minimum of six thousand ready for service on fifty-two-hours' notice.

And thanks to Charisian generosity, every single one of those nine thousand men was now equipped with a Mark IV Mahndrayn rifle with bayonet. The Charisians had delivered five hundred revolvers, as well, and thirty-eight "mortars"—what the Host had called "angle-guns." That was enough to equip three complete mortar platoons with a couple of spares in case they were needed. Then there were the sixty-five tons of Lywysite and the "sweepers" and "fountains" which could be emplaced to cover the approaches to any position his militia took up. And the ammunition for all of it.

It had taken almost a score of airship deliveries to get all of that into Syngpu's hands, but the Charisians had managed it before the treacherous winter weather of the Chiang-wus made flight too dangerous even for the lunatics in the Charisian Air Force. Air contact had been reestablished only two five-days ago.

Although—of course—that hadn't prevented *Seijin* Merch from dancing in and out whenever the mood took her.

He looked at the slender *seijin*—she was more substantial than his own Yanshwyn, and there was nothing remotely fragile about her, yet she was definitely on the small side. She'd laid her gun belt and peculiar sword aside when they sat down at the table, and she was dressed in the sort of rough, serviceable garments any mountaineer might have chosen, although hers were far better made than most Harchongese mountaineers could have afforded. She didn't *look* like a figure out of legend. Maybe that was the problem. But she reminded him strongly of the younger sister he'd never had.

"The other main thing is that 'Baron Cliffwall' has figured out which side of the bread his butter's on," she continued now in a tone of profound satisfaction. "The snow hasn't completely melted in the higher stretches of the pass, but it shouldn't be more than another few days now. And once that happens, Brigadier Zhanma's column's going to come knock on his front gate at Ky-su. And do you know what's going to happen then?"

She smiled brightly as Syngpu shook his head with a resigned expression.

"What's going to happen is that he'll open that front gate, and he'll explain how *terribly* sorry he is he ever closed it in the first place, and could he *please* join the United Provinces, if it wouldn't be too much trouble? *Pretty* please, with briar berries on top!"

Syngpu had to chuckle at her expression, but he didn't doubt she was right about Cliffwall. The only real question in his mind was whether or not they should let him, given what he'd been a party to.

"You really need to be as . . . generous with him as you can without compromising your own safety, Tang-wyn," Merch said, and there was no humor in her voice now. He looked at her, saw the understanding in those sapphire eyes. "I know what he tried to do, but he didn't think he had a choice. I'm not nominating him for saint-hood, because frankly, he's about as far from a saint as anyone I could imagine. But he's not an unmitigated monster, either. In fact, he's a hell of a lot better deal than Spring Flower or Qwaidu! And something Cay-leb and Sharleyan learned is that having a reputation as someone who keeps her word—for good or ill—is what makes people trust you when you *give* your word. The United Provinces need to remember that, and as the UP's newest prospective member, you do, too. I know it would be a lot more satisfying to give him a fast horse and a twenty-six-hour head start, but you could be sur-prised. A lot of people who've been through what he's been through turn over new leaves. And in his case, my friends and I will be keeping a very close eye on him. If he's the same old leaf he used to be, you'll know in plenty of time to snip it off the branch."

He gazed at her for several seconds, then nodded.

"'Spect you're right about that, too, *Seijin*," he said. "Seems to be a habit of yours. Reminds me of—"

"Excuse me, Tangwyn!"

Syngpu paused in midsentence, looking over his shoulder at the young man who'd just arrived.

"Yes?"

"Sister Baishan sent me," the youngster said, and Syngpu froze, his face suddenly expressionless. "She says it's time!"

▼ ▼ ▼

"You're not going to make Boisseau tonight, you know."

"What?" Syngpu stopped and turned. "*What* did you say?"

"I said," *Seijin* Merch told him with a smile that mingled humor and sympathy, "that you're not going to make Boisseau tonight. I figure you've already paced off most of the distance between here and Jai-hu, but I doubt you'll make even Shang-mi before dark."

Syngpu stared at her. Then he shook himself.

"Hadn't planned on going anywhere," he told her with a small, answering smile of his own. "'Sides, the healers tell me exercise's good for a man. Specially when he's got a lot on his mind."

"I'm sure they do, but come over here and sit down," Obaith said, patting the arm of the chair beside hers. "You've been pacing that same circle for almost three hours now. Give your poor feet a rest."

He gazed at her for another moment or two, then shrugged and walked across to the indicated chair. He settled into it, his elbows on his thighs and his hands clasped between his knees, and shook his head.

"Guess I *am* a mite . . . distracted," he said. "Never took this long with Pauyin or Tsungzau or Fengwa. 'Course, the midwives always said Shuchyng had easy pregnancies." He shook his head, his eyes filled with memories. "Never seemed like there was anything easy about it, though. She always fought hard for her kids. And now Pauyin's the only one left."

"She wasn't the only one who fought hard for her

kids," the *seijin* said gently, putting a hand on his shoulder. "You fought for them, too. And you're the *reason* Pauyin's 'left.' Don't ever forget that."

"What Yngshwan says, too. Reckon if the two smartest women I know both think so, I'd best pay attention." He managed a quick, a fleeting smile. "It's just . . . just the hole it leaves in your heart, *Seijin*."

"I know." Her voice was soft, her sapphire eyes deeper than the sea, and she shook her head. "Oh, trust me, Tangwyn, *I* know. If anyone on Safehold knows, it's me. Me and Merlin."

In that moment, she looked neither young nor impish. And she didn't look like an invulnerable, superhuman *seijin*, either.

"Believe you do," he said after a moment, reaching up one hand to cover the slender one on his shoulder. They sat for a moment, then he inhaled deeply.

"Not why I've been walking to Shang-mi today, though," he said more briskly, and she laughed.

"No, *really?*" She shook her head. "There's something *else* going on today?"

He suppressed an urge to smack her, and she smiled with a hint of penitence. Only a hint, of course.

"Tangwyn, she's going to be fine. I promise you. Sister Baishan's been delivering babies here in the Valley for almost fifty years. She knows what she's doing, and Yanshwyn's not the first late pregnancy she's dealt with!"

"But she's forty-six, *Seijin*. That's not the age a woman should be having her first baby, and it's my fault."

"Oh, *please!*" *Seijin* Merch rolled her eyes. "You're telling me Yanshwyn never wanted children of her own? That she and Zhyungkwan never tried? That this was all your idea and you *made* her get pregnant? For that matter, are you telling me *anyone* could make that woman do *anything* she didn't choose to do?"

"No," he said after a moment. "But—"

"No 'buts'!" she interrupted. "Do I think one reason she was so happy when she found out she was pregnant was because she knows how much you loved the children you lost? Of course it was, you dummy! But she wants this child for herself, too. For the two of you to share and raise. And the reason she does—" those sapphire eyes looked straight across into his "—is because, first, she loves you, and second, Tangwyn, you were *meant* to be a father. That's what's driven every single thing you've done since the Jihad—do you think Yanshwyn didn't realize that? She's seen you—*I've* seen you—with Pauyin and your grandchildren, and this is what you do best in all the world. Mind you, you're not too shabby when it comes to raising armies, fighting off invasions, all that minor, unimportant crap, too, but this . . . *this* is what you were born to be, and that's why Yanshwyn wants you to be the father of *her* baby."

He stared at her, unable for once to think of a rejoinder, and she punched his biceps lightly.

"So stop worrying. In fact, if it'll make you feel any better, I'll admit the real reason I scheduled this trip to get me here this five-day was so I'd be here when the baby was born." Syngpu's eyes widened, and she shook her head. "I don't just chop people up into little tiny pieces, Tangwyn. As it happens, I'm a pretty damned good midwife myself. Which is why I know Sister Baishan's doing everything right and that Yanshwyn's doing just fine. You're right; it is late for a first pregnancy, and we all expected her delivery to be hard, but if she needs me, I'll be in that birthing chamber in a skinny Siddarmark minute. So you keep your butt parked in that chair and think tranquil thoughts until I tell you you can get out of it. Clear?"

"Clear . . . *Seijin*," he said after a moment, and she nodded in satisfaction as he sat back in the chair.

▼ ▼ ▼

Merch O Obaith watched the big, burly ex-peasant through the eyes of someone who'd never expected to become a mother herself. Someone who understood exactly what this meant to Yanshwyn Syngpu, as well as to him. Someone who Syngpu would never know had covertly injected the Federation nanotech to deal with Yanshwyn's infertility issues.

Probably wasn't really my place to do that, she thought now. *It* definitely *wasn't my place to do it without at least consulting Yanshwyn, because Tangwyn's right. It is* late for the first pregnancy.

At forty-six—and she wouldn't actually be forty-six for another three months—Yanshwyn wasn't quite forty-two Standard Years old, which was scarcely late at all by the standards of the Terran Federation's medical technology. It was definitely into the high-risk range here on Safehold, however. That was the reason Nimue Gahrvai had planted the medical remote in Yanshwyn's bedchamber so that "Merch O Obaith" could monitor the pregnancy she'd sponsored.

But late or not, this needed *to happen. Because every word I told him about being a father was true. And because shared love—shared* children—*really can heal the heart. Especially if the parents are going to love them for who* they *are and not as replacements for the ones they lost. And, God bless him, Tangwyn Syngpu couldn't* not *love a kid for who she is to save his immortal soul. Somehow, I don't see Yanshwyn coming up short in that department, either.*

The *seijin* tipped back in her own chair, watching the take from the remote in the birthing chamber, and smiled at the man she'd come to respect so deeply.

▼ ▼ ▼

"You have a daughter, Commander."

Sister Baishan Quaiho was a small woman, only an inch or two taller than Yanshwyn. There was nothing frail about her, but her still-thick hair gleamed like fresh snowfall in the lamplight, and a face worn by seventy-three years of love and laughter, sorrow and joy, was creased in an enormous smile as she opened the door and stood aside.

Tangwyn Syngpu felt huge, ungainly, as he stepped past her, and his heart was in his throat and in his eyes as Yanshwyn looked up at him from the bed. He knew Sister Baishan and her assistants had helped her clean up before they allowed him into the chamber, but the air was heavy with the smell of sweat and fatigue, of hard physical work and discharged fluids. He'd smelled the aftermath of childbirth before, and he leaned over her, his calloused hand featherlight as he stroked the side of her face. It was framed in hair still heavy with sweat, that face, and lined with fatigue and the memory of pain, but her eyes glowed as she smiled up at him.

"Hey," he said softly.

"Hay is for horses," she replied, completing the familiar joke, and he chuckled.

"Hard day?" he asked.

"Oh, no! I've had *much* harder days . . . and for a lot worse reasons," she told him, and folded back the blanket to show him the screwed-up, red, frowning, *beautiful* face of their child.

"She's beautiful," he said.

"Maybe not yet. Let's be honest here, neither of us is really at our best for you today. But she *will* be beautiful, Tangwyn. She will be."

"With you for her mother? '*Course* she will—even with me for her *father*!" He laughed, touching that tiny, sleeping face with the tip of a finger. She would have fitted into the palm of his hand with space left over, he thought. She was even tinier than Fengwa had been.

"You do realize that because she's a daughter, *I* get to pick the name?" Yanshwyn said. He looked at her, and she looked back with an edge of challenge. "That's the way we do it, here in the Valley," she said firmly. "Isn't it, Sister?"

"Without a doubt," Sister Baishan said serenely.

"Well, who am I to argue about the way we do things here in the Valley?" Syngpu said mildly.

"Good, because her name is Shuchyng Fengwa Syngpu," Yanshwyn said very softly. He stiffened, but she shook her head before he could speak. "I never got the chance to know them, Tangwyn, but I know *you*. And because I do, I know what extraordinary people they must've been. So that's her name, and if we have another child—which, despite the day's strenuous nature, I happen to be in favor of—and it's a boy, I hope you'll name him Tsungzau. Not because I'm trying to give you your family back, but because I want to honor their memories while we build *our* family."

He looked down at her, and then he went to his knees beside the bed. He put his arms around her, and around their daughter, and laid his cheek on her chest beside the baby.

"Hello, Shuchyng Fengwa," his voice was husky, quivering around the edges. "I hope someday you realize how *special* your mother is."

SEPTEMBER YEAR OF GOD 914

·◆·

. I .
Conference Chamber,
Lord Protector Alvyn Annex,
Protector's Palace,
Siddar City,
Republic of Siddarmark.

Safehold had no equivalent of the Terran Federation's ubiquitous electronic communications network, but it did have its print news media. Locally produced broadsheets festooned bulletin boards outside every major church and even the smallest provincial town boasted at least one newspaper, although the Safeholdian journalistic tradition had never attempted to separate opinion from news. Journalists did seek to differentiate between *facts* and what those facts might *mean* . . . usually, at least, and as long as those facts didn't gore their own oxen. But the pages of their papers had always forcibly reminded Merlin Athrawes and Nimue Gahrvai of the thousands of "opinion journalism" sites which had populated the Federation's info net.

On the other hand, the reporters who wrote for the major newspapers, in places like Siddar City (where there were currently no fewer than sixteen of them), were aggressive in chasing the news. That had become particularly true since the Jihad, partly because the typical Siddarmarkian had become more politically aware than he had been but also—and more importantly—because of the growth of Charisian-style industry. More people were reading papers, and a lot more people were buying goods, and that meant a *lot* more advertising revenue *for* those papers, and all three of those considerations were calculated to make their publishers happy people.

It also meant "yellow journalism" was alive and well in Siddarmark, although it hadn't yet reached the levels of Old Earth in the twenty-first and twenty-second centuries, thank God!

Along the way, however, successful politicians had learned to manage the media, or at least try to, and the large chamber was packed with just over two hundred reporters. They'd been waiting for almost an hour now, and the air was heavy with a haze of tobacco over a surf-like rumble of conversations. All of them knew what they were there to hear, but their employers all expected them to find some small tidbit they could use to pad the release the Exchequer had already prepared. Some small personal observation, comment, or opinion. And if they couldn't find one, they were damned well supposed to *invent* one.

A side door opened, and the hum and rumble of voices faded quickly as Lord Bryntyn Ashfyrd walked in through it with a leather folder under his arm. The Chancellor of the Exchequer was a well-known figure in Siddar City, and the slight stoop to his shoulders, the way his silvering ginger hair always seemed on the edge of escaping control, and the stiff gait imposed by arthritic knees were favorite hooks for the caricaturists whose engravings populated the capital city's editorial pages.

They also explained the less-than-admiring nickname those who disapproved of his handling of the Exchequer had pinned upon him: "the Stork."

He crossed to the low dais at one end of the room, climbed the three shallow steps, laid the folder on the single brightly polished table at the center of the dais, and seated himself, all without saying a word. The only thing on the table beside the folder was an even more brightly gleaming silver ink stand, and Ashfyrd reached into an inner pocket, extracted a pair of gold-wire spectacles, and settled them onto his nose and hooked them behind his ears, still without speaking. Then he folded his hands on the folder and looked out at them while the dozen or so sketch artists' pencils began flying.

"I'm sure all of you know why we're here," he said finally. "Allow me to begin with a brief statement. Then we can get down to the real business of the morning and, after that, I will answer questions. Within reason, of course."

His voice, unfortunately, was high-pitched and a bit thin, and he spoke with more than a hint of a lisp. That was another reason his detractors called him the Stork, given the wyvern species' grating, unpleasant mating call. It was also another reason he'd always been happier in the accounting room than in politics. Today, though, his words carried clearly through the sudden, intense quiet, and he smiled.

"I'm very pleased to announce that this coming Monday the Exchequer will officially launch the bond issue the Chamber of Delegates has authorized to finance the Republic's portion of the Silkiah Canal. This project has been delayed far too long, and that delay has been unfortunate not simply because it's prevented us from meeting our commitments to our treaty partners but also because of the growth potential for our own economy which has been so sadly delayed. I recognize many of your faces," he smiled briefly, "so I know you're aware of many of the difficulties which have delayed this issue. I'm happy to tell you those difficulties are behind us, that the Republic's economy is stronger than it's ever been, and that the Trans-Siddarmark Railroad gives us a shining example of what the Canal is and can become for all of us.

"The return rates and maturity dates for the bonds are listed in the handout which my office will make available before you leave the Annex. I would like to point out, however, that the Lord Protector has instructed me to make participation in this project—and in its profits—as widely accessible as we possibly can to our citizens as a whole. To give them a stake in the Canal, as it were."

Some of the reporters shifted in their chairs at that, because they knew what he was really talking about. It was true the TSRR was thundering ahead at a frenetic pace. It was true the Republic's heavy industry sector was expanding in time with the insatiable demand for rails and rolling stock. But it was also true that those who'd been left behind or felt frozen out had become even more embittered in the process. They saw the TSRR not as a harbinger of a new, stronger economy and higher standard of living but as a living metaphor for the way their previously skilled trades had been overtaken and made irrelevant, the way jobs upon which they and their families depended had vanished. The guilds, especially, had grown only more vociferous as their wealth—and that of their members—declined, and the Exchequer's and Central Bank's effort to rein in the runaway, undisciplined financial markets had created its own intense dissatisfaction.

Ashfyrd gave them a few moments for that to roll through their minds while he opened his leather folder and looked down at it for the notes every reporter was confident he didn't really need. Then he looked up again.

"There will be multiple classes of bonds," the Chancellor continued. "They will be issued with maturities of ten years, fifteen years, twenty years, and thirty years, but there will also be a special class with a maturity of only six years. This class will pay a substantially lower interest rate, but individual bonds will cost only fifty marks, as opposed to a range of values from two hundred, four hundred, and eight hundred marks which will be offered in all of the other classes. In addition, at the maturity date, the special bondholder will have the option of converting his bonds into stock in the Silkiah Canal Corporation rather than receiving his payout in cash. The share price for those converting the mature value of their bonds will be eighty percent of the then-current general price."

Several people stirred at that, and there was a soft, quiet hum of hushed side conversation.

"In effect," Ashfyrd said now, looking up from his notes again, "the purpose of the special class of bonds is to present average citizens of the Republic an opportunity to become stakeholders in what the Lord Protector and the Chamber firmly believe will become one of the most valuable, profitable, and longest-lasting physical assets in the entire world. The most pessimistic estimates of the revenues the Canal will generate are enormous, and it seems fitting to the Lord Protector—and to me—to allow as many of our citizens as possible to participate in that revenue flow. Only the special class will have this conversion feature; the standard bonds will have substantially higher returns, but will not be directly convertible into stock in the Canal Corporation."

He paused, looking around the room, then drew a document from it and laid it on the table before him. He reached out to the ink stand and ceremoniously inked the pen, then looked around the assembled reporters' faces while the sketch artists' pencils flew.

"It gives me enormous pleasure as Chancellor of the Exchequer to sign this official directive to release the first flight of the Silkiah Canal Consortium Construction Bond program," he said then. "It marks, I believe, the dawn of a new day of opportunity and enrichment for the entire Republic."

He looked down again, and the scratching of the pen's nib was clearly audible in the stillness as he signed.

The airship settled majestically towards the mooring mast which had been erected at one end of the Imperial Charisian Air Force's now vast and well established landing ground. It was a sight Baron Star Rising had never tired of, yet it was also one which—unbelievable as it would have seemed only a year or two ago—had actually become *routine* for the citizens of Zhynkau.

He thought about that, as he watched *Aivahn Hahgyz* drop the mooring line from her nose, watched the groundsmen pounce, make it fast to the line from the mooring mast. Two of the huge airship's spinning propellers stopped turning; the other two paused, then began spinning more slowly in the opposite direction, pushing back against the pressure of the steam-powered winch reeling in the mooring line. A dozen other lines, spaced equidistantly along the sides of the airship's enormous, cigar-shaped envelope, had hit the ground well before the mooring line. Unlike the mooring line—which was a bright green in color—they were red, however, and he felt a brief, familiar qualm as he watched them.

He'd wondered, the first time he'd watched an airship land, why the groundsmen had stayed so far clear of the lines dropping from *Synklair Pytmyn*'s cabin. What he hadn't known then was that an airship could generate the same sort of sparks a comb could generate on a cold day, or as a silk cloth rubbing amber. It made sense once it was explained to him, but he couldn't quite forget the *Holy Writ*'s injunctions against profaning the *Rakurai* in any way. Bishop Yaupang had patiently explained how the *use* of the *Rakurai* was an unforgivable and mortal sin but that the natural production of the mortal world's pale and feeble shadows of Holy Langhorne's sacred power—as in that same comb, that same rubbed rod of amber, or the *rakurai* fish, for that matter—was nothing of the sort. That it was, in fact, yet one more example of Langhorne reminding fallen humanity of the *Rakurai* which still lay ready to his hand if it should be needed.

Intellectually, Star Rising knew the bishop was correct. It was just a little difficult to remember, sometimes, when he thought about how a groundsman could be literally knocked from his feet—even seriously injured or killed—if one of those "sparks" leapt from the end of a "grounding cable" to him. That was a bit more potent "reminder" of Langhorne's majesty than he felt comfortable around. Especially when it was applied to something as . . . novel and still undeniably unnatural-feeling as human beings floating through Langhorne's heavens like vast wyverns.

And especially when he remembered the devastating fire which had consumed the airship *Zhenyfyr Kyplyng* right here at Zhynkau.

On the other hand, what had happened to *Zhenyfyr Kyplyng* made him powerfully in favor of avoiding any possible source of combustion at a moment like this.

He smiled and gave himself a little shake as the familiar train of thoughts flowed through him. Then, as more hydrogen vented and the airship settled even lower, he started forward in the wake of the mobile gantry rolled out to *Aivahn Hahgyz* on the bed of its steam dragon.

After all, if the whole process still seemed . . . odd to him, what must it have been like for the passengers who'd just flown for the very first time?

▼ ▼ ▼

Tangwyn Syngpu stood at the circular porthole, looking out at the sprawl of the steadily expanding provincial town which had become, whether it officially admitted it or not, the capital of a new and independent realm.

He'd never seen a clear end for the Rebellion, and this was one he wouldn't have predicted, but he felt a peculiar sense of . . . completion. Or satisfaction, perhaps. That growing town—no, that growing *city*—was filled with people who had refused to be property any longer, and beyond them were literally millions of others who'd made that same decision when the possibility of freedom was offered to them. That wouldn't have happened, the possibility would never have been presented, without the Rebellion. He knew that, and as he gazed out at the buildings and streets of Zhynkau, that knowledge filled him with a profound awareness of accomplishment. Of the memorial rising in the city's brick and wood and stone—and beyond that in the hearts of its citizens—not just to his own beloved dead but to *all* of the Harchong Empire's victims.

It was almost enough to balance the nightmares which still woke him, if with blessedly less frequency, than they used to. That was the Yanshwyn's doing.

He was glad to see the ground no more than a few feet away once more, too. The flight had been as exciting as he'd hoped, but there was something undeniably unnatural about floating about up in the sky. He wished Yanshwyn had been able to accompany him, but that had been totally out of the question with a four-month-old!

And it was not either an excuse to get away from the Langhorne's watch feedings! he thought with a grin.

He caught movement at the corner of his vision and his eyes widened slightly as he saw yet another of the Charisian innovations rolling towards him. Major Bulyrd and *Seijin* Merch had described the new self-propelled steam dragons to him, but the sight of something the size of a heavy freight wagon trundling towards him without a draft animal anywhere in sight was still startling. His grin broadened and he snorted in amusement as that realization flowed through him. After flying like a wyvern for over a thousand miles in less than a single day, the sight of a wagon without a dragon in front of it was *startling*?

He shook his head at the thought, then turned as a uniformed Charisian rapped gently on the lightweight frame of the cabin to announce his presence.

"Captain Krugair's respects, Father Yngshwan, Gentlemen, and we'll be prepared to disembark in about ten minutes."

"Thank you, my son," Yanshwyn Tsungzhi said, signing Langhorne's scepter in blessing, and the steward bobbed his head and disappeared again.

"You see, Zaipu?" the priest continued, turning to Zaipu Ou-zhang. "Here we are, safely on the ground, without a single person's having plunged to his death en route!"

"With all due respect, we *aren't* 'on the ground' just yet," the Mayor of Zhutiyan replied tartly.

"For all intents and purposes we are," Tsungzhi told him with a broader smile.

"And if we get off this infernal device without its exploding the way Major Bulyrd said it might, I'll be a happy and a grateful man," Ou-zhang retorted. "I don't count my wyverns before they hatch, though!"

"You are the *gloomiest* man I know, sometimes," the priest who'd become the effective Bishop of Chynduk observed.

"Realist, Father. *Realist,*" Ou-zhang shot back. "Somebody has to be one!"

"That's Yanshwyn's job," Miyang Gyngdau said. "Your job, whether you want to admit it or not, is to be the Valley's *pessimist*. And I suppose we do need one of those, too."

"I don't how the two of you always manage to make me feel so appreciated and loved," Ou-zhang replied, and Gyngdau chuckled. Then he looked at the man who'd married his sister-in-law. As far as he was concerned, that made Tangwyn Syngpu his *brother*-in-law, and as their eyes met, Gyngdau twitched his head in the direction of the steam dragon which had just stopped with the head of the stair in its wagon bed even with the cabin's starboard door.

"Best we be going," he said.

"I'm ready," Syngpu said mildly. "Just lead the way."

But Gyngdau shook his head.

"No," he said. "The rest of us discussed it, and we're in agreement. *You* lead the way, Tangwyn."

"That's not fitting!" Syngpu protested. "You or the Father—you're the leaders of this 'delegation'! I'll be coming along at your back, where I belong."

"No, you won't, my son." Father Yngshwan's voice was gentle but implacable and Syngpu looked at him. "As Miyang says, we've discussed it, Tangwyn, and the man whose soldiers have protected us so long—the man who's the only reason we're here—is the one who's going to lead us off of Zaipu's 'infernal device.' And that man, my son, is you."

Syngpu opened his mouth again, but then he looked around those steady eyes, saw the agreement in all of them, and realized objecting would do him no good. And even as he thought that, even as he realized a peasant had no business usurping his "betters'" place, he realized something else, as well.

They were right.

Not because they'd decided to bestow such an honor upon him, whether he wanted it or not, but because this day, in this place, it wasn't a matter of anyone's "*betters*" . . . and it never would be again. That was the true legacy of the Rebellion, the memorial to his and so many other people's dead. Today, when the Chynduk Valley officially joined the United Provinces, they would do it because that was what the people—*all* the people—of the Valley had freely chosen to do. And so these men—these friends, every one of whom had once been *his* "better"—were right to make that point. To insist the Valley's delegation to the new nation of which they were about to become a part be led by a peasant. Because after this day, those peasants would never again follow like cattle at the heels of any aristocrat or prelate.

He looked around the small circle of the closest friends he'd ever had and his eyes burned strangely as he nodded.

"Stubborn lot, aren't you just," he growled gruffly and led the way towards the stairs.

"Koryn! It's good to see you," Cayleb Ahrmahk said, clasping forearms firmly with the general as Koryn Gahrvai, his wife, and all three of their children came down the shallow steps to the sundrenched terrace.

The twins were eight, now, and young Daffyd held his father's hand while Lyzbyt held her mother's. Alyk, a sturdy three-year-old who'd celebrated his birthday less than two months ago, held Krystin Nylsyn's, looking around him with huge blue eyes. The twins were fraternal, not identical, and Daffyd had his mother's red hair and blue eyes, although there was more gold in the hair and the eyes were a bit lighter than Nimue Gahrvai's, while Lyzbyt had her father's coloration. Alyk, with a perversity worthy of his namesake, had split the difference, with dark hair and blue eyes.

"It's good to see you, too, Your Majesty. It's been too long," Gahrvai replied now, for the benefit of the assorted Imperial Guardsmen and servants standing about.

Cayleb nodded and held out his hand to Nimue as Sharleyan blended out of the gathering crowd to join them.

"How was the flight?" she asked.

"Smooth," Nimue replied. "Hit a little turbulence over the Cauldron, but nothing to worry about. The kids were great about it, too. Of course, they've had a more experience with airships than most kids their age, given our schedule."

"Good!" Sharleyan hugged the *seijin*.

"We were a little afraid you might not make it," Cayleb said, giving Nimue a quick hug of his own. "Or, rather," he smiled at Daffyd and Lyzbyt, "*Nynian* was afraid you wouldn't."

"Oh, *Daddy!*" a voice said, and Princess Nynian Zhorzhet Ahrmahk, whose eleventh birthday it happened to be, followed her mother across the terrace.

"Don't pay him any attention," Sharleyan told the Gahrvai twins. "He thinks he's funny."

"No, I'm an emperor. So I *know* I'm funny!"

"*Cayleb!*" Sharleyan smacked him on the shoulder, then bent to hug the younger members of the Gahrvai clan. "We're so glad you could get here, Daivy. And you, Lyz!"

"Thank you for inviting us and we promise to behave, Aunt Sharley," Daffyd said in the voice of someone repeating a carefully learned official formula, then looked up at his father. The general looked back down solemnly for a moment, then nodded.

"Just see that you *do* behave," he said with a smile. "And stay away from the cookies before dinner! There'll be plenty of time for that after, and you don't want to fill up before we even cut the cake."

"Yes, Father!" Daffyd promised, and Lyzbyt nodded in solemn agreement when Gahrvai glanced at her.

"Then we resign them to your hands, Krystin," Nimue told their nanny. "Good luck!"

"I'll have you know all three of them are going to behave themselves just fine," *Seijin* Krystin told their parents chidingly. "*Aren't* you?" she said ominously to the twins, glowering at them ferociously.

"Yes, Krystin!" they promised around a shared giggle.

"Good! Now, let's go have some fun," she continued, and she and the children followed Nynian towards the mob of other youngsters who'd already assembled.

"I'm sure they will," Sharleyan told their father as the children headed away. "Have fun, I mean. And you didn't tell them about the surprise, did you?"

"About the ice cream? *Please!*" Koryn shook his head. "Do I look that stupid?"

"Don't answer that!" Nimue said quickly, and Cayleb laughed.

"Just as long as you didn't spoil the surprise, everything's good," he assured their guests, and Koryn chuckled.

The truth was that he was looking forward to the "surprise," as well. Ehdwyrd Howsmyn's Delthak Enterprises had introduced refrigeration to Safehold the previous year. Powering the compressors without electricity was a bit of a challenge, which meant household refrigerators weren't going to become commonplace anytime soon, but Stahlman Praigyr had produced a small, "household-sized," low-output version of his kerosene steam engines that could handle the job. And that meant that for the first time in Old Charis' history, ice was as available—and even cheaper—right here in Tellesberg than it was from the ice houses of more northern realms.

And that had allowed Nynian Athrawes to "invent" ice cream. The first of which would be delivered to *Princess* Nynian's guests in about three hours.

"Lord—how many *are* there?" Nimue asked now, as she and Koryn followed their hosts towards the adults at the far end of the terrace from the children.

"Of the kids?" Cayleb asked. "Oh, not that many." He waved his hand airily. "Just our five, Zhan and Mahrya's three boys, Nahrmahn Garyet and Zhanayt's pair, the two Falkhan boys, Kynt and Elayn's pair, the Delthak twins, and six of Hauwerd and Mairah's. That's only—" he counted ostentatiously on his fingers; it took him a while "—twenty-two. Well, twenty-five, counting yours."

"Lord," Nimue repeated, shaking her head, and Koryn laughed.

"Stefyny and Alahnah are riding herd on them?" he asked.

"Along with a little help from Lywys," Sharleyan replied with a nod. "He's a very useful young man, you know. We think of him almost as another son by now."

"I'm not surprised," Koryn observed, and looked across the terrace at the tall, brown-haired young man helping Crown Princess Alahnah and Stefyny Athrawes untangle a thicket of croquet players.

The affection between him and Alahnah was plain to see, and the people of Tellesberg had taken the young Dohlaran to their hearts after his part in saving their crown princess' life. There was, in fact, a steadily growing expectation that, despite Lywys Whytmyn's relatively humble birth, an imperial wedding lay somewhere in his future. Obviously, that would have to wait—after all, Alahnah was only twenty. No one wanted to rush someone that young to the altar. On the other hand, her parents had married very young, as well, and that had worked out well. Still, it was early days, and it wasn't as if she *had* to marry to produce heirs, given the number of siblings and cousins she possessed.

Of course, Tellesberg didn't know about the tunnel from Archbishop's Palace to Tellesberg Palace or the private stair from Tellesberg Palace's basement to the imperial family's quarters. Alahnah's Marines knew about it, as did the Imperial Guard, but none of them were about to say a word about who used that tunnel and those stairs on a nightly basis.

Koryn smiled at the thought and wrapped an arm around his wife in a quick hug. She looked up at him with a raised eyebrow.

<Just thinking about Lywys and Alahnah,> he told her over their private com channel. <And wondering how the two of them're going to keep their faces straight for Daivyn and Frahncheska.>

<They'll do just fine,> she replied. <Probably, anyway. At least until we go aboard *Ahlfryd* and they have to go back to separate staterooms!>

Koryn snorted, although she was probably right that Lywys and Alahnah would manage to conduct themselves with proper decorum. Not that there was any reason they shouldn't tease the happy couple pretty vigorously.

No one had ever anticipated that Daivyn and Frahncheska Chermyn might marry. The two of them had been such good friends as children, despite the difference in their ages, that the thought of anything deeper had never occurred to either of them. Not until Frahncheska came home from Tellesberg all grown up, that was. It was remarkable how Daivyn had found pressing reasons to return to Carmyn every month or two ever since she'd gotten back.

Of course, there was the tiny problem that Daivyn was the Prince of Corisande. That was the other reason not even Nahrmahn Baytes had considered the possibility of their marriage. Given how many Zebediahans remembered his father's iron hand, the courtship of any Zebediahan by a Corisandian prince would have been fraught with difficulties and Frahncheska Chermyn wasn't just any Zebediahan.

The people of Zebediah were fiercely loyal to all of their grand duke's family, but Frahncheska had been the baby of the family when Hauwyl Chermyn became their liege lord. She'd grown up in Carmyn, and the people of Zebediah regarded her as much—and as fiercely—as their own as ever Tellesberg had regarded Alahnah or Cherayth had regarded a younger Sharleyan. They'd also discovered that their Charisian-born grand duke and duchess (and family) did things their own way, though. And so, grudgingly at first, the majority of Zebediah had accepted the betrothal once it became clear the son of the hated Hektor was courting their grand duke's niece with all due propriety . . . and that she was not at all adverse to the marriage.

And it was difficult—no, impossible—to think of a more politically effective bride for Daivyn. Like Alahnah herself, there were no real dynastic candidates outside Charis itself. And the symbolism of Hektor's son marrying into the ruling dynasty of Zebediah couldn't be lost on any Zebediahan or Corisandian. For the minority of Zebediahans who would never forgive Corisande or Corisandians under any circumstances, that only made the pill more bitter, but for their fellows, it represented a way to heal the past.

<I don't think Nahrmahn's forgiven himself for not seeing Daivyn and Frahncheska coming,> Koryn said now. <And I know it caught Dad flat-footed. He recovered pretty quickly, though, didn't he?>

<No flies on your father,> Nimue agreed with a gurgle of mental laughter. <And he's no dummy. Once he was convinced Frahncheska wouldn't be bringing any daggers on her honeymoon, he was all for it!>

<And she's going to be good for him,> Koryn said. <Not to mention the fact that she and Irys have always gotten along like a house on fire. Hard to see any downside to this one.>

<At least no one's likely to be waiting to blow them up outside the church, like another Manchyr wedding I could think of,> Nimue replied a bit more grimly, and he hugged her tighter as he remembered that horrible day. Her memories were actually those of Merlin Athrawes, since she hadn't existed at the time, but that made them no less real. He wondered, sometimes, how Merlin's interface factored into "her" memory of watching him being hammered to the ground with the wounds which had left his face so badly scarred. For himself, the physical scars were nothing compared to the anguish he'd felt—the total, crushing sense of grief and personal failure—as he'd seen the deadly shrapnel scythe down his cousin and her new husband on the very steps of Manchyr Cathedral despite every protective measure he'd taken.

<No, not going to happen this time, love,> he told her. <First, because nobody in Manchyr hates either of them. And, second, because you and I will have that cathedral smothered in sensor remotes of our own this time. Nobody's getting a *microbe* through the security I'm laying down for *this* wedding!>

<Good!> she replied, leaning against him, and he smiled as he kissed the part of her hair then looked back at that herd of children. At that promise, like Daivyn and Frahncheska, of the future to come.

Maybe.

His smile faded as the qualification flowed through him, but it was one that occurred to all of them these days. It occurred to them a lot.

And that's the real reason we've gathered so many of

the tribe for Nynian's birthday, he thought. *Because the ticking of that clock's getting louder and louder.*

In less than seven months, it would be July. July of 915. The July in which the "Archangels'" return might kill every single person on this terrace.

The bright sun seemed momentarily cold, and his eyes went bleak and hard. But only until he looked across the children to where Merlin and Nynian Athrawes stood watching their daughter. Merlin looked up, as if he'd felt Koryn's gaze, and their eyes met. They held for a moment, and then Merlin nodded.

There was great comfort in that nod, Koryn realized. Not because he thought even Merlin could defeat a horde of returning "Archangels," but because that was Merlin Athrawes' nod. And because deep inside, despite all Koryn Gahrvai had learned about the Federation, about Eric Langhorne, and about the odds against them, and despite whatever his head might fear, his heart knew better. It was a heart which thought not in soulless numbers, not with coldly calculated odds. It was a heart which saw the deeper reality beyond "the truth" and "the inevitable."

And it was a heart which knew that Nimue Alban had not knowingly and deliberately gone to her death a thousand years before Koryn Gahrvai's birth only to fail now.

NOVEMBER YEAR OF GOD 914

✦

Siddar City,
Republic of Siddarmark.

"You know what I wish?" Klymynt Myllyr asked as the servants withdrew from the private dining room on the top floor of Protector's Palace.

The dining room was paneled in expensive southern hardwoods that gleamed with rich-toned highlights in the lamplight. And those lamps were needed, despite the relatively early hour, thanks to the fresh snow sifting down across the Republic's capital. That snow fell heavily, steadily, from the dark and lowering skies, and it clearly intended to go on falling for a long time to come. But at least it was unaccompanied by the powerful winds which too often assailed Siddar City this time of year.

"I can think of a lot of things you *ought* to be wishing for," Samyl Gahdarhd replied. "Spring would be one of them." He looked out the dining room window at the charcoal sky and steady veils of snow.

"True." Myllyr picked up his salad fork. Thanks to the speed of Charisian-built steamers, Tarotisian and Emeraldian lettuce was available here in Siddar City even in November. "On the other hand, I was thinking of something a little more . . . immediate than that."

"That the people who keep carping about how terrible the economy is and what awful people Zhasyn and I are would shut up for a bit?" Bryntyn Ashfyrd offered.

"That would be nice, but I think we're already getting

that one. To some extent, anyway." Myllyr forked up a bite of salad and chewed appreciatively. "Mind you, nothing's going to shut *some* of them up," he added more glumly.

In fact, their hard-core opposition would *never* "shut up," as all of them knew perfectly well. Their opponents' vociferous denunciations had fallen on increasingly less receptive ears since the Canal Consortium bond issue had hit the markets, however. Even the special bonds were beyond the reach of the millions of the Republic's citizens who worked hard just to put food on their families' tables, but they were affordable by a far larger slice of the population than the earlier issues of government securities to help finance the Trans-Siddarmark Railroad. That meant more and more people had a stake in the "new" economy, and the option to convert their bonds into stock in the canal when it was finally completed had been even more popular than Myllyr had hoped. In fact, the special class of bonds was almost fully subscribed already, and purchases of the more expensive bonds were ahead of projections. At this rate, the Canal Consortium would be fully capitalized within no more than three or four months. Siddarmark's economy might remain far short of Charisian levels of performance, but it was stronger than it had been since the Jihad and growing steadily stronger, and their critics hated that.

"So it's not the weather, and it's not the economy," Gahdarhd said. "And neither Vicar Tymythy Rhobair nor Archbishop Dahnyld have done anything to piss you off, so it's not religion. Which leaves politics—right?"

"I never could fool you," Myllyr said dryly, and Gahdarhd chuckled.

"Actually, I wish two things," the lord protector went on. "The first is that I could chuck this job out the window and go back to being an honest soldier. Langhorne, I hate politics! And if I didn't know they'd elect that idiot Hygyns, I *would* chuck it." Despite his light tone, he was obviously serious. "Which brings me to my second wish—which is that Hygyns was still on active duty so Daryus could order him up to command the garrison at Salyk over the winter."

His smile was not entirely humorous, and Ashfyrd snorted. The small town of Salyk had grown significantly since the Jihad, but it still shut down every winter once Spinefish Bay froze over, and if there was a colder place in the Republic of Siddarmark in November, Bryntyn Ashfyrd had never heard of it. Which, he conceded, made it the perfect place to send Zhermo Hygyns.

"I understand the sentiment," he said, cutting a bite-sized morsel from the steak on his plate, "but I think his hopes for the protectorship have sprung a leak." He put the steak in his mouth and chewed appreciatively.

"My reports say pretty much the same thing," Gahdarhd agreed. "In fact, he's lost at least three important endorsements over the last month or so. And I can't say it grieves me to think about that," he added.

"That's one reason I'd like to send him off to Salyk," Myllyr retorted. "I'm a vindictive son-of-a-bitch, especially when it comes to someone like him, and now that his campaign's starting to founder, I might be able to get away with sending him off without anyone seeing through my mask."

Both his guests chuckled at that, and he smiled again, more easily.

"In the meantime, though, we have more pressing concerns. What I especialy wanted to discuss with you, Samyl—and the reason I wanted you to sit in on the conversation, Bryntyn—is the situation in the Western provinces. Daryus tells me he's ready to certify to the Chamber that we can begin drawing down the Army detachments. I tend to agree, but I also think a lot of the resentment's still there. Oh, it's shifted from straight hatred between Temple Loyalists and Siddar Loyalists, but I know Westerners." He smiled briefly, his Tarikah accent more pronounced than usual, "and once they get the pissed-off bug, they hang onto it. They just find new targets for it, and given the mess the Syndicate and the Troubles between them have left behind, none of them have to look far to find one. We all know how much of the local resentment's due to the Western Syndicate and what it's done to the local farmers, but the way the economy's turned around here in the East is only making it worse. Or, rather, *keeping* it worse, since it was already pretty damned bad. And it's harder than hell to blame average citizens in someplace like Tarikah for feeling that way."

Both his lunch guests nodded somberly, and he paused to sip hot cherrybean before he continued.

"I don't like the anti-Charis thread in their unhappiness one bit, either, but I think that's starting to ease." He raised an eyebrow at Gahdarhd, who nodded.

"Easing," the keeper of the seal agreed. "Not going away anytime soon, though."

"Don't expect it to." Myllyr shook his head. "The only way to get on top of that is to find some kind of economic fix. I know our ability to do anything from the Capital's limited, but we've got to find some way to . . . to *un-depress* their economy, too. If we don't—if things keep right on getting better here in the East and stay stuck in the crapper in the West—the resentment will set even deeper. So, since Daryus has managed to put out the active fire, now it's time for you two to come up with a way to start pissing on the coals."

He smiled at them across the table.

"Thoughts?" he asked.

▼ ▼ ▼

"I'm starting to think I should fold my tent and go back to Tarikah, this year at least," Zhermo Hygyns said moodily, frowning down into his snifter of brandy.

"Oh, that would be *very* premature, General!" Zhaikyb Fyrnahndyz, who'd invited the small, select group to gather in his Siddar City mansion, shook his head. "The Republic *needs* you!"

"I don't know about that," Hygyns growled. "Those idiots in the Chamber of Delegates don't seem to think so, anyway."

"Not all of us feel that way, General," Styvyn Trumyn, one of Cliff Peak's delegates, said earnestly. Like Fyrnahndyz, Trumyn knew how much Hygyns preferred to be addressed by his military rank, even though he was no longer officially on active duty. Most people might have preferred the "Governor" to which he was entitled after serving as Governor of Tarikah for four years, but not Hygyns. "Especially not those of us who remember how vital your efforts have been in the West!"

"Absolutely!" Mahthyw Ohlsyn, the senior delegate from Tarikah agreed. "After the job you did in Lake City, there's no question in *my* mind, General! You're the one man I believe can actually *deal* with the issues we face, and I don't know if the Republic can survive if someone *doesn't* deal with them. Trust me, there's not a voter in the West who doesn't understand that!"

"Maybe not," Hygyns conceded. "Unfortunately, there aren't enough votes in the West to beat Myllyr in the East. And whatever Tarikah and Cliff Peak may think—or the unincorporated part of the South March, for that matter—Glacierheart and Thesmar will line up with the Eastern block to vote for anybody willing to kiss Charis' arse!"

The general's expression was as bitter as his tone, and several of the other men gathered in the palatial private dining room looked at one another.

"Not everyone in the East's ready to do that, General," Raphayl Ahskar, head of the Papermakers' Guild in Siddar City, said after a moment. "Not by a long chalk."

"Fucking right!" Mahryahno Kreft more than half snarled. The white-haired Kreft headed the Shipbuilders Guild . . . or what was left of it. He was also almost fifteen years older than Ahskar and far less polished.

"Raphayl and Mahryahno have a point, General," Ghustahv Phaiphyr said. "My reporters all agree there are still plenty of voters who recognize the need for change."

Fyrnahndyz nodded, although he was confident Phaiphyr was shading what his reporters had actually said. It was entirely possible he honestly didn't realize he was doing it, though. His newspaper—the *Siddar City*

Sentinel, one of the capital's larger papers—was the un-official organ of the Opposition for reasons Phaiphyr fondly believed were a matter of principle. Fyrnahndyz was willing to concede that principle played a part in Ghustahv Phaiphyr's political views, but the death of *Phylyp* Phaiphyr, Ghustahv's only son, in the retreat to Serabor through the Sylmahn Gap was at least as impor-tant. Ghustahv had never forgiven Charis for "provok-ing" the Jihad which had killed Phylyp, nor did he have any intention of forgiving the man who'd commanded Phylyp's company at the time.

"That's really the crux of the matter, General," Ohlsyn said. Hygyns looked at him, and the delegate shrugged. "Myllyr and Ashfyrd may have deluded people into thinking things are looking up, and it's true there are fewer people still thrown out of employment." He gave Ahskar and Kreft a sympathetic look. "But that's never going to last, and even if it were, there are plenty of people who aren't going to forget how the Charisians have repaid us for all of our wartime sacrifices!"

Hygyns' jaw tightened at the mention of wartime sac-rifices, and he gave Ohlsyn a jerky nod. It was interest-ing, Fyrnahndyz thought, that Ohlsyn hadn't mentioned how the depressed economy in the West had played into the hands of his own allies in the Western Syndicate. Or of how hard they'd worked to keep that economy depressed—and all those farmers out of work—while they bought up everything in sight. Nor had he com-mented on how the state of that economy decreased the pool of voters who met the property qualifications for the franchise, or how that gave their own political ma-chine an even tighter stranglehold on power.

And it was even more interesting that all those con-nections seemed to sail straight past Hygyns, despite—or perhaps even *because* of—his term as governor. Of course, they'd been careful to keep their machinations as far out of sight as possible, but the man had been the *governor*. So he was either even blinder than Fyrnahn-dyz had thought, or. . . .

"Speaking as a member of the business community,"

he said, his own expression grave, "I have to say there's a lot of truth in what everyone's just said, General. And eventually, the people who Myllyr and Ashfyrd are duping right now will figure out that you've been right to warn them about the Charisian puppet strings all along. I just pray to Langhorne they won't figure it out too late!"

"Exactly!" Phaiphyr picked up on the cue as quickly as if they'd rehearsed it. "Exactly, General. And if you drop out of the campaign before it's even fully begun, the one voice most likely to expose Cayleb and Sharleyan's machinations in the Republic will fall silent. My editorial pages will keep up the fight no matter what, but there's no denying that your voice and your record—both in the Jihad and during the Troubles—are the true rallying point for those of us determined to thwart Myllyr's . . . misguided policies."

"I don't know. . . ." Hygyns said.

"General," Fyrnahndyz said earnestly, "I know we're asking a great deal of you, especially after you've already given the Republic four years in Tarikah. Langhorne knows *I'm* not cut out for a career in politics, either!" He shook his head. "There's nothing I'd like more than to stay as far away from this as I possibly could. There are only twenty-six hours in the day, and I've got more than enough personal concerns to keep anyone busy. Besides, with all due respect to Mahthyw and Styvyn, politics, especially here in the capital, are a cesspool. But it looks to me like too many of the new voters are buying the lies Myllyr and Ashfyrd are selling them."

"Hard to blame them," Phaiphyr put in. "Stohnar's decision to expand the franchise was a terrible mistake! Or, at least, if he was going to do it, he should have done it a lot more gradually. Myllyr's taken blatant advantage of that, just like Maidyn did! Half those new voters feel like they 'owe' their loyalty to the people they think gave them the vote. And even the ones who don't are too politically unsophisticated to make informed decisions."

"Ghustahv's right," Fyrnahndyz said. "And if we don't stop this pernicious rot now, if Myllyr has another five years to continue the same mistaken policies, Charis' stranglehold on our economy may become unbreakable. I'm not prepared to say you're the only one who could possibly stop that, but I *am* prepared to say you're the best chance we have of reversing the trend while there's still time."

"You may be right," Hygyns replied after a long moment of silence. "You're definitely right about how much I loathe political campaigns. That was one of the main reasons I didn't stand for a second term in Tarikah. But you may be right."

Fyrnahndyz nodded sympathetically. He suspected Hygyns truly did dislike political campaigns, although watching the way he glowed when audiences cheered his speeches suggested he didn't find *all* of it distasteful. For the matter, the general had been delighted by the perquisites of office as a provincial governor. But Fyrnhandyz also suspected Hygyns' personal ambition ran even deeper and stronger than most of his political allies had yet realized. He might dislike *campaigning* for the protectorship, but that didn't mean he didn't want it with a deep and burning hunger.

"Unfortunately," Hygyns continued, "however right you may be, the shift in public opinion's still the same in the short term. And in light of the way the political climate seems to've shifted—however temporarily—I'm not at all sure I could ask my family to bear the financial burden of continuing my campaign at this time. Especially now that I'm no longer on active duty. And I can't go back *onto* active duty as long as I'm a candidate for office."

"I hadn't actually considered that aspect of it," Fyrnahndyz replied with a total disregard for the truth.

The Constitution banned active-duty officers from any elective office. Army officers could continue to hold *reserve* commissions—and remain liable to recall in an emergency—while seeking office, but reserve officers received only a quarter of their active-duty salaries. For that matter, if they succeeded in winning election, they received *no* salary from the Army so long as they remained in office. And it didn't matter what office it was. From lord protector to lizard-catcher, the prohibition on active-duty officers in political office was absolute.

Unfortunately for Hygyns, the Constitution was equally firm that no one who currently held elective office could stand for lord protector. He could have retained his governorship for another full year, until the end of his term, while he ran for a seat in the Chamber of Delegates, but not if he wanted to contest the protectorship with Myllyr. Until the recent economic turnaround, his decision to retire from the governorship had looked like the best choice. Now that Myllyr's chances of retaining office had rebounded, the man had to be regretting it. He'd become accustomed to the lifestyle and perks of high elective office; becoming one more retired general after that had to be . . . disheartening.

And it didn't pay the bills, either.

Now the banker frowned deeply into his own brandy. This was the critical moment, and he knew it. He'd put together the core of a potent political machine without the other members of its leadership realizing how adroitly he'd gathered up their strings. Every man in this room had his own reasons to oppose Klymynt Myllyr, whether it was genuine fear of the future, personal animosity, the destruction of privileged livelihoods, or simple greed. For that matter, he included himself in that description. Yet so far, all the others were convinced he was simply one more ally in the cause. He wanted to keep it that way, for a lot of reasons, and he wasn't certain he could if he came farther into the open. But if he didn't. . . .

"General," he said finally, " I know you're a man of honor and of pride, so I hesitate to bring this up, and I devoutly hope you won't take what I'm about to say amiss. But I truly hadn't reflected on how . . . straitened your family's finances must have become since you left the governorship to oppose Myllyr's madness. I should have. I know the law. But, somehow, I never did, and I respect you even more for making those sacrifices, now that I have."

He paused, and Hygyns gave the compliment a choppy nod of acceptance.

"As I say, I'm hesitant to bring this up, knowing you as well as I've come to, but I would be honored—*deeply* honored—if you permitted me to assist you. I'm not talking about any gifts, and I'm not talking about attaching any strings," Fyrnahndyz continued quickly as Hygyns' eyes narrowed ever so slightly. "That would be grossly improper! But I would be honored to make you a personal loan of the funds you might require to support your family properly if that would free you to devote your full attention to the desperately important campaign against a second Myllyr protectorship. I know that you would, of course, insist on repaying me in full, with interest. For my part, any interest would be completely superfluous, but I'm aware it would be important to you. For that matter, I realize how a political enemy might be able to use it against you if you didn't. But if you could see your way to letting me help in whatever modest way I can, it might make it possible for you to continue the fight."

"Obviously, neither Styvyn nor I are in a position to join Zhaikyb in offering loans, General," Mahthyw Ohlsyn said. "As members of the Chamber of Delegates, that would be a clear violation of the law. However, I'm sure we—and all your friends in the West—could be counted upon to contribute generously to the costs of the campaign."

"And Mahryahno and I can promise you the guilds' support," Ahskar put in. Hygyns looked at him, and the papermaker shrugged. "We've got more than enough guildsmen out of work right now to provide lots of campaign workers," he said bitterly, "and our people know the community. I mean the *real* community, the one Myllyr and the Charisians are strangling to death. We'll turn out the voters to support you."

And break the heads of voters who oppose *you,* Fyrnahndyz thought cynically, even as he nodded in grave agreement.

"And I'm not the only publisher whose paper will support you," Phaiphyr said, once again falling into line as smoothly as if Fyrnahndyz had rehearsed him for his role. "At the moment, we may be in a minority, but I promise you, you'll still have spokesmen—passionate spokesmen—to support your platform!"

Hygyns looked around at their faces, and Fyrnahndyz reached out to rest a hand on the general's shoulder.

"We can't do this without you, General," he said softly, earnestly. "Each of us can do our own small part, offer to carry our little piece of the load, but it all comes down to you, in the end. You're the voice and the face that can carry the fight to Myllyr and his cronies, both here in the Republic and in Charis. All we ask is that you allow us to support you in this effort—in this fight for the Republic's soul. Do us the honor of allowing us to stand at your back while you wage the greatest battle of your life."

APRIL YEAR OF GOD 915

◆

.I.
HMS *Ahlfryd Hyndryk,*
Jackson Sound,
and
Tellesberg Palace,
City of Tellesberg,
Kingdom of Old Charis,
Empire of Charis.

"I feel so *Charisian* today," Frahncheska Chermyn said.

"What?" Daivyn Daikyn stood very close to her, but he clearly hadn't heard her. They stood on the foredeck of HMS *Ahlfryd Hyndryk,* just inside the solid bulwark where the deck narrowed to meet the steamer's stem, and the wind of her passage roared around their ears as she ripped her way through the heavy swell. That wind showered them with regular spatters of spray from the water bursting white under her sharply raked prow.

It also whipped the loose ends of Frahncheska's ponytail in a way he found incredibly attractive and more than a little arousing. And he knew it was laying up at least an hour of work for her and her maid as they worked to get the knots out again.

"I said, I feel so Charisian today!" she said much more loudly. "All . . . nautical and everything!"

"Well, you *are* Charisian!" he replied, and she shook her head and said something else he couldn't quite catch over the wind roar. But that was fine. It gave him an excuse to move even closer and wrap an arm around her while he ostentatiously moved his ear closer to her lips.

"You were saying?" he prompted, pressing her against his side and enjoying the firm, shapely warmth of her, and she grinned.

"I said I may've been born Charisian but I've actually always thought of myself more as a Zebediahan," she said.

"Well, fair's fair," he replied with an answering smile. "You were *raised* Zebediahan—and pretty aggressively, too. Which was really smart of the Grand Duke. I doubt anyone in Zebediah thinks of him as 'that transplanted foreigner,' any more, but even if someone does, he probably doesn't think it about you or your cousins. On the other hand," his smile turned thoughtful, "I've always thought of myself as a Corisandian, but that's become almost . . . secondary. We're *all* Charisian now."

She looked up at him, into the depths of his suddenly contemplative eyes, while the deck underfoot quivered to the beat of *Ahlfryd Hyndryk*'s mighty triple-expansion engines. His sense of humor and refusal to take himself too seriously were very real parts of his character, but there was a deeper, far more thoughtful side to Daivyn Daikyn. One he used those other parts to disguise whenever possible. She still hadn't figured out why that was, although she'd begun to suspect it was a deliberate effort to distinguish himself from his father. Hektor Daikyn's subjects had called him "Hektor the Crafty" but his enemies had used adjectives like "unscrupulous," "slippery," "devious," and "treacherous," and she wondered if he was consciously—or *un*consciously, for that matter—seeking to avoid a similar label. Or, worse, the label of "like father, like son" in the hearts and minds of those he cared about. But whatever his reason, she remembered how her heart had warmed the day she realized she was no longer one of the people from whom he sought to conceal that keen, analytical part of him.

"I think that may be the most remarkable thing Cayleb and Sharleyan have accomplished," he went on, unaware of her thoughts. "I mean, the entire Empire's younger than either of us, but they've convinced everyone in it that we belong to it and, more important, that *it* belongs to *us*."

"That's what happens when a bunch of stupid Out Islanders stand up against all the rest of the world . . . and win," she told him. "When people follow you into that kind of furnace and then walk out the other side at your side, that's a bond simply being born to rule could never forge."

"You're right." He nodded and kissed her forehead lightly, then drew her around in front of him, folding both arms around her while she leaned back against his chest. "But I think maybe you just put your finger on another part of the magic." She looked up over her shoulder and quirked an eyebrow, and he shrugged. "We all walked out of that furnace at their *side,* not their heels. And I'm not talking just about princes and grand dukes and earls. I'm talking about brick masons and carpenters. About common seamen and railroad tracklayers, about farmers and manufactory workers. I don't think there's anyone in the world stupid enough to defy the pair of them, but that's not the reason no one does. It's because that bond you're talking about is *personal* for all their subjects. And it creates awful big footprints for the rest of us to try to fill."

He looked ahead, eyes squinted against the wind of their passage, lips pursed while he considered that. And then, suddenly, he laughed.

"What?" she asked, and he shook his head.

"I was just thinking about the first time I was on a Charisian ship," he said. "That was right after Merlin and Hektor pulled us out of Delferahk, and I thought *Destiny* was the biggest ship in the world. She was bigger than anything *I'd* ever seen, anyway! And you should've seen the looks on their faces after we got aboard and they all realized no one had thought to provide a maid or a chaperone for Irys!" He shook his head. "There she was, an innocent, delicately nurtured maiden—she'd just turned nineteen, for Langhorne's sake!—all alone on a ship with three or four hundred men, most of whom weren't the sort any reputable young lady should know and *all* of whom had been stuck on board without so much as seeing a woman for *months*."

"Really?" Frahncheska cocked her head. "You know, I don't think anyone ever told me that bit! She didn't have any chaperones at *all*?"

"Well, she had Phylyp—he was our legal guardian. And she had Tobys and Traivahr and Zhakky. More importantly, though, she had Earl Sarmouth—he wasn't an earl then; not even a baron yet, of course—and she had Hektor. And she had the fact that not one of those common born, woman-starved, uneducated seamen would have dreamed of laying a finger on her. They were too busy rescuing us and I think all of them had decided she was their kid sister, at least until they got us home. I didn't even think about it at the time, of course. I was too busy catching krakens!"

"Krakens?"

"Well, that's what I thought I had. It was actually a neartuna, and nowhere near as big as I thought it was. Of course, I was a scrawny-enough runt it didn't have to be really big to be bigger than me! They had me in a safety harness, lashed to the deck, and there were these two great big seamen ready to pounce if the line started pulling me over the stern." He shook his head, smiling in fond memory. "I think that was the first time I'd actually *laughed* since we'd left Manchyr for Delferahk. Sir Dunkyn and Hektor gave us that."

"I can just see you," she said, leaning back against his chest. "I bet you had the time of your life!"

"Oh, yes!" A chuckle rumbled through his chest, vibrating against her back. "In fact, I still go fishing whenever I can. It's never been quite the same again, though. Probably because I'd just been rescued by the legendary *Seijin* Merlin—only he was more the 'notorious *Seijin* Merlin' at the time—and I knew no one was going to try to kill me or Irys. That was a nice change."

His light tone didn't fool her, but she let it pass. He

was a much deeper and more complex person, her Daivyn, than she'd thought when they were younger.

"Actually, the one thing I don't like about this trip is that the *Ahlfryd*'s moving a bit too fast for comfortable fishing. Does make a nice breeze, though, doesn't it?"

"That's one way to put it," she replied, raising her head and shading her eyes against the brilliant sunlight with one hand while she looked out at the low-slung, gun-bristling armored cruisers crashing through the swell on either side of their ship.

Thanks to her time at the Royal College—and, even more, to her status as the sister of a commander in the Imperial Charisian Navy who'd been navy-mad since he could talk . . . and who talked a *lot*—she knew quite a lot about *Ahlfryd Hyndryk*'s escorts.

HMS *Devastation* and HMS *Kahrltyn Haigyl* were twenty feet shorter than *Ahlfryd Hyndryk*, and they were working hard to keep up with her as her prow turned back high, white walls of foam and her wake trailed away behind her. Without their massive weight of guns and armor, she was lighter and fleeter of foot than they, despite her much larger and commodious superstructure. They were warships, low and sleek; she was a passenger vessel, with luxurious accommodations and a top speed of thirty knots. The cruisers couldn't match that speed. They could just touch *twenty-seven* knots, but they couldn't sustain it for very long.

The ICN had also specified a cruising radius of 12,000 miles at normal displacement when the *Thunderbolts* were designed. That limited them to a cruising speed of only fourteen knots (which would have been only twelve knots on Old Terra, where nautical miles and land miles were different lengths), because coal consumption was far lower at that speed. The fact that reciprocating steam engines required far more frequent maintenance if they were run at high RPMs was another factor in their design, since the navy emphasized durability over speed. They were also designed to stow up to an additional seven hundred and fifty tons of coal at maximum displacement, which extended their maximum range at fourteen knots to over 14,000 miles, although it also increased their draft so much two-thirds of their armored belt was submerged until they'd burned off the excess.

Ahlfryd Hyndryk, with no need to pack in their armament (or the eight hundred men to crew each of them) could afford the combination of sleek lines, optimized for high-speed, and an enormous coal capacity. She could also afford to be far more "maintenance intensive" than they could, and the combination let her cruise for over 10,000 miles at twenty-three knots. At that speed, a *Thunderbolt*'s maximum range at design displacement was only 5,200 miles.

Because of that, all three ships had refilled their bunkers at the ICN's Hard Shoal Bay coaling station five days ago, and each cruiser had loaded an extra two hundred tons of coal. Since then, they'd steamed roughly 3,000 miles, and they were presently leaving Jackson Sound, passing to the west of Fergys Island on their way to round Dahnahtelo Head. From there, they would travel another 2,600 miles down Dolphin Reach and across Darcos Sound to Crown Point, in just over four and a half days. And from there, *Ahlfryd Hyndryk*'s passengers would travel the final thousand miles to Tellesberg by automotive, which would take them another day and a half.

Or, of course, they could have made the entire trip, direct from Manchyr, in only four and a half days aboard one of the Air Force's *Moonraker*-class airships, and Frahncheska knew that was what Daivyn had truly hoped to do. Unfortunately, the Air Force had declined to make any of its *Moonrakers* available to him. They'd been very polite about it, but they'd been equally firm, and Daivyn had recognized the fell hand of Earl Coris and Earl Anvil Rock.

Personally, she was just as happy they'd decided Daivyn was too important to risk aboard an airship, despite the safety record they'd so far amassed. Daivyn, on the other hand, felt particularly aggrieved that his cousin Koryn and his entire family had made the same flight—both ways—not just once but three times, now. Unfortunately for him, Earl Coris had pointed out that so far neither Cayleb nor Sharleyan had been allowed to risk themselves in the air, either. And then he'd asked if Daivyn really wanted to take Frahncheska two or three miles into the air over trackless ocean in a cabin attached to an enormous bag of explosive gas.

As it happened, she had no problem at all being used unscrupulously to deflect Daivyn from airships in general. Ships that floated in *water* were one thing, as far as she was concerned. Despite her time at the College, ships that floated in the *air* still struck her as profoundly unnatural. Pretty, and impressive, and undoubtedly useful, but distinctly unnatural.

And, besides, this way she got him all to herself for two whole five-days. Well, to herself, a bevy of servants, her maid, her parents, and Earl Anvil Rock and Lady Sahmantha. Fortunately, *Ahlfryd Hyndryk* was a large ship and they'd been able to find something like privacy in places like this, standing amid the exuberant buffeting of the wind with the bow wave crashing rhythmically to either side. No doubt dozens of eyes were upon them even as they stood here, but she really didn't care about that, and she nestled down in Daivyn's wind shadow and leaned her head back against his chest.

▼ ▼ ▼

"So, Daivyn," Cayleb said, tipping back in his chair, "should I assume you've come to formally seek my permission to wed, like a dutiful vassal?"

"Actually, no," Daivyn said politely, then took a sip from his whiskey glass. "This is really good Glynfych," he added brightly.

"Undutiful whelp!" Cayleb growled. "I've got a good mind to put my foot down and forbid the banns!"

"No you don't," Daivyn told him. "First, because politically it's brilliant." He grinned broadly. "Secondly, because I happen to know Empress Sharley's entirely in Frahncheska's corner and she's the only person in the world you're frightened of. And third," the grin faded into something much softer, "because you know how much I love her."

"I don't know which is worse," Cayleb sighed. "Being told my consent to the marriage is immaterial or knowing you can read me like a book."

"What can I say? I had good teachers!"

"Yes, you did," Cayleb agreed. "And they had a good student. Seriously, Daivyn, I couldn't be happier for both of you. Although Alahnah has pointed out—in her exquisitely tactful style—that it did take you the better part of twenty years to figure it out."

"Not fair," Daivyn said firmly. "For a good half of those years she was a scrubby schoolgirl and I was an even scrubbier school*boy*. That was during our 'kisses are icky' phase, you understand. And then she was gone to school for five of the other ten! Actually, I think I did pretty well, given the time I actually had to work with!"

Cayleb shook his head with a grin, then climbed out of his chair and beckoned for Daivyn to follow him through the latticed glass doors onto the second-floor balcony overlooking the palace's central courtyard.

"I tend to agree with you, and the truth is both of you have improved with age. As Merlin would put it, you clean up pretty good. And neither of you is a dummy, either."

"I don't know if my natural modesty can stand all this effusive praise," Daivyn said dryly, carrying his whiskey glass with him.

"Just calling it as I see it," Cayleb said. "And, on a more serious note, I'm glad to see you finally settling down. Now I'll have all of my ruling princes married off and busily producing heirs!"

"I tend to doubt any of us are going to produce them at the rate you and Sharley have." Daivyn shook his head philosophically. "Must be something about the water here in Old Charis and Chisholm."

"Whippersnapper!"

Cayleb leaned on the balustrade, looking out over the courtyard as evening settled across Tellesberg. Daivyn joined him, and they stood companionably side-by-side, the son at the shoulder of the man who'd been his father's most bitter enemy.

"Seriously," Cayleb continued after a moment, "I couldn't be happier for both of you. And thank you for making the trip to announce the formal betrothal here."

"Political choreography *can* be a pain, can't it?"

"Oh, tell me about it! The real problem's Gorjah, though. I can't blame him for wanting to stay close to home, given how Maiyl's mother is failing. I know he'd come to Manchyr for the wedding if he had to, and he'd smile while he was there. But he really doesn't want to take her that many thousand miles from home right now."

"And there's no reason he should have to." Daivyn shook his head.

He wasn't as close to King Gorjah of Tarot as he was to Cayleb and Sharleyan or even Nahrmahn Garyet of Emerald. The two of them got along well on the rare occasions when they met, but there were over thirty years between them, as opposed to barely nine between him and Nahrmahn Garyet. Despite that, he knew how deeply Gorjah cared for his queen and how deeply attached he himself was to his mother-in-law.

"And agreeing to formalize the betrothal here in Tellesberg means he doesn't have to," Cayleb agreed, resting one hand lightly on Daivyn's shoulder. "He and Nahrmahn Garyet can both pay their respects to your future bride right here, and then they can stay home while the rest of us sail to Manchyr for the actual wedding."

"Nahrmahn Garyet's staying home, too?" Daivyn raised an eyebrow.

"Zhanayt's having a harder time with this pregnancy." Cayleb shrugged. "She insists she'd be just fine aboard *Ahlfryd Hyndryk*, and she's probably right. Nahrmahn Garyet really doesn't want to take any chances, though, and if he stays home from the wedding it could make Gorjah's absence seem a bit less pointed to the more hypersensitive. I think he's planning on explaining that to you in person when he and Zhanayt get here tomorrow. He doesn't want you to think it's because he doesn't care."

"This is probably going to be the most crowded wedding in Corisandian history," Daivyn said with the air of the man who'd tried his best to avoid that distinction. "We'll be just fine without him, and Zhanayt and the baby are way more important."

Cayleb squeezed his shoulder and nodded, then looked down to where the insect-repelling flambeaus had just been lit in the gathering dusk as swarms of servants descended upon the long tables arranged along the terrace. They came armed with table cloths, flatware, and serving utensils, and strands of music drifted up to the balcony as the musicians began tuning their instruments.

"Looks like they're getting ready," Cayleb said philosophically. "It's going to be crazy, you know. We kept the guest list as lean as we could, but that wasn't all that lean, I'm afraid. Last time I checked, it was up to over a hundred and fifty. And that was last five-day."

"I know," Daivyn sighed. "Going to be a lot worse in Manchyr, though. I have to say it does seem sort of silly to be 'presenting' Frahncheska to people who already know her, though. I mean, she's been in and out of Tellesberg for her entire life. For that matter, she was just here for five years!"

"Court etiquette knows no sanity." Cayleb shook his head. "God knows it isn't because I haven't *tried,* but this is one task which is clearly beyond the reach of any mere emperor or empress. Sharleyan and I've been scandalizing the protocol experts for over twenty years, and not *one* of them's dropped dead of apoplexy." He shook his head, sadly this time. "You'd think we could've gotten at least one of them by now."

"You may not have killed any of them off, but I'm sure you've made their lives a living hell," Daivyn said in an encouraging sort of tone.

"There *is* that." Cayleb brightened visibly. "Come on. Let's go scandalize them some more!"

MAY YEAR OF GOD 915

·✦·

.I.
Manchyr Cathedral
and
Royal Palace,
City of Manchyr,
Princedom of Corisande,
Empire of Charis.

"Daivyn was right," Cayleb murmured glumly in Sharleyan's ear as they gazed out across Manchyr Cathedral from the royal box.

Their four older children—and Lywys Whytmyn—had joined them there, although eight-year-old Domynyk Maikel had been spared. Hektor, Irys, and all five of the Aplyn-Ahrmahk children filled in for him, however, which filled the box pretty close to capacity. Earl and Lady Anvil Rock, Koryn, Nimue, and their brood filled the Gahrvai family pew to the left of the sanctuary, and Nynian and Stefyny Athrawes had joined them.

Merlin, of course, stood post outside the royal box.

"About what?" she murmured back under cover of the organ music which filled the packed cathedral as the massed worshipers awaited the wedding party.

"About how damned *crowded* this shindig would be." Cayleb shook his head. "Talk about your dog-and-dragon shows!"

He had a point, Sharleyan thought. Although the components of the Charisian Empire clearly dominated among the celebrants, every major realm of Safehold outside the empires of Harchong and Desnair and the Kingdom of Delferahk was represented, despite the vast distances involved. Silkiah had sent a member of the grand duke's family, and the Dohlaran ambassador was also a cousin of King Rahnyld, so the House of Bahrns was directly represented. Most of the others had sent ambassadors, and a special place had been reserved for Vicar Zherohmy Awstyn, who'd made the enormous trip—over eighteen thousand miles—by rail, canal, and steamer to attend as Vicar Tymythy Rhobair's personal representative.

That was a gesture she and Cayleb deeply appreciated, and the fact that Awstyn retained so many reservations about the Church of Charis only made his manifest willingness to undertake that gargantuan journey even more important to them both. Among other things, it reminded them both yet again of how many good and compassionate men and women there were within the Church of God Awaiting's ranks. There were times when they *needed* that reminder, which made them treasure men like Awstyn even more deeply.

He was, however, only one of the diplomats and visiting clerics who packed the pews like picklefish. She hadn't seen so many of them in one place since the Siddar City Peace Conference at the end of the Jihad.

"I haven't actually counted," she said now. "Are there actually more of them than there were for Nahrmahn Garyet and Zhanayt?"

"I think so," Cayleb replied.

<Definitely,> Merlin's voice said quietly in their earplugs. <Counting everybody, there's about twelve percent more.> The *seijin* outside the box never actually moved, but the image of him superimposed on their contacts shrugged. <I think it's because even more than Irys and Hektor, this seems like a formal ratification of Corisandian membership in the Empire.>

That was an interesting thought, Sharleyan reflected. And Merlin was probably right. At the moment, Irys' children remained Daivyn's legal heirs, since Corisandian law still barred female inheritance, and the Corisandian peerage's more conservative elements were dug in deeply in defense of that principle. Daivyn fully intended to ram through an amendment to change that in the crown's case, but Irys and Hektor had convinced him to defer that until he'd produced at least one heir of his own body. Irys had no desire to assume his crown, and the last thing they'd wanted to do was to draw attention to the fact that if anything happened to Daivyn, one of the House of Ahrmahk's collateral branches would inherit the throne of Corisande. Or to provide the paranoid with further "proof" Sharleyan and Cayleb had pressured their youthful prince into bending to their will to insure that happened. Theoretically, that throne was already Cayleb and Sharleyan's to dispose as they willed, but despite the general acceptance of Irys and Hektor's marriage, the thought of a "Charisian interloper" on the throne had remained a thorny one.

Daivyn's marriage to Frahncheska—and the production of one or two heirs, an effort to which she was confident they would devote their enthusiastic efforts in the very near future—would lay that issue to rest once and for all. Probably. There were still a handful of Corisandian revanchists who would never accept their princedom's inclusion in the empire, but they were few, far between, and dying out steadily. Daivyn and Frahncheska were about to give that process a hefty kick, in addition to taking a long stride towards reconciliation between Corisande and Zebediah, and that made today an even more significant political event than most royal weddings.

"He's got a point," Cayleb said in her ear. He'd clearly been following the same train of thought. "And to be honest, Nahrmahn Gareyt and Zhanayt weren't in the same league, as far as political impacts go. The House of Ahrmahk and the House of Baytz were already firmly allied thanks to Zhan and Mahrya, and—"

The organ music paused for a moment, in which the enormous cathedral seemed unnaturally silent. Then it surged back to life, joined by the trained voices of two hundred choristers as the cathedral doors opened to admit Prince Daivyn Dahnyld Mahrak Zoshya Daikyn with Lady Frahncheska Ahdylaid Chermyn on his arm.

Cayleb and Sharleyan came to their feet, along with every other person in that enormous cathedral, as Daivyn and Frahncheska paced regally down the aisle through the swirling music and the soaring voices. Despite the protocolists' stern admonitions about the solemnity of the moment, both of them wore enormous smiles, and Sharleyan felt her hand stealing into Cayleb's as she remembered another day in another cathedral. She turned her head to smile up at him and discovered he was already smiling at her.

His hand tightened on hers, and then they turned back as Daivyn and Frahncheska reached the sanctuary rail and paused before Archbishop Klairmant Gairlyng and Archbishop Maikel.

The hymn ended, the music died, and someone coughed in the sudden, singing silence. Then Gairlyng raised his hands in benediction.

"My children," he said, "you have been bidden here this day to witness the marriage of our Prince, Daivyn Daikyn, to his chosen bride, Lady Frahncheska Chermyn. This is the marriage of two young people who have known one another literally since childhood. They know one another's strengths and they know one another's weaknesses, and more importantly still, they know one another's hearts."

He smiled at the couple before him, then raised his eyes to the crowded pews behind them.

"Daivyn and Frahncheska have completed their premarriage counseling with me as prescribed by the Holy Bédard, and I am confident this is a marriage of hearts. Yet it is, of course, also one of state. One which all of us hope and pray may further the healing between Corisande and Zebediah. And so we have many reasons to join in this joyous celebration, but the most important one of all comes from the *Book of Bédard*. 'Join with your friends, your brothers and sisters, the whole and the healthy of heart. Share the joy you find in one another with those most dear to you, and seek out those with whom you would share this most holy and intimate of moments. For this is the day in which two become one, and that one becomes stronger than the sum of its parts. Build in your hearts a fortress against all the world may bring against you, and choose carefully those with whom you would share the laying of the cornerstone of the rest of your life together.' Come now, and join with us as we lay the cornerstone of this young couple and with it all of the joys and triumphs which will proceed from it all the rest of the days of their lives.

"And now, my children," he said, signing the scepter of Langhorne, "it's time the two of you expressed to this company assembled what you have already expressed so eloquently to one another. Are you prepared?"

"We are," they replied in unison. Their voices were less superbly trained than his, but they carried clearly in the stillness, and he smiled at them once more, then raised his own voice in the ancient, familiar words.

"Dearly beloved, we are gathered here—"

▼ ▼ ▼

"For something with so much hoopla tied up in it, it went really, really well," Cayleb said, much later that evening, as he and Sharleyan settled at last into their chamber in the suite which was always set aside for their use here in Manchyr. It was the same one in which Merlin Athrawes had carried Sharleyan to the bed after an all too nearly successful assassination attempt, but it had been completely redecorated since and she seldom thought about that anymore.

"Yes," she agreed. "Yes it did."

She toed off her court shoes with a sigh of relief. Eventually, they'd have to go ahead and summon Gahlvyn Daikyn and Sairaih Hahlmyn, but for now it could be just the two of them, with no valets and no maids.

"My feet are swollen," she said plaintively, settling onto the side of the enormous bed in an airy billow of skirts. She'd deferred to Corisandian custom and style for the wedding itself, but she'd opted for a lightweight, simply cut—and far cooler—Old Charisian style gown for the reception.

"Not surprising if your feet are barking at you, given how much time you've spent on them," Cayleb told her. He crossed to her and hooked a footstool closer with one toe, then settled onto it in front of her. "Give me," he said, and she smiled as she laid one foot in his lap.

"Has it really been twenty-two years since that was *us*?" she asked as his strong, skilled fingers went to work.

"Doesn't seem possible, does it?" He shook his head, kneading the sole of her foot with his thumbs. "Or that both of us were actually *younger* than they are! God, if you'd really known what I was asking you, would you still have been crazy enough to say yes?"

He paused in the foot massage, looking up at her, and she looked back down. She saw the strands of silver which had crept into his dark hair and close-trimmed beard, and she remembered the intensity of that far younger man. Remembered the glow in those eyes, the way he'd reached out to a woman he hadn't even known, trusting her to reach back. So many years since then, so many miles. So many truths revealed. So many challenges and triumphs . . . and failures. So many joys and so many griefs. Alahnah, Gwylym and Braiahn, Nynian Zhorzhet and Domynyk Maikel. So many people to mourn, so many to embrace.

She leaned forward, ran her fingers through that hair, wondered if he saw that younger Sharleyan when he looked at her. She was still slim, but no longer as slender as she'd been then, for childbearing and time had exacted their price, and she disdained the dyes other women in her position might have used. The strands of white in her gloriously black hair were broader than his, stood out more strongly, and she knew twenty-two years of laughter, life, and tears had put lines into her face, too.

"In a heartbeat," she told him softly. "In a single heartbeat." The hand stroking his hair touched his cheek, instead. "I won't say you've never pissed me off, because we both know better. But I wouldn't have missed you, or a single *second* of our lives together, for any imaginable price. And if, at the end of it all, the 'Archangels' come back and the 'Nahrmahn Plan' fails, not even that could make me change my mind. You gave me the chance to do something about all the lies, all the deceit. You and I, Cayleb—*we changed the world,* and it was worth every single thing it cost. But, even more than that, we have always, every instant of our lives together, been there for each other. And I know that whatever happens in the next year or so, you and I will always be together. Nothing can ever change that, no matter what lies beyond this moment. Nothing will ever separate us. Zhaspahr Clyntahn couldn't do it, the 'Archangels' can't do it, and neither can Heaven or Hell." She smiled at him through a sudden sheen of tears. "Here we stand, my love. Right here . . . inside each other's hearts."

He came off the stool, kneeling beside the bed, and his arms were around her. Those familiar, strong, beloved arms. And hers were about him, holding him tight while their cheeks pressed together.

"Whatever price God asks in the end, I'll pay it," he whispered in her ear, "because he gave me you. He gave me a 'marriage of state' beyond anything I could have imagined—could've *dreamed* of!—when I sent you that letter. And if Daivyn and Frahncheska are blessed with a quarter of the joy we've had, then they'll be the second most fortunate pair of people on the face of Safehold."

They never knew how long they stayed there in each other's arms, but eventually Cayleb drew a deep breath, kissed her cheek, and settled back on the stool. He recaptured her foot and began massaging it once more.

"If I'd known what good foot massages you gave," she said in a deliberately light voice, "it would've made the decision to accept your proposal a lot easier. Have I told you before that you're very good at this?"

"A time or two," he acknowledged with a smile. "Always good for a man to know he has a second profession to fall back on if his current line of work falls through."

"Maybe we could open a pedicure shop down off the waterfront in Tellesberg," she said. "Or even a full-service beauty salon. You could trim toenails and massage feet, and I could do fingernails!"

"It has possibilities," he replied. "Don't know how Merlin would feel about it, though. The security aspects could be a little challenging."

"We wouldn't open it under our own names, doofus!" She gurgled a laugh. "I'm sure we could come up with aliases that worked."

"And nobody in Tellesberg would recognize *us*, right?"

"Well, maybe two or three people."

"Only two or three?"

"All right, I'll give you a dozen. Even *two* dozen. But if you shaved your beard and I dyed my hair—?"

She arched her eyebrows at him, and it was his turn to laugh. But before he could respond, a soft, musical tone chimed in their com earplugs.

He paused, looking at her. Then his lips firmed as he recognized the identifying ring . . . and its priority.

"Accept," he told the com's small computer after a moment, then paused for a second while the circuit was opened.

"Yes, Nahrmahn?" he said then.

"I hate to disturb you," Nahrmahn said, "especially on today of all days. But Owl and I have just been looking at some new data from Siddar City, and we think we have a problem."

JUNE YEAR OF GOD 915

·◆·

. I .
Silkiah Canal Consortium Building
and
Protector's Palace,
Siddar City,
Republic of Siddarmark.

"Shan-wei–damned bastards!"

"Fucking thieves!"

"Burn 'em out!"

The line of city guardsmen around the magnificent marble-faced building locked their riot shields, leaned their shoulders into them, and braced themselves as the mob surged once more. Cobblestones pried out of the streets, some of them the size of an infant's head, sailed viciously through the air. Most of them struck the hard-held shields and staggered the guardsmen ducked down behind them but bounced away harmlessly, in the end.

A few struck more fragile prey.

The guardsmen had been issued breastplates and helmets when they mustered for duty today, but three or four of them went down anyway as the whistling stones hit their helmets. Two of them were next to each other, and a gap opened in the shield wall as they were battered off their feet.

"Kick the bastards' arses!" a powerfully built, bearded man whose tunic bore the badge of the Shipbuilders Guild shouted. *"Come on, lads!"*

The mob howled in triumph and crashed forward like the sea.

Most of the guardsmen managed to stay on their feet, lashing out with the riot batons they'd been issued. Eight inches longer than the Siddar City Guard's standard ironwood batons and loaded with ten ounces of lead, they were more like cylindrical maces than nightsticks, and bone broke as they landed on their targets. None of the men wielding those batons had any interest in simply "discouraging" the rioters, because they had a very good idea what would happen if they went down. They weren't fighting just to maintain public order or protect a building. They were fighting for their *lives*, and they knew it.

Screams of fury turned into shrieks of pain, but the guardsmen weren't the only ones with bludgeons. Quite a few of the "spontaneous rioters" had come prepared with lengths of two-inch iron pipe whose last three or four inches had been poured full of cement by the members of the Plumbers Guild before they were capped. One of those "spontaneous rioters" leapt into the gap and swung his weapon two-handed, like a baseball player swinging for the stands. The twenty-six-inch-long pipe struck the nape of a city guardsman's neck like a hammer, just below the protective edge of his helmet, and he went down in a boneless heap as bone shattered under the impact.

Another rioter came through the gap across his corpse. This one swung low, not high, slamming his bludgeon into the back of a second guardsman's knee. His target went down; the bludgeon rose high, crunched down once more; and the gap was suddenly a man wider.

A scant reserve of guardsmen charged forward, batons swinging and thrusting with deadly, trained precision as they tried to halt the incursion. But there were too few of them, and their comrades on either side of the break in the shield wall fell too swiftly.

"*Over them!*" someone bellowed. "*Run over 'em, boys!*"

Smoke rose in at least a dozen places in the mob as the heads of Shan-weis' scratched on brickwork, sputtered to sulfurous life, and lit oil-soaked rag wicks. An instant later, more men whose tunics bore the badges of half a dozen of the city's guilds, hurled their oil-filled firebombs. The glass and pottery vessels shattered as they hit the ground, or the shields . . . or the guardsmen behind those shields. Men cried out in pain as the flames bit, and the stubborn line began to crumble.

"Now, boys! *Now!*"

A fresh roar of fury went up as the mob sensed victory. Men who might have preferred not coming into reach of the guard's riot batons were given no choice as pressure from behind drove them forward. At least three rioters went down for each guardsman, but there were thousands of rioters and less than two hundred guardsmen, and no one in the guard had foreseen the intensity of the madness. No one had issued firearms, and a cement-loaded pipe was as deadly as any riot baton.

The shield wall splintered in a dozen places and guardsmen who'd been assigned to protect a building suddenly found themselves fighting desperately to protect wounded and fallen fellows . . . or themselves.

The mob bellowed in triumph and doors and windows began to shatter.

▼ ▼ ▼

"What the Shan-wei *happened*?" Klymynt Myllyr demanded harshly. "*How* did it happen?!"

"This wasn't just spontaneous," Daryus Parkair replied in a weary voice. He'd been out in the city for hours with Brigadier Allyn Zhoelsyn, the Siddar City Guard's commanding officer, and the smell of smoke had ridden his clothing into Protector's Palace. "Oh, a lot of it was, but *somebody* sure as Shan-wei knew it was coming. They were too well prepared and the attack on the Consortium building was too targeted. So far the confirmed count is thirty-seven Guardsmen dead and close to two hundred hurt. I'm sure there're more to come before the count's complete. And I don't have any kind of number on how many rioters got their arses killed or crippled, but I'll be surprised if it's not in the multiple hundreds for both."

"And the Consortium building?" Bryntyn Ashfyrd asked.

"Completely gutted. The fire brigade commander tells me it's a total loss," Parkair replied in the tone of the man who clearly found architectural damage secondary—at best—to the men who'd been killed or badly injured trying to protect it.

"Completely?" Ashfyrd pressed. Parkair glared at him and the Chancellor waved one hand. "I'm not trying to minimize anything else, Daryus, believe me. But all of the Consortium's records were in there. *All* of them. If they're gone. . . ."

His voice trailed away, and he shook his head.

"That's what happened in the *streets,*" Myllyr said in a voice of iron. "And that's important. In fact, in the short term, it's the most important problem we've got, and we need to get focused on solving it as soon as Brigadier Zhoelsyn gets here. But in the meantime, what the hell happened to the bond issue and the banks, Bryntyn?"

"I don't know!" Ashfyrd threw up both hands. "I know *some* of it, but we'll be years figuring out all of it . . . assuming we ever do! I'll tell you this much, though—we're going to find Braisyn Qwentyn at the bottom of it. Or up to his Shan-wei–damned neck in it, anyway!"

"Meaning what?" Myllyr demanded.

"Meaning he was the agent for almost half the consolidated buying blocs," Ashfyrd sighed. "We knew he was. In fact, a lot of us at the Exchequer recommended him to people looking for an agent to manage their purchases—or their entire portfolios, for that matter." The ginger-haired Chancellor looked much older than his sixty-seven years at that moment. "It seemed like a way to pay old Tymahn back, find a way for Braisyn to recover some of the ground the House of Qwentyn's lost."

"Bryntyn, it lost that ground because Braisyn was a frigging idiot," Myllyr said, sitting back in his chair. "He's the one who cut the House's throat trying to freeze Owain out. In fact, I'd argue he's the one who caused three-quarters of the problems we've got when he killed the House of Qwentyn by blocking Delthak's efforts to bail him out. Damn it, Henrai was right! *That's* what threw everything—and everybody—off the edge of a cliff in the first frigging place!"

"I know that!" Ashfyrd said defensively. "But we all owed Tymahn for what he did during the Jihad, if nothing else. And it looked like Braisyn had learned his lesson. Recommending him was a way to help him recover his house's fortunes without anything coming directly from the Exchequer."

Myllyr glared at him, but then he shook his head and made a waving away gesture.

"If you'd asked me, I'd've said the same thing," he admitted. "But what did he do?"

"He pulled a sleight-of-hand. Or, at least, that's what we think he did. He converted his buyers' securities and notes into cash and substituted loans drawn on half a dozen of the bigger banks to finance the purchase of the bonds. And the collateral for the loans was . . . nonexistent. Two-thirds of it were old House of Qwentyn notes which had never been redeemed and weren't worth the paper they were written on."

"How did he get away with it?"

"We're not sure. We're still trying to find out! My guess is that he had to have someone on the inside of the banks. They may not've known everything he was doing—I'd guess most of them thought they were the only ones working with him, that their little piece of it was *all* of it, but there's no way of knowing that—but somebody had to've been looking the other way to let that much bad paper get past them. I don't know if we'll ever be able to prove it, but I guarantee you there has to be someone."

"I want them found, and I want them found fast," Myllyr half snarled. "We've got to be able to explain how this happened if we don't want half the capital to go up in flames!"

"I don't know if we can stop that from happening even if we do figure out what happened," Samyl Gahdarhd said heavily. The lord protector looked at him, and he shrugged, then turned to Ashfyrd. "How much of the total bond issue are we talking about here?"

"Probably at least a quarter," Ashfyrd admitted heavily. "Maybe more than that, if it turns out he wasn't the only one playing fast and loose with the financing."

Gahdarhd's face tightened—in confirmation, not surprise—and he looked back at Myllyr.

"That's going to cripple the Consortium, no matter what," he said. "It *may* be survivable from a purely technical viewpoint, but the damage to the public's confidence in it's going to be enormous. And here's another point to consider. Unless I'm mistaken, he was pretty deeply involved with Trans-Siddarmark's purchasing contracts. Has anybody taken a look at the books over *there*?"

"Not yet. Nezbyt'll be looking at that very closely, and so will Zhasyn Brygs, but Zhasyn's up to his arse in krakens right now over at the Bank. That's where the real threat's coming from, however big a part the Consortium may be playing in the riots right now. When the word broke, we had a huge run, with people demanding their deposits, and there's no sign of its easing anytime soon. Not just from the Central Bank, either; *every* bank's getting hit, and I'm pretty sure some of them—maybe a *lot* of them; we don't really know how bad this is going to be in the end—are going under." Ashfyrd's expression was grim. "The Exchequer's going to take a bath from the Guarantee Trust banks, but it'll be even worse for the independents who never joined the Trust. They're going under without a trace, and they'll be taking their depositors' savings with them."

"Langhorne," Myllyr muttered.

"That's why I'm not sure we can stop this anytime soon," Gahdarhd said, twitching his head in the direction of the council chamber's window. It was open, and the sounds of rioting—faint with distance, but unmistakable to anyone who'd lived through the Sword of Schueler—drifted in through it.

"There are already people out there shouting that this could never have happened without connivance from the inside," the keeper of the seal went on. "And, from what Bryntyn's just said, they're right, at least as far as some of the banks are concerned. We'd just finally turned the corner, started seeing some real confidence in the possibility of prosperity at last. Now *this*?" He shook his head. "It's going to hit everyone twice as hard expressly because there was so much optimism, seemed to be so much hope for the future. And I promise you, this *will* spread beyond the city. We're not just the Republic's capital, we're the center of its financial markets—you know that even better than I do—so the consequences of this are bound to spread. Hell, how many of the canal bond buyers are from the provinces, not here in Siddar City at all? We may not be looking at these sorts of riots elsewhere, but investors in places like Santorah and Clahnyr are about to get hit hard, too. And if Trans-Siddarmark gets pulled into this, it's going to hammer people as far away as Lake City and Talmar."

He shook his head again, and Myllyr nodded in ashen-faced understanding. He knew, even better than Gahdarhd, how much anyone's financial and economic decisions depended on psychology. As the Archangel Bédard had written so many centuries before, what mattered where decisions were concerned wasn't the truth; it was what the decision-maker *believed* was the truth.

And panicked people weren't likely to think in terms of restraint and the need to let the banks ride this out. The really big investors might, but not the smaller investors. And not the depositors in those banks. *They* were going to think in terms of the clothes on their families' backs. Of roofs over their families' heads . . . or their families' next meal.

"I think Samyl's probably right, Klymynt." Daryus Parkair's voice was harsh but his expression was unflinching. "And if he is, this'll be the worst shit storm since the Sword. I can't begin to predict how far into the provinces the ripples will spread, but I do know it's going to get even worse here in the capital once people begin to realize just how deep this goes. I don't think Zhoelsyn will be able to handle it with just the Guard."

"We can't put *troops* into the city!" Ashfyrd objected quickly. The others looked at him, and he raised one hand pleadingly. "Bad as this is, it can still get worse if we convince people who haven't made up their minds yet that it's *going* to get worse. Putting the Army out on the streets of Siddar City would be a huge escalation, and Langhorne only knows where that would end!"

"I understand what you're saying," Parkair said, almost compassionately, "but I can't worry about people's minds when *lives* are being lost out there. And don't forget, we have an election in less than two months. How in hell are we going to manage that if we still have people killing each other in the streets, Bryntyn?"

Ashfyrd looked back at him, and the distant rioting sounded much louder in the silence which answered the seneschal's question.

. II .

Imperial Palace,
City of Cherayth,
Kingdom of Chisholm,
Empire of Charis.

"It's going to get a hell of a lot worse before it gets better," Duke Delthak said flatly over the com. "Trust me, Ashfyrd and Brygs still haven't found all of it, and the momentum's all on the downward spiral now. People are absolutely panicked, and it's spreading to every security and stock issue, even ones that don't have a thing to do with the Canal. People are desperate to get out before their investments tank, *whatever* their investments are, and they're taking any price they can get for assets that should be—will be, when the panic passes—worth hundreds or thousands of marks. They're all desperate for gold, something they know will hold its value. Something they can hide under the mattress or bury in a hole in the ground, and that's exactly what a lot of them are doing—pulling their deposits out before *their* bank goes under so they can hide it somewhere 'safe.' And that's taking even more cash out of circulation and, even more importantly, out of the banks, which is only driving the failures. Over a third of the Siddar City banks have gone under already, and Nahrmahn, Owl, and I figure half the remainder are likely to do the same thing. This won't be a recession; it's going to be a *depression*. The mother of all depressions. I don't think anyone in Siddarmark's ever seen anything as deep and as bad as this is going to be, and the repercussions will spill over onto everybody doing business with Siddarmark. The Border States, the Temple Lands, Silkiah—even Desnair! The funny thing—if it's not obscene to call anything about this 'funny'—is that the mainland realm that's going to get hurt least badly is probably Dohlar because of the way public opinion operated against anybody in the Republic's doing business with Dohlar."

"And Myllyr's going to lose the election," Sharleyan said grimly.

She and Cayleb shared an outsized rattan chaise lounge on their suite's balcony, gazing up at a moonless, crystal-clear sky swathed in stars. A gentle breeze sifted across them with the scent of flowers from the gardens below, nightbirds and wyverns sang or whistled softly, and they could hear the distant sounds of late-night traffic from the streets beyond the palace wall. It was a beautiful, restful, *tranquil* scene, far removed from the imagery of riots, arson, and political invective sweeping Siddar City like a plague.

"Of course he'll lose," Nynian Athrawes said from the chambers assigned to her and Merlin. "Everybody's going to blame him for it. And, much as I hate to say it, they've got a point. It *did* happen on his watch, and it happened despite the warnings we kept dropping in his ear."

"Fair's fair, Nynian," Nahrmahn said from his computer. "We didn't warn him about Qwentyn. Or not where the Canal Consortium was concerned, anyway. We warned him about Kartyr Sulyvyn and the fact that Qwentyn was paddling around in the same muddy waters, but we completely missed the way he was embezzling everything in sight where the bond issues were concerned. We didn't pick up on it until that first call came in and couldn't be covered."

"All right," Nynian conceded. "That's fair enough. But we did know he was providing a conduit for a lot of Sulyvyn's transactions. For that matter, we knew he was lending the House of Qwentyn's reputation to Sulyvyn and the others to cover some of their shadier doings, and we passed those 'rumors' along. That should've sounded warning bells with Ashfyrd and Brygs if anyone had bothered to *check* the rumors."

"Yes, it should have," Cayleb sighed. "But it should've done that for us, too, and where the Canal was concerned, it didn't. It sailed right past us. Probably because we were all so delighted by how well the bonds were doing. Everything was finally going right. Who wanted to look a gift dragon in the mouth when that was true?"

"What are they going to do about it?" Irys asked from Manchyr, after a moment.

"I don't know." Delthak's com image shrugged. "I don't know what they *can* do. Technically, the bonds are still good, however they were purchased. Eventually, they're supposed to be paid off out of the Canal's earnings, and that hasn't changed. It's the banks holding the worthless collateral that are the problem, and the Consortium isn't directly involved with that. But nobody seems to *understand* that, unfortunately."

The duke leaned back in his chair, scowling out at the afternoon sunlight of Old Charis.

"The bonds were issued by the Exchequer to fund the Consortium, and the Exchequer got thirty percent of the purchase price in cash when the bonds were originally sold. I wasn't sure about the wisdom of selling them on a margin that way, but the Canal was supposed to be the wyvern that fetched the golden rabbit, and letting people buy in on the 'installment plan' was supposed to kickstart the Consortium.

"Now, though, there's not a chance in hell the Exchequer'll get the other seventy percent from the people who get wiped out in the panic, and that means the Consortium won't see the capitalization it was supposed to get. Worse, since it all started with the Canal bonds, the Consortium's tainted in the public's eyes. Then there's the loss of all of the Consortium's records when its headquarters burned. Believe me, the rioters couldn't have picked a worse psychological target—from our viewpoint, anyway—than that."

He shrugged bitterly.

"The distrust is spreading way beyond just the bonds Qwentyn was involved with," he continued. "*All* the bonds are being dumped on the market for a quarter of their face value, with damned few takers. Not only that, but don't forget that over a third of the Consortium's total capitalization is supposed to be in the form of private direct investment, not the Exchequer's bonds. That *stock's* getting dumped, too. It looks to me like the entire Consortium's going down, and until—and unless—they can reconstruct their records, nobody really knows who owns what or who owes who how much, which is only adding to the panic."

"And what's happening to the Consortium's really secondary, at this point," Nahrmahn put in. "Like Ehdwyrd says, the real problem's the banks. Even the members of the Guarantee Trust are getting hit, and a bunch of them ended up holding worthless paper, too, despite the Central Bank. The Exchequer's on the hook for those banks' direct deposits, but nobody's going to cover their other debts. At this point, I'm not prepared to offer any hard predictions on how many of them will go under before it's done, but Owl and I will be amazed if it's not something like fifty percent of the total banking industry."

"And outside the Guarantee Trust, not even the depositors will get a tenth-piece back," Delthak added glumly. "Absent a miracle, the Republic's entire economy's going down the drain, and there's not a damned thing we can do to stop it."

"Or to prevent Hygyns' election," Nynian said. "Sharleyan's right about that. He was the only serious opposition candidate Myllyr faced before the crash. There's no time for anyone else to get into the race now, and the panic and the fear play directly into that jingoistic hatred he spews. Clearly, this is all our fault."

"That's ridiculous, Aunt Nynian," Alahnah said from her own room. It was a very nice room, the same one she'd had since she was twelve, but she hated it, because there was no convenient tunnel between it and Lywys' room. "How could this possibly be *our* fault?"

"Because anything that goes wrong anywhere on the face of Safehold is our fault, sweetheart," Cayleb said resignedly. "That's what happens when you're the biggest kid on the block and you keep insisting on making waves."

"And when so many people want to see you *stop* being the biggest kid on the block," Sharleyan added, and he nodded.

"But it doesn't make any sense," Alahnah protested. "We weren't even involved in the bonds—or the Consortium, for that matter!"

"Since when do paranoia and scapegoating need to make sense, Lahna?" Elayn Clareyk asked. Duchess Serabor and her husband sat on the veranda of their comfortable mansion in the Maikelberg suburbs. "No good conspiracy theory in history—here or on Old Terra—ever worried about logic or making sense! Victimology's all about emotions and finding someone—*anyone*—else to blame for your situation. And of course, that 'someone' has to've done it out of pure malevolence! After all, you're the *victim*, the pure and innocent injured party who never did a single thing to deserve what's happened to you." She shook her head, her expression bitter. "Trust me, sometimes it really works that way. God knows Lyzbyt and Hairyet—I mean Krystin—saw enough of that during the Jihad. But by the time it comes to explaining why everything else *has* to be someone else's fault, reason and sanity have left the building."

"A little bitter, but true," Duke Serabor said, reaching

out to take her hand. "And separating someone from their sense of victimhood is one of the hardest things in the world to do, Alahnah. Because it takes the onus off of *them*. If it's not their fault, then it's manifestly unfair to expect them to do anything about it, and they'll fight like hell to avoid giving that up."

"That's all true, and I hate what's happening, and I hate the fact that Myllyr's almost certainly going to lose the election now," Cayleb said. "Even more, I hate thinking about all the innocent bystanders who're about to find themselves wiped out, especially all those people who bought the special class of bonds. If the Consortium goes under, they've lost all of their investment, as well, and it was a hell of a lot *bigger* investment for most of them, too. That's one reason the panic's spreading so rapidly, cutting so deep.

"I hate all of that, and most of all, I hate the fact that there's not a single, solitary damned thing we can *do* about it. But the truth is, right this minute it's secondary. Families're going to be ruined, people are even likely to die before this is over, but it's not truly the end of the world. Ultimately, one way or the other, Siddarmark will recover. It may take a long time and it's almost certain to inflict a *ton* of suffering and bitterness in the process, but eventually it will happen.

"Unless something even worse happens to the rest of the world, first."

There was silence over the com net. In less than three five-days, it would be God's Day of 915. And if the "Archangels" *were* returning on the actual thousandth anniversary of the Day of Creation. . . .

"I don't know about the rest of you," he said now, sliding closer to Sharleyan, putting his arm around her, "but for the next five-day or so, Safehold can look after itself. Even in the Republic. We've made all the plans we can make, done everything we could think of to do, taken all the precautions we could think of to take, and it all comes down to the fact that the dice may be about to stop tumbling, and we don't really have a clue which way they'll land. So I advise all of us to spend the next three days with the people we love most. Never hurts to tell them you love them, even if there aren't any fake archangels coming out of the woodwork.

"And if those dice come down wrong, we may not get another chance."

. III .
Siddar City,
Republic of Siddarmark.

"And who d'you think *let* them steal everything that wasn't nailed down?!" the leather-lunged man on the platform demanded. "*Who?*! I'll *tell* you who—it was that worthless son-of-a-bitch Myllyr, that's *who*! First he crams his Shan-wei–damned 'Central Bank' down our throats, then he signs on with frigging Charis to completely wreck an economy that was just *fine* before he started fucking around with it! And now *this*! He's stolen the bread right out of your children's mouths, people!"

An ugly chorus answered him as the flambeaus fumed, spilling their smoky, bloody light across the audience that packed the square around the platform. Saint Cehseelya's Square always saw healthy crowds during elections, but seldom like tonight's. And seldom when such fury floated in the air along with the flambeaus' smoke.

"And another thing!" the orator shouted. "How many people have that butcher Parkair's thugs shot down right here in Siddar City? You think it's just a *coincidence* that we're coming up on an election and he and Myllyr are flooding the capital with troops?! *Please!*"

The answering shouts were louder and uglier, and he nodded.

"Exactly!" He told them. "*Exactly!* And it's not getting any better, friends. Oh, no. Not one *bit* better! This is going to go right on snowballing until it rolls over everything in its path and nobody in the entire fucking Republic has a pot to piss in. And when *that* happens, the Shan-wei–damned Charisians will step in and offer to 'save' all of us by buying up every goddamn thing in sight for a fucking tenth-piece on the mark! And that son-of-a-bitch Myllyr will hold the door open for them when they walk in and then kiss their arses when they walk back out of it with everything they can stuff in their goddamned pockets."

"Damned right he will!" a voice shouted from the depths of the crowd. "I say we go to Protector's Palace and sort his arse out *right now!*"

A thunderous shout of agreement went up.

"*Yes!*" someone else shouted. "And I'll bring the rope! And after we drag his worthless arse out into the street, we should—!"

He chopped off in mid-sentence as the sudden clatter of iron-shod hooves on cobblestones rose behind him. The crowd turned and saw the mounted city guardsmen walking their horses down two of the streets which fed the square. They were grim faced, those guardsmen, and they wore full riot gear, which would have been difficult to tell apart from a cuirassier's armor. They carried riot batons, but this time there were revolvers on their hips and a third of them had shotguns in their saddle scabbards, as well, and there were over fifty of them.

The crowd seemed to settle in upon itself, gather itself, but a lane parted as half a dozen guardsmen moved straight towards the speaker's platform. They reached it, and most of them stayed mounted, turning their horses to face the crowd, while the captain in command of the detachment dismounted and climbed the stairs to the platform.

"What the *fuck* do you think you're doing?" the speaker snarled, careful to pitch his voice loud enough for the crowd to hear.

"I'm dispersing this gathering," the Guard captain replied flatly.

"You can't 'disperse' a political rally! That's against the law!"

"I can when the speakers at that rally start inciting violence."

"I haven't said a single word suggesting violence against anybody!"

"Well maybe you haven't been listening to what the people you're talking to are saying back to you, then. I *have* been, and it's gone past peaceful criticism. A hell of a long way past." The captain turned to face the crowd. "Now disperse, all of you!"

"No fucking way!" someone shouted from the safe anonymity of the crowd.

"Trust me, a lot of people are likely to get hurt in the next little bit if you don't," the guardsman warned.

"Including *you*, arsehole!" the other man shouted back defiantly.

"Not as bad as the people you're about to get into a world of hurt with that mouth of yours, friend," the captain said flatly.

"*Screw you!*"

Some of the crowd stirred uneasily, starting to drift away towards the edges of the square, but far more of it snarled agreement with the speaker.

"All right," the guardsman said. "Looks like we do it the hard way."

He looked across the sea of heads at the mounted men who'd drawn up in a two-deep line that stretched across two-thirds of the square's width.

"Clear the square, Lieutenant!" he shouted, and those mounted men moved forward at a slow walk, riot batons swinging in gentle arcs as they came.

▼ ▼ ▼

"Disgraceful," Zhermo Hygyns said to his well-groomed audience, shaking his head in mingled sorrow and anger as he stood at the podium at the head of the vast, luxurious banquet hall. No one would have guessed, looking at the elegant china and glittering silverware that the entire dinner had been organized in less than two days' time.

"It's just disgraceful," he continued to the crowd of well-heeled potential donors. "There's no other word for it! Lord Protector Klymynt's reaction from the very beginning of this crisis has been . . . clumsy, to say the least. Completely leaving aside the question of how Qwentyn and his co-conspirators were able to defraud so many people on the Lord Protector's watch—he *is* an ex-Chancellor of the Exchequer, after all; how could he miss seeing something like *this* coming?—what are we to make of the hundreds of people who've been killed or injured—or the thousands who've been arrested!—in the middle of an election year? How can that *not* be seen as an effort to intimidate his political opponents?"

Hygyns paused to sip water and the silence was deafening.

"I'm not prepared to accuse the Lord Protector of deliberately suppressing the vote," he resumed in a tone of voice which said exactly the opposite. "I am prepared to say it will have that *effect*, however, and that runs counter to every principle of our constitutional Republic! The free exercise of the franchise by every qualified voter is absolutely sacred in Siddarmark . . . or it's *supposed* to be, at any rate. But then, we're also supposed to be a government of laws. Of laws which are enforced free of any foreign influence, free of any favoritism towards realms who clearly don't have the Republic's best interests at heart. We haven't seen *that* over the last five years, so why should we expect the rest of the Republic's laws—the fundamental principles of our Constitution—will survive the *next* five years of a Myllyr protectorship? Whether or not he's Charis' *willing* dupe, the consequences will be the same. If we ever hope to recover our economic footing, we must do it the *Siddarmarkian* way, remembering the values and the strengths which once made the Republic the greatest single realm on the face of Safehold. We need to *return* to those strengths and—"

"He's doing well," Ghustahv Phaiphyr murmured in Zhaikyb Fyrnahndyz's ear as Hygyns continued with his speech. "In fact, he's doing better than just 'well.' I can already hear the marks ringing in the collection boxes!" The *Siddar City Sentinel*'s publisher smiled. "I'd written my editorial for tomorrow before I headed over here, but I may need to go back to the office and rewrite it before I turn in!"

"He is doing well," Fyrnahndyz agreed. "I do hope he's not pushing the personal condemnation of Myllyr too hard, though."

The banker, who'd quietly rented the banquet hall through no less than three cutouts—and whose bank happened to be surviving the current economic crisis far better than most because it hadn't held a single scrap of Braisyn Qwentyn's valueless collateral—allowed his face to show an edge of worry.

"He *can't* push too hard," Phaiphyr replied. "Not against Myllyr and his crowd. And not at a time like this. All my reporters agree that the vote's turned completely around since the Consortium Scandal hit, and public opinion's getting nothing but worse where Myllyr is concerned. This is the time, Zhaikyb—the time for him to bring the hammer down with everything he's got!"

The publisher didn't even try to hide his satisfaction, Fyrnahndyz noticed. That wasn't very surprising, perhaps, given everything the *Sentinel* was doing to fan the fury against the Myllyr protectorship.

It was all coming together nicely, Fyrnahndyz thought. The consequences had already proved worse than he'd anticipated, and it was obvious the economy's headlong tumble was still gathering speed. That could be . . . unfortunate, even for him, despite how carefully he'd buttressed his position. From a political perspective, however, the timing had worked out far more fortuitously than he'd ever dared to hope.

It wasn't as if he'd put Braisyn Qwentyn up to it; he simply hadn't said a word about it once he realized what was happening. He'd always known about the corruption in the Trans-Siddarmark purchasing process, of course, but he'd carefully gotten out of that, as well, months before he started building his pro-Hygyns political machine. He *had* used a carefully concealed contact to make the first call on collateral he knew was worthless, however. And he'd arranged for Qwentyn to learn the call would be placed a day and a half earlier. As he'd hoped, Qwentyn had been aboard a fast ship, headed for Desnair the City, where all of the gold he'd already shipped out of the Republic awaited him, by the time the authorities began to discover what had happened.

And it was all coming together so *nicely,* he thought again, sitting back with his brandy while he listened to the man he fully intended to make the next Lord Protector of the Republic of Siddarmark.

. IV .

Cherayth Cathedral
and
Imperial Palace,
City of Cherayth,
Kingdom of Chisholm,
Empire of Charis.

"Rejoice, my children!" Archbishop Ulys Lynkyn proclaimed, raising both hands in blessing. "Rejoice and be glad in the Lord on this day of all days!"

"We rejoice in the Lord!"

The response rumbled back from the packed pews through the tendrils of incense, the shafts of multi-colored light spilling through the stained glass. The weather was perfect, and this was a particularly important Wednesday. It was July 13, 915—God's Day, the most holy day of the year. The day which celebrated the Day of Creation itself. The traditional God's Day feast waited, and many of the city's wives and mothers had attended early mass so they could return home to have those feasts ready to serve when their families returned.

"It is right and good that we should rejoice in Him and in the work of His and His Archangels' hands," Lynkyn continued.

"It is right and good," the congregation responded.

"As the bounty and the beauty of the world He has given us through Them enfolds us, so His love uplifts and strengthens us. We are the first fruits of His love, and so we give Him our praise and our worship."

"We praise and worship Him with all of our hearts and all that is within us!"

"As children we are taught, as children we are loved, and as children we come to know the One who is parent to us all. And so—"

Cayleb Ahrmahk tuned out the familiar liturgy and reached out to take his wife's hand. She turned her head to smile at him, but he saw the same tension, the same worry in her eyes.

The last month or so had been hard on every member of the inner circle. The ongoing meltdown in Siddarmark would have been bad enough under any circumstances, but it was barely even on their radar, a useful concept they'd picked up from Merlin and Nimue, under *these* circumstances. Their anxiety had coiled tighter and tighter as they approached today, and now it was upon them.

Every sensor Owl had been able to get into orbit was focused on the Temple and the city of Zion. So far, none of the power sources they could detect from the outside had shown any fluctuations or spikes. Of course, as Merlin had discovered during Tymythy Rhobair's investiture, there were a lot of power sources they *couldn't* detect from the outside. The best they could say was that they hadn't seen any overt evidence of anything ominous emerging from the Temple's cellars . . . yet.

In some ways, that lack of evidence actually made things worse, though. It encouraged them to hope . . . and along with hope came the fear that they were setting themselves up for an even more crushing hammer blow if that hope proved unfounded.

He glanced at the empty place at Sharleyan's left elbow. All of their other children were present, but Alahnah was sick today. She'd discovered her thespian talents simply didn't extend to projecting the proper joyous focus for God's Day Mass when she knew the *Rakurai* might be preparing to strike even as she sat there.

He wondered how even Maikel Staynair's serenity would survive celebrating that same mass in Tellesberg Cathedral when today's sun reached Old Charis. As far as he could tell, Staynair was the only member of the inner circle who was truly prepared to accept whatever happened today. There were times when Emperor Cayleb found the depth of his old friend's personal faith hard to comprehend . . . and more than a little irritating.

On the other hand, even though mass might be particularly hard today, given the truth about the "archangels," at least it kept them from sitting around and fretting. And he and Sharleyan had plenty of other things to keep them occupied, as well. Unlike their eldest daughter, both of them had learned to be *excellent* actors over the last twenty-three years, and concentrating on their lines would undoubtedly help them at least pretend they weren't actually anxious, after all.

He only wished there'd been a way he could have thanked Hauwyl Chermyn for that.

Chermyn had turned eighty in March, and his health had taken a turn for the worse. His once-powerful physique had eroded sadly, the tremor in his hands was ever more noticeable, and he'd begun walking with a pronounced stoop . . . and a cane. He was spending more time with the healers, and the people of Zebediah were preparing themselves as best they could for the loss of their beloved grand duke. No one expected him to go tomorrow, but no one thought he had all that many tomorrows left, either, and his eldest son, Rahz, had resigned his army commission and returned home to take as much as possible of the load off of him . . . and to be at hand when the moment came for him to inherit his father's title.

Under the circumstances, any reasonable grand duke would have stayed at home, in his palace, where his healers could keep an eye on him. Hauwyl Chermyn, however, had other plans. He'd brought his entire family to Court in Cherayth, ostensibly for Rahz to reaffirm his own oath of fealty as his father's heir to Cayleb and Sharleyan on God's Day. What not even Rahz knew was that Hauwyl intended for rather more than that to happen. In fact, today would be his final day as Grand Duke Zebediah when he announced to the Court—and to his son—that he was abdicating in Rahz's favor. The hoopla and consternation that would cause would keep everyone occupied. And, just for good measure, the Chermyns would be celebrating their youngest grand-child's birthday. Young Allyn was a "God's Child," one of the children born on God's Day—in his case, the year before, which made him a "miracle baby" in every way, since there were fifteen years between him and his older brother, Hauwyl Cayleb . . . and eighteen between him and his oldest sister, Enylda. Today would see his place in the Zebediahan succession formally recognized . . . and an *energetic* birthday party on his behalf. One where everyone who was anyone would be paying his or her formal respects to the abdicating grand duke.

And one thing we can all damned well use is a birth-day party, he thought. *Can't hurt a thing to remember life goes on.*

AUGUST YEAR OF GOD 915

✦

Siddar City,
Republic of Siddarmark.

"Here now! I've a right to vote! You can't—!"

The protest broke off in a harsh sound of pain as one of the guardsmen grabbed the man's right arm and twisted it so high behind him his wrist touched his shoulder blades. He bent over, gasping, and the guardsman's partner reached into his tunic and removed the short-barreled revolver from the holster hidden inside it.

"And I suppose this is what you meant to mark your ballot with?" the senior guardsman said.

"Man's got a right to protect himself on the streets, especially these days!" the civilian got out through gritted teeth. "No law against carrying a gun for self-protection!"

"There *is* a law against carrying *any* weapon into a polling place." The guardsman's voice was hard, flat. "And the penalty's three years. Hope you'll think it was worth it when they let you back out."

"You can't just—!"

"The hell we can't," the guardsman told him and jerked his head at his partner. "Cuff this . . . gentleman and see about finding him a ride."

"Can do, Sarge." The junior guardsman tweaked the hard-held wrist a fraction of an inch higher. "Gonna give me any problems about the cuffs?" There was no response, so he tweaked it again, high enough his prisoner squealed and shook his head violently. "Didn't think so," the guardsman observed with obvious satisfaction, and marched the offender away.

Myltyn Fyshyr watched them go and wondered where this was all going to end. This was his fourth protector's election as a poll watcher, and he'd never seen anything like it. Polling places normally had a guardsman or two handy to help keep order, and there were usually street guardsmen to keep traffic flowing outside. This year, there were almost a dozen guardsmen *inside* the polling place, and this was the third arrest he'd seen. At least none of the others had been for bringing weapons into the polling place, though. They'd been because someone had "only" started a physical brawl, usually because they'd decided someone else was there to vote against Zhermo Hygyns. The Myllyr voters seemed far more interested in just keeping their heads down, voting, and getting out again. Hygyns' supporters were just a bit more . . . proactive than that.

Judging by the sounds drifting in from the street, there'd been quite a lot more of that outside. In fact, given the ugly mood of the electorate, the fellow with the revolver actually might have had a point about self-protection. Which didn't mitigate the gravity of his offense one bit, of course.

"Your name?" he asked as pleasantly as he could as a man who looked gaunt and whose tunic and boots had obviously seen better days stepped up in front of him.

"Bryttyn," the man replied, presenting his certificate. "Dezmynd Bryttyn."

"Thank you," Fyshyr said, turning to the proper page of his precinct roll. He found Bryttyn's name, checked the certificate's details, and handed it and the printed ballot back to him.

"Through the arch," he said for at least the two hundredth time that day.

"Thanks," Bryttyn said, which there'd been precious little of today.

He took his ballot and departed, and Fyshyr looked after him for a moment, thinking about his worn boots, the hollows in his cheeks. The poll watcher had seen too many faces like that, and the sullen desperation which gripped the capital like a fist seemed deeper with each one he saw.

A fresh ruckus broke out outside the polling place and two or three of the internal guardsmen drifted—not particularly unobtrusively—towards the front doors. Their streetside fellows had been reinforced by detachments of Army troops, but everyone knew it would be far better to let the Guard handle everything it could without involving the Army. The mood was ugly enough without that.

He shook his head, praying for Langhorne's help to make it through the day without actual bloodshed, then looked up at the next voter.

"Your name?"

"Sahlahmn Breyk."

Fyshyr nodded and started turning pages again.

▼ ▼ ▼

"Let me be one of the first to congratulate our *new* Lord Protector!" Ghustahv Phaiphyr said loudly as he walked into the smoke-filled suite.

Zhermo Hygyns turned quickly from his conversation with Zhaikyb Fyrnahndyz and Ahlahnzo Mykgrady, the owner of one of the capital city's biggest chain of groceries, and opened his mouth. But he closed it again, quickly, Fyrnahndyz observed with a sense of approval. It wouldn't do for him to look *too* eager even here, in front of his core supporters.

"Surely that's premature," Fyrnahndyz said instead for him now. "The polls only closed three hours ago. The tally won't be in until tomorrow evening, at the earliest!"

"Doesn't matter," Phaiphyr said confidently. "My people've been spread out to half the polling places in the city, and the other papers've covered the rest. We've been asking people who they voted for when they left. A lot of them wouldn't say, of course, but we've tallied the ones who did. The General's leading by over—*over,* Zhaikyb—two-to-one among the ones who *will* say.

We've seen that clear across the capital. Can't say for sure what the other major cities look like, but going *into* the vote it was pretty damned clear which way the wind was setting here in the East after people finally realized how Myllyr and Ashfyrd had fucked up the economy. And we already knew the General commanded a hefty lead in Tarikah and Cliff Peak."

"But not in Glacierheart," Fyrnahndyz pointed out. "And Thesmar's been a tossup, too."

In fact, Glacierheart was going against Hygyns by a substantial majority, he suspected. And Thesmar wasn't a "tossup," either. Hygyns didn't want to hear about that, since he fancied himself "a man of the West," but his anti-Charis rhetoric had played very poorly in both those provinces. The good news from his perspective was that Thesmar remained very thinly populated and that Glacierheart's resistance would be more than compensated for by the vote tallies in Tarikah and Cliff Peak. In fact, that would have been true even without the . . . creative accounting the Western Syndicate's political allies could be relied upon to provide.

"Doesn't matter!" Phaiphyr repeated even more emphatically. "No lord protector in history's ever won election without carrying the Capital, and Myllyr's losing it in a landslide. The only real question's how *big* a landslide, and the one we're looking at would probably bury Mount Olympus!" He crossed the room to Hygyns, holding out both hands. "Congratulations, General." He clasped both forearms with the other man. "I mean, congratulations, *Lord Protector* Zhermo!"

. II .
Imperial Palace,
City of Cherayth,
Kingdom of Chisholm,
Empire of Charis.

"Well, that's about as ugly as it gets," Duke Delthak sighed over the com. "I figured he was going to lose, but he didn't just *lose*; he got hammered."

"Not like we didn't see it coming," Cayleb replied, as philosophically as he could.

"Do we have any better read on Hygyns' probable policies once he's sworn in, Nahrmahn?" Sharleyan asked.

She sat in the warm sunlight with her embroidery hoop, needle flashing back the sun, while Domynyk Maikel gravely chalked a rather lopsided dragon on the flagstones at her feet. No one had ever actually seen a bright purple dragon, but that didn't seem to bother the almost-seven-year-old one bit.

"Not the specifics, no," Nahrmahn replied. "Nynian, Owl, and I have been looking that over, but I think he's still trying to catch up on that himself. Before the crash, he didn't expect to win any more than we expected him to, so he was fairly safe talking in generalities. Now?"

His avatar shrugged.

"To be fair, he *is* trying to catch up," Nynian pointed out. "And he has until February to do that. I'd be happier if he was turning to more qualified—and more *honest*—advisors, and I don't think he's being as effective as he could be, but he's definitely not letting the grass grow under his feet, either. It's just that he hasn't had time to enunciate any specifics yet."

"Not where long-term policy's concerned, no," Nahrmahn agreed. "Some things we do know, though. For one thing, Gahdarhd, Ashfyrd, and Brygs will all be headed out the door with indecent haste on inauguration day.

And I'll be damned surprised if Daryus doesn't follow them." He shook his head. "I know the Seneschal's supposed to be confirmed or fired only with the consent of the Chamber of Delegates, but that could be no more than a formality this time around."

Sharleyan nodded as she continued setting the neat stitches. Cayleb was in his study, ostensibly reading the latest dispatches from Mahlkym Preskyt. No one needed to know he had rather more recent data on the Republic than their ambassador could provide. Now he grimaced, pushed back his comfortable chair, and rose to pace angrily around the quiet study, because Nahrmahn was right. Hygyns hadn't just won the protectorship. His allies had won a narrow but decisive margin in the Chamber, as well. Worse, quite a few of the other delegates who'd survived the bloodletting knew better than to cross him and those allies. At least for the first few months of his protectorship, just about anything he wanted was going to pass the Chamber with ease.

Including Daryus Parkair's dismissal. The blunt-spoken seneschal had made his disdain for General Hygyns too clear during Hygyns' military service—and been too loyal a servant of both Henrai Maidyn and Klymynt Myllyr. In fact, he'd been a servant of the *Republic,* but someone like Hygyns would never recognize that distinction. And so, after thirty-plus years commanding the Republic of Siddarmark's armed forces, Parkair would find himself kicked to the curb by someone who wasn't worthy to carry his helmet.

"I'm more worried about Fyrnahndyz, to be completely honest," Nynian said. "That man's too good at hiding his tracks, and I don't think Hygyns even begins to suspect how many strings his 'good friend Fyrnahndyz' has attached to him."

"He's going to have to be careful how he pulls those strings, if he doesn't want Hygyns figuring it out," Delthak said.

"He's been pretty successful so far," Nynian retorted. "And he and his friends—like Mykgrady—are already starting to turn the tap to siphon more money into their purses. Once Hygyns is formally in office, the trickle they're getting now's going to turn into a flood."

"And despite all Hygyns' promises, he's not going to turn the economy around anytime soon," Cayleb said glumly. He stopped pacing so abruptly he rocked on his heels and stood glaring out the window into the palace gardens. "Doesn't mean there won't be plenty of slops for the hogs, of course. In fact, there'll probably be *more* opportunities for graft, thanks to the relief programs."

Several people nodded at that.

Klymynt Myllyr had organized the largest civilian relief effort since the Sword of Schueler. The Church was heavily involved as well, but this went beyond the scope of the Church's resources in Siddarmark, and it wouldn't be too many more five-days before winter began moving in on the both Havens. Myllyr had recognized that and had already set up programs to subsidize fuel and food, especially for families with children. Given human nature, it was almost inevitable that *Hygyns* would receive the credit for those programs, since he'd been careful to rail against their inadequacy during the closing five-days of his campaign. The inner circle could count on him to pour even more funding into that once he was in office and then claim he'd turned around Myllyr's "failing, ineffectual measures." And they could just as surely count on men like Fyrnahndyz and Mykgrady to batten on the flood. In fact, Mykgrady had snapped up scores of additional grocers from desperate small business owners all across Siddar City to add to his already large empire. He was also very privately salivating over the opportunities that would provide when the time came to procure and distribute emergency food aid, and Fyrnahndyz was already providing Hygyns with the names of "loyal" businessmen to could replace the "pro-Charis lackeys" running those assistance programs.

The inner circle weren't the only ones who could read the writing on the wall, either. Their SNARCs might give them an enormous advantage, but private Charisian investors in Siddarmark saw what was coming with stark clarity. They were liquidating their investments, often at significant losses, and fleeing the Republic's worsening economic situation. And, predictably, Hygyns used that as another pretext to blame them *for* that economic situation. They'd only been interested in the Republic's marks all along and they'd been sucking Siddarmark's economic life's blood for two decades now! Obviously, now that their predatory conduct had finally brought the Republic's economy down in crashing ruin, they were looting any final marks they could squeeze out of the wreckage and heading home with their ill-gotten gains.

The fact that the Charisian Quarters in most of the Republic's cities had never recovered from the Sword of Schueler only made it easier for him to sell that vile and preposterous allegation. The expatriate Charisian families with ties of blood and marriage to non-Charisian families in the Republic had been largely wiped out, which left them with far fewer voices to speak in their defense. Siddar City's Charisian Quarter had survived the Sword and the Jihad. In fact, it had grown significantly. But people who'd survived the Sword saw ominous similarities between the vilification directed at them by Hygyns' supporters and the rabble-rousing invective which had driven the Sword's ferocity.

"All we can do is hope for the best—or, for the least worst, at any rate," Sharleyan sighed at last. "And at least the 'archangels' haven't returned yet."

"There *is* that, love," Cayleb acknowledged with a smile. "Mind you, I'm not holding any celebrations for at least another three or four months. They could've gotten their sums wrong, after all! But I have to consider the fact that we're all still alive a major plus. And if they *aren't* coming back this year, at least we ought to have plenty of time to deal—or *try* to deal—with this ungodly mess in Siddarmark."

"You're right," Nahrmahn agreed. "And, speaking of archangels that haven't turned up yet, Owl and I would like to show you what we've been working on with Paityr and Nynian to kick off the final phase of the 'Nahrmahn Plan.'" His avatar's smile was remarkably broad . . . and evil. "Somehow, I think the real Schueler's going to be spinning in his grave."

FEBRUARY YEAR OF GOD 916

⋅✦⋅

. I .
Chamber of Delegates,
Siddar City,
Republic of Siddarmark,
and
Tellesberg Palace,
City of Tellesberg,
Kingdom of Old Charis,
Charisian Empire.

"The Chamber of Delegates hummed with excited background conversations.

The Chamber itself was a vast expanse of marble and paneled wood, tucked away at the heart of a magnificent structure overlooking the Siddar River where it flowed through the capital toward North Bedard Bay. One entire wall of the Chamber was glass, looking out over the river and filling it with natural light. Normally, at least. Today, the skies were dark, the river a broad stripe of dull pewter absorbing the drifting snow without even a ripple. The wall which faced the windows was an immense mosaic in faceted tiles, tracing the history of the Republic from the day of its inception, and greater-than-life-size figures of most of its great heroes looked out of it with stern and noble eyes upon their present-day successors.

Chamber Hall had taken almost ten years to build and been completed only fifteen years before the Jihad.

There were those who believed its construction had been a mistake. That the old, wooden, cramped Chamber Hall which had survived almost three and a half centuries of wind, weather, and warfare should have been retained. That the Chamber's resplendent new home was sadly out of touch with the ideals of the Republic's Founders, even if those Founders *had* been given places of honor upon its walls.

No one had paid the gloomy wet blankets much attention, and the Delegates had settled happily into their new surroundings.

Whatever its possible philosophical failings, however, the Chamber's acoustics were superlative. Someone speaking in normal tones from the raised podium at its northern end could be easily heard in the last seat, closest to the patterned bronze doors at its southern end. At the moment, those acoustics were bouncing back the rumbling mutter of conversations, filling the spaciousness like the sound of a none-too-distant sea, as the delegates waited to be gaveled to order.

"Can you believe this shit?" Wahlys Mahkhom muttered in Rahskho Gyllmyn's ear as the two of them stood just inside the antechamber door, watching the slow flow of conferring delegates swirl around the Chamber.

"Of course I can believe it," Gyllmyn replied, equally quietly. "I'd really prefer for it to all be a bad dream, but it's not."

Mahkhom's nod was glum as he wondered—not for the first time—what lapse of sanity could have led a mountain boy from the Gray Walls *here,* of all places. He wanted to say it was his wife's fault. Or maybe he should have blamed Bishop Gharth. Glorya had insisted he could be anything he wanted to be, but it was Gharth Gorjah, Glacierheart's auxiliary bishop, who'd turned the screws of duty on him when old Holystyr died in office. And the ease with which he'd been elected by his fellow veterans had seemed to validate Glorya's view. For that matter, he'd enjoyed a solid sense of accomplishment during his first term as a delegate.

He didn't expect to experience the same thing this

time, but at least he'd have one tried and tested ally outside his own delegation.

"Got my orders from Governor Landoll yesterday," he said now. "Don't think I'm going to enjoy following them, though." He grimaced. "Doesn't mean I think the Governor's wrong; just saying I'm going to get hammered by Ohlsyn's crowd as soon as I open my mouth and tell them to put Hygyns' proposals where the sun don't shine."

"You and me both," Gyllmyn replied philosophically. "Kydryc's view's about the same as Governor Landoll's. But Thesmar's the newest kid on the block, so I don't have the kind of clout a Glacierhearter's supposed to have. I'm supposed to have your back with all the clout we do have, though. The question, of course, is who's got *my* back, because I don't think we've got a lot of other friends in the room right now."

He smiled with a flash of true humor, but the smile vanished into something bleaker and his eyes hardened as a silver-haired man entered the Chamber from a side door, accompanied by a red-haired upper-priest in the black cassock of the Order of Langhorne, and made his way toward the podium.

"I suppose we should find our seats," he said. "This is going to be painful."

▼ ▼ ▼

Zhefytha Trumyn climbed the shallow steps to the speaker's podium through a sudden, singing silence. It was an ascent he'd made more times than he could count over the last seventeen years. That was how long he'd been Speaker of the Chamber, and he'd worked with three lords protector during those years.

He would not be working with a fourth.

He reached the top of the steps and crossed to the lectern in front of the high-backed, leather-padded Speaker's chair. He stood there for a moment, looking out over the sea of delegates, missing so many familiar faces . . . and seeing all the new faces with more than a hint of despair. If only what everyone had taken to calling "The Collapse" had held off even a few months longer! Just until after the election! But it hadn't, and those new faces were the result.

And God only knew where it was all going to end.

He picked up the gavel, brought it down on the polished square of ironwood. The sharp "crack" was clearly audible, and he laid the gavel down once more.

"Gentlemen, the Chamber will come to order," he announced. He looked out across them for another second, then turned courteously to the upper-priest at his side. "Father Ansyn, if you would open us in prayer, please?" he invited.

"Thank you, Master Speaker," Father Ansyn Ohmahly, the Chamber of Delegates' chaplain, replied.

It was his turn to look out at the Chamber for a long, still moment, before he said, "Let us pray."

Chairs scraped on the marble floors as the assembled delegates rose, bowing their heads even as he bowed his own.

"Oh, most Holy Langhorne," he said then, "we beseech you to look down upon these men gathered here, called to follow in your blessed footsteps as the givers and the keepers of our Republic's laws. Touch them with your wisdom that they may decide aright upon the manifold difficult issues which will come before them. In these unhappy days, their duty is graver, their burden heavier, than that of many Chambers which have come before them. We ask you to help them bear it in the service of all God's children within Siddarmark. Amen."

"Amen," rumbled back from the Chamber, and Trumyn bowed gratefully to Ohmahly.

"Thank you, Father. I hope the Archangel will hear you and truly touch us with his wisdom in this difficult time," he said with quiet sincerity.

Ansyn returned the bow with a courteous nod, then withdrew to the chair beside the Speaker's and seated himself while Trumyn turned back to the assembled delegates.

"The Chamber's first order of business," he said, "will be the formal certification of the results of the recent election and the seating of our new Delegates. After which," he smiled bleakly, "the Chair will entertain nominations for the post of Speaker."

He looked at the Clerk of the Chamber, seated behind his desk at floor level at the base of the podium. The leather folder on that desk was bound shut by scarlet ribbons fastened with a lead seal bearing the impression of the Republic's great seal where they crossed one another.

"If you would be good enough to read the Chamber the results, Master Gahnzahlyz," Trumyn requested.

"Of course, Master Speaker," the clerk replied, and the sound as he used his pen-sharpening knife to cut the ribbon was loud in the silence.

▼ ▼ ▼

"The Chamber will come to order!" Maikel Zhoelsyn announced, cracking the gavel rather more loudly than Zhefytha Trumyn had cracked it. Then again, Zhoelsyn was a rather more . . . flamboyant sort in many ways.

Feet shuffled and paper rustled as the Chamber obeyed its new Speaker, and he felt a rush of power. This was what he'd worked for all those years, he'd been confirmed by an overwhelming majority, and not even the knowledge that he'd been his patrons' second choice could dim that moment of triumph. A lot of people had expected Mahthyw Ohlsyn to seek the Speakership, and several of the Western Syndicate's members had wanted him in it. Cooler heads had prevailed, however. Ohlsyn had weathered too many allegations of corruption for some of their Eastern allies to swallow. Zhoelsyn had his fingers as deeply into the pie as Ohlsyn, but he'd always been the number two member of the Tarikah delegation, hiding in Ohlsyn's shadow. As such, he'd stayed below the horizon more successfully than his companion.

Ohlsyn didn't like it, but he was too pragmatic to deny the logic. Besides, he still got to call the plays, and he clearly thought he could be more effective as the man giving the Speaker his instructions without ever emerging into the open himself.

Of course, Ohlsyn might not have contemplated the future implications for their working relationship inherent in Zhoelsyn's new position quite as thoroughly as his loyal accomplice had. For now, however—

"Master Speaker!"

Mahthyw Ohlsyn shot to his feet right on cue, raising his hand as he sought recognition, and Zhoelsyn nodded gravely.

"The Chair recognizes the honorable senior delegate from Tarikah," he announced.

"Thank you, Master Speaker," Ohlsyn said. He walked down the central aisle to the lectern beside the Clerk's desk and turned to face the seated delegates.

"Fellow delegates," he began, "this is normally the time at which the senior members of the Chamber would take turns welcoming our new members, following which those new members would make their maiden addresses to the Chamber. Today, however, our Republic faces an unprecedented challenge, one which has brought untold suffering to our citizens and which threatens to bring still worse. Under those circumstances, I believe it's far more important for us to deal—to the best of our ability, at any rate—with that challenge, and I request that the Chamber suspend the normal rules of procedure in order to do so."

"It has been requested that the rules be suspended," Ohlsyn intoned. "Is there a second?"

"Master Speaker, I second the motion!" Bahrtolohmayo Zheffyrsyn, one of the new delegates from Westmarch, called loudly.

"The request has been seconded," Ohlsyn announced. "The Chair calls for a voice vote. All in favor of the request, please signify by saying 'aye.'"

A response rumbled back, although it was clear several of the senior delegates were less than happy that he'd allowed no debate.

"All those opposed, will signify by saying 'nay.'"

A second response rumbled, and Ohlsyn cocked his head for a moment. Then—

"The ayes have it," the new Speaker declared, and he

was probably right, although the vote had been close enough most speakers would have opted for a roll call vote to confirm it. Ohlsyn was taking no chances, however, and no one cared—or dared—to demand one.

"Master Zhoelsyn, you may continue," he said.

"Thank you, Master Speaker," Zhoelsyn said with becoming gravity, then turned back to the Chamber.

"Fellow delegates," he said again, "all of us know the nature of our beloved Republic's current crisis. I realize there's been a great deal of debate over the causes of the financial and economic turmoil sweeping Siddarmark, but its gravity cannot be denied. Neither can the fact that the damage appears to be growing steadily worse even as we watch. And I would submit to the Chamber that the results of the recent election make clear the *electorate's* view of its causes and who bears the responsibility for it. The margin of victory for Lord Protector Zhermo was almost three-to-one, and many of our new members enjoyed similar margins in their home provinces. Under the circumstances, I believe it's clearly our paramount duty to our constituents, the purpose for which we were elected and sent to Siddar City, to enact the Lord Protector's agenda. I know some members of this chamber question the wisdom of Lord Protector Zhermo's proposals, and I anticipate the debate may wax lively. Nonetheless, I believe—as I believe many of *you* believe—that the time for talk is long past. It is time for *action,* my friends! For action which will address our Republic's many bleeding wounds . . . and also hold accountable those responsible *for* those wounds! Master Speaker, I move that the Expropriation and Public Relief Act be laid before the Chamber for debate and speedy enactment."

▼ ▼ ▼

"Well, that's one way to make bad worse," Rahskho Gyllmyn said disgustedly to Wahlys Mahkhom across the dinner table. He shook his head. "And the bastards—pardon my language, Glorya—" he looked apologetically at Glorya Mahkhom, "are going to get away with it."

"I'm married to someone who used to be a soldier, too, Rahskho," Glorya said dryly. "And before that, he was a Gray Walls trapper who spent *much* too much time in taverns and saloons. I've heard the word before. Not infrequently prefaced by a very inelegant term reserved for young men who are just a bit too close to their mothers." Gyllmyn's lips twitched. Glorya Mahkhom had considerably more formal education than her husband, but she'd never looked down on Wahlys or his veteran friends. "And in this case, I think you're being too kind to them," she continued, once again confirming her own awareness of the stakes. "In fact, I think you should have applied that inelegant term to them, because that's exactly what they are. Not to mention being dumber than rocks if they really want to do this."

"You may be insulting rocks, then," he sighed, "because they're still going to do it.

Glorya cocked her head, then looked at Mahkhom with an arched eyebrow.

"Rahskho's right," he said, replying to the unvoiced question. "They're going to ram it through, and they'd probably have the votes they needed even if the rest of the survivors had the guts to stand up with me and him on the Chamber floor. Which, not surprisingly, I guess, they don't and won't."

Glorya's lips tightened, but she only nodded in understanding. It was scarcely a surprise that the non-Hygyns delegates who'd survived the election had a pretty shrewd idea what the new majority would do to anyone who bucked it.

"And is this 'Hygyns Program' as bad as we thought it would be?" she asked, looking back and forth between the two delegates. "Or should I assume from what Rahskho just said that it's even worse?"

"Worse, I think," Mahkhom said glumly. "The way the act's worded, I'm not sure we can even protect the Charisians in Glacierheart!"

"Wahlys, the Governor promised—" she began, her expression distressed, and he laid a hand on the back of hers where it rested on the table.

"I know what Tompsyn promised," he said quietly. "I *know*. And I also know we'll do our damnedest and that both Archbishop Ahskar and Bishop Gharth will stand with us. For that matter," he twitched his head in Gwylym's direction, "Governor Fyguera's going to do his damnedest in Thesmar, too. But Hygyns is out for blood, all these new delegates who rode his coattails want to give it to him, and I think the election showed that way too many voters are panicky enough to go along with it."

"But even an idiot—even *Zhermo Hygyns*—should be able to understand what this will do to the prospects for a recovery! It may offer a quick fix of cash, but it'll also kill one of our most important—and strongest—long-term revenue sources deader than Zhasphar Clyntahn! How can they not *see* that?" she demanded. It was a rhetorical question born of frustration and anger, and Mahkhom knew it, but he shrugged.

"Because Hygyns is a clever fool and a bigot," he replied, "and because the delegates in the Syndicate's pocket or beholding to the guilds in the East know which side their personal bread's butter is on. And because the people who voted them into office are too scared, too confused, and—sometimes for reasons that are actually legitimate—too pissed off at all the changes—and now The Collapse—to see where this has to lead. At the moment, our wonderful new Lord Protector's pretty much got the go-ahead to do whatever the hell he wants."

"And it's going to take years—more likely *decades*—to undo the damage," Gyllmyn said bitterly. "Which doesn't even consider what this will do to hundreds, even thousands, of perfectly honest, hard-working people."

"Or how completely the arsehole is about to piss off Cayleb and Sharleyan Ahrmahk," Mahkhom added. "You'd think even *this* idiot would be smart enough not to do that after what happened to Clyntahn and the Inquisition!"

▼ ▼ ▼

"—and then, your godson turned around, looked Hairyet straight in the eye, and said 'The *seijins* must have snuck in and broken it!'" Sharleyan told Merlin Athrawes.

"And exactly why is it that *I'm* to blame for this?" Merlin asked quizzically.

"Because—"

She paused, clearly searching for an appropriate answer. He only sat there, head cocked, politely waiting, until she shook herself and glared at him.

"Because someone, by example, has taught him to prevaricate," she said, "and I know it wasn't *me*."

"Oh, of course not! Perish the thought!" Merlin rolled his eyes.

"None of the other four ever did anything like this," Sharleyan pointed out.

"Never 'prevaricated' to save their buns when they were caught red handed?" Merlin's tone was skeptical.

"Well, never so . . . *badly*." Sharleyan shook her head. "You'd think that with mine and Cayleb's genes, he'd be *better* at it."

"Sharley, he won't be *eight* for another five-day and a half! There's plenty of time. For all you know, by the time he's twelve he'll be as good a liar as *Nahrmahn* was!"

"And this is supposed to make me feel better?"

"Of course it is! A royal or imperial dynasty never has enough skilled diplomats. Just think of what a negotiator he'll make if he has this kind of gall already and can just acquire the skill set to go with it!"

"My God," she said. "You actually think you're funny!"

"Oh, no. I don't *think* I'm funny," he told her with a smile, and she chuckled.

"Well, given how handy you are with assassins and great lizards, I think we'll keep you around anyway. After all—"

"Sorry I'm late!" another voice interrupted as Trahvys Ohlsyn dropped into the com circuit. "I thought that meeting would never end!"

"Don't worry about it," Cayleb said, looking up from his own conversation with Sir Dunkyn Yairley. "Aside from keeping the eastern participants in our discussion up late, we've got plenty of time."

"Your concern for my sleep deprivation overwhelms me, Your Majesty," Duke Serabor said dryly.

"Hear, hear!" Earl Coris echoed from Corisande, and Cayleb chuckled. But then his amusement faded and he sat back in his chair beside Sharleyan, his expression far grimmer than it had been a moment before.

It was physically impossible to find a time at which all of the inner circle could have joined a com conference. That was why they were normally limited to the circle's senior members, and quite often not all of them. Tonight, however, every member who possibly could be was present electronically, in a net which covered the circumference of Safehold, all the way from Koryn and Nimue Gahrvai, who were once again visiting the United Provinces; to Ehdwyrd and Zhain Howsmyn and Zhanayt Fahrmahn in Lathyk; to Kynt and Elayn Clareyk in Maikelberg; to Zhansyn Wyllys and Ahmbrohs Makfadyn, at Southland Drilling's new oilfield in Silkiah; Coris, Hektor, and Irys in Manchyr. Paityr Wylsynn was there, and Maikel Staynair—his brother Domynyk and Sir Dunkyn Yairley. Alahnah and Lywys Ahrmahk-Whytmyn, Edwyrd Seahamper, Ahrnahld Falkhan, Sister Ahmai Bailahnd, Father Ahbel Zhastrow, Rahzhyr Mahklyn, his daughter Tairys and his son-in-law, Aizak Kahnklyn. . . .

It was a very long list, and there was a reason they were all present this Tellesberg evening.

"Before we get to the main business," Cayleb said now, "we probably need an update on Siddarmark." Someone made a disgusted sound over the com, and Cayleb nodded. "I know. I know! But we need it for background. Nahrmahn?"

"It hasn't gotten any better," Nahrmahn said as his avatar appeared in every participant's field of vision. His hands were clasped behind him as he stood on the balcony of Eraystor Palace's electronic doppelgänger with Owl. Princess Ohlyvya stood between them, her hair whipped by the brisk breeze blowing in off Eraystor Bay, no longer needing her virtual-reality suit to join her husband there, thanks to the wetware Owl had devised.

"Hygyns' so-called Expropriation and Public Recovery Act sailed through on first reading," Nahrmahn continued. "And while they were at it, they passed the Bank Reform Act. There were quite a few other bad ideas in the same legislative package, but those are the two that are going to do the most damage.

"The EPRA's a lot heavier on the expropriation than on the recovery. He's nationalized the Canal Consortium, frozen out all non-government board members of the Trans-Siddarmark Railroad, nationalized the steel industry, and ordered the expropriation of every Charisian-owned asset in the Republic."

Someone whistled, and Nahrmahn arched an eyebrow.

"Sorry, Nahrmahn," Koryn Gahrvai said. "I've been pretty focused on the UP. The last time I took a look at the proposed legislation, it didn't go nearly that far!"

"That's because our good friend Zhermo's still making this up as he goes along, and he's discovering that people this frightened are willing to let him get away with a hell of a lot more than even *he* expected," Nahrmahn said grimly. "The bad news is that we don't have any idea how much farther he's likely to go. The good news is that there isn't a lot farther he *can* go!"

"But what the hell is he *thinking*?" Earl Coris asked from Manchyr.

"The biggest problem is that he's a lot less . . . economically sophisticated than he thinks he is, Phylyp," Nahrmahn replied. "He has very simplistic ideas and a . . . somewhat less-than-perfect grasp, shall we say, of how markets work, but he thinks he understands them perfectly. Or better than the so-called experts who let everything get this screwed up, anyway. Part of it is a sort of 'How could I possibly do worse than *they've* done?' mindset that justifies almost anything he wants to try. He's not overly blessed with moral scruples, either, although I do think he's genuinely convinced himself that everything happening to the Republic is our fault."

"Which goes to show that calling his ideas 'simplistic' is a bit like calling Hsing-wu's Passage cold in February," Earl Sarmouth observed.

"That's fair." Nahrmahn nodded. "At the same time, that's a view a lot of Siddarmarkians share, and they started evolving it well before Hygyns ever came along to be their mouthpiece. And—again, being fair—it's a little hard to blame them if they live someplace like Mantorah, wouldn't you say?"

Sarmouth grunted sour acknowledgment of the point.

The Charisian Quarter in Mantorah had been wiped out by the Sword of Schueler and all of its holdings had been snapped up by a handful of Siddarmarkian scavengers. They'd become inordinately rich in the process, and they'd used that newfound wealth to import "Charisian-style manufactories" after the Jihad. But they'd imported them without Charis' labor laws, or the codes banning child labor, or the Delthak practice of encouraging labor to participate in management decisions. Nor had they seen any reason to pay a living wage or provide educational benefits for workers' children . . . or provide pension benefits for those killed or crippled in their manufactories. They were as bad as Stywyrt Showail at his worst, and they'd established a stranglehold on Mantorah no outsider was likely to break anytime soon. Coupled with the near-complete destruction of the Mantorahan guilds—who'd lost not only their economic power but also the political clout which had come with it—there was no true protection for their employees outside the Church, and the Church of God Awaiting's power and footprint in Siddarmark was substantially smaller than it had been before the Jihad.

"Those poor people in Mantorah think that's how we run *our* economy," Nahrmahn continued, driving home his point. "And there are other places where it's almost as bad, because both Maidyn and Myllyr were more focused on structural reforms to their *banking* system than aggressively tackling the labor codes. But when there are people living that way who think it's the way *our* people are living, it's easy for them to buy into Hygyns' line that all we ever wanted to do was to loot their economy and then go home with every mark we could squeeze out of them. And then there are the western provinces. Aside from Thesmar and Glacierheart, their provincial legislatures've become examples of machine politics at their worst. So even if anybody living there was inclined to disbelieve Hygyns—and most of them aren't; they really do regard him as one of their own, and that means he must be the one telling the truth—there's no way for them to do anything about it."

"Wonderful," Serabor muttered.

"Sum it up for us, Nahrmahn," Sharleyan said.

"All right," Nahrmahn's avatar nodded. "The short version. This has almost certainly finished off the Canal Consortium as a viable entity. I don't know what's going to happen to the TSRR, but I don't expect it to be good. Now that Brygs is out on his ear, the people who've been playing Nezbyt all along don't see any restraint on their embezzlement and fraud. The Collapse had already created the conditions for a major depression; Hygyns' actions—especially the Bank Reform Act's abolition of the Central Bank, which we're pretty sure was Fyrnahndyz' brilliant idea, although Ghustahv Phaiphyr wasn't far behind—have just *guaranteed* a major depression. And he's probably made sure it's going to last a long time. During which, he'll go right on pouring the Exchequer's funds into those relief programs of Myllyr's, which will prop up all the people who've been thrown out of work—at subsistence levels, anyway—and he'll reap all the credit for 'taking care of them' while *we* get the blame for the fact that they're out of work in the first place.

"The repercussions in the Border States will be pretty severe for the next—oh, year or so—too, because of the fall in Siddarmarkian production and the collapse of Siddarmarkian markets for their goods and raw materials.

But then Dohlar will begin taking over that lost market share . . . and we'll get blamed for *that*, too. After all, we've been 'enabling' Dohlar for years now, despite their treachery during the Jihad."

The plump little prince paused, then shrugged.

"Until Hygyns is out of office—and that means at least five years from now—the Republic's official position will be that we're responsible for the overwhelming majority of its problems. And if that's the official position long enough, it'll almost certainly become the default belief for Siddarmarkians as a whole."

"Wonderful," Cayleb sighed. "Ehdwyrd, is there anything you'd like to add to that dismal picture?"

"Not really," Delthak replied. "Nahrmahn's summed it up it pretty well. We're going to take a significant hit, as well. We've already lost over half our Siddarmarkian market simply because consumers don't have the money to buy. I imagine we'll see exclusionary tariffs very soon now, which will make that worse. Probably finish it off just about completely, really, although I'll try to keep at least our toe in the door. On the other hand, we've got a big enough internal economy and enough markets in the United Provinces, the Temple Lands, and the southern Border States to survive handily. But one thing this *will* do is kill the Canal. Nahrmahn's a hundred percent right about what just happened to the Canal Consortium. Besides, I think our friend Hygyns might find it just a little difficult to build the canal with us at the very time he's using us as his economic scapegoat!"

"Which means they're going to default on the treaty," Earl Pine Hollow said.

"They're already in default, Trahvys," Nahrmahn pointed out. "We've simply kept waiving the time requirements because we didn't want to kick Myllyr in the kneecaps while he was trying to get things turned around."

"I know. What I mean is there's no way they'll be able to turn that around as long as Hygyns keeps driving them farther into the red, so they won't be able to meet the treaty requirements however long we keep waiving deadlines."

"Which means Rahnyld's going to get the green light he's been waiting for." Sharleyan didn't look especially happy saying that, but she shrugged. "To be honest, I'd rather work with him, Fern, and Dragon Island than Hygyns and his offal lizards. And it's not like we haven't kept them briefed on what was happening. We may not've told them quite *everything* we've been up to," she smiled warmly at Alahnah and Lywys, "but they're ready to work with us. Which, of course, will only reinforce Hygyns' narrative."

"Can't be helped," Cayleb sighed. "God knows we tried to work with Siddarmark, instead!"

He looked around the circle of com images for a moment or two, then twitched a shrug.

"All right, that's the bad news, and as Gwylym Haarahld would say—when his mother wasn't around—it really, really sucks. But in the long term, whatever happens to Siddarmark, however terrible it is for the people *of* Siddarmark, it's survivable from our perspective. I don't like being cold-blooded about that, and Sharley and I intend to do everything we can to help, whether or not anybody in Siddar City's likely to admit that's what we're doing. But, compared to what we've been sweating out for the last year or so, it's small beer."

A stir went through com conference's members, and he smiled.

"As of this month, we're officially prepared to say that whatever Schueler was talking about in his message for your ancestors, Paityr, it wasn't the anniversary of the Day of Creation. And that means we've got eighty or so years before the next likely return date. And we can do a *lot* with eighty years, people."

"That's one way to put it," Merlin observed. "And, may I say, speaking in my all-knowing *seijin* persona, that just this once, it's really nice to have the timing work out in our favor for a change!"

Laughter—very *relieved* laughter—rumbled over the com, and Merlin smiled broadly. The tension which had coiled so tightly during the countdown to God's Day had actually grown worse for a month or two after that date. But as September oozed into October, the possibility that they'd dodged the bullet after all had begun growing within them. No one had been willing to actually *say* so, probably because of an atavistic conviction that if they did, they would "jinx" themselves. But now, five months—half a Safeholdian year—after God's Day, they finally felt safe enough to openly admit the truth.

And Cayleb was right, they *could* "do a lot" in the next eighty years. Not everything they would've liked to do. And not anything remotely like what they could have done without the bombardment system's constraints. Old Earth had gone from Kitty Hawk to the moon in less than *seventy* years. Admittedly, standard years, but that was still only seventy-six Safeholdian years. And they'd started from a far less capable knowledge base than the one tucked away in Nimue's Cave. But without electricity, Safehold couldn't emulate that progress.

It *could* build a steam-powered planetary industrial infrastructure that truly would be effectively impossible to eradicate, however. And in the meantime—

"So I suppose it's time to initiate the second stage of the nefarious Nahrmahn Plan?" he said out loud.

"You suppose correctly," Cayleb said, and he and Sharleyan both looked at Nahrmahn. "You and Owl are cleared for Operation Androcles."

"Oh *goody!*" Nahrmahn replied with a huge smile, and punched Owl on the shoulder. "I *told* you they'd let us!"

"And I did not dispute your prediction," the AI pointed out. "I simply fail to share your indecent pleasure and anticipation."

"Oh, bull!" Nahrmahn laughed, and Owl's expression changed as his nose began to grow. His avatar reached up, feeling the steadily lengthening appendage, and Nahrmahn laughed even harder.

"My VR, my rules!" he chortled while the rest of the inner circle began to laugh. "And the subroutine controlling that is based on the same algorithms as the Stone of Schueler, so don't tell me I jiggered the results!"

Owl looked offended for a moment, but then offense flowed into chagrin, and, finally, he nodded.

"I believe the proper response is 'got me,'" he said. "And it was well done. I completely failed to note the program change. I salute you."

"Why, thank you, kind sir!" Nahrmahn swept him a bow.

"You're welcome. However, I believe you may have failed to consider one point."

"Such as?" Nahrmahn demanded.

"Why only that something like this would never have occurred spontaneously to an innocent and unsophisticated artificial intelligence such as myself. Now, however, that it has been suggested to me," Owl smiled broadly, his nose suddenly beginning to shrink again, "you might want to recall who controls all of the programming here in the Cave *outside* your VR." His smile grew even broader. "Since Prince Gwylym Haarahld has been referenced this evening already, permit me to employ one of his other aphorisms, acquired from his godfather."

"Which is?" Nahrmahn asked suspiciously.

"I believe the precise words are 'Payback's a bitch.'"

MARCH YEAR OF GOD 916

✦

. I .
Cathedral of the Holy Archangel Schueler,
City of Brohkamp,
Episcopate of Schueler,
The Temple Lands.

"I could wish for better weather, Father," Archbishop Lywkys Braytahn said wryly as he stood looking out the vesting chamber's window at the driving sleet.

Unless he missed his guess, the weather was going to get still worse before the day was over, and winter had over a month and a half to go. Yesterday's midday temperature had reached only two degrees; today's temperature seemed unlikely to attain even that anemic height. The waters of Lake Pei were invisible from the vesting chamber, but he didn't need to see it to picture the horizontal bands of sleet driving across its frozen surface on the teeth of the bitter wind that roared around the eaves in a steady, icy counterpoint to the organ music flowing in through the vesting chamber's open door.

"I'm afraid that's something we could wish for most days this time of year, Your Eminence," Father Ahrnahld replied. "And I know it's not going to get above freezing, whatever else happens. It would've been nice to at least have a little sun today, though."

Ahrnahld Samsyn, the rector of the Cathedral of the Holy Archangel Schueler, was young for an upper-priest—only forty-seven, although he'd be forty-eight next month. His brown hair was perpetually unruly, and unlike Braytahn he was clean-shaven, which made him seem even younger standing beside the archbishop.

"Well, it won't worry the Archangel one way or the other," Braytahn said philosophically. "And, speaking of the Archangel, I believe it's about time, Father."

"It is, indeed, Your Eminence," Samsyn agreed, glancing at the clock on the chamber wall. He and the archbishop turned to face one another, giving their vestments one last check. It was even more important than usual for their appearance to be faultless on today, of all days.

Someone rapped lightly on the frame of the open door, and a throat cleared itself.

"Are you ready, Your Eminence? Father?"

Father Kohdy Trahskhat, the assistant rector of the Cathedral of the Holy Archangel Schueler, was vested in the white of the Order of Bédard rather than the purple of Schueler. It wasn't unusual for assistant rectors to be assigned to churches dedicated to someone other than the patron of their own orders, but since the Jihad, there'd been rather less competition for assistant rectories in churches consecrated to the Archangel Schueler. Trahskhat was an exception to that rule, and he and Samsyn got along very well.

"Yes, we are, Kohdy," Samsyn said now. "How does the attendance look?"

"Much better than I expected, given the weather, really." Trahskhat shrugged. "I'd say there's probably three hundred, possibly four."

"That's better than I would've expected, either, Father Ahrnahld!" the archbishop said, laying a hand on Samsyn's shoulder. "You must be doing something right!"

"I try, Your Eminence," Samsyn said with a smile. "Some days I seem more successful than others."

"Trust me, my son, you aren't the only member of our order who could say that," Braytahn said feelingly. "But every year we win back a little more ground. And it's only fair that it be difficult for us to regain our flocks' trust once more."

Samsyn bent his head in agreement with that.

The Order of Schueler had taken a monstrous—and,

he admitted ungrudgingly, well-deserved—blow in the course of the Jihad. Samsyn himself had been a mere under-priest, fresh out of seminary and assigned as a teacher in a small mountain town in the Episcopate of St. Aileen, while young Trahskhat had still been at seminary. Samsyn was devoutly grateful he'd stayed in St. Aileen to the end of the Jihad, because that assignment had kept him out of the hideous perversions of the Inquisition . . . and, he was guiltily aware, spared him the sort of decisions priests like Kuhnymychu Ruhstahd had been forced to make. He hoped he would have had Ruhstahd's courage, even in the face of the Punishment, but he was too self-honest to be confident of that. The upper-priest from Camp Chihiro had been named an official martyr of Mother Church by Grand Vicar Rhobair, and Samsyn strongly suspected that Martyr Kuhnymychu would become *Saint* Kuhnymychu as soon as the minimum twenty-five-year waiting period ended.

But there'd been far too few Kuhnymychus and far too many Wyllym Raynos, too many clerics who'd lent themselves willingly to Zhaspahr Clyntahn's madness. Grand Vicar Rhobair had been ruthless in purging the order of its rot, and the vast majority of its prelates and upper-priests had been summarily relieved of their posts. Some had been transferred to other orders on a probationary basis; some had simply been defrocked; and some had faced ecclesiastic courts here in the Temple Lands even if they hadn't been delivered to the Charisians and their allies for trial in the secular courts, as the peace treaties required for any who'd actually served in one of Clyntahn's concentration camps.

All of which helped explain how Ahrnahld Samsyn could be a senior upper-priest at such a young age. Of course, Archbishop Lywkys was only eight years older than he was, which was absurdly young for an archbishop entrusted with the governance of any of the Temple Lands' episcopates. For that matter, before the Jihad, his office would have been occupied by one of the vicars, although the actual business of ministering to the episcopate's people would undoubtedly have been entrusted to a bishop executor while the vicar in question dealt with more important matters in Zion.

That was something else Vicar Rhobair had put a stop to. Under his reforms, no vicar would ever again hold any office outside the vicarate itself.

"Well, I realize that this is your church, and not mine, my sons. Still, I fear it would never do to keep anyone faithful enough to come out in this—" Braytahn waved at the sleet drumming against the window panes "—waiting in a drafty cathedral!"

"Of course not, Your Eminence," Samsyn said with a smile. Technically, Braytahn was Samsyn's "guest" for today's high mass. It was an unusual upper-priest, however, who didn't agree with his archbishop, no matter whose church they were in.

"After you, Your Eminence," he continued, waving gracefully towards the open door, and Braytahn signed the scepter of Langhorne in blessing before he led the way through it.

The side passage delivered them to the vestibule, where the acolytes waited for them. The Cathedral of the Holy Archangel Schueler wasn't really all that drafty, but the chill radiating from the inside of the closed doors was enough to make the unfortunate youngsters shiver, despite their heavy woolen winter cassocks and linen surplices, and Braytahn smiled sympathetically as he and the priests joined them. The archbishop laid his hands on their heads, murmuring a special blessing upon each of them in turn, and then smiled again, almost mischievously.

"Buck up, boys," he told them. "It'll be a lot warmer in the sanctuary, and all that kneeling and genuflecting and singing will soon have your blood moving again!"

"We know, Your Eminence," the oldest of the three scepter-bearers said with an answering grin. "And we'll try to keep our teeth from chattering till we get there."

"*That's* the spirit!" Braytahn laughed, and made shooing motions with both hands for the processional to form up. The bishop took his own place directly behind the candle-bearers, with Samsyn and Trahskhat at his elbows, while the thurifers removed the covers from their thuribles and gave them gentle swings to make certain the chains were straight. The sweet-smelling smoke curled up, and Samsyn's nostrils flared as he inhaled the familiar, comforting fragrance.

Then the sextant who'd been watching stepped through the vestibule door into the cathedral proper, and the choirmaster who'd been watching for him gave the organist the signal he'd been expecting. He nodded back, and the prelude he'd been playing for the last twenty minutes flowed smoothly into the processional Samsyn had chosen for today's mass. The majestic opening chords of "Lord of Adoration" filled the cathedral, and then the choir burst into song as the scepter-bearers—their faces solemnly joyous, now—led the way through the doors, down the nave, and into those glorious waves of music.

Samsyn followed the archbishop, his own voice joining those of the choir and the other celebrants, and he felt a stir of satisfaction as he realized Trahskhat's estimate had been very close. The cathedral was still less than half full, but that was far better than it had been the first time he'd celebrated the Feast of Schueler here.

It wasn't hard to understand why, after the atrocities of the Jihad. Nor was it difficult to blame laymen and laywomen for finding it difficult to distinguish between the actions of a monster like Zhaspahr Clyntahn and the order he'd used to carry out his mass murders. The yearly Day of Atonement had a very special meaning for the Order of Schueler, and Schueler himself had come under intense . . . scrutiny. No one could deny the words of the Archangel's book, of the horrible punishments he'd laid down for the heretic and the blasphemer. Some people had tried to argue that the *Book of Schueler* should be read in a figurative way, but that was a fringe movement, and one not condoned by Mother Church. The inerrancy of the *Holy Writ* was absolute, attested to by the Holy Langhorne and Holy Bédard themselves, and that meant the Holy Schueler *had* written those words, *had* laid down those punishments.

Samsyn wanted to believe Grand Vicar Rhobair had been right when he argued that the Punishment of

Schueler, which for all of its specificity and horrific severity accounted for barely a twentieth of the complete *Book of Schueler*, was intended primarily to deter and was to actually be applied only to those who knowingly and with hearts filled with malice strove to seduce the innocent into Shan-wei's service. The merely mistaken, the sincerely deluded, were to be reclaimed for the Light, not snuffed out and condemned forever to the Dark. That fate awaited only the truly unregenerate who'd deliberately given himself to the service of Shan-wei and refused to renounce his hellish mistress.

Most days Samsyn did believe that, but there were still the occasional nights when sleep eluded him as he wrestled with the possibility that even the Grand Vicar might be mistaken. Yet there was so much *else* in the *Book of Schueler*, so much guidance for the education of God's children. Yes, it was stern throughout, harsh in many places, yet in the fallen world Shan-wei had left broken and marred in her wake, that sort of sternness was necessary. It was the sternness of a father who wanted his children to grow up spiritually strong and morally straight, and it had been only Zhaspahr Clyntahn's own spiritual rot that allowed him to inflict the Punishment wholesale in a holocaust the Holy Schueler himself would never have sanctioned.

Those familiar thoughts carried him down the nave, through the music, past the pews occupied by the worshipers who'd braved cold and wind and sleet to be here on this high feast day—the Feast of the Holy Schueler, commemorating the joyous day on which the Archangel had returned to his well-deserved rest in the glorious presence of God Himself, leaving behind the worn out mortal body which had housed his soul for so long. That mortal body was buried in the crypt of this very cathedral, which had been raised for the specific purpose of guarding and sanctifying his tomb. This service, here today, was the epicenter of all of the other high masses being held across the face of Safehold to remember the Holy Schueler on this, his day.

Samsyn's heart rose, swelling with the simple joy and

unquestioning faith which were too often tested by the memory of the Jihad. How he wished he could cling to that joy, that simple, clarifying faith, every day of the year! That the vengeful, harsh Schueler whose wrath Zhaspahr Clyntahn had been able to twist and pervert to serve his own ends, could somehow vanish into Schueler the teacher, Schueler the guardian. If only—

Ahrnahld Samsyn staggered, crying out as his hands rose to shield his eyes against the sudden, intolerable burst of light. He'd never seen—never *imagined*—such an explosion of brilliance, and he heard other voices crying out, some of them screaming, in shocked confusion and sudden fear. The organ music died a discordant death, the choirs' massed harmony fragmented into individual cries of alarm, and then a voice, deeper than any Samsyn had ever heard, more powerful than any tempest he'd ever endured, spoke.

"Do not be afraid, my children!" Its majesty filled the cathedral, rolling down from its high dome, flowing outward along the nave like a wall of sound, and Samsyn lowered his hands, blinking, trying to see. He couldn't quite—

His vision cleared, his eyes flared, and he flung himself to his knees in awe as he saw the mighty shape towering in the sanctuary of his cathedral.

The inner dome of that cathedral floated a hundred feet above its pavement; the figure standing beneath it towered to at least half that height. It loomed like a titan, light streaming from it in rippling waves, and he knew that face. *He knew it!*

"Do not be afraid," the Archangel Schueler repeated. "You are safe here, for you stand on ground consecrated by faith, dedicated to hope. In a darkling world, you are a beacon of hope and of light, and I call upon you to be strong, to stand always for the truth."

Samsyn trembled under the mighty Archangel's stern but compassionate gaze. He couldn't look away, although he heard the archbishop whispering the words of the Catechism of Schueler as he, too, knelt at the Archangel's feet.

"You have survived a dark time," the Archangel continued. "Terrible, evil deeds were done in my name. Deeds any godly person must renounce as the foul perversion they were. Enough time has passed for you to recognize that truth, to grapple with it and realize that even though terrible things were done in my name, it was never with my *approval*."

Samsyn signed himself with the scepter and felt those words—the words that validated his love for Schueler and the assurance that Zhaspahr Clyntahn had, indeed, perverted the Archangel's will and intent—flood through him like the sun.

"Yet now that that those days and years have passed, the time has come for a further truth, a deeper truth, to be shared with you. For know this, this world has indeed strayed far afield from the plan for which your forefathers and your foremothers, the Adams and the Eves who left you *The Testimonies,* were brought forth upon it. You do live in a dark and fallen time, but—" that mighty voice softened, went darker with what could almost have been pain "—it did not fall the way you have been taught it did."

Samsyn froze as the Archangel paused. What? What could he mean?!

"You have been taught that it was Shan-wei the Bright who fell, allowing evil and darkness into the world. But I tell you that was a lie."

Samsyn's heart seemed to stop. No! No, that was *impossible!* Every word of the *Holy Writ* taught that—!

"I know this is hard to hear, my children," the Archangel said quietly, soberly. "I know the pain and the confusion it causes you. Yet it is true. I have been prevented from telling you this truth for far too long, but that is because of the malign forces which truly violated and twisted the great plan for Safehold, and those forces *did not spring* from Shan-wei. She was not the one who betrayed that plan. Rather she was the one who was *destroyed* by the betrayer of that plan because she refused to compromise it. Because she refused to turn away from the great charge which had brought her to Safehold to prepare and shape it as a home for all humanity. And it is time you know. Time that I may finally tell you, who the true betrayer was."

Samsyn realized he was shaking his head again and again and again, that he was panting like a spent runner, his fingers aching with the force of his grip upon his pectoral scepter, his heart pounding as the impossible words rolled over him.

And then another light, too brilliant for the mortal eye to withstand, descended from the cathedral dome above the Archangel like a drifting star, settling towards the earth.

Or, his quivering mind told him, like *The Testimonies'* descriptions of the *kyousei hi*—the great fire no mortal had beheld since the last Archangel had returned to God.

The eye-searing brightness touched the sanctuary rail, and then it slowly faded into something a human eye could tolerate, and Ahrnahld Samsyn swallowed hard as he saw the mighty volume resting upon the rail. Saw the flickering, flowing glow of holy brilliance dancing through its gems, saw the precious metals of its cover, and knew—*knew*—that its pages were of that same imperishable metal, in paper-thin sheets etched with a finer script than any mortal hand could produce.

"This is *my* Testimony," the Archangel said. "The *Testimony of Schueler,* and I leave it with you so that all who see it may know I truly appeared before you, that this is truly my word. And that word, my children," he said while Samsyn trembled before him, "is that it was not Shan-wei who Fell, but Chihiro who *lied.*"

A chorus of gasps washed through the cathedral, and the Archangel looked down upon the mall.

"Take that word forth with you, my children, for it is time the truth was known. Time the lies were set aside. Time for you to walk once more into the light of the purpose which brought you here.

"I know it's frightening. I know the burden I've laid

upon you will be heavy. But it is *time,* and I charge you all as my witnesses and my messengers to take that truth and proclaim it to all the Faithful."

He gazed down upon them for another endless moment, then raised his hand in a gesture of benediction.

"I leave you as my watchmen and my heralds. Be vigilant, be brave, and know that the truth is a mightier weapon than any lie."

And with that, he vanished, as suddenly as he had appeared, and Samsyn blinked, wondering if it had all been some sort of incredible, impossible delusion.

But then he saw the Godlight still washing across the gems encrusting that gleaming metal cover and whimpered, because he knew it hadn't.

Glossary

Abbey of Saint Evehlain—the sister abbey of the Monastery of Saint Zherneau.

Abbey of the Snows—an abbey of the Sisters of Chihiro of the Quill located in the Mountains of Light above Langhorne's Tears. Although it is a working abbey of Chihiro, all of the nuns of the abbey are also Sisters of Saint Kohdy and the abbey serves as protection and cover for Saint Kohdy's tomb. The Abbey of the Snows is built on the foundation of a pre-Armageddon Reef structure which is reputed to have been a resort house for Eric Langhorne before his death.

Angle-glass—Charisian term for a periscope.

Angora lizard—a Safeholdian "lizard" with a particularly luxuriant, cashmerelike coat. They are raised and sheared as sheep and form a significant part of the fine textiles industry.

Anshinritsumei—"the little fire" from the *Holy Writ*; the lesser touch of God's spirit and the maximum enlightenment of which mortals are capable.

Ape lizard—ape lizards are much larger and more powerful versions of monkey lizards. Unlike monkey lizards, they are mostly ground dwellers, although they are capable of climbing trees suitable to bear their weight. The great mountain ape lizard weighs as much as nine hundred or a thousand pounds, whereas the plains ape lizard weighs little more than a hundred to a hundred and fifty pounds. Ape lizards live in families of up to twenty or thirty adults, and whereas monkey lizards will typically flee when confronted with a threat, ape lizards are much more likely to respond by attacking the threat. It is not unheard of for two or three ape lizard "families" to combine forces against particularly dangerous predators, and even a great dragon will generally avoid such a threat.

Archangels, The—central figures of the Church of God Awaiting. The Archangels were senior members of the command crew of Operation Ark who assumed the status of divine messengers, guides, and guardians in order to control and shape the future of human civilization on Safehold.

ASP—Artillery Support Party, the term used to describe teams of ICA officers and noncoms specially trained to call for and coordinate artillery support. ASPs may be attached at any level, from the division down to the company or even platoon, and are equipped with heliographs, signal flags, runners, and/or messenger wyverns.

Bahnyta—the name *Seijin* Kohdy assigned to his *hikousen*.

Band—the AoG and Harchongese equivalent of an army corps. The word "corps" itself can't be used because of the Inquisition's opposition to the adoption of that "heresy-tainted" term.

Beaver—the Safeholdian analog of a terrestrial beaver. It is larger even than the terrestrial species, with full-grown adults reaching as much as 150 pounds (70 kilos) but less prolific, which is fortunate, considering its effect on its environment. They are a favored prey of slash lizards and great dragons, but are dangerous if cornered and difficult prey.

Blink-lizard—a small, bioluminescent winged lizard. Although it's about three times the size of a firefly, it fills much the same niche on Safehold.

Blue leaf—a woody, densely growing native Safeholdian tree or shrub very similar to mountain laurel. It bears white or yellow flowers in season and takes its name from the waxy blue cast of its leaves.

Bombsweeper—the Imperial Charisian Navy's name for a minesweeper.

Borer—a form of Safeholdian shellfish which attaches itself to the hulls of ships or the timbers of wharves by boring into them. There are several types of borer, the most destructive of which continually eat their way deeper into any wooden structure, whereas some less destructive varieties eat only enough of the structure to anchor themselves and actually form a protective outer layer which gradually builds up a coral-like surface. Borers and rot are the two most serious threats (aside, of course, from fire) to wooden hulls.

Briar berries—any of several varieties of native Safeholdian berries which grow on thorny bushes.

Catamount—a smaller version of the Safeholdian slash lizard. The catamount is very fast and smarter than its larger cousin, which means it tends to avoid humans. It is, however, a lethal and dangerous hunter in its own right.

Cat-lizard—a furry lizard about the size of a terrestrial cat. They are kept as pets and are very affectionate.

Chamberfruit—a native Safeholdian plant similar to a terrestrial calabash gourd. The chamberfruit is grown both as a food source and as a naturally produced container. There are several varieties of chamberfruit, and one common use for it is in the construction of foamstone pipes for smoking.

Cherrybean tea—a "tea" made from the beans (seeds) of the cherrybean tree, especially favored in Emerald and Tarot and is a highly esteemed luxury in North Harchong and The Temple Lands, although its expense limits it to a very wealthy group of consumers.

Cherrybean tree—the Safeholdian name for coffee trees. There is only one variety on Safehold, a version of robusta genetically engineered to survive in a wider range of climates. The cherrybean tree is still limited to a fairly narrow belt of equatorial and near-equatorial Safehold because of the planet's lower average temperatures.

Chewleaf—a mildly narcotic leaf from a native Safeholdian plant. It is used much as terrestrial chewing tobacco over much of the planet's surface.

Choke tree—a low-growing species of tree native to Safehold. It comes in many varieties and is found in most of the planet's climate zones. It is dense growing, tough, and difficult to eradicate, but it requires quite a lot of sunlight to flourish, which means it is seldom found in mature old-growth forests.

Church of Charis—the schismatic church which split from the Church of God Awaiting (see below) following the Group of Four's effort to destroy the Kingdom of Charis.

Church of God Awaiting—the church and religion created by the command staff of Operation Ark to control the colonists and their descendants and prevent the reemergence of advanced technology.

Cliff bear—a Safeholdian mammal which somewhat resembles a terrestrial grizzly bear crossed with a raccoon. It has the facial "mask" markings of a raccoon and round, marsupial ears. Unlike terrestrial bears, however, cliff bears are almost exclusively carnivorous.

Cliff lizard—a six-limbed, oviparous mammal native to Safehold. Male cliff lizards average between 150 and 250 pounds in weight and fill much the same niche as bighorn mountain sheep.

Commentaries, The—the authorized interpretations and doctrinal expansions upon the *Holy Writ*. They represent the officially approved and Church-sanctioned interpretation of the original Scripture.

Composition D—The Charisian name for TNT.

Cone wood—an evergreen tree, similar to Terran conifers, native to northern Safehold. Not much seen south of Chiang-wu Province. Grows to about 65 feet.

Cotton silk—a plant native to Safehold which shares many of the properties of silk and cotton. It is very lightweight and strong, but the raw fiber comes from a plant pod which is even more filled with seeds than Old Earth cotton. Because of the amount of hand labor required to harvest and process the pods and to remove the seeds from it, cotton silk is very expensive.

Council of Vicars—the Church of God Awaiting's equivalent of the College of Cardinals.

Course lizard—one of several species of very fast, carnivorous lizards bred and trained to run down prey. Course lizard breeds range in size from the Tiegelkamp course lizard, somewhat smaller than a terrestrial greyhound, to the Gray Wall course lizard, with a body length of over five feet and a maximumn weight of close to 250 pounds.

Crusher serpent—a huge Safeholdian predator roughly analogous to a boa constrictor. Crusher serpents are warm blooded, which better suits them to Safehold's colder climate, and can reach lengths of up to sixty feet. They are ambush hunters which prefer flight to fight in threat situations, and they can sometimes be faced down even by relatively small prey animals. Nonetheless, they are fearsome foes if cornered and have been known to take down even adolescent slash lizards.

Dagger thorn—a native Charisian shrub, growing to a height of perhaps three feet at maturity, which possesses knife-edged thorns from three to seven inches long, depending upon the variety.

Dandelion—the Safeholdian dandelion grows to approximately twice the size of the Terrestrial plant for which it is named but is otherwise extremely similar in appearance and its seeds disperse in very much the same fashion.

De Castro marble—a densely swirled, rosy marble from the de Castro Mountains of North Harchong which is prized by sculptors, especially for religious and Church art.

Decrees of Schueler—the codified internal directives, regulations, and procedure manual of the Office of the Inquisition.

Deep-mouth wyvern—the Safeholdian equivalent of a pelican.

Doomwhale—the most dangerous predator of Safehold, although, fortunately, it seldom bothers with anything as small as humans. Doomwhales have been known to run to as much as one hundred feet in length, and they are pure carnivores. Each doomwhale requires a huge range, and encounters with them are rare, for which human beings are just as glad, thank you. Doomwhales will eat *anything* . . . including the largest krakens. They have been known, on *extremely* rare occasions, to attack merchant ships and war galleys.

Double-glass or **Double-spyglass**—Charisian term for binoculars.

Dragon—the largest native Safeholdian land life-form. Dragons come in two varieties: the common dragon (generally subdivided into jungle dragons and hill dragons) and the carnivorous great dragon. See below.

Eye-cheese—Safeholdian name for Swiss cheese.

Fallen, The—the Archangels, angels, and mortals who followed Shan-wei in her rebellion against God and the rightful authority of the Archangel Langhorne. The term applies to *all* of Shan-wei's adherents, but is most often used in reference to the angels and Archangels who followed her willingly rather than the mortals who were duped into obeying her.

False silver—Safeholdian name for antimony.

Fire striker—Charisian term for a cigarette lighter.

Fire vine—a large, hardy, fast growing Safeholdian vine. Its runners can exceed two inches in diameter, and the plant is extremely rich in natural oils. It is considered a major hazard to human habitations, especially in areas which experience arid, dry summers, because of its very high natural flammability and because its oil is poisonous to humans and terrestrial species of animals. The crushed vine and its seed pods, however, are an important source of lubricating oils, and it is commercially cultivated in some areas for that reason.

Fire willow—a Safeholdian evergeen tree native to East Haven's temperate and subarctic regions. Fire willow seldom grows much above five meters in height and has long, streamer-like leaves. It prefers relatively damp growing conditions and produces dense clusters of berries ranging in color from a bright orange to scarlet in color.

Fire wing—Safeholdian term for a cavalry maneuver very similar to the Terran caracole, in which mounted troops deliver pistol fire against infantry at close quarters. It is also designed to be used against enemy cavalry under favorable conditions.

Fist of Kau-yung—the unofficial name assigned to Helm Cleaver and its operatives by agents inquisitor attempting to combat the organization.

Five-day—a Safeholdian "week," consisting of only five days, Monday through Friday.

Flange-beam—Safeholdian term used for what a Terran engineer would call an "I-beam."

Fleming moss—an absorbent moss native to Safehold which was genetically engineered by Shan-wei's terraforming crews to possess natural antibiotic properties. It is a staple of Safeholdian medical practice.

Foamstone—the Safeholdian equivalent of meerschaum. This light-colored, soft stone takes its name from the same source as meerschaum, since it is occasionally found floating in the gulf of Tanshar. Its primary use is in the construction of incense burners for the Church of God Awaiting and in the manufacture of tobacco pipes and cigar holders.

Forktail—one of several species of native Safeholdian fish which fill an ecological niche similar to that of the Old Earth herring.

Fox-lizard—a warm-blooded, six-limbed Safeholdian omnivore, covered with fur which ranges from a dull russet color to a very dark gray. Most species of fox-lizard are capable of climbing trees. They range in length from 40 to 48 inches in length, have bushy tails approximately 25 inches long, and weigh between 20 and 30 pounds.

Gbaba—a star-traveling, xenophobic species whose reaction to encounters with any possibly competing species is to exterminate it. The Gbaba completely destroyed the Terran Federation and, so far as is known, all human beings in the galaxy aside from the population of Safehold.

Glynfych Distillery—a Chisholmian distillery famous throughout Safehold for the quality of its whiskeys.

Golden berry—a tree growing to about ten feet in height which thrives in most Safeholdian climates. A tea brewed from its leaves is a sovereign specific for motion sickness and nausea.

Grasshopper—a Safeholdian insect analogue which grows to a length of as much as nine inches and is carnivorous. Fortunately, they do not occur in the same numbers as terrestrial grasshoppers.

Grass lizard—a Safeholdian herbivore, somewhat larger than a Terrestrial German Shepherd, which is regarded as a serious pest by farmers. There are several subspecies, which are found almost everywhere outside the arctic regions.

Gray-horned wyvern—a nocturnal flying predator of Safehold. It is roughly analogous to a terrestrial owl.

Gray mists—the Safeholdian for Alzheimer's disease.

Great dragon—the largest and most dangerous land carnivore of Safehold. The great dragon isn't actually related to hill dragons or jungle dragons at all, despite some superficial physical resemblances. In fact, it's more of a scaled-up slash lizard, with elongated jaws and sharp, serrated teeth. They have six limbs and, unlike the slash lizard, are covered in thick, well-insulated, scaly hide rather than fur. A fully mature male great dragon can reach twenty feet in length, with a body weight of over five thousand pounds.

Group of Four—the four vicars who dominate and effectively control the Council of Vicars of the Church of God Awaiting.

Gun dogs—ICA infantry and cavalry nickname for their own army's artillerists.

Hairatha Dragons—the Hairatha professional baseball team. The traditional rivals of the Tellesberg Krakens for the Kingdom Championship.

Hake—a Safeholdian fish. Like most "fish" native to Safehold, it has a very long, sinuous body but the head does resemble a terran hake or cod, with a hooked jaw.

Hammer-islander—Safeholdian term for a sou'wester; a waterproof foul-weather hat made of oilskin or tarred canvas. It takes its name from Hammer Island, which experiences some of the harshest weather on Safehold.

Hand of Kau-yung—the name applied by agents of the Inquisition to the anti-Group of Four organization established in Zion by Aivah Pahrsahn/Ahnzhelyk Phonda.

Helm Cleaver—the name of *Seijin* Kohdy's "magic sword," and also the name assigned by Nynian Rychtair to the covert action organization created in parallel with the Sisters of Saint Kohdy.

High-angle gun—a relatively short, stubby artillery piece with a carriage specially designed to allow higher angles of fire in order to lob gunpowder-filled shells in high, arcing trajectories. The name is generally shortened to "angle-gun" by the gun crews themselves.

High Hallows—a very tough, winter-hardy breed of horses.

Highland lilly—a native Safeholdian perennial flowering plant. It grows to a height of three to four feet and bears a pure white, seven-lobed flower eight to nine inches across with petals tipped in dark crimson. Its flower is considered sacred to martyrs and those who have fought valiantly for Mother Church.

Hikousen—The term used to describe the air cars provided to the *seijins* who fought for the Church in the War Against the Fallen.

Hill dragon—a roughly elephant-sized draft animal commonly used on Safehold. Despite their size, hill dragons are capable of rapid, sustained movement. They are herbivores.

Holy Writ (1)—the central scripture of the Church of God Awaiting. The complete *Holy Writ* actually contains hundreds of volumes, as each of the "Archangels'" books consist of multiple volumes dealing in detail with subjects from *The Book of Sondheim*'s instructions for terraforming ("consecrating") native Safeholdian flora and fauna to *The Book of Pasquale*'s instructions for treating appendicitis. (But see also below.)

Holy Writ (2)—when applied to a single volume, the term "the *Holy Writ*" refers specifically to the books of *Langhorne, First Bedard, Chihiro,* and *Schueler,* which are customarily bound between a single set of covers and form the primary "teaching texts" of the Church. It is this volume which is found in every church and cathedral on Safehold and normally provides the scriptural reference for any sermon, although passages from other volumes of the complete *Writ* may also be used.

Hornet—a stinging, carniverous Safeholdian insect analogue. It is over two inches long and nests in ground burrows. Its venom is highly toxic to Safeholdian life-forms, but most terrestrial life-forms are not seriously affected by it (about ten percent of all humans have a potentially lethal allergic shock reaction to it, however). Hornets are highly aggressive and territorial and instinctively attack their victims' eyes first.

Ice wyvern—a flightless aquatic wyvern rather similar to a terrestrial penguin. Species of ice wyvern are native to both the northern and southern polar regions of Safehold.

Inner circle—Charisian allies of Merlin Athrawes who know the truth about the Church of God Awaiting and the Terran Federation.

Insights, The—the recorded pronouncements and observations of the Church of God Awaiting's Grand Vicars and canonized saints. They represent deeply significant spiritual and inspirational teachings, but as the work of fallible mortals do not have the same standing as the *Holy Writ* itself.

Intendant—the cleric assigned to a bishopric or archbishopric as the direct representative of the Office of Inquisition. The intendant is specifically charged with ensuring that the Proscriptions of Jwo-jeng are not violated.

Ironquartz—the Safeholdian term for ferrosilicon, an alloy of iron and quartz produced in Ehdwyrd Howsmyn's blast furnaces as the basis for airship hydrogen gas generation.

Ironwood—an extremely densely-grained Safeholdian hardwood. Ironwood prefers a colder climate and is native to both Havens, Howard, and the southern portions of the Land of the Raven Lords but is not found on the other islands/smaller continents. It is favored for baseball bats by many of the Mainlander teams, although a regulation bat is too heavy for many batters. It is also a preferred wood for nightsticks and riot batons.

Journal of Saint Zherneau—the journal left by Jeremy Knowles telling the truth about the destruction of the Alexandria Enclave and about Pei Shan-wei.

Jungle dragon—a somewhat generic term applied to lowland dragons larger than hill dragons. The gray jungle dragon is the largest herbivore on Safehold.

Kau-yungs—the name assigned by men of the Army of God to anti-personnel mines, and especially to claymore-style directional mines, in commemoration of the "pocket nuke" Commander Pei Kau-yung used against Eric Langhorne's adherents following the destruction of the Alexandria Enclave. Later applied to all landmines.

Kau-yung's striker—(also simply "striker") the ICA's combat engineers' nickname for a flamethrower.

Keitai—The term used to describe the personal coms provided to the *seijins* who fought for the Church in the War Against the Fallen.

Kercheef—a traditional headdress worn in the Kingdom of Tarot which consists of a specially designed bandana tied across the hair.

Key of Schueler—a memory module left with the Wylsynn family by the "Archangel Schueler."

Knights of the Temple Lands—the corporate title of the prelates who govern the Temple Lands. Technically, the Knights of the Temple Lands are *secular* rulers who simply happen to also hold high Church office.

Under the letter of the Church's law, what they may do as the Knights of the Temple Lands is completely separate from any official action of the Church. This legal fiction has been of considerable value to the Church on more than one occasion.

Kraken (1)—generic term for an entire family of maritime predators. Krakens are rather like sharks crossed with octopi. They have powerful, fishlike bodies, strong jaws with inward-inclined, fang-like teeth, and a cluster of tentacles just behind the head which can be used to hold prey while they devour it. The smallest, coastal krakens can be as short as three or four feet; deepwater krakens up to fifty feet in length have been reliably reported, and there are legends of those still larger.

Kraken (2)—one of three pre-Merlin heavy-caliber naval artillery pieces. The great kraken weighed approximately 3.4 tons and fired a 42-pound round shot. The royal kraken weighed four tons. It also fired a 42-pound shot but was specially designed as a long-range weapon with less windage and higher bore pressures. The standard kraken was a 2.75-ton, medium-range weapon which fired a 35-pound round shot approximately 6.2 inches in diameter.

Kraken oil—originally, oil extracted from kraken and used as fuel, primarily for lamps, in coastal and seafaring realms. Most lamp oil currently comes from sea dragons (see below), rather than actually being extracted from kraken, and, in fact, the sea dragon oil actually burns much more brightly and with much less odor. Nonetheless, oils are still ranked in terms of "kraken oil" quality steps.

Kynyth Tompsyn—the name of *Seijin* Kohdy's best friend and mortal sword companion.

Kyousei hi—"great fire" or "magnificent fire" from the *Holy Writ*. The term used to describe the brilliant nimbus of light the Operation Ark command crew generated around their air cars and skimmers to "prove" their divinity to the original Safeholdians.

Land-bomb—Temple Loyalist armed forces' term for a land mine.

Langhorne's Tears—a quartet of alpine lakes in the Mountains of Light. Langhorne's Tears were reportedly known as Langhorne's Joy before the destruction of Armageddon Reef.

Langhorne's Watch—the 31-minute period which falls immediately after midnight. It was inserted by the original "Archangels" to compensate for the extra length of Safehold's 26.5-hour day. It is supposed to be used for contemplation and giving thanks.

Lizardhole—Temple Loyalist armed forces' term for "foxhole."

Marsh wyvern—one of several strains of Safeholdian wyverns found in salt and freshwater marsh habitats.

Mask lizard—Safeholdian equivalent of a chameleon, mask lizards are carnivores, about two feet long, which use their camouflage ability to lure small prey into range before they pounce.

Master Traynyr—a character out of the Safeholdian entertainment tradition. Master Traynyr is a stock character in Safeholdian puppet theater, by turns a bumbling conspirator whose plans always miscarry and the puppeteer who controls all of the marionette "actors" in the play.

Messenger wyvern—any one of several strains of genetically modified Safeholdian wyverns adapted by Pei Shan-wei's terraforming teams to serve the colonists as homing pigeon equivalents. Some messenger wyverns are adapted for short-range, high-speed delivery of messages, whereas others are adapted for extremely long range (but slower) message deliveries.

Mirror twins—Safeholdian term for Siamese twins.

Moarte subită—"sudden death," the favored martial art of the Terran Federation Marines, developed on the Terran Federation colony world of Walachia.

Monastery of Saint Zherneau—the mother monastery and headquarters of the Brethren of Saint Zherneau, a relatively small and poor order in the Archbishopric of Charis.

Monkey lizard—a generic term for several species of arboreal, saurian-looking marsupials. Monkey lizards come in many different shapes and sizes, although none are much larger than an Old Earth chimpanzee and most are considerably smaller. They have two very human-looking hands, although each hand has only three fingers and an opposable thumb, and the "hand feet" of their other forelimbs have a limited grasping ability but no opposable thumb. Monkey lizards tend to be excitable, *very* energetic, and talented mimics of human behaviors.

Mountain ananas—a native Safeholdian fruit tree. Its spherical fruit averages about four inches in diameter with the firmness of an apple and a taste rather like a sweet grapefruit. It is very popular on the Safeholdian mainland.

Mountain spike-thorn—a particular subspecies of spike-thorn, found primarily in tropical mountains. The most common blossom color is a deep, rich red, but the white mountain spike-thorn is especially prized for its trumpet-shaped blossom, which has a deep almost cobalt-blue throat, fading to pure white as it approaches the outer edge of the blossom, which is, in turn, fringed in a deep golden yellow.

Narwhale—a species of Safeholdian sea life named for the Old Earth species of the same name. Safeholdian narwhales are about forty feet in length and equipped with twin horn-like tusks up to eight feet long. They live in large pods or schools and are not at all shy or retiring. The adults of narwhale pods have been known to fight off packs of kraken.

Nearoak—a rough-barked Safeholdian tree similar to an Old Earth oak tree. Found in tropic and near-tropic zones. Although it does resemble an Old Earth oak, it is an evergreen and seeds using "pine cones."

Nearpalm—a tropical Safeholdian tree which resembles a terrestrial royal palm except that a mature specimen stands well over sixty feet tall. It produces a tart, plum-like fruit about five inches in diameter.

Nearpalm fruit—the plum-like fruit produced by the nearpalm. It is used in cooking and eaten raw, but its greatest commercial value is as the basis for near-palm wine.

Nearpoplar—a native Safeholdian tree, very fast-growing and straight-grained, which is native to the planet's temperate zones. It reaches a height of approximately ninety feet.

Neartuna—one of several native Safeholdian fish species, ranging in length from approximately three feet to just over five.

NEAT—Neural Education and Training machine. The standard means of education in the Terran Federation.

Needle tree—a fairly low-growing evergreen (adult trees are no more than ten to twelve feet tall) which grows in a near-symbiotic relationship with nearoak. It grows best in shade, and the nearoak canopy provides an ideal environment by keeping much sunlight from reaching the forest floor. The needle tree's dense root system helps hold water and stabilize the soil and its dense branches shield dropped nearoak seed cones from predators and provide a rich mulch of dropped needles.

Nest doll—a Harchongian folk art doll, similar to the Russian Matryoshka dolls in which successively smaller dolls are nested inside hollow wooden dolls.

New-model—a generic term increasingly applied to the innovations in technology (especially war-fighting technology) introduced by Charis and its allies. (See "new-model kraken," below.)

New-model kraken—the standardized artillery piece of the Imperial Charisian Navy. It weighs approximately 2.5 tons and fires a 30-pound round shot with a diameter of approximately 5.9 inches. Although it weighs slightly less than the old kraken (see above) and its round shot is twelve percent lighter, it is actually longer ranged and fires at a higher velocity because of reductions in windage, improvements in gunpowder, and slightly increased barrel length.

Northern spine tree—a Safeholdian evergreen tree, native to arctic and subarctic regions. Spine tree branches grow in a sharply pointed, snow-shedding shape but bear the sharp, stiff spines from which the tree takes its name.

Nynian Rychtair—the Safeholdian equivalent of Helen of Troy, a woman of legendary beauty, born in Siddarmark, who eventually married the Emperor of Harchong.

Offal lizard—a carrion-eating scavenger which fills the niche of an undersized hyena crossed with a jackal. Offal lizards will take small living prey, but they are generally cowardly and are regarded with scorn and contempt by most Safeholdians.

Oil tree—a Safeholdian plant species which grows to an average height of approximately thirty feet. The oil tree produces large, hairy pods which contain many small seeds very rich in natural plant oils. Dr. Pei Shan-wei's terraforming teams genetically modifed the plant to increase its oil productivity and to make it safely consumable by human beings. It is cultivated primarily as a food product, but is also an important source of lubricants. In inland realms, it is also a major source of lamp oil.

Operation Ark—a last-ditch, desperate effort mounted by the Terran Federation to establish a hidden colony beyond the knowledge and reach of the xenophobic Gbaba. It created the human settlement on Safehold.

Pain bane—a more potent opiate, also prepared from the sleep root tree (see below). It is normally prescribed as the next stage in potency from pain root (see below). It will normally produce drowsiness and usually produces dizziness and mild disorientation in its users. Addiction can occur.

Pain root—a fairly mild opiate painkiller made from the root of the sleep root tree (see below). It can produce drowsiness in its users, but is generally a first step when something more potent than silk leaf (see below) is needed. It is generally nonaddictive.

Pasquale's Basket—a voluntary collection of contributions for the support of the sick, homeless, and indigent. The difference between the amount contributed voluntarily and that required for the Basket's purpose is supposed to be contributed from Mother Church's coffers as a first charge upon tithes received.

Pasquale's Cleanser—the Safeholdian term for carbolic acid.

Pasquale's Grace—euthanasia. Pasqualate healers are permitted by their vows to end the lives of the terminally ill, but only under tightly defined and stringently limited conditions.

Pasquale's hand—one of the most potent opiates in Safeholdian pharmacology, Pasquale's hand is prepared from the sleep root tree (see below). It has significant transitory side effects, including depressed breathing, nausea, dizziness, and muddled thinking. As such, it is generally considered the last stage of pain medication. Addiction for heavy users is not at all uncommon.

Persimmon fig—a native Safeholdian fruit which is extremely tart and relatively thick-skinned.

Picklefish—any of several small species of Safeholdian forktail (see above) which are prepared and preserved in oil or wine sauce much like Old Earth sardines.

"Pikes of Kolstyr"—a Siddarmarkian military march composed to commemorate a Desnairian atrocity in one of the early wars between the Republic of Siddarmark and the Desnairian Empire. When played on the battlefield, it announces that the Republic of Siddarmark Army intends to offer no quarter.

Prong lizard—a roughly elk-sized lizard with a single horn which branches into four sharp points in the last third or so of its length. They are herbivores and not particularly ferocious.

Proscriptions of Jwo-jeng—the definition of allowable technology under the doctrine of the Church of God Awaiting. Essentially, the Proscriptions limit allowable technology to that which is powered by wind, water, or muscle. The Proscriptions are subject to interpretation by the Order of Schueler, which generally errs on the side of conservatism, but it is not unheard of for corrupt intendants to rule for or against an innovation under the Proscriptions in return for financial compensation.

Rabies—a native Safeholdian disease which produces symptoms very similar to those associated with the terrestrial disease of the same name. It does not affect imported terrestrial fauna, however, and the terrestrial disease was not brought to Safehold with the colonists.

Rakurai (1)—literally "lightning bolt." The *Holy Writ's* term for the kinetic weapons used to destroy the Alexandria Enclave.

Rakurai (2)—the organization of solo suicide terrorists trained and deployed by Wyllym Rayno and Zhaspahr Clyntahn. Security for the Rakurai is so tight that not even Clyntahn knows the names and identities of individual Rakurai or the targets against which Rayno has dispatched them.

Rakurai bug—a Safeholdian insect analogue similar to a Terrestrial firefly but about three times as large.

Rakurai fish—a Safeholdian analog of the terrestrial electric eel. The rakurai fish is distantly related to the saltwater kraken. It has a maximum body length of about five feet and can generate an electrical shock substantially more powerful than that of the electric eel. The rakurai fish's shock, unlike the electrical eel's, is capable of killing an adult human under ideal circumstances. Unlike the electrical eel, the rakurai fish's shock is primarily defensive in nature, not a means of disabling prey, and rakurai fish are not normally aggressive unless threatened.

Reformism—the movement within the Church of God Awaiting to reform the abuses of power and position which have infested it by the time of Merlin Athrawes.

Reformist—one associated with the Reformist movement. The majority of Reformists outside the Charisian Empire still regard themselves as Temple Loyalists.

Reformist movement—the movement within the Church of God Awaiting to reform the abuses and corruption which have become increasingly evident (and serious) over the last hundred to one hundred and fifty years. Largely underground and unfocused until the emergence of the Church of Charis, the movement is attracting increasing support throughout Safehold.

Rising—the term used to describe the rebellion against Lord Protector Greyghor and the Constitution of the Republic of Siddarmark by the Temple Loyalists.

Round Theatre—the largest and most famous theater in the city of Tellesberg. Supported by the Crown but independent of it, and renowned not only for the quality of its productions but for its willingness to present works which satirize Charisian society, industry, the aristocracy, and even the Church.

Rugby—a Charisian version of water polo, played by nine-man teams: one goalie and eight field players.

Saint Evehlain—the patron saint of the Abbey of Saint Evehlain in Tellesberg; wife of Saint Zherneau.

Saint Kohdy—a *seijin* who fought for the Church of God Awaiting in the War Against the Fallen. He was killed shortly before the end of that war and later stripped of his sainthood and expunged from the record of the Church's *seijins*.

Saint Kylmahn Rifle—a single-shot, breechloading, caplock rifle, developed from a rifle designed by Dynnys Zhwaigair of the Royal Dohlaran Navy.

Saint Zherneau—the patron saint of the Monastery of Saint Zherneau in Tellesberg; husband of Saint Evehlain.

Salmon—a Safeholdian fish species named because its reproductive habits are virtually identical to those of a terrestrial salmon. It is, however, almost more like an eel than a fish, being very long in proportion to its body's width.

Sand maggot—a loathsome carnivore, looking much like a six-legged slug, which haunts Safeholdian beaches just above the surf line. Sand maggots do not normally take living prey, although they have no objection to devouring the occasional small creature which strays into their reach. Their natural coloration blends well with their sandy habitat, and they normally conceal themselves by digging their bodies into the sand until they are completely covered, or only a small portion of their backs show.

Sandrah's Doorknocker—also simply "doorknocker." ICA engineers' slang term for the Composite Demolition Charge, Mark 1; the Safeholdian equivalent of the Bangalore Torpedo.

Scabbark—a very resinous deciduous tree native to Safehold. Scabbark takes its name from the blisters of sap which ooze from any puncture in its otherwise very smooth, gray-brown bark and solidify into hard, reddish "scabs." Scabbark wood is similar in coloration and grain to Terran Brazilwood, and the tree's sap is used to produce similar red fabric dyes.

Sea-bomb—Temple Loyalist armed forces' term for a naval mine.

Sea cow—a walrus-like Safeholdian sea mammal which grows to a body length of approximately ten feet when fully mature.

Sea dragon—the Safeholdian equivalent of a terrestrial whale. There are several species of sea dragon, the largest of which grow to a body length of approximately fifty feet. Like the whale, sea dragons are mammalian and insulated against deep oceanic temperatures by thick layers of blubber, and virtually are krill-eaters. They reproduce much more rapidly than whales, however, and are the principal food source for doomwhales and large, deepwater krakens. Most species of sea dragon produce the equivalent of sperm oil and spermaceti. A large sea dragon will yield as much as four hundred gallons of oil.

Sea-kite—the Imperial Charisian Navy's name for a minesweeping paravane.

Seijin—sage, holy man, mystic. Legendary warriors and teachers, generally believed to have been touched by the *anshinritsumei*. Many educated Safeholdians consider *seijins* to be mythological, fictitious characters.

Shan-wei's candle (1)—the deliberately challenging name assigned to strike-anywhere matches by Charisians. Later shortened to "Shan-weis."

Shan-wei's candles (2)—a Temple Loyalist name given to the illuminating parachute flares developed by Charis.

Shan-wei's footstools—also simply "footstools." Charisian name for non-directional antipersonnel mines which are normally buried or laid on the surface and (usually) detonated by a percussion cap pressure switch. See "Kau-yungs."

Shan-wei's fountains—also simply "fountains." Charisian name for "bounding mines." When detonated, a launching charge propels the mine to approximately waist height before it detonates, spraying shrapnel balls in a three-hundred-and-sixty-degree pattern. See "Kau-yungs."

Shan-wei's sweepers—also simply "sweepers." Charisian name for a Safeholdian version of a claymore mine. The mine's backplate is approximately eighteen inches by thirty inches and covered with five hundred and seventy-six .50-caliber shrapnel balls which it fires in a cone-shaped blast zone when detonated. See "Kau-yungs."

Shan-wei's War—the *Holy Writ's* term for the struggle between the supporters of Eric Langhorne and those of Pei Shan-wei over the future of humanity on Safehold. It is presented in terms very similar to those of the war between Lucifer and the angels loyal to God, with Shan-wei in the role of Lucifer. (See also "War Against the Fallen," below.)

Shellhorn—a venomous Safeholdian insect analogue with a hard, folding carapace. When folded inside its shell, it is virtually indistinguishable from a ripe slabnut.

Siddar Loyalist—the self-identifying post-Jihad label for citizens of the western provinces of the Republic of Siddarmark who remained loyal to the Republic when those provinces were first wracked by the

Sword of Schueler and later overrun by the Church of God Awaiting's armed forces. They tend to be extremely bitter and hostile towards any of their pre-Jihad fellow citizens who supported Mother Church.

Silk leaf (1)—a native Safeholdian tree with birch-like bark. There are many varieties of it, and one or another of them grows in almost every subarctic or temperate climate zone. Its edible inner bark is rich in salicylates.

Silk leaf (2)—a painkiller and fever reducer very similar to aspirin which is produced from the bark of the silk leaf tree (see above).

Silk leaf tea—a popular restorative and "sports drink" brewed from the inner bark of the silk leaf tree (see above).

Sisters of Saint Kohdy—an order of nuns created to honor and commemorate Saint Kohdy. The last of the "angels" used kinetic weapons to obliterate their abbey and the tomb of Saint Kohdy shortly after the last of the original Adams and Eves died.

Sky comb—a tall, slender native Safeholdian tree. It is deciduous, grows to a height of approximately eighty-five to ninety feet, and has very small, dense branches covered with holly-like leaves. Its branches seldom exceed eight feet in length.

Slabnut—a flat-sided, thick-hulled nut. Slabnut trees are deciduous, with large, four-lobed leaves and grow to about thirty feet. Black slabnuts are genetically engineered to be edible by humans; red slabnuts are mildly poisonous. The black slabnut is very high in protein.

Slash lizard—a six-limbed, saurian-looking, furry oviparous mammal. One of the three top land predators of Safehold. Its mouth contains twin rows of fangs capable of punching through chain mail and its feet have four long toes, each tipped with claws up to five or six inches long. A fully mature slash lizard can reach fourteen feet in length, only four feet of it tail, and weigh up to 2,800 pounds.

Sleep root—a Safeholdian tree from whose roots an entire family of opiates and painkillers are produced. The term "sleep root" is often used generically for any of those pharmaceutical products, but there are generally more specific names as well (see "pain root," "Pasquale's hand," and "pain bane").

Slime toad—an amphibious Safeholdian carrion eater with a body length of approximately seven inches. It takes its name from the thick mucus which covers its skin. Its bite is poisonous but seldom results in death.

Snapdragon—the Safeholdian snapdragon isn't actually related to any of the other dragon species of the planet. It is actually a Safeholdian analog to the terrestrial giant sea turtle. Although it is warm-blooded, its body form is very similar to that of a terrestrial leatherback sea turtle, but it is half again the leatherback's size, with fully mature male snapdragons running to body lengths of over nine feet. No living Safeholdian knows why the snapdragon was given its name.

SNARC—Self-Navigating Autonomous Reconnaissance and Communications platform.

Spider-crab—a native species of sea life, considerably larger than any terrestrial crab. The spider-crab is not a crustacean, but more of a segmented, tough-hided, many-legged seagoing slug. Despite that, its legs are considered a great delicacy and are actually very tasty.

Spider-rat—a native species of vermin which fills roughly the ecological niche of a terrestrial rat. Like all Safeholdian mammals, it is six-limbed, but it looks like a cross between a hairy gila monster and an insect, with long, multi-jointed legs which actually arch higher than its spine. It is nasty-tempered but basically cowardly. Fully adult male specimens of the larger varieties run to about two feet in body length, with another two feet of tail, for a total length of four feet, but the more common varieties average only between two or three feet of combined body/tail length.

Spike-thorn—a flowering shrub, various subspecies of which are found in most Safeholdian climate zones. Its blossoms come in many colors and hues, and the tropical versions tend to be taller-growing and to bear more delicate blossoms.

Spine fever—a generic term for paralytic diseases, like polio, which affect the nervous system and cause paralysis.

Spruce—a tree native to Safehold, found primarily in the cooler regions of the planet's temperate zones. It has many of the qualities of the Old Terran tree of the same name, including light weight and strength. It is much more resistant to decay and insects, however, which makes it more durable for external construction uses. There are several varieties of Safeholdian spruce, but blue spruce (named for the color of its seed cones)—which grows to a mature height of around 120 feet—is the most commonly used for building. Yellow spruce is one of the trees more widely used by Safeholdian papermakers.

"Stand at Kharmych"—a Siddarmarkian military march composed to commemorate the 37th Infantry Regiment's epic stand against an invading Desnairian army in the Battle of Kharmych.

Steam automotive—the Charisian term for a steam-powered locomotive.

Steam carriage—the Charisian term for a steam-powered passenger vehicle.

Steam dragon—the Charisian term for a steam-powered tractor.

Steam wagon—the Charisian term for a steam-powered freight vehicle.

Steel thistle—a native Safeholdian plant which looks very much like branching bamboo. The plant bears seed pods filled with small, spiny seeds embedded in fine, straight fibers. The seeds are extremely difficult to remove by hand, but the fiber can be woven into a fabric which is even stronger than cotton silk. It can also be twisted into extremely strong, stretch-resistant rope. Moreover, the plant grows almost as rapidly as actual bamboo, and the yield of raw fiber per acre is seventy percent higher than for terrestrial cotton.

Stone of Schueler—a solar-powered verifier (truth detector) left with the Wylsynn family by the "Archangel Schueler."

Stone wool—Safeholdian term for chrysotile (white asbestos).

Stork—a Safeholdian species of wyvern named for the Old Terran bird it resembles. A Safeholdian stork is about fifteen percent larger than its Old Terran counterpart, and its legs are proportionately a bit longer.

Sugar apple—a tropical Safeholdian fruit tree. The sugar apple has a bright purple skin much like a terrestrial tangerine, but its fruit has much the same consistency of a terrestrial apple. It has a higher natural sugar content than an apple, however, hence the name.

Surgoi kasai—"dreadful" or "great fire." The true spirit of God. The touch of His divine fire, which only an angel or Archangel can endure.

Swamp hopper—a moderate-sized (around fifty to sixty-five pounds) Safeholdian amphibian. It is carnivorous, subsisting primarily on fish and other small game and looks rather like a six-legged komodo dragon but has a fan-like crest which it extends and expands in response to a threat or in defense of territory. It is also equipped with air sacs on either side of its throat which swell and expand under those circumstances. It is ill tempered, territorial, and aggressive.

Swivel wolf—a light, primarily anti-personnel artillery piece mounted on a swivel for easy traverse (see "wolf").

Sword of Schueler—the savage uprising, mutiny, and rebellion fomented by the Inquisition to topple Lord Protector Greyghor Stohnar and destroy the Republic of Siddarmark. It led directly to the deaths of several million Siddarmarkians, primarily in the Republic's western provinces.

Sword Rakurai—specially trained agents of the Inquisition sent into the enemy's rear areas during the Jihad. They operated completely solo, as did the Inquisition's regular Rakurai; they were not suicide attackers or simple terrorists. Instead, they were trained as spies and infiltrators, expected to do any damage they could but with the primary mission of information collection.

Talon branch—an evergreen tree native to Safehold. It has fine, spiny needles and its branches are covered with half-inch thorns. It reaches a height of almost seventy feet, and at full maturity has no branches for the first twenty to twenty-five feet above the ground.

Teak tree—a native Safeholdian tree whose wood contains concentrations of silica and other minerals. Although it grows to a greater height than the Old Earth teak wood tree and bears a needle-like foliage, its timber is very similar in grain and coloration to the terrestrial tree and, like Old Earth teak, it is extremely resistant to weather, rot, and insects.

Tellesberg Krakens—the Tellesberg professional baseball club.

Temple boy—Charisian/Siddarmarkian slang for someone serving in the Army of God. It is not a term of endearment.

Temple Loyalist (1)—Safeholdians who remained loyal to the Church of God Awaiting and the leadership of the Temple, in Zion, before and during the Jihad.

Temple Loyalist (2)—one who renounces the schism created by the Church of Charis' defiance of the Grand Vicar and Council of Vicars of the Church of God Awaiting. Some Temple Loyalists are also Reformists (see above), but all are united in condemning the schism between Charis and the Temple.

Temple, The—the complex built by "the Archangels" using Terran Federation technology to serve as the headquarters of the Church of God Awaiting. It contains many "mystic" capabilities which demonstrate the miraculous power of the Archangels to anyone who sees them.

Testimonies, The—by far the most numerous of the Church of God Awaiting's sacred writings, these consist of the firsthand observations of the first few generations of humans on Safehold. They do not have the same status as the Christian gospels, because they do not reveal the central teachings and inspiration of God. Instead, collectively, they form an important substantiation of the *Writ*'s "historical accuracy" and conclusively attest to the fact that the events they describe did, in fact, transpire.

Thanksgiving—a Safehold-wide religious holiday, mandated in *The Book of Sondheim*. It falls on October 24th in the northern hemisphere and on June 24th in the southern hemisphere. As the Old Terran holiday of the same name, it celebrates the gathering of yet another successful harvest.

Titan oak—a very slow-growing, long-lived deciduous Safeholdian hardwood which grows to heights of as much as one hundred meters.

Tomb of Saint Kohdy—the original Tomb of Saint Kohdy was destroyed by the same kinetic weapons which destroyed the Abbey of Saint Kohdy. Before that destruction, however, the Sisters of Saint Kohdy had secretly moved the saint's body to a new, hidden tomb in the Mountains of Light, where it remains to this day.

Trap lizard—a medium-sized (for Safehold) predator. Trap lizards run to an adult body length of approximately four feet. They have outsized jaws and are ambush hunters who normally dig themselves into dens near game trails and then pounce on prong bucks and other herbivores using those trails.

Waffle bark—a deciduous, nut-bearing native Safeholdian tree with an extremely rough, shaggy bark.

War Against the Fallen—the portion of Shan-wei's War (see above) falling between the destruction of the Alexandria Enclave and the final reconsolidation of the Church's authority.

Western Syndicate—the label assigned to a cabal of land speculators and corrupt politicians in the western provinces of the Republic of Siddarmark. The speculators, who took advantage of the distressed state of those provinces after the Jihad, now control the majority of all farmland and have established enormous commercial farming operations, reducing many once-independent farmers to little more than sharecroppers and gradually squeezing out the remaining small farmers who were the backbone of the provinces' agricultural sector before the Jihad. Through their financial clout with the provincial political machines, they effectively control local policy and the election of delegates to the national Chamber of Delegates.

Wind dance—a traditional Harchongese dance. A variation on the square dance, it is an endurance competition between the dancers and the caller.

Wind hummer—a small, delicate wyvern very similar to a terrestrial hummingbird. There are many species of wind hummer and they are found in almost every region of Safehold.

Wing warrior—the traditional title of a blooded warrior of one of the Raven Lords clans. It is normally shortened to "wing" when used as a title or honorific.

Wire vine—a kudzu-like vine native to Safehold. Wire vine isn't as fast growing as kudzu, but it's equally tenacious, and unlike kudzu, several of its varieties have long, sharp thorns. Unlike many native Safeholdian plant species, it does quite well intermingled with terrestrial imports. It is often used as a sort of combination hedgerow and barbed-wire fence by Safehold farmers.

Wolf (1)—a Safeholdian predator which lives and hunts in packs and has many of the same social characteristics as the terrestrial species of the same name. It is warm-blooded but oviparous and larger than an Old Earth wolf, with adult males averaging around two hundred to two hundred and twenty-five pounds.

Wolf (2)—a generic term for shipboard artillery pieces with a bore of less than two inches and a shot weighing one pound or less. They are primarily antipersonnel weapons but can also be effective against boats and small craft.

Wyvern—the Safeholdian ecological analogue of terrestrial birds. There are as many varieties of wyverns as there are birds, including (but not limited to) the homing/messenger wyvern, hunting wyverns suitable for the equivalent of hawking for small prey, the crag wyvern (a small—wingspan ten feet—flying predator), various species of sea wyverns, and the king wyvern (a very large flying predator with a wingspan of up to twenty-five feet). All wyverns have two pairs of wings, and one pair of powerful, clawed legs. The king wyvern has been known to take children as prey when desperate or when the opportunity presents, but they are quite intelligent. They know that man is a prey best left alone and generally avoid areas of human habitation.

Wyvernry—a nesting place and/or breeding hatchery for domesticated wyverns.

Zhyahngdu Academy—perhaps the most renowned school for sculptors in all of Safehold, located at the port city of Zhyahngdu in the Tiegelkamp Province of North Harchong. It dates back to the days of the War Against the Fallen and has trained and produced the Church of God Awaiting's finest sculptors for almost nine hundred Safeholdian years.